Fitzwilliam Darcy

An

Honourable Man

Fitzwilliam Darcy

An

Honourable Man

A Pride and Prejudice Adaptation

Brenda J. Webb

DarcyandLizzy@earthlink.net

ISBN-10: 1461073146
ISBN-13: 978-1461073147

First Edition: July 2011

Front cover photographs courtesy of Wikimedia Commons, Abovian Portrait, 1831 and Wikipedia, Chatsworth House.

Back Cover photographs courtesy of Wikimedia Commons, George Romney's Portrait of Lady Hamilton, 1782, and Wikipedia, Chatsworth House.

Cover and internal design by M. K. Baxley 2011

Dedication

To Debbie Styne

Without your help and support during the writing process, this book would not have been possible. Nevertheless, your friendship means more to me than all your skills. Your encouragement, advice and ability to make me smile when I am at my lowest are invaluable. I am so glad we crossed paths.

Acknowledgement

I must acknowledge my longtime friend and beta, Karin Loebbert, who is always a member of my team because of her attention to details, and newcomers, Beth Cochran and Gayle Mills, who lent their time and talent to the story and to whom I am greatly indebted. Lastly, I'd like to acknowledge M. K. Baxley for all her work in design and structure of this book.

Chapter 1

Netherfield
1814 March

Charles Bingley nervously ran his hands through his hair, trying to make sense of what had just happened. Lizzy was supposed to be in her rooms, but once again they had found her on the terrace staring out into the night. "Is she asleep?"

"I think so. I cannot tell anymore." Jane sighed wearily, her blue eyes filled with worry. "She pretends to sleep, but Mrs. Drury informed me that she gets out of bed as soon as I leave."

"It is difficult to judge if it is any better. She does not speak, and she clutches that doll..." Charles' voice trailed off. He did not want to add to the upset his wife was already suffering.

Jane took a ragged breath. "True, she does not speak, but what concerns me more is that she will not look me in the eye. She seems to be in a daze. The only time I have been able to elicit a response is when she does not want to do something. Then she will resist, shaking her head no and pulling back. As for the doll, she will not let anyone take it from her. Mrs. Drury has tried to remove it while she sleeps, but she panics if she wakes, and it is not in her arms. I truly do not understand the significance of the doll... nor any of it."

Silent tears slid down her cheeks, causing Charles to take his wife in his arms and gently rock her back and forth. "Calm yourself, my love. It will not help for you to get so distressed again."

"If only I knew what happened. It breaks my heart to make Lizzy do anything she does not want, after that savage..."

She could not continue, and Charles held her tighter, whispering words of comfort until she sniffled and pulled back to look into his face. "I do not know how much longer we can hide her, and if he were to find out that she is still alive..." she shuddered. "I would simply die if he came for her."

"I know. We have to think of a safer arrangement. Your mother has almost found her several times, since she persists in coming to the house unannounced. Then there was the dance at the assembly hall. How in the world did Lizzy get out of the house and walk that far without having anyone come upon her?"

"I have no idea how she eluded Mrs. Drury to escape the house that night, but Lizzy is used to walking. You know that, Charles."

"Is there something else we can do? More locks on the doors?"

"We have locked her doors, but she just knocks one of the small window panes out of the balcony door and unlocks it. I refuse to board up the windows. It would break her heart not to be able to see outside, and I would be fearful of a fire. I think she goes out of doors because she misses the freedom of walking."

Charles ran his fingers through his hair in exasperation. "But we cannot let her walk about just anywhere. She might be seen and now there are all these silly rumours about a ghost outside the assembly hall, all because Lizzy walked about in plain view, howbeit at a distance, and Miss Paulson saw her. If she had not screamed and run back into the room, scaring Lizzy away, well, I fear she would have been discovered that very night!"

"I realise that we came close to being found out, but we have managed to keep her safe here at Netherfield for five months. It is hardest on Mrs. Drury, poor thing. She hardly gets any sleep. Lizzy is just as likely to ramble around in the middle of the night as during the day, but we cannot risk bringing anyone else into our confidence."

Jane began to cry softly. Charles slipped his arms around her, pulling her to his chest and patting her on the back. "We will find a way. Lizzy shall be safe, even if I have to buy a house far out in the country and hire someone to care of her."

"I do not want her to be where I would worry over her safety. If only we could get Mr. Darcy to . . ." Jane's whispered hopes ended abruptly.

Charles stiffened and pulled back to look in her face. "I cannot believe I have not heard from Darcy. Even if he could not help us, he could at least have answered my letters."

Suddenly his eyes flashed. "Why did I not think of this before? I shall write to his cousin, Colonel Fitzwilliam, and ask whether or not he knows if Darcy is in residence at Pemberley."

"Charles, I told you that Lizzy was truly sorry for refusing Mr. Darcy's proposal, and I imagine that he was very hurt too. Do you think he did not return because he thought he would have to see her? She was so sure that he hated her."

"I do not think Darcy has it in him to hate anyone and especially not Lizzy, but perhaps he felt it better not to open old wounds. After all, he had no idea she was missing."

Charles seemed to mull over the reason he had not heard back from his oldest friend. "It is unlike Darcy not to give me an answer. I have heard nothing since that letter he sent last year from Scotland. Surely he has returned to Pemberley by now."

"I would be willing to move elsewhere in order to keep Lizzy safe."

"And I would move anywhere for you, my love." Charles leaned in to give her a kiss. "Now it is late, and she is safe for this night, at least. Let us get some rest, as young Master Peter will be up early looking for his mama."

Jane slipped her arms around his neck and kissed him back. "Yes, and his mama will want to see him, too."

Onboard a ship from Ireland
1814 April

It was eerily dark aboard the creaking vessel, the moon having gone behind ominous black clouds. Rain, which he could smell already, was headed their way, but it had not begun just yet, and Captain Burris was thankful for that as he pulled his cap down over his ears. The wind, however, had picked up, and he had trouble keeping his balance as he moved along the starboard side. Just as he stepped around a load of cargo lashed to the deck, he was startled to see someone, a passenger judging from his clothes, leaning on the rail, bracing himself against the rocking of the ship. It was a rare occurrence to find a passenger awake at this time of the morning, much less above deck, where the waves washed over the sides of the ship in stormy weather.

Shaking his head in annoyance, he moved to warn the man of the danger before stopping abruptly. *It is Mr. Darcy.*

Though Fitzwilliam Darcy had never been outgoing, over the years, they had become acquainted and shared a few conversations regarding the stars, currents and navigation as the taciturn man travelled to Ireland and back, visiting his estate. However, the gentleman from Derbyshire had been so reclusive on this voyage, keeping to his cabin even during the day, that Burris had wondered about his apparent change of character. Deciding he had better leave well enough alone, the elderly captain moved on towards the bow.

He never takes kindly to my warnings. I hope the man can take care of himself in the coming storm.

~~~*~~~

Fitzwilliam Darcy was going home. It had taken a long time, but he was certain now of one thing—he could meet her as an indifferent and common acquaintance. He had conquered the steady ache in his heart, and he no longer thought of her every waking moment. He could go for days without waking in the middle of the night, wet with sweat and heart pounding, as dreams of their last argument tormented him anew. He was almost free of her at last!

He had decided that when he arrived home, he would write Bingley. Perhaps Charles might mention her without any prompting, since she was probably his sister now. It had been almost two years, and she was most likely married…quite possibly a mother. Those circumstances would only strengthen his resolve, and he half hoped to have it confirmed. Knowing with certainty that she was lost to him forever would reinforce what he had determined in his heart.

I no longer love you, Elizabeth!

Taking a deep breath of the sea air, he turned to go back to his cabin. Tomorrow they would dock in England, and within a week, he would be at his beloved Pemberley.

Pemberley
One week later

"Oh, William!" Georgiana exclaimed as she slid gracefully off her horse, throwing the reins to a nearby footman. Her feet had barely touched the ground before she sprinted towards him, her golden hair flouncing about her shoulders and her dark blue eyes sparkling with joy. "You are home! You are home!"

Her actions and demeanour were so reminiscent of her as a child that William could feel tears filling his eyes. Unaware of the effect she was having, she never slowed, eventually running into him. Having braced himself against the impact, he caught her flying form and whirled around with the momentum, then sat her back on her feet as she giggled and he pulled her close.

"Evan will be furious with you," he murmured in her hair as his head lay atop hers. "Does he know you are here? I heard him say often enough that he does not want you riding so far on horseback, and it is ten miles to Rosewood." Without waiting for an answer, he pulled back to look at her with an expression of unabashed love. "Just let me look at you! Do you know how much I have missed you?"

He leaned in to kiss her forehead and then promptly clasped her in another tight hug before she could answer, content just to have her in his arms. They stood that way for a long time before he straightened.

"Have you been well?" The tone of William's voice asked the question he could not. Georgiana had suffered two miscarriages since her marriage three years ago and had not been with child again.

Schooling herself not to show any concern, she answered as happily as she could muster, "As I have answered each query in each letter since you went away, I am well and happy... except for missing you."

William chuckled. "And that scoundrel of a husband of yours?"

Georgiana giggled. "The scoundrel is well. I imagine Evan will be along shortly to find me."

Her face quickly sobered when she pulled back to look at him closely. She realised at that moment what had not been obvious at first sight. He had lost weight, causing his clothes to hang on his large frame. He had lines across his forehead and around his eyes, which were dull and without the sparkle that had been there before. Even more shocking was the recognition that his almost black hair was beginning to gray dramatically around his face. It took everything she possessed to speak without letting her voice quiver.

"And you?" She took his hands, and her eyes searched his to find the truth. "Are you well, truly?"

"I am," he responded almost too quickly, his eyes darting away. Then he began to shift from one foot to the other, feeling self-conscious under her steady gaze.

"You have aged," she said solemnly.

"Well, that is a fine thing to say on my first day home!" He forced a smile, trying to cheer her. "Thank you for making me feel as old as I obviously look!"

He actually felt years older—unresolved heartache having taken its toll, physically as well as mentally—nevertheless, he had hoped Georgiana would not notice so readily. When he glanced back, he was surprised to see her eyes flash in annoyance.

"I care not if you are offended. I knew it would not be good for you to spend all that time alone, and I can see that I was correct." Softening her voice, she reached up to cup his face. "Have you come home for good? No more running away?"

William started to protest that he had not run away, but he checked himself. That would be a lie. His face fell at the revelation.

"Will, promise me that you will stay home—or at least stay for a long time."

He stood silently contemplating his next words, then sighed heavily. "I have come home to stay. Except for trips to London or those necessary for business, I will be at Pemberley." She watched the corners of his mouth lift slightly. "What say you, Gigi, to settling in the drawing room with a cup of tea to review our accomplishments while we have been separated?" The use of his pet name for her made her smile, in spite of her frustration.

"I say lead on, Fitzy!" He grimaced at the appellation she had given him when she was too young to pronounce *Fitzwilliam*.

"I wish you would come up with another term of endearment."

"Oh, but that would not be you! You will always be *Fitzy* to me!"

Giggling at his discomfiture, she took his offered arm and stepped onto the first of the many steps leading to the front door. As they attained the top and crossed the portico, Mr. Walker, the elderly butler, threw the door open, greeting them and taking their coats.

"Good morning, Mrs. Ingram," Mr. Walker said enthusiastically. "It is so good to have you back again! I know you are just as thrilled as we are to have Mr. Darcy home."

"Yes, Mr. Walker," Georgiana said, leaning her head against William's shoulder, "I am extremely pleased to have my brother home."

~~~*~~~

They spent the better part of the afternoon sitting side-by-side, holding hands. Georgiana listened raptly as William told her about his eight-month stay at the estate their father had purchased years before in Scotland and the subsequent twelve months he had spent in Ireland at the estate he had inherited from their grandmother.

He related all the particulars—the repairs and improvements to the mansions, the various servants and the changes he had made in staff. She marvelled as he rattled off names of people and places and then figures, including the number of servants, tenants, crop yields and income. She was not actually absorbing the information as much as she was silently admiring his ability to remember so much. It was a long time before she interrupted him to speak.

"Oh, my poor, dear brother," she murmured, stretching towards him to kiss his cheek. "It is a miracle that you can keep it all straight. You have so much to attend."

"I do not mind." He seemed dispirited, even as he tried to smile. "I would rather keep busy."

She cupped his chin, pulling him around to face her, and the sadness in his sky blue eyes broke her heart. "I fear I must ask. Will you ever tell me why you felt compelled to leave?"

He stood and walked over to the windows, clasping his hands behind his back. It was quite some time before he spoke softly. "The reason no longer exists, and I would prefer not to speak of it, as I do not want to be dragged down into that well of despair again." He turned to look over his shoulder. "Can you understand, Ana?"

She nodded, standing to move beside him and slipping an arm around his waist. "I understand, but please know that if you ever feel you need to tell someone the reason, I will listen. I love you, William, and I am so truly happy you are safely home."

"I love you, too." He turned then, taking her into his arms and kissing the top of her head. "Having you for a sister was the best thing that ever happened to me."

She smiled. "I surely hope you have better things happen to you in the future— like finding the right woman and getting married."

"Georgiana Ingram! What are you about? Do I now have to contend with your playing matchmaker as well?" He asked in mock horror, his hand over his heart.

"Well, you know Evan's step-brother died over a year ago in a hunting accident. His widow, Cecile Preston, is coming to stay with me next week. We are having a dinner party and . . ."

"Stop!" he retorted. "I think you are getting too far ahead! Let us go back to *I am truly happy you are safely home!*"

Rosewood Manor
One week later
The dinner party

Evan Ingram was very much his own man. Tall, blond, blue-eyed and quite handsome, he was muscular from years of fencing and riding. He had been quite the eligible bachelor when he stumbled upon a rider-less horse one afternoon on the road to Lambton. Looking around, he found that Fitzwilliam Darcy's little sister had been unseated by a disagreeable animal. At that point on, the man who had fancied himself never marrying but living the life of an adventurer, changed course. Tonight was just one of many occasions that he thanked his lucky stars that he had.

He watched as his wife proved, once again, to be the consummate hostess, moving among their guests and making everyone feel special and welcome. She looked especially beautiful tonight in her new blue gown, and his chest swelled with pride to know that she was his.

He turned then to locate her brother among the crowd. Darcy had just returned from almost two years in Scotland and Ireland, and Evan wondered what demons had driven him that far from home. He had known the man all his life, not that they had ever been close. He was two years younger than Ana's brother and was always too ill-behaved for Darcy's taste. Always so serious, Darcy was the kind of boy who tried to please his father, whereas Ingram was the kind who tried his father's patience. Only since he had been drawn to the beautiful Georgiana, had he finally gotten to know the man he once considered dull. His brother could be reserved, but he was also kind, generous and sometimes very witty.

Evan Ingram smiled over the top of his glass of punch as he located him among the crowd. His brother seemed to be trying not to appear interested in any of the women eyeing him. In fact, he had found a convenient corner in which to hide just as soon as dinner was finished. So far, he had danced only with Georgiana and two older married women and was trying to fade into the wallpaper. Seeing his disconcertment, Evan decided to join him and do what Georgiana asked him to do— but only on his own terms.

As he came to a stop by Darcy, his eyes roamed the room to locate Cecile, and finally he found her standing on the other side of Georgiana. Her face was turned towards his wife, but her eyes were on Darcy. Evan smiled to himself. His step-brother's widow was no beauty, but she was not ugly. In truth, she was pleasant though mostly plain, and at six and twenty, she was eager to find someone interested in offering marriage.

When Cecile appeared on their doorstep two days ago, her year of mourning had ended several months before. With Georgiana's letter touting her brother's return to England, Cecile had made hasty plans to visit. There were eligible men in London, but the most recent gentlemen to take notice of her had only been interested in her fortune. Besides, the opportunity to be in the company of Fitzwilliam Darcy was just too tempting. Though never introduced, Cecile spoke often of seeing him at the theatre and opera years before and told Georgiana that she had been captivated by his tall, dark figure even then.

"Ana is hopeful that you will form an attachment with Cecile, I believe," Evan said quietly.

William shifted uncomfortably. "Your sister is lovely, but I am in no hurry to form an attachment." Afraid that he might have offended his brother, he added, "Not to say that I never will be."

Evan barely nodded. "I understand, Darcy. Though Georgiana is rather hopeful for a match, I only want you to know that I would be most pleased if you were inclined in that direction. Cecile has had too many suitors interested in her fortune, I fear. It is disheartening when one's sister is sought after by one cad after another, only out to pay his gaming debts."

"How well I remember." William stared pensively at some point straight ahead. "I believe you were the only man I considered worthy of Georgiana." His eyes flew back to Ingram. "Not that you were perfect!" Both men laughed.

"Oh, of course not! I was too much like you—accustomed to saying what I thought and getting away with it! I thought you would toss me out of the house when I asked permission to court her."

"I was quite shocked. She had always said she would never marry...That is until you came along. I remember telling you that I had not formed an opinion about you."

"And I retorted that I was not worried about your opinion, only Ana's!"

"Yes," William said wistfully, his mind recalling his sister's joy at discovering Evan was at Pemberley to ask permission to court her. "I remember it well."

Straightening even taller, he punched Evan on the arm. "You should be thankful that I overlooked your impertinence and granted my permission."

Just at that moment, Georgiana began to stroll towards them, her blue velvet gown hugging her lovely figure and tendrils of gold trailing down her back from a crown of curls atop her head.

She was so lovely that Evan's breath hitched. "I will forever be thankful, Darcy! I could never love another as I love her!"

William could not but smile as he watched their eyes lock and Evan move to meet his wife. Georgiana took her husband's outstretched hands and leaned towards William, whispering sweetly, "Come, Brother, you must not stay hidden in this corner. Many are eager to speak with you, and I promised Cecile that you would play a selection on the pianoforte."

William grimaced as his sister grinned. "I knew that I should have stayed in Ireland!"

"Shhh, Fitzy! People will hear you!"

~~~*~~~

Chapter 2

Pemberley

Pulling back on the reins, William halted his stallion at the top of the ridge, taking in the beauty of Pemberley nestled in the valley below. He always enjoyed pausing at this particular spot before heading back to the stables and today he was not surprised to hear Mrs. Preston's mare trot up beside him. The view never failed to inspire and, apparently, it delighted Mrs. Preston as well.

She sat staring at the vista for a few seconds before exclaiming breathlessly, "It is beautiful!"

"Thank you," he stated quietly. "I think so."

He and Mrs. Preston had ridden out quite early that morning on an excursion planned by Georgiana, who decided at the last minute that she had something that required her attention, leaving him and this new acquaintance alone. William was worried about the impropriety of their ride and the fact that he had no idea what he was going to say to the woman. He had counted on Georgiana to carry the conversation.

After several moments, he dismounted, tying Onyx to a tree, and walked around to take the reins of Mrs. Preston's horse. As he tied up her mare, she slid off to the ground, not waiting for him to help her as most women interested in securing him would have done. That action alone made him begin to think of her as more than just another woman out to gain his approbation. Perhaps it was worth the effort to become better acquainted with Evan's sister.

"You ride well," he offered shyly. "Have you always ridden?"

She smiled warmly. "Yes, but I was not very good at it until a few years ago, though I dearly love horses. My husband insisted that I become a more accomplished rider. His estate was quite large, and it was impossible to get to the more remote areas in a carriage—too rocky, I suppose." She looked as if she were reminiscing. "In order to visit the tenants, I had to ride."

William nodded in agreement. He was beginning to admire her character. "I am sure Mr. Preston appreciated having someone to help him in that regard."

Her head dropped, and she studied her riding boots for a moment before looking back up to meet his eyes. "Did you know my late husband well, Mr. Darcy?"

"I would not say I knew him well. He was three years behind me at university, so I knew who he was, though we hardly talked. Afterward, I saw him occasionally at my club." William wondered at the sudden expression of sadness that washed over her.

"Yes." She sighed, sitting down on a huge boulder and staring across the valley. "White's, I believe it is called."

8

"That is correct." William looked puzzled. "You seem unwell, madam. Do you need to return to the house?"

"I am well, I assure you, sir." Her attention was fixed on a point somewhere straight ahead. "It is just—my husband spent most of his time there whenever we were in Town."

William did not know what to say, so he did not reply. He knew Owen Preston was a gambler when he was at Cambridge and was later known as a drunkard. Furthermore, when he ran into him at White's, Preston often bragged of frequenting the local courtesans. Georgiana had confirmed his opinion of the man when she confided that Evan had often confronted his brother about fulfilling his obligations to Cecile. Rumour was that he had deserted Cecile's bed shortly after the honeymoon, preferring his mistress and the courtesans.

When he did not reply, she cut her eyes back to William. "I—I am sorry. I should not have said anything. I have cast a pall upon our lovely ride. Forgive me."

For the first time, William truly studied the woman. She was certainly plain, but not ugly. Her light brown hair had been streaked blond by the sun, and her eyes were light gray. She was tall like Georgiana, but her figure was even leaner. She was not voluptuous like Elizabeth.

Where did that thought come from? Why must she invade my every consideration of another woman?

Focusing anew on his riding companion, William began to wonder if she would make a pleasant partner for a marriage like that of most of his peers—a marriage of convenience. She had experience as mistress of an estate, and in addition to being an excellent rider, she was intelligent and did not blatantly try to please him. Knowing her husband's failures during their marriage, he had no qualms about her ability to provide an heir. Still, he reasoned, he did not want to raise her expectations. He simply wanted to get to know her better.

He did not love her, and he would not lie to her. If she accepted an offer knowing he could only offer friendship, perhaps, in time, a familial love would grow.

"There is nothing to forgive, Mrs. Preston. Would you like to race back to the stables? Then, perhaps, we could see if Mrs. Winters has finished the muffins she was baking this morning while we await Georgiana."

Cecile beamed. "I would love that. Perhaps Georgiana will join us before long, and she and I could play one of the duets we have been practicing."

"Perhaps." William forced a smile. "May I assist you in remounting?"

"You may."

He held her mare still, positioning her stirrup and taking her arm as he helped her up. Then handing her the reins, he turned to focus on his stallion. He mounted with the practiced, fluid movement of an experienced rider. His strong, athletic body sat astride the horse as if they were one entity. His physical attributes were mesmerizing, and Cecile gazed at him as if spellbound. She startled when he spoke, motioning for her to take the lead.

"Ladies first!"

Cecile nodded absently, kicking her mare into a canter, leaving William staring after her as she quickly put distance between them. He shook his head in wonder as he realised that she was the first woman he had given any consideration to since he met Elizabeth Bennet. Frowning, he remembered his vow not to compare every woman to her and kicked his stallion into a gallop.

Rosewood Manor
Weeks later

"Oh Cecile! I knew William would admire you! It was just a matter of getting to know who you are. You do realise he is very shy."

Cecile smiled, more confidant of William's esteem now. They had spent a considerable amount of time in each other's company in the last two weeks, almost always in the company of Georgiana or Evan.

"I think your brother is the most handsome, interesting man I have ever met."

At Georgiana's gasp, Cecile covered her mouth and blushed. "I—I realise how terrible that sounds, but you must understand that my marriage was arranged. I never respected Owen, and over the course of our marriage, I grew," her voice softened, "to care less for him."

Georgiana reached out to take her hand. "Evan disclosed some of your ordeal. I am so sorry that your marriage was so unfulfilling. I cannot imagine..." Georgiana could not continue.

"Do not grieve for me. It seems a lifetime ago." Cecile's sad face suddenly changed as a small smile began and grew larger. "And now I have a wonderful sister, and she has a wonderful brother!"

Georgiana laughed with her. "Yes, my brother is wonderful, is he not? And if I remember correctly, he will be here for dinner in less than two hours, so we had better begin our preparations. I am hoping that soon he shall have something important to talk to my husband about."

They giggled and hugged like schoolgirls. This was the scene that greeted Evan as he entered the drawing room. Seeing the scheming looks on both their faces, he turned and went right back out the door. Smiling to himself, he heard them laugh even louder as he hurried down the hallway to his study.

Darcy had best be on his guard or else he shall be betrothed before he knows it!

Pemberley

The knock on his study door was so light that William wondered if he had imagined it. The second knock convinced him he had not, and he called, "Come!"

Mr. Walker pushed opened the door, and seeing William at his desk, hurried in that direction with another basket loaded with mail. Setting it on the desk, he bowed and turned to leave.

"I thought Mrs. Ingram said she answered all the mail, except for my personal letters, while I was away. I know I have gone through a large stack already."

"Mrs. Ingram did go through the mail, sir, but she found these in another place and asked me to deliver them to you."

William sighed loudly. "I suppose I have no choice but to read them."

Mr. Walker smiled. "You may do with them as you wish, even discard them."

Now William smiled. "That is an excellent idea! Thank you, Mr. Walker."

"You are very welcome, sir," Mr. Walker smiled in spite of trying to maintain his serious mien and turned to leave.

"One other thing." The elderly butler stopped, once again turning to face William. "While I was away, did my cousin Richard Fitzwilliam stay at Pemberley?"

"Why, yes sir. He was here a few times, but Mrs. Ingram always approved his visit first."

"I suppose that explains the depletion of my stock of French brandy." William shook his head in wonder as a small smile lifted the corners of his mouth. "Thank you, Mr. Walker, that is all."

After the butler departed, William returned to reading the letter from his aunt, Catherine de Bourgh. Just before he left England, he had learned that Anne was married. Never close to his cousin, he prayed it was for the best; but lost in his own pain, he had no interest in following her situation. Besides, he knew Lord Matlock was certainly able to look after his sister's family.

Scanning the months old letter, he was surprised to find Lady Catherine demanding he come to London immediately to help in locating Anne's husband. She wanted him to find the man, demand the cad return Anne's dowry, and then force him to have the marriage annulled. William chuckled at the irony. He clearly recalled that the last time he saw his aunt, she demanded he leave Rosings and never return because he would not do his "duty" and marry Anne.

Richard had related that Lady Catherine was estranged from Anne ever since her daughter impulsively married this charming stranger. She had been living in London with her aunt, Margaret de Bourgh, Sir Lewis' sister, when she had fallen under his spell, and they had apparently married after a whirlwind courtship.

According to the letter, Lady Catherine had only recently gotten word that Anne's husband had depleted her accounts and abandoned her, leaving her penniless and heartbroken in their London townhouse. Anne had been loath to share this information, but her sister-in-law, had grown tired of supporting Anne and had gotten word to her mother. Now Lady Catherine intended to make William straighten out the debacle.

William shook his head. He could only wonder why Anne's husband had not forced his aunt into the dower house, claiming Rosings too. There were certainly a lot of questions to be answered, but he was under no obligation to get involved and felt no burden to do so.

I imagine my aunt lives in fear of what the man will do next, but that problem will fall to my uncle, as I have no intention of intervening. As I so aptly explained to my aunt the night she asked me to leave Rosings, I will only accept responsibility for the woman I marry—if I marry at all.

Immediately Mrs. Preston's face appeared before him. As he recalled her nondescript grey eyes, they changed into two brilliantly sparkling, dark chocolate orbs with long black lashes. Frustrated that Elizabeth materialized whenever he tried to picture Mrs. Preston, he tossed the letter in his hand towards the fireplace.

Impossible woman! He was not sure whether he referred to his aunt or Elizabeth.

Shuffling through the rest of the pile, the neat hand of his cousin, Richard Fitzwilliam, caught his eye. William marvelled at receiving anything from Richard, as he truly loathed writing letters. Opening it immediately, he found that it contained a short note asking after his health, related that Richard was quite busy with his duties, and said he hoped to see him soon. His cousin then indicated the reason for his letter was to enclose a letter he received from Bingley, who was eager to know whether William had returned to Pemberley.

I wonder why Bingley would take the time to write to Richard. Perhaps I should see if I have any letters from him in this pile.

Rifling through the remainder, he immediately recognised Charles' untidy handwriting. Tearing the seal, he was surprised to find it dated about six months after he had left for Scotland—*six months after Elizabeth's refusal.*

Quickly scanning the missive, he smiled. Bingley was to be married to Jane Bennet!

William's heart lightened knowing he had righted a wrong. When he had finally confessed to Charles his part in keeping him apart from Jane, his friend had been kind enough to forgive him. Yet, William had worried that his interference might have caused irreparable damage, and this letter laid those fears to rest. Suddenly it occurred to William that, while he was happy for Charles and Jane, knowing that Elizabeth would be pleased was the catalyst that lifted his spirits.

That knowledge brought to mind why he had returned—his declaration of being free of her. He simply must not think of Elizabeth! Shaking off the melancholy that always accompanied her memory, he picked up where he had left off reading. Charles' plea for him to stand up with him at the wedding began to tug at his conscience.

All of a sudden, William bolted upright in his chair! He was stunned to read that Mr. Bennet had died of a heart ailment two months after Elizabeth returned to Meryton from Kent. Charles related that the family had been expelled from Longbourn because Mr. Collins insisted on occupying it immediately. The letter ended with a plea for him to come to Netherfield for the wedding and advise him on a matter of great importance, one that he did not want to relate in a letter.

William's heart sank when he realised the letter did not mention Elizabeth specifically, so he began rummaging through the stack of mail looking for similar letters. It was a simple matter to find two more. Breaking the seal on both, he looked at the dates and took the next one in order, which was dated about six months after the first.

In this letter, Charles stated that he and Jane were married and expecting their first child. He expressed sorrow that William had not come for the wedding nor sent word that he could not attend. He declared that he was now desperate for help with the situation he had mentioned in his last letter, though he did not specify what it was, and knew of no one else he might ask for assistance. He requested William come to Netherfield as soon as possible.

The third and final letter was dated about eight months after the second, which meant it was four months old. In this letter, though Charles mentioned the birth of a healthy boy, he did not seem as joyful as one would imagine a new father would be. He seemed resigned to the fact that William was not going to help him, but made it clear that he was still desperate for advice and begged for mere correspondence in lieu of his actual presence. He seemed most hurt that William had never replied.

William sighed heavily. He had not meant to injure his friend. When he left England, it was all he could do just to get out of bed each morning and breathe in and out. Hearing from Charles would have been like hearing from Elizabeth, and that he could not abide while trying to purge her from his heart, mind, and spirit. He laid the last letter atop the first two and stared into the gardens just beyond the windows, gathering his thoughts.

Can I put my feelings aside and come to the aid of my friend?

He concluded that this would be a good test of his ability to treat Elizabeth as a common and indifferent acquaintance.

If I still want to call Bingley my friend, I must offer to help him, no matter the problem he faces.

Pulling out a sheet of paper, he began a reply.

Netherfield

Charles found Jane in the solarium, sitting side-by-side with Lizzy on a settee. The contrast of golden and chocolate curls never ceased to amaze him—that the sisters could look so different. Thinking then of the equal differences in their personalities, he remembered sadly that Lizzy was no longer the outgoing, gregarious woman she had been years ago.

Also very noticeable were the worry lines that always seemed to run across his wife's forehead now. He did not regret trying to help Lizzy, but he hated that Jane had less time for him and their son as she tried to coax her sister out of her mental prison.

Seeing their son Peter the first day she arrived at Netherfield, had made Lizzy hysterical, so the child was not allowed near her. This forced Jane to choose between spending time with her sister and her child. In the end, she tried to spend part of every day with each of them, but the choice was readily taking a toll on her.

The sun streamed in the flower-bedecked room, and Lizzy had the familiar doll tightly in her grip, her face turned to catch the rays of light and her eyes closed. Glancing at her with trepidation, Charles did not draw closer. Whenever a man came in sight, Lizzy would begin to draw back, her breath would become rapid and her eyes would glaze over. There were few servants that they trusted to keep the secret of her residence at Netherfield, so since her arrival, she had not been exposed to anyone other than him, Jane, Mrs. Drury, or Mr. Mercer, the butler. He and Mr. Mercer kept out of view whenever possible.

"Jane," he whispered.

She glanced over to him, and he watched as she patted Lizzy's hand before rising. She received no acknowledgement of the endearment from her sister. Jane rose and crossed to him. They exited the room, standing just outside, so Jane could still see her sister while they conversed quietly.

"I have finally heard from Darcy. He has been gone most of the last two years and has just now read my letters." Charles shook his head in astonishment. "It seems he has only been concerned with business affairs. I can hardly believe it of him—leaving his personal correspondence unanswered."

"You know he could not have been himself after Lizzy's rejection," Jane responded softly. "And he was always such a private man."

"Well, no matter. I am going to ask him again to come."

"How shall we handle this? We cannot just tell him of Lizzy straight away, as I do not want him to know if he cannot or will not help."

"No. We need to see how he reacts to the news of her *death*. Only after we are sure he still has feelings for her, will we reveal the secret and ask for his help."

"And if he has no feelings left in his heart for her?"

"Then he will return to Pemberley no more the wiser and with no added burden."

Jane wrung her hands as she glanced back at Elizabeth who was oblivious to the drama unfolding around her, sitting silent as always.

"I pray he will want to help her, or God help us all."

Rosewood Manor

"Mr. Darcy, sir. It is so good to see you."

"Thank you, Jenkins. Is my sister in?" William smirked as he kept moving through the house, knowing the frustrated butler was on his heels. He smiled to think of how Richard played the same trick when he was here. Hearing the sound of the pianoforte, he headed towards the music room, knowing he would find Georgiana there. He wanted to speak to his sister alone.

"She is in the music room," Jenkins called after him, finally slowing and no longer trying to get ahead of the tall gentleman. He shrugged. The Ingrams were used to the Mistress' brother appearing unannounced and never seemed upset with him when it happened.

Stopping at the door, William took in the sight of Georgiana in full concert mode, her head down and fingers flying over the keyboard. He was always amazed that she could coax such beautiful melodies from the same inanimate object that he played so poorly. Never had he been prouder of her or more pleased with the money spent on the music masters.

For these few precious minutes, he propped against the doorframe and listened. Until she finished, it was almost as if she were a child again, and they were at Pemberley. When she concluded the lovely concerto with a flourish, he stirred from his reverie and began applauding. She turned, blushing at his approbation.

"What are you about, sneaking up on me?" She stood and walked into his embrace. "You could have had Jenkins announce you, so I would have been aware of your presence."

"And spoil all my fun?" They both laughed. "You know I never give him the opportunity to announce me. It has become a game."

"You are getting as bad as Richard! I assure you Mr. Jenkins does not think it a game, Brother. He is rather staid."

"Well, I enjoy it, and besides, he should be used to it by now. Not to change the subject, but I understood that Mrs. Preston would leave for London this morning, and is your loving scoundrel still out of town?"

"Yes and yes. Evan will not return until Friday, and my sister left hours ago. Did you need to speak with either of them?"

"No. I actually wanted to speak to you...alone."

Georgiana's eyebrows rose, but she said nothing as she went about closing the door. Then she moved to take his hand and pulled him to sit next to her on one of the overstuffed sofas. Making herself comfortable with a pillow behind her back, she turned her full attention on him. William smiled at the grim expression on her face.

"I am afraid I have been lax in my duties to my friends. I am going to go to Netherfield for a few days to help Bingley with some problem with which he is still contending."

Georgiana tried hard not to show her disappointment. "Will you be gone long? You have just come home, and I have enjoyed having you with me again, and Evan loves having a man around to talk to, and Cecile will be coming back from London just as soon as she has met with her steward."

He laughed. "Slow down and catch your breath!"

She chuckled in spite of her sadness at the revelation he was leaving. "I am sorry. I am being silly, I know. But I love that I have my brother back, and besides, I was hoping you were about to settle down." She searched his eyes. "You realise Cecile is coming back to stay with us again only because you have led her to believe there is hope."

He looked away and then back with a steady gaze. "I like her. She is witty, fun and engaging, and she has become a friend. I have told her I would like to explore where our friendship might lead, but I have tried not to raise her expectations for more just yet."

"That is all I can ask." Georgiana said soberly. "I wish to see you happily married and living here, and I believe Cecile would further both my wishes. I cannot bear to lose you again to melancholy."

He pulled her into a hug. "I promise you will not lose me ever again. And for your information, I plan to stop in London on my way to and from Meryton. Since Mrs. Preston will be in London at the same time, I will call on her, so our getting to know each other will still progress. Besides, I will probably stay no more than a week at Netherfield, unless Bingley has gotten himself in too big of a pickle!"

She pulled back to giggle and exclaimed, "I remember that he was always prone to get into trouble and then call for you to rescue him." She shook her head. "One would hope that he had matured by now."

"I do think he has matured. He is married and has a son—but we are talking about Charles Bingley."

"I am glad to hear it. He was always a pleasant man, though so often needy."

William sobered. "He lost his father when he was quite young, and he has no uncles, so I am like an older brother to him. I only regret that I thought I had to stay away from him in order to avoid..." His voice trailed off as he realised that Georgiana had discerned the significance of his words. He had said too much.

"To avoid?" she whispered with bated breath. She had never gotten this close to understanding why her brother had felt it necessary to leave England.

"To avoid a person related to him."

William's eyes shifted away from her, and Georgiana knew he was close to retreating again. She did not want to impede the confession that had bubbled to the surface, but a part of her worried that he would return to the place of his torment.

"And you think you will be safe even if you cannot *avoid* this person now?" She heard, as well as observed, his deep intake of breath.

"I came back because *I know* I have overcome," he paused, "what I could not before. As for seeing her," he quickly corrected, "*them* again, I must face my demons to prove I have conquered them. Then I will be more than willing to consider marriage and a family."

Georgiana heard his correction. Deep down, she had known all along that only a woman could have broken his spirit. Taking solace in the fact that he had confessed to thinking of marriage, which was not something he would ever tell her unless he was seriously considering it, she squared her shoulders. Standing, she pulled him to stand with her.

"If you feel you must go, then go! Be done with it, and come back to me. I will be waiting right here for you when you return."

William leaned down to kiss her forehead. "And you will be the first person I see when I return. I love you, Gigi."

Pulling him into a tight hug, she responded, "I love you, Fitzy."

Holding him close, Georgiana could not keep her thoughts from drifting to the woman William must have encountered in Meryton.

And I will hate you forever if you hurt him again, no matter who you are!

Chapter 3

London
Darcy House

"Colonel Fitzwilliam, so good to see you, sir," Mr. Barnes declared, bowing imperceptibly as he reached to take the coat being discarded as Richard Fitzwilliam walked past.

"Thank you, Barnes. I understand my elusive cousin is in."

Not expecting a reply, Richard continued in the direction of the library. He opened the doors and seeing no one inside, closed them and proceeded towards the study with Mr. Barnes on his heels.

"The Master is in his—" The butler's words were cut short.

"Study!" Richard announced boisterously as he opened the door and spied William behind stacks of papers at his huge desk. Before William could react, Richard charged into the room.

"Darce! It has been an age! Why did you not tell me you would be in Town? Or mother? She will be furious!"

Though he had hoped for a day to catch up on business before anyone, even family, knew he was in Town, William had to grin at his cousin. Richard could always brighten his spirits. Standing, he walked around the desk to greet him with a warm hug and pat on the back.

"I only just arrived yesterday. How did you know I was here?"

"I have my spies!" Richard wagged his eyebrows. "You cannot reside at Darcy House without my knowledge."

William looked surprised, and seeing his cousin's enquiring look, Richard chuckled. He would never let on that Mrs. Barnes' rush to order from the butcher whenever Darcy was in residence, alerted the neighbourhood gossips to his presence. One particular servant at Matlock House made sure to inform him whenever his sources confirmed that William was in London. This type of diligence always garnered him great favour with the colonel.

"I shall not give away my secrets. Where would an officer be without the element of surprise?"

Choosing to ignore his cousin's jest, William backed away to look Richard up and down. According to his letter of months ago, Richard had been slightly wounded in the leg during a training manoeuvre.

"It seems you are well, as I cannot tell which of your legs was injured."

"My left! But I assure you that it is completely healed. Nevertheless, if you see me limping when we are in public, think nothing of it!" William's eyebrows raised in question. "I find that it elicits the most wonderful responses of concern from the ladies, and then I have the chance to expound on my heroism." Richard smirked, causing William to chuckle.

"You have not changed in the slightest."

16

"And you had better be thankful for that. I am the only relative you have that can make you laugh, and you dearly need to laugh!"

Precisely at that moment, Richard stopped to study his cousin. They corresponded infrequently, and he had seen William very little in the last two years—twice while he was in Scotland, and again when he met with him briefly before he made his way to Ireland. Richard realised with a start that time had not been kind, as William was thinner, and his hair was beginning to grey. His perusal continued for so long that William began to feel self-conscious.

"Richard, you are staring!"

"Sorry, Darce, but you look as though you have had a rough time of it since... well, since everything changed." No longer glib, he continued, "You left England with no notice to your family, and you stayed away nearly two years. Had I not had my duty to perform, I would have collared you and brought you back. Is there anything I should know?"

The smile left William's face as he walked back to his desk, taking his seat, and motioning for Richard to sit. Richard dropped down into one of the leather chairs in front of the desk and leaned forward, waiting for an accounting.

Seeing he would not be put off, William sighed. "It is simply that I needed to get away for a while. Get another perspective. Now, I have returned, and all is well."

Richard stared at him in disbelief for several moments before shrugging. "Very well, if you are not going to tell me what is bothering you, then tell me how Georgiana and that dandy she married are faring?"

"His name is Evan! And you know he is not a dandy. He is a gentleman and a damn fine person. You have just never forgiven him for dumping you in the creek the summer you turned sixteen."

"He did no such thing!" Richard protested. "I jumped in the creek to cool off!"

William tried not to smile. "Well, in any event, he and Georgiana are both well."

"But, alas, still no children?" William shook his head, causing Richard to continue, "I know they want a family. It is a shame that they have been unsuccessful thus far."

William's gaze toward Richard was steady. "Evan confided something that I know will cheer you, but you have to promise not to repeat this, not even to your mother."

"As an officer and a gentleman, you have my word."

William smirked. "Well, I suppose the officer portion will have to suffice!" Richard chuckled, waiting for the revelation. "Georgiana has finally agreed to seek an orphan to raise as their own. For so long, she believed that if she accepted someone else's child, it meant she was giving up the idea of having her own, and she would not hear of it." William studied something in front of him that only he could see. "I pray that she will follow through as she promised Evan. She would make a wonderful mother."

"Yes. Georgiana was born to be a mother, and I am sure there are children who need homes."

They both sat in silent contemplation for a few moments before Richard spoke excitedly. "Oh! I forgot! You are in luck! Mother is having a ball day after tomorrow for my homecoming, now that my leg," he stuck his foot out and wiggled it, "is well enough to dance. I insist you come!"

William groaned loudly, provoking Richard to laugh. "Come on, Darce! You have not been in polite society for most of two years. It will not kill you, and besides, I need your help."

"My help?"

"Yes. If you will just stand beside me, flashing those dimples that all the ladies love, I shall be put in the way of the most beautiful women in London. Surely one or two of them will find me, shall we say, interesting!"

"Richard! You are incorrigible!"

"I am not! I am in need of a beautiful lady with a large dowry to support me in the style to which I have become accustomed." At William's laugh, he declared, "I am! Just ask Mother. She has been pushing one woman after another at me for the last five years. And I mean to tell you some of them were WELL-endowed, as well as having a large dowry!"

"Then why have you not been captured by one of these *well-endowed* ladies?"

"I was not ready to abdicate my independence."

"But you are now?"

"I am ready to agree that I need to abdicate my independence." They both laughed. "Will you promise to come? I know Mother has already invited Mrs. Preston because Georgiana has instructed her to do so. Does she know something I do not? Am I to wish you joy?"

"Mrs. Preston and I are only friends. Georgiana would like us to be more."

Richard blew out a breath in relief. "Good. You can have your choice of the most beautiful women in England. Why should you choose someone so painfully plain and boring?"

Frustrated, William sighed heavily. "I am not interested in any woman at this time, Richard, but if I decide to marry, it will not be simply for beauty."

"Well, then you would certainly be safe with Mrs. Preston on that count!" William started to protest, and Richard held both hands up. "I am sorry, but I have never lied to you, and I will not begin now."

"Richard! That is enough about Mrs. Preston!"

"I assure you, not another word, if you agree to come." He pouted and William smiled.

"If I can finish my work," William motioned to the pile of papers on his desk, "I will come. But I can only stay a short time. I have to leave the next day for Meryton."

"Meryton? Why Meryton?"

"I am going to help Charles Bingley with some estate matters at Netherfield. I will not be staying long, as I have much to do at Pemberley."

"Bingley? Oh yes, the chap who married Miss Elizabeth Bennet's sister."

He watched a light turn off in William's eyes. "Did I say something wrong, Darce?"

"No." William said softly, turning so as not to face him. "Not at all."

William's countenance declared something entirely different, and it was not lost on Richard. He decided to test a theory that had been brewing in his mind for some time.

"I wonder what has become of Miss Elizabeth."

William did not answer. Instead, he diligently studied his pen as he let it roll slowly over his fingers and back again.

Richard tried anew. "I suppose she is probably married by now."

William shifted in his chair, taking a deep breath, but still did not speak. Just as Richard gave up hope of a response, he replied solemnly, "I imagine I will discover the truth of your speculation when I am at Netherfield."

Surprised to get this much from his taciturn cousin, Richard offered, "I know you admired Miss Elizabeth when we were at Rosings, and shortly after that you went away. Is she the reason you left? The reason you are going to Meryton now?"

William stood abruptly, irritated at Richard's queries. "Charles is a friend, and I have neglected him. He needs my help, and that is the only reason I am going."

"It was only a question, Cousin."

William's frame relaxed, and when their eyes met, he barely smiled. Richard moved to him, clasping him around the shoulders as they moved towards the door.

"I suppose I should leave so that you can finish and attend my mother's ball. I will see you in two days."

"Two days," William repeated.

"See that you are there, or I shall come fetch you!"

The sound of Richard's raucous laughter as he made his way through the foyer caused the corners of William's mouth to lift into a small smile, and it was not until he recalled his questions about Elizabeth that it faded away. Frowning, he went back to his desk and slumped down in his chair. Picking up the next letter, he began doing as he had always done, burying his feelings beneath the weight of his responsibilities.

London
Hurst's Townhouse

The door slammed, and Caroline flounced into the room, throwing packages on the floor. "Can we not afford a footman to carry these? Really, Louisa, it is embarrassing not to have someone to do these things for me!"

"Then I suppose you should marry a rich man who has a large number of servants. Mr. Hurst cannot afford another servant just to follow you about. Besides, have you not spent all your allowance this month?"

Caroline shrugged. "I shall have to ask Charles for more. He has plenty. Besides, I must have a new gown and accessories, as I have just heard the most wonderful news! Mr. Darcy has returned to London, and you are aware of the significance of that!"

"No. Suppose you tell me." Louisa replied sarcastically, knowing her sister would not notice her disgust.

Caroline began unwrapping the new bonnet she had bought, holding it up to inspect it in the light. "Mr. Darcy will surely visit Charles. They were always such good friends, and when he does, I shall be present."

"Caroline, the man disappeared for two years, and Charles told Mr. Hurst that he has not heard from him, so perhaps their friendship is over. Besides, he had ample opportunity to court you before he left, and he never gave you a second look."

Caroline turned to give her sister the evil eye. "When I am Mistress of Pemberley, do not think you will be invited!" She picked up her packages and bounded towards the door. "I shall be in my room writing a note to let Charles know that I am to visit."

At her departure, Louisa Hurst sank down into the sofa. "All your devious planning will come to nothing, Sister. Would that you had accepted that fool tradesman who offered for you, and I were rid of you for good!"

Matlock House
Richard's Ball

"I say, Margaret, he is even more handsome than I remembered. The gray in his temples makes him even more appealing. If I were not married . . ."

"And when has that ever stopped you, Henrietta?"

Both ladies laughed behind their fans, straining to keep watch over the handsome gentleman from Derbyshire who stood next to Colonel Fitzwilliam in the receiving line along with Lord and Lady Matlock.

"I could desire him for myself, if only I were five years younger."

Five years? Margaret Courtland thought to herself. *You would have to be twenty years younger. You are fifty, if you are a day, and Fitzwilliam Darcy is only thirty, much nearer my age.* Of course, Mrs. Courtland was past forty, though she did not like to be reminded of it.

"Oh, look!" Harriet Robbins exclaimed. "That Preston woman is greeting Mr. Darcy!"

Just at that moment, Cecile Preston had made her way to him. William smiled warmly at her, making her the envy of the entire female population of the ball. His mouth actually widened into a smile, revealing two deep dimples, and there was such a collective sigh, that many a man turned to see what the woman on his arm was going on about. Subsequently, several gentlemen removed their companions to the far corners of the room—all the better to resist temptation.

Mrs. Preston curtsied impeccably, her eyes locked on her intended prize. "I am most happy to see you again, Mr. Darcy."

"And I am equally pleased to see you, Mrs. Preston. Are you well?"

"I am in excellent health, sir. I had hoped to see you while in London. I wished to continue our discussion of the best species of ornamental plants for gardens in the northern counties. Perhaps we can do that while you are in Town."

"Unfortunately, I will be leaving tomorrow for Meryton. I will, however, come back to London before I return to Pemberley. Perhaps, if I may have the second set, we can take up our discussion where we left off and then continue when I return."

Her smile was brilliant, though it hardly improved her ordinary features. "The second set is yours, sir."

Cecile Preston moved confidently into the ballroom on the arm of her uncle, the Earl of Whiteshall. She was quite pleased to see the looks of scorn on the faces of the women who had watched her interact with Mr. Darcy. She met each set of eyes head on, nodding to let them know she was assured of her place in Mr. Darcy's company. Since her return to London, she had been diligent in spreading the news that she and the handsome bachelor had been keeping company while she stayed at her brother's estate in Derbyshire and that she was a great confidante of his sister. By this, she hoped to stave off any ladies thinking to compete for his attention now that he was back in England.

She might not be a beauty, but she prided herself on being very clever. From Georgiana, she knew the way to Mr. Darcy's heart was to let him think she was unaffected by his wealth and position. She dearly needed all that his money and connections could provide, but he must never suspect her baser motives. Thus far, she had been able to foster the impression that she had adequate wealth, but those funds were now dangerously low. If she was able to marry Fitzwilliam Darcy, she would have no trouble convincing him that her fool of a husband gambled away everything. She had already begun to disparage Owen Preston whenever given the opportunity, and she knew that he was sympathetic to her situation.

Once she secured Mr. Darcy, she could breathe easier, knowing that between her allowance and the household accounts, she could secret away enough to cover her gambling debts. Perhaps she could even sell some of the more obscure Darcy jewels she would undoubtedly inherit with her position. How she had ever gotten so far in debt to that scoundrel was beyond her, but she would curb her enthusiasm for the horses until she was Mrs. Darcy. Smiling with satisfaction, she made her way toward a group of her contemporaries. This evening was going to be a triumph. She could feel it.

"Ornamental plants?" Richard smirked, leaning in to whisper to William as they both watched Mrs. Preston depart. "You discuss plants? How romantic!"

"Hush!" William said, elbowing his cousin to shift his attention to the next person in line. There was such a throng in attendance that the receiving line took nearly an hour. With every mother having available daughters, every widow, and quite a handful of married ladies all vying for Mr. Darcy's attention, it took an extraordinary amount of time for everyone to be properly acknowledged.

For his part, William had forgotten just how painful it was to be introduced to almost every available female in London, and seemingly half of England, in one evening. However, firmly planted by his side, Richard never ceased to appreciate the magnetism of his dour cousin. While the ladies were waiting to address Mr. I-am-too-bored-to-smile Darcy, Richard carried on lively conversations with one prospect after the other, and by the end of the spectacle, had been granted a set for every dance. Finally, the last person was greeted, and the ball began in earnest.

As they moved into the room to the sound of the musicians tuning their instruments, Richard kidded, "Oh, come now, Cousin! That was not so painful." He elbowed William. "At least you are assured of one set with your botanist friend!"

William's voice was low and controlled. "Richard."

"Perhaps, you shall even discuss the need for a male and female of each species!" With that, Richard chuckled and moved toward the lovely lady who had granted him the first set, just as everyone lined up for the dance.

~~~*~~~

"Well, I do not see what he sees in that wallflower!" Mrs. Courtland sneered, having seen Mrs. Preston elicit another smile from Mr. Darcy as they danced. "She has no beauty, no figure. Why, her bosom is as flat as a child's."

"Perhaps her accomplishments lie elsewhere." Mrs. Walton retorted. "Perhaps she is proficient in the bedroom." Their cackling laughs brought several pairs of jealous eyes in their direction, all of whom were thinking the same thing but were not imprudent enough to voice it aloud.

"Look how Louise Grant is following Mr. Darcy with her eyes and likewise, Millicent Martin. If her husband turns around, he will be quite shocked."

"Oh, I doubt that, Henrietta," Mrs. Courtland retorted. "He is too busy eyeing Mrs. Pickens."

Another round of ribald laughter garnered them even more notice, so they removed themselves to an obscure corner where they could do as they pleased. As they passed Lady Flanders, they heard her berating her daughter.

"Did I not tell you years ago, Agatha, to befriend Georgiana Darcy? But did you heed my advice? No, and now she is married, and you have no entry into his circle. You might have had the rich, handsome Mr. Darcy instead of being married to your poor excuse of a husband."

Agatha responded acidly, "One would think you wanted Mr. Darcy for yourself!" She watched her mother's eyes light up at the thought. "Mother! You are twice his age!"

"I am still a woman! Besides, wisdom in certain areas can put one at greater advantage, my dear."

~~~*~~~

As William escorted the Widow Preston to supper, Richard changed his mother's seating arrangements so that he was able to sit across from them and listen in on their conversation. As a result, he learned that Mrs. Preston was quite conversant on every subject William broached. Nevertheless, as he studied William's conversation and interaction with the woman, he could see no evidence that his cousin had any feelings towards her other than friendship.

And so it went all evening, Richard following William around and making sport of his relationship with the plain Mrs. Preston, while at least a dozen handsome women openly salivated, hoping William would recognise the naked desire in their eyes. Richard sighed, thinking of how he would have loved to have had the opportunities that his cousin ignored.

I could just as easily love a rich, beautiful woman, as a rich, ugly one, and it would be much easier to take her to bed.

As if he had walked from the dark into the light, suddenly everything became perfectly clear, and Richard knew what attraction the Widow Preston held for William—she was not handsome, thus he would not fall in love with her. His stoic cousin, who had rejected every entreaty to align himself with this or that heiress for the last decade, was giving up, or at least giving in to a marriage of convenience.

But what would cause Darcy to capitulate? Of course—Georgiana! She told Mother that she is insisting that he marry and have a family because she is worried that he will fall back into melancholy. AND what caused the melancholy in the first place? Why a woman... it has to be a woman!

Richard's mind began spinning with ideas. *A woman he still loves but cannot have. That is it! He will marry someone he does not love, because he is still in love with someone he cannot have. And since it all seemed to have begun after we returned from Rosings two years ago, what woman was at Rosings that year that had never been in attendance before? Elizabeth Bennet!*

Smiling smugly, Richard looked up to see that he was all alone near the balcony. Amazingly, the people milling about him were totally unaware of the great conundrum that he had just solved. Gazing around the room, he noticed, however, that his mother was looking at him quizzically from her position among a group of ladies. He gave her a grand smile, which she immediately returned. Walking in her direction, he passed William, who was now dancing a second set with Mrs. Preston, much to the chagrin of the other ladies.

Evelyn Fitzwilliam excused herself from the group and held out her hands to her son as he approached and whispered, "I am so glad your father was civil to Fitzwilliam tonight. He has been simply inconsolable since our nephew went to Scotland instead of marrying Anne. I suppose now that she is with Catherine at Rosings, things have quieted down." She glanced at her son. "You know your father does not talk to me of his sister and her problems, since we always disagree."

"Well, I am happy my cousin did not marry that lunatic woman!"

"Richard! Watch your manners," she hissed, looking about to see if anyone heard. She leaned in to whisper, "I agree, but we do not need to make our opinions public." Richard nodded. "Besides, it is Catherine's fault that Anne is a candidate for Bedlam."

Abruptly, his mother changed the subject. "I find it difficult to grasp that Fitzwilliam is really in my house and seems so happy! I do not remember him ever dancing twice in one night with anyone not family and surely not with the same woman!" Richard dutifully turned to peruse his cousin as his mother exclaimed, "I expect we will be wishing them joy shortly!"

"I certainly hope not, Mother!"

Her brow knit in consternation. 'Why ever would you say such a thing? I thought you wanted him to be happy."

"That is why I object! Mrs. Preston will never accomplish that, as he is not in love with her. He will be without any prospect of felicity."

"How can you say that? She is an excellent choice. She is a respected member of society with wealth and connections, and she knows how to be mistress of an estate. True, she is no beauty, but he may come to care for her. Love is not necessary in a marriage!"

"I know all her qualifications, Mother! If she were a horse, she would suffice!"

"Richard!"

"It is true! I know my cousin better than anyone. He is of a peculiar kind, and he needs a woman he loves and who loves him. As it is, he is heartbroken over another, and if he marries that woman, it will be only to make Georgiana happy, while it will make him utterly miserable."

"How do you know he is heartbroken over another?"

"Why do you think he has hidden away the last two years, and now, suddenly, agrees to consider marriage to that—to someone he does not love?"

"Why indeed?" she replied, awaiting Richard's explanation as her eyes returned to Fitzwilliam with new insight.

"He thinks it will help him to forget the one he regrets."

"And you know this woman?"

"He was in her company when last we were at Rosings together, two years past. He was not himself the entire time, and I began to see how he stared at the young lady, even becoming tongue-tied in her presence. Something happened between them the last day we were there, but he would not confide in me. After we returned, I had to report for duty, and he disappeared."

Lady Matlock stopped to thoroughly study her nephew for the first time tonight. She observed the now obvious grey in his hair, the lines around his light blue eyes, and she saw that the smile on William's face did not reach those eyes. When no one was looking, his face always fell back into the same, solemn mien.

"I hope you are not correct."

"Would that I was not, Mother, because he seems determined to seal his fate."

~~~*~~~

As William's carriage pulled into position in front of Matlock House, Richard stayed his cousin by grabbing his arm. "Darce?"

William halted and turned back to face him. He was tired and really did not want to answer any more of Richard's questions. Though he meant well, his cousin was just too inquisitive.

"Are you truly well?" Richard searched for the right words. "You seem so distant. I could not be with you after we returned from Rosings. I had to be at camp for manoeuvres shortly after that, and when I returned, you had already departed for Scotland. I feel as though I failed you."

William grasped Richard's shoulder and hugged him tightly, as they used to do when they were boys. Neither let go for a long period, but finally William drew back to lock eyes with his cousin.

"You have never failed me, Richard. I have always known I could count on you and that means everything to me. You are the brother I never had, and I love you."

"I love you, too. I just wish I knew how to help you."

"You do help me. You make me smile, and that means a great deal." William shook his hand. "I will call on you when I come back from Netherfield, if you are still in Town."

"Oh, I will be here! I have to get to bed quickly because Mother has several more ladies she is anxious for me to charm, beginning tomorrow."

Shaking his head, William entered the carriage but leaned back out the window to add, "Far be it from me to interrupt your beauty rest, and you will need all your strength, I imagine! Good night, Richard." Tapping the roof of the carriage with his cane, it began to roll forward.

"Good night, Darce! Call on me when you return!"

As the conveyance got smaller in the distance, Richard whispered, "And may you find what you need at Meryton, my friend."

~~~*~~~

Chapter 4

Jane carefully closed and locked the door to Charles' study before speaking. It took great effort to remember not to say anything loud enough that a servant might overhear and have his suspicion raised. According to Mrs. Watkins, there was already plenty of speculation among the servants that Netherfield was haunted. They had spirited Lizzy into the mansion at night, keeping her isolated in rooms on the third floor. When she first escaped her room, she was seen walking about the grounds by one of the maids and with her pale skin, dark hair, and white gown, she certainly looked ethereal, almost ghostlike. The Bingleys were hopeful that talk of apparitions would cover the truth of her existence.

"Charles, I have instructed Mrs. Drury that it is imperative Lizzy stay in her rooms while Mr. Darcy is visiting. I pray she is able to keep her in bed during the night and calm during the day with the herbal potion Mrs. Watkins created. If she sleeps a goodly amount, we may be able to keep him from suspecting anything."

Charles nodded. "Mrs. Watkins swears by those herbs. Let us hope they work."

"I pray you are quickly able to ascertain the likelihood of Mr. Darcy's help. I do not know how long we can keep her hidden with him under our roof."

Seeing the worry in Jane's eyes, Charles pulled her into his embrace and rested his head atop hers. "Have faith. I believe Darcy may be the answer to our prayers. Pemberley is very remote, tucked away in the mountains with acres of land comprising the estate. If Lizzy were there, she could be hidden practically forever, both from society and those who would do her harm."

"As if she were dead."

The catch in Jane's voice pierced his heart, and Charles leaned down to kiss her forehead. Lizzy's situation had taken a great toll on his wife, and he would do anything to find a solution.

"Surely, sweetheart, you know it was best that everyone thought Lizzy died in the fire."

"My mind knows that." She began to cry. "But with her present condition, my heart breaks. I feel as though I have lost my sister already."

"Jane, look at me," he whispered, tipping her chin up and waiting until her teary blue eyes met his. "You worry that she will never get better, but I believe that she will. Love can make all the difference in the world. We must have faith that love will bring Lizzy back to us. We must believe for her... be strong for her."

He waited for her to acknowledge his words. "I will try, Charles. Remind me when I falter."

"I will. Now Darcy will be here shortly, and we cannot have him suspect anything." He kissed her gently on the nose as one hand played with a tendril of her hair. "How good an actress are you? Are you going to be convincing?"

"I will try for Lizzy." She took a lace handkerchief from her pocket and dried her eyes. "There." She nodded her head sharply. "I am ready." Charles smiled at her red nose and swollen eyes.

"My brave wife. I want you to know how much I respect your loyalty to Lizzy. It is admirable how you care for our sister." Jane's face softened. "It makes me proud to know you are my wife and the mother of my child."

"Oh, Charles!" She began to weep anew. "Now see what you have done."

~~~*~~~

William's coach was late, and it was not until darkness began to fall that it pulled up in front of Netherfield. After being greeted warmly by his hosts, he immediately retreated to his room to prepare for dinner. Bathed and dressed, he made his way back downstairs to find Charles alone in the drawing room. As he entered, Bingley stood to pour two small glasses of brandy and studied his friend's appearance as he handed one to him. He took note of William's weight loss, greying hair, and the deep lines around his eyes. Oblivious to his perusal, William asked a question.

"Did my presence keep Mrs. Bingley from coming down for dinner?" His voice sounded teasing, but the look on his face showed true unease. Charles was quick to respond, realising William might think Jane held a grudge for his part in separating them initially.

"Peter was fretful, and she had to attend him. She will be down shortly, and then we shall dine."

Having seen Charles' son when he arrived, a smaller version of his father with the same red curls, William said pensively, "You have a fine boy. He looks very much like you."

At Charles' pleased nod, he stated quietly, "You seem truly happy and content."

"I am. Jane made me the happiest of men when she became my wife, and now she has given me Peter."

"That is indeed a wonderful gift." William added a little wistfully, "Would that I had a son." Swirling the liquid in his glass, he studied it seriously before adding, "I am exceedingly sorry that I only recently read your letters, Charles."

William took a deep breath. "I had... I was trying to solve a problem for which I could find no resolution. I decided, quite impulsively, to visit my property in Scotland. From there, it seemed only natural to check on my estate in Ireland before returning home. I never meant to be away so long or neglect my friends."

Charles responded sympathetically. "I understand, truly I do. Sometimes life brings problems our way that seem insurmountable at the time, and we must do whatever it takes to get through them."

William studied his friend with new appreciation. "I am thankful for your understanding and insight." Charles could only nod, very aware that William had no idea how the last few months had lead to that epiphany.

"Once I read your letters, I realised how selfish I had been to stay away so long without a word, but at the time I was blind."

"I believe you," Charles offered, moving to pat his back. "Do not apologise. You have explained why you were out of touch and why I did not receive a reply from you. We are friends, so all is well."

"Once again, I have asked forgiveness, and you have been generous in granting it." William reached to clasp Charles' hand. "You are a true friend."

Jane walked into the room to see her husband and William with hands clasped and could not help but smile at the scene. "We are so glad you have come at last, Mr. Darcy."

"William," he said softly.

"And you must call me *Jane*."

William nodded just as the dinner bell sounded, and Charles moved to offer his arm to his wife.

"Come, Darcy! You must be starved—spending days on the road with only the inns to rely on for meals. Our cook does wonders with pheasant and bakes an apple tart to rival any I have ever eaten!"

~~~*~~~

The last course was being served and the Bingleys and Fitzwilliam Darcy had managed to talk about anything and everything, without touching on the subject of the Bennets. During the entire meal, William had hoped Charles would mention them, so he could learn what had happened to Elizabeth. Instead, his host had rattled on and on about the problems he was having with proper land drainage and the solutions his newly hired steward had suggested.

Whenever William chanced to look at Jane, she was usually watching Charles. She was perfectly amiable when spoken to, but he got the impression she was trying not to say anything amiss.

The dinner was nearing the end, and they were enjoying the apple tart Charles had bragged about earlier, when William ventured to ask after the Bennets. He had no way of anticipating the floodgate of emotions that question would release as he addressed Jane nonchalantly.

"Are your mother and sisters in good health? Do they still reside in Meryton?"

Jane's fork stopped in midair, and he thought he saw her hand tremble. She glanced to her husband but did not reply, so Charles answered in her stead.

"They are well. Mrs. Bennet purchased a home here. Mary is now married to Mr. Phillips' law clerk and Lydia and Kitty are... well they are still silly, just older." William noticed Charles' smile fade but saw it quickly replaced with a forced one.

As William looked between the couple, he surmised that something was wrong, but he could not help asking, "And Miss Elizabeth? I assume she is married with a child of her own by now."

A sob escaped from Jane, as she rose and ran from the room. Both men stared at the door through which she disappeared.

"Charles, I am sorry if I said—"

Charles' hand in mid-air stopped William. "You are not to blame, Darcy. Let us go into my study, and I will explain." They stood, and William silently followed his friend out of the room, puzzled by what had just transpired.

~~~*~~~

After Charles had poured each of them a full glass of brandy, he motioned for William to have a seat and wearily sank down on the sofa across from him. Their eyes met, but Charles looked away, trying to gather his thoughts. He could relate only what had happened to Lizzy up to a certain point, then he would lie to protect her until he was sure of William's cooperation.

Taking a deep breath, Charles looked back at his friend. His drink had not been touched, and his eyes were still locked on him. The decisive moment had arrived. *Does he still care enough for Lizzy to help her?* Charles wondered.

No longer patient, William slid to the edge of his seat, leaning forward. "Where is she, Charles?"

"I suppose, being out of England, you have not heard." William's head slowly moved back and forth. "Steel yourself, my friend."

"Charles!" William sounded more desperate than angry.

"Elizabeth is dead."

The glass of brandy William was holding hit the floor.

William started to speak, looked about dazed and then stood. Showing no concern for the broken glass, he managed to walk to a window, where he clung to the frame, looking faint. Charles rang for a servant to clean up the spill, and afterward poured another glass of brandy and brought it to him. Without turning, William took it and drank the entire glass, grimacing as it burned his throat.

With much anguish he forced out, "How?"

"It is a long story and not very pretty. You have had a long trip today, my friend. Why do we not get some sleep, and I will explain everything tomorrow?"

"No!"

Charles startled at the ferocity of the outburst. Then he relaxed as, head hanging down in defeat, William pleaded in a defeated whisper, "Please! I must know. I will not sleep until I know."

Charles squeezed his friend's shoulder. "Then let us sit down. It will take some time to tell everything." Charles led William, who seemed in a fog, to a chair near the fireplace, taking the one next to it.

"It began right after I left for London. Lizzy went to visit her friend, Charlotte Collins, in Kent." He saw William's jaw tighten. "According to Jane, while she was gone a gentleman leased Monteagle, supposedly to use it as a hunting lodge. He was half-English and half-Italian, Count Stefano Gianni Montalvo de Cavour, if I have pronounced his name correctly."

William said nothing, but his eyes burned into Charles as he continued. "He is about eight and thirty, blond and quite handsome, I am told." William frowned at the description.

"Jane said that, at first, he appeared very amiable, and after it was bandied about that he was wealthy and unmarried, her mother and every other mother in Meryton set about pushing their single daughters in his path. Count Stefano began to attend the assemblies and danced with many an available lady. He even danced with my Jane, but to Mrs. Bennet's chagrin, after he spied Lizzy, he singled her out for his attention."

William stiffened and turned as if to study the flames leaping from the charred logs in the fireplace, but Charles was convinced that he was listening by the white of his knuckles as he gripped the arms of the chair.

"Jane thinks the count was drawn to Lizzy because she wanted no part of him. She told me that when Lizzy came back from Kent, it was with a deep sadness. She was not the impertinent, teasing girl who had left. She had no tolerance for flattery, his least of all. She saw right through his easy manner and was quick to point out his inconsistencies. It seems the more she resisted the man, however, the more Count Stefano pursued her. When he could get no satisfaction with his attentions, he asked Mr. Bennet's permission to court her, even without Lizzy's consent."

"Mrs. Bennet, of course, was eager to force the match, but Mr. Bennet would not make Lizzy agree to a courtship. Jane said Mr. Bennet did not trust the man; thus, he was thwarted. With Mr. Bennet's untimely death, however, Mrs. Bennet went absolutely mad. She fretted and cried over Mr. Collins' taking possession of Longbourn. You remember him, do you not?"

William nodded, recalling the simpering idiot his aunt had named as her rector.

"I suppose she was right in that regard. That worm barely waited until Mr. Bennet was cold in his grave before he appeared to claim his inheritance. He said Lady Catherine de Bourgh encouraged him to immediately take what was rightfully his."

William stood and began to pace, clenching and unclenching his fists, livid that his aunt had interfered so cruelly. "Vicious woman!"

Witnessing William's ire, Charles swallowed a large lump in his throat to continue. "After that, Mrs. Bennet would not cease lamenting that if Lizzy had performed her duty and married Mr. Collins, they would not have found themselves in such a quandary. Jane tried to point out that she, too, could have married Collins, but Mrs. Bennet would not hear of it. She said Jane was too beautiful for him, and that she was destined for a rich man, but that Lizzy should have been sensible."

Charles shook his head in wonder. "It could have been my Jane forced into a loveless marriage with either of those... I should never have left." Unspoken was the fact that William was largely responsible for the departure that left the Bennets so vulnerable. Lost in unpleasant memories for the moment, Charles rose and walked over to stare into the darkness outside, trying to compose himself.

"Jane says it was right after Lizzy turned down the count a second time that she disappeared."

At this, William stopped pacing. "Disappeared?"

"Yes. Lizzy just disappeared, and suddenly Mrs. Bennet was rich, five thousand pounds richer, if her bragging is to be believed. She even began shopping for a house. Knowing all of this, Jane was almost hysterical... fearful of what might have happened to her sister."

Charles shuddered in remembrance. "Her mother was totally unconcerned for Lizzy. It was only after Jane threatened to go in search of her, that Mrs. Bennet admitted she had given her permission for the count to marry her. She claims Lizzy consented, and they left immediately for Gretna Green. Jane says it is impossible for Lizzy to have consented, as she loathed him."

William scowled and his face became even more sombre at the revelation that Elizabeth had been taken away against her will. It was not lost on Charles.

"I promised Jane I would do everything in my power to locate Lizzy. Right after we married, I hired a retired investigator from the Bow Street Runners, but he could find no trace of either of them. If the count was still in England, he was not in London. I had my investigator look throughout the surrounding counties, but I simply did not know where else to begin searching." He shook his head as if remembering. Then Charles' face hardened, and he barely resembled the amiable man William knew.

"We had just about given up, when it happened."

William's voice was rough with emotion. "What?"

"A man appeared at our door, carrying a letter for Jane. It happened that his aunt had worked as a housekeeper for the count." William tried to brace himself as Charles turned away, not willing to look William in the eyes, while he lied to protect his sister.

"She informed us that Lizzy had been living near Sheffield, at an estate owned by Count Stefano—Northgate, it is called. There was some type of altercation, Lizzy was harmed and the mansion set afire. Lizzy died either from her injuries or the fire."

William groaned and sank down onto a sofa, head in hands. "Oh, God!"

Charles moved to him, squeezing his shoulder as William continued to cradle his head in his hands, shaking visibly.

"We retrieved the body and buried Lizzy here in the churchyard, next to her father." William barely nodded, still hiding his face in his hands.

"I... I will leave you to your grief." Charles walked over to the door and looked back to see him in the same position.

Time will reveal the truth of the situation. Did Darcy love Lizzy? Does he still? Not sure he was doing the right thing, Charles left William alone.

That night William finished the rest of the bottle of brandy and finally fell into a fitful sleep, lying on the sofa. Nightmares of Lizzy raced though his troubled mind, and he awoke frequently with tears in his eyes. Finding himself wide awake just before dawn, he struggled to his room to change clothes. He had to see her grave, or he would never accept she was gone.

Thus, the first rays of daylight found him walking through the mist hovering near the ground as he made his way to the stables.

~~~*~~~

John Williamson resided in a cottage behind the Meryton church he had served as vicar for forty years before his retirement. The present vicar, Mr. Clary, had a large family and needed a bigger house, so he lived in town. Mr. Williamson, in addition to filling in for Mr. Clary when the need arose, kept watch over the building and grounds in exchange for being allowed to stay in the smaller house. He dearly loved living near the church where he preached his first sermon and where his dear wife, sister and parents rested in the cemetery beyond.

As was his habit, he rose before dawn to go into the church to pray. He found he was disturbed in his morning prayers less often at that hour, since so many of his parishioners still stopped by the cottage to talk with him if they had a need or were just in the neighbourhood. Mr. Clary was not jealous of his relationship with the parishioners, and frankly, was glad for his assistance. With the growing number of people in the parish, his help was gratefully accepted.

On this particular morning, the sky was still quite dark. Streaks of orange, red and purple were just beginning to appear on the horizon, and Mr. Williamson shivered a little in the chilly air. As happened every morning, the mist rose like a fog from the ground, hiding his shoes as he came down his front steps. Swiftly making his way around to the front of the chapel, he could barely discern the outline of a horse tethered to a tree on the opposite side, near the cemetery. Unused to anyone being about at this hour, he walked toward the animal, hoping to find the rider. As he drew nearer, he heard an anguished cry coming from somewhere in the cemetery. It sounded so distraught that he wondered if he could be of help and thus moved in that direction.

Daylight now began to illuminate the headstones, and he carefully picked his way back to the corner where someone knelt near one of the newer graves. Just recently a stone had been set, engraved with a name that he knew well.

Ah, he is visiting Lizzybet! Immediately the image of a dark-haired imp with laughing eyes made his eyes glisten with tears. *How well I remember you, my sweet girl.*

In his grief, the young man did not hear Mr. Williamson approach, so the old vicar stopped to observe, trying to determine when or if to intervene.

Suddenly the younger man cried out, "Oh Elizabeth! Why could you not have accepted me? I would never have let anyone harm you!"

Then he lowered his head into his hands, crying, and new tears appeared in the old vicar's eyes as well.

He ventured softly, "She was my favourite, too."

William jerked his head around at the sound. A tall, lanky, white-haired man with kindly brown eyes stood behind him. Turning back around swiftly, he began wiping his eyes self-consciously.

"Do not mind me, son. Cry all you want—she is worthy of your tears. I have cried for months, ever since I was notified of her death. Lizzybet was a great pal of mine."

William got to his feet, brushed the dirt from his knees and turned to face the man. His voice was barely audible. "Lizzybet?"

"That was how she pronounced her name when she was just beginning to talk." He chuckled. "I never called her by any other."

William whispered hoarsely, his voice quivering and tears threatening again. "You knew her well then?"

The vicar stared past him then into the darkness. "She was like my own child." Then looking back to the man who now needed his comfort, he forced himself to continue in spite of his own pain.

"I was vicar here when she was born. I christened her. She had the prettiest chocolate curls even then. I watched her grow into a precocious child who sat in my lap and tried to read from the Bible." Shaking his head in awe, he continued, "Later, she became quite the fearless adventurer, leading the likes of my son, John Lucas, and David Watts into battle with sticks for swords, and God forbid one of them should try to be the leader." This elicited a small smile from William.

Then his face softened. "Before I realised, she had become a beautiful young woman. She would talk with me quite often. She asked about everything—how to sketch a man's character, how to know you were in love. She had begun to garner attention from some of the young men, and I think she wanted a man's perspective. She could not talk to her mother, and her father would make a joke of her concerns." He glanced at William and saw the face of someone deeply mourning a woman.

Looking back to her grave, the vicar sighed. "I looked forward to marrying her to a man worthy of her." They both stood silent for some time, each with his own regrets.

"After her father died, those who should have loved my Lizzybet failed her. It broke my heart when I was asked to conduct her funeral." He shook his head as his own tears flowed unchecked. "Such a waste of a precious, delightful life."

He looked up then to see an expression of unadulterated pain on the gentleman's face. *This man surely loved her.*

"Would you care to have a cup of tea? If you do, I could tell you how she talked Charlotte and Jane into helping her to christen a cat and ended up wrecking the altar right before Easter."

William could not hold back a little chuckle, though tears still slid down his face.

The elderly man put an arm around the younger man's shoulder, and they walked together towards the cottage. "Perhaps you would like to hear about the time the green snake she caught just that morning, waited until my sermon to crawl out of her pocket and onto Frances Bennet's lap? I thought quickly and asked her to bring the snake up front—not lying, mind you—but letting everyone assume I asked her to bring it to church as an illustration for my message. I promptly changed my sermon to expound on that deceitful snake, Satan."

The vicar laughed wholeheartedly now and felt William take a shaky breath, then shudder as it was released. Morning prayers could wait. Ministering to the suffering took precedence this morning.

~~~*~~~

Chapter 5

Netherfield

Charles and Jane ate mostly in silence, each lost in his own thoughts of what would happen when they told William about Lizzy. Charles had related the discussion he and William had that morning, after William's return from the cemetery.

"Darcy, I was just about to mount a search party to go look for you." He put an arm around his friend, leading him into the drawing room and pulling the door shut. *"You have been gone most of the day. Are you well?"*

"I had to visit Elizabeth's..." Charles knew what William could not voice. *"It was not real to me until I saw for myself. Forgive me if I was inconsiderate in being gone so long, but I was invited to Mr. Williamson's home, and we talked at length."*

Charles nodded his understanding. He was beginning to think he should have just told Darcy the entire truth and asked for his help—but no! He and Jane had agreed to wait until they were absolutely sure.

"I enjoyed meeting Mr. Williamson." William ventured as he stared straight ahead, focusing on something only he could see. *"He was very kind."*

His small smile almost reached his eyes. "He told me tale after tale of Elizabeth as a child and young girl. He called her Lizzybet, because that is how she pronounced her name when she was small." He shook his in head in wonder. *"She was really quite unique."* A sad expression crept across his face as he stated wistfully, *"He misses her, too."*

"Mr. Williamson is a good man. I do not know how Jane and I would have coped without him."

"He mentioned Jane, Charlotte Lucas and many others. It seems he christened most of Meryton." William tried to chuckle, but did not quite succeed. *"I have much to ponder. If you do not mind, I would like to rest in my room today. If you want a consultation on your estate matters, I will make myself available in the morning."*

Finally Jane broke the silence. "I imagine William will want to return to Pemberley soon."

"Yes. He mentioned talking over the estate problems in the morning, and I got the impression he was eager to finish and be gone. So if we decide to tell him, it must be done quickly."

"From what you say, William seems devastated. Does that not signify that he would be willing to help us?" Jane's heart began pounding rapidly. She was not sure her reaction was relief that he might help them or regret for having to involve him.

"I believe we have to go with our instincts and trust Darcy. After what I have observed, he must have been in love with her and still cares deeply."

"I feel dreadful that we had to deceive him." She studied her plate, pushing the food about with her fork but not eating. "And even worse to use his feelings to entrap him in this ordeal. I wish we could have handled it on our own."

33

"Sweetheart, we have done our best, but circumstances dictate we must find another residence for her. Can you imagine being able to keep this from Caroline, and she is determined to come. Besides, I truly believe Darcy would want to know she is alive and help her in every possible way."

"But that will effectively sentence him to ..."

She hesitated, and Charles finished for her, "Possibly a lifetime of caring for her. He would, most likely, never marry, as no woman would accept a man who keeps another woman at his estate—and a married one, at that."

He threw his napkin down in disgust. "And if the truth is ever revealed, people will assume she is his mistress."

"It is a lot to ask." Jane laid down her fork. "I am not hungry."

Charles pushed back from the table. "Neither am I."

He stood, reaching a hand out to her. "We will tell him tomorrow. Come, let us visit Peter. Perhaps that will lift our spirits."

~~~*~~~

William lay on his bed, staring at the ceiling and trying to sort his feelings. He had seen her name carved in stone; it was real. Nevertheless, what his mind acknowledged, his heart still refused.

Every time he was left alone to contemplate, Elizabeth appeared—laughing and teasing. His memory replayed every conversation they had ever had. If only he had known during their earliest acquaintance that her witty replies were veiled digs at his arrogance—instead of learning her true feelings at Kent.

I wish I knew if she had at least believed my explanation for separating Jane and Charles.

His thoughts drifted to Mrs. Preston. Try as he might, he could find no feelings for her other than friendship. Though she was pleasant enough, there was nothing extraordinary about her. When she smiled, her grey eyes faded into her light complexion. They did not light up, tugging at his heartstrings, as a dark brown pair had. He realised then that her greatest appeal was the fact that, other than being an acceptable match, Mrs. Preston would not expect his love...for he would never love another woman.

Georgiana's laughing face came to mind then. She would be greatly disappointed if he did not follow through with a courtship of her widowed sister. Did he owe her feelings at least some consideration? After all, Georgiana only had his welfare in mind, and he already knew what she would advise: The past is behind. Settle for what is right before you.

Settle. How does one teach a heart to settle for someone it does not want?

He blinked away hot tears as a pair of fine eyes came to mind, and he heard the music of her laughter. Turning on his stomach, he buried his head in a pillow just in case anyone could hear.

~~~*~~~

Stormy weather woke William hours later. It was night, and though he tried, he could not fall back into his restless dreams. For over an hour, he lay watching the deluge clearly visible through the French doors leading to the terrace. Fierce winds blew rain, leaves, and twigs sideways across the portico and bent smaller trees in half. Every so often, a succession of intense lightning strikes would flash across the sky, followed by thunder that shook the windows and doors ferociously. Nevertheless, the storm raging outside was nothing compared to the one raging inside him. Immediately upon awakening, his mind had raced to a single thought. *I will never see her again.*

Most painful was the realisation that Elizabeth had been dead for months, and he had not known. Over the few months since he had decided to come home to England, he had worked out what he would say were they to meet—how he would act—only to find out it had all been pointless. She was already dead, even as he practiced his lines.

His father had told him once that he knew the exact moment his mother passed. He explained that he had risen from his bed and gone into her bedroom, knowing she would not be there. The only evidence of the woman he loved was the body she had occupied while on earth. Tears rolled from the corners of William's eyes. He remembered that night well. He had felt as though his heart had been ripped from his chest when his father awakened him to go into her room and say his goodbyes. He had experienced that feeling once more when his dear father died, but never again, until now.

How could I ever have thought I was over you, Elizabeth!

No longer able to bear it, William slipped out of bed, grabbed his robe and found the shoes he wore in his bedchamber. Adding more logs to the waning fire, he stoked it until it burned hot again, then moved to the French doors, hoping to be distracted by watching the display of nature.

However, just as he reached the door, a bolt of lightning lit up the terrace, and William found himself staring into the face of a woman on the other side. Her white gown was wet and clung to her body. Some of her long dark hair was plastered around her face, but the rest blew wildly in every direction. She was extremely pale, and as her dark eyes met his, a strangled cry escaped his throat.

"Elizabeth!"

Just as quickly as the lightning subsided, it was pitch black. The encounter shocked him enormously, and he took a step back, his heart beating wildly.

Am I hallucinating? He rubbed his eyes with the palms of his hands before fixing his gaze once more on the glass separating him from the tempest raging beyond. *It must be my imagination! She cannot be there!*

Another brilliant flash of lightning appeared, and this time when the terrace lit up, he saw a flash of white flying down the steps towards the garden. Without hesitating, he unlocked the doors, throwing them open, and ran in the same direction. With his long legs it did not take him long to catch sight of her again, and in another seventy-five feet, he stopped abruptly. She had stilled, her arms stretched overhead, eyes closed and face turned skyward. Streams of tears mingled with the rain flowing down her face.

Suddenly lightning struck a tree not too far away, causing a limb to break and come crashing down. Recognising she was in harm's way, William closed the gap between them, quickly catching her in his arms. Finding that she was truly flesh and blood and not a fantasy come to haunt him, his heart filled with joy. It took all his strength to keep from crying as he clutched her to his chest, his head buried in her hair. Then, gaining his senses, he quickly stirred, carrying her towards safety.

Elizabeth began flailing at him, trying to escape his grasp, which induced him to tighten his grip and try soothing her as he had a young Georgiana when she had nightmares, whispering in her ear. "Shhh, Elizabeth. It is Fitzwilliam. I will not hurt you. Hush, Lizzybet, calm yourself. All will be well. You are safe, sweetheart."

He continued his soothing words, and as they reached the terrace, something seemed to register in Elizabeth's subconscious. She quit fighting him, looking up as if she were seeing him for the first time. Then her arms went around him, and she hid her face in the crook of his neck and sobbed as if her heart would break. Stunned, he stilled for just a moment. Then recovering, he continued on through the open doors. Once inside, he kicked the doors shut and tried to set her down, but she would not let go, clinging to him fiercely.

Thus thwarted, he moved to the settee nearest the now roaring fire. Sitting down, Elizabeth in his lap, he grabbed the blanket lying across the back and wrapped it around her, taking note of her cold, bare feet. He knew she could not stay in wet clothes for long, but he hoped to gain her trust, and then summon Jane. His mind was full of questions, but his heart was so full of love, that all he could focus on was the woman in his arms. He held her tightly to his chest, rocking her gently back and forth, continuing to whisper words of comfort, even as everything he had heard and seen in the last two days raced through his mind.

Eventually he felt her grip on his robe loosen and her breath become steady. Allowing her head to slide back into the crook of his arm, he peered into her sleeping face and his breath caught. She was still beautiful, but this was not the face he remembered. She was thin and pale, which made her dark lashes and eyebrows appear black. She had blue circles under her eyes and her lips, which he remembered as the colour of berries, were pale. She looked much older than her years, and his heart broke for what she must have endured since last he had seen her.

Able to think more clearly with her asleep, he seethed with the knowledge that Charles had deceived him. To what end? And why would Elizabeth be running around outside in the middle of the night, apparently ill? His thoughts were interrupted by soft moans and his eyes darted back to her. Gathering her to his body, he lifted her gently, and carried her over to the bed. She must have been exhausted, as she did not wake when he moved her or laid her on the soft sheets.

Pulling the blanket and counterpane over her, he quickly shed the wet robe and night shirt he was wearing, replacing them with others from his closet and sat on the edge of the bed, not ready to relinquish the sight of her just yet. For several minutes, he let his fingers trace the planes of her face, pushing wet curls away from her eyes and playing with the long tendrils of hair lying on her pillow. Lifting one lone curl, he brought it to his nose. It smelled of lavender. Tears threatened as he remembered that the only time he had smelled that fragrance in a woman's hair it had been Elizabeth's.

Sudden loud voices in the hallway interrupted his reverie, and he realised it was time to declare her presence, as they needed to get her into dry clothes and her own bed. Then he would have a confrontation with Charles.

Charles' Study

"You let me go through hell, thinking her dead!" William paced back and forth in front of Charles and Jane, who were also standing. "I…. I grieved at her graveside." A strangled cry tried to escape, and he covered his face with his hands and turned, not wanting them to see his tears.

Charles and Jane exchanged tortured glances as William struggled to compose himself. Finally able to continue, he swung around.

"And you call me your friend, Charles! What evil possessed you to send for me, only to carry out this hateful charade?"

"I am so sorry, Darcy. We felt it best—"

"**Felt**?" William fumed as he stalked towards Charles, coming to a halt in his face. "What about what *I* felt? You do not know how I have agonised over her in the last two years, how much I have wanted to see her, to hear her laugh again."

Jane pushed in between the two men, causing William to step back. "I know exactly! I was without my sister for those two years as well!"

"Then, if you know the extent of my agony, why would you put me through this...this pretence? Telling me she was dead and leaving me no hope!"

"She was taken from me, without so much as a goodbye, and I could not find her! Only through the kindness of a servant was she recovered, gravely ill. I would not chance **that man** learning Lizzy was still alive, so I insisted we tell only those necessary...those we could trust."

"And you could not trust me?" William retorted, waving his arms about in disgust. "What a recommendation! Why did you even condescend to invite me here?"

"Go ahead! Rage at us, if it makes you feel better! But I would do it all again to protect my sister!" Jane shouted, tears now coursing down.

Charles moved beside Jane, sliding his arm around her shoulders and declaring, "We are truly sorry to have lied to you, but we felt we had no alternative. We have fostered the lie that she is dead for her own good. The Count is ruthless!"

Fearlessly, Jane stepped forward again, pleading, "You saw what we are up against, trying to keep her in her rooms. We do not have enough trusted servants to have her watched night and day. God knows Mrs. Drury cannot do it around the clock, and I cannot while also tending to Peter. Most of our servants are local people, and they have family in Meryton. Can you imagine what would happen if my mother found out? I fear that she might have sold her to that tyrant! And just today, we learned that Caroline is coming to Netherfield."

Taking another ragged breath, she declared, "Count Stefano may stop at nothing if he finds she is alive. He thought he had killed her when he left her to burn at Northgate, so will he try to finish the job?" Having exhausted all arguments, she covered her face with her hands, and her body shook with uncontrollable sobs.

Charles turned Jane around, pulling her into a tight embrace and patted her back, trying to soothe her. His eyes locked with William's, and calmer now, he stated with resignation, "We have tried, but we cannot keep her hidden. With Caroline determined to visit, it is inevitable that she will be exposed."

William turned to gather his composure, feeling shame that he had taken his anger out on Jane and Charles. While their deception had been cruel, it had been done to keep Elizabeth safe. Besides, was he not, even now, thinking of how to accomplish the same thing? Taking a deep breath, he turned to face them.

"I apologise. I should have listened to your explanation before I spoke. It was just such a shock to see her. I.... I thought Elizabeth was gone forever."

Hope appeared for the first time on the faces of Jane and Charles, and William's voice was kinder as he ventured, "Does the woman who informed you of Elizabeth's plight know where the count went?"

"No." Charles sighed. "He apparently set the fire and then left the county, perhaps the country. He has not returned, as the housekeeper promised to alert us if he should. We do not know where he is now. He could be anywhere, perhaps even in Italy, where his mother was born, and he might be using another name."

"Or perhaps he is, even now, aware that he did not succeed in killing her and is trying to find Lizzy," Jane whispered fearfully.

Her words made William shiver. The thought of such evil ever having control over Elizabeth made him sick to his stomach.

"If it makes any difference, we had decided we would tell you the truth in the morning." Charles' words penetrated William's thoughts, and he turned to see both Bingleys studying him. "It seemed you—we prayed you still cared enough about Elizabeth to..."

William knew what they intended. "You want me to take Elizabeth to Pemberley." It was a statement, not a question.

Jane shared a glance at Charles. "Yes. Her reaction to you was astonishing. Elizabeth will not let any other man near her, not even Charles. Somewhere inside, she must feel safe with you. Even if she should escape the manor, Charles says Pemberley's holdings are so extensive that the likelihood of her being seen by someone outside the grounds is small. Here in Meryton, she remembers all the places she used to walk, and she tries to go back there, even to Longbourn."

William turned back to the windows and studied the storm outside. He was full of questions that needed answering.

"The last time I saw Elizabeth, she said I was the last man on earth she could ever be prevailed upon to marry. What is to prevent her suddenly remembering that she does not like me and trying to leave?"

"I can answer that truthfully, as my sister told me of your ill-fated proposal."

William dropped his head, somewhat embarrassed that Jane, and probably Charles, knew everything that had transpired between them.

"When Lizzy returned from Kent, she was heartbroken. She told me of your proposal and admitted that her temper had controlled her response. Her wounded pride had coloured her opinion of you from the very beginning, and she was ashamed of her behaviour. After reading your letter, she understood why you felt as you did about Charles and me, though you were mistaken."

William glanced over his shoulder to meet her steady gaze. He nodded.

"She regretted what she said. She realised too late that she was in love with you."

William's head lifted as his heart sank. *She loved me. If only I had returned to Meryton instead of leaving for Scotland, how different our lives would have been.* His thoughts flew immediately to Georgiana. *She is counting on my courtship of Mrs. Preston, of my marrying and having a family.*

If he took Elizabeth to Pemberley, he would be giving up the prospect of a future with another woman, and there would be no future with Elizabeth as his wife, as she was already married.

Could I settle for another woman, knowing that Elizabeth is alive? Can I live with the prospect of caring for her for a lifetime without being able to marry her?

Remembering the way his heart leaped upon seeing her, the sense of elation that overtook him and the sweet sensation of her in his arms, he had his answer. "I will take Elizabeth to Pemberley."

Jane rushed to William, taking his hand and kissing his knuckles, as she broke into tears of joy. "Thank you, William! I shall forever be grateful to you."

Embarrassed, William gently pulled his hand out of her grasp and took both her hands in his. Looking steadily into her eyes, he stated, "I love Elizabeth. I can do no less."

Charles moved to put an arm around his shoulder. "We agonised over bringing you into this nightmare and are truly sorry at how you learned the truth. You have many questions, I am sure, but we are all exhausted, and for now, Lizzy is safe and sound. Why do we not meet here in the morning and discuss everything?"

William nodded, covering a yawn with his hand. "I will be able to think more clearly then, I believe." Charles and Jane watched as he departed wearily. Stopping at the door, he glanced back over his shoulder.

"We need to have our talk very early in the morning, as I must get Elizabeth away from here before Caroline arrives."

Jane replied, "Caroline is to arrive the day after tomorrow. I shall have Mrs. Drury's and Elizabeth's things packed first thing tomorrow. If you want to leave immediately after we talk, it will be possible."

"Thank you."

~~~*~~~

"What an awful way to discover the truth," Jane said softly, as she reached a hand towards Charles.

"The worst," was all he could add, as he took her hand and began leading her back to their bedroom. Lizzy was safe and all was well.

In his own bed, William rolled over to grab the still damp pillow Elizabeth had laid her head upon, breathing in the lavender scent. He held it tightly to his chest as his eyes closed, and he slept soundly for the first time since Charles had told him she was dead.

~~~*~~~

Chapter 6

Netherfield

Trunks littered the hallway as footmen moved back and forth loading them aboard the coach in front of Netherfield. Nodding to Charles who stood just out of Lizzy's sight, William entered the small sitting room adjoining Lizzy's bedroom. He could hear Jane, who knelt in front of the chair where her sister sat, patiently explaining what was about to happen.

"Lizzy, dearest, do you understand what I am trying to say?"

Elizabeth showed no reaction, and Jane glanced over her to William and Charles before her eyes returned to her sister. "All of us—William, Charles and I—agree that it is best if William takes you to his home... to Pemberley. It is very lovely there, and you will be safe. You know how you love to walk? Well, you can walk about the estate to your heart's content." She smiled, patting her sister's hands.

"While you will be under Mr. Darcy's protection, Charles and I will be kept informed of your health and well-being. You and I will exchange letters frequently, and God willing, we shall come to visit you there as soon as possible. Would you like that?"

She waited a moment, but with no response, she continued. "We love you, Lizzy, and I would not have you think we are abandoning you. We would never do that."

Jane searched her face, but Elizabeth only stared at her, barely blinking. William moved to kneel in front of Elizabeth and took the hand that Jane released.

"We all love you, Elizabeth, and together we will see you through this. Not one of us will allow anyone to hurt you. You will be safe at Pemberley, I promise."

Elizabeth looked down to watch as his thumb made a small circle on the back of her hand, and everyone followed her gaze. No one moved or spoke, recognizing that this was the first time since Elizabeth had been recovered that she had actually followed anything with her eyes.

Seeing her reaction to this small touch, William felt hot tears fill his eyes. He glanced at Jane and saw that she was crying silently. He lifted Elizabeth's hand slowly, letting his eyes adore her as he placed a soft kiss on the back of her fingers. He was rewarded with her eyes following this gesture as well. Though this was the extent of her response, there was a wave of emotion coursing throughout the room, and tearful eyes met and heads nodded in silent acknowledgement of this milestone.

Thus, it was with renewed hope for Elizabeth's recovery that the trip to London began.

On the road to London

Mid-morning found William, Elizabeth and Mrs. Drury in Darcy's coach, slowly making their way to London through a thick fog that cloaked the countryside and slowed their journey. Elizabeth had been given a draught to calm her before they left

Netherfield, and almost immediately upon entering the coach she had removed her pelisse and laid her head back against the seat, closing her eyes. William worried that she should have kept the pelisse on, as she was likely to become cold the further they travelled.

With every sway of the coach, her head moved from side to side, and by the time they were several miles out of Meryton, Elizabeth leaned heavily against Mrs. Drury. Seeing that she was asleep, William motioned for Mrs. Drury to help him, and he picked up Elizabeth's feet, laying them on the seat, causing her head to slide down into the woman's lap. He then removed her pelisse to his side of the coach and reached under the seat to secure two warm blankets. One he used to cover Elizabeth, and the other he handed to Mrs. Drury. The companion smiled, nodding her appreciation, and closing her eyes, rested her head against the side of the coach.

With both ladies asleep or resting, William availed himself of the opportunity to study Elizabeth. As much as was possible, Jane had taken good care of her. She was fashionably dressed in a very becoming green gown and half boots of dark blue kid. Her hair looked beautiful, arranged with small butterfly pins scattered throughout. The pelisse, which she had immediately discarded, was dark-blue twilled cotton with a light blue silk lining, trimmed in fur. Examining her face, William noticed that she looked almost peaceful as she slept.

As the long ride progressed with his companions napping, William's thoughts turned to the meeting he had had with the Bingleys that very morning. All of them had Elizabeth's best interests at heart, and each was painfully aware of the importance and consequences of the actions they were taking.

Netherfield
The Drawing room
Earlier That Morning

"You realise that for Elizabeth to be sheltered at Pemberley, I will have to close the estate to almost everyone else? And until her condition improves, I think it best for no one—not even you—to visit."

Jane nodded thoughtfully. "We could correspond regarding her, keeping abreast of her progress, could we not?"

Charles interjected, "What if one of our letters fell into the wrong hands?"

"We can establish a name to refer to Elizabeth in our letters," William responded.

"When we were small, we pretended to be grand ladies, and we would make up names to go with our new identities. Lizzy used to call herself Elise Lawrence."

"Then if we speak of her in correspondence, we shall refer to her as Elise. However, it would probably be less confusing to Elizabeth if she is addressed by her Christian name in conversation at Darcy House and Pemberley. She shall from this time forward be called Elizabeth Elise Lawrence while she is under my protection. Now, we must decide on her background."

"Can she not be a distant cousin of yours? You remarked of having cousins in Sussex—a few of which you had met only once," Charles offered. "I could feign having met her at Pemberley in years past, thus the enquiries into her health in my letters."

William considered the suggestion. "That is probably as good a story as any. Are we in agreement?" Jane and Charles nodded.

"I have other concerns. I met Mrs. Drury this morning in the hallway, and she seems very refined, more so than the average servant. Is she the one primarily responsible for caring for Elizabeth?"

"Yes. She is Lizzy's nurse. Until circumstances forced her into service, Mrs. Drury was a gentlewoman. She was our nurse at Longbourn when Lizzy was born, and as we got older, she did not agree with Mama's treatment of Lizzy." Jane looked away.

"She left Longbourn and found work elsewhere. When Charles and I married, I learned she was available and convinced her to come here. Naturally, when Lizzy was recovered, we needed someone we could trust, and she has been a godsend. She loves Lizzy. I assure you she will think nothing of accompanying her to Pemberley."

"I believe familiarity will be helpful. Mrs. Drury does not have to assume another name, but at Darcy House and Pemberley, she will take on the role of Elizabeth Lawrence's aunt and chaperone, which she seems capable of doing. If you will, Elizabeth will be a proper young lady being chaperoned by her aunt, in case others learn of her presence."

William frowned as he addressed other concerns. "Of course, in order to truly keep her safe, some of my trusted servants must know her true identity and why she is with me, and I will not lie to my cousin Richard, my sister or her husband."

"We understand completely. Do what you must."

"Now, tell me everything from the first time she met this blackguard. I want to understand how this could have happened."

"I believe Charles has already told you how Count Stefano came to be in Meryton." Jane ventured, and seeing William nod, she continued. "Lizzy was not impressed at all by the count's smooth conversation and charm. Used to having his choice of female companions, he could not comprehend why every woman was taken with him—except Lizzy. He became obsessed with her."

She shivered. "If only I had listened when Lizzy said there was something evil about him! Finally, she persuaded Papa to tell him to leave her alone." She added softly, "Lizzy was Papa's favourite."

Taking a deep breath to strengthen herself, Jane continued. "Then Papa died unexpectedly, we had to move into a small cottage behind Aunt Phillips' house, as Mr. Collins demanded that he take possession of Longbourn at once. Mama went mad with grief and worry. She began inviting the count to our small house every night. Elizabeth begged her not to encourage him, but to no avail. One day when I came home, Lizzy was gone, and no explanation was offered."

Jane stood and began pacing as she relived the horror. "I tried to find her myself. I had Mr. Hill drive Mary and me throughout Meryton and half the county, asking if anyone had seen her. I enquired at posting inns, I talked to the constable," she struggled, "but it was hopeless." Silence filled the room.

Whirling around, her eyes blazed in anger. "Then Mama purchased a bigger house, began hiring servants, buying clothes, as though she had gained a fortune. I suspected then that she had profited by my sister's absence. It was only by chance that I heard her bragging to my Aunt Phillips that she had given her consent for Lizzy to marry Count Stefano!"

She dropped her head in her hands and began to cry, then lifted it to vent her rage. "LIZZY WOULD NEVER CONSENT TO MARRY THAT MAN!"

Charles moved to hold her, and she calmed somewhat. "We would have left Meryton long ago, but I feared Lizzy would make her way back, and I would not be here to help her!"

Trying to gain control of his temper, William walked over to stare into the gardens. The set of his shoulders, the clenching and unclenching of his fists, were the only evidence of his barely contained fury.

Charles took up the tale. "I returned to Netherfield just after Lizzy disappeared. We were married shortly thereafter, and I immediately hired a man to help in the search. After a year, he had found no trace of Lizzy or the count. Then about four months ago, a young man came to Netherfield, saying he was the nephew of the housekeeper of an estate in Sheffield. His aunt, a Mrs. Browning, asked him to deliver a letter to Elizabeth's sister, Jane. He asked a few questions in Meryton and was directed here."

Charles held up the missive. "The letter was precise. We were to come straightaway to retrieve Lizzy, but cautioned not to inform anyone, especially Mrs. Bennet. We did as she asked and found Lizzy being cared for by a relative of Mrs. Browning. She, her husband and a few other servants were living in a fire-ravaged mansion. Though the damage was extensive, it was confined to one wing."

"And the cause of the fire?"

"A maid told Mrs. Browning that she had heard the count shouting and then a gunshot before she saw the smoke. She assumed that he had set it. Mrs. Browning said the maid found Elizabeth on the floor, just inside the door to the burning room, still alive but with a wound to her head.

Lizzy's personal maid and a child appeared to have been killed instantly by other shots. They had time only to remove Lizzy to safety before the flames spread. Had a thunderstorm not been raging that night, the entire mansion would probably have been consumed by the blaze."

William's brow furrowed as he turned to face Charles. "A child? Whose child?"

"It seems the maid had a child who lived in the servants' quarters with her."

"I see." He relaxed his stance a little. "Does the estate where Elizabeth was found belong to the count?"

"The estate is owned by the count's father. Apparently, the count was only in residence sporadically before the fire and has not been heard from often since then.

William eyes narrowed. "Who is the father?"

"Frederick Warren Stanton, Earl of Essex. Do you know of him?"

"I have heard the name." William considered for a moment. "And the son goes by an Italian surname?"

"Evidently he chooses to go by the title he inherited from his mother's father, who was an Italian count." William's eyebrows rose in question.

Bingley nodded, his thoughts taking the same direction. "Yes, I had wondered about it myself. As he is so difficult to find, he may use various names to confuse those whom he knows to be looking for him."

"Tell me about Elizabeth's injuries. Has she been seen by a physician?"

"A private surgeon from London, Mr. Callahan, examined her. In his opinion, she was grazed by a gunshot, and he says that could explain why she does not talk and could also account for her odd behaviour. He assumed that it was an accident, and I did not correct him."

"Martin Callahan?" William enquired and Charles nodded. "He is a colleague of my own surgeon, Farnsworth Towson, is he not?"

"Yes. I learned that he and Towson are versed in head injuries, and that is why I sent for him. They were commissioned by the Crown to do research on soldiers returning from battle with such injuries. Most of them have been shuffled to Bedlam, but he believes that they could have been helped, given time and patience."

"Time and patience," William murmured. "One I cannot control and the other I lack."

~~~*~~~

William was thankful that Charles had sent a servant ahead to arrange for fresh horses along the way and that Jane had packed a basket of food and drink, as it allowed William and his party to arrive at Darcy House just after dark in spite of the thick fog that slowed their coach. Elizabeth was still sleeping, probably because of the draughts. He was relieved to think he would be able to get her into his home without contending with the prying eyes of his neighbours. He vowed to leave the same way when they removed to Pemberley.

As the coach came to an abrupt stop, a footman appeared seemingly out of nowhere to open the door. Gently lifting Elizabeth from Mrs. Drury's lap and clutching her tightly to his body, William stepped out on the walk in front of his home. He glanced up at the three-story façade as he always did when he came back to his London home. The front door's immediate opening brought his attention back to the situation at hand.

"Good evening, Mr. Darcy! A pleasure to see you again, sir!" Mr. Barnes exclaimed as he stepped back for them to enter.

Mr. Barnes had been the butler, and his wife the housekeeper, at Darcy House for the last five and twenty years, and William knew he could rely completely on the man's discretion.

The butler averted his eyes to keep them on the young man. "Mrs. Barnes has your rooms prepared, and supper is waiting."

The smell of roast beef and fresh bread filled the foyer as William moved towards the staircase—his eyes still fixed on the butler. "Thank you, Mr. Barnes. Please remember not to put the knocker on the door tomorrow. I do not wish for anyone to know I am in Town."

Mrs. Barnes was at the foot of the stairs as he turned. "Mr. Darcy, would you like Perkins," she motioned to a footman, "to assist the young lady to her room?"

Eyeing the tall young man with caution, William replied. "I will carry her myself. Just show Mrs. Drury to the rooms you have prepared, and I will follow."

"Yes, sir. Madam, please follow me."

Mrs. Barnes started up the grand staircase and everyone followed. Glancing back over her shoulder, she addressed the weary party, "After you are refreshed, I will send each of you a supper tray, as I know you are most likely famished. Cook has prepared Mr. Darcy's favourite meal."

"That is so kind of you," Mrs. Drury replied as she continued her trek up the stairs, William following.

Leading the procession, Mrs. Barnes made no remarks about the circumstances that brought the young woman to Darcy House. She and her husband along with Mr. Noble, Mr. Darcy's valet, had been informed only to expect Mr. Darcy's cousin, who was travelling with him to Pemberley, as she needed to recuperate after a severe illness. William trusted them implicitly and intended to explain everything to them later. He knew they would guard Elizabeth's secret just as tenaciously as he.

Arriving at a large bedroom, tastefully decorated in gold and green, Mrs. Barnes motioned for them to enter. Two maids stood at attention, awaiting instructions, and showed no astonishment at seeing the Master come into the room with a woman in his arms. They were well-versed in their duties and kept their eyes cast down.

"This is your room, Mrs. Drury," Mrs. Barnes said, looking to one of the maids. "Agatha, will you attend Mrs. Drury. Lula, come with me." With quick curtsies, the maids complied.

Crossing the room to a door, Mrs. Barnes opened it to reveal a sitting room and continued through and into a second bedroom, decorated in lavender and white.

"This is Miss Lawrence's room."

William followed his housekeeper into the second bedroom and carefully placed Elizabeth on the large white counterpane covering the bed. He perceived that she was awakening, so he sat down on the side of the bed. A flick of his hand sent the servants out of the room.

"Elizabeth?" Her eyes flew open and locked on his. "You are at my home in London. We will rest here for just a few days before travelling to Pemberley." He took both her hands in his, remembering how she had reacted to his touch that morning.

"I will leave you in the care of my trusted employees, who will see to your comfort. You will have a nice hot bath and something to eat before you have a good night's rest in this soft bed."

Elizabeth seemed to study his face and he smiled. Leaning over, he placed a kiss on her forehead before pulling back.

"Mrs. Drury will be in the next room, and Lula will be sleeping on a cot in the sitting room in between. If you need anything, you may ring this bell." He reached over and picked up a small bell on the bedside table, ringing it a bit and smiling.

"I will see you tomorrow. Most likely, you will want to tour the house, and I will be happy to escort you. Would you like that?"

As quickly as he stood, the young maid reappeared, and he nodded towards Elizabeth. As she came around the bed, he slipped out the door and found Mrs. Barnes standing just inside the sitting room. She said softly so that Lula could not hear, "I thought that having them in adjoining rooms would ensure that Mrs. Drury is able to keep close watch over Miss Lawrence."

William nodded, glancing back to Elizabeth, and speaking equally as quietly, he gave further instructions. "Keep the doors to the hallways locked. I do not want her to encounter any men—footmen or otherwise—in the house." Then he said wearily, "I will retire to allow you to take care of Miss Lawrence so that she and Mrs. Drury may eat and rest."

As he made his way out of the room, he could hear Mrs. Barnes speaking. "Mrs. Drury, Agatha will assist you with a bath if you would like. Rest assured that Lula will see to Miss Lawrence's every need."

Mrs. Barnes had been informed that if anyone should enquire, Elizabeth Lawrence was a distant cousin of Mr. Darcy, and a debilitating illness had triggered an invitation to Pemberley to recuperate. Of course, Miss Lawrence was being chaperoned by her aunt, Mrs. Drury. Though this explanation was plausible, it was certain that nothing would satisfy the gossips of the *ton* if they got wind of the young woman's presence in Mr. Darcy's homes, either here or at Pemberley.

William's Study
The next day

Attending to some problems with his steward the next morning, William was startled when Mr. Barnes announced his cousin. "Colonel Fitzwilliam to see you, sir."

Sighing, he stood. *Richard warned me that he had ways of knowing when I was in Town.* "Send him—"

"Darce!" Richard entered without waiting for William to finish. "You were not joking when you said you would not be staying at Netherfield long, were you?" Then looking back at the departing butler he chuckled, "Old Barnes is getting faster. He was able to catch me this morning!"

Shaking his head at Richard's antics, William replied, "It is good to see you too, Richard, but I do have much work to accomplish before I return to Pemberley. Perhaps we could meet later today?" As he spoke, he motioned towards the pile of papers on his desk and his steward still sitting in the chair in front.

"And this is the thanks I get for coming to warn you, Cousin?"

William immediately dismissed the steward, waiting until he closed the door on his way out before asking, "Warn me?"

"Yes. Mrs. Preston is on her way to Darcy House, even as we speak."

"Mrs. Preston? How would she—" He stopped at Richard's smirk. "What would possess her to call on me uninvited and unaccompanied?"

"Oh, she is not unaccompanied. Mother is with her!" William sat back down with a groan. "It seems the two of them have become quite cosy since you danced with the *Black Widow* at my ball. She has convinced Mother that you shall offer for her any day now."

Another louder groan filled the room, and Richard guffawed in response. "Oh, come now, Cousin! Did you really expect to pay even the slightest amount of attention to that wallflower and not raise her expectations?" At William's scowl, he sobered and spoke candidly. "It is true! She has been seen picking out her trousseau, and I have a firsthand account that she has been commenting on where you might go on your wedding trip."

"I...I never gave her any expectation of—" William turned to grab the bottle of brandy behind his desk and poured a large glass.

"Pour me one as well," Richard declared, taking the seat formerly occupied by the steward and reaching out to take the proffered drink. "I think we will have to plan our strategy quickly, before they get here."

At that precise moment, a loud commotion upstairs interrupted their conversation, and William hurried out the study door without explanation, Richard on his heels. William reached the first floor landing quickly, having ascended the steps two at a time, to find Mrs. Drury struggling to keep Elizabeth from escaping her grip.

"Please, Miss Elizabeth. Do you not remember that we are in London now? You cannot walk out this morning. Besides, it is much too cold, and the wind is fierce," her companion begged.

Elizabeth pushed away from Mrs. Drury, trying to get past her. Immediately, William moved to fold her in his arms, pulling her solidly against his chest. She stilled, taking hold of his coat lapels, and relaxed into him, laying her head on his chest. As she did, she took a deep breath, seeming to calm at the familiar sandalwood cologne permeating his clothes.

Mrs. Barnes had arrived by then and shared a look of astonishment with Richard, before composing herself into her normal head housekeeper mien. Richard's expression never changed.

William whispered into her hair, the lavender scent making his heart beat faster.

"Shhh, Elizabeth. All is well, but it is still quite cold outside. London is much colder than was Meryton, and I would prefer you do not go walking about today."

He nodded slightly to Mrs. Drury and then to the maid. "Come. Let Lula direct you and Mrs. Drury to the conservatory where you may enjoy the sunshine and flowers this morning. You can even eat breakfast there, if you like."

Elizabeth did not move, still holding tightly to his coat. He smiled as he gently unclasped each hand, taking them in his own, and pushed her slowly back to create some distance between them.

Mrs. Drury came to Elizabeth's side, taking one arm, while the maid stepped up to take the other. William lifted her chin, willing her eyes to focus on his. "I shall join you there in a short while, and we shall have that tour of the house I promised. Then perhaps we shall share a book." Though there was no recognition or emotion in her eyes, her gaze never varied. He smiled lovingly at her and then stepped back.

"Please take Miss Elizabeth to the conservatory by the back staircase. Mrs. Barnes, please go before them, and see to it that there are no footmen in her view."

"Yes, sir," the elderly woman said as she hurriedly led the others down the hall. Soon they were all out of sight.

Having forgotten about Richard during the crisis, William was startled by a low whistle.

"If I had not seen it with my own eyes, I would never have believed it! What in the world is going on, Darce? Is that not Elizabeth Bennet? Whatever has happened to the poor girl?"

William motioned for Richard to be quiet. Looking about and seeing no other servants, he replied worriedly, "I find it hard to believe myself. Come, and I will explain it all, as I will most likely need your help."

~~~*~~~

Thus, it was with Richard's assistance that Lady Matlock and Mrs. Preston were thwarted in their attempt to encounter William at Darcy House. Richard met the two ladies as they ascended the steps, while he was coming out the front door.

"Mother!" he declared heartily, "imagine meeting you here. And Mrs. Preston, it is a pleasure to see you again so soon." He bowed and the ladies nodded. "Alas, if it was your wish to visit with William, I regret to inform you that I was just inside, and William is not here. I would not take Mr. Barnes word for it at first." He turned to address the widow. "My taciturn cousin sometimes has Mr. Barnes say he is not in when he has work to finish. Thus, I always confirm it for myself."

Mrs. Preston was not quite sure what to make of the colonel's revelation, but turned as he began to escort her and Lady Matlock back down the steps towards their carriage.

"I am on my way to White's to confront him. Shall I tell him that you expect him for dinner tomorrow, Mother, and that the lovely Mrs. Preston will be in attendance as well? Will that suffice for the inconvenience of your finding him not at home?"

"Yes, thank you, Richard," Lady Matlock answered, patting Richard's cheek affectionately as he helped her into the carriage.

"Mother!" Richard blushed and said mockingly, "not in public!"

Watching his mother's carriage wend its way down the street, he breathed a sigh of relief before remembering what he had just learned from William. A frown crossed his face as he turned to go back into the house.

Somehow, I must talk Darce out of this madness!

~~~*~~~

Chapter 7

London
Preston House
The next evening

Cecile Preston lifted the steaming cup to her lips, contentedly admiring the general splendour of her drawing room. The townhouse had been left to her in her late husband's will, provided she remained a widow. If she remarried, the house would pass to Owen's youngest brother, Marvin; but for now, it was hers. She mentally inventoried the room's valuables for possible use as payments on her debts, and her head tilted in reflection.

Though I dearly love it here, I shall not repine the loss of it, for I shall have even grander houses when I marry Mr. Darcy.

Reflecting on Darcy House, she recalled her one visit there before she married Owen Preston, and how she was smitten with Fitzwilliam Darcy from that point on. Her uncle, Lord Tierney, the Earl of Whiteshall, had been invited to a dinner party hosted by Mr. Darcy and the Fitzwilliams, and she had convinced him to ask if he might bring a guest. They had been detained and arrived rather late. Due to the large crowd in attendance that evening, she had never actually been introduced to the man she had most wanted to meet. She still flushed at the memory of seeing him that night—she a tongue-tied two and twenty, too shy to coax an introduction with a dashing man of six and twenty.

For his part, Mr. Darcy had ignored her, as he had most of the women in attendance. She shrugged. She knew she was no beauty—even Owen had married her for her dowry. Though Mr. Darcy's inattention may have hurt then, her present good fortune had certainly made up for her former disappointment.

Yes! All is well now. I am free of Owen Preston, and I have encountered Fitzwilliam Darcy just when he is most vulnerable. His sister is insisting he marry, and he is tired of beautiful women throwing themselves at him. He seems ready to settle for a marriage of peers, and I am his peer. How providential that I am finally in the right place at the right time.

The lengthening shadows on the wall served to remind her that she would have to begin dressing for the dinner party at the Fitzwilliam's residence before long. She poured herself another half cup of tea and finished it off with brandy.

If I were a man, I would dispense with the tea altogether, but drinking tea is more ladylike than gulping down a glass of brandy.

Mr. Potts suddenly appeared at the door. "Madam, a Mr. Wickham to see you."

Quickly looking to the doorway, she observed that no one was behind Mr. Potts. Putting a finger to her lips to silence him, she motioned for him to come forward. Glancing behind as though he thought she might be talking to someone else, the portly man saw no one. Realising then that she indeed meant him, he moved in her direction as quietly as possible.

As he drew nearer, she whispered, "Is Mr. Wickham aware that I am available to receive him?"

The butler said softly in reply, "No, madam. I told him to wait, and I would see if it was convenient."

"Then, please tell him I am not able to see him today, and it would be best if he return later this week."

The butler frowned. Mr. Wickham was not an easy man to put off, and he had become noticeably more surly in the last few weeks. Having no choice in the matter, he responded, "Yes, madam."

Listening as his footsteps crossed the foyer, Cecile cringed when they abruptly stopped, and she could hear the raised voice of Mr. Wickham addressing Mr. Potts. Though she could not tell what he was saying, she could discern anger in his tone. Finally, the closing of the front door allowed her to breathe again. She was not surprised to see Mr. Potts reappear at the drawing room door a few seconds later.

He coughed self-consciously, and his eyes studied the floor as he delivered a message. "Mr. Wickham asked me to tell you that he will be here tomorrow evening, quite early, and he will expect you to be available."

"Thank you, Mr. Potts."

As the butler made his way back to his post, he wondered at the strange relationship between Mrs. Preston and the flashy Mr. Wickham. No gentleman would act or dress that way, nor would he think of addressing a lady in the manner in which he addressed Mrs. Preston.

Mr. Wickham had begun calling on the Mistress immediately following Mr. Preston's death, though his visits had become more frequent in the last few months. Shaking his head, Potts decided he would think of it no more tonight.

Nothing done by the wealthy surprises me!

~~~*~~~

Cecile Preston's hands shook as she fingered the delicate diamond creation, trying to fasten it about her neck. She sighed at the thought of having to hand it to Mr. Wickham in payment of her latest promissory note. This was the last costly piece of the Preston jewels, as she had used all the rest to pay previous bets. How would she ever appear at proper social functions without her jewels? Then remembering that she could always borrow from her friends under the pretence of admiring one thing or another, she relaxed.

Her light-heartedness did not last. Wickham's bold declaration had dashed her hopes of putting him off until she could become Mrs. Darcy. When he arrived tomorrow, she would have to admit her inability to pay what she had lost or his excessive usury—at least not at present. She would assure him that if he gave her a little more time, she would have sufficient resources to settle her debts and perhaps even to make an occasional bet in the future.

Surely the prospect of my future wealth and further wagers will convince him.

The truth was that she was so far in debt that she feared being able to settle the balance, even if she secreted money from her allowance and household accounts as Mrs. Darcy. No, she would have to ask Mr. Darcy for the ten thousand pounds, pretending the debt was for something legitimate. As long as she laid the responsibility on Owen Preston, Mr. Darcy would feel pity for her.

Perhaps tonight will be the night Fitzwilliam Darcy realises that we would be an excellent match. God knows he has had enough encouragement from his family and plenty of time!

She tried to study her reflection in the mirror, but her thoughts drifted back to the handsome rogue who held her debts. From the start, she knew Wickham was not to be trusted. After all, he had been Owen's gaming partner before becoming hers. It was not a month after her husband's death that she became involved in a torrid love affair with him. He had convinced her to make more and higher wagers until she was, for all practical purposes, impoverished. She stamped her foot in frustration.

Now that I am destitute, I hold no interest for that blackguard! Well, no matter. I shall be Mrs. Darcy ere long and shall look down my nose at him!

Throwing the necklace onto her dressing table, she screamed, "Martha!"

Grabbing the combs that were to adorn her hair, she began putting them in place. "I should never have let Suzette go to save money. Martha knows nothing of being a lady's maid."

A young woman quickly appeared behind her, curtsying and holding out the freshly pressed gown she had gone to retrieve.

"What took you so long? I do not have all night."

"Yes, mum—I mean, no, mum," Martha sputtered.

"Help me with this gown and then fasten my necklace. I do not want my uncle to be kept waiting."

Martha did her best, albeit, not as efficiently as Suzette, and Cecile was finally ready. She was waiting in the parlour when her uncle came to escort her to the dinner party. Cecile thanked him for accompanying her, and he assured her he was delighted to do so.

As usual when she was in her uncle's company, all she could focus on was the fact that, with her aunt dead, she would be one of his heirs. He had no children and only eight nieces who would inherit his wealth. However, the man was in good health, and at eight and fifty, he could live another ten years. Cecile sighed as he offered her his arm, and they left the house.

As they settled into his carriage, she was thankful that Lord Tierney could not hear well and, thus, was not very talkative. The silence that ensued gave her ample time to ponder just how she might force Mr. Darcy's hand on the matter of marriage as she needed immediate relief, and her uncle could not provide that.

~~~*~~~

In another carriage negotiating the route to Matlock House, William fidgeted with his cravat.

I should not have let Mr. Noble stay on as my valet. He should have retired long ago. He always ties my cravat too tightly!

Sighing, he realised that it was not the cravat or Mr. Noble who raised his ire, but the situation with Mrs. Preston. He chided himself for getting into this quagmire. *I should never have encouraged the woman. Even to please Georgiana.*

How does one explain? I am sorry to have raised your expectations, Mrs. Preston? It was foolish of me to think I could settle for someone I do not love."

Having dinner tonight with the Fitzwilliams was the price he must pay for Richard's help in keeping his aunt and Cecile Preston away the day before, but as

William drew closer to his uncle's home, his apprehension increased manifestly. He had found no time to plan a workable strategy concerning Mrs. Preston.

Even though he had explained to Elizabeth that she was in London, she was still confused when she awoke. She had reacted to the strange house, first by getting upset with Mrs. Drury; and second, by trying to leave—from her room and then the house. As at Netherfield, William was the only one able to calm her, so he spent most of the day doing just that, not that he minded. Quite the opposite, just being able to hold her close to him was a balm to his tortured soul. He found himself longing for the day when holding her would be by mutual desire and not because she was sick.

His thoughts drifted back to Mrs. Preston. There was no doubt she was a fine match for someone seeking a marriage of convenience. She was intelligent, able to converse with ease in social settings, she was wealthy and her connections were above average. Nevertheless, she was not the desire of his heart—**Elizabeth was.**

Acknowledging that brought him a peace he had not known since he left Kent. Truly smiling from the heart now, he grasped the truth of it—even if Elizabeth never fully recovered, he would thank God for the chance to care for her as long as he lived.

Satisfied that he finally knew his own heart, William resolved to do whatever was necessary to discourage the widow. After all, he was taking Elizabeth home to Pemberley, and Mrs. Preston would likely never be there again. It was just as well that he made that clear tonight.

The abrupt motion of the carriage's stopping brought him back to the present, and with a new determination, he descended from the coach. Stopping to take a deep breath, he straightened his waistcoat and turned to see Richard as he came down the steps to greet him.

~~~*~~~

Cecile could not believe it. Not only had Mr. Darcy been cool to her when she addressed him after going through the receiving line, but he had not asked her to dance even once. The Matlocks had had the large music room cleared of furniture, so everyone that wanted to dance would have room to do so. She had situated herself next to him several times during the evening, giving him the opportunity to talk, but Mr. Darcy had acted as though they were barely acquainted.

She was livid, though she could not let anyone know. Determined to get to the bottom of this puzzle, Cecile decided to try another tactic. Near time for dinner, she walked over to William who was engaged in conversation with Richard, and smiling as pleasantly as possible, declared, "Mr. Darcy, I find myself free for our dance now, sir."

William raised his eyebrows, but unwilling to embarrass her, bowed slightly and offered his arm. As Cecile turned, William shared a look with his cousin that signified something dreadful was about to happen. Richard blew out a breath as he watched William escort the lady to the dance floor. Suddenly feeling the presence of someone beside him, he turned to see his mother.

"What in the world is wrong with my nephew? Last he was in Town, he could not smile at Mrs. Preston enough, and now he acts as though he hardly knows her."

"Perhaps now he regrets his attention to her," Richard replied, never taking his eyes off William. Lady Matlock raised one eyebrow and turned to study her son.

"Because…"

"Perhaps, because he has found his true love."

With that Richard left his mother watching Fitzwilliam and the widow Preston going through the steps of a dance as though they were strangers. Sighing, she rushed to find the butler to direct him to rearrange some of the place cards before dinner.

"Mr. Darcy, would you mind telling me why you have been avoiding me?" Cecile said calmly, a pleasant smile that did not adequately represent her feelings, plastered on her face.

"I do not follow you, madam."

Madam? "That is so formal for friends, is it not? Come now, sir. We both know of what I am speaking. You said you would call on me as soon as you came back to Town. Tonight I overheard Colonel Fitzwilliam say you have been here two days already. And, you have barely spoken two words to me this evening."

William began to feel some guilt, but he knew it would be best to come right out and tell her the truth. "I am sorry, Mrs. Preston. I wanted to speak to you before now, but I have not had the opportunity."

The dance separated them, and Cecile held her breath, wondering what excuse Mr. Darcy would give for his inconstancy. As they made their way back down the line, finally facing each other again, he continued, "I should have asked for a private audience to discuss something of importance."

Cecile released a huge sigh of relief. *He is probably just nervous because he is going to offer for me.* "Then let us find the time now." She nodded in the direction of the balcony. "If you will follow me, we should have sufficient privacy outdoors."

William groaned to himself.

On the other side of the room, Richard followed the development with a frown and began to make his way toward the same balcony.

As the door to the balcony closed behind them, Cecile whirled around and moved to stand so close to William that he could feel her breath on his face.

"Mrs...Mrs. Preston," he began as he took a step back. "I feel I must tell you—"

Cecile leaned in and kissed William on the lips, and he pulled back abruptly. "Madam, what are you doing?"

"Oh, Fitzwilliam! You looked so solemn, and this should be a happy occasion, should it not?"

"I do not take your meaning, madam. I was only going to tell you that I have decided that I have too many responsibilities at this time to consider a courtship."

Cecile's sharp intake of breath was followed by an angry scowl. "You what?" She turned, wringing her hands and began to pace. "You have decided—*you* have decided! And what about me? You have given me every indication that you would be offering for me but now..." Her voice faded away.

"I have tried not to raise your expectations. I have never asked to court you."

"No. But you have shown preference towards me—asking me to dance to the exclusion of all others."

"And for that I apologise profusely."

She turned and faced him, her head held high in disgust. "Well! I do not accept your apology, sir. Unfortunately, I shall have to write to your sister and tell her what a cad her beloved brother has become." With that she exited the balcony, slamming the door loudly behind.

William took a ragged breath and turned to look into the gardens. As usual, a low whistle announced his cousin's presence, as he did not hear him come through the door.

"The Black Widow did not take that well at all!"

"Richard!" William was not in the mood for his kidding.

"I am sorry to have to say this, Darce, but I, for one, am entirely happy! That ugly woman was not for you."

William frowned at him but he continued. "Not because she is ugly *outside*, but because she is ugly *inside*. There is something about her that I have never liked, much less trusted, and she was entirely wrong for the likes of you."

William shrugged. "Well, it is done. Now I shall be able to return to Pemberley with Elizabeth."

"Do you really know what you are about, Cousin? You have just freed yourself from an entanglement with one woman and are immediately jumping into another, proposing to take charge of a young woman who may never be well. I know you fancy yourself in love with her—" His words were cut off by an angry retort.

"You know nothing of my feelings for her!"

Richard stiffened at William's reproof. He had never known his cousin to react with such emotion.

"I should not have—" Richard began but stopped short.

William stared into the starry sky, closing his eyes and conjuring the image of his beloved. "Richard, have you ever needed someone so much that you felt as though you could not breathe without them…could not exist if they no longer existed?"

He hesitated, though he did not expect Richard to answer.

"I have. I have eaten, breathed and lived with Elizabeth since the day I met her. It is her face that haunts my dreams, and it is she who fills my every waking moment. I stayed away for two years, trying to put her out of my mind," he searched for the right words, "which, in the end, was futile. When I thought her dead for those few hours at Netherfield, something inside me died, and when I found her in the rain that night, it came alive again. I came alive again."

William turned to face his friend, willing him to understand. "Now that I have her back, I do not believe I could survive if something happened to her."

Richard stared at William for a long time, and then made a decision. He clasped William on each shoulder. "I am sorry, Cousin. I can say with assurance that I have never known that kind of love." He tilted his head and smiled. "I do not think I ever want to know a love that deep, but in any event, I will support you in whatever you decide. Come hell or high water, you can count on me."

William smiled wanly. "I am afraid it may very well come to both before this is over. But I am most humbled and forever grateful that you have chosen to be on my side."

Richard smiled. "I always have been, just as you have always been on mine." They shook hands and moved towards the French doors, intending to rejoin the party. "Come, let us face the enemy as a united front!"

Both chuckled softly as they entered the room, catching the attention of Lord and Lady Matlock.

"Is there something I should know about our son or our nephew, dear heart?" the earl whispered to his wife.

"Not that I know of, Husband." Not wishing to have him upset with William once again, she decided not to tell him what Richard had divulged earlier. Reaching for his hand, she said sweetly, "But one never knows about these young people. Why do we not dance and forget all about them for the evening? I am sure tomorrow will bring enough troubles of its own."

And she was correct.

Preston House
The next day

"But I **do not** have your money, Mr. Wickham!" Cecile wrung her hands in desperation. "Surely you can understand that I am trying to acquire it, but all I have at present is the necklace you now demand. If I do not have this piece, I will have to borrow jewels so that I can attend the best soirées. If I am not seen on the town, then my chances of remarrying, as well my ability to repay my debt to you, will be diminished."

Wickham smirked. *Who would want you, especially now that you are penniless?*

"My associates do not take excuses, madam. Give me the piece." Wickham held out his hand, and she reluctantly placed the diamond necklace in his palm. He began inspecting it, holding it to the light. "You do know that this will not cancel all your debt?"

"Surely there is some other way." She touched his hand, and his eyes met hers. "I would do *anything*! Can you not see the advantage of working with me?"

Wickham rubbed his chin as Mrs. Preston's words played over in his head. "Perhaps there is a way."

"Marvellous!" Cecile batted her rather sparse eyelashes. "At one time, you were fond of me."

"Yes, but that was when you had money," Wickham sneered, causing her to frown. "Oh, come now. You surely did not think I was enamoured of your beauty."

"No. Of course not," she replied testily.

"So, now that we are being honest with one another, I think I could use someone with your—shall we say—connections, to help me in my other line of work."

Her brows rose in unison. "And what *work* would that be, sir?"

"I procure valuables."

"What do you mean '*procure*'?"

"Burglary, madam."

"Oh!" Cecile dropped down in the nearest chair, shocked into silence for a moment.

"I have several people who aid me in procuring valuables. When I have accumulated enough, I have a buyer who spirits them overseas and resells them to the rich in his country. I make a fair profit, and he makes an even bigger one." Wickham shrugged. "And we are both happy."

"But I cannot. It would be illegal and..." Cecile sputtered.

"Madam! Do you or do you not wish to get out of debt? Besides, you could probably fully settle your debts and have some leftover for yourself, depending on your willingness to work hard." Wickham saw her mind begin to turn. The idea of acquiring money beyond paying her debts was evidently appealing.

"I would be paid?"

"Yes, you would be paid a commission—let us say ten percent of what I get for the merchandise. For instance, one necklace I procured was worth ten thousand pounds. I sold it for approximately one-half, or five thousand pounds. Your commission would have been five hundred pounds." Her eyes became large and round, so he continued. "And they always have more than one necklace, my dear. I also take anything else of value—silver and gold pieces—such as candelabrum, cigar boxes, jewellery cases, brushes, and combs."

"What would be required of me?"

"Certainly nothing dangerous. You would do just what you mentioned earlier. You would borrow pieces of jewellery from your friends and relations. While you were doing so, you would take note of the layout of the house, the rooms where their valuables are located and, if possible, what they had to offer. I would rather try for very valuable jewels and not waste my time on cheap imitations!"

"I certainly could not steal the items loaned to me. It would be too obvious."

"No, you would borrow some of the lesser jewels, perhaps under the pretence of modesty, as we would not want them to suspect your interest in the more expensive items. As soon as I know which house to target and where the safe is located within the house, I can make my plans—*our* plans." He looked as though he was getting another idea. "And you may be valuable in keeping me informed as to the time they will be out of the house or even out of town, as you ladies do so love to gossip."

"I suppose that would not be hard for me to do. I would not be directly involved in the burglaries, so I would be safe from suspicion." She smiled then. "I would be able to keep my necklace and perhaps make enough to redeem myself and accumulate some funds."

"Indeed!" Wickham proclaimed. "We have an agreement then?" He stuck out his hand. "Of course, you will have to start soon, or I shall be forced to take this necklace to appease my partner."

Cecile shook his hand. "I shall have a prospect for you this week."

"Splendid." Wickham rubbed his hands together now. "I shall look forward to hearing from you." At that, he bowed and walked towards the door.

"One thing, though." At the sound of Cecile's voice, Wickham turned. "Do not try to cheat me. I will be keeping track of what was stolen."

"Your mistrust has wounded me," Wickham declared, clasping his hand to his heart.

"I thought you said we were being honest." Cecile retorted, lifting her head in disdain.

"*Touché*, my dear, *touché*!"

~~~*~~~

Chapter 8

Darcy House
The Conservatory

The two men, Mr. Darcy and a stranger, stood at the open door to the conservatory, trying to remain unnoticed. Mrs. Drury was aware of them straightaway but gave no indication of their presence to the lady who was being watched, whose back was turned to the gentlemen. She and Miss Elizabeth were enjoying the tea and cakes that Mrs. Barnes had been so kind as to provide, and she hoped that it was enough to keep the young woman from noticing that they were being observed.

Mr. Darcy mentioned a doctor who was coming today for a consultation.

Elizabeth had been quiet for nearly an hour, seemingly mesmerized by the beautiful flowers about her as Mrs. Drury read aloud from a book of poetry by William Blake. The companion was very much aware that her voice could not command Elizabeth's attention so well as Mr. Darcy's mellow baritone, but at least the reading kept her calm while she waited for him. Since they had been in London, Mr. Darcy had spent time talking or reading to Elizabeth every afternoon.

Thirty minutes later, Elizabeth began twisting in her chair, turning so that she could see the door—a clear indication that she was expecting him. Mrs. Drury prayed that either Elizabeth would settle down or that Mr. Darcy would appear soon, as her charge's present state of agitation usually portended another struggle to get her to cooperate, one which only Mr. Darcy was able to allay.

William's Study

Mr. Towson paced back and forth across the expanse of William's study, his head down, one hand on his chin and the other behind his back. Trusting his old friend implicitly and believing it was the only way in which he might understand and help Elizabeth, William had recounted her story to him.

Using only her Christian name, he explained how she was hurt, how Jane and Charles found her and his encounter with her that night in the rain. He extracted a pledge from the good physician that he would tell no one, as it might put her life in jeopardy. Finally done with pacing, Mr. Towson drew himself up to his full height and faced William.

"You say that she has been in this state since the gun shot grazed her temple?" Mr. Towson enquired, rubbing his chin as if in great deliberation.

"According to her brother and sister, she has been uncommunicative and unable to focus on anything or anyone since they recovered her about four months ago. However, while I was staying at their home, she did show some signs of improvement."

His bushy eyebrows rose in question. "In what way?"

"She was calmer," he explained. "Less combative. She allowed her sister to take the doll that she clings to, and place it on her bed. Jane, her sister, convinced her that it needed to rest."

"Does she think it is a child?"

"Jane believes it is so, but since she does not talk..."

"And does she still look for it at times?"

"Sometimes she still walks around with it, and Mrs. Drury says that she insists on having it before she will sleep."

"Were there any other signs?"

"Right before we left for London, she focused on something for the first time."

"What was that?"

William hesitated only a second, knowing he would have to be honest with the doctor. "I was holding her hand and unconsciously made a circle with my thumb on the back of it. She looked down to follow the movement. Seeing this, I raised her hand to bestow a kiss, and she followed my actions."

The grey haired physician studied his long-time friend and sometime patient for a few seconds. "May I ask a personal question, Fitzwilliam?"

William teased the man who had treated him since childhood. "Have you ever asked any other kind?" Then throwing up his hands, he replied, "If it will help Elizabeth."

"Does she care for you as much as you care for her?" He watched William's face flush.

"Her sister assured me that she does. I had no chance to discover the truth of it before this tragedy happened."

"And she began to focus on you, your touches, even though you told me earlier that she grew agitated when any man came near her."

William nodded. "After she clearly had figured out who I was, she was never afraid of me. In fact, she clung to me."

"That seems reasonable. With my work on head injuries, I have observed that my patients usually respond to someone who loves them or with whom they were in love, more often than to other relatives or just a caregiver."

"What do you make of Elizabeth's injuries?"

"In my opinion, she was debilitated by two things—something she witnessed and the bullet that grazed her head. Though a head wound such as she suffered can cause shock initially, I truly believe that because the wound was not deep, there will be no lasting damage, but the possibility of both happening at once could explain why she is so troubled." He looked back to see the worry on William's face and walking over to him, slid an arm around the younger man's shoulder.

"Nevertheless, we have had great success with this type of injury. I am convinced we can help her overcome this adversity if she is given the correct help. We could admit her to the clinic that Callahan and I operate, but that would not be appropriate as it houses soldiers."

William was already shaking his head. "I will care for her at Pemberley. Nothing will be overlooked in her treatment."

William's resolve impressed the physician, but he had to be pragmatic. "I believe you will try with all your heart, Fitzwilliam, but you have no idea what it will involve, the extent to which you must devote yourself to the task. Are you willing to let your family, your business affairs, your pleasure, even Pemberley, become secondary to implementing her recovery?"

"Elizabeth is everything to me. I will do whatever is necessary, for however long it takes, to see her well again."

Staring into his young friends eyes, Mr. Towson recognised the determination needed for this type of commitment and nodded.

"Tell me what I am I to do," William pleaded.

"The most essential thing you must do is dedicate as much time as possible to being with her. These patients have returned to an earlier stage of life, unable to handle reality. You must stimulate her senses, making her focus on the world outside, even if it is just having her sit beside you as you read aloud or as you answer your correspondence. Ask her opinion, though she may not answer. Speak to her as though it were a two-sided conversation. Point out a new rose or a starry sky. Make her focus!"

"Are there things that I should not do?"

"Yes. Try never to let her see you frustrated, angry, or dejected, if possible. She needs for you to be happy and encouraging. Never let her hear anyone say she will not recover. She may not be able to speak at the present, but I am certain that she is listening. Do not hurt her feelings, as any blow at this stage would be twice the grief."

The kind physician looked away. "I suppose that she has seen enough of that already."

Shaking off his gloomy thoughts, he continued. "I apologize. I have seen so many individuals with this type of injury that sometimes it boggles the mind to think what they have been through."

"I can only imagine," William ventured. He continued after some hesitation, "I must ask, though, are there those who do not recover?"

"There are some. But I do not believe this will be her fate—not with you by her side." William could not help but smile.

"However," Mr. Towson cautioned, "do not undertake this challenge unless you can do it wholeheartedly, fully believing that she will recover. *Your* faith will have to sustain her until she can have faith in herself. She shall rely on your belief in her. Tell her she is going to be well, that you have faith in her ability to recover, and if it be true, tell her you love her. Love works miracles for which no man of science can account."

William replied soberly, "I shall endeavour always to remember that."

"It would serve you well in every aspect of your life. Now, if she is going to be at Pemberley, I suppose we shall handle her progress by correspondence. Of course, I might be talked into visiting once or twice to observe her." His smile was warm and wide. "I did so enjoy visiting when your father was alive. He used to invite me to all the hunts."

William looked down, ill at ease. "I am sorry I have not continued his hospitality. After Father died, I was not in the mood for company for many years, and I have just returned from two years out of the country."

"I know. I have heard the laments of my wife and her sisters over your sudden absence from the balls and dinner parties in Town. They had great hopes for their unmarried nieces and daughters." The physician chuckled as William smiled and looked down, embarrassed. "At least, it seems you may have been better occupied outside England."

It did not go unnoticed that William's smile faded. "Things are not always as they seem."

The wise old physician nodded, grabbing his bag and preparing to leave, he squeezed William's shoulder. "Well said, my boy. Well said."

~~~*~~~

A pile of correspondence was spread out before him, but William's mind was on something else entirely. He had just spent two hours with Elizabeth. She had grown tired, as she was prone to rising before it was light, and he had suggested she rest before dinner. Though she clung to his hands as before, she consented to a nap when he declared that he would personally escort her to her room.

He smiled as he remembered how she had looked up at him and closed her eyes as they stopped just outside the door. She had wanted him to kiss her forehead, as he had done on several occasions this past week. He was only too pleased to comply, though he knew of the impropriety of the kisses.

Impropriety be damned! If Elizabeth needs a kiss to reassure her, then a kiss she shall have.

At that moment there was a knock on the door. "Come," William called.

Mr. Barnes opened the door and stepped just inside. "Lady Matlock to see you, sir."

William straightened, afraid of what she might do if she were to see Elizabeth in his home. Sighing, he realised he had no choice. "Send her in, please."

Rising from his chair, he moved in the direction of his aunt who was just entering the room. "Aunt, so nice to see you again." He took both of her out-stretched hands and guided her to a chair. "Please, sit down."

She complied, taking the measure of her nephew as he walked around and sat down behind his desk again.

"And, I am happy to see you, Fitzwilliam. I hope you will forgive me for coming without an invitation, but I was afraid you would be away to Pemberley before I had the chance to talk to you." She saw the trepidation in her nephew's face. "Oh, come now. You cannot fear what I have to say that much."

William smiled. "You can be a fearsome person when you want. I well remember the punishment you administered when Richard and I broke your rules."

Evelyn Fitzwilliam suppressed a smile. "And the punishment was well deserved, though that was five and twenty years ago at least!"

"At least! But well remembered!" Easy smiles faded as each examined the other expectantly. Finally, his aunt broke the uncomfortable impasse.

"I have come because I feel I have lost touch with you, nephew. All those months you spent in Scotland and Ireland, with only an occasional letter…" Her voice softened and trailed off as she observed his discomposure.

"I am sorry." Affectionately she patted his arm. "I did not come to chastise you. I love you as my own child, and I find I still tend to treat you as that young boy who used to climb into my lap."

A sparkle returned to William's eyes, and his lips lifted at the corners as he teased, "Richard claims my dimples bring out the mother in every woman."

She laughed. "That Richard! Well, you brought out the mother in me long before you were a handsome, eligible bachelor with captivating dimples!"

The smile faded as she suddenly grew solemn. "I could not help but notice that your attitude toward Mrs. Preston has drastically altered in the short time you were away from London." William shifted in his chair and refused to meet her eye. "Am I correct?"

After a few moments, he nodded without looking up.

"You are a grown man and that is your business, but I did notice that you seem to be more preoccupied," she paused, "or should I say troubled? So I am here to remind you that if you ever need a woman's—a *mother's* perspective, you have only to ask."

William sighed, pinching the bridge of his nose as he grimaced. "I am sorry. I thought your visit might involve my duty to marry Anne now that she has been abandoned."

"Lord no! I would never wish that for you, though I would love to see you married and content. God only knows it would have been easier to agree with your uncle than champion your right to choose the woman you want."

"I...I am not thinking of marriage at this point, but you would support my choice, if I decided to make an offer?"

Evelyn Fitzwilliam stopped short. *He is questioning my resolve already? Has he someone in mind as Richard believes?*

Straightening her shoulders she declared, "Yes. Though you are well aware that I would prefer you to choose someone of your station, the most important thing is that she be the woman you desire."

William's lips curved into a small smile. "And my uncle will not approve unless she is a member of the *ton.*" It was not a question.

"My Edward is stubborn and opinionated, but he loves you. He was wrong to become angry about Anne and he knows it, though he would never admit it. He has even yet to admit his error in insisting that Edgar offer for Jacqueline." She wrung her hands. "That decision proves his ability to err, and my poor Edgar is suffering the consequences. It has turned into an unimaginable disaster."

"Richard mentioned that they have had no more children after their son was stillborn."

"Jacqueline refuses to try for another child. She is staying here with her father. When I last talked with her, she firmly declared that she no longer wished to live with Edgar. Her father has always spoiled her, and he refuses to interfere. I suppose it is a lost cause." She shook her head as if to clear her mind.

"And the viscount is still living alone at Montrose Estate?"

"He is."

William's voice was sympathetic, as he realised it could just as likely have been him. "I see."

"But that is a discussion for another time. Speaking of Anne, Edward visited her here in London after her hasty marriage and the equally hasty disappearance of her husband. He was appalled at her mental decline. He said it was no wonder the cad had seen an opportunity to take what he wanted and then leave."

"What has been done to recover her dowry and dissolve the marriage?"

"Edward has men looking into everything—the possibility of having Anne secretly committed to a hospital for the insane in Ireland, the possibility of an annulment due to her mental defects, and the whereabouts and background of the man she married. Thus far, there is much confusion as to his real identity. He apparently has used several titles, count....Viscount, and we have no idea where he may be. Anne, of course, is of no help." She shook her head in bewilderment. "It has been most puzzling, and I am afraid it will become more so before this is settled."

She smiled wanly. "I suppose we should be grateful that the man left so soon after the wedding and has not tried to oust Catherine from Rosings. Can you imagine what a debacle that would be? She might reside here in London, near me for God's sake, for the rest of her life."

William could not help but smile at his aunt's words. "Well, I am glad that Uncle is handling that chaos, as I have no stomach for it after Aunt Catherine's diatribe when I refused to marry Anne."

"I am glad you did not let them place that burden on you. She is, after all, Edward's niece and his responsibility, not yours." She studied his face. "Is there anything you would like to tell me, Fitzwilliam?'

William toyed with the pen on his desk for a moment before lifting his eyes. "No. Not at this time, Aunt."

"Then, may I assume you will tell me, all in good time?" she asked, standing to take her leave and reaching to take his hand.

William smiled warmly. "You may rely on it."

Rosewood Manor
The Library

"Oh look, Evan! A letter from Cecile!" Georgiana was practically walking on air as she ran into the room, holding the letter aloft. "She must have some wonderful news to share for us to receive a letter this quickly!"

Evan laid the book he was reading aside, trying not to laugh. His wife's enthusiasm was exhilarating. Her light blue eyes, a match set to her brother's, sparkled as she plopped down across from him to begin reading. He was admiring the way the sun bounced off her golden curls, when he saw her countenance go from pleased to distressed in a matter of a few seconds.

"Darling, is everything all right?" Georgiana did not answer, her eyes never leaving the crisp linen stationery. "Ana?"

Slowly she appeared to focus on him. "I...I do not understand."

"Understand what, love?"

"Cecile writes that William was indifferent to her when he returned to London from Netherfield. She saw him at a dinner party at my aunt and uncle's home and..." She looked back at Cecile's words, a puzzled expression, causing her brows to knit.

"And?"

Georgiana responded, reading word for word. "He acted as though we were barely acquainted!"

Mumbling to herself, Georgiana began again to read the short letter, as if by doing so, she would find she had been mistaken.

Evan shrugged. "Well, your brother can certainly be aloof, especially in crowds, but never to those with whom he is familiar. I have never known him to be less than a gentleman where a lady is concerned. What do you suppose would give her that impression?"

"Cecile writes that he told her he has too many responsibilities to think of marriage at this time." She stood, beginning to pace back and forth with great agitation. "I thought he had decided to marry, to begin a family...I thought we had it settled before he left!"

"Ana." Evan stood then, grabbing her arm as she walked past and pulled her into an embrace. With great exasperation, she blew away a curl which had fallen into her eye. He pulled back to laugh at her, gaining him a glare in return.

"Georgiana Celeste Darcy Ingram! Your brother is a grown man, and you cannot insist he marry." As she started to protest, he held up his hand. "He never forced you to marry." Her eyes dropped to her shoes. "He supported your decision not to marry, and you managed quite well until you met a dashing, charming rogue whom you simply could not resist."

Her smile returned and she hit his arm. "Oh, you! You make me feel so guilty." She kissed him quickly and pulled back to look at his face. "I cannot help but worry. I love him so much, and I know he is lonely. You may not be able to tell, but I can. It tears me apart to realise how much love he has inside, yet he is all alone. I want him to have someone to love, like I have you."

Evan hugged her close. "I agree, love. However, having known Darcy since I was a lad, I understand his intensity. He will not be happy unless he finds the deepest kind of love—the kind we share. As much as I care for Cecile, I could never imagine his marrying her for love. For convenience perhaps," he said, "but not love."

Georgiana shook her head. "You are right. All this time I have pushed him to court Cecile, when she may not be his choice. Perhaps I should just make sure that more of my unmarried acquaintances are invited here so that he is thrown in company with them. Perhaps, then he might meet someone he could love!"

"That sounds like a splendid idea, sweetheart." He kissed the tip of her nose. "As long as you do not push, and you allow him to decide!" He sat back down, pulling Georgiana into his lap in one smooth motion.

"Now, when shall we learn what Cecile has up her sleeve? I do not think she will give up the Master of Pemberly without a fight. She seemed too enamoured of him, and if I know anything of my sister, I know she is a determined woman."

Even as he talked, Evan began to kiss just below her ear, trailing down her neck and making his way across her décolletage. Georgiana squirmed in response, sliding back and forth against his now hardening groin.

Breathing heavily, she sighed, "I have no idea, but I imagine she will tell me, as she means to return for your birthday dinner in a fortnight."

"How fortunate then that we have so long before she arrives," he responded, kissing that spot at the base of her neck—the one that always made her moan. Today was no exception.

Hearing her response, he stood with her in his arms and hurriedly crossed the room, exited into the hallway, and strode towards the grand staircase that led ultimately to their bedroom. One of the downstairs maids walked out of the drawing room just ahead of them and, seeing the spectacle, made a complete circle, heading back into the room from whence she came. They both chuckled.

"Mr. Ingram! In broad daylight!" Georgiana teased. "What will the servants think?"

He nuzzled her perfumed hair, his ardour beginning to take control, and whispered hoarsely in reply, "They will think the Master loves his wife, Mrs. Ingram."

As the seasoned maid peeked out of the drawing room, the sound of laughter could still be heard continuing up the stairs and then echoing down the hallways above. Seeing no one about, she cautiously continued on her way, trying to suppress the wide grin on her face.

Chapter 9

London
A Townhouse

"You had no right!" Count Stefano bellowed, his green eyes flashing, the veins in his neck were distended as he hurled a candelabrum across the room where it smashed into a liquor cabinet. The sound of crystal shattering brought a servant rushing to the door, who upon seeing the commotion quickly retreated. "I should have been the one to decide when my wife was to be informed of my activities!"

"The contessa is the mother of your son, Stephen. She deserves to know the truth! You are in no position to have Eduardo join you here. At any time, you might be confronted by an angry father or brother. Do you want to place the life of your son at risk?"

"What *truth* did you tell her, *Father*? Have you told her that I have taken several more wives in England or that I make my living by thievery, as you have cut off my allowance?"

Frederick Stanton, Earl of Essex, recoiled, making his son sneer.

"Surely, if you are aware of the number of women I have supposedly married, you must know what enables me to live so lavishly, though you have for all practical purposes disowned me."

"All the more reason to keep Eduardo away from you."

"You have made it your mission to keep those I love from me. I loved Elizabeth, but you took her away from me." He began to pace, mumbling incoherently before halting abruptly. "She was the only one I chose because I loved her. She had no fortune." Whirling around, he moved to stand face to face with his father. "You ruined it! You told her everything!"

"No! I should have told her, but for her sake, I could not. It was your failings that caused her to leave."

"Lies! You are lying!"

At the look on his father's face, Stefano began laughing hysterically, causing Stanton to declare, "You are mad!"

"You only want to be rid of me. Was that not your plan when you schemed to have me committed when that wench died! Do not think you can fool me again. I now have with me men from my mother's country that will stop you—men whose loyalty was to my grandfather and now to me. If you are smart, you will go back to your comfortable life and keep your nose out of my affairs."

The earl grabbed his cane and stalked towards the door but was halted as Stefano ran to step in front of him, grabbing his forearms tightly.

"Consider this your last warning, *Father*. If I learn that you have interfered in my life again, I will not hesitate to have my men hunt you down."

Stanton shook his arms free and walked around his son, not looking back until he stood outside the front door. Taking a shaky breath, he descended the steps and entered his carriage.

Mr. Scroggins, his long-time servant now serving as his bodyguard, enquired, "What did he say?"

"The usual threats," Frederick Stanton replied, not meeting the other man's eyes. Mr. Scroggins studied him for a few moments.

"You should have let me accompany you." Stanton shrugged. "You did you best, sir. You tried to rear him right, but that mother of his and his grandfather filled his head with so much rubbish that—"

"Please, Scroggins! Do not try to absolve me. I knew what he was—what he was capable of many years before I tried to right the wrongs he had committed. If only I had acted sooner! He has deceived two women that I know about, not counting that mentally unbalanced one."

"Miss de Bourgh?" the servant ventured.

"Yes. That is the one." He shivered. "She is probably as disturbed as my son. At least I got him out of the country before he could carry out his threat to take Rosings. Her mother, Lady Catherine de Bourgh, would have seen him dead first. I was barely able to convince him to remove himself from England before Lord Matlock got word that he had depleted all the money from Miss de Bourgh's accounts. Edward Fitzwilliam is very influential and not to be crossed."

Stanton turned to study the scenery outside the window for a long time before lamenting, "Why did he have to return? And why to London? If word reaches Fitzwilliam..." He sighed.

"He was never one to listen, not to you, nor to anyone else. It is a wonder he is not involved in more trouble."

Stanton met Mr. Scroggins' gaze. "I am sorry to report to you that he is. I did not want to believe it, but he confirmed my fears today.

"He pays accomplices for stolen gold, silver and precious stones. He smuggles the contraband aboard the ships in which I have invested—those that sail to and from Italy, hiding the items inside other goods that are being legally exported. I imagine he can then sell the pilfered goods for a substantial amount on the Continent."

"How did you find out?"

"The agent that I hired reported to me several days ago. Mr. Burger is an excellent sleuth—very expensive, but he uncovers the information that he is employed to find. He also stated that a man has been enquiring after Stephen in Town." He dropped his gaze to his boots. "It may be some relative of one of the ladies he has ruined. I am amazed he has evaded justice this long."

He sat silently as the carriage swayed back and forth, carrying them to his townhouse. Mr. Scroggins knew from his expression not to question him further. Frederick Stanton was lost in memories of a fair-haired boy who was always eager to be with his father, a boy who loved to ride with him across the meadows at Northgate. As always, his heart began to ache with regret. Perhaps if Maria had not abandoned their marriage and listened to her father's pleas to return to Italy, Stephen would have turned out differently. As it was, his son was taken from him when he was barely seven, and he had not seen him again until he was twenty. It had caused an irreparable breach in their relationship.

Neither man brought up the fact that had Stephen's mother not spirited him back to Italy the year he was nine and twenty, he now would have been residing in a place where he could not hurt anyone again—in Bedlam.

Journey from London to Pemberley

This journey home was unlike any William had made before. He was determined to lessen the travelling time by one day because he had decided not to give Elizabeth the herbal brew that kept her calm and sleepy unless it proved absolutely necessary and he was concerned that she would not adjust well to being on the road. They had left London at dawn in his best coach with a basket of food and drink—enough to allow them to traverse many miles, making stops only to change horses.

When they finally stopped at a small coach stop, he helped the women out so that they could stretch their legs and take care of necessities. He escorted Elizabeth inside before handing her off to Mrs. Drury and heading back outside to check their progress. A short while later, he returned to inform them that they were ready to resume their journey.

This course of action was repeated several times over the course of the day until they reached the inn William had chosen for their first night. The establishment was well cared for, provided hot baths, served adequate food and had several larger bedrooms available for those who had the means to pay for them. As weary as they were when they arrived, he was pleased that he had heeded Mr. Barnes' suggestion that he send a servant ahead to arrange lodging and horses along the entire route.

It was not lost on William that Elizabeth was exhausted. She leaned heavily on him as he helped her from the coach. With her hand on his arm, they entered the inn, and she immediately froze as several men, all sitting around one table in a dark corner, stopped their conversation to gawk at her. Glancing in the direction of the men, William slid his free hand over hers protectively and looked back over his shoulder to nod at Mrs. Drury. She quickly moved up to stand next to Elizabeth, effectively shielding her on the other side. Thus, with Elizabeth in between, they moved to the inn's desk.

"Mr. Darcy, how pleased we are to have you with us!" the proprietor, Mr. Gates, gushed. He glanced at Elizabeth and appeared to wonder if she were Mrs. Darcy. When no presentation was forthcoming, he recovered briskly. "As you requested, hot baths will be readied immediately, and I shall send dinner trays to your rooms. If you will follow Gertrude," the innkeeper gestured to a plump young woman with red hair and freckles, "she will show you the way."

William nodded his acquiescence and began to guide Elizabeth towards the stairs. Gertrude, who was not only round but short, had to run to get ahead of the party. As she assumed the lead, she occasionally cast glances back at Elizabeth and Mr. Darcy. She had been enamoured of the handsome gentleman since she had come to work for her uncle, Mr. Gates, at four and ten years of age. That year, the object of her admiration was a dashing fellow of one and twenty. She knew his exact age because she had overheard Colonel Fitzwilliam, who often travelled with him then, remark about his upcoming birthday.

As the years passed and Mr. Darcy had not married, she began to pretend that he had not taken a wife because he secretly admired her. It was only whimsy, but it gave her something to dream about amid the dullness of her existence. Barely a fortnight ago, Gertrude had been thrilled to see him again after a two-year absence, but his appearance tonight, with a beautiful woman in tow, caused only disappointment. As she guided the party up the stairs, her mind raced. Had Mr. Darcy married? She tried to determine if the lady wore a ring, but gloves covered the evidence. Sighing heavily, she faced forward knowing that the way Mr. Darcy looked at the young woman, her flight of fancy had been just that.

Reaching the second landing, she guided them down a little-used corridor lined with larger rooms. Stopping in front of the first door on the left, she barely lifted her eyes to address the gentleman she had long admired. "We have reserved this single room," she informed him, and then she motioned to the right side of the hall, "and these two rooms, which are connected. They share a small dressing room with a sitting area in between."

Without replying, William motioned for the footman following them to put his trunk in the single room on the right, then signalled the other footman with a slight nod of his head to carry the remaining trunks into the suite on the left hand side. After the footmen had carried in the luggage and departed, he led Elizabeth into the suite.

"You and Mrs. Drury shall occupy these rooms." He glanced to see Elizabeth's reaction, and from the corner of his eye caught sight of Gertrude standing just inside the room. Annoyed, he turned to direct her elsewhere. "Please have a bath prepared right away."

Gertrude took a few steps towards the hallway door, stopping when William's attention focused on Elizabeth again. As he led her into the small sitting area, Gertrude turned and slipped closer to the door through which they had exited, quite envious of his tender words to the young woman she now envied.

"Elizabeth?" William raised her face with one finger under her chin, waiting until she looked up. When she did, he smiled warmly and could not help but cup her face with his hand. "The small table in the corner will suffice for you and Mrs. Drury to have your dinner. After you bathe and eat, you must go to bed, as we will leave early. Mrs. Drury will leave all the doors open between your rooms so she can hear if you call her. I shall be just across the hall. Do you understand?" She did not respond, but he was encouraged by her serene countenance.

Gertrude was fascinated. She had never heard any man speak to a woman so lovingly, and she was sure that she would never enjoy the experience. Sighing heavily, she turned and ran into Mrs. Drury. Elizabeth's companion had taken longer to come up the stairs and had observed the maid's eavesdropping. Gertrude coloured and practically ran from the room.

Observing the servant's hasty exit and frowning in disapproval, Mrs. Drury debated mentioning it to Mr. Darcy, but seeing that he was talking to Elizabeth, she thought better of it. The man had enough to worry about as it was.

~~~*~~~

George Wickham could not believe his eyes. Fitzwilliam Darcy with a woman—and a beautiful one at that!

He had been seated at a table with a few inebriated men when the Darcy party entered the inn. He liked to provide plenty of liquor, as it was much easier to relieve drunks of their valuables. One of the men made a bawdy remark about the woman with Darcy, causing the rest to laugh uproariously. Wickham, however, did not join in the laughter as he was engrossed in studying the Master of Pemberley and the lady close by his side. The dimly lit corner provided enough cover to prevent his being recognized as he took in the woman's fine figure and lovely face. And as she turned towards Darcy, he felt his ire rise.

He could have had such a woman, had George Darcy provided for him as he had promised that he would. Suddenly, a new thought emerged from his hatred. *Perhaps he left me more than the meagre three thousand pounds I was given, but Darcy withheld it. I could certainly believe it of the bastard!*

Observing the obviously devoted couple anew, he searched his memory, trying to remember if he had heard or read that his old friend had married or was even engaged. With his new enterprises claiming his attention, Wickham had been too busy to keep up with London society. Smiling, he considered for just a moment that the woman was a whore. The smile vanished just as quickly as the thought that provoked it.

No! She did not dress the part, and she had a chaperone. Besides, Darcy would never be seen in public with such a woman. Hell, he is hardly seen in company with any woman. Perhaps he likes men!

Chuckling to himself, Wickham knew that it was not true, but enjoyed the thought just the same. His reflections were interrupted by the sight of Gertrude leading Darcy's party up the stairs. A wide smile creased his face. He had ingratiated himself to the unattractive redhead during the last year, paying her compliments and bringing her paste jewellery, and now she was primed to do his bidding. On his last stay, she had agreed to obtain keys for him to the rooms occupied by the rich and to alert him when a woman was staying alone.

He intended to wait until the early morning hours, slip in and relieve them of their best jewels, leaving the cheaper items. He hoped that by leaving some baubles, the thefts would not be discovered until much later. In any event, he already would have vanished by daylight, leaving Gertrude a few pounds richer and himself considerably more so.

Rising to go to their usual meeting place behind the inn, Wickham could not remove the smirk from his face. He wondered if the beautiful woman with Darcy would be alone tonight. Perhaps he would take more from her than just her jewels!

Later that night

The room was ablaze, and smoke was filling her lungs. There was a blinding pain in her head, and her ears seemed to ring from the loud blast as Elizabeth tried to sit up. From the corner of her eye, she could see the child lying on the floor next to her mother, both with red stains spreading across their muslin gowns. Elizabeth tried again to move, but could not, so she began to scream for someone—anyone. Suddenly, she realised that she could not hear anything—not the sounds of the fire or even her own cries.

Sweating profusely, Elizabeth bolted upright in the bed, reaching for her baby, but it was not beside her. She felt around for it frantically, but as her eyes adjusted to the darkness, she realised that she did not recognise the room either. Beginning to panic, she slid from the bed and ran to the door. Trying the knob, she found it locked and turned to run through the open door into the sitting room. Just at that moment, that door opened and a tall, dark-haired man stood outlined in the doorway, holding a small candle. She stopped and stood deathly still, wondering if it was he—the only one whose face she remembered, the one who was so kind to her.

George Wickham had already relieved an older female guest across the hall of her jewels and had just slipped open the door to the sitting room, when he was confronted by the sight of Elizabeth, standing still and quietly watching him. The flickering light of his candle revealed that she wore nothing but a nightgown. Wickham stood perfectly still, anticipating her scream, but he began to relax when she did not cry out or try to run. He thought it odd that she did not attempt to cover herself, though clad only in thin cotton. Holding the small candle higher to see more clearly, George was more surprised by the strange look in her eye.

Does she think I am Darcy? I suppose in the darkness, we look somewhat similar.

Quickly, he blew out the candle and walked towards her. He was mesmerized by her lack of fear. She did not react as a normal lady would have; in fact, she seemed confused or perhaps not in her right mind.

He smiled. Perhaps taking advantage of her would be easier than he had thought. Slowly, he reached out to take her hand and began to lead her from the room. He was surprised when she followed without protest. Once out of the room, he caught sight of a door at the end of the hallway and led her in that direction. He was delighted to find it opened onto a small porch.

~~~*~~~

Tossing and turning, William had not been able to sleep. Yet again, he turned and closed his eyes tightly, knowing that he would likely fall asleep in the carriage tomorrow if he did not sleep at least a few hours tonight. Just as he was drifting off, he heard a whisper in his ear. *Something is wrong!*

"Elizabeth!"

Sitting up, he looked about the room, and realising that no one was there, wondered at the sense of foreboding that gripped his heart. He could stay in bed no longer. Grabbing his robe and sliding on his slippers, he jerked the door open. The hallway was dark and quiet. Standing perfectly still, the only sound he heard was his rapidly beating heart. He waited. After a few seconds, he began to feel foolish and stepped back, preparing to close the door. Just as he did, the voice spoke once more. *See to her.*

Without hesitation, he stepped across the hall and tried her door. It was locked. Looking down the hall to the sitting room door, he moved to it and was surprised when it opened easily. Panicking, he entered and crossed to her bedroom. Instantly, he knew she was gone. As if drawn by an invisible cord, he found himself back in the hallway, his gaze at once falling on the door at the end.

A muffled sound reached his ears, and he shouted, "Elizabeth!"

Reaching the door in a few long strides, he pushed it open to find a man running down the steps to the ground and Elizabeth softly crying. She was alone, her hair blowing wildly in the wind and her eyes wide in fright. Immediately he pulled her into a tight embrace, whispering words of comfort as she trembled. She melted into him, sobbing.

Shouting her name had brought everyone into the hall. Servants, guests, and Mrs. Drury all stared at the open door to the porch and the couple locked in an embrace. Oblivious to their audience, William picked Elizabeth up and carried her past them without acknowledging anyone or stopping until he had laid her down on her bed.

"Sir, is there anything I can do?" Mrs. Drury asked as she leaned over the bed from the opposite side.

"Please have someone tell Mr. Gates to meet me in the sitting room, and order some tea so that you can mix in the herbs that help her to sleep. After you return, I will leave her with you while I meet with Mr. Gates." She quickly left to find one of the servants.

"Elizabeth?" She would not look at him, so he cupped her face until she did. He could see the tears pooled in her eyes. "Did he hurt you?"

She did not reply, only closing her eyes, but he noted that her gown was not in disarray, and there were no marks on her skin. He prayed that he had arrived in time.

"We will not leave you alone as you sleep again. I promise. Until we get you to Pemberley where you shall be safe, Mrs. Drury or I shall stay in your room every night to guard you. Would you like that?" She opened her eyes, and he felt the pressure of her hands squeezing his. He was comforted to think she answered in her own way.

He squeezed her hands in return and saw a flicker of recognition in her eyes. "Yes, you understand what I am saying, sweetheart."

William started to stand, but Elizabeth refused to loosen her grip. He brought both her hands up to his mouth, kissing first one, then the other, just as Mrs. Drury walked back into the room.

"I shall return, Elizabeth." He glanced to the companion. "Mrs. Drury will stay with you until then."

Mrs. Drury moved to take his place on the edge of the bed, carefully pushing Elizabeth's hair from her eyes. Finding the doll on the floor, she placed it next to her. She soothed Elizabeth as if she were a child. William walked to the sitting room, stopping in the doorway for one last look at his beloved before he stepped inside to confront Mr. Gates.

It was nearly a half-hour before William returned to find Elizabeth's eyes closed. Mrs. Drury promptly stood.

"Shhh," he said, lifting a finger to his lips. He motioned for her to follow him to the sitting room. He stood in the doorway, one eye on Elizabeth as he spoke quietly. "I do not want her to hear."

Mrs. Drury nodded. "Mr. Darcy, I am so sorry. I blame myself for not being aware of what was happening earlier. If she had been hurt—"

"Madam, it is not your fault. There was nothing to hear. The blackguard had a key to the room."

She gasped. "But how?"

"It is the only logical explanation. There was no forced entry. I checked all the doors before going to bed, and they were secure. Somehow the thief acquired keys. He had already stolen jewels from another room." William's expression hardened as he continued. "What I do not understand, though, is why he did not run when he saw Elizabeth instead of taking her with him." He shook his head. "If I find the—"

"Do you know who it is?"

"No. But a man of that ilk will continue his mischief until he is caught, and I fear that a servant in this establishment might have aided him since he had keys. Mr. Gates has promised a thorough investigation." He sighed, wearily rubbing his eyes with his palms before speaking again. "I do not intend for her to be alone ever again at night while we travel. What happened proves she is incapable of protecting herself against anyone who would do her harm."

Mrs. Drury murmured, "Poor child."

"I need you to stay with her for the first few hours after dark. Then when everyone else is asleep, I shall slip into the room for my watch, while you get some rest. At first light, I will return to my room, dress and go downstairs to arrange our departure and a basket for the journey. You shall, of course, be with her until we are ready to leave."

"But, sir, that will leave you very little time for rest."

"I have slept in many a chair—even on the ground when necessary—so it will not affect me very much, especially as it will only be for a few days." He smiled. "You are the one who will find no rest while watching her, I fear."

It was her turn to smile. "Lose no sleep over me, sir. I may be old, but I am of sturdy stock!"

William stepped over to open the door to the hall and seeing no one about, closed it quickly. "For tonight I shall stay, as there is no one about to know. Please try to rest. We leave in a few hours."

Mrs. Drury bobbed a curtsy and entered her room, closing the door.

William turned to enter Elizabeth's room, checked the door to find it secure, and then pulled a large upholstered chair over to the bedside. However, after dropping tiredly into its cushions, his eyes refused to close. Instead they sought Elizabeth. Thoughts of what might have been her fate had he not listened to the inner urgings made his stomach churn. No matter the reason, he had failed her.

Gently he moved to sit on the edge of the bed. She looked peaceful, her dark curls fanned out across the white linens, and the lines on her face smooth in sleep. The doll she normally clutched lay on a pillow nearby. Memories of the young woman he had met at the assembly in Meryton came flooding back as he drank in her features. He was powerless to stave off the same fear that overwhelmed him as he had searched for her. His heart began to throb with such force that it seemed it might leap from his chest, and against his better judgment, he reached out to caress a lock of her ebony hair.

Her eyes opened sleepily. She reached to caress his face, and in spite of his weariness, he smiled and covered her hand with his. Then she slid over in an attempt to make room for him to lie down. Hesitating only a moment, he lay alongside her, and she turned to snuggle into his chest, closing her eyes. Though it was difficult to ignore the feel of her body next to his, he would not deny her the safety of his arms. Steeling himself not to react, he wrapped his arms around her, pulling her closer and closing his eyes.

They remained entwined until the first rays of light prompted him to rise, before the rest of the inn and any prying eyes awakened. Elizabeth still slept as he slipped out of the room, and he encountered Mrs. Drury coming into the sitting room. He acknowledged her slight curtsy.

"She had a restful sleep, no doubt from the herbs. I hope you did as well?"

"Yes, I managed to sleep a little, thank you."

"I am glad. I will return to my room before the servants bring around the warm water I requested and our trays of food. After you both have eaten and dressed, send word and I shall escort you to the carriage. I would like to leave as soon as possible."

"Very well, sir."

~~~*~~~

Wickham sat on his horse for some time, still in sight of the inn but hidden by the trees. He grinned at all the lights suddenly flickering inside, the sounds of loud voices, then chuckled to see men running to and fro, inside and out. Suddenly sobering, he cursed the luck that had brought Darcy out onto the porch so quickly that he had not the time to steal even a kiss from the captivating vixen.

How did Darcy know that he was just about to discover what was under that thin gown? Hell, the man must be a wizard!

It was Darcy's shout that had interrupted his pleasure and sent him flying down the stairs. He would know that voice anywhere, and he was not about to let Fitzwilliam Darcy apprehend him. The man could be ruthless when it came to those he loved. Once he had threatened his life, just for stopping by Pemberley when Georgiana was alone. Wickham laughed. There had never been any danger of Georgiana Darcy falling for his charms. She was much too intelligent to believe his lies.

His thoughts returned to the mysterious woman that travelled with Darcy. *Elizabeth. The name suits. She is clearly a beautiful woman, if a little odd. But who am I to tell Darcy what kind of woman he should pursue. Perhaps only one who is not in her right mind would have him!* Chuckling, he tipped his hat and kicked his horse into a canter.

I hope we meet again soon, Miss Elizabeth!

~~~*~~~

As they crossed the highest point along the drive to the front of the house, the sight of Pemberley in the distance caused William to smile. The prospect never failed to inspire and never more so than today. He tapped his cane on the ceiling, bringing the coach to an abrupt halt. Opening the door, he lightly dropped to the ground before a footman could lower the step, and he turned to assist Elizabeth. Without hesitating, she let him place his hands around her waist, lift her from the coach and deposit her on the ground. Then he guided her to the place where large boulders marked the edge of the road. He watched her expression until she seemed to focus on the house before speaking.

"This is my home, Elizabeth. This is Pemberley, and it is to be your home now. I hope you will love it as much as I do." He felt the now familiar squeeze of her hand, though her gaze never left the scene, and he returned the gesture before guiding her back to the coach. Mrs. Drury had been taking in the view from the window and was suitably impressed. She spoke as they settled back into their seats.

"Your home is lovely, Mr. Darcy."

"Thank you, Mrs. Drury. But there is so much more of it to admire than just this view." He watched Elizabeth. "I hope you both will be very happy here."

Smiling at the way his gaze never left Elizabeth as he spoke, Mrs. Drury responded, "I am sure we will, sir."

For a moment, William thought Elizabeth might say something, but in the end, the only sign of her approval was a very slight upturn of her lips. His heart sang. This was the first sign of a smile since he had found her that night in the rain, and he could not tear his eyes away.

You are home, my love, and I hope to make you smile for the rest of your life. You will never be unhappy again, if it is in my power to make it so.

Chapter 10

Pemberley

"Mr. Darcy! I was hoping to find you out early today!" Cecile Preston's greeting caused William to turn Onyx around from the view at the top of the mountain and watch her manoeuvre her mare up the steep trail behind him. He frowned to think she might have followed him to Derbyshire. Her appearance at this place, sacred to him since he had come here first alongside his father, raised his ire.

He wondered whatever had possessed him to show it to her. This outlook was his destination each time he rode out seeking sanctuary, and now she knew just where to look for him. Seeing the unnatural smile on her face, he wondered at her presence on his property at all. He had assumed that Cecile had been sufficiently offended by his actions that he would never see her again by her own choice.

Fears of a compromising situation intruded on William's thoughts as well as the realisation that she must still be hopeful of gaining his admiration. If that were true, she would likely want to follow him back to the manor. Trying not to raise her suspicions, he summoned his best manners and assumed a pleasant mien.

"Mrs. Preston, I am surprised to see you! I thought you were enjoying the advantages of Town."

"Oh, I decided to leave London shortly after..." She coloured and looked down demurely. "I decided I simply must apologize for what I said at your aunt's ball. I do not know where my manners were, but I assure you that I did not mean a word of my," she looked up through her pale eyelashes, with what she believed was a most seductive expression before continuing, "my little show of temper."

William showed no emotion, so she quickly continued, "I still want for us to be friends and maybe, when you have all your responsibilities well in hand—"

"Speaking of those responsibilities, I am supposed to meet with my steward in a half-hour, so I must beg your leave and return to the house. I wish you a very pleasant day." He pulled the reins and nudged Onyx to turn, but at the dejected look on her face, felt somewhat sorry and added, "You understand that I have been gone a great deal lately, and I have much to do."

"I understand completely. You have much resting on your broad shoulders. However, I wonder if I might ride back to Pemberley with you? I need to rest my horse for a bit before I return to Rosewood Manor, and surely you would not deny a thirsty lady a cup of tea."

At the sight of a frown appearing on his handsome face, she continued pleadingly. "You will not even know I am there, as I know you have a meeting to attend, and I must return to Rosewood shortly or Georgiana will worry." She tried to be more cheerful. "I cannot wait to inform her that you are already home. She mentioned your return to me, and from the intended date of departure, we believed that you would arrive tomorrow."

He wondered at Georgiana's discussing his letters with her and that she rode all the way to Pemberley this morning if she believed he was to arrive tomorrow, but he kept those thoughts to himself.

"Of course. You are welcome to rest and have some refreshments."

They rode back to the stables in silence, and he was able to keep a short distance ahead the entire way. His thoughts were occupied with planning how best to keep Cecile from seeing Elizabeth. Once they attained the paddocks, William dismounted, throwing the reins to a groom, and began surveying the house to see if he could espy Elizabeth on the balcony outside her room.

"Mr. Darcy?"

William looked over his shoulder to see Cecile holding out her arms, obviously waiting for his assistance in dismounting. She had never required his help before, and he stood transfixed until suddenly remembering his manners and moving to lift her down. The smile she bestowed as she slid down, purposefully trying to move closer to his person caused him to shiver in disgust. It was the exact smile he had seen on innumerable ladies of the *ton* throughout the years. How wrong he had been to ever think she was not one of them!

After setting her on the ground, he offered her his arm, and they walked swiftly towards the manor. It was all Cecile could do to keep pace with his long legs, as William wished to gain the house as soon as possible and be done with her company. He cut across the lawn to enter the house via the portico. The French doors in the parlour already stood open, letting in the morning air.

As they entered, William startled to see a flustered Mrs. Drury walk hurriedly past the door in the direction of the front of the house. Forgetting about Cecile, his only thought was that something might have happened to Elizabeth, as her companion rarely left her alone.

"Mrs. Drury?" he called, leaving Cecile behind as he stepped briskly ahead. Mrs. Drury's footsteps stopped and became louder as she hurried back toward him. Upon reaching the door, she timidly peered inside, and seeing Mr. Darcy, sighed audibly.

"Mr. Darcy, I am so glad you are here. Elizabeth—" She stopped, as he held up his hand to silence her, and Cecile materialized from behind him. In his concern, William had almost forgotten his unwanted guest was right behind, so now he sought to isolate her.

"I am sorry, Mrs. Preston. Would you excuse me? If you will continue to the dining room, I am sure cook has set out breakfast and will see to it that you have your tea and perhaps something more filling."

Although she must have realised from the way Mr. Darcy quieted the woman that something had to be amiss, Cecile's face showed no disquiet.

"Oh, do not concern yourself about me, Mr. Darcy. I know just how to make myself at home here." She started out of the room, a simpering smile on her face that caused his stomach to turn. With Mrs. Drury's sudden appearance, he was beginning to regret allowing the woman to visit.

William followed her to the doors, closing them and turning to Mrs. Drury. He had no way of knowing that Cecile had quickly moved down the hall and through the music room next door, then out onto the portico, where she inched towards the still open doors of the parlour they had entered just moments ago. She was able to hear their entire conversation from her hiding place.

"Mrs. Drury, what about Elizabeth?" William enquired, now quite alarmed.

"As is her habit, Elizabeth arose before dawn and was on the balcony as the sun rose this morning." The elderly woman brought her hand to her forehead as though she was trying to remember precisely. "I was with her when I saw you ride off quite early. After the sun was up, I requested the maid bring her breakfast. She ate a muffin and drank a cup of tea, and I read to her. Shortly afterward, you returned and," the woman blushed, "I was not trying to spy on you, but I did notice you helping that woman down from her horse."

"Yes, and?"

"Out of the blue, Elizabeth dropped her cup. As I went to pick it up, she stood and hurried into her bedroom. She locked the door, and I have not been able to get her to open it. I returned through the door into my bedroom. I was afraid to alert your staff, as I did not know how much you wanted them to know."

"I was planning to discuss our strategy after breakfast. I would like to keep her presence a secret from outsiders, of course, but not every servant here will know about her special problems either—only those that I trust implicitly. I will discuss it with you today."

At that very moment, a footman appeared on a nearby balcony, and still eavesdropping, Mrs. Preston was obliged to hide behind a large potted plant. Sure that she had heard quite enough to alarm Georgiana, she decided not to wait for tea, but to return to Rosewood immediately. She stood perfectly still until the footman went back inside and practically ran down the path towards the stables.

Meanwhile, William paced the parlour, running his hands through his hair. He knew Elizabeth was beginning to rely on him completely, and he recollected Dr. Towson's warning not to hurt her feelings. "Do you have any idea what caused the spell? Could she have seen me with Mrs. Preston?"

"I am not sure. She never seems to pay attention to anything in particular, but this is her first morning at Pemberley, and to see you with any woman, particularly one holding onto you the way the lady…well, I would have assumed she was your wife, if I did not know better."

"Return to her, and I shall come as soon as I wash the dirt off and change clothes." She bobbed a curtsy, and he bowed imperceptibly before hurrying past. As she reached the doorway, she caught sight of him as he reached the staircase and took the steps two at a time. Being not so nimble herself, Mrs. Drury followed at a more sedate pace.

Stalking back to the stables, Cecile was seething.

So, he has thrown me over for some chit, and he had the audacity to bring her to Pemberley. He is a fool to believe he can hide her!

She stopped abruptly when another theory came to mind. *Of course! She is probably his mistress! And what special problem could she have? Is she with child already? Well, Mr. Darcy, we shall see exactly what Georgiana and Evan will say when they learn of this!*

The groom already had her horse prepared, and she was on the way to Rosemont Manor before William had even remembered to check on his visitor in the dining room. Having washed and changed into clean clothes, he returned downstairs to find she was not in the house. Checking with Mrs. Reynolds, he learned Cecile had never entered the dining room, and a footman had seen her hurrying to the stables.

William had a niggling suspicion why Cecile might have left without a word but no way of confirming it, so he convinced himself that it made no sense to worry about something that might not be true. He had intended to offer his sister and brother a full accounting of Elizabeth's situation; now that would have to become a priority for this day. If Cecile stayed in Derbyshire for any length of time, she would likely learn of Elizabeth's presence, so he would need to seek Georgiana's thoughts on telling her sister, in confidence, the story they had invented about Elizabeth's being a distant cousin. Perhaps Cecile would feel bound by familial duty to Georgiana and Evan to keep it private.

He shook his head, trying to clear all negative thoughts and assume a pleasant countenance. At this very minute, there was a beautiful young woman that needed some reassurance from him, and William was eager to be of service. As he hurried to her room, he distinctly heard a small still voice. *Remember, she is married.*

He stopped for a brief moment before dismissing it as he had at every other instance. He was too deeply in love to consider that.

~~~*~~~

"Elizabeth! Please open the door!"

For the fourth time, William put his ear against the smooth wood, but Pemberley's doors were so thick it was impossible to discern any movement within the room. His eyes met Mrs. Drury's and he shrugged. "I shall have to get inside via the servant's hall."

At her expression of surprise, he explained. "All the bedrooms have hallways behind the walls that allow the servants to come and go without disturbing the guests." While he talked, William went into Mrs. Drury's bedroom, walked over to one of the walls and pressed a panel. She gasped as a door opened, revealing a narrow space wide enough for one person to enter. He lit a candle sitting on a nearby table and holding it, disappeared inside. She walked over to look down the narrow corridor in the direction of a light that was getting dimmer the farther he walked.

Entering Elizabeth's bedroom through a similar door, William blew out the candle and stood still for a moment. He did not wish to frighten her, and she had all the curtains drawn, rendering the room almost black. As his eyes became accustomed to the dark, a small sigh caught his attention, and he stepped silently towards a form, now visible on top of the white counterpane.

She hid her face in a pillow and only an occasional sound escaped. She looked so vulnerable, still in her white, lace-trimmed nightgown, barefoot, her dark hair dishevelled. It was entirely void of pins and hung down like a child's. For several seconds, his starving eyes drank in the sight of her. She must have detected his presence, because she raised her head from the pillow.

"Elizabeth?"

She rolled in the opposite direction, hiding her face in the pillow once more.

"Please, Elizabeth!" He went around to the side she now faced, sat down and took one hand in his. "Will you at least let me explain?"

When he finally coaxed her to open her eyes, he was devastated to find the distant look that harkened back to his first memories of her at Netherfield. He cupped her face, but got no reaction. Finally, as a last resort, he leaned down and placed a lingering kiss on her forehead. When he pulled back, she was studying him with a puzzled look.

"The woman you saw with me, the one I helped down from the horse, is only a guest who wished to rest here for a bit before resuming her journey. I could not refuse her request for a cup of tea." He longed to see her features relax. "She is only an acquaintance."

Once again, Elizabeth focused somewhere off in the distance, so he continued.

"Today I would like to show you Pemberley's walking paths. We have short ones through the gardens and longer ones around the lake and ponds. Would you like that?" He thought he felt a squeeze of her hand. "All right then. I will open the door for Mrs. Drury and your maid to assist you in getting dressed."

With a heavy sigh of relief, he stood and opened the door, finding Mrs. Drury waiting patiently just outside. "I shall have Mrs. Reynolds send Maggie to help her get dressed. Send for me when she is ready, and I shall take her walking."

"Very good, sir. I feel sure it will raise her spirits." Mrs. Drury could not contain her smile as she entered Elizabeth's room.

Rosewood Manor
A Drawing Room

"And you say this woman is living at Pemberley?" Georgiana's voice got higher as she questioned her sister.

"I am only repeating what I heard," Cecile stated resolutely. "He said he wants to keep this woman, *Elizabeth,* a secret, and he mentioned her special problem."

Evan Ingram frowned at his wife. "Ana, you should wait until your brother explains. I am sure he will come today. He always sees you as soon as he gets home. Cecile may have been mistaken."

Cecile looked between the two with barely concealed irritation. By the time Evan had joined them, she had practically convinced Georgiana to storm Pemberley, demanding that Mr. Darcy throw the whore out. How she wished that he had been out of the house when she returned! He was being the voice of reason, and she could not let him prevail.

"Mr. Darcy did not seem eager to visit today. In fact, he seemed more worried about the problem Mrs. Drury was having with the woman."

"And just how did you happen to hear a private conversation between Darcy and this Mrs. Drury?"

Evan's question made Cecile colour, but she had become quite used to producing excuses since she had partnered with Mr. Wickham. She needed plenty of them in order to borrow her friends' jewels and visit their homes to learn their configuration.

"As I explained to Georgiana, I left my riding crop in the parlour and was going back inside to find it, when I accidentally heard them talking. I was shocked by the scandalous topic and froze to the spot. But I could do nothing but wait on the portico until they left the room, then retrieve the crop and hurry here." She slowly lifted her eyes to Evan's, but his face was as expressionless as Mr. Darcy's had been.

"I see," was all he managed to say, though his manner clearly showed his disbelief. He turned back to Georgiana. "I have my steward and a tenant in my study as we speak, but if you will wait, I will ride over in the carriage with you after we conclude our business."

Georgiana would not be gainsaid. "I believe it would be better if I talk with my brother alone. He will speak more freely with just the two of us present, and if he has really brought a—someone he needs to hide…" Georgiana could not go on, as she was overcome with emotion, thinking of the implications.

Evan frowned, as he took in Cecile's satisfied smirk. He tried once more. "If you go now, alone, I fear you will only make matters worse."

"Nevertheless, I shall ride over and see what he has to say."

Evan scowled at her insistence on doing as she pleased, even knowing that he disapproved. She was just as stubborn as her brother. "I only wish to reiterate that you should wait, but if you are determined, good luck! You will need it."

With that, Evan stalked out of the room, clearly annoyed, leaving Georgiana flustered and Cecile with a wicked smile on her face, one which instantly sobered when Georgiana looked her way. She offered encouragement.

"If it means anything, I believe you should go alone as well. Mr. Darcy would feel the need to defend himself in front of Evan."

"I believe you are right, and I must know for my own peace of mind if what you heard is true."

"I will ride over with you and wait in the garden, if you desire."

"No, it is best that I go alone." With that, Georgiana hurried toward her bedroom, eager to change into her riding habit.

Pemberley

"Do you see that rock over there?" William pointed to a large boulder that was about fifty feet out into the lake. Elizabeth stood with him on the bank, staring in that direction. "There is a terrapin that suns itself on it every day in the summer. He is larger than any I have ever seen, and his is so colourful that Georgiana used to sit on this bank and draw likenesses of him."

His heart leapt as she smiled wanly—only the second time that he could remember her doing so. "Do you remember when I talked about my sister, Georgiana?" She squeezed his hand, and he continued excitedly. "She lives nearby—she and her husband, Evan Ingram. They are very good people, and I know they will love you. Perhaps Gigi—that is what I call her—will bring some of her drawings to show you."

They were almost at the end of the path around the lake, and Elizabeth seemed to be tiring. So as they neared the house, William planned to escort her back to her room to rest until the afternoon meal was served. Instead, a calico cat trotted past them on her way to the stables, the evidence of her newborn kittens very noticeable. As she passed, she mewed a greeting to William.

"Good day, Stockings!" William called after her, causing Elizabeth to glance up at him. He smiled at the evidence of her attention.

He squeezed her hand. "Georgiana named her that because she looked as though she wore four white stockings." She still wore a blank expression, and a thought crossed his mind.

"Do you want to see her kittens?"

Elizabeth's eyes showed a spark of interest, so he pulled her off the path and across the lawn in the direction of the stables. Once there, they went around to the back of the building and entered a door. The last stall was filled with so much hay that there was no room for a horse, but atop several bales, sat four kittens in various hues of black, brown, orange and white on an old blanket. As they stood there, Stockings hurried inside to plop down among her brood, and the kittens began to nurse hungrily.

Elizabeth was mesmerized, and William had no intention of suspending her enjoyment. They observed the kittens until the last one was satisfied with his meal, and then William gently pushed her towards them.

"Go ahead. You may hold them."

She eased forward, sitting down gingerly on the straw, gently lifting first one and then another. She gave each a thorough rubbing and a quick kiss before she set them down. With the last kitten, an orange stripe, she lay back on the straw and held him overhead. All the kittens began to walk around and across her, and as one brushed her face, she closed her eyes and smiled. Her peaceful expression warmed William's heart.

"When they are old enough to leave their mother, would you like to have one? Georgiana used to have a cat in her room. They make excellent pets."

Elizabeth barely nodded as he held out a hand to help her stand. He tried brushing the straw off her dress and from her hair, but was not successful. "I am afraid Maggie will have to remove the straw, as all I shall accomplish is to rake the pins from your hair."

He laughed as she seemed to blush, and they hurried back to the house. "Mrs. Reynolds will wonder where I have taken you, if I do not return you shortly! She always provides a light snack at this time, as I am usually famished by then."

Once at the house, he could find no one about as he led Elizabeth to her room, so he walked her out onto the balcony.

"Stay right here, and I will send Maggie to help you get the straw out of your hair and change clothes. I would like you to join me for refreshments, if you feel up to it." He squeezed her hand and left.

As he exited, he went through the sitting room and knocked on Mrs. Drury's door. There was no answer, so he continued into the hallway where he was met by an exasperated Mrs. Reynolds.

"Mr. Darcy, there are two tenants downstairs who almost have come to blows in the foyer. I asked Mr. Walker to escort them to the east drawing room and stay with them to assure they do not resort to fisticuffs until I could locate you."

"What do they—never mind. Please ask Mr. Walker to escort them to my study where I shall hear their dispute. Also, have Mr. Sturgis come to the study, as I am sure he knows more about their argument than I do at the moment."

Mrs. Reynolds looked frustrated. "I am sorry you have to deal with this now, with the young lady here and all."

"Oh, I nearly forgot! I left Elizabeth out on her balcony, and I could not locate Mrs. Drury or Maggie. One of them needs to go to her immediately."

"Maggie is helping to train a new maid downstairs. Mrs. Drury is in the east wing drawing room. I shall send her back to Miss Lawrence straightaway."

"Thank you." William touched her shoulder. "I can always count on you." She blushed and bobbed a small curtsy.

"I shall have Mr. Walker send the men to your study right away and locate Mr. Sturgis."

William watched her walk away and for a moment considered whether Elizabeth would be safe alone for a few minutes. Increasingly loud voices below caught his attention, and deciding Elizabeth would surely be safe on the balcony, he hurried down the stairs towards the angry men.

Meanwhile, Georgiana arrived at the front door of Pemberley to find the place seemingly deserted. While there were footmen outside, there were none to be seen once she stepped inside the doorway. Neither was Mr. Walker about to greet her. She waited for Mrs. Reynolds to appear as usual, but even she did not come, so she continued on through the foyer and stood looking up at the grand staircase. A young maid whom she had never met, came swiftly down the stairs with an armload of dishes on a tray. Georgiana addressed her.

"I am Mr. Darcy's sister, Georgiana Ingram. Do you know where I might find my brother?"

She bobbed a curtsy. "Yes, ma'am. I heard Mr. Walker say he was taking two tenants to Mr. Darcy's study where the Master is to hear their dispute."

Just at that moment, loud arguing could be heard from the direction of the study, and Georgiana determined she might as well take this opportunity to assess the mysterious woman for herself.

"Yes, well, I have actually come to see the visitor Mr. Darcy brought back from London. Can you tell me where I might find her?"

The young girl studied the older woman, and believing that she was Mr. Darcy's sister, answered her question. "The young lady is staying in the family wing—the third room on the right."

"Thank you," Georgiana replied through gritted teeth. She tried not to show her disgust. "You have been most helpful."

In the family wing! How could William put her in our family quarters?

Opening the designated door without knocking, Georgiana stalked inside to find no one about. She turned to leave but noticed that the curtains covering the French doors were billowing in the wind. Walking to the doors, she looked upon a sight that made her cringe. Elizabeth sat in a comfortable chair, her shoes off and her feet propped upon a stool. She was watching a pair of horses gallop in perfect synchronization across a nearby meadow, oblivious to the fact that her dress and hair were littered with hay. Her chocolate curls were half out of the pins from William's attempts to get the straw out.

Georgiana walked around in front of her. "I am Georgiana Darcy Ingram, and you are?"

Elizabeth's gaze drifted to her shoeless feet, and she began to wring her hands, but she did not answer, causing Georgiana to become even more agitated.

Putting her hands on her hips, Georgiana exclaimed, "Have you no manners? And just what are you doing with hay in your hair? Did the tenant's dispute interrupt a roll in the hayloft with my brother?"

"Georgiana!"

She turned to see William striding towards her, Mrs. Drury fast on his heels.

"William, this creature will not even introduce herself! And look at her appearance, what kind—"

William said nothing but took his sister by the arm, and none too gently dragged her from the balcony into the bedroom. Then is a low, barely controlled voice, he hissed, "Go to the drawing room and wait for me." Just as quickly, he turned on his heel and hurried back to Elizabeth.

Raising her head in indignation at his callous treatment of her over an obvious strumpet, Georgiana marched to the door. She intended to go directly home without waiting to hear him out, but at the door, she turned to see William kneeling in front of the woman, gently stroking her hands as he talked to her in a comforting manner. She had never seen her brother look at any woman the way he was looking at this one. With a start, she realised that the woman did not seem to be paying much attention to him either.

The lump in her throat refused to be swallowed, as she recognised that perhaps there was more to the situation than first she had thought. As she quit the room and descended the stairs, it was with much more meekness than she had ascended them minutes before.

Fitzwilliam would never speak to me in that manner, unless…

A multitude of possible reasons for his actions began to rush through her mind, and she began to regret her impulsiveness. Mortified, she wondered how she could justify accosting his guest.

Entering the empty drawing room, she found a comfortable seat. She would wait for her brother, regardless of the time or inconvenience. She knew she deserved whatever chastisement she would receive.

~~~*~~~

Chapter 11

The minute Georgiana returned from Pemberley she had retreated to their bedroom, flinging herself on the bed and weeping. It had been almost a half-hour before she was composed enough to recount what had happened in a rational manner. There were no secrets between them, and Darcy was aware that anything he told Ana she would relate to her husband, so Evan was not worried about breaching a confidence as he sat in stunned silence while Georgiana described the events of that day.

Having been acquainted with Fitzwilliam Darcy since they were mere lads, he knew him to be an honourable man, albeit proud, reserved, aware of his station and driven by duty to uphold his heritage, but honourable nonetheless. It had been very puzzling when, two years previously, that same man had thrown caution to the wind, leaving Pemberley in his and Georgiana's hands while he visited his estates in Scotland and Ireland. That impulsiveness, for which Darcy had never really offered an explanation that made sense, had *definitely* been out of character. In fact, it went against his very nature!

So, to finally learn that the Master of Pemberley had fallen in love with a penniless woman with no connections and that he had offered for her was almost hard to believe. Further, it shook him to the core to hear her recount Darcy's story of spending the last two years trying desperately to overcome his love for this mystery lady. How had his brother managed to keep this much heartache hidden? He had had no inkling of Darcy's torment.

There was no doubt now that Darcy had considered marriage to Cecile, not because of her wealth or connections, but because he wanted to purge the woman at Pemberley from his heart. My God, how close he had come to making a tragic mistake.

In all our conversations before he left for Scotland, Darcy never betrayed his feelings, never once sought my opinion. Perhaps I have been too selfish in my own happiness to wonder if he was content.

"And then," Georgiana's sob captured his attention, "William told me how devastated he was to find she was married and that her husband was such a blackguard that he left her to die in a fire."

Once again, she dropped her head into her hands, crying as though her heart would break. "That poor girl! And to think William was deeply in love with her, and I never knew!"

"Do not blame yourself. I had no idea, and I thought we talked about everything." He knelt in front of her, bringing her hands to his heart and waiting until she looked into his eyes. "Do you think he wants to help her because he **was** once in love with her, or does he love her still?"

"Oh, he definitely loves her. It is obvious in the way he touches her and how his eyes light up when he speaks of her. It is so difficult because I truly wish Miss Elizabeth to get better, and I know William can help her if anyone can—he is so gentle. But there is so much room for heartache in this situation, if not danger. It will be complicated to be supportive of her recovery without supporting what I know he truly wants—a relationship with her."

"But it is his choice, Ana."

She took a ragged breath, standing as big tears rolled down her cheeks. "I know that, Evan!" she protested, stomping over to stare out the window.

After a few moments, her shoulders slumped, and her voice broke with a sob. "In my heart I know that," she whispered, "but he is my brother. When he is sad, I am sad, and when he hurts, I hurt. I could not bear for something—*someone* to hurt him that much again."

Evan moved to her, and she turned to fall into her husband's arms. "For so many years we had only each other. That is why I swore that I would never marry, because I could not bear to leave him alone. Can you not see that he is longing for someone to love and to love him? It pains me to see his heartache."

He ran his hands over her back. "I know, darling, I know. You are very close."

"And now that he is home ..." She hiccupped. "I dreamed that when he returned, he would find that person to love. I would have a new sister and a house full of nieces and nephews. Mostly, I would have the brother I love back. That dream was so real to me."

He tipped his head to look into her teary eyes. "You have not lost him, Ana."

"Not yet, but I fear I shall! The last two years were lost to me, and I know now that she was the reason he left—the reason I lived without him for so long. Will I now be forced to watch him die a little each day because he cannot have her? Even should she recover completely, she belongs to another man."

"Darcy loves deeply, Ana; it is just the way he is. That will never change, and I am glad, as I admire that about him. I have known him almost my entire life, but it was only when I came back to Rosewood Manor at my father's death that I began to fully understand the man—when I observed his devotion to you."

She pulled back to look up at her husband and smiled wanly. "I know. I love that about him too. He is fiercely protective of those he loves."

"What you did today was terribly foolish and irresponsible, and you may have caused an awful setback for the young woman. I can only imagine that Darcy is heartbroken that the cause of her suffering was his own sister."

Georgiana practically moaned as she dropped her head to his chest. "I know! It was so stupid of me, and I was so very sorry when I realized what I had done. I asked if I might go to her and apologise right away, but he would not hear of it. William said he will have to judge how much damage I have done before he will let me near her." She moaned the last few words and began crying again.

Evan sat down, pulled her onto his lap and kissed the top of her head. "There, there. Do not cry, sweetheart. Darcy is a forgiving man, and he loves you very much. He will forgive you. Eventually."

"Oh, why did he not just rage at me? It would have been easier to accept than the disappointment in his eyes! He was so disheartened that he could not look at me, and I do not blame him. I fear he may never forgive what I did or my lack of trust in him."

"He will. You just have to give him time." He kissed her again. "Perhaps there is some way you may help Miss Elizabeth when he does allow you to see her. Since she is withdrawn, you might take your art supplies and entertain her by drawing. I know I enjoy watching a picture come to life at your hands. Or better still, teach her to draw if she seems interested."

Georgiana brightened. "I would love to do that if Brother and Miss Elizabeth will allow it. Though she may not be the woman that I had dreamed of for William, I will be kind to her, and I will help her to the best of my ability."

"They will allow you to visit in time, I am sure. Now, there is something else we have to discuss. Have you examined why this debacle occurred in the first place?"

Her eyes widened as she considered his question. "I have not had time to dwell on it."

"I believe your desire to do something right away was a result of Cecile's influence. By the way she framed her tale, we were intentionally led to believe that Darcy had installed Miss Elizabeth as his mistress at Pemberley."

"She did encourage me to confront him without delay and without waiting for you, though that does not excuse my behaviour. I should have stopped to think or," she smiled sheepishly, "just listened to you."

"And she emphasised Miss Elizabeth's *problem* as though the woman were with child. At least, that was the impression that I got."

"As did I." Georgiana rubbed her forehead, feeling the beginnings of a headache. "Nonetheless, we shall not let Cecile have the pleasure of knowing she succeeded in her plot. William wants us to confirm his story that this woman is our distant cousin Elizabeth Lawrence, here to recover from a debilitating illness, and I shall tell her that is what I learned today at Pemberley."

"It is good then that she was in her room when you returned and did not see your distress, but will she question why Miss Lawrence is staying with him and not us?"

"I will tell her that since I entertain often and he does not, Pemberley will be a more restful place, and besides, she has a companion in Mrs. Drury."

"I do not believe we shall have a problem getting Cecile to agree to keep Elizabeth's presence a secret. She does not know that Elizabeth is married already and will think that William could be in danger of a forced marriage if the gossips get wind of her being there."

Georgiana stiffened. "Where is Cecile? How is she to be trusted? How do we know that she is not eavesdropping as we speak?"

"From now on I shall feel the need to make absolutely sure our conversations are confidential," Even grumbled. "And I despise the necessity of that in the privacy of my own home."

Georgiana sighed. "Perhaps we should *suggest* that she return to London after your dinner party on Saturday."

"The party! I had forgotten all about it." Evan seemed lost in thought. "I wonder if your brother will come after everything that has happened."

"He just might overlook my failings and come in honour of your birthday. Would you please ask him?"

Evan rolled his eyes. "I will ask, but I will not press him. Is that understood?"

Georgiana kissed his nose. "Yes, dearest."

"And what will you do with all the eligible young women you have already invited to celebrate my birthday. You realise that they will be swarming around Darcy as if he were honey and they the bees."

"I can do nothing at this point as the invitations have gone out. The truth is that regardless of his devotion to her, Miss Elizabeth is married, so my brother is still available. What he is doing for her is admirable and I will support him. But that does not change the fact that he may meet a woman who can be his wife and the mother of his children."

"Ana!"

"I am just stating the obvious, Evan. I will try never again to pressure him, but I will not cease hoping that he finds love. He cannot have that with Miss Elizabeth, regardless of how much he wishes it to be so. I hope he helps her to recover and when she is able, she leaves."

Evan shook his head, his voice lowering in warning. "Your brother is a grown man and you must accept his decisions. She may leave and she may not. It is not for us to decide."

Georgiana flinched at the severity in his manner. "I—I was only ..."

Pulling her back into an embrace, he hugged her tightly. "I love you, Ana, and it pains me to admonish you, but I am resolute! Let Darcy decide what is right for him."

"Yes, *Fitzwilliam*."

"Do I really sound like him?"

"Only when you force me to realise how wrong I am."

Pemberley
William's study
One week later

"Well, it seems, once again, that you are too preoccupied to notice my arrival."

Richard's entrance had gone undetected by William until he stood before him. He had entered quietly to find William leaning back in his chair, his feet propped upon the edge of his desk, his gaze firmly fixed out the window and his mind obviously elsewhere. Richard had stood perfectly still for some time until realising that his cousin was not going to notice his presence unless he spoke.

For William's part, his thoughts had not been on the problems of his estate, but were, as usual, on Elizabeth's situation. Startled by Richard's greeting, he swung his feet to the floor and sat up straight, agitated at the interruption.

"Perhaps if you were announced as any other visitor—"

"Visitor?" Richard guffawed, plopping down in the chair directly in front of William's desk. "Is that all I am, a visitor?"

"You know what I mean, Cousin! Mr. Walker would be happy to announce your presence, should you slow down enough for him to get ahead of you."

Richard smirked. "You know my penchant for alarming the servants with my impropriety! It is my only entertainment when I visit the wealthy, especially as I have no servants of my own to bother. Besides, I hear you have learned this same trick from me." He raised his brows and wagged them. "I was told that you make Mr. Jenkins very nervous when you call on Georgiana."

William tried not to smile, but remembering Georgiana's butler following him in the same manner, he did in spite of himself. However, just as suddenly as it appeared, it faded. He did not wish to be rude to his cousin, but he had hoped to have no company for a time, praying Elizabeth would return to her previous state of mind—before Georgiana's visit.

"How is it you are here without any notice?"

"General Winston has decided that I am his emissary so I am sent here and yon without notice. I was in London before I was sent to Derbyshire to consult with the local militia leader regarding a new recruit who once served here. However, the commander is out of town until next week, so I am forced to await his return. I hope it is not an inconvenience for me to stay with you until such time as I return to my unit which is now stationed in York. It should not be more than a week."

"Of course not, Richard." William sighed, feeling somewhat guilty for his earlier tone of voice. "You know you are always welcome here. It is only ..."

"Only?"

"Miss Elizabeth has not been ..."

"Oh, come now, Cousin. Surely the young lady has lightened your disposition now that she is in residence." Richard's voice softened as a look of sorrow flashed across Darcy's face.

"Did I say something to upset you? She is well, is she not?"

Richard watched William stand and walk to the windows, locking his hands behind his back. That was never a good sign!

It was several more seconds before he answered. "Everything was going well, I believe, before Mrs. Preston arrived uninvited. And furthermore, she gave Georgiana the impression Miss Elizabeth was my mistress."

"That busybody! Why was she even at Pemberley? After her threat to you in London—to suggest that she would tell Georgiana that you were a cad!" He tossed the riding crop with which he had been slapping his leg, down on the desk. "What nerve to show her face here!"

William smiled slightly as he looked over his shoulder to find Richard pacing across the rug now. It warmed his heart to see his cousin so concerned for his sake. He returned to take his place behind the desk.

"Calm yourself, Richard. It will serve neither us, nor Miss Elizabeth, if we get angry at this point. I must focus my energy on determining how to help her."

Richard nodded and sat down again, crossing his legs. The constant twitch of his foot was the only visible sign that he was still irritated. "Pray explain to me what happened."

It was some time before William was done with the tale of Mrs. Preston's appearance and quick departure from Pemberley and then Georgiana's unfortunate call on Elizabeth. When he was finished, both men sat in silence, contemplating the possible effects of the incident on the young woman. Finally, Richard broke the silence.

"You realise that Georgiana was worried sick over your absence for the last two years. I am sure her reaction was partially due to her concern for you."

William's hand in the air stopped his cousin's defence. "I am not angry anymore with Georgiana. I do own to the fact that I am hurt that she did not trust me, and because she did not, she has caused a setback in Miss Elizabeth's recovery."

"But, Darce, you must be aware of how it appeared to Georgiana—having a woman living at Pemberley, a married woman, I might add, and Mrs. Preston implying that she was with child." He whistled, shaking his head. "If the gossips of the *ton* ever discover that, I daresay even the fact that they may believe she is your cousin and Mrs. Drury her aunt, would not save you."

William fiddled with the pen in his grasp, twirling it back and forth over his fingers. "We went over this in London, Richard. I know the cost and, in the end, if everything becomes common knowledge I do not care."

Richard sighed. "No, I suppose not." He sat up straighter. "What does Georgiana plan to do now?"

"She wants to befriend Eliz—Miss Elizabeth, but I will not allow it until Elizabeth regains the progress she had made before this incident. I fear, though, that Georgiana will never truly accept Elizabeth. My sister is intent on seeing me properly married."

Richard studied William's face. "And you cannot marry her."

William's gaze met his and held it. "I am acutely aware of that."

Just at that moment, the door to the study flew open again. "Well, well, what have we here?" Evan Ingram strolled in casually, smiling at his brother and cousin. "You have arrived just in time for my birthday dinner party, Richard!"

Richard's face lit up, and he smirked at William. "I would love to attend. Unlike some, I am not averse to meeting single young ladies. Please say there will be some in attendance?"

Evan's eyes sought William as he shook his head in resignation. "Of course, you know my wife! Ana is the consummate matchmaker." Only Richard laughed as Evan continued. "She has invited most of Derbyshire, and we have friends coming from London. Some will stay with us, and others will stay with their own families in the area. There should be perhaps fifty friends and relations, if not more."

Noting the scowl on William's face, Evan hurried with his mission. "I am truly sorry to have invited myself in, Darcy, but your man was not in the foyer."

William waved his hand in dismissal. "It seems anyone is welcome to walk into Pemberley unannounced today."

Evan lifted his brows as he cast a glance to Richard, who sheepishly volunteered, "I am afraid I was not expected or announced either." Richard eyed William as he enquired of Evan, "When is this event? My dour cousin has said nothing."

"Tomorrow night. I was sent to learn if Darcy would still attend." His eyes locked with his brother's. "Ana is very sorry for her actions. She hopes that what transpired will not cause you to abandon my birthday dinner and the dance afterward."

William lowered his gaze. "You are aware that I dislike associating with a gathering of people I do not know."

"I understand completely, though I think you have met most of them. All Ana asks is for you to say you will come."

A look of resignation swept over William's face and Evan and Richard exchanged worried looks as the seconds passed. Finally, William answered in a voice so low it could barely be heard, "I will come."

~~~*~~~

In the middle of that night, Richard awoke to the sounds of the rain pounding against the windowpanes and winds howling. Looking about the room, the glow from the dying fire gave off just enough light for him to recognise his favourite room at Pemberley. Suddenly lightning flashed, illuminating it entirely. He relaxed. Perhaps it was only the storm that made him uneasy.

However, being the consummate soldier, he lay quietly, intently listening a while longer. At once he realised that the sound he thought had been the wind howling was actually a woman crying. Quickly, he threw back the covers, slipped from his bed and donned his dressing gown. Opening the door as quietly as possible, he looked out into the dark hall, lit by sparse candles along the walls. Stealthily, he moved in the direction of the noises that were coming from across the hall and several rooms nearer the grand staircase.

As he neared the rooms once occupied by Georgiana, he noticed that one door was not fully closed and at that second heard a moan and someone speaking. He hurried to peer inside. A lone candle illuminated the room enough for him to see his cousin sitting in the window seat, holding Miss Elizabeth. She leaned into him, her cries muffled against his chest. His arms were about her, one hand held the back of her head, while the other stroked her back. William's deep baritone was easy to make out, even as he whispered words of comfort to her.

"Do not cry, sweetheart. It is only a storm. You are safe. William is here."

As he soothed her, William rocked her gently back and forth and occasionally kissed the crown of her head. Embarrassed to be watching so tender a scene, Richard slipped quietly away from the door, closing it as he did so.

You are lost, my friend. Totally, hopelessly lost.

~~~*~~~

Chapter 12

Georffe Wickham felt ill. Not only had the dreary weather, constant rain, and lightning brought down his spirits, but also the sway of the carriage as it lumbered along the uneven streets did not aid his queasy stomach either. His unsettled constitution might have reflected the excessive amount of brandy he had consumed the night before, but more than likely was due to his dread of this afternoon's meeting.

Lately his business associate, Count Stefano, had become quite hard to anticipate. Exceedingly cheerful one day, he could be equally gloomy the next, and his temper was violent when stirred. In addition, the man was either trying to swindle him or had begun to experience lapses in memory regarding their agreements on monetary matters. This was quite irritating to Wickham, as he had bargained with his own associates based on what he expected to be paid.

The man is certainly peculiar! But then again, any man who would abandon wealth and privilege for life as a rake and a thief has to be peculiar. Could he not have pretended to be a gentleman for his father's benefit and carried on with his amusements in secret?

When the charismatic man had first made Wickham the temping offer of becoming rich with hardly any effort on his part, he had identified himself only as Count Stefano. Nevertheless, thieves are not a trusting lot, and Wickham trusted no one, especially not this *count*. Thus, before throwing his lot in with the stranger, howbeit a seemingly wealthy one, Wickham put word on the street that he would pay for information leading to the count's identity. What he had discovered was astonishing.

The man who called himself Count Stefano was actually Stephen Stanton, Viscount Glascomb, heir to Lord Stanton, a former diplomat and well-liked member of the *ton*. Apparently, father and son were estranged, and whatever their disagreement, it had resulted in the son's return to Italy to reside with his mother's family as he neared thirty. Upon returning to England years later, he called himself Count Stefano Gianni Montalvo de Cavour, a title apparently inherited when his maternal grandfather died.

Wickham's sources also uncovered evidence of the Count's many liaisons with wealthy widows and heiresses, each dalliance mysteriously increasing his coffers. There was proof that he had married at least one extremely wealthy widow, a Lady Marlton, who had died soon after the wedding. However, most surprising was the rumour that he had never bothered to rid himself of one wife before acquiring another.

The final report, which was unproven, suggested he had married Anne de Bourgh, taken her dowry and then abandoned her. Wickham smiled to himself, remembering his meeting Miss de Bourgh and the imperious Lady Catherine de Bourgh once at Pemberley. The old bat had practically spit on him when she learned he was the steward's son.

Just at that moment, the carriage came to an abrupt halt, jarring him from his contemplations. Sighing audibly, Wickham stepped from the carriage, instinctively peering up at the three-storey Georgian facade of the townhouse the Count was renting. It always put him in mind of Darcy's residence only a few streets away. His head naturally turned in that direction as feelings of deprivation rushed over him. If old George Darcy had been a decent godfather or his son a better man, he might also be living in this elite section of town. Determined not to be distracted by old wounds while there was business of import to conduct, Wickham turned and pasted a smile on his face as he briskly ascended the steps.

To his surprise, the elaborate front door opened before he could knock, and a small, dark-skinned butler immediately reached for his coat and hat, nodding, though he did not say a word. A maid, arranging a vase of flowers on a table under an elaborate mirror, lowered her eyes and turned away. Wickham tried to recall if he had seen these servants on his last visit, as the count's servants seemed to change regularly. Instantly, his thoughts were halted by the sound of Stefano's voice reverberating throughout the house via the open drawing room door.

"Do not make excuses!" Stefano bellowed. "I do not want to hear them. You have had ample time! You were hired to tell me if she is alive, and if so, where she is at present! You take my money, but you bring me no satisfaction!"

After exchanging worried glances, the butler moved into a dark corner near the front door, while a maid scurried out of sight. Observing the servants' discomfort, Wickham was amazed that the count had not at least closed the door, though the outburst was just as likely heard in the park across the street.

"It seems as if she disappeared from the face of the earth. I cannot find evidence that she lives or conclusive evidence that she died in the fire. The housekeeper feigns no knowledge of her after the catastrophe. She says there were numerous bodies that were burned beyond recognition. And, you know of the marked grave in Meryton."

"I am not convinced of her death, even though her mother assures me it is true! Someone knows more than they are saying! Question everyone—present and former servants, and the locals! Pay them to talk! Do not come back to me without accurate information again! Do you understand?"

The voices and footsteps kept getting closer, and Wickham distinctly heard someone say, "Yes. Yes. I understand," just as a man backed out of the drawing room, the count following close behind.

Wickham had never seen Stefano so angry—face contorted and shaking with rage— but the count stopped abruptly when he became aware of his presence. Somewhat embarrassed to find he had an audience, Stefano carefully adjusted his waistcoat, while waving his hand in dismissal at other man. "Get out of my sight until you have what I want!"

With that pronouncement, the little man turned and hurried towards the now open front door. Grabbing the coat and hat offered by the equally fearful butler, he never slowed down or bothered to don them as he ran down the front steps.

"Mr. Wickham," Stefano turned now to him, his green eyes still flashing angrily, "I hope at least you have some good news for me."

Wickham bowed slightly, trying not to let his uneasiness show. "I believe you will be pleased with my report."

"Come then." Stefano waved towards an open door. "Tell me something that will make me smile." As Wickham moved in that direction, Stefano addressed an older woman who emerged from a nearby doorway. He was curt. "Signora Giovanni, send a tray of refreshments to my study."

She bobbed, cutting her eyes towards Wickham before they settled on the count again. "Yes, sir."

Entering the study, Wickham began perusing the well-appointed room as any thief would, noting that it was expensively furnished with rich wood furniture, oil paintings, imported carpets, silver services and china figurines. All their previous talks had been in the drawing room, and it was not nearly this well appointed. His examination abruptly ended with the sound of the door closing, and he followed the count with his eyes as he moved to sit behind the desk and motioned for him to take the chair in front. As Stefano leaned back in his chair, seeming to relax a bit, he fixed his steely gaze on Wickham.

"Now, what do you have for me?"

Wickham pulled a piece of paper from inside his coat and leaned across the desk to place it in front of Stefano. "This is an inventory of the objects that I delivered this very morning, signed by your contact at the wharf."

Listed were several cases of silver serving pieces, silver candelabrums, gold and silver boxes, gold pocket watches and numerous necklaces, brooches and bracelets with precious stones and pearls. The count's face lit up, and he looked pleased for the first time that day.

"I am suitably impressed with your inspiration to use this woman for her connections and knowledge of their valuables. She has made a great difference in the number and quality of items procured. What did you say her name was?"

"As I said before, she wishes to remain anonymous." Wickham knew it would anger him, but he did not trust the count. What was to keep him from dealing directly with Mrs. Preston and cutting him out of the arrangement altogether?

Stefano's smile did not change, though his eyes betrayed his displeasure. "She must be a lady of some means, I suppose, since she has the ability to gain access to the homes of people of quality."

"Precisely."

Stefano stood and turned to a picture behind his desk as if studying it. "You have doubled your profit in the last month. I would have liked to have had the lady's cooperation much earlier or that of others like her."

Wickham shifted in his chair. Mrs. Preston had fallen into his lap due to her love of the horses, inability to curb her habits and no ready income. However, all of the other ladies indebted to him had sufficient future income to pay their notes. "I have no other prospects. She agreed only because she was indebted to me and had need of extra income since her husband's death."

"A widow?" Stefano turned, rubbing his chin as a wicked grin spread across his face. "I have had great luck with widows."

The smile vanished as quickly as it had appeared, and he seemed to sober, taking his seat again and beginning to play with a crystal paperweight. "I want you to know that I am going to leave England in the near future—perhaps several months, perhaps mere weeks. Whatever goods we acquire until then will have to suffice. Our partnership will end at that point, as I intend never to return."

Wickham was taken aback. He had never given a thought to the end of their venture and, for a moment, he pondered how he would live without this source of income. He had just concluded that he would merely have to find another person to buy the stolen goods, when his thoughts were interrupted.

"You see, I am at present attempting to locate my wife, and when I find her, I shall finish my business ventures here and return to Italy with all due haste. She is very important to me, and I will not leave England without her."

"Your wife?"

"Oh yes. I have been married for some time."

Wickham's thoughts returned to the report he had read, recounting the marriage to the very wealthy Lady Marlton a few years ago, and her subsequent death months later.

"And she is missing?"

"For several months now, though I was only recently informed." Stefano appeared lost in thought before he spoke again. "I sent a personal representative to my father's estate a while back, as I wanted him to look into some matters on my behalf. That was when I discovered she might not be ..."

His voice trailed off, and he stared into space as though there was something only he could see. Wickham had begun to wonder if the man had gone completely mad when he seemed to improve. "I have men looking for her even as we speak, and I have offered a handsome reward for knowledge of her whereabouts."

"How handsome?" Wickham ventured.

"One thousand pounds for her location."

"That is a substantial amount just for information. If you do not mind my asking, who is she?"

"No one of consequence—a penniless gentleman's daughter from Hertfordshire. I daresay no one but I would want her." He sighed heavily. "We were very happy until," his voice took on an angry edge, "well, my father interfered. I fear whatever he told her must have had some bearing on her ... disappearance. Nevertheless, if I can find her, bring her home, I am certain we can be happy once more. In Italy, my mother's family is well respected." He smiled genuinely now. "You must think me daft pining for a woman, but she is the only person I have ever loved. She belongs to me, and if she is alive, I will not stop until I have her."

"If she is alive?" Wickham repeated with some trepidation. "What do you mean?"

Realising his mistake, Stefano recovered. "I meant to imply that since she left my home unescorted, anyone could have harmed her. I hope to find her alive and well."

Satisfied with that explanation, Wickham ventured, "Would you mind if I put word out among my various associates and see what pertinent information I can discover?"

"I appreciate all assistance, and I would just as soon pay you as anyone else." He sat back down, and at the knock on the door called, "Come!"

Signora Giovanni entered noiselessly and set a tray of tea and cakes on the edge of his desk.

"Leave us!"

She quickly bobbed a curtsy and was out of the room by the time the count stood to pour himself a cup of tea.

"Let me tell you of the love of my life, Elizabeth."

Rosewood Manor
Evan's Birthday Dinner
Saturday Evening

Colonel Richard Fitzwilliam looked quite dashing in his regimentals, standing between Evan Ingram and Fitzwilliam Darcy in the receiving line. Georgiana had insisted that he and her brother join them in welcoming the guests, many of whom were their neighbours, to Evan's birthday celebration. Evan was dressed in dark blue, in pleasant contrast to his wife's light-blue silk-velvet gown, trimmed in white satin, overlaid with lace along the hem, sleeves and bodice. William, as usual, was impeccable in black, though tonight he wore a dark gold waistcoat embroidered with black thread in an intricate design, attributable to Mr. Adams, his valet. He had insisted that William needed to dress in a festive manner for Evan's birthday celebration.

Richard was delighted to be in the receiving line, as he was at ease conversing with strangers, and his position of honour enabled him to meet eligible women. Normally he would arrange dance sets before all were spoken for, but tonight he intended to stay beside William, except when he danced with Georgiana. Glancing sideways at his dour cousin, he had to smile. There had been a steady stream of love-struck women trying to catch the eye of his handsome friend, and at this point, William looked as though he wished the earth would open up and swallow him. In fact, only Richard's promise to stay close had persuaded him to attend when his courage had failed earlier that day.

Just as there was a fortuitous break in the never-ending trail of people, Richard leaned over to tease him. "Smile! You look exactly like one of the statues in your garden."

William murmured under his breath, "At this moment I wish I were!"

Richard chuckled at William's jest, glad that he was taking the attention in stride. "Do not worry, Cousin. I have good news. Evan told me that the *Black Widow* is returning to London with her uncle. And if there are other harridans present tonight, they will soon learn that I am on duty!"

~~~*~~~

A few feet away, a group of said harridans were discussing how **very** happy they were that the elusive Mr. Darcy had decided to brave society once again.

"I think it is just criminal that a man of his wealth and good looks is not married," Mrs. Gunter, a tall brunette, declared cutting her eyes to take in William's handsome figure in the receiving line. The other women in the small circle were already looking in that direction.

"I would like to have had him myself," Mrs. Madison retorted, her pink blush complimenting her red hair. "I certainly would have tried a compromise, but he hardly attended any of the soirees during my debut year. Then he disappeared off the face of the earth, and Father insisted I accept Mr. Madison's offer." She sighed heavily. "I would have waited forever, if he had so much as smiled at me."

"Any of us would have, Pauline." Mrs. Harding interjected, unashamedly undressing Fitzwilliam Darcy with lustful eyes. Mrs. Harding, the wife of one of Mr. Darcy's classmates from Cambridge, had been thrown in his company often before her marriage. Though quite pretty with light brown hair and hazel eyes, she had never been able to draw the attention of Mr. Darcy.

"I admit to being attracted to him, but we should not be voicing such thoughts," Mrs. Martindale, a short strawberry blond responded, glancing about to see if anyone outside their circle was listening. "He is exceedingly handsome, but we are all married."

"I may be married, Abigail, but I am not dead!" Mrs. Nicholson exclaimed, her blue eyes focusing on the cut of William's breeches. "Besides," she whispered knowingly, her gaze fixed, "it is the accepted custom in our society for men to take mistresses and for us to take lovers. Just because one is on a diet does not mean she cannot read the menu." She giggled.

"Julia!" Mrs. Martindale cried, quickly lowering her voice as several people turned to look. "That is not something one should discuss in public."

Julia Nicholson tossed her dark curls saucily. "You are correct, Abigail. I intend to find somewhere private to discuss it—with Mr. Darcy." Abigail gasped as the others giggled.

"If you have no objection, I will too!" Mrs. Madison added. "I have not had a real man since I married."

Mrs. Nicholson smirked. "The more the merrier, I always say."

~~~*~~~

At that moment, another simpering mother stopped to address Richard and push her pretty daughter ahead of her in line. Said daughter, of course, ended up standing directly in front of William, and as she did, the wrap around her shoulders began a slow slide down her arms. Before long, it was obvious that she wore an extremely low cut dress. Also obvious was the fact that she was well-endowed, and William could not help but notice. Both women were delighted to see his gaze dip to her cleavage. Just as quickly though, he brought his eyes back to her face, discomfited as he coloured. In return, she brandished a most provocative smile.

Being a man of normal appetites, William was not immune to a pretty face. Accordingly, he conceded that her light blue eyes and dark auburn hair were pleasing, but the look in her eyes mirrored the other women he knew in the *ton*. She did not look away, and his posture became rigid at the suggestiveness in her gaze. Noticing his reluctance to speak, her mother abandoned her idle chitchat with Richard in an attempt to salvage the opportunity.

Stepping towards William without taking her leave of Richard, she pulled her daughter closer. Richard shook his head as she exclaimed, "Mr. Darcy, you remember my Henrietta? I am sure you were introduced at Lady Matlock's home a few weeks ago. Your aunt asked her to entertain at the pianoforte, and she was pleased to sing as well. My daughter is very accomplished and will make some man a wonderful wife."

"I am afraid I did not have the honour." William stated flatly, cutting his eyes to the mother. "In fact, I do not remember ever making your acquaintance either, madam."

Those within range of his voice began to titter, drawing Georgiana's attention. Flustered, the woman's hands fluttered as if she were about to fly and was only able to utter, "Oh ... oh."

Evan and Richard tried not to laugh aloud at William's put-down, though their shoulders were shaking. Each slid a hand over his mouth as Georgiana glared at them and leaned over to address William.

"Brother, would you move this way, please? I need to confer with you on a matter of some import." With a huge sigh of relief, William bowed slightly to the women before him and stepped behind Richard and Evan to take the place next to his sister.

"Thank you," he breathed, slipping his arm around her waist and giving her a slight hug before releasing her.

Georgiana tried not to smile too as she looked toward the next guests. She gave his arm a small squeeze. "You are welcome."

~~~*~~~

After dinner, Richard stood at the ballroom entrance with William trying to decide which corner his cousin should occupy while he had his dance with Georgiana. As William looked about to find his sister and brother, Richard leaned in to whisper, "Enemy at three o'clock."

William frowned. "Speak plainly. I am not in the mood for riddles."

"Then, by all means, let me explain. Your classmate's wife, Mrs. Harding, and the little hens with her are having a grand time ogling you—or parts of you. If you imagine this room is a pocket watch, and we are standing at six o'clock, then they are at three o'clock. From the looks of it, I suspect you will have more than one offer tonight and from the remark you made earlier, I just imagine you can handle them quite well!"

Without thinking, William looked in that direction, which caused the ladies' murmurings to increase. They all seemed to be speaking at once and looking his way. "Good Lord, Richard! They are all married!"

"I hate to be the one to inform you, but married women do have affairs." Richard raised an eyebrow when William shot a glare at him.

"I am not so naïve as to be ignorant of that fact, Cousin, but it repulses me. What kind of man do they think I am?"

"Apparently, a damned fine specimen!" Richard crowed with a smirk.

William valiantly attempted to restrain the smile threatening to curl his lips, but when Richard slapped his back, he lost his vaulted control. The steely reserve collapsed and a beautiful smile appeared with both dimples clearly visible. Quickly exiting onto a nearby balcony, both men laughed openly the minute they were out the door.

~~~*~~~

"Look! Oh, ladies, did you see!" Frances Madison turned back to her friends. "Is he not the handsomest man you have ever seen when he smiles? Oh, if only he would look at me like that!" She sighed, as did the others.

"It was worth the trip to Derbyshire just to see that man smile!" Her fantasy was interrupted by a firm hand on her shoulder, and the looks on the faces of her companions told the rest of the story.

"That is quite enough, Mrs. Madison. I believe it is time we danced."

Twenty years her senior, Thurgood Madison was bald and almost as round as he was tall. The smile left her face as Frances placed her hand on her husband's forearm, and he led her to the dance floor. Her great disappointment was promptly replaced with pleasure, however, when Mr. Darcy approached to stand next to her husband in line and Georgiana Ingram stood next to her, across from her brother. As the music began, Mrs. Madison raised her eyebrows towards the coterie observing her extreme fortune, and they acknowledged her good luck with nods of approval.

Perhaps if I am lucky, in this dance, we will change partners several times, and I shall have the opportunity to make my proposal.

~~~*~~~

William's dance with Georgiana led to unavoidable dances with several wives and daughters from nearby estates. Afterward, two of his former classmates introduced their wives, and he felt obligated to dance with them as well. Having thoroughly exhausted every topic he could think to bring up in polite conversation, he had managed to retreat to the safety of a dark corner where Richard swiftly joined him.

Having just settled into his normal detached mien, William was beginning to relax a bit when he caught sight of a beautiful woman making her way across the room, eyes fixed on him. He groaned loud enough to attract Richard's attention. He turned to study his cousin.

"What is the matter, Darce? You sound as though you are ill."

"I may very well be shortly."

Richard followed his gaze, and his thoughts flew to the time he had caught his cousin with this woman in his father's library. "Oh, my Lord! I cannot believe she is back and has turned up here."

Gwendolyn, Lady Waltham, now seven and thirty, was once the most beautiful woman in London, and she was still striking with her dark blond hair and cornflower blue eyes. At the time of Richard's recollection, she was a recent widow of only seven and twenty. Even so, at that age, she was a seasoned huntress, and she had honed in on his handsome cousin for her next husband. Although he had just turned twenty, William was essentially an innocent when it came to women and had been ensnared by her schemes.

When George Darcy had learned of the affair, he had made quick work of rescuing his son, as well as shaming him for falling into her clutches. Not many months later, Mr. Darcy had died forcing Fitzwilliam to grow up overnight. Gwendolyn was left to move on to another—Lord Waltham—whom she married. She had moved to the southernmost part of Ireland, and as far as Richard knew, William had never dallied with another woman.

Now, Gwendolyn strolled directly to William as the conversations around them dwindled. Richard moved in closer to his cousin, an icy stare fixed on the intruder. Even those that were not old enough to remember the rumours of ten years before, realised that there must be something afoot and held their breath. "Mr. Darcy ... Fitzwilliam. I had the great pleasure of meeting Cecile Preston before I left London and learned that she was related to dear Georgiana. She said you had returned to England, and well, I just had to come tonight to welcome you back. I regret I was delayed by carriage trouble and have only just arrived."

William managed to appear indifferent. "Lady Waltham, I hope you have been well."

She held out her hand, and he hesitated before realising that everyone was waiting to see what he might do. Taking it, he bowed slightly over it without raising it to his lips. Gwendolyn was vexed but pretended not to notice as she continued.

"I am well, Fitzwilliam. I lived in Ireland until Lord Waltham died." She raised her brows as if waiting for his reply, and when he said nothing, she leaned in to murmur in a low voice, "I must say, the young boy I knew has become a very handsome man. I have missed our," she paused as her eyes travelled down his body, "*friendship.*"

Cecile Preston appeared beside them out of nowhere. "Gwendolyn, darling, I had no idea *you* would be here." The venom in her voice was unmistakable. "However did you manage to get here so quickly, and if I remember correctly, without an invitation?"

The ice in Gwendolyn Waltham's voice balanced the fire in her eyes. "I was invited, Cecile, dear, to accompany Lord and Lady Greenwich, Evan Ingram's great aunt and uncle to Derbyshire. It is fortuitous that my aunt, who is leasing my estate just outside Lambton, and Lady Greenwich are best friends, is it not?" Not expecting an answer, she went on. "Lady Greenwich insisted that I attend the party with them."

"I see." Mrs. Preston declared, glaring first at the interloper and then at William. "I see." She flounced away to Lady Gwendolyn's chuckle.

"What a wallflower! It will be a miracle if she marries again!" She looked back to William and sobered at the look on his face. "Do not tell me you have feelings for that mousey little thing."

"No, madam. I have no feelings for her or for you. Now, if you will excuse me, I need to find my sister." He turned and walked away. Richard did not bother to hide his amusement as he followed.

Looking around to find every eye upon her, Gwendolyn's lips curled into a determined smile as she walked in the opposite direction.

Humph! I do not give up so easily, darling. I am sure you have not forgotten our lessons.

A balcony

Looking into the clear night sky dotted with seemingly millions of stars, William sighed as he recalled last night. He had gone to Elizabeth's room to make sure she was well and say goodnight. Instead of finding her abed, waiting his usual visit, he had found her on the balcony, dressed only in her nightgown, staring at these very stars.

"Elizabeth?" Her head turned, but she did not move. "You should not be out here dressed like that!"

She did not reply, only turning back to her study. He moved behind her, unbuttoning his coat and pulling her into the warmth of his body before folding the coat around her. She melted into him as always, and he had to fight his desire for more.

They stood that way for far too long as he talked of the constellations and stars, and she looked wherever he pointed in the velvety darkness. It took great effort for him to finally pick her up and bring her back into the house, depositing her on the bed. As she sank into the soft mattress and pillows, he kissed her forehead and began to massage first one cold foot, and then another, her eyes closing in response to the pleasurable feelings he elicited.

As her breath settled into a continuous rhythm, he watched the steady rise and fall of her chest for a bit, dreaming of a time when he could stay with her the entire night. Then standing, he pulled a blanket and the counterpane over her, tucking it in. He leaned in for one last kiss on the forehead, but paused. She looked so beautiful that instead he brushed her lips lightly with his. Unaware of the stolen kiss, she slept on.

"It is difficult at best to dance out here."

He startled as Georgiana's voice broke through his thoughts. William chuckled a little, though he kept staring into the darkness, refusing to face her. "I am glad to hear it, as I was hoping that was the case."

"And you are not likely to meet any eligible women out here either."

"Is that why you invited me?"

"Not truly, at least not anymore. But I cannot deny I want you to fall in love and marry."

She studied him as he studied the stars. "I assume, since you are out here, that the group of ladies shadowing your every move, all married if I remember correctly, made some offers."

William chuckled softly, shaking his head. "Only two, and they are married to men I admire, not that I would ever be tempted to accept."

Georgiana squeezed his arm. "Of course you would not, but do not let these women dissuade you. There is someone who will make you the perfect wife."

"What if I have already met the only woman I will ever love?"

Georgiana felt hot tears fill her eyes. "But, Fitzy, you cannot marry her. And what of the children you always wished for?"

"I would be happy with her alone, if she just recovers and will have me."

"You would give up your wish for an heir?"

"You do not have children, and your marriage is happy."

"Yes, yes it is." She faltered. "Though Evan and I are still hopeful."

"I am sorry, Gigi. I was not thinking. I should not have said that."

"No apology needed. It is just a fact. But you would not even have what Evan and I have—a marriage. How can you exist being near her but not being able to have her, to make love to her as your wife?"

"I do not know. I only know that I cannot let her go." He turned away and his head dropped. Swiftly she stepped close behind him, wrapping her arms around his waist and laying her head against his back. She held him tightly until he stopped shaking.

Finally letting go, she took his hand and pulled him around to face her. "I have not really thanked you for coming tonight. I would not have blamed you for staying home after what I did."

"Let us not mention it again." William said softly. "I wanted to come to honour Evan and to see you."

"Dare I ask how my distant cousin, Miss Lawrence, is faring?"

"She is," he searched for words that would be truthful but not upsetting to his repentant sister, "she has not responded as well as before. But I have hope that she will improve."

She dropped her head and leaned into his chest. "I am so sorry. So very sorry."

"I know."

She pulled back to look up at him. "Evan and I talked about taking my drawing supplies to Pemberley to show her a little of how I learned to draw, or I could even draw a picture for her—that is, whenever I see her again." She spoke rapidly as if any minute he might stop her, then smiled sheepishly. "I am rambling."

He smiled. "Yes, you are, but I like your suggestion. Elizabeth has always shown a keen interest in learning." He saddened a little. "When I knew her before, at Meryton, she was a voracious reader and knowledgeable about so many things. I feel certain she would be interested in whatever you would be willing to show her, though it may take time and effort."

"But I have plenty of time and want to make the effort. Please let me."

William pulled her into a hug. "Soon."

~~~*~~~

Chapter 13

Pemberley

Richard Fitzwilliam walked into the dining room very early, hoping to find his cousin available for a private conversation. Instead, he found no one, save a servant arranging copious amounts of food on every available surface of the sideboard. The smell of freshly baked sweet rolls permeated the air, and unable to resist the temptation, he followed his nose until he stood directly in front of the delicious creations.

A half-hour later, he was uncomfortably full, and he groaned as he stood and loosened some buttons on his waistcoat. *I shall not be able to mount my horse if I tarry in this idle luxury much longer.*

Since Darcy had never appeared, Richard quit the room and immediately encountered the butler, who was instructing two footmen in the foyer. Mr. Walker straightaway dismissed the men to acknowledge his favourite Fitzwilliam relation.

"Colonel, may I say how pleased I am that you are at Pemberley once more."

"Thank you, Walker. You are most kind. Has my taciturn cousin taken to lying abed until the late hours of the morning?"

"No, I can assure you that the master arises quite early, sir. He is already out and about this morning."

It was evident from his expression that Mr. Walker was withholding some pertinent information, and Richard wondered if Darcy had gotten in the habit of accompanying a certain young lady who loved morning walks. Not wishing to interfere, he made his decision.

"I see," he stated. "Then I believe I shall just change into my riding clothes and go out without him."

"Very good, sir!"

~~~*~~~

A while later, Richard sat astride his horse, letting the animal make its way slowly back down the path that led to the paddocks and stables. Having ridden for quite some time, he had not encountered anyone, save some guards, so he assumed he had been right about the morning walks. Unexpectedly, he caught sight of a patch of light blue and pulled his horse up short. In a nearby copse of elms a woman sat perfectly still atop her horse, almost entirely hidden from sight by the foliage. It was obvious that she was involved in studying something, as her attention was so focused that she had not heard or seen him. Richard followed her gaze to two figures in the distance, walking around the lake.

Ah! She is spying on Darcy and Miss Elizabeth!

As he looked back to the woman, she turned slightly, and he recognised Lady Waltham. A strange feeling invaded his stomach. From what Richard remembered, she could be a formidable foe.

Years before, he had overheard his father and George Darcy discussing her relentless pursuit of Fitzwilliam. It seemed she had been determined to have his cousin in spite of the objections of his family. He could still hear the concern in his uncle's voice as he related the tale of hiring private investigators to peruse every area of her life and his relief at having found damning information, which Mr. Darcy used to end her designs on his son. It was most unfortunate that she still owned Ravenbrook, her first husband's estate, only miles from Pemberley.

Richard's contemplation was interrupted by the lady, who edged her mount forward, ostensibly to get a better view. He waited to see if she had intentions of riding towards his cousin or would leave unobserved. When it was obvious she had no plans to make her presence known, he kicked his horse into a trot, coming to rest beside her.

"Spying does not become you, my lady."

Lady Waltham's head swung around, but seeing Richard, the tight line of her mouth relaxed into a catlike grin, and her blue eyes softened.

"*Colonel Fitzwilliam*," she purred in an exaggerated manner, "I should have known you would be lurking somewhere nearby. You always had a gift for stealth, uncovering Fitzwilliam and me in ... shall we say ... delightfully compromising positions." She smirked at his frown, pleased to have reminded him of her indiscretions with his cousin. "What is the matter, Colonel? Have you nothing to say?"

"As I am an *invited* guest here, it appears you are the one lurking," Richard retorted. To his delight, Lady Waltham's smile evaporated.

"Do not be so distrustful," Lady Waltham challenged. "It does not become you." Her eyes sought and found William again while she explained. "I accompanied Lord Greenwich, who is here to examine the colt he wants to purchase."

"I understood that he was to come tomorrow."

"That was his intention until I mentioned how much I would love to accompany him to Pemberley—but it had to be today."

Richard looked towards the stable to see the earl conversing with the head liveryman. "But you are not with Greenwich," Richard stated matter-of-factly. "You are hidden in this copse."

"You are correct. When I saw that Fitzwilliam was not alone, I moved into these trees." Her eyes stayed locked on the two at the lake. "As I sat here trying to decide whether to interrupt, I was reminded of just how rewarding it is to renew old *friendships*."

"What a coincidence! I was just thinking that my cousin is no longer the smooth-faced boy you manipulated, but rather a man who has strong feelings regarding those who would try to steer him one way or another."

She threw him her most seductive look as she cooed, "I *love* men with strong feelings."

Richard's eyes narrowed, and he hissed, "That does not surprise me at all, madam. But I can assure you that you will have no success with my cousin this time."

"And what makes you so sure? I know Fitzwilliam to be a *very* passionate man. I was surprised to learn on my return to England that he never married." She smirked. "Such a waste!"

"As he matured, he learned not to let his emotions rule him. He is an honourable man, not a curious boy."

"Oh, but I believe I could pique his curiosity again."

"Then you are deceiving yourself."

Gwendolyn Waltham squared her shoulders. She was not one to give up easily. "I was going to see if Fitzwilliam wanted to ride out with me, but it seems he is *occupied* with that sickly cousin of his," she uttered scornfully. "Miss Lawrence, I believe Cecile called her. I have to wonder why she chose Pemberley as the place to regain her health."

"Her physician prescribed quiet and rest. Our dear cousin's family suggested Pemberley, and Fitzwilliam was kind enough to consent."

Richard's reply caused her to regard him, and her eyes travelled up and down his body admiringly. "Perhaps you would care to accompany me on a ride instead?"

Richard stiffened. "One lesson I have learned well in the service of His Majesty, Lady Waltham, is to avoid fraternizing with the enemy. Besides, you shall have to go home if you want to ride. Pemberley's guards have been instructed to stop anyone who trespasses." At that precise moment, one of the guards rode across a nearby pasture, and Richard pointed him out. "You would not have gotten very far."

She laughed. "My, my, Colonel! I would never have dreamt that you or your cousin would be afraid of a mere woman."

"Not afraid, madam, just wise enough to see you for what you are—trouble. Why do you not leave my cousin alone? Target another man with wealth and connections."

"There are men of my sphere who are available, but none as pleasing to the eye as Fitzwilliam. I want him." She kicked her horse to move beside Richard and looked him squarely in the eye. "And I always get what I want. Now, if you will excuse me, I shall rejoin my friend."

With those words, she laughed haughtily and kicked her horse into a trot in the direction of the stables where Lord Greenwich was mounting his own horse. As she left, he let go of the breath he had unconsciously been holding.

Then you had better prepare to be disappointed, milady!

At the Lake

William's melodious baritone could be heard clearly near the lake. "And just as soon as the kitten is weaned, you may bring him into your room. Would you like that?"

Elizabeth held the orange stripped kitten to her chest and closed her eyes, a small upturn of her lips the only reaction. William smiled at the scene. It had been his idea to bring the kitten before they began their walk, as she seemed to care for it very much. Continuing to guide her with a hand on her elbow, he kept up his part of the one-sided conversation.

"Old Man Turtle was out yesterday when I rode around the water, so perhaps he shall be lying on that same rock when we get to the other side. Have you thought about sketching his likeness? I am sure we have plenty of art supplies, as Gigi leaves supplies here so that she can draw anything that catches her fancy. Have you ever had opportunity to draw, Elizabeth?"

Stopping, he turned towards her to find she was staring wide-eyed at him. The look reminded so much of the young woman he had met at Netherfield that tears involuntarily welled up. Forcing a smile, he rubbed the kitten's head, making its eyes close as it began to purr. "Perhaps you would like to draw your friend here."

Elizabeth did not answer, though her eyes returned to the kitten, and she immediately brought it to her lips, bestowing several kisses on its soft head, then nuzzling its soft fur. This gesture made William's heart ache. Would there come a time when she would bestow her kisses on him as willingly?

A horse whinnied in the distance, and William's attention was drawn to a couple on horseback near the stables. He recognised Richard, but it took a moment for him to ascertain that Lady Waltham was the woman beside him. Fury washed over him, and his first thought was to go directly to the stables and demand to know what she was doing on his property.

However, a sudden nudge by Elizabeth drew his attention back to her. She was holding the kitten up as though she wanted him to take it. Without a second thought, he knew that she was his first priority. This day would not be ruined, as Richard could be trusted to handle the matter with Gwendolyn. With all his love shining in his eyes, he reached for the small, furry creature and held it to his chest. With his other hand he took her elbow, and they began their walk again.

"Look over there, darling. See that red mare with a white blaze on her head? I thought she might be a good mount for you, as she is very gentle. That is, only if you decide to ride with me when you begin to feel better. I would dearly love to show you parts of the estate that can only be seen on horseback."

Thus, the conversation continued all the way around the lake.

Later in William's Study

After the unwanted visitors departed, Richard decided not to interrupt his cousin but to return to the house and await him there. Less than an hour later, Richard was relating the news of Lord Greenwich's unexpected appearance and Gwendolyn's manipulation to William in his study. Angrily throwing his gloves on the desk, William caused the papers lying there to flutter about and land on the floor. He seemed unconcerned at their fate, as he relentlessly paced back and forth, rubbing his forehead as another headache loomed.

"What possessed Greenwich to change our plans! And for God's sake, why did he bring her?" William hissed. "The guards were alerted that Greenwich would be coming to see the colt, but he was due tomorrow!"

Picking up his unfinished brandy, William downed it in one swallow and threw the empty glass into the fireplace. "For her to have come along is outrageous!"

"Calm down, Cousin! Do not work yourself into a frenzy! Gwendolyn would love that!"

"I placed ten extra guards around the grounds in addition to the twenty that normally patrol! Still I am invaded! Greenwich was the last person with unfinished business here, and I shall bloody well see to it that NO ONE else comes through those gates unless they are on the list I post! Even Lady Greenwich will not be able to accompany her husband without an explicit invitation!"

"You can bar the whole world if you wish, but that will not stop everyone," Richard protested. "You cannot monitor every acre of Pemberley—it is too extensive. And, unfortunately, Gwendolyn Waltham is an excellent rider, skilled enough to take her mount over the fences and hedges that surround the outermost property lines. The most you can hope for is to secure the house."

"I have posted guards at every door—two on the front! I wish I had never laid eyes on the woman. Why did I ever succumb to her schemes?"

"You were an innocent, Darce. Before you met her, your father had managed to protect you from such predators by keeping you at Pemberley and instilling in you that damn sense of duty!" Richard grinned as William's scowled. "You know it is the truth. You always abided by your father's wishes and tried to live up to the standards he set before..."

"Go ahead and say it! Before Gwendolyn! If I had had any sense at all, I would never have gone to her estate alone, even if it was with the best of intentions."

"What actually happened, if you do not mind telling me? I heard rumours, but all these years, I have wondered."

William studied Richard for a moment before answering. "You must never repeat what I am going to say. I am heartily ashamed and never want Georgiana to hear of it."

Richard sobered at the expression on William's face. "You have my word."

"Lord Milton, Lady Waltham's first husband, had died the week before harvest. Father mentioned that at the funeral he had offered Gwendolyn his help in determining what must be done. By this point, I was handling these things at Pemberley, as Father was growing steadily weaker. He and I both knew he did not have the strength to handle her problems." He paused for a moment, as if reliving the event. Richard waited silently.

"I ... I thought I would help Father by taking on this task; so one afternoon while he was resting, I rode over to offer my services." He shook his head and smiled wanly before sobering. "Gwendolyn was very eager to take advantage of my *services.*"

"I can only imagine," Richard interjected.

"In any event, she locked the door to the study and proceeded to undress. I had never before seen a naked woman, and she was very beautiful. I was mesmerized. Foolish youth that I was, I was flattered when Gwendolyn proclaimed that she had been in love with me for some time. Her husband had been at least thirty years her senior, so I suppose it was easy enough to believe." William looked sheepish and refused to meet Richard's gaze. "I suppose it was my sense of duty that brought me back to reality, because I tried to protest. I knew that Father would be very disappointed in me. I even confessed to her that I had never ... but Gwendolyn quieted my protestations very effectively."

William's gaze fell, and he shuddered. "It was not long after, that I realised I was not in love but only in lust. By that time, however, I felt obligated."

"Obligated! My God, Darce, you were young, and she enticed you. You owed her nothing!"

"I know that now, but then ..." He stood and paced again. "It was Father who made me see reason. He was very upset, but he told me I was not the first young man to be entrapped by an older woman, nor would I be the last. He expressed confidence in my ability to do what was right." William shook his head in awe. "Then he hugged me. I do not remember his hugging me often, but I will never forget that time."

"Uncle George was a fine man."

William blinked back tears. "Yes. Yes, he was." He walked over to a side table and poured a glass of brandy and looked to see Richard's nod. Pouring another, he handed one to his cousin before sitting down.

"Why would Gwendolyn assume I want to see her now? She must know that I am not the foolish boy she exploited years ago."

"Vanity, my friend. She has not seen you since you were twenty. She wants to believe she can still turn your head and probably believes you to be like most men—eager for the thrill of illicit sexual encounters at a moment's notice."

William sneered. "Indeed! If she only knew how little ..." His voice trailed off as he realised what he was saying, and he glimpsed the beginning of a smile on Richard's face.

Seeing Darcy's discomfort, Richard felt sympathetic and changed the subject. "Well, now that you are sufficiently warned, let us talk of other more pleasant things. How is Miss Elizabeth faring this morning?"

William's bearing sobered, and he looked away. When he finally spoke, his voice was so low that Richard had to strain to hear. "She does not respond as well as she did before Gigi confronted her. Today was only the second time she has agreed to walk out with me, and I believe it was only to escape the house. She does not seem to hear what I say anymore. I try to carry on a conversation as Mr. Towson suggested, though she hardly gives any indication that she understands me."

"So what does Mr. Towson recommend if she does not improve?"

William sighed heavily. "He has suggested that I confront her with something or someone that might force her to remember what happened to induce her current state."

"Could that not do more harm than good?"

"Possibly, but what other choice do I have?"

A knock on the door interrupted their conversation. "Come!" William said loudly. The door opened, and Mr. Walker came in holding a silver salver, an envelope upon it.

"This express just arrived, sir."

William reached for the post. "Thank you." The elderly servant bowed and hastily left, closing the door.

A puzzled look accompanied William's perusal of the address. "What could Bingley possibly need to send me in such a hurry?"

"I do not suppose you will know until you open it!" Richard declared, receiving a withering look for his attempt at a witty retort.

William broke the seal. His face remained blank, though his entire body tensed as he proceeded to read. Much to his companion's chagrin, he did not share the contents.

Richard could stand it no longer. "What does he say, Darce?"

William's eyes flicked to Richard and then back to the letter. Finally he replied, "It looks as though I will have the unexpected opportunity to find out what happened to Elizabeth."

William resumed reading until he reached the end, then sitting up straighter, he blew out a long breath of air. "The housekeeper who initially contacted the Bingleys to come for Elizabeth has sent another letter begging them to come immediately. They cannot make the trip themselves because little Peter is ill, but Bingley sent word to her that I will come in their stead. After all, Sheffield is less than a day's ride from here. I shall set out tomorrow."

"If you are going, I am going with you."

"I appreciate your concern and your company, Cousin, as I am not sure what to expect. I hope I do not meet the count while I am there, as I believe I would kill him with my bare hands."

"All the more reason for my company."

On the road to Sheffield the following day

They were almost in Sheffield, and thus far, the trip had been uneventful. Darcy's coach was very comfortable, and the weather had been unseasonably sunny, resulting in roads that were, for the most part, easily traversed. William glanced over to the corner of the carriage where Richard's snores confirmed his deep repose. He shook his head in wonder. Being a true soldier, his cousin could fall asleep anywhere.

William, however, was too full of Elizabeth to sleep. He remembered how exquisite it felt to envelope her in his arms. Though he knew he had often crossed the bounds of propriety since finding her alive, he was determined to show her his deepest feelings. Long over the pride that declared her beneath his station, he needed her to remember a different man, a man who loved her. His greatest fear was that she might never recover. Almost as great was his fear that she might recover and recall only the cruel way they had parted at Hunsford and not the bond they had shared since he had brought her to Pemberley. Knowing Richard would not wake, he closed his eyes to relive once again the events of that morning.

Elizabeth was in the habit of waking before dawn with Mrs. Drury. As he wished to tell her in person that he would be away, William made his way to her sitting room immediately after dressing. She was already on the balcony, leaning against the rail and staring up into the heavens as the sunrise painted the grey skies with patches of purple, orange and red. A gentle wind blew about the wisps of hair which had escaped her braids.

Taking in her dishevelled appearance—curls blowing about, a silk dressing gown that the breeze occasionally parted to reveal a lace nightgown—he could resist no longer. Knowing he should not, William stepped behind her, slipping his arms around her waist. At his touch, she inhaled sharply; then recognizing his scent, she relaxed into his body, turning her head to lie against his chest. He was nearly undone. Willing his hands not to move up and cup her breasts, he closed his eyes and buried his face in her scented hair. They stood like that for a short while, and in those tender moments, William pretended she was his. It was only with great effort that he released her, turning her to face him.

"Sweetheart, I must go away today, but I will return very soon. I leave in a few minutes and will be gone until the day after tomorrow. Mrs. Drury, Mrs. Reynolds and all my servants will care for you and protect you while I am away."

He searched her dark chocolate orbs for some sign of recognition, some spark of the lively Elizabeth he had fallen hopelessly in love with at Netherfield. But there was nothing to indicate that that woman still existed.

He sighed heavily. "Do you understand?"

He held her hands, longing for her to squeeze his in reply as before, but she did nothing. So he gently cupped her face and leaned in to place a warm kiss on her forehead. She sighed at the touch of his lips and her long dark lashes fluttered down as she closed her eyes.

"I shall return to you as quickly as possible."

Out of the corner of his eye, he saw Mrs. Drury discreetly waiting inside the sitting room door and nodded for her to come. He addressed her even though his gaze never left his love.

"Mrs. Drury, as I explained last night, I shall return Friday. If there is anything you or Miss Elizabeth have need of, you have only to ask Mrs. Reynolds or one of the other servants."

She tried to hide her smile. "Thank you. I am sure we will be well taken care of by your kind staff."

He gently drew the back of his fingers across Elizabeth's cheek, and she focused on him. "Take care of her...please."

"You need not worry, sir. I will."

He stilled, memorizing Elizabeth's face, before leaving the balcony and heading out of the room. At the sitting room door, he looked back at her one last time before exiting.

Mrs. Reynolds and Mr. Walker waited in the foyer, as the master had requested. Seeing him descend the grand staircase, they exchanged glances and stood taller, awaiting his instructions. Looking between the two, William reiterated how to contact him should an emergency arise. In that event, they were to send a trusted footman on horseback to locate him in Sheffield and another servant to Rosewood Manor to fetch Evan and Georgiana. Days before, he had extracted a pledge from them to be available if Mrs. Reynolds needed any help if he was away.

Thus, it was with a heavy heart that he had left Elizabeth at Pemberley while he travelled to Sheffield.

"Are we close?" Richard's enquiry abruptly ended William's meditation. He tried to recover from his memories of Elizabeth while Richard rubbed his eyes, groaned and sat up straight. Groaning again as he flexed his back, Richard then settled his gaze on William, waiting for an answer.

William smiled at his cousin's dishevelled appearance. "I believe we have only a few more miles to suffer."

Richard guffawed. "Riding in this fine coach is not suffering, Darce. Travelling for days on horseback, only to sleep in tents every night—that is suffering." He absent-mindedly scratched his chest. "Where are we staying?"

"The Rose and Crown. We are to wait there for further instructions."

Richard nodded. "I suppose that it is best to be careful. No need to ride into trouble unknowingly."

William nodded his assent. "To be sure."

~~~*~~~

Chapter 14

Sheffield, England
Rose & Crown Inn

It was nearly noon on the day after William and Richard had arrived in Sheffield, and still no one had come to meet them. Having reached the Rose and Crown in the afternoon, they had gone to bed at dark, as they were exhausted from their long journey. In addition, they had arisen early, dressed and eaten, fully expecting someone to arrive promptly at eight o'clock as the letter indicated. As the hours slipped away, William kept pulling the missive out of his pocket to read it through again, wondering if he had missed some detail. Nevertheless, upon each reading, the instructions were the same—to wait at the inn for someone to contact them.

"I cannot sit here one minute longer!" Richard declared, standing and striding towards the door. "Besides, I am getting hungry, so I shall order us something to eat."

Just as he turned the knob on the door, someone began to knock on the other side. Richard pulled it open. Standing there was a skinny, red-headed young man of about eighteen with his fist still raised in the air.

Surprised, Richard stuttered out an apology and stepped back at the frightened look on the intruder's face. "Excuse me. I—I was only ... Are you here to see us?"

The boy, eyes wide now, swallowed hard and nodded. "Then, do come in!"

Stepping barely inside the room, he squeaked up at Richard, "Mr. Darcy?" If Richard and William were not previously aware of his nervousness, his voice betrayed it now.

Richard forced himself not to smile, replying in his most officious voice, "I am Colonel Fitzwilliam." He motioned towards William, who had been sitting on the edge of the bed, but was now beginning to stand. "This is my cousin, Fitzwilliam Darcy." William nodded.

"I—I am Arthur Fielding, sir," the boy managed to get out. "My aunt, Mrs. Browning, requests that you come with me."

At that, the boy did a perfect about-face, walking away as though he fully expected them to obey his aunt without question. Realising that the young man was not waiting, neither was he leaving the establishment by way of the front door, William and Richard grabbed their coats and hats and made haste to catch up to him. By the time they exited the back door, he was holding open the door to an old carriage and motioning for them to enter it. They exchanged quick glances and did as directed.

Their escort assumed the driver's position and whipped the horses into motion, quite oblivious to the silent exchanges between the two men being transported in the shabby carriage. With a slight lift of the corners of his mouth, William nodded to Richard. One had to admire the ingenuity of the person who had sent for them. They had been secreted out of the inn by way of the rear entrance, and rushed into this miserable conveyance without drawing the least bit of attention from anyone, servant or guest. In addition, it was highly improbable that anyone would desire to know the identity of whoever travelled in this dilapidated carriage or his or her destination.

Long past serviceable, the interior of the carriage was in even worse condition than the exterior. The old cushions, with little or no padding, were ripped in several places. Being used to more comfortable means of travel, William felt every rut in the road down to his very bones. For his part, Richard had put up with worse in his career with the army, so he was unfazed and focused on the passing scenery. Pleasantly surprised at the loveliness of the landscape, he turned to look out the window on the opposite side of the coach and noticed that William was not as agreeably occupied. His wealthy cousin was concentrating on a tear in the seat cover, unconsciously fiddling with a piece that was hanging loose.

Waiting until William noticed his observation, Richard wagged his brows and chuckled. William shook his head, smiled knowingly and looked away. Leaning towards him, Richard spoke just loud enough to be heard over the noise of the road. "Come on, Darce, you have to admit this is hilarious! Can you imagine what gossip would ensue if the *ton* caught sight of the illustrious *Master of Pemberley* riding in a carriage so dilapidated? Good Lord, it may disintegrate at any moment, depositing us upon the ground with little or no ceremony."

A small smile began at the corners of William's lips, and then blossomed into a wide grin before he could suppress it. Richard relaxed—satisfied. If only he could coax a smile from his dour cousin more often.

They had not travelled many miles before the carriage turned off the main road and passed through an old rusted gate. Then they continued for perhaps another quarter-mile through some lovely woods before a modest estate was seen in the distance. As the carriage negotiated the last hundred feet towards the front entrance of the house, the front door flew open and two older women emerged, each waiting on the portico. The carriage came to an abrupt stop and their young driver unceremoniously hopped down and opened the carriage door, motioning for them to alight. As they did, the women began to descend the steps, not pausing until they stood directly in front of them, bobbing slightly.

"I am Gertrude Browning, the housekeeper at Northgate Manor," the first declared and nodded towards the other. "And this is my sister, Mary Sweeten." She swept her hand towards the dwelling. "It is her home we are using for our meeting." Beaming now at the red-haired boy, she continued. "And you have already met my nephew, Arthur."

Richard usually took the lead in conversations with strangers, and this time was no different. "I am Richard Fitzwilliam, and this is my cousin, Fitzwilliam Darcy." Both men bowed. "We are pleased to make your acquaintance and wish to thank you for agreeing to meet with us in place of the Bingleys."

Mrs. Browning nodded, smiling pleasantly. "Please come inside. We shall have a cup of tea while I explain the reason I asked you to make this journey."

The smell of freshly baked bread instantly enticed their senses as they entered the foyer, and Richard inhaled deeply as a blissful look swept across his face. It did not go unnoticed by his hostess.

She enquired cleverly, "A bit of bread and jam with your tea would not be unwelcome, I suppose?"

"You are too kind, madam. That sounds lovely," he quickly responded, trying to keep his growling stomach from being heard.

"It would be most welcome," William confessed. "We have not had time to eat since early this morning."

"Oh?" Mrs. Browning frowned. "Then we shall have to remedy that. Follow me."

~~~*~~~

After they had enjoyed a much-appreciated repast of hot soup, cold meats, cheeses, jams and the newly baked bread, everyone, including Mrs. Browning's sister and nephew, settled in the parlour with fresh cups of tea. However, all attention was focused on Mrs. Browning, who cleared her throat self-consciously.

"First, let me apologise for Arthur not being at the inn earlier as planned and for requiring you to ride in that eyesore." Her eyes lit up as both men smiled. "I felt your coach would draw unwelcome attention to your presence at my sister's home. In our small town, as in any other, I am sure, there are eyes and ears eager to find some gossip. Let them think that the person who arrived in that fine coach was only at the inn to rest before continuing his journey and not here for some specific purpose. Likewise, it would be best if you leave as soon as possible after we conclude our business. The less attention you command, the better."

"I agree completely," William stated solemnly.

"The reason for the delay in meeting you earlier was due to some problems at Northgate Manor. We have had a great deal of trouble keeping servants, and just this morning we lost another. To put it simply, we do not have the required number of people to maintain the up-keep of the house, and when someone leaves without notice ..." Her voice trailed off as she sighed. "I am sorry. I should not bother you with my concerns."

William spoke up, "If I may ask, how far is Northgate Manor from the village?"

"The entrance is only six miles to the north of the village, but after you enter the gates, the drive winds a half-mile before reaching the mansion."

He nodded. "Are the lands extensive?"

"They once were, but Lord Stanton sold many hundreds of acres in the last few years. I believe I heard him say it now consists of less than four hundred acres."

"I see." William glanced at Richard, both knowing that this was not enough land to support a large estate.

Mrs. Browning began to reminisce, unaware of their silent exchange. "At one time, Northgate was thriving, with nearly a hundred servants and tenants tending the grounds and the house. It was quite a showplace. Now much of the up-keep, as well as the management are left to Cliffton, me, and the few others who are left."

Seeing the question in their eyes, she offered, "Cliffton is my husband. He has been the butler at Northgate for nearly as long as I have been there, almost thirty years now, though his duties are so much more extensive than that. At present, he is watching the house so I can meet with you. Mr. Johnston, the Stanton's steward, has arrived, and I overheard him tell his assistant that Lord Stanton would be coming to Northgate in the near future, I suppose to approve the final repairs."

She sulked. "I am never notified of his comings or goings anymore, so it behoves us to hurry, just in case he arrives later today. I would not have him wondering where I am."

Mrs. Browning saw the men glance towards her sister and nephew. "You may speak freely in front of Mary and Arthur. Arthur was the one I sent to Meryton to find Miss Elizabeth's sister, and Mary hid her in this house while she recovered from her injuries. You can trust them."

William apologised. "I am sorry if we offended anyone. We are just fearful for Elizabeth's safety."

"No offense was taken. I am glad that you are careful, as you are correct to fear. The young master can be cruel, and I believe him capable of doing great harm if he feels threatened."

William ventured, "May I ask why you continue to work for such a man?"

"I do not work for the son, I work for the father," she replied defensively. "The old master, Lord Stanton, is a good man, though he is rarely here anymore. He suffered a great heartache years ago when his foreign wife left him, taking their son back to Italy with her. He was but seven at the time. Afterwards, the master lived here only about four months a year, preferring to live in London the rest of the time." She shook her head. "I think Northgate Manor held too many memories.

"When Stephen, Viscount Glascomb, returned to England at almost twenty, he and Lord Stanton moved back here. I understand that Lord Stanton had hopes of grooming him to take over the estate after university. However, the viscount was no longer a sweet-tempered boy. In fact, he had a volatile temper, and they disagreed often and forcefully. After he entered Cambridge, Stephen refused to visit, and Lord Stanton returned to London. In the last few years, I have seen them sporadically and usually separately."

"You called him Stephen, though he calls himself Stefano," Richard interjected.

"Yes, well he was born Stephen Anthony Stanton, Viscount Glascomb. However, when he returned from Italy, he preferred the name and title he had inherited from his maternal grandfather, Count Stefano Gianni Montalvo de Cavour. He is quite taken with his perceived importance and refers to himself as Count Stefano. Naturally, the rejection of the family name broke his father's heart."

"You seem to care for the father. Why would you risk making him angry by seemingly betraying the son?"

"There are two reasons. First, Lord Stanton does not approve of most of his son's activities, though it is plain he chooses to ignore some of his faults. After all, Stephen is still his son, even if he is estranged from him."

William ventured, "And second?"

"I truly care for Miss Elizabeth. She is a very kind young woman who has been ill-used. She puts me in mind of my youngest sister, Grace." For just a moment, Mrs. Browning seemed to reminisce as she played with the fringe on a pillow. "We lost her to a ruthless cad many years ago." Then shaking her head as if to clear her thoughts, she resumed her narration.

"I was surprised when the young master arrived with Miss Elizabeth, as he had hardly been in residence in the previous six months. In any event, he arrived unannounced in the middle of the night, carrying this young woman in his arms—his wife, he insisted. I assumed she was ill, as she was definitely not conscious. She did not stir for days, and I began to worry that she never would."

William closed his eyes, taking several deep breaths before rising to take his usual stance at a window. His discomposure was noticed by the other occupants of the room, Mrs. Browning especially. She had suspected all along that this wealthy gentleman would not have taken Miss Elizabeth into his home, as the Bingleys had explained, unless he was very much in love with her. Seeking the colonel's eyes, his nod gave her permission to resume her story.

"Stephen rattled on almost incoherently—they had been married in Gretna Green—she was ill—he hoped their marriage would be incentive for her to recover. The next day I was given very precise instructions as to her care. I was to administer powders, mixed in tea, every morning before she had eaten." She began to sniffle, her voice almost a whisper. "I truly did not know she was being drugged to keep her submissive until much later."

Richard's eyes cut to William, who had initially clasped his hands behind his back. Now his arms hung down futilely, the only sign of his discomposure being the curling and uncurling of his fingers into fists. Mrs. Browning's next exclamation brought Richard's attention back to her.

"Almost immediately, Stephen left! He received an express from London the day after and set off for Town, staying away three full months. This became his practice, arriving and staying for two or three days, then leaving and staying away for months on end. It continued this same way for almost two years ... until the fire.

"Dutifully, I gave Miss Elizabeth the powders every day for weeks, since he had left explicit instructions, and I believed her to be ill. However, the truth always comes out in the end! My sister, Mary, was terribly sick and had no one to care for her, so I had to leave. I left it up to Addie, Miss Elizabeth's maid, to administer the powders, and being a flighty young thing, she forgot. By that evening, her charge was awake and talking. So the next day, Addie withheld the powders again—deliberately—and she improved even more astonishingly. By the time that I returned several days later, it was obvious that the powders were being used only to keep her immobile and mute. But, of course, this discovery brought its own set of problems."

"She realised she had been trapped," William ventured from his perch by the windows. His voice sounded hoarse, and though he kept his gaze fixed on something in the distance, Richard noted that he had begun to run his hands through his hair. This had always been a sure indication that William was trying to control his temper.

Mrs. Browning's head swung around, astounded at William's understanding. "Precisely!"

William continued, his voice eerily calm. "And she could not remember how she came to be married."

"You are correct, sir. Miss Elizabeth could not remember anything beyond entering her home to find her own mother entertaining the man she had vehemently refused—Count Stefano ... Stephen. She began to cry hysterically, telling me she would never have consented to marry him and asking for my help. But what remedy did the poor child have? She could not return home if her own vile mother had pushed him upon her daughter, mind you. And if she left now, her reputation would be ruined anyway. She had no hope of escape."

All was quiet in the small parlour for several seconds, each person present considering Elizabeth's cruel fate. Mrs. Browning pulled a large white handkerchief from her pocket and dabbed her now red eyes. "Addie and I came to believe she had been drugged and kidnapped with her mother's consent."

"When did she become resigned to her fate?" The flat tone of William's enquiry belied the turmoil he felt, and even Mrs. Browning was not fooled.

"Not many days later, I found her staring into space. She no longer carried on much conversation with Addie or me, preferring to be alone. We worried for her sanity and her person, thinking once she had given up, she might harm herself."

William shuddered, dropping his head. "What happened when Stefano returned to find her awake?"

"We had all decided—Addie, Miss Elizabeth, and me—to let him think she was still taking the powders. So whenever Stephen was here, we would take note of his whereabouts and warn her when he came towards her rooms. We thought she could feign sleep if he went near her."

"That makes no sense!" Richard said vehemently, causing everyone to jump. "What man wants a wife who sleeps all the time? What would be the sense in that?"

He became aware of William's glare and softened his demeanour. "I am only saying, Cousin, that any man who wants a comatose wife is obviously not sane."

"You are correct in both your assertions, Colonel," Mrs. Browning replied. "Our plan began to unravel when he decided he wanted Miss Elizabeth to be awake, at least whenever he was in residence. About eight months after he brought her here, he arrived unannounced, as usual, and more irritable than I had ever seen him. I remember the strong smell of liquor on his breath when he gave me his instructions."

William turned questioning eyes towards her, and seeing the dread on his face, she dropped her gaze. "He ordered me to stop administering the powders."

She continued, barely audible. "Perhaps Elizabeth will tell you what transpired between them, if she recovers." Glancing at William's pained expression, she offered, "Never once did she confide in me—or Addie, to my knowledge—what happened during those times he was in her room."

William stiffened now, holding on to the window frame to brace himself. "What do you know of the fire?"

"Very little actually. I had gone to visit my aunt and returned a day and a half later to find that several rooms in one wing had burned—parts of it were still smouldering. The servants who were still there were trying to salvage what they could from the ruins. I feel sure the entire house would have burned had it not been storming that night."

"Elizabeth is terrified of storms." The soft whisper did not seem to belong to the tall gentleman poised at the window, though those exchanging worried glances knew the truth.

Her eyes tearing up at his obvious pain, Mrs. Browning continued with some difficulty. "I immediately sought word of my Cliffton and was told that he was well and at my sister's home. When I enquired about Miss Elizabeth, I was informed that she had perished in the flames, along with Addie. Addie's little girl had survived and was being cared for by another servant, and there were other servants missing, some found later in the rubble."

At the mention of Elizabeth's death, William sunk into a chair, his head propped on one arm, a hand covering his face.

"But," she quickly explained, "my nephew arrived directly afterward to inform me that Cliffton had spirited Miss Elizabeth to my sister's home under cover of darkness. Her lungs had been injured by the smoke, and she suffered some burns, but her head wound was her most serious injury. The local physician is a kindly old man we have known and used for years, and when I explained her circumstances, he treated her in secret.

"We pretended one of the bodies found in the rubble was Miss Elizabeth, though I knew it to be another young servant who had no family. That girl is buried in Elizabeth's grave in Meryton."

"I saw her grave," William offered with barely controlled emotion, causing Richard to ponder how on earth his cousin had kept secret so deep a devotion.

"As you are aware, once we were confident Miss Elizabeth would survive, we set out to locate the sister she had mentioned—Jane."

William nodded. "Yes. The Bingleys were most appreciative of your kindness towards Elizabeth and them, and you can rest assured, I will forever be indebted to you."

"There is no debt, young man, as we are all very fond of Miss Elizabeth." The truth of her statement was evident in the faces now observing him. His blue eyes shined as he looked around the room, offering, "Then I thank each and every one of you."

Mrs. Browning sat up straighter and took a deep breath, trying to gain her composure. "Now we come to my reason for asking you here today. I mentioned that the steward is here now, but a few weeks before he came, a strange little man arrived. He carried a letter of introduction from the young master. Mr. Chaney, he called himself. He said he was supposed to prepare an estimate on the cost of repairs, and he asked many questions, but not many were pertaining to that purpose. He wanted a list of everyone who died in the fire and where they were buried. After I gave him the list I had falsified, he specifically questioned me on my claim that Miss Elizabeth died in the fire and was buried in Hertfordshire, near her family. I do not think he believed me."

Richard and William exchanged worried glances.

"My friends tell me he spread quite a bit of money around town, trying to loosen tongues. I cannot vouch for everyone who works at Northgate, other than those I trust. I fear that someone could have learned the truth and passed it on to him. Before he left, he made it clear that he was not convinced that all the people who died had been accounted for, and he intended to get to the bottom of it."

"So it begins," William muttered to himself, glancing to see everyone's eyes on him. "I cannot let him find Elizabeth." No one replied, each knowing that the undertaking would be easier said than done. Even Richard did not reply, as he was already mentally engaged in planning how to help his cousin.

Suddenly, Mrs. Browning exclaimed again. "Oh! I almost forgot. Arthur, bring me the chest!"

The red-haired boy hurried out of the room, and the housekeeper's voice became a little more animated. "I discovered a small chest belonging to Miss Elizabeth in the room the young master frequents when he is at Northgate. I knew when I saw it that it was hers, as it had arrived with her and was usually left in her room. I peered inside, just to be sure, you understand." She looked about to see everyone nodding in approval. "And Elizabeth's Bible was on top, so I knew it was her property. I thought it might bring her some happiness to have returned the few small items that belong to her."

At that moment the door flew open, and an elderly woman shuffled in holding a crying child of about two and a half years of age. William's first thought was that the child was the image of Georgiana at that age. In fact, he reflected, if she stood next to a portrait of his sister as a child, it would be difficult to tell them apart. Her hair was light blond, and though her eyes were filled with tears, they were obviously light blue.

"I am sorry to disturb you, Gertrude, but she will not be comforted. I thought you might—"

Mrs. Browning reached for the child, pulling her into her lap and kissing the top of her golden curls. The child leaned into her chest, instantly quieting and closing her eyes. "Never mind, Clara. I have spoiled her." With a smile and a wink, she dismissed the other woman, who retreated into the room from whence she came.

She spoke quietly, stroking Millie's hair. "Gentlemen, this is Millie, Addie's child. Addie was just a young girl when she came to Northgate. I trained her to be a maid, and she served as Miss Elizabeth's personal maid while she was at Northgate. You will remember that Addie," she stopped realising the child might hear, "well, you know the results of the fire already." She rubbed the child's back protectively. "Millie has been living here since the woman who took her in had to move back home with her parents."

"A maid with a child?" Richard ventured, almost afraid to ask but curious just the same.

"Yes. She was taken advantage of by a heartless cad, who paraded about as a valet for Lord Stanton. I would not dismiss her, though I did influence the old master to rid himself of that vile man!" She sighed heavily. "In any event, we are all too old to begin raising children again, and Millie needs to be with a young couple."

Suddenly, a solution to her problem came to mind, and William almost withered as she turned a penetrating gaze on him. "Mr. Darcy, did you mean it when you said you were indebted to us?"

He paled and Richard tried not to smile at the look his cousin was desperately trying to hide. Swallowing the lump in his throat, William tried to sound nonchalant, wondering what she was about. "Yes, madam, every word."

"Then I have a request. Millie has no living relations, and her mother would have wanted her to have a mother and a father—not be condemned to an orphans' home. Do you know of any people, good folk, among your acquaintance that might take Millie and raise her as their own? I ask because, to be honest, you are wealthy and have connections. Anyone you recommend, I am sure, could offer Millie a much easier life than those with whom I am acquainted. She has had such heartache in her short life. I wish to give her every chance for a good future."

William exchanged glances with Richard and saw him nod. "I think I know the perfect couple."

"I can tell you are a good man with a kind heart, Mr. Darcy, but I must insist on one thing before you take this precious child from my guardianship."

"You have only to state your conditions, madam."

"I would have your solemn promise that no matter who you deem worthy of raising Millie, you will take an interest in her affairs for the rest of your life—take on the role of a godfather, if you will. Since there is no parent to designate you as such, I will do so here and now, in front of all these witnesses. Do you accept?"

William's eyes flicked to Richard, then back to Mrs. Browning's steely gaze. "I accept most heartily, and I assure you, I will be in close proximity to Miss Millie as she grows. Her welfare will be my utmost concern."

Large tears filled the housekeeper's eyes. "I knew you were an honourable man, Mr. Darcy, the minute Mrs. Bingley told me what you were doing for Miss Elizabeth."

"You are too kind. I am only doing what anyone would."

"No, sir. You are doing what few men of your station would, both for Miss Elizabeth and now Millie."

Her handkerchief now soaked, she swiped at her tears with the back of her hand and leaned down to kiss the top of Millie's head. "It will be best for the child to get things settled quickly. When you leave, you shall take Millie with you. Arthur will go along to see after her, as she is as comfortable with him as he is with her. Once you are home, you may put him on a coach back here."

Just at that moment, Arthur returned with the chest. As he walked into the room, every eye fixed on him, causing him to blush as red as his hair.

"What?"

~~~*~~~

Chapter 15

Rosewood Manor
Evan's Study

"I say, Ana, if you do not stop leaving your books ..."

Evan Ingram's words died on his lips as he stood, the offending tome that he had just tripped over, in hand. Georgiana sat behind his desk, smiling provocatively. His eyes followed her long delicate limbs to her perfectly shaped feet propped on the edge of his desk. She wore no shoes and her skirts were pulled up enough for him to see that she wore no stockings either. His mouth hung open for so long that she had time to slide her feet off the desk and glide over to place her arms around his neck.

"Breathe," Georgiana whispered as she leaned in to capture his lips in a searing kiss. Finally coming to his senses, Evan pulled her into a tight embrace, his mouth answering hers in a battle for dominance, even as he hardened with desire.

Pulling back for air, he leaned in to whisper, "I locked the door." He could feel her smile against his cheek.

"I knew there was a reason that I married you, Evan Martin Barrett Ingram." She slipped his coat off, and it fell to the floor unnoticed. "You are a very considerate man."

While they kissed, she began undoing the buttons of his waistcoat as his hands ran up and down her bare arms. Done with the waistcoat, it joined his coat on the floor. "I think I might be persuaded to keep you," she purred. Her delicate rosewater perfume wafted over him, fanning the flames of desire.

"So you MIGHT keep me, Mrs. Ingram?" Evan retorted, sounding as though he had more self-control than he did. Quite easily picking her up, he headed to the nearest sofa. Stopping to capture her mouth once more, his tongue found hers and they duelled until he broke away to lay her down on the soft cushions. Quickly he joined her, lying down beside her, then rolling on top. She felt some cool air as the hem of her gown was slowly raised, and then the warmth of a hand as it slid up her legs to the junction of her thighs.

"When will you know for sure?" Evan murmured, his voice as smooth as warm syrup.

"Hmmm," she murmured dreamily. "I—I think I shall know very shortly, if you keep to your present occupation."

And he did.

Afterwards they lay in contented bliss, neither wishing to break the spell by parting even to straighten their clothes. Lying with his head in the crook of her neck, he began to kiss the softness available to his lips.

"I love you so much, Ana. I cannot imagine my life without you. You are all I need to be happy for the rest of my life."

Georgiana's reply, whispered in his ear was barely audible. "Wh—what if we never have children?"

He pulled back to study her. Tears slowly rolled down her face as uncertainty crept into her heart. Running the backs of his fingers over her cheek, he whispered, "I would rather live with you and have no children, my darling, than to live without you. However, you were born to be a mother, and a mother you shall be. We have excellent people employed to find a child to be ours. Somewhere out there is a small creature in need of parents, and the good Lord is working to bring him or her to us at this very minute. I have no doubt."

Ana sniffled, smiling now. She ran her fingers over his beloved face, the stubble of a beard barely beginning. "Do you really think so?"

Evan's face split with the most amazing smile—the same smile that had stolen her heart the day he found her thrown from a too spirited mount. His even, white teeth contrasted with the tan of his skin, and his bright blue eyes sparkled with adoration—all for her. Once again Georgiana was reminded of how blessed she was to have him in her life.

Unaware of her observations, Evan exclaimed, "Absolutely! I have no doubt that somewhere out there a child is making its way to us at this very moment."

On the road home

William studied the face of the child destined to be his niece while she sat enraptured by the fanciful tale his cousin was weaving to entertain her. For one so young, she paid attention almost as well as Arthur, and her humour had been excellent for most of the journey, becoming irritable only when she tired. Fortunately, Richard's masterful talent for creating stories—a skill honed beside many a campfire—saved them. Of course, the stories William recollected that Richard composed for his fellow soldiers were a lot bawdier!

"And so it was that Sir Richard, the noble knight, arrived just in time to save the beautiful Princess Millie from that old dragon—the evil Queen Catherine. Afterwards, that ugly, slimy toad, Collins, hopped into a deep hole and was never seen again in England!"

Millie giggled and clapped her hands in delight. This was the third story Richard had completely fabricated, using distinct voices for each character and a plethora of hand movements. Arthur, who was holding the girl, seemed almost as spellbound as his charge and continued to stare at Richard with his mouth open, as if expecting him to continue or begin another.

William's lips curved involuntarily. "An evil Queen Catherine and a toad named Collins?"

Richard smirked. "I call them as I see them, Darce! Besides, it is never too early to teach Millie who can and cannot be trusted."

"I am afraid the child will have to be kept away from Aunt Catherine and Rosings until she is old enough to know not to repeat your stories."

"Every child should be kept away from our Aunt Catherine. Would that I had been!" Richard smirked, then sobered. "Besides, Georgiana goes near her about as often as you do, which is never!"

William shook his head at his cousin's comments. Even if he did agree with Richard's assessment of Lady Catherine, he hated that the family had come to such division. Sighing, he turned just in time to recognize a small post inn—a landmark that signified they were only a few miles from Rosewood Manor. Once there, the weary child would be able to rest, and they would have a respite from the long journey.

Unfortunately, he reflected, it also meant that he would have a great deal to explain. His sister and brother were completely unaware of Millie's arrival, and though he felt sure that they would be delighted, he felt uneasy just appearing on their doorstep with a child in tow. He had considered sending an express, but gave up that idea when he had tried three times to compose a logical explanation for his impulsiveness. Talking with them face-to-face seemed to be the only sound alternative.

He shook his head as if to clear his mind. Since there was nothing he could do at this late hour, he closed his eyes, hoping to think of more pleasant things ... such as home.

Home—Pemberley—Elizabeth!

William paused at the thought. The word *home* had always evoked images of Pemberley, but now thoughts of home brought to mind *Elizabeth*. Closing his eyes, he envisioned the way she looked when last he saw her on the balcony. He allowed his head to fall back, sinking into the cushion. He could almost feel her in his arms. *How I have missed you, my love.*

Abruptly, his daydream was interrupted. "Mr. Darcy, I think she wants you to take her."

William opened one eye to see Arthur looking from him to Millie. She was perched on the edge of his lap, holding out both arms towards him, while the boy was trying not to smile. Apparently, he had no trouble seeing the apprehension William felt reflected in that one eye.

"It has been a long time ... I do not know if I remember how to—" William stammered, sitting up straighter. He was interrupted by her protector.

"Millie does not bite."

Richard's chuckle drew a pointed glare from William. He quickly covered his mouth with his fist, and his shoulders shook as he tried not to make a sound while he continued laughing.

William's gaze flicked back to Arthur in time to see Millie fall towards him, and he had no recourse but to grab her. Awkwardly, he tried holding her on the very edge of his lap, but she would not be satisfied and squirmed about until she sat snuggled against his chest. Then slowly, she raised her head to study him. Immediately, his gaze was captured by two intense blue eyes, and it was as though another small girl with the same blue eyes and golden curls stared back at him. Long forgotten memories overwhelmed his senses and he swallowed hard.

He knew just where to look—the heavy curtains in the library always had been her favourite hiding place.

"Why are you hiding, Gigi?"

"I ... I am not hiding, Fitzy."

"Then why are you here?"

"I cannot be still. Papa is cross."

"It is only for a little while."

"But I would have a tea party."

"I know; however, Mother is sick, and this is all she asks for her birthday. Will you not do it for her?" He held out his hand. "Or for me? You can sit still for a little while longer. The artist is almost finished."

"I—I guess so, if you promise to play tea party with me after."

"I will. I promise."

"Thank you, Fitzy. I love you."

"I love you, too!"

He led his three-year-old sister back to the drawing room where his father and mother waited patiently, while the artist patted his foot impatiently. As his father sat Georgiana in her mother's lap, he and his father took their places alongside them. He felt the familiar squeeze of his shoulder, signalling that his father was pleased.

Even though he was but six, William had understood his father's unspoken communication—this portrait could possibly be the last likeness of his mother. Though he had watched her grow weaker and weaker with each child she had lost, he chose to believe her health was improving, as his father always assured Georgiana. So it was on the occasion of his mother's thirtieth birthday that he pasted a faint smile on his lips, and stood perfectly still, willing his heart not to break. Fortunately, he had no way of knowing that two summers later, it would.

Unbidden tears filled his eyes, and William looked up through his dark lashes to see if anyone was looking. Finding Richard observing him, he turned to the window, hoping the offending tears would not spill and give him away as his thoughts returned again to that painful memory. Had it truly been four and twenty years since his family was complete?

Millie's small hand on his face brought his thoughts back to the present, and he looked down at her. Several small teeth gleamed as she crinkled her nose and smiled at him. Then satisfied, she laid her tired little head back on his chest and instantly fell asleep. As feelings he had long suppressed came rushing back, William's arms wrapped protectively around her.

Richard had not missed a thing—from the initial fear of holding the child, to the remembrances of long hidden hurts and the unsolicited tears, and finally the comfort of the child's caress. Rarely had he seen his cousin so exposed. Without the usual expressionless mask, there was nothing but a very vulnerable man.

You have seen much heartache, my brother. Would that you find equally as much happiness with your Elizabeth.

Arthur looked on in awe. "She does not usually take to strangers." He cocked his head to the side. "It looks to me like you have done this before."

Pemberley
The Library

Mrs. Reynolds peeked in the door, pleased to see Elizabeth sitting quietly among the books, as Mrs. Drury read from Donne's sonnets. Elizabeth held another leather covered book in her hands, sliding her fingers up and down the spine. Stopping to admire the beauty of the wood panelling, thick rugs over polished wood floors, and the cream and green sofas and chairs spaced throughout the vast space, the housekeeper sighed with contentment. This library was one of Mr. Darcy's delights, and she had no doubt that when he returned, he would be pleased to know that Miss Elizabeth had agreed to join Mrs. Drury here in lieu of staying in her room all day.

Marvelling that due to the considerable size of the room the companion's voice could barely be understood from the doorway, Mrs. Reynolds entered, confidently striding towards the duo with a tray of tea and refreshments. Since Miss Elizabeth had unquestionably accepted her as a friend while the master was away, she was determined to become better acquainted. It was obvious that her boy cared a great deal about the young woman, and she intended to let her know that she cared as well.

"Good morning!" she said, a bit louder than necessary and in a decidedly cheerful tone. She was pleased to note that when Elizabeth looked up to study her, a very slight smile lifted the corners of her mouth.

She set the tray on a table directly in front of the young woman, leaning down to address her. "I brought your favourite, Miss Elizabeth—apple muffins!" Elizabeth's eyes studied the lid the housekeeper was removing, and the smell of apples wafted through the room as they were uncovered. "I hope you and Mrs. Drury will enjoy them."

When Mrs. Reynolds' eyes flicked to Mrs. Drury's, and she noted that Elizabeth's companion was nodding her approbation.

"Thank you, Mrs. Reynolds. You have been so kind to us," she murmured. Her voice almost cracked as she added, "You have taken on so much by having us here."

"It has been our pleasure to have you and Miss Lawrence as our guests. Never think it has been anything but a delight. I am thrilled that you both," she cut her eyes to Elizabeth, "have begun visiting other areas of the house. I am sure you will love the conservatory and the music room just as much, should you care to spend time there. Mr. Darcy will be so pleased, when he returns to learn that you have ventured from your rooms."

Both women watched as Elizabeth leaned forward, took a small plate and placed a small muffin on it before placing it in her lap.

"Would you like some tea?" Mrs. Reynolds hurried to pour a cup of the steaming liquid. "Sugar and cream, I believe, is your preference." She prepared the tea and held out a saucer, carefully balancing the delicate china cup on top.

"Thank you."

It was weak, barely audible, but both women gasped and exchanged glances, aware that they must have heard the same utterance. Mrs. Reynolds' hand shook, and she placed her other hand on the cup to keep it steady. Elizabeth's eyes met hers before accepting the proffered refreshment and taking the cup to her lips.

"You—you are most welcome, my dear," Mrs. Reynolds breathed.

Mrs. Drury sat transfixed. Had she been alone, she might have thought it just her imagination, but the look on Mrs. Reynolds' face confirmed what had occurred. She took several deep breaths, trying to calm herself. Finally, she recovered enough to ask, "Miss Elizabeth, are you well?"

Elizabeth's face had settled into her former indifference, and no answer was forthcoming when she met her guardian's gaze. Then resuming her enjoyment of the delight, she took a bite as if nothing had happened.

Mrs. Drury sighed, and with a nod to Mrs. Reynolds, patted her charge's hand. "After you finish eating, perhaps we shall walk in the garden. Would you like that, dear?"

Knowing there would likely be no reply, she suppressed the tears that threatened. At least this was a beginning.

Elizabeth's mind was whirling. She was not at home—at Longbourn. No. Wherever this room was situated, it was beautiful beyond her wildest imagination. She began to admire the abundance of polished wood on the walls and recognised a smell she had almost forgotten—the smell of her father's library.

She could hear someone reading, and it comforted her. Looking to both sides, she was amazed at the sight of more books than she ever had seen in one place. This was definitely not Longbourn's library. She reached for a book that was lying on a nearby table, running her fingers down the spine.

Suddenly her eyes settled on two women, one sitting and one standing. Their countenances were so kind that she was not afraid, though she wondered who they might be. Abruptly, one woman lifted a lid to reveal golden brown muffins on a plate directly in front of her. The smell of apples filled her nostrils and, tentatively, she reached for a delicate china plate and placed a warm treat on it. She scarcely had set it in her lap when someone handed her a cup of steaming liquid—tea it was.

Instinctively she murmured, "Thank you."

Rosewood Manor
Evan's study

The sound of a carriage pulling up in front of the house brought Evan to his feet and directly after, to the window of his study. "Oh no, Ana, it is your brother's coach. They have returned sooner than expected."

The unmistakable sound of an approaching carriage had propelled him into action, and he had begun to right his clothes—tucking in his shirt and buttoning his breeches—even as he stalked towards the window to see who had arrived. Returning to the place where he had been deliriously happy only minutes before, he picked up his coat, waistcoat, and cravat along the way.

Equally alarmed, Georgiana quickly smoothed her skirts and began putting her clothes into some semblance of order. She then twisted her hair into one long strand before swiftly fashioning it into a bun, mumbling under her breath the entire time. Evan grinned at the sight of his beautiful wife's discomposure.

"What are you saying, dear?"

"Why does William always show up without notice?" she whined.

Never once stopping, she continued to complain as she stooped to retrieve a pin, then haphazardly stuck it into the bun. "Inconsiderate!"

Spying one more just a few feet away, she squatted to pick it up and glimpsed another. "Thoughtless!"

Falling to her knees, she crawled towards the last pin which was nearly unreachable under a table. Completely unaware of the pose she presented in her pursuit of the pins, she was surprised to hear her husband's voice from behind her.

"If your brother were not on the verge of discovering us, I would show you how enticing you look from this point of view." Still on her knees, she blew out an exasperated breath and looked back over her shoulder.

"You should not be thinking of that at a time like this!" She held out her hand. "Help me make myself presentable!" His wonderful deep laugh filled the room as he reached to take the offered hand, pulling her to her feet and into a warm hug, before planting a quick kiss on the tip of her nose.

She stomped her foot. "One of these days, I shall just send him away without an explanation!"

"Of course, you will, my love! And tell me, when has Darcy ever given us notice of his arrival? Here!" He held out three more pins. "Put these last few in your hair, and we shall be perfectly respectable!"

Once she had finished, he turned her around in a circle. "Lovely, as usual. He will be none the wiser!"

She reached out to smooth his ruffled hair. "Do not think for a moment that we shall fool Richard—my brother, maybe, but never Richard!"

They both laughed, falling into each other's arms for one last hug before going, hand-in-hand, to unlock the study door. As they did, they shared a knowing smile. Richard had discovered a locked door once before, and they still had not heard the end of it.

Just as they reached the foyer, the front door was thrown open by Mr. Jenkins, and Richard's large frame filled most of it as he strode into the house. "Good Lord, it is good to be back in Derbyshire!"

A young, red-haired boy followed close behind him, and then Ana's beloved brother came through the door carrying a blond-haired child of about two. Shocked at the sight of Millie, both Ingrams froze, neither able to move or offer a word of greeting. For just a moment, William wondered if he had made a mistake, and even Richard threw him a questioning look.

Instantly, his attention was drawn back to Millie as she began crying and wiggling so forcefully that William was obliged to set her down. She took off like a flash, small shoes tapping out a cadence on the polished marble tiles as she ran towards Georgiana.

"Mama!"

As in a dream, Georgiana stooped to catch her as she neared, and the crying child flung herself into her arms. There were tears in every eye as the crying child clung to Georgiana, and she soothed the child with calming reassurances. Evan looked from the scene before him to his brother with a puzzled expression.

"She is an orphan in need of a good home. I thought—" William began, before being interrupted by Arthur's reverent voice.

"I—I cannot believe it. You look so much like her mother, ma'am. She was tall and blond, like you and ..." His voice faltered, and he shook his head in wonder. "I am Arthur Fielding. I have been helping to care for Millie since ..." His voice trailed off. "I think she believes you *are* her mother. She has not seen her since—since the fire."

He stopped, suddenly realising what he was saying and fearing the effect it might have on the child. However, Millie was too emotional to notice anything but Georgiana. Pulling back to study the small, teary-eyed child clinging to her, Georgiana soothed, "Shhh, little one, all is well." She swayed from side to side in a rocking motion as Millie laid her head against her chest.

Meeting Evan's eyes, now as bright with tears as her own, she brushed an unruly curl from the cherub's face. Then Georgiana flashed a confused smile at him before setting her gaze on her brother. "Of all the people in the world, how did this child come into your care? Is she truly in need of a home? Can this be happening?"

William's head bobbed up and down. "Yes, she is, and before you become alarmed, let me assure you that I would never have brought her here without careful consideration. Arthur's aunt has charged me with finding her a good home, and though you are my sister," his eyes flicked to Evan, "and my brother, I know of no couple with greater capacity for loving her than the two of you."

Slowly Georgiana let out the breath she had been holding, her eyes coming to rest on Millie. "This is real. No waking up tomorrow to find out it was all a mistake?"

"You have always trusted me, Gigi. Trust me now." Big tears rolled down her face as she met her brother's gaze, nodding solemnly.

Georgiana and Evan then focused on each other, and without words, he moved to slide his arm around his wife's waist, while slowly bringing the other up to cradle Millie's head. Two large, blue eyes opened, studying him intently for a moment, and as if in acceptance, closed again, causing Evan to struggle not to weep.

William ventured tiredly, "I will be glad to explain all the particulars, but I had hoped it would not be necessary to do so tonight. She ... we are all exhausted."

Georgiana nodded in acquiescence. Though there were a thousand questions she wanted to ask, now was not the time. For at this moment, she had a small person in her arms that needed a bit of supper and plenty of rest. Her words were barely audible as she focused on William. "Thank you for your faith in us."

She seemed about to cry, and not waiting for his reply, raised her chin and looked to her other guests. "Please come back with Fitzwilliam tomorrow, Richard. We have had little time to visit lately, and," glancing to Arthur, "I look forward to hearing everything you have to tell me about Millie."

Turning, she began to mount the grand staircase, speaking softly to the little girl in her arms. "And so, sleepy angel, would you like to see a room I decorated for someone just like you? You know, it has stood empty for far too long." She deposited a kiss on the top of the child's head just before she disappeared at the top of the stairs.

The men below followed the loving scene until the participants were gone. Then Richard and William hurriedly composed themselves, turning to wipe all evidence of their tender hearts from their faces. However, when they turned to Evan, they found that he had not tried to hide his own tears in the least. Looking to first his brother and then his cousin, he did something totally out of character—he pulled both men into a tight hug, an arm around each friend. He whispered roughly, "Thank you seems so little a sentiment."

Then swiftly stepping away from them, the Evan of old returned, and each pretended nothing out of the ordinary had occurred. "Will you entertain yourselves, while I join my wife for a little while? Dinner should be ready shortly, and I ask that you please start without us. You know how to make yourselves at home."

Nothing more was said as they watched Evan take the steps two at the time on his way to the nursery. William was deep in thought again when he was roused by Richard's teasing of the butler.

"Mr. Jenkins, I have every faith in your ability to locate Mrs. Jenkins swiftly. Would you please tell her there are two very hungry bears and one cub waiting in the drawing room?"

Mr. Jenkins had been fighting to control his own emotions, and Richard's playfulness was just what he needed to recover. "No need, Colonel Fitzwilliam. I was just about to announce dinner. Mrs. Jenkins is awaiting everyone in the dining room. Will the young man be eating with you?"

"Yes. Yes, he will."

Richard and William began to make their way in the direction of the dining room, the smell of delicious food now wafting through the house, making them exceedingly hungry.

They had not gotten very far when Mr. Jenkins called out, "Sir, if I may." Richard and William stilled to look back at him as he addressed Georgiana's brother. "I would like to say you have made this household very happy."

With that he lifted his chin, assumed his normal emotionless expression, and more quickly than usual, disappeared down the hall.

Richard grinned, putting an arm around Arthur's shoulder. "Come, my boy. Let me show you how a soldier eats when he is unsure of his next meal!"

"Unsure of his next meal?" William chided, chuckling softly.

"Shhh, Cousin. Do not interrupt me when I am training a future recruit!"

~~~*~~~

Chapter 16

Rosewood Manor

Pushing back from the table, Richard patted his stomach and groaned. "I feel as though I could use a nap. I am entirely too full!" His pronouncement made Arthur laugh and he almost choked on a mouthful of water.

"Richard, where are your manners!" William chided.

"I do not know where I left them, Cousin, and I am too tired to look for them at the moment!"

William chided, "Then we must get you back to Pemberley, so you can rest, and I hope, find your manners. I, for one, cannot wait to spend an entire night in my own bed. Excuse me while I find my brother and sister and have a word with them before we depart."

"And I cannot wait to impose upon your hospitality and enjoy a night in one of your fine beds!" Richard retorted, winking at Arthur. Then he whispered loudly enough to be heard, "A soldier takes every opportunity to impose upon those who lead lives of leisure."

William shook his head at Richard's antics and headed for the door, almost clearing the room before remembering a concern. Turning, he enquired of Arthur, "Will Millie be well if I leave her here tonight? I mean, without anyone with whom she is familiar? Do you need to stay with her?"

Arthur had already finished eating, so he stood and stepped closer to William, eager to explain. "No, sir. She is used to a number of people caring for her, and she is content as long as she is not by herself. She is especially frightened, though, when she awakens alone." He concluded, beaming proudly, "But other than that, she is a very good child."

William could not suppress a smile at the young man's obvious pride in Millie. "You are very kind to take care of so young a charge."

Raising his chin, the youth replied confidently, "It is my Christian duty to care for widows and orphans, so the Bible teaches. Moreover, I am used to children, as I helped with my younger brothers and sisters. My mother says it will serve me well when I have children of my own."

William clasped his shoulder. "You are correct, and your mother is a wise woman. Still, you are a good man to take such prodigious care of her."

Arthur flushed as red as his hair, dropping his head in embarrassment. "I thank you."

William stepped into the hall then, moving in the direction of the grand staircase. He glanced up the stairs to see Evan already half-way down and waited for him at the bottom.

Grabbing his brother's hand as they met, Evan absently shook it as he proclaimed, "I have not seen Ana this happy in—I cannot remember how long! How did you ever accomplish this miracle? Is Millie really ours?"

William's smile was kind but weary. "As her newly commissioned godfather, I can assure you that she is most definitely yours. However, we agreed to talk about it all tomorrow."

Evan held up both hands as if in surrender. "Of course. I am walking on air, and I forget that you are tired. Forgive me!"

"No apologies needed. But I would like to tell Gigi I am leaving, if it would not be an inconvenience."

"None at all. You will find your sister in the nursery rocking an already sleeping child to sleep." They both chuckled. "But I will not mind if she stays there all night—and she may. She is entitled to be thrilled about the child." Evan continued, "She is perfect, and not just because she is the very image of my Ana."

"That was the first thing I noticed about the girl. She could be the child in the portrait at Pemberley, the one painted when Gigi was three."

"Yes! I had not thought of it, but you are right," Evan exclaimed, "the portrait of your entire family, where Ana is sitting on her mother's lap!"

William's face fell just a little. "Yes, that is the one." Patting Evan's back as he passed him, he added, "I pray she will bring you both joy."

"She already has," Evan said hoarsely. "How can we ever thank you?"

"Just love her as you would your own."

"You know I will ...we will."

"That is why she is here."

~~~*~~~

The sound of Georgiana's clear soprano caught William's attention long before he reached the door to the nursery. She often sang as a child, and even as a young woman, she accompanied herself on the pianoforte. However, it had been years since he had heard her sing and never something so simple, so heart-warming.

Stopping just outside the door, he peered in to find her sitting in the chair he had given her when she was expecting her first child, still rocking Millie. Fortunately, for him, her head was bowed so she could not see his struggle. He was finding it hard to keep his composure as she sang a nursery rhyme their own mother had sung to them.

> Lavender's blue, dilly dilly,
> Lavender's green
> When you are King, dilly dilly,
> I shall be Queen
> Who told you so, dilly dilly,
> Who told you so?
> 'Twas my own heart, dilly dilly,
> That told me so.
> Call up your friends, dilly, dilly,
> Set them to work
> Some to the plough, dilly dilly,
> Some to the fork
> Some to the hay, dilly dilly,

Some to thresh corn
Whilst you and I, dilly dilly,
Keep ourselves warm.
Lavender's blue, dilly dilly,
Lavender's green
When you are King, dilly dilly,
I shall be Queen
Who told you so, dilly dilly,
Who told you so?
'Twas my own heart, dilly dilly,
That told me so.[1]

Hearing a deep sigh, Georgiana glanced up to find William in the doorway. She waved him forward as she stood and placed the child in her own small bed, laid a stuffed rabbit beside her, and pulled the satin counterpane over both. Having endured the tiring journey, Mille did not awaken, instead she turned to clasp the toy and snuggle deeper into the soft pillow.

Georgiana leaned in to caress the soft curls around her face and placed a kiss on her forehead. Straightening, she contemplated the child for a second before turning, walking to William, and immediately falling into his arms. Her body shook as she cried quietly against him. Tenderly he held her, rubbing her back until she calmed, then he led her out into the hallway so they could speak without fear of waking the sleeping child.

"Arthur assures me Millie will be well if he does not stay, but I will leave him here if it will ease your mind." Georgiana was shaking her head no even before he finished.

"Forgive me if I frightened you by crying. I am sure she will do well. I was just overcome with joy as everything is just so perfect," she managed through her tears. "I have longed to see a child in that bed for so many years and tonight…" A sob caught in her throat, and William pulled her back into a hug.

He murmured reassuringly, "You will be a wonderful mother."

"I will do everything in my power to be the mother Millie needs."

William lifted her chin to look into her eyes. "Of that I have no doubt." She beamed. "I came to tell you that we are leaving. As I said earlier, I shall explain everything tomorrow, but tonight I wish to go home and sleep in my own bed."

Standing on her toes to kiss his forehead, she then playfully pushed him back a bit. "Go home, Brother. You have done so much, and you will need your rest, as I have many unanswered questions. Tomorrow will come soon enough."

He winked at her and turned. She took another step towards his retreating form. "I know you are anxious to learn how Miss Lawrence has fared while you were gone. We have not heard a word from Pemberley, so I can only assume all is well." For the first time that evening, she saw worry cross his face.

"I have heard nothing either, but I am hopeful she is progressing."

---

[1] *Lavender's Blue* is a traditional song often used as a lullaby. Its composer is unknown, but it dates back to at least the 1680's. Like many lullabies, it was probably passed down through generations and has been changed many times. An alternative opening is, *"Lavender's blue, dilly dilly, rosemary's green."* *Lavender's Blue*, Walter Crane, 1877. *4815*

"I wish that as well, for your sake as well as hers. I have my art supplies ready. Perhaps I could call on her soon?"

"Perhaps."

Pemberley

As the coach bearing its tired travellers stopped in front of Pemberley, it was already quite late, which deeply disappointed William. He had harboured hopes of arriving in time to say goodnight to Elizabeth. But as late as it was, she was most likely in her room preparing for bed if not asleep already. His glum expression was duly noted by Richard.

"Heavens, Darce! You look as though we have just arrived at Rosings! I thought you would be giddy with relief to be home!" His loud guffaws as they exited the coach caused the footmen standing at attention to steal glances at each other, then just as quickly, resume their stance as they saw Mr. Darcy's frown.

"I am tired, Richard! That is all!"

"And I am the Prince Regent!"

William groaned as he proceeded up the steps to find Mr. Walker opening the door. "Mr. Darcy, sir, Colonel Fitzwilliam, it is so good to have you both back so soon. I hope your trip was pleasant."

"Yes, Mr. Walker," William responded. "The trip was not as difficult as I imagined it would be." By that time, Mrs. Reynolds had joined them, and he addressed her. "Please have a room prepared for my friend here, Arthur Fielding." He nodded in the direction of the boy. "Richard will, of course, be staying in his usual rooms."

The elderly housekeeper smiled at the young boy before promptly returning her attention to William. "Very good, sir. I am so pleased you are home."

William took note of the meaningful look Mrs. Reynolds gave him. Nearly a lifetime spent with her had taught him what that look meant. She needed to speak to him in private.

Before he could say anything, however, she gave instructions to the maid that had followed her to the foyer. "Constance, show Mr. Fielding to the green bedroom, the Colonel knows where his rooms are located—they are always kept ready."

As the maid bobbed a curtsy in reply, Mrs. Reynolds focused on William. "I shall order hot baths prepared for you immediately and send everyone a tray with supper afterwards, if that meets with your approval."

Before William could answer, Richard crowed, "Mrs. Reynolds you are a mind reader!" Then motioning for Arthur to join him, he slung an arm over the boy's shoulder, and they ascended the stairs behind the maid. "Come, young man, as a future soldier, you have much to learn about enjoying the kindness of generous people."

William and Mrs. Reynolds both watched with amusement as Richard continued his banter up the stairs and on down the hallway, his voice still loud enough to be heard long after he was out of sight. Turning to each other, they smiled and shook their heads in mutual acknowledgement. Then the housekeeper's mien sobered.

"Would you have just a moment, sir?"

"Of course. Shall we go to my study?"

Without any further words, she followed Mr. Darcy down the hall.

~~~*~~~

Elizabeth had fallen asleep rapidly, but the scenes running through her unconscious mind brought worse night terrors than she had experienced in the past. This time she could see him clearly.

A tall, blond-haired man, obviously drunk, his face distorted with rage. He was waving a pistol, yelling obscenities, and accusing her of disloyalty. He grabbed her arm, twisting it painfully behind her as he hissed, "You plotted to leave me—your husband! After all I have done for you, this is the thanks I get!"

Her hands gripped the sheets tighter, twisting the linens first one way and then another, as in her dream she tried to break free of him.

"You shall learn what happens to those who betray me!"

Suddenly a young woman holding a child came from somewhere behind, interrupting his fierce rant and trying to distract him. He swung the gun in her direction.

"You! You were the one who assisted her! I should kill—"

Elizabeth stepped in between them just as a loud blast reverberated through the room. Her head exploded with pain at the same time she caught sight of the mother and child being splattered with blood. Was it hers? Suddenly a large red stain began to spread across the mother's breast. Horrified and unbelieving, she watched as the woman and the child sank to the floor. Abruptly rough hands were grabbing her arms, pulling her back around. The madman's face was only inches from hers, and he appeared to be shouting, though Elizabeth could hear nothing as the darkness claimed her.

Bolting up in the bed, Elizabeth's breath came in great gasps. Immediately, a certain phrase broke through the chaos—***your husband.***

With that horrible revelation, the veil that had begun to lift since she had been at Pemberley slammed shut, and Elizabeth slipped back into the abyss she had occupied after the fire.

In her current state, she now believed that Pemberley was Northgate, and she reached for the doll lying by her pillow and slipped out of the bed. She ran from the bedroom into the sitting room and finding it locked, went on into Mrs. Drury's room. The elderly companion, asleep for hours, did not hear Elizabeth slip through her room and into the hall. Completely unaware of her state of undress, Elizabeth ran through the house, her sole focus on escaping from **him.**

The household was asleep except for the servants patrolling the halls and William, who was completely unaware of her distress. Swiftly she navigated the long hallway to the grand staircase, only encountering the footmen once she got that far. She eluded the first by swiftly sitting down on the stairs as he passed below and another by rushing into the lone room downstairs that was familiar—the library. Going straight to the doors that opened onto the terrace, she worked for some time before she managed to unlock one. Flinging it back, she ran out onto the terrace unsure of which way to go. The familiar gravel path to the stables caught her eye, and she began to run.

~~~*~~~

The hour was late by the time William finished bathing and eating, and though he was weary, sleep would not come. Mrs. Reynolds' account of how Elizabeth had thanked her for pouring a cup of tea intrigued him. Could it be that she was coming to her senses? And, if she was, what would it mean for their relationship? If she truly remembered everything, would she hate him as she had after Kent? Every dreadful thing he could imagine kept him from finding any rest.

After two hours of staring blankly into the flames still flickering in the hearth and consuming two glasses of brandy, the overwhelming desire to see Elizabeth overrode his better judgment. Pulling his robe on over his nightshirt, he opened the door to the servants' hall, and grabbing a candle, advanced in the direction of her bedroom. Since he was well familiar with the house, it took little time for him to arrive at the secret opening. He blew out the candle and stepped inside, standing perfectly still until his eyes adjusted.

It was several moments before he realised she was not in the bed or even inside the room. Moving closer, he touched the mussed sheets, evidence that she had lain there earlier, and found them cold. His eyes flew to the French doors, which were closed. Moving swiftly to them, he tried the handle but found it locked. Something compelled him to go onto the balcony, and as he stepped into the cool night air, he caught sight of something moving across the manicured lawns below, but he could not see it clearly.

A paralysing fear washed over him. Was it Elizabeth or was she elsewhere in the house? And if it was Elizabeth, why would she wish to escape? Had someone or something scared her? Had he been foolish to believe she was improving because she had not once tried to escape Pemberley as she had Netherfield?

Twirling around, he reached the servants' hallway in a few long strides and began the trek back to his room. Arriving there swiftly, he pulled on his boots and grabbed his coat off the back of a chair, racing into the hallway. Reaching the grand staircase, he cleared the stairs faster than ever before, slowing down only when approached at the bottom by a footman.

"Have you seen any guests downstairs since you have been on duty?" William asked a little too forcefully, his composure almost spent.

Taking in the Master's unkempt appearance and never having seen him in such a state, the footman replied nervously, "No, sir." He swallowed a large lump in his throat, wondering if he might not have been diligent. "I have been on duty since dark and have seen no one."

"Carry on," William declared in his Master of Pemberley voice, and the footman, eager to be out of sight, bowed and hurried back the way he had come.

As the footman scurried away, William noted that the library door was the only one not entirely closed and hurried there. Once inside, he found the door left open and ran through it onto the terrace. Now convinced that the figure he saw earlier must have been Elizabeth and that she had escaped via that door, he followed the gravel path, zigzagging through the gardens towards the stables. Not slowing, he reached the tree-lined lawn in front of the stables and stopped abruptly, scanning his surroundings with no sign of her. He began to question his decision not to alert the staff straightaway.

No! If Elizabeth sees strange men combing the grounds, looking for her, it would only exacerbate her fears.

It was a moonlit night, but a cloud passed over at that moment, making it impossible to see anything other than the outline of the barn. William cursed the fact that he had not thought to grab a lantern but as he waited for the light to reappear, suddenly Elizabeth's destination became clear. Moving swiftly around the barn to the back, he entered the same door he had used to show her the kittens. Silently, he stepped inside and stood deathly still, praying he did not frighten her.

At last, the sound of hay being moved about assured him she was indeed in there. With very few steps, he stood at the entrance of the stall that held Stockings and her kittens. He waited for the moon to illuminate the barn through the tall windows that ran along the walls, and when it did a moment later, Elizabeth was clearly visible. She was sitting atop a large pile of hay in one corner, her knees pulled towards her chest, clutching the doll she had previously given up. She had all the kittens about her, as though they might afford protection from whatever demons pursued her.

Even in her dishevelled state, she was beautiful, and it took his breath. In her haste to escape, her loose braid had become undone, and her tresses hung down her back and across her shoulders—unrepentant dark curls flying in all directions. A white cotton gown with blue satin trim along the neck, sleeves, and under the bosom was all she wore. One thin cap sleeve had fallen off her shoulder, causing the neckline to slip lower on that side, exposing the top of a breast. If not for the frightened look in her dark eyes and the way she scooted further away when she saw him, he would have thought this the most beautiful vision he had ever beheld.

"Elizabeth?" His voice sounded more composed than he felt.

She violently shook her head. Then wrapping her arms around her knees, she buried her face there, atop the doll, and wept. His heart broke.

"Elizabeth, it is Fitzwilliam Darcy ...William. I will not harm you." He took a small step forward, and she whimpered.

Knowing he must take control, he commanded stridently, "Look at me!" Adding in a much softer tone, "Please, Elizabeth." Slowly she raised her tearful eyes to study him.

"I am not *him.* I am Fitzwilliam ...your William. Say my name, Elizabeth. Say William."

Time stood still until she murmured, "William."

Letting go of the breath he held, William deliberately moved closer, one step at a time. He soothed her as he neared with tender words. "That is right, sweetheart. It is William, and I have *never ...nor will I ever* hurt you. In your heart, you know that."

Her eyes never leaving his, he finally got close enough to extend his hand, palm up. Elizabeth's eyes flicked from his face to his hand and back. He nodded and cautiously she extended her hand until it lay in his larger one. He smiled reassuringly and brought his other hand to cup her small one.

"You are safe with me, sweetheart. Now, let us get you back to the house."

Helping her to her feet, he noticed for the first time that she was not wearing any shoes, and her feet were scratched and bleeding. He adjusted her sleeve back where it belonged, took off his coat and draped it around her as she clasped the doll. Buttoning two buttons to keep it around her, he slipped his arms under her knees and picked her up.

Meeting her dark eyes from only inches away, he pleaded, "Trust me, Elizabeth. I will protect you with my life."

Her only answer was to lay her head against his chest.

London
Lady Rutherford's Ballroom

Lady Gwendolyn Waltham surveyed the ballroom from the doorway. Her dark blond curls, swept up into an elaborate display, were interspersed with ruby-encrusted combs. Her burgundy velvet gown was of the latest style, cut exceptionally low, displaying her ample cleavage and still-small waist. A single large ruby, surrounded by diamonds, dangled dangerously between her breasts, while the matching earrings adorned her ears, both had been presents from her late husband. Every eye turned to stare, before returning to their conversations.

Now that she was no longer the single centre of attention, she despised these events. At one time, her entrance would have stopped the music and the conversations. Now, there was a new crop of debutantes every season, all younger than she, if not more beautiful, and it forced her to work harder for male attention. Her inspection of the occupants of the room ended with the sight of Cecile Preston at the other side of the ballroom, locked in an animated discussion with two women.

So, the ugly duckling has returned to London. Perhaps, Gwendolyn thought, she would glean some information from Cecile regarding Fitzwilliam, since she had so little luck in Derbyshire. That accursed Georgiana had been no help at all!

With a great deal of practiced theatrics, she crossed the room, meeting the eye and nodding to every man in her path. Her lips were barely lifted in a knowing smile as she skilfully conveyed her availability. Only the swift poke of an elbow by a diligent wife kept some of the men from returning her greeting, and she suppressed a laugh. Now it was up to them to make a move.

If she could not convince Fitzwilliam to share her bed, she was not above securing another man's devotion—even one with a boring, stupid wife—but only if he were wealthy enough to merit the trouble. However, until someone more tempting came along, she still meant to concentrate on the most devastatingly handsome man of her acquaintance. Moreover, though Fitzwilliam seemed impervious to her machinations at present, she felt confident that he would eventually surrender to his baser instincts. As she considered this pleasant development, she slowly made her way to Cecile Preston.

Oblivious, Cecile was in the middle of a lament over the same handsome man. "And I am sure this cousin has used her illness as an opportunity to seduce him. Otherwise, why would Fitzwilliam's feelings have changed so drastically after having practically courted me for weeks? Why would a man, who is known for his reticence, take in this mysterious cousin, allowing her to reside at his beloved Pemberley? No, I am convinced there is something more than meets the eye in **that** relationship."

The other ladies nodded in agreement, which only encouraged Cecile to continue boldly. "Knowing Fitzwilliam as I do, I imagine he feels he is under some obligation to this woman. I would be very surprised if an announcement of their engagement is not forthcoming."

Meanwhile, Gwendolyn had positioned herself behind the trio and overheard this bit of news. She was incensed! Surely, the Fitzwilliam she knew was not enamoured of that small, dark creature. Why, she was not even beautiful! Promptly burying her annoyance under an abundance of boldness, Gwendolyn stepped in between the ladies, facing Cecile.

"Cecile, darling!" She took the mouse's hand without its being offered. "How good to see you again!"

Noting with satisfaction the ire in her expression, Gwendolyn continued. "I had no idea you were back in London. I had to return for business, and imagine my surprise to walk in here and find you holding court!"

Cecile barely hid her disgust. "Oh, Gwendolyn, darling," she parroted her nemesis, her smile never reaching her eyes. "I was hardly *holding court*." Motioning to the women Gwendolyn had ignored, she added, "Have you met Lady Matthews and Lady Dawson?"

Gwendolyn's pasted smile froze. She would be forced to acknowledge the ones she had so callously disregarded moments before. Turning, she eyed the women suspiciously. After all, were they not all jealous of her?

Cecile continued the introduction. "Ladies, allow me to introduce Lady Gwendolyn Waltham."

Before either of them could speak, Gwendolyn retorted, "Charmed," and quickly faced Cecile again. Somewhat amused by her single-minded rudeness, the other ladies threw sympathetic looks at Cecile over Gwendolyn's shoulder and walked away.

When the two were no longer within hearing range, Cecile said boldly, "In answer to your greeting, I cannot possibly convey my feelings at seeing you again so soon."

Understanding her meaning, Gwendolyn smirked. "I can assure you the feeling is mutual."

She waited for another retort and when none was forthcoming, ventured, "I wondered if you had heard from our dear Georgiana of late. The last I heard, she was truly worried about her dear cousin—the one staying at Pemberley for her health." Gwendolyn would never admit that her source was a maid paid to collect gossip and not Fitzwilliam's sister. Cecile's face was an unreadable mask as she kept silent.

"I understand she is not progressing as well as they would have liked because *someone* tried to turn Georgiana against her from the very beginning of her stay."

Cecile stiffened slightly before slowly smiling. "I have it on good authority that Mr. Darcy is very enamoured of his lovely cousin, and they plan to marry."

"And that sits well with you because..."

Cecile continued to smile and lied. "I am fond of Fitzwilliam, but ours was a friendship, nothing more. If he finds happiness with his cousin, then I will wish him joy."

Gwendolyn drew herself up straight. "I thought surely you would be devastated if he did not offer for you."

"No, I believe it is you who will be devastated when the inevitable happens, Gwendolyn, dear." With that, Cecile swept past her and joined her true friends.

Flushing with ire, Gwendolyn realised that several people standing nearby were studying her. Lifting her chin in defiance, she started to move forward, when a warm baritone voice and a firm hand on her arm stopped her.

"I have never seen a more beautiful..." Gwendolyn turned and Count Stefano's gaze drifted from her face to the ruby and back again. "Gown," he concluded.

Gwendolyn smiled at the tall, regal-looking, blond-haired gentleman, taking in his toned body and exquisite clothes. "And do you often go around admiring 'gowns,' sir?"

"No. I actually admire the woman in the gown, but I was afraid to admit as much so soon. Not proper, you see." His green eyes laughed and a flash of white teeth split his tanned face. Her breath caught, as he bowed over the hand he had stolen, brushing it with a kiss.

"Count Francesco Benso de Martino, at your service, madam."

~~~*~~~

Chapter 17

Before daylight, Richard made his usual solitary trip to the dining room. Mrs. Lightfoot, Darcy's cook, always had something prepared very early just for him. Years in His Majesty's service brought him out of bed before nearly everyone else. Only this morning when he reached the foyer, a dim light down the hallway brought him up short. Though his cousin was an early riser, he knew it was not like William to be up at this hour—it was still dark. Even so, following the mysterious light, he indeed found his cousin in his study, laid back in his chair, feet propped on the edge of his desk and eyes closed.

Since he made no move to stir and seemed to be sleeping, Richard decided to have some fun at William's expense. However, a lone candle in the room was not enough light, and he tripped over a stack of books on his way towards his victim.

William startled, sitting upright and planting his feet firmly on the floor. "What the devil!"

Even to someone used to seeing men at their worst, Richard noted that William looked a fright—eyes red-rimmed with dark circles underneath, hair dishevelled, unshaven and not fully dressed. It was obvious that he had gotten very little sleep. With the Colonel's experience in questioning enemy soldiers and William's state of sleep deprivation, Richard was sure it would be an easy occupation to find out what had happened to effect this change in his normally fastidious cousin. Instead, as he attempted to get answers to his questions, William left him standing in front of the desk as he walked to the tall windows to observe the sunrise. Determined not to be denied his explanation, Richard joined him.

Neither cousin spoke—standing silently side-by-side. They shared identical stances: hands clasped behind their backs, eyes trained on the horizon. From behind, they looked very much like brothers, except that William was a bit taller and had darker hair. Not a word passed between them as the sun slowly rose over a distant line of trees. Hues of greys and purples gave way to brilliant reds, oranges and yellows, before finally settling on a shade of blue so light that it unexpectedly reminded William of his mother's eyes. Unbidden, his eyes filled with tears, and he struggled for control by taking a deep breaths.

Richard noticed. Though he had appeared to watch the sunrise, his eyes had never left William. He not only had heard his cousin's heavy intake of breath, but he had seen his jaw clench. Evidently, the usual demons William wrestled with had gotten reinforcements. Weariness had finally overcome his cousin's vaulted willpower.

Perhaps now he will be willing to talk.

For his part, William was weighing his options. If he answered a few of Richard's questions, then he might be able to keep some of his interactions with Elizabeth a secret. "Go ahead! You will not be satisfied until you ask."

"What happened to leave you in such a state?"

"Elizabeth tried to leave Pemberley last night. I heard her as she ran down the hallway, so I quickly dressed and went after her. Once I was sure she had escaped the house, I knew she must be at the stables. That is the only place she is familiar with on the grounds. I found her inside with the kittens and brought her back here."

I can hardly believe I slept through anything so remarkable. My army experience has taught me to sleep with one eye open. I cannot imagine how you, Mister Sleeps-like-a-rock, heard someone as light as Elizabeth running down the halls of Pemberley."

"I was not sleeping. I was reading in my bedchamber."

Richard walked to the middle of the room, pacing in his interrogator's posture. "So what of Mrs. Drury? Would she not have heard the door opening? And why would Elizabeth run away in the first place? Did someone scare her?"

"I learned that Mrs. Drury is sick with a cold, and Mrs. Reynolds had given her a draught that made her sleep more soundly. As to why she ran, from the fear in her eyes I believe Elizabeth must have had a nightmare and thought she was escaping Northgate—escaping **Stefano**." A look of distaste crossed his features as he repeated that name. "At the stables, I had to convince her that I was not the count."

"And that is all? She came back with you just as if she had not run from here as though the building were on fire?"

Wearily, William rubbed his eyes, trying to decide how much to tell. He had begun to feel guilty for the way he conducted himself—going in and out of Elizabeth's room unchecked, kissing her whenever he desired and holding her in his embrace, though she was often only in her nightclothes. His mind recalled the events earlier that evening.

As he neared the house with Elizabeth in his arms, he went to enter the still open door to the library. She cringed, uttering a small sound, and buried her face in his shoulder. Her arms tightened around him, crushing the doll between them. He stopped, clasping her even more securely.

"This is my home, Elizabeth. This is Pemberley. You are safe here. No one can harm you inside these walls. Do you understand?"

When she did not reply, he whispered in her ear, "Look."

Barely turning her head, she gazed at the familiar façade. "Pemberley," she repeated.

Blowing out a deep breath, he began walking again. "Yes, Pemberley. My home—your home now."

She seemed to relax, and he almost regretted that she loosened her grip on him. Continuing through the door, across the room and into the foyer, he encountered Mrs. Reynolds, whom he addressed even as he kept moving. "Please bring your bag of remedies. Miss Lawrence has some injuries to her feet."

Richard repeated his point. "And once you got Elizabeth back to the house, she entered just as if nothing had happened to make her fly out of here in the first place?"

"Not exactly."

Richard smiled. "And what exactly does *not exactly* mean, my friend?"

William groaned, sank into the nearest chair and looked away.

"Oh come on, Darce. You have not been able to keep any secrets from me since you were five, when you lost my favourite whistle. Confession is good for the soul! Besides, nothing you do in regards to Miss Elizabeth would surprise me."

William glared at him. Seeing his glower, Richard only succeeded in making things worse. "Do not take offence so readily. I am only saying that you have already broken all the rules of propriety where she is concerned."

Richard held up his hands in surrender as William stood, hands now clenched into fists. "I know you had no choice but to take her in, and I am convinced that you truly care for her. I know that you would never take advantage of the situation, so sit back down, Cousin!"

William did as he was asked—not because of Richard's request, but because he knew he **had** taken advantage of Elizabeth's response to him. It had been like a dream for the woman he loved to welcome his touches, his kisses. Convinced that it had been for her benefit—after all, the doctor said that her recovery depended on her ability to trust in him—he had done everything to strengthen their bond. Thus, he had treated her as though they were betrothed, and praying that when she recovered, she would remember the man he was now and not the arrogant man she rejected in Kent.

A pronouncement interrupted William's reflections, and he looked up to see Richard smiling from ear to ear. "Do not spare my feelings. Tell ol' Richard everything!"

William had never been good at keeping things from his cousin, as they had been best friends all his life. Thus, he retold the story of what happened, revealing *almost* everything.

"I had gone to Elizabeth's bedroom to check on her." Richard's smirk caused him to frown. "That is how I knew she was missing. Providence must have intervened, however, as I felt led to go out onto the balcony and caught sight of her running towards the stables. I have already told you how I found her in a stall with the kittens. She thought I was *him*." Richard nodded, no longer smiling.

"The other significant development is that she was once more grasping that doll—the one she brought from Netherfield." Shaking his head with resignation, William admitted, "But you guessed correctly. When we returned to the house, she was afraid to come in. Just as, at first sight, she believed I was Stefano, I imagine she thought this was Northgate. I had to reassure her that it was Pemberley."

"I see."

"I met Mrs. Reynolds as I entered the foyer and learned that she had awakened to check on Mrs. Drury. I explained what had happened and asked her to tend Elizabeth's feet as soon as she looked in on her companion."

At his cousin's quizzical brow, he explained, "Elizabeth's feet were scratched and bleeding from running shoeless."

William's eyes darkened as he studied the floor. "After Mrs. Reynolds finished and departed, I honestly meant to leave her, but whenever I moved from the bed, Elizabeth became upset. So, I sat on the edge, which seemed to placate her and ended up staying until she fell asleep."

As she closed her eyes once again, I brushed the hair from her forehead and ran the back of his fingers over her cheek until her breathing came in even measures.

"When I was convinced she was asleep, I went to leave. But as I opened the door, I heard her call my name. Before I could turn completely, she had thrown the covers back and was sliding out of bed."

Hearing his name, he turned just as she threw her arms around him, burying her face in his chest, weeping. He knew he could never leave her like that, so he held her, and with promises to stay, she quieted. Then picking her up and cradling her in his arms, he gently carried her back to her bed, where she immediately reached for the doll. Covering her, he pulled a chair next to the bed and lay his head down on the counterpane. He felt the touch of her hand in his hair, and soon both were fast asleep.

"I decided that it was best if I tried to sleep in the chair in her room. I woke up several times in the next two hours. The last time, she was still sleeping soundly, so I came down here."

Richard studied him for a moment, weighing his confession. Seemingly satisfied that he knew all but the most intimate details, he moved on to another concern.

"So what do you do now, since it seems she has relapsed? Has Towson been any help?"

"He has, but as he said from the beginning, each case is different. What works for one person, may not work for another. Recently, though, he wrote to me of some success with a most stubborn case—a soldier. The patient was helped by confronting him with people and things that reminded him of how his injury occurred."

"Such as..."

"Towson brought in another soldier who was with him when the injury was inflicted, as well as his own torn and bloody uniform and his sword—even his horse was brought to the yard just outside his window. Of course, we are speaking of a soldier injured performing his duty, which is not what happened to Elizabeth."

"So what would you use to prod Elizabeth's memory? Surely you cannot take her back to Northgate?"

"No, and short of taking her there, I do not have a clue as to what would trigger her memories of the event. Mrs. Browning mentioned that the count and her maid were present in the room on the night that Addie died in the fire."

Richard walked to one of the comfortable sofas and sank down. "I understand that Millie and her mother normally stayed in the servants' quarters at Northgate, and unless she was needed by Miss Elizabeth, Addie would not have been in Elizabeth's room."

"That is what I understood as well."

"I cannot imagine why Addie would have been there during the melee. Perhaps she heard an argument and tried to intervene in Elizabeth's defence."

William sighed. "It certainly seems possible."

"What about Arthur? Do you suppose he might have an idea?"

William straightened. "I had not thought of that. Where is Arthur now?"

Richard chuckled. "Still sleeping like a baby! My future recruit is worn out from the gruelling travel of only one day's journey!"

"As soon as he comes down to break his fast, I should like to speak with him."

"I will see to it."

William nodded, turning and lifting his feet up on the sofa. "If you would excuse me, I am just going to rest my eyes..." His voice trailed off as he lay back, and in a few breaths, he was asleep.

Richard shook his head, and he stood up and slipped out of the room. "Rest, Darce. After last night, you deserve it."

He went to find Mrs. Reynolds to have her keep everyone out of the study for as long as possible.

139

Rosewood Manor
The Nursery

Evan poked his head in the door to find Ana sitting in the rocking chair watching Millie as she slept. "She probably will not awaken for some time, darling," he whispered as he drew nearer, trying to be quiet. "Did you get any sleep at all?"

"I slept a little. I hope I did not wake you when I arose so early this morning."

"Not at all," he chuckled. "I was dead to the world. But once I awoke and realised that you were no longer in bed, I had no trouble knowing where to look."

Georgiana rolled her eyes at him, nodding towards the woman sitting in the upholstered chair in the corner. Chosen to act as Millie's nurse until further arrangements might be made, Mrs. Calvert was pretending not to listen. Evan grinned, and not in the least concerned about the servant, leaned in to plant a kiss on his wife's brow.

"She was a very tired little girl when she arrived last night. I imagine she will sleep late."

Georgiana looked sheepish. "I—I just wanted to be here when she woke—at least for the first time."

Evan's heart swelled with love. "I completely understand. Why do we not both wait for her to awaken? We can have a tray of food and drink brought here and wait until she does."

"You would do that?" Georgiana grinned. "In all the years we have been married, first thing every morning you have exercised your horse, broken your fast with me, and then reviewed your books before Mr. Corvin appears with his concerns—all in that order."

"And now we have a child, which will, of necessity, change our carefully designed order." He flashed the crooked grin that always melted her heart, and unbeknownst to him, Georgiana felt as though she were falling in love with him all over again.

"It will not be long until Miss Millie is rising with the chickens and starting her day with her parents. No child of mine will stay in the nursery all day, and I just imagine she will be riding out with me before too long." He grasped Ana's hand as he looked over at the sleeping angel. "We shall work out a schedule that takes her needs into account."

Looking to the elderly woman, he declared, "Mrs. Calvert, I apologise for not having a small bed moved in here earlier. It will be done before the day is out. Now, would you please take this opportunity to break your fast, and while you are in the kitchen, have trays sent up for Mrs. Ingram and me."

The elderly nurse stood and stretched her back. Having slept all night in the chair, she was a little stiff. "Thank you, Mr. Ingram. After I have eaten, I shall be in my room in case I am needed." She nodded towards the adjoining room and then slipped out of the nursery.

"I believe Mrs. Calvert would work out splendidly! Why not keep her on as the nurse?" Evan enthused as he took the chair she had vacated. "She is a grandmother several times over."

"Yes," Georgiana joined in. "And anything I do not know, I am sure she would. But I am not sure she would have the patience for a small child."

"She seems patient with you!" Evan teased.

"I have to admit that she does have patience with me. I can be quite a handful when I get excited."

"I love it when you get excited, Mrs. Ingram." A small pillow flew past Evan's head. He successfully dodged it, but was hit by the one that followed. "I was only agreeing, sweetheart."

"Do not be so agreeable about certain things, Mr. Ingram. In addition, for now, I think you should be warned to have patience with this new mother. I have enough on my mind, and it will do you well to remember to be kind and supportive."

Evan grinned and stood to grab her hands, pulling her out of the rocking chair and into his arms. "I can be **very** kind and supportive under certain circumstances." He kissed her until her breath quickened.

"Mama?"

The small voice penetrated the fog of their desire and both pulled back to consider the towheaded child, now sitting up and watching them. Georgiana pulled from Evan's grasp to sit on the side of the bed. He followed, standing beside her with his hand on her shoulder.

"Yes, Millie, Mama is here." Two little arms reached for Georgiana, so she lifted her onto her lap and gave her a hug. Once situated, Millie buried her face in Georgiana's chest.

"Are you hungry?"

The small head bobbed up and down.

"Would you like to eat with Papa and me?"

Millie looked up into Georgiana's blue eyes, and then around her, to consider Evan who stood behind. "Can you say Papa?"

Quickly the little head was buried in her chest again, where it shook side-to-side. Georgiana squeezed her tighter and exchanged a knowing look with Evan. There probably had never been a father in the poor child's life.

"Well, no matter, sweetheart. I am sure you will get used to Papa in time."

Then Georgiana stood with Millie, taking her over to the large dressing table and setting her upon it. "Let us see what you shall wear today. I am sure we will need to go into Lambton and order you lots of clothes, but for now..."

Digging though the small bag that Arthur brought with him, there were four dresses, some undergarments, and a worn coat and an old pair of shoes. Pulling out the dresses, she noted that they were all serviceable, though they looked quite used, as if the child wore them often. In contrast, the dress in which she had arrived, which was now in the wash, was a very pretty blue muslin, with ruffles around the neck, and the shoes she had had on were almost new. Included, was a small bag filled with items that looked as though they had been fashioned for a doll—tiny clothes, shoes and such, but no doll.

As she pulled out the nicest of the plain dresses, Georgiana murmured, "I suppose this will have to do, but we definitely must go shopping today." The last was said as she looked directly at Evan.

He grinned. "I would be glad to accompany my girls to the modiste." He reached over to ruffle Millie's curls, making her burrow into Georgiana once more, though she peeked at him shyly.

"I shall have the carriage readied as soon as we finish eating. Does that suit my lovely wife and daughter?"

"Yes, Papa," Georgiana teased.

Evan grinned ear to ear. "Papa ...I think I could get used to that!"

Pemberley
One day later

Georgiana and Evan swept into the foyer with Millie in tow. "Where is my brother?"

Mr. Walker and Mrs. Reynolds were there, but both failed to answer as their eyes came to rest on the child in Georgiana's arms.

"Oh, forgive me. I should have...this is..." A little flustered as she realised the way Millie was dressed, she turned the child in her arms, so that the elderly couple could see her pretty face. "This is our daughter, Millie!"

"Oh my!" they both exclaimed, before Mrs. Reynolds declared. "She is beautiful—the very image of you, Mrs. Ingram. Master William mentioned your good fortune briefly this morning, and we are all so delighted."

Mr. Walker shook his head in agreement. "Indeed! Both of you!" he echoed, nodding to Evan who beamed.

Georgiana hurriedly explained. "We have been to the shops in Lambton, buying new clothes and such. She is in need of everything!"

"That is perfectly understandable." Mrs. Reynolds assured her, patting the little girl's back. "I am sure she has outgrown everything. Children grow so fast."

Mr. Walker intervened, bringing the conversation back to what he and Mrs. Reynolds had been discussing before their arrival. "I am loath to deliver bad news amidst your happiness, but we have just now received this message from the Hazelton's estate." He held up a paper. "Of course, we did not open it, but the servant who delivered it confided that Mr. Hazelton has died. He strongly suggested that we should inform the Master as soon as possible."

Georgiana and William had known Lord and Lady Hazelton all their lives, as they had been the good friends of George and Anne Darcy. And while Howard Hazelton had not been well, his sudden passing was unexpected. Well aware of the Darcy's high regard for the Hazeltons, Mr. Walker sighed in relief when Georgiana indicated she already knew.

"Yes, I came to tell William that I heard of it while we were in Lambton."

Mrs. Reynolds offered, "We were discussing sending a footman to the far pasture to fetch Mr. Darcy. He was summoned by one of the workers this morning to inspect a shed that was in danger of collapsing after the last storm."

"And my cousin, Richard?"

"He received a letter by special messenger early this morning from his commanding officer, requesting his immediate return to camp. There was a stroke of good luck in that the man he had been waiting to see in Lambton, sent word that he was back. He and young Fielding left straightaway to meet the fellow in Lambton, then to return the young man to Sheffield on the Colonel's way north. Though Colonel Fitzwilliam insisted they could ride, Mr. Darcy had them take his coach as far as Sheffield for the boy's sake.

Georgiana nodded, perturbed that she had not had the opportunity to see Richard again or to talk with Arthur. Seeing the frustration on her face, Mr. Walker added, "It was unexpected, madam, but young Fielding did leave this letter for you. He said it included his address so that you may write with any questions you might have."

Taking the missive, she replied sadly, "It seems that is always the case with Richard. I hardly ever have a chance to talk with him anymore. Nonetheless, I am glad Mr. Fielding left his address." Seeing her disappointment, Evan leaned down and kissed Georgiana on the cheek, then addressed the butler.

"I will go fetch Darcy." He donned his hat. "Ana, you and Millie should probably wait here, as I am sure you will want to discuss with your brother how to be of help to Mrs. Hazelton."

She cast a questioning gaze to Mrs. Reynolds. "Will we disturb Miss Lawrence if we wait in the music room?"

"I think not. She has not been out of her rooms since—well, for some time. If you will proceed to the music room, I shall find Mrs. Lightfoot and order tea and refreshments. You and the little one can enjoy it while you wait for your husband and the Master to return."

~~~*~~~

Barely an hour later, William and Evan had already returned and instantly set off for the Hazeltons' estate, as the widow's letter had requested William's presence immediately. He asked Evan to accompany him and suggested that Georgiana and Evan stay for dinner, so they could discuss what he learned. Nonetheless, as the hours wore on, Georgiana was beginning to wonder if she should not have taken the carriage home. Millie was getting tired and irritable and really needed a nap. Rejecting the idea of putting her down to sleep in one of the guest rooms, Georgiana had decided to let her sleep on one of the sofas in the music room.

However, Millie had managed to get berry stains on her hands, face, and the front of her dress after she discovered the sweet treats on a plate of fruit Mrs. Reynolds had sent along with some other refreshments. Georgiana was not concerned about the stains on the dress, as it would be thrown out as soon as her new clothes arrived, but she wanted to clean her face and hands of the stains before she fell asleep.

Since Mrs. Reynolds had not reappeared, she picked up her child and quietly made her way out of the room and up the stairs, intent on using William's dressing room. There was sure to be a fresh pitcher of water, soap and clean towels inside there, and she knew that she would not encounter anyone inside his private quarters.

Tiptoeing down the hall, she was unaware that Millie was beginning to suffer a stomach-ache because of all the fruit she had consumed. The little girl's tiredness, combined with a now aching stomach caused her to begin to whimper. Not long after they had entered William's dressing room, the whimpers escalated into crying, and, before she could decide whether to abandon her plans to clean up her daughter, Millie's sobs had turned to wails. The sound of footsteps in the hallway signified that the servants were trying to locate the source of the disturbance, so, in exasperation, she abandoned her efforts and went towards the door to reassure the servants. Just as she re-entered the hallway with her crying child, the door just across the hall flew open and Georgiana cringed.

Elizabeth stood in the doorway, frozen in place at the sight of Georgiana holding a screaming Millie, who sported red stains over her hands, face and gown. Before Georgiana could utter anything in the way of explanation, Elizabeth fainted.

The sound of her hitting the floor with a sickening thud caused Georgiana to scream as well, and servants began rushing towards them from every direction.

~~~*~~~

Chapter 18

London
The Royal Academy of Art
Somerset House
The Summer Exhibition

George Wickham was thoroughly enjoying his stroll through the summer display in the Great Exhibition Room of the Royal Academy of Art. Having had the good fortune of being born to the steward at Pemberley, he was raised almost as a member of the illustrious Darcy family after his father's death, so faking his suitability to be among this crowd was no hardship. He was an expert at parroting the manners of the *ton*.

It mattered little that he might not have the funds necessary for a room at an inn. The money that he did have went towards the purchase of clothes that mimicked those worn by Fitzwilliam Darcy—his coats, gloves, hats and even his boots were of the same style. A good first impression was essential to one's livelihood when one lived by one's wits. Even though there were times he had not eaten well, he had always cut a dashing figure. Fortunately, with his new partnership with the count, the lean times seemed to be in the past. A small smirk lifted the corners of Wickham's mouth as he surveyed the unsuspecting throng.

Hobnobbing with the wealthy, well-connected, cream of society—this is where he belonged!

Truth be known, though he may have been a little awed by the display of hundreds of paintings hung on the walls at every conceivable level, he was more impressed by the sheer number of jewels conspicuously hung about the necks of the women perusing the art. If he played his cards right, perhaps he might be able to find his next victim—either someone whose jewellery would make a fine addition to his collection for the count or a vulnerable woman he could manipulate, as he had Mrs. Preston.

Suddenly his eyes came to rest on a beautiful pair of breasts, adorned by a lovely drop pearl surrounded by diamonds, all prominently displayed in a gown the colour of a summer sky. As his eyes journeyed upward, Wickham found that the breasts and the necklace belonged to a beautiful woman who looked to be in her thirties, with honey-blond hair and eyes the same shade as her frock. She was watching him, too, and a slight smile flickered across her face before she turned to address a man to her left. This man was half-hidden in the crowd, and Wickham could not make him out.

Not one to be put off by a woman's husband, fiancé or family, Wickham sauntered across the room in her direction. He was within twenty feet of her, when the crowd thinned and the man who accompanied this vision turned. It was Stefano! The count caught sight of him at the same time, and his smile fell away. He had made it clear that Wickham was never to approach him if they met in public.

Wickham halted. His eyes wavered between the woman and Stefano as he quickly evaluated the situation. Then tilting his head slightly, he nodded curtly at the count, and turning on his heel, quickly retraced his footsteps to disappear into the crowd. Lady Gwendolyn Waltham watched the exchange, apparently amused that an admirer had been warned off by the count. She had no way of knowing that he and Stefano were partners in enterprises that would eventually involve her.

Meanwhile, satisfied that Wickham had done as instructed, the count turned to whisper to his next target, even as his eyes searched the room for an even bigger catch. "Gwendolyn, darling, why do we not go on to the next gallery? This one is so very crowded." Taking her arm without waiting for a reply, he skilfully guided her through the next door and into yet another room teeming with opportunities for him.

Pemberley
Three days later
Evening

William slipped into Elizabeth's bedroom to find Mrs. Drury asleep in the large upholstered chair beside her bed. He reached to touch the companion's arm, and she startled before remembering where she was and why she was there. Glancing to Elizabeth and finding no change, she looked to Mr. Darcy and smiled sympathetically. Motioning with his head towards the door, he started in that direction, and she rose to follow, neither speaking until they were outside in the hallway.

She knew what he would say before he asked.

"Has there been any change?"

His weary eyes pleaded for hope, but she had none to give, not even for the man who was so obviously in love with Miss Elizabeth.

"No, sir."

His shoulders slumped as his head dropped, and he studied the floor for a moment. Her heart went out to him as he was obviously distraught. His appearance, which had always been faultless, was now unkempt, and he looked as though he had not slept at all in the last three days. She did something she normally would not do—she reached out to pat his arm sympathetically. He took a shuddering breath.

"Do not give up! You are all she has; you must be strong!" As his eyes rose to inspect her, she could tell that he was starving for a ray of hope.

"She needs you to have faith in her. Tell her you expect her to recover. I have always felt that people in her condition hear much more than we realise that they do."

William's countenance changed immediately, and he straightened, standing tall and pulling his shoulders back. Mrs. Drury had no way of knowing that her advice had reminded him of Mr. Towson's almost identical words. How could he have forgotten?

"Do not undertake this challenge unless you can do it wholeheartedly, believing she will recover. Your faith will have to sustain her until she can have faith in herself. She shall rely on your believing in her. Tell her she is going to be well, that you have faith in her ability to recover, and, if it be true, tell her you love her. Love works miracles for which no man of science can account."

William patted the woman's hand and tried to smile. "Thank you. You have given me excellent advice. Now, it is time you rest in your own bed. I shall sit with her until Mrs. Reynolds takes another turn. Please get some sleep, as you may be needed again."

She nodded and with one last smile, turned and proceeded down the hall. As she arrived at the door to her room, she turned to see him waiting in the dim light of the candles along the wall, making sure she was safely inside. Both smiled at the shared encouragement.

Back in Elizabeth's room, William replaced the almost burned out candle with another and then slumped down in the large, soft chair. Elizabeth looked so small in the large bed that he reached out to take hold of her hand. It was cold, so he began rubbing it, hoping to return some warmth. As he focused on massaging the soft skin, he reflected on what had happened in the last seventy-two hours.

Richard and Arthur had departed, but not before he had learned that the boy had no other knowledge of Elizabeth's time at Northgate and could offer no suggestions to help her recall the ordeal she had been through. Shortly after they left, William was summoned to a far pasture to look over a shed that needed repair, and it was there that Evan found him and delivered the news of Mr. Hazelton's death. He and Evan had immediately gone to the Hazelton's estate and upon returning to Pemberley, found it in an uproar.

Downstairs, Mrs. Reynolds was trying to soothe a crying Millie. Evan immediately took charge of the child and his whispers of comfort immediately calmed her and she fell asleep in his arms. Meanwhile, he had found Georgiana with Mr. Woodwright, a physician newly settled in Lambton, in this very room with Elizabeth—she lying unaware of the drama surrounding her. As he entered, Georgiana was explaining Elizabeth's history to the man.

As it turned out, Mr. Woodwright was well versed in head injuries, as his father had been an associate of Mr. Towson before his death. William was immediately impressed by the tall, thin, red-haired man. Learning of his connections with Towson, William's hope rose, only to be dashed with his analysis—this new injury could be the last straw, assuring she would never recover her right mind.

He explained that while the small knot on the back of her head would normally heal with no further complications, adding that insult to her previous injuries made the outcome uncertain, and the fact that she had not awakened since she fainted was not a good sign. It was with a comforting pat on William's back that he returned to his office, promising to return every day. The physician had been as good as his word, coming early the next two mornings to find no change in her condition.

At his departure, Georgiana had been inconsolable. Even as William held her and assured her that she had done nothing wrong, she insisted that her impulse to come to Pemberley without notice had caused the tragedy. He tried to reason with her, pointing out that there was no way she could have known this would happen and that Pemberley was still her home, so she did not have to give notice of her visits.

Nevertheless, William understood Georgiana's guilt. He was filled with guilt, too. He had promised to protect Elizabeth, and she had received this injury while under his watch. He wondered what the Bingleys would say. How would he tell Jane?

He groaned. This was the first time he had thought of Elizabeth's sister. In Charles' last letter, he disclosed that Jane was with child again. She had been planning to visit Elizabeth just as soon as William thought it was advisable, but her doctor had put her on bed rest because of complications with her pregnancy. Her distress over Elizabeth was likely exacerbating her problems, and William had tried to keep his subsequent letter cheerful and positive, short of deceiving them as to the progress of her sister's recovery.

He rubbed his head for a moment as another headache threatened. Suddenly the door opened and a maid came in with a tray of hot tea. Agatha bobbed, setting the tray on a nearby table and reaching into her pocket to produce a packet of powders.

"Begging your pardon, sir, but Mrs. Reynolds asked me to bring this to you when you relieved Mrs. Drury. The powders relieve headaches."

William chuckled as he took the proffered packet. "Thank you. Please inform Mrs. Reynolds that she is indeed a mind reader." The young maid unsuccessfully tried to suppress a chuckle and bobbed slightly askew before exiting the room.

"Kind, thoughtful woman," William said, shaking his head in awe.

~~~*~~~

Several minutes later, his headache abating, William gave his full attention to Elizabeth. It was time to begin practicing what Mr. Towson had preached. Nervous as a schoolboy, he moved to sit on the edge of the bed, taking her small hands in his.

He drank in her appearance—dark brows and long lashes contrasted against her pale complexion. Her ebony tresses, now wildly out of control, were spread out like silk on the pillow. He could not suppress a smile. God help him, he did not think he could ever look at her without smiling. Even as she lay unaware, her presence here brought tears of joy, and he found himself struggling for control. If only the Elizabeth he loved would return, he would grant her anything within his power.

He took a ragged breath. *Nothing ventured. Nothing gained.*

Leaning in close to her, he picked up one dark tendril lying across her shoulder and caressed it. With great difficulty, he forced his eyes to her motionless face, swallowed hard, and compelled his voice to steady.

"I love you, Elizabeth Bennet. I think I have loved you from the first moment that I saw you. Do you remember the night that I walked into the assembly at Meryton and the entire crowd parted like the Red Sea?" He tried to chuckle, but it sounded joyless.

"I could hear their whispers—single ...ten thousand a year ...half of Derbyshire. But I knew there was no way I could avoid the gauntlet, and my heart beat furiously as I began to walk in my eyes focused straight ahead."

He smiled down at her now and brushed a stray curl from her forehead. "I swear that only the grace of God allowed me, from the corner of my eye, to catch sight of a slip of a girl with ebony eyes and a head full of chocolate curls. When your eyes locked with mine, it felt as if a fire ignited within me. Did you feel it as well, my love?"

He ran the back of his hand across her cheek. "If only I had known then what I know now, I would never have denied the connection and turned away." He took a deep breath.

"If it were possible, I would apologise for my actions. I was angry with Charles for trying to force me to dance, and I took it out on the people there—on you, especially. The insult you heard, *'tolerable, but not handsome enough to tempt me,'* was uttered without thought and was utterly false." He quieted, contemplating his next confession.

"Of a truth, from the moment I saw you, Elizabeth, I was drawn like a moth to a flame, and it frightened me. I had been hiding behind this mask for so long ..." His voice trailed off as he cocked his head towards her, as if expecting her to say something. The slow rise and fall of her chest was his only answer.

"It took years, but I am now acutely aware of all that my mask accomplished. Yes, it often kept me from the schemes of those who would use me for their own reasons, but it also kept me from those for whom I truly might have cared." He clasped her hand, placing a soft kiss on the palm, then held it to his cheek.

"I pray that when you awaken, and I have no doubt that you will, that you remember our time together. That is all I ask. If you remember Pemberley, you will remember how much I love you." He leaned in to place a chaste kiss on her forehead.

"I will spend the rest of my life loving you, if only you will stay with me. *Please, Elizabeth.*"

~~~*~~~

It was early evening when Elizabeth became aware of her surroundings. First, she was conscious of the unique feel of satin sheets and pillows. Then heavy-lidded eyes opened to scan an elegantly appointed room. The walls were covered with images of delicate flowers, gossamer curtains hung at the windows. The canopy above the intricately carved bed seemed vaguely familiar. A soft snore revealed a woman sleeping in a large chair nearby, and though she recognised her, Elizabeth could not quite remember her name.

She started to rise, but a sharp pain in her head and neck made it impossible, so she gave up the attempt. A great weariness washed over her, and she closed her eyes, preferring the twilight realm where she no longer felt anything. It could have been minutes or hours afterward that a deep baritone voice awakened her once more. He spoke so softly that it was difficult to make out every word, but some of his declarations seeped into her consciousness before she slid back into the darkness.

...Of a truth, from the moment I saw you, Elizabeth, I was drawn like a moth to a flame, and it frightened me. I had been hiding behind this mask for so long...

...I will spend the rest of my life loving you, if only you will stay with me. Please, Elizabeth.

~~~*~~~

"Brother?"

William was being jostled from his sleep, and his unconscious mind leapt to the wrong conclusion.

"Elizabeth?" he exclaimed, jumping from the chair to lean over the small figure lying still on the bed. His bloodshot eyes refused to focus for a moment.

"It is I," Georgiana whispered from behind as she touched his arm. "Elizabeth is unchanged. I apologise for frightening you."

Finding everything the same, he released a heavy sigh and sank back down into the cushions of the chair, rubbing his eyes before allowing himself to concentrate on his sister. She motioned for them to leave the room and moved towards the door. He stood and followed her into the hall.

"I left Millie with Evan this morning. I want to sit with Elizabeth, if I may." Her voice was full of regret. "I hurt her, once intentionally and again unknowingly.

Please say that I may help." Her blue eyes swam with tears, and William knew he could not deny her request.

"Of course, you may," he whispered, pulling her into a hug.

In his embrace, she felt his desperation and slipped her arms around him. Their respite was suddenly interrupted by a strangled cry, and they pulled back to stare at each other in confusion. Suddenly, what was happening penetrated William's weary mind, and he rushed past her towards Elizabeth, Georgiana right on his heels.

Elizabeth was screaming, crying and lashing out as if she were fighting for her life, though her eyes were closed.

"He killed them! He killed them!" she cried, her face contorted with grief, as her arms lashed out at an invisible enemy.

Though she longed to be of help, Georgiana backed into a corner. With Elizabeth in such turmoil, she feared her presence might cause even more harm.

Elizabeth's movements brought her perilously close to the edge of the bed, and afraid she might hurt herself further, William immediately reached for her, pulling her squarely back to the middle of the large bed. Her eyes opened and now she lashed out at him.

Sensing that she was in some kind of traumatic stupor, he shouted over her cries. "Elizabeth! You are safe! He is not here! He cannot harm you!"

Still Elizabeth fought, managing to roll free of his grasp and onto the other side of the bed. Before he could catch her, she slipped out of the bed and ran through the unlocked door to the balcony. William was right behind, and Georgiana slipped near the opened doors to watch, fearing she might have to step in at any time. She peered around the curtain as William approached the frightened woman. Seeing Elizabeth's terrified expression, she began to pray.

Elizabeth slowly stepped backwards until her calves touched the wall surrounding the balcony. Realising that she had reached the end of her escape route, she quickly turned and climbed upon the wall where she balanced precariously on the top rail. William's heart almost stopped. He knew that if she fell, she would surely die.

"Do not move, Elizabeth!" he ordered in his most commanding voice. "Stand perfectly still." He took a step towards her, and she began shaking her head, turning it so she did not have to look at him.

"Nooooo!" The plea came out as a sob.

Immediately William stilled and backed away with his hands held up in surrender, the pain of her rejection clearly evident on his face. Georgiana started to move onto the balcony, only to freeze in horror as Elizabeth wobbled and almost fell. William started as though he was going to keep her from falling, but immediately halted as she righted herself.

Feeling she had no choice, Georgiana slipped in between the two, whispering as she passed him, "Will you let me try, Brother?"

Heartbroken, William looked between Georgiana and Elizabeth. "It seems I cannot help." His voice broke. "Please ...she is in your hands."

Stoically, he backed up until he stood in the doorway leading to the bedroom. Leaning dejectedly against the frame, he had barely gotten situated before Mrs. Drury, Mrs. Reynolds and two footmen rushed in behind him, hoping to be of assistance. Looking over his shoulder, he motioned them out. They hurriedly retreated to the hallway, while he turned his attention back to Elizabeth.

For a moment, Elizabeth was wild-eyed as she took in the grounds below, then slowly her gaze came up, and she focused on Georgiana. An expression of disbelief crossed her face.

"He ...he killed you ...you and Millie. I remember it all." She took a ragged breath, seeing something only she could see, before settling her gaze again on William's sister.

"I saw the count raise the gun, and it went off. You fell!"

Georgiana stopped, realising now why Elizabeth had fainted previously when seeing her with Millie. "I may look like her, but I am not Addie, Elizabeth. I am Georgiana Ingram, Fitzwilliam's sister."

"Not Addie?"

"No. It would seem I strongly resemble her, but I am not Millie's mother."

Elizabeth said nothing, though she studied her thoughtfully.

"You may remember that we met previously. I was very rude to you at our first meeting. In fact, it was right here on this very balcony. I wanted to apologise sooner, but we were afraid that it might upset you even more, so I waited. Please believe me ...I am here only because I truly want to help you."

Elizabeth's face crumpled. "Addie was my friend, and she was only trying to help me. I ...I should never have agreed for her to help me." She sobbed now, causing her to sway dangerously. William took one step forward. "Poor Addie! Poor Millie!"

Praying under her breath, Georgiana stepped closer. "It was not your fault. Addie would not want you to blame yourself, and you need to know that Millie did not die." Elizabeth looked up, her eyes growing larger.

"It is true. Though Addie was lost, Millie was saved. My husband and I are going to raise her."

Elizabeth blinked several times in confusion. "But ...but I saw the blood. I saw Addie fall with Millie."

"Miraculously, Millie was not harmed."

Elizabeth's eyes lowered, and she seemed to be considering this revelation. Georgiana took the opportunity to step closer. "I would love for you to see her, to see that she is well." She held a hand out, palm up. "Please come down. Brother and I would be heartbroken if you fell and were hurt."

Elizabeth stared at her hand. "No, I must go. If he finds me here, he will kill everyone."

Every opinion Georgiana had held about the woman changed at that moment. She had been helping Elizabeth solely because her brother was in love with her, but now she felt admiration welling up. Anyone who put the safety of others above their own interests was a woman worth getting to know.

"No one knows you are here, except your sister and brother. You are safe in my brother's home and in mine, and you are welcome at both."

Elizabeth considered her for some time before slipping her hand in Georgiana's and allowing herself to be guided to the floor. William blew out the breath he had been holding and sank back against the doorframe, so weak he hoped his legs would not give out. Then, praying not to garner Elizabeth's attention, he hurried through the room and out into the hallway where his slight smile and nod met with sighs of relief from the members of his staff.

Leading Elizabeth slowly back into the bedroom, Georgiana tried to think what she should do next. A question brought her out of her reverie.

"Where am I?"

"This is Pemberley."

Elizabeth gasped, whispering almost to herself, "Mr. Darcy's home." She turned to Georgiana. "Why am I here?"

"Only Fitzwilliam can explain, but your sister Jane and my brother felt that it was necessary."

Elizabeth was unable to meet her eye. "I ...I need time ...alone."

Georgiana stepped to her, taking both of her hands and causing Elizabeth to look up through her lashes. "It is Fitzwilliam that you do not wish to talk with, is it not?"

Shyly Elizabeth nodded. Georgiana sighed, knowing how much this would hurt William.

"I will tell him that you do not wish to speak to him at this time if that is truly what you want." Another nod sealed the agreement, but Georgiana could not leave it there. "But at some point, you will need to talk to him. I want you to know that Fitzwilliam is truly the best of men. He would never harm you—you must know that."

A soft voice came from the now lowered head. "He must hate me."

So, that was the crux of the matter—memories from their past. "You are greatly mistaken. In fact, he has taken great pains to see to your welfare. I can assure you that he does not hate you."

"He always looked down on my situation, and now that I am married to a...a murderer." Her voice trailed off, and she began to cry. Georgiana wrapped her arms around her, rocking her from side to side.

"Shhh. Crying will only make you feel worse, and you have to improve so I can bring Millie to see you. You want that, do you not?" She felt Elizabeth nod against her shoulder.

"Let us get you settled in bed. The physician does not want you walking until he thinks you are ready. You will need something to eat and—" She smiled at Elizabeth's attempts to wipe her tears on her sleeves. "Here!" she said offering her a handkerchief from her pocket. "Now that I have Millie, I have learned to have several in my pocket at all times."

Elizabeth tried unsuccessfully to smile as she climbed back into the large bed. Georgiana took pillows and piled them behind her, so that she sat upright. Once settled, Georgiana took her hand and squeezed it affectionately. "I will not leave you. Rest for a moment while I send a servant for some broth and tea."

Standing, she backed towards the door. "I shall be right outside, and I shall return in just a moment."

Once she was alone, Elizabeth closed her eyes and took a ragged breath. *Please God. Do not let him find me.*

~~~*~~~

Chapter 19

Later that evening

Elizabeth devoured the broth Mrs. Reynolds sent up as though she were starved. Then for the next half-hour, Georgiana sat with her, making conversation and doing everything possible to alleviate any fears she might have about being at Pemberley. Finally, sleep beckoned.

Mrs. Drury slipped into the room not long after Elizabeth began to show the signs of drowsiness, and fortunately, Elizabeth recognised her companion, accepting her company without hesitation. As sleep claimed the weary young woman, a drained Georgiana relinquished her place as Mrs. Drury insisted that William's sister also retire to sleep. Confident that the elderly woman could manage the situation if Elizabeth awoke, Georgiana went in search of her brother.

She did not have to go far, as William was just outside, standing in the hallway, shoulder propped against the wall, head down and eyes closed. When she opened the door, he did not stir, so she quietly stood in front of him. Sensing her presence, he opened his weary eyes, and she smiled tenderly, running a hand over his stubbled cheek.

"I feared you were asleep in this position."

Standing up straight, he stretched and returned her smile, though it was forced. "I might have dozed a little." Quickly he got to the point. "Elizabeth?"

Georgiana took his hand and pulled him into the sitting room next to Elizabeth's bedroom before beginning. "She is improved, but still very weak. I will leave word with Mrs. Lightfoot to cook something appropriate for her in the morning, perhaps eggs and toast—she needs something besides broth. Elizabeth should be hungry by the time Mr. Woodwright departs, as he always arrives so early."

William nodded, seemingly preoccupied. His expression resembled a small child requesting a favour. "I would like to speak with her ...not tonight, of course, but tomorrow. That is, if you think it would not upset her."

Georgiana sighed at his eager expression. The truth would hurt tremendously. "I—I am afraid Miss Elizabeth does not wish to see you." His reaction was to blink continually, so she added, "For now."

His eyes closed. The pain he felt was palpable, and Georgiana reached out to squeeze his arm in sympathy, struggling not to cry herself. She hated to see him suffer.

"She may not want to see you at present, but she is sure to change her mind at some point." He shook his head all during her words of consolation.

"Did she say why—why she will not see me?"

"Her exact words were, '*He must hate me.*'"

"Hate? Why would I—"

"She mentioned that you looked down on her. I suppose during your stay at Hertfordshire you displayed your *duty-and-station-above-all-else* persona."

William shuddered, murmuring, "And it has haunted me ever since."

"She feels she is even more of an anathema, now that she is married to that despicable man."

He stood still for some time, as if he were weighing the situation, then forced a slight smile as if to appear recovered. "I suppose it would be kinder to leave her alone, at least for a time. Would it be too much to ask that you check on Elizabeth every day or so until I return? Mrs. Reynolds and Mrs. Drury are quite capable, but I would feel better if you looked in on her."

"Of course I will, but where are you going?"

"London. Aunt Evelyn has implored me to attend the Viscount's ball on Saturday—I know you received an invitation as well." Georgiana nodded. Just as with every previous invitation from her family in London, she had never considered attending.

"She was so kind when last I saw her in London that I hate to disappoint her, though I do not care to socialize with most of the family, save Richard. I had not intended to go, but since Elizabeth wants time alone ..."

"Viscount Leighton's birthday celebration—that should be quite a soirée," Georgiana exclaimed sardonically.

"I imagine so. Lord Matlock spares no expense when it comes to his firstborn. I do wonder how it will feel to be in their company again. I have not seen Edgar in years."

Georgiana blew an imaginary curl off her forehead in exasperation. "Frankly, other than Aunt Evelyn and Richard, the separation could never be long enough to suit me."

"Edgar should never have brought Lord Hamilton's offer of marriage to the earl's attention, even if he and the rogue were the best of friends. It was obvious that Hamilton only wanted your dowry to pay for his gaming debts. Lord knows, I will never forgive him for that."

"I would not have accepted Lord Hamilton for any reason," Georgiana huffed.

"And I told Edgar and Lord Matlock that I would never allow it. For all his wealth and connections, Hamilton was always a reprobate hiding in a gentlemen's clothing. Besides gambling and drinking excessively, he kept a mistress and still found time for the brothels. My uncle could not see beyond his standing with the *ton*, but you, my darling sister, were not meant for that demented vulture."

Georgiana hugged William. "I love you too, Brother." Pulling back to consider him, she sobered. "I have two warnings to impart. First, from what little Elizabeth said of her husband, I gather he is quite dangerous. Please promise me that you will be careful. I cannot bear the thought of losing you."

"He seems to be in hiding, but from what I learned from the Bingleys and Mrs. Browning, the housekeeper at Northgate, he may indeed be insane. So you may rest assured that I will be wary. Your other warning?"

"I have heard from Cecile that Jacqueline has returned to Edgar and is acting the dutiful wife. Our aunt and uncle are treating her as though she never left."

William's brows knit in interest, so she continued. "Rumour has it that her father grew tired of her *friendships* with other men, so he sent her away, resulting in her decision to return to her marriage. Keep well away from her—her kind never changes. Jacqueline was trouble before, and she is trouble now."

"I imagine our aunt and uncle had no choice. As for Lady Leighton, she has probably not thought of me in years. Her infatuation—"

"Infatuation! She threw herself at you the night her engagement was announced! If I had not seen it with my own eyes ..." Georgiana grew so infuriated that she could not continue.

William smiled at his sister's indignation. Pulling her back into his embrace, he tried to calm her by teasing. "Gigi, you must try to let go of this anger, else soon there will be no one in the family with whom you are on speaking terms."

"*Let go!* She had her breasts clearly displayed to tempt you, and Edgar was in a room nearby! If I had not gone to find you—" She shook her head, as though trying to excise the memory. "I can only imagine what would have transpired if, instead of me, her fiancé had walked in on you. Though you were clearly backing away, and the look on your face mirrored your disgust, Edgar would have insisted on pistols at dawn."

He patted her back. "I know, sweetheart. I know."

"Despite my having spoiled her scheme, all she could do was smirk at me when I rebuked her. That is why I despise her so!" She sniffed indignantly. "Besides, Aunt Evelyn, Richard, and Amelia will suffice for family as far as I am concerned!"

"Yes. Poor Amelia! Richard said she hardly comes to London anymore since her marriage. I have to wonder if she is as unhappy as Edgar, since Uncle arranged her marriage as well."

Georgiana retorted, "I know I would be unhappy with a man thirty years older than myself, even if he were kind."

William seemed to ponder that for a brief time before responding. "Let us think no more on it tonight." He pushed her out to arm's length. "You will sleep here tonight, will you not?"

She grinned. "Yes. I imagine Evan and Millie are already abed, as Mrs. Reynolds was seeing to their comfort. I will not be missed."

"Then I shall see you in the morning before I leave for London." He kissed her forehead and began to lead her from the room and down the hallway, pausing at the bedroom she always occupied when at Pemberley.

"If you will excuse me, I am exhausted." As he turned to leave, the set of his shoulders revealed his discouragement.

"Brother." He stopped.

"Give her time." A nod was Georgiana's only answer.

Why had he insisted on seeing her when he came back to England? Georgiana wondered. Just when the brother she knew and loved had returned, he fell in love again with the one woman who could only bring him heartache.

How can I possibly help you and her?

Shaking her head in resignation, Georgiana entered the bedroom where Evan lay sleeping, snoring softly. She smiled.

Millie was asleep on a small cot across the room—the child-sized bed having been brought into their room, since the nursery had not been used in years. She ran a hand over the sleeping girl's hair before continuing through the bedroom to the adjoining sitting area where candles still burned. Dropping into a large upholstered chair, she began reviewing the conversation she had with Elizabeth only a short while before.

"Are you feeling any better?"

Elizabeth's face crumpled, and she almost cried. "I am afraid to tell anyone how I truly feel."

"Oh, Miss Elizabeth! Please do not be afraid to talk to me. I will never divulge a confidence. I promise."

Elizabeth's voice cracked. "I—I have so many thoughts running through my mind, and sometimes I cannot discern what I remember from what I might have imagined." A sob escaped, and Georgiana's heart broke for the young woman. She moved to sit on the bed, pulling her into a hug.

"I expect that is normal with the terrible experiences you have had. We can certainly ask Mr. Woodwright tomorrow morning if you like." Elizabeth nodded, pulling back to speak.

"I do not wish for anyone else to be harmed because of me. I want to leave as soon as I am able." Georgiana knew Elizabeth would never be safe outside Pemberley or Rosewood Manor.

"You have to understand that Pemberley is, and has been for years, a secure fortress. William has a multitude of guards and servants to ensure that it is safe, and my husband has done the same at our estate, at my brother's insistence." She smiled tenderly at Elizabeth. *"You are out of harm's way here."*

*"No, you do not understand how **he** thinks. The count is not like most men—he is like two different men. One is spoiled, but charming; the other is very cruel. Once, he struck me when he found a letter that I had written to my sister. He forbade me to ever again contact anyone and declared that I could never leave. There was no place on earth that I could hide—no place he could not find me."*

Elizabeth eyes widened as if picturing him. Her voice was barely audible when she continued. "He swore he would kill everyone I care for and see me dead before he would let me go."

Georgiana could not form a reply in the face of Elizabeth's certainty.

"I would rather die than have something happen to Fitzwil—" She caught herself. *"Mr. Darcy."* Then added softly, *"Or anyone."*

Suddenly, everything made sense to William's sister. "Miss Elizabeth, may I ask you a somewhat indelicate question?" Elizabeth met her gaze but said nothing. *"You may ignore it if you do not wish to answer."*

When Elizabeth did not look away, she ventured. "I believe you were once in love with my brother. Are you still?"

A lone tear slipped from Elizabeth's eye, the only sign of her discomposure. Dropping her head, she nodded.

"Is that why you did not want him to touch you? You seek to protect him by keeping him at a distance ...by keeping him from caring?"

"For a brief moment I imagined him to be Stefano, but when I realised—" She stopped.

"No. He cannot care for me. I am too far beneath him, but Stefano would never believe he does not have some feelings for me if I stay." This revelation was followed by fresh tears.

"Please do not cry. All will be well. Trust me. We will care for you—Fitzwilliam and I, Mrs. Drury, Mrs. Reynolds, and your sister and brother, Jane and Charles. Together we will keep you safe."

Elizabeth continued to cry, as Georgiana ran soft hands over her face and hair.

"Shhh, you will make yourself more upset. Try not to cry."

Finally, Elizabeth sobbed, "Do not tell him." She looked up. "Please, you promised."

"I will keep your secret, though I think you should tell him what you have told me."

"I cannot."

"I understand."

London
Matlock House
The Viscount's Birthday Ball

As at every party in London, a group gathered in a corner to critique the participants of the Matlock's ball. These little get-togethers were a source of delight to this coterie, as they, themselves, were of little consequence. Thus, following the comings and goings of those who **were** important, made them feel somewhat important, too, especially when they were the first to learn the latest gossip.

Each lady in the circle was beyond the flower of youth, and none had ever been called a beauty, so they were resigned to being ignored by most of the male populace. Gentlemen of their acquaintance were mainly interested in the gullible debutantes, pretty young widows and lonely wives. Even their own husbands preferred the company of other men in the smoke-filled card rooms to partnering them in a set.

Thus, left to their own devices, the ladies formed a club of sorts recently. Their favourite activity thus far was wagering on the likelihood of one lady or another capturing the attention of a certain gentleman, always designated to be the most eligible one in attendance. Tonight the man who captured their interest was not only the most eligible man at this ball, but quite possibly, in all of England—Fitzwilliam Darcy.

"Oh, ladies, I am so excited. We do not often have a man of Mr. Darcy's calibre, so shall we begin? Tonight my wager is on Lady Waltham," Mrs. Graham exclaimed, trying to be heard over the din of conversation surrounding her circle of friends. "Lady Leighton is not even in the receiving line, though I had understood that she was to attend with her husband, the viscount, so perhaps she has given up her designs on Mr. Darcy."

Even as she spoke, Mrs. Graham's eyes combed the receiving line to see who might be next, seeing that Lady Gwendolyn Waltham had made her dramatic entrance moments before, and the murmuring amongst the crowd at her appearance had just now quieted. On the far end of the line were, of course, Lord and Lady Matlock, followed by the Viscount Leighton, his brother Colonel Richard Fitzwilliam, and lastly, Mr. Darcy. But still, Lady Leighton had not appeared.

"I have never seen a more daring gown than Lady Waltham's! I would never wear something as bold as red satin and certainly not one so revealing. I expected her bosom to fall out at any moment. And those rubies! The necklace must have cost a fortune, let alone the earrings."

Mrs. Mumford finally had her say. "I hear she has had plenty of experience in, *shall we say*, arts and allurements." Then remembering her own failed attempt to engage Mr. Darcy in suggestive conversation at the Matlock's dinner for Richard, she chuckled. "I could certainly use some advice."

"I could as well!" Mrs. Trentholm sighed, glancing again at Mr. Darcy. Her attempt at seduction came on the heels of Mrs. Mumford's and had been quickly thwarted by the dark-haired Master of Pemberley.

Mrs. Hinds stated decidedly, "Gwendolyn Waltham does not stand a chance if Jacqueline Leighton decides to attend. You know the rumours as well as I—how they were found in the library together the night of her engagement dinner and by his own sister!" As several began to voice disagreement, it forced her to concede, "I know—I know. Mr. Darcy was never implicated as being anything but an innocent party, but that is all the more reason to suspect she will try again. She set her sights on him once, why would she not try again with her marriage in tatters? Certainly there is no love lost between the viscount and her."

As the ladies nodded in agreement, Janet Mumford brought in another name. "I believe Cecile Preston has given up her quest to be the next Mistress of Pemberley and rightfully so. Lord knows she is too plain to compete with Gwendolyn or Jacqueline."

"Or most women!" Martha Harris interjected to everyone's delight.

"I never saw any logic for Mr. Darcy's attraction," Patience Trentholm added.

"I agree entirely," Gertrude Hinds confided enthusiastically, then adding, "I have it on good authority that dear Cecile has now set her cap for Lord Farthington."

"Farthington!" The rest exclaimed in concert.

"Why he is at least eight and fifty!" Janet Mumford gasped.

"Yes," Mrs. Harris rejoined, "but there is something to be said for early widowhood when the dearly departed has so much wealth and so few heirs."

"Hear! Hear!" Margie Graham chuckled. "Would that Mr. Graham was twenty years older!"

That remark set off a new round of giggles until everyone around them turned to see what had provoked such merriment. These observations caused the ladies to reign in their high spirits somewhat. They certainly did not want their little musings to get back to their husbands.

"Oh!" Patience Trentholm declared. "There is Lady Leighton now!"

They all followed her gaze toward the entrance to the ballroom where the woman in question stood as if posed, obviously very pleased with herself. Shockingly, she had waited until most of the guests had arrived before appearing ...alone. The viscount hurried towards his wife, though those who suspected her intent could see that her eyes were trained on Mr. Darcy.

Renowned for her beauty, Jacqueline Fitzwilliam enjoyed taking centre stage. She wore a deep emerald green gown and a necklace consisting of several strands of diamonds and emeralds, along with matching earrings. Her lustrous dark red hair was piled high on her head and two emerald-encrusted combs held it in place. The green of her gown served to enhance her green eyes and exquisite complexion. One perfect brow rose as Edgar came towards her, and when he held out his arm, for a moment she stared at him, making him and everyone else uncomfortable. Finally, a delicate hand came to rest lightly upon his arm, and he began to escort her. Once situated in the receiving line, she leaned over trying to catch Mr. Darcy's eye, making her husband livid. Then she straightened to welcome the next guest.

"That went well, I think," Richard smirked, speaking out of the corner of his mouth so Edgar could not hear. "At least you will not have to worry about Edgar's speaking to you."

Instead of turning towards William, which might draw attention, he flicked his eyes over to see his cousin's unease. "Relax, Darce! If your jaw clenches any tighter, you will break a tooth."

William was fuming as he leaned slightly towards Richard and whispered so only he could hear, "I had hoped she would behave with more decorum than the last time we were in company."

Richard chuckled, causing his mother to lean forward and glare, while he only smiled at her. "I would say you have hoped in vain."

"Richard," William's voice was low but authoritative, "you are not helping."

"On the contrary, I plan to be a great deal of help tonight. Mother was thrilled that I was sent back to London in time to attend this soirée and she has charged me not to leave your side. So you will not be suffering the attentions of the harridans—I mean, *ladies*—alone. I shall sacrifice myself to keep them at bay!"

At that William smiled, leaning forward to get his aunt's attention and giving her a full smile, dimples and all. "Thank you," he mouthed. She smiled and nodded.

"I say!" Richard enjoined, watching the exhibition. "Why is it I got a glare and you got a smile? She is *my* mother, after all!"

Unfortunately, Mr. Darcy's charming smile was seen by all the ladies who were ogling him, and it set hearts racing; among them were Lady Waltham's, Lady Leighton's and Mrs. Preston's. Seeing the expressions of desire upon the women standing around him, Colonel Fitzwilliam shook his head.

"You are not making it easy for me, Cousin! Cease smiling!"

~~~*~~~

Chapter 20

The ball continues

Leaving this madness was beginning to appear to be the only solution. The Fitzwilliams had invited scores of people who were unfamiliar to William due to his two-year absence from society, and his aunt, with single-minded purpose, had insisted on personally introducing him to half of them. The other half insisted on introducing themselves—and their single daughters.

Mrs. Preston had at last been led away, albeit unwillingly, by Lord Farthington, but Lady Waltham and Lady Leighton were determined to stay close by William, who flatly refused to dwell on the number of other women, married and widowed, who had offered suggestions for his afternoons in the coming week. Sometimes, it seemed as if it was pointless to leave Darcy House when he was in town.

Richard blew out a deep breath as the latest debutante and her mother ambled away, disappointed. "What does that make ...ten ...twelve? I swear I do not know how, with that scowl, you attract so many mothers *and fathers* with marriageable daughters!"

Glancing to William, he did not find the customary smile at his jest. Instead, his cousin appeared to be in lower spirits than he had ever seen him, so he tried another tack. "Some of them would do nicely for me, you know. What do they think I am? A vagabond?"

Finally William chuckled a little. "I am sorry, Richard. I realise that I have not been good company. This cannot have been a very pleasant evening for you. Why do you not ask that young lady you have been smiling at all night to dance? I shall be fine."

Richard lifted one brow and leaned in to whisper. "You promise to stay in plain view, so I can assure that you are not accosted by my demented sister—or your demented ex-lover—while I take a turn with Mrs. Largin?"

William grimaced at Richard's language but recognised that, essentially, he was correct. Instead of bothering to comment, he enquired about another matter entirely—"Mrs.? The lady you have been paying your attentions to is married?"

"Of course not! She is a widow with two small children and, yes, she is older than she looks!"

William turned to get a better look at the tall woman with light-brown hair that his cousin had been keeping in his line of vision even as he tried to be discreet. "Far be it from me—"

"Oh, for heaven's sake, I know you were thinking she looks very young. She does not look a day over four and twenty, but she is thirty. Her husband, a member of my prior unit, was killed a year or so ago in an accident, and I accompanied his body home. I was reintroduced to her last week when she was with one of mother's many friends at the theatre. The only good thing to come from mother's many introductions!"

"Ah! Then why are you waiting? Go!" William replied, pushing Richard towards the woman.

"Well, if you think ..." Richard turned to find the lady who had captured his interest standing only a few feet away, smiling shyly at him. He moved closer and bowed. "Mrs. Largin, I had hoped that you would save me a set."

"Oh, Colonel Fitzwilliam, you should not have doubted," the pretty woman replied. "Did I not say that I would?"

Richard held out his arm, and she placed her slim hand upon it, captivating him with her sparkling blue eyes as they moved towards the dance floor. Taking their places in line, the looks on their faces made William smile in spite of himself and his thoughts turned to the one that he missed most severely. What he would not give for Elizabeth to look at him that way!

Lost in watching Richard and the widow, it was a moment before he realised that other women had noticed that he was stripped of his guard. Looking around to see every eye following him, William began searching the room for his aunt when his gaze fell on Lady Waltham. Her come-hither look caused him to take a frustrating breath and turn to go in the opposite direction—almost running into Lady Leighton in his haste to escape.

"My goodness! Who are you fleeing, Fitzwilliam?" Jacqueline Fitzwilliam's voice was low and seductive, her smile calculating, as her eyes danced gleefully between William and Lady Waltham.

An image of her came to William from out of the blue. *Like a spider cornering a fly.* Suddenly he had had enough of being polite. Not bothering to address her question, he declared haughtily, "What concern is it of yours, madam?"

"Come now? *Madam?* Why so formal? After all, we are cousins." As she spoke, her jealous green eyes slowly travelled down his body and back up before coming to rest on his light blue ones. She leaned in to whisper sensually, "Care to look over the library while Edgar is dancing with his mother? There is something I would love to show you."

William drew himself up to his full six feet, two inches, not bothering to conceal his displeasure. "I assure you, *madam*, there is nothing that you have that interests me!" Abruptly stepping around her, he walked away, leaving the crowd surrounding them tittering and staring.

Instead of being angry at his rejection, now Lady Leighton definitely resembled the spider William had conjured only moments before—only this spider wore a smile. *This is perfect. He must still be attracted to me, or he would not be afraid to meet me alone.*

Refusing to be intimidated, Jacqueline unashamedly met every eye in the circle that stood round about her, until she came to Lady Waltham's questioning gaze and openly smirked. To that woman who dared try to gain Fitzwilliam's attention, she nodded knowingly before heading in the direction of the refreshment table.

And that aging whore need not think she is any competition for me.

~~~*~~~

Lady Gwendolyn Waltham was elated that she had managed to attend the ball without being escorted by the count. Fortunately, he had business to attend out of Town and would be gone for another day, so she had come with friends. Count Francesco was an accomplished lover with many and varied skills, she had to admit, but she still had reservations about him. For all his talk of wealth and property, he rented a residence in Town that could not compare to Darcy House—or Matlock House, for that matter. She had been inside both of those homes and their opulence was almost beyond compare. If she were to ever marry again, this was the type of wealth to which she would aspire—old money, hopefully tucked inside a younger man's breeches.

The count always bragged of his father's estate in northern England and his mother's property in Italy, but from the gossip circulating in Town, little was known that would confirm his wealth, and she was not willing to risk her future on mere speculation, even if the count was a good lover. Thus, when she learned that Fitzwilliam Darcy had returned to London and would be at the ball tonight, she knew she simply must garner an invitation to attend.

After all, Fitzwilliam was the more handsome of the two—and much younger. She was convinced that she could entice him into her bed once more and then claim she was with child. Honourable man that he was, he would, of course, insist on marriage to legitimize his heir. She smiled. This time his father would not be there to save him!

Recalling the chatter that spread throughout the ballroom when she arrived with her friends, Gwendolyn smiled. It was satisfying to know that every eye in the room had focused on her, just as when she was younger. The only difference was that she could no longer hold their interest over the course of an evening. The younger men eventually returned to the simpering debutantes and the henpecked husbands to their controlling wives. The rest—men eager for scintillating company—had once been her exclusive domain. Now she had to share them with the likes of Jacqueline Fitzwilliam.

She consoled herself with the thought that there was really only one man she deeply desired—Fitzwilliam Darcy. When she was not dancing, she stayed close by him, looking for the opportunity to speak privately. Therefore, it was with a sense of great satisfaction that she witnessed the unpleasant confrontation between Lady Leighton and William. Seeing William challenge Jacqueline, Gwendolyn had looked around.

Surely that idiot husband of Jacqueline's saw it, too!

Running her eyes over the crowd, she found the viscount with his mother and father in a far corner, surrounded by guests. They seemed blissfully ignorant of the drama that had just played out. Annoyed, her eyes came to rest on Richard. He was engrossed in conversation with his dance partner. With the colonel occupied and Jacqueline rebuffed, this might be her only opportunity.

She began to follow her *objet d'amour* through the crowd, losing sight of him for a moment before catching a glimpse of his head clearing the doorway to the terrace. Quickly she made her way to the same door and, seeing no one watching, slipped out after him. There was no one on the terrace. She turned in a circle. Nothing. She was pondering the situation when a dog's bark caught her attention, and she looked to see a dark, ghostlike figure striding across the lawn, towards a gazebo. She knew that confident stride, and so she followed.

Caught up in his thoughts, William had no idea anyone was behind him as he reached the structure. Wearily he slumped down onto one of the benches and began to rub his forehead, trying to stave off a threatening headache. There was enough moonlight to illuminate a pair of swans on the pond behind the structure, and he became engrossed in their graceful movements, oblivious to all else. The swans were performing mating rituals, their heads bobbing up and down in a dance as old as the rhythm of the sea.

"Even they realise they need a mate."

Recognising that voice, he stood abruptly. Neither could see clearly in the shroud of the gazebo, so his scowl was not evident to Gwendolyn as she continued, "You must have seen that I was following you."

William had to quell his temper before attempting to reply, so Gwendolyn took this as an invitation to come closer. "I take it you do not disapprove of my presence."

Before William could move or reply, a sharp screech rang out. "Just what the devil do you think you are doing?" Lady Leighton hurried up the steps and stomped across to push herself in between William and Lady Waltham.

"I could ask you the same thing!" Lady Waltham retorted, moving to stand only inches from her rival. Face-to-face they argued.

"What right have you to follow my cousin like a common whore?"

"Whore? You call me a whore? At least I am not married! What would happen if your fool of a husband found you here?"

"You have no right to question me. What Fitzwilliam and I share is private—between family."

"Family? Is that what you call it?"

"This is ridiculous!" William interjected. "Both of you must leave at once!"

He grew more livid as the two women kept arguing, paying no attention to his attempts to quiet them. Fearing that shortly other guests would hear their bellows and they would all be exposed, he stepped between them.

"Enough! What must I say to convince you that I do not desire to keep company with either of you?!"

A military commander's voice rang out in the darkness. "What the deuce are you women doing?" Richard stepped up to grab each of the harridans by an arm, looking from one to the other.

"I am personally escorting you both to the house this minute. You will go inside as though you are the best of friends who stepped out for a bit of air ...**together.** DO YOU UNDERSTAND ME?"

In the face of his anger and authoritarian behaviour, both ladies nodded. Immediately, he jerked them roughly towards the house, one on either side. They had to walk briskly to keep up with his long strides and when he reached the terrace, he halted abruptly.

"You **will** lock arms and start your charade, or so help me God ..." They shrunk back.

"NOW!" he barked, pushing them forward. He observed them as they re-entered the room, giving a performance worthy of the London stage. Lady Matlock was just inside the door and glowered as they passed, then hurried out onto the terrace to address her son.

Running a hand along Richard's cheek, she noticed that he was trying to calm himself by taking deep breaths. "Are you well, my boy?"

He kissed her fingers and smiled wryly. "I am now, Mother. In fact, I rather enjoyed confronting those two."

"And Fitzwilliam?"

"I shall find him and make certain he is well."

"I hated to interrupt your evening to ask you to intervene. You looked as though you were thoroughly enjoying Mrs. Largin's company, and I must add that she seems a fine person."

"Mrs. Largin is a wonderful woman, and I very much enjoyed our dance, but I failed in my duty to my cousin. I should never have left Darce alone. I should have known that one or both of those vipers would pounce at the first opportunity and I regret giving it to them."

"No, no. It is not your fault. I should never have asked you to forego your pleasure to guard your cousin. You are entitled to enjoy yourself. It is the fault of those—those—I cannot bear to call them 'ladies!' Would that they would leave the poor boy alone!"

"I fear that is not likely to happen as long as Darce is unmarried and possibly not even then. I have never seen anything like the effect my dour cousin has on women." He shook his head in wonderment.

"And he is totally unaware of it. How he resists all that—" Realising who he was speaking to, Richard stopped abruptly. "I am sorry, Mother. I did not mean to be crass. I will just say that the man is a saint!"

"We must convince him to marry soon, Richard."

"We will need plenty of luck for that! Now," he leaned down to plant a kiss on her forehead, "if you will keep an eye on those two, I shall see how Darce is faring."

Netherfield

Caroline Bingley was more than miffed. She had arrived in this Godforsaken country weeks ago, only to learn that Mr. Darcy had already returned to Pemberley. Had she known that the gentleman from Derbyshire would not be in Meryton, she would have stayed in Town. As it was, her sister and brother, the Hursts, had taken the opportunity of her absence to plan an extended visit with his relatives in Sussex. They did not intend on returning to London for months, effectively abandoning her to the heathens.

For days after she arrived, she had held out hope that a reciprocal invitation would be issued for the Bingleys to visit Mr. Darcy's estate—naturally, she would travel with them. But alas, none came, even though she had glimpsed letters in Mr. Darcy's elegant script being delivered to Charles. To make matters worse, Charles had actually asked her to help with that brat, Peter, because his angel, mealy-mouthed Jane, was with child. Again! Lord, did they not know what caused that!

A most unladylike snort from one of her guests drew her attention back to the present and the occupants of the drawing room—the most disgusting people she had ever met—the Bennets.

How utterly cruel to be exiled here with these chits!

Lydia snorted as she slapped Kitty's leg. "La! I would much rather be in Town. At least there are men in red coats there." This set off a new round of guffaws between the two of them.

Mrs. Bennet ignored her daughters' banter, preferring to whine. "I should like to go to London, but my brother is not very accommodating anymore. I have told my Jane that she should insist Mr. Bingley buy a house in Town. Then, at least, I could spend part of the season there."

Caroline's eyes narrowed, and she was about to disabuse Mrs. Bennet of that notion in language even she could understand when her brother walked briskly back into the room. "I am sorry, madam, but I have checked on my wife, and she is still asleep. She will not be receiving company today."

Mrs. Bennet stood, waving her handkerchief about. "Well, I shall just see about that!" She started towards the door, but Charles stepped in front, effectively halting her progress.

"Mrs. Bennet, I must ask you to leave my wife to her rest. She is truly unable to receive you or her sisters. Perhaps if you will come back in a few days ..." His voice trailed off, but his cold eyes never left hers.

Mrs. Bennet could feel Mr. Bingley's animosity, though she was not sure just why he was angry. "I—I suppose I must. Tell Jane I shall return on Saturday."

Then she addressed her other children. "Come along, girls. There is still time to visit Mary." She glared at Bingley. "At least I have one married child who always wants to see her mother."

The two youngest girls clapped and jumped up with glee, ready to leave. Since Mary had married Toby Faulk, Mr. Phillip's clerk, and moved into the small cottage behind the law firm, there had been more opportunities for trips into town than ever before. Mrs. Bennet began moving towards the door before remembering Caroline. She looked back over her shoulder.

"Thank you for your hospitality, Miss Bingley. We shall see you again soon, I hope." She bobbed a curtsy.

Good Lord, not another visit! "You are welcome I am sure, madam." The words almost stuck in Caroline throat.

She watched as her brother escorted them to the door, as though he was making sure that they left. When he returned to the room, Charles turned to regard her.

"Caroline, I will be having dinner with my wife in our rooms tonight. I shall see you in the morning." With those terse words, he stalked off.

Caroline followed him with her eyes as he mounted the stairs and quickly disappeared above. She was absolutely amazed at the change in her once docile brother. *When did he become so quarrelsome?*

Recovering from her wool-gathering, she realised there were no servants about, so she took the familiar key from her pocket and studied it. Dear Jane had not even noticed its disappearance from her dressing table weeks before. Caroline considered with a smirk that Jane's indisposition must have affected her memory.

She suppressed a smile as she moved stealthily through the halls, not stopping until she stood at the door to her brother's study. Glancing left and then right, she slid the key into the lock, opened the door and slipped inside. Locking it behind her, she moved to sit in the large chair behind Charles' desk. Weeks ago she had been relieved to find the desk unlocked, as that had afforded her the opportunity to read all his business papers and correspondence. After all, she reasoned, she might have to depend on Charles' support for the rest of her life—well, that was if she did not secure Mr. Darcy. Thus, she needed to know the particulars of her brother's holdings.

Caroline felt a little thrill at defying Charles in this manner. He had gotten stricter and stricter with her allowance, and God forbid if she should say anything untoward about dear Jane or that Peter. He had no tolerance for any perceived slight to his wife or child, so she had had to watch her every move. Knowing that she was doing something that he would definitely not approve of empowered her; it was almost as good as talking back to him.

For a long moment, she enjoyed the feeling of power that came from being in his chair. Then she leaned forward to move the papers about on the desk. Suddenly a bit of familiar handwriting caught her eye. Once she had spent an entire afternoon watching Mr. Darcy write letters of business, so she was well acquainted with his script. Sliding the already opened letter out from underneath some of the other papers, she basked in the knowledge that Fitzwilliam Darcy had written this missive to the Bingleys ...and she was a Bingley. As she examined it, she pretended he had written to her personally and wondered what he would think if he knew she was reading it.

As the content became clear, a frown formed, and her brows knit in concern. Apparently Charles knew this cousin Mr. Darcy was so concerned about, else why would the Master of Pemberley pass along news of her to the Bingleys? Most disturbing was that Miss Elise, as he called her, seemed to be staying there ...at **her** Pemberley.

Her ire rose. No one, not even her own brother, had bothered to tell her that Mr. Darcy had a female cousin living at his home. It was most disturbing, even if the woman was chaperoned. It was common among the wealthy to marry their cousins and keep the wealth in the family. Was Mr. Darcy contemplating marriage to this particular cousin? She read on impatiently, her anxiety mounting until she reached the part where he mentioned that she was there for her health!

Caroline sighed in relief. It was obvious that something was seriously wrong with this Elise Lawrence. Perhaps she would die soon, and she would not have to worry about her. *Yes! That was probably the only reason Mr. Darcy allowed her to stay. She is dying.*

The letter was brief, and there was no more mention of the woman, so Caroline carefully placed it back in the stack. Then shuffling through the rest of the papers, she decided there was nothing that she had not studied before. Taking every precaution, she quit the room just as she had in the past, quietly moving through the halls unnoticed, until she was safely ensconced in her own bedchamber.

Once inside, she plopped down on her bed, losing herself in her daydreams of being Mrs. Darcy. That always caused her to smile, and she did so until she remembered her dissatisfaction with Charles. If only he would force his hand—make Mr. Darcy invite them to Pemberley. Then that gentleman would see her suitability to be the Mistress of Pemberley. Yes! She must devise a way to have Charles invited. She sat up.

Of course! A letter! She could mimic her brother's handwriting, splotches and all, and with any luck, Mr. Darcy might not mention her letter when he extended the invitation, but if he did, Charles would likely think he was referring to some earlier post. After all, they exchanged letters frequently. Yes, that is the solution!

~~~*~~~

"Charles, we cannot keep Mama away with frivolous complaints. At some point, she will understand that I do not really want to see her and then—then I shall have no peace." She sniffled, and Charles tightened his hug and kissed her forehead.

"I am sorry, love. I suppose I should have brought her up for just a moment, and she would have been satisfied for a while. It was just that she was so overbearing, pushing her way into the house, ordering our servants around. Sometimes—"

"We have only a short while longer to bear it. We have agreed to move just as soon as the baby is born. Have you asked Mr. Darcy to keep watch for an estate in the area of Derbyshire?"

"Not yet. Are you sure it would be in Lizzy's best interest if we move near her? I mean, if your mother came to visit, she might accidentally see her."

"Charles, when we move, I am determined to break all ties with Mama. I do not want to ever see her again—not after what she did to my sister."

"I know you say that, sweetheart, but you may change your mind."

"No! No, I will not. If not for Lizzy's situation, I would have moved north before now. I feel better about her now that she is in Mr. Darcy's care, and once we move, Mama will have no idea where I have gone. I shall see to that."

~~~*~~~

Chapter 21

Richard strolled in unannounced. "I have come to see if you have recovered?"

His cousin's voice drew his attention from his business papers. William knew very well to what Richard referred, but chose to act as though it had not affected him. "I beg your pardon?"

"Come now, Darce! It is I! Richard—your omniscient, omnipresent cousin. You remember—the one who saved you from the clutches of those two wicked harridans!" The smile left Richard's face, replaced by a more serious countenance. "Tell me, are you well?"

How William hated Richard's ability to make him smile when he wished to scowl. Standing, he dropped his papers and walked around the desk to lean against it, facing the one person he could never fool.

"I am well. It is just that I hate for Edgar to think—"

Richard placed a comforting hand on his shoulder, effectively silencing him. "Edgar said things he should not have. He knows Jacqueline is a liar, but he is jealous of you. He always has been. Surely you know that."

"But I never—"

"Look, Darce, the women love you! Hell! Even I am jealous of you sometimes. Then I remember that you cannot help what you are, and you certainly do not vie for anyone's attention." Richard tried not to smirk as he added, "You are perfect through no fault of your own."

William shushed him. "I am no such thing."

"When it comes to looks, you are! But you came by it honestly. Uncle George was a handsome man, and I was told he had his share of women chasing after him."

"He did?" William brightened. "He never mentioned anything."

"My mother told me once that Aunt Anne had to beat the women off Uncle George with a stick."

William smiled widely. "You jest."

"Well, about the stick perhaps, but not about the women who harassed him or his being a handsome man. I remember that he was still a fine looking fellow when you graduated from university."

The thought of how young his father had appeared only a year before his death caused an ache in William's chest. Forcing himself not to dwell on it, he feigned a smile. "I appreciate that you are trying to lift my spirits, Richard, but I fear it is useless. Only this morning, Mrs. Barnes informed me that one of the maids heard rumours of last night's happenings when she went to pick up an order at the market. I can only wonder at how it became common knowledge overnight."

"It appears there were others in the gardens during the melee. I saw no one when I escorted the *ladies* to the house, but naturally, the gossips scurried like rats from a burning building to spread the news."

William dropped his head and groaned. "This is a disaster!"

"Not for Edgar! You did him a favour." William's head shot up and a quizzical brow lifted.

"With Jacqueline's blatant display of shameless regard for you, Father has finally seen what Edgar has said all along—that their marriage is hopeless. And since she had no intention of providing him an heir, last night was further incentive for them to separate permanently. As I see it, the only problem is that she may pursue you even more vigorously afterward."

"I never sought her attention. There is only one woman's attention I want, and right now she does not want even to talk to me."

"Miss Elizabeth does not want to talk to you? Why ever not? You were so close just weeks ago. What happened?"

"Her memory is returning." He laughed mirthlessly. "I believe she has remembered what she did not like about me."

"You and she had such lively debates when we were at Rosings. I would never have guessed she did not like you. How did you come to find out?"

"I made her an offer of marriage." At Richard's look of astonishment, he shrugged. "In Kent."

"You did not!"

"I most certainly did, and she refused me."

"My word! What reason did she give for refusing one of the most eligible men in England?"

"Among other things, my selfish disdain for the feelings of others—of a more personal nature, the separation of her sister and Charles Bingley."

"Separate Bingley from Miss Bennet? She was the one?" William did not reply, but the guilt on his face was confirmation.

Richard realised his part in the misunderstanding and groaned. "All of this—your exile, Miss Elizabeth's ordeal—should be laid at my feet! I had no idea that Miss Bennet was the woman Bingley was enamoured of in Hertfordshire, and I told Miss Elizabeth of how you were his advisor—how he valued your opinion. My purpose was just to impress her with the way you look after your friends and family. Can you ever forgive me for betraying a confidence and causing you both pain?"

William patted Richard's arm. "It is in the past, Richard. And the truth would have come out eventually, so do not be distressed. Besides, Elizabeth had such a poor opinion of my character that that alone would have been reason enough. She said I did not act like a gentleman."

"I can undoubtedly see where your shyness might appear as disdain, but I have never known you not to act the part of a gentleman."

"Believe me, my proposal was not kind as I ended up insulting her family. And though I did not specifically tell Bingley to leave Meryton, I discouraged him in his pursuit of Miss Bennet. I—I thought the Bennet family, other than Elizabeth and Miss Bennet, were vulgar. So when he asked my opinion—"

"You pointed him in the opposite direction."

"Precisely."

"But he married her anyway, did he not?"

"After I left Rosings, I went straight to Bingley and told him what Elizabeth had said of her sister's broken heart. Charles returned to Hertfordshire, and they were married."

"And you were off to Scotland to lick your wounds." William stood silent. "The mystery of your disappearance is solved at last—a broken heart." Richard's next words contained not a hint of joviality. "What will you do now? You cannot very well stay away from Pemberley just because she is there. You must go home at some point."

William sighed heavily. "I promised Georgiana I would return before the week's end. Pemberley has ample space, and I see no problem with being able to keep well away from Elizabeth."

Looking as though he was considering the prospect of being near but not with the woman he loved, William's mien darkened. "I pray that at some point she will—at the very least—consider me a friend."

"Surely that would not suffice with the way you feel about her. It seems you will only torture yourself with this *friendship*."

"Right now being friends with Miss Elizabeth would be a vast improvement."

On a balcony at Pemberley

"I am almost finished. You may talk, but keep perfectly still."

Elizabeth sat stroking the sleeping kitten in her lap as Georgiana worked her magic with the coloured pencils. She could see the strokes Georgiana made from her vantage point but could not make out the image.

"How long will Millie nap?"

"Oh, she normally rests for at least an hour, maybe more. I believe you quite exhausted her while playing," Georgiana teased, "And she was delighted to have her doll returned."

Staring wistfully in the distance, Elizabeth recollected. "Addie used to bring her to see me when ..." She was unable to continue for a moment, but just as Georgiana was about to speak she added, "Millie was not allowed in my private quarters, but Addie would sneak her in when I was at my lowest."

Georgiana nodded, not sure what to say, but trying to be a good listener. She had done so each day since her brother's departure, and it was plain that Elizabeth's memory was returning. The results were oftentimes painful to watch.

Taking a ragged breath, Elizabeth continued with even greater emotion, "I believe Addie ... I believe she would be very happy that you and your husband are raising Millie. She would want her to have a father and mother who love her."

Georgiana had ceased drawing when Elizabeth began speaking of Addie, and tears filled her eyes. She leaned over to catch Elizabeth's hand and their eyes met. "I—I can only hope that somehow she is watching over Millie and that she is pleased." Elizabeth nodded tearfully.

Trying to lighten the mood, Georgiana held up the drawing. "It is not entirely finished, but I believe you can recognise yourself! I give you, Elizabeth and—" She stopped. "What is the kitten's name?"

Elizabeth picked up the calico kitten, touching her nose to its pink one. "Jade. Her name is Jade because that is the colour of her eyes."

"Very well then, Elizabeth and Jade! How do you like it?"

"It is lovely! You draw beautifully, and it looks exactly like Jade, though I think that you have flattered me."

"You are too modest, Elizabeth. You are very pretty."

Elizabeth smiled knowingly. "You are mistaken. I have no delusions about my appearance, but I do have a sister Jane who is beautiful—hair the colour of summer wheat and the bluest eyes." Suddenly her face crumpled though she did not cry. "I miss her so much."

Georgiana moved to hug her. "I am sure you shall see her soon. Just mention it to Brother, and he will invite Mr. Bingley and your sister to Pemberley. There is nothing that he would not do for you."

Elizabeth's gaze dropped to her shoes. "I really do not understand why he would do anything for me."

Georgiana stilled. "What do you remember of Fitzwilliam?"

"When I told you there were many thoughts going through my mind and sometimes I cannot discern what I remember from what I might have imagined, I was referring to him."

"Fitzwilliam?"

Elizabeth's head bobbed up and down.

"Would you like me to tell you a little about my brother? After all, he can be quite the mystery."

"I would like that very much."

Georgiana spent the next hour extolling the man she knew and loved, explaining how he had had to become the master of Pemberley at a young age because of their father's passing, and how he had become more reticent as his every action was critiqued. Then tenderly, she recounted their relationship.

"Fitzwilliam and I have always been close. Our mother died when I was quite young, and I think my brother tried to make everything right by keeping me close to him." She smiled almost to herself. "If he was riding, I sat in front of him; if he was swimming, I was on his back. I even begged to fence when he began lessons." She laughed. "His friends *despised* me!"

Shaking her head in wonder, Georgiana said wistfully, "If I remember my childhood fondly at all, it is only because of him."

Seeing Elizabeth's puzzlement, she explained. "You see, my father was heartbroken at my mother's passing. Though he was a good man, after she died, he spent much time away from Pemberley, leaving us on our own. Fitzwilliam took it upon himself to see to my happiness."

Georgiana giggled. "You know, my brother vetted all my suitors. Never tell Fitzwilliam this, but Evan said his greatest fear in falling in love with me was having to approach Fitzwilliam. They were old acquaintances, but they were not good friends then. I cannot begin to tell you how Brother behaved when Evan asked for my hand."

Elizabeth could not help but laugh. "I can only but imagine."

"And it would take days for me to tell you of all the women who have chased or been pushed towards my brother. No less than seven attempts have been made to compromise him that I know about. He is so handsome that many desired him, while not a few coveted his wealth and connections. That is why I shall wager that when you met him, he did not appear friendly in the least."

"He was not personable when we met, no. Nor did he improve on subsequent meetings."

"One would have to know all he had been through, all the hypocrisy he had witnessed and the 'duty and honour' driven into this head by our uncle to understand fully why he invented that mask of indifference everyone sees. It was in self-defence."

"Thank you. You have helped me to understand why Mr. Darcy acted as he did in Hertfordshire," Elizabeth ventured. "I daresay my mother was not the only mother pushing her daughters in his direction."

"And if I am correct, you met him again in Kent?"

Elizabeth coloured but did not have to reply as Georgiana continued. "When he returned that year, he was a different man—*defeated* is the only word that comes to my mind that would describe him at that point. I had never seen him so dispirited, and it frightened me. Then only a few days later, he was gone—in his self-imposed exile. I was broken-hearted.

"Though we corresponded, it was two years until he returned, and naturally, I was thrilled to have my brother near me again. Each day I pray that he will marry and start a family, as I believe that would give him peace of mind as well as a reason to stay."

Georgiana halted, realising what she had said might hurt her new friend. "I am sorry if I said anything to upset you."

Elizabeth shrugged. "There is no need to apologise. I would not want a beloved brother to bring **me** home either." At Georgiana's sympathetic look, she tried to smile. "The truth hurts sometimes but it does not make it any less true."

Georgiana changed the subject. "Do you remember anything of your arrival at Pemberley?"

"Yes. It was almost as though I were in a thick fog. I could hear people talking, but they were far, far away, and I could not understand what they were saying." She smiled wanly. "I am slowly regaining my senses, but there is one thing I would dearly like to ask you."

Elizabeth stood then, setting down the kitten and walking to the wall around the balcony. For a moment she took in the view of the pastures full of sheep and horses galloping in the distance, but her mind was not on those. Her thoughts were of soft hands and firm muscular arms ... the smell of sandalwood cologne ... soft lips brushing over her forehead and being held tightly to a man's chest because her feet were without slippers.

"I think I remember being reassured by your brother's embrace—more than once. Is that true?"

Georgiana took a deep breath. "Yes, but in fairness to Fitzwilliam, his touch was the only thing that calmed you when ... when you had one of your spells. He was only trying to help—to comfort you." She stood silent so long that Georgiana became worried. "Elizabeth?"

"Only now that I can think more clearly, have I realised how very kind Mr. Darcy has been to me. Taking me into his home without reservation and showing nothing but compassion for my plight. I repaid him cruelly."

"No. You—"

"Yes." Elizabeth interrupted. "It was unkind to refuse to see him. I owe him my life, the least I can do is thank him." Looking over her shoulder, she enquired, "Is he to return soon?"

"He is expected home in a day or two."

"Then I shall have a chance to make amends before I leave."

"You must not leave, Elizabeth. It would not be safe."

"It would mean his ruin if I stay." She gestured across the expanse of Pemberley. "More importantly, everyone here, even your own family nearby, would be in mortal danger. That would be an unkind way to repay such benevolence. I will find employment, and that shall dictate where I go."

At Georgiana's frown, she smiled. "Do not worry. I shall sort it out. I must."

When she turned back to truly study the magnificent view, her quiet resolve kept Georgiana from replying.

London
Preston House

"I insist your people go through with this!" Stomping across the room, Cecile Preston poured herself another glass of brandy and turned to confront Wickham again.

"I went to a great deal of trouble having my maid befriend her maid so we would know when she was out of town. There is an enormous amount of money at stake."

"INSIST! *You* insist! Who are *you* to tell *me* what to do?"

Wickham angrily rose from his chair. "I am not going to say this again. The man we are aligned with does not wish to relieve Lady Waltham of her valuables. He did not explain his reasons to me, and I did not ask. He is not someone you wish to make an enemy, whether you know it or not. Move on to another target."

"But why? She has many expensive pieces. What reason could he possibly have to object?"

"It is purely speculation on my part, but I assume he had targeted her already for his own reasons. He was doing this sort of thing long before I joined him."

"Targeted her? How delicious! An international thief involved with Lady Waltham!"

"If it is true—" Wickham interjected, but was quickly interrupted by Cecile.

"That is likely the only rationale that would appease me. I hope he is, and she loses everything!"

"My, my, you sound like a woman scorned! Has Lady Waltham stolen your lover perhaps?" At the look of annoyance on her face, Wickham cackled. "That is it! She stole your lover. Who is he? Some old gentleman with one foot in the grave?" He bent over laughing, as she seethed.

"I will have you know that the men I favour would never give her a second glance. I just do not care for the woman because she had an elevated opinion of herself—she thinks she is so beautiful."

"She is!" Wickham smirked at Cecile's glare. "I have seen her about town, and while she may be getting older, she is still a beauty. I would not mind dipping my pen into that."

Huffing in disgust, Cecile threw her glass into the fire, breaking it. "So, our profits rest on the whims of men whose only concern seems to be getting whores into their beds."

Wickham scowled and started to the door, turning to impart a warning. "You had better watch what you say about certain people. It could get you into more trouble than you ever imagined." He stared menacingly for a moment.

"Send for me as soon as you find less dangerous baubles to pilfer."

Rosewood Manor
The Nursery

Evan peered into the nursery to see Georgiana rocking slowly, her eyes fixed upon the small bed which held their daughter. Quietly, he entered without her notice, leaning down to plant a kiss on her perfumed hair and announcing his presence.

"She finally sleeps?"

She gave him a smile. "Yes. She was exhausted but determined to fight sleep." Chuckling, she added, "After Elizabeth caught sight of Millie today, I barely got to hold her. It was heart-warming to see her take to Elizabeth so quickly and then squeal with delight at the sight of her doll. Now I know why there were doll clothes in her bag. It seemed to lift Elizabeth's spirits so much to see Millie and to give her the doll."

Just then, Mrs. Calvert stepped into the room, and Georgiana rose to vacate the rocking chair. "I shall stay with the little Miss now. You need your rest, Mrs. Ingram," the nurse whispered, giving Evan a slight smile.

Even before she had taken her seat, Evan was pulling Georgiana towards the door. "Thank you, Mrs. Calvert, you are invaluable to this household," he pronounced, quitting the room with his wife.

The elderly woman could not suppress a smile. Rosewood Manor had always been a delightful place to work, but now that the Ingrams had their new daughter, the atmosphere had grown even brighter. *Children bring such joy!*

A few feet down the hall, Georgiana chastised her husband, "Evan! What will Mrs. Calvert think—you practically dragged me from the room?"

He stopped walking and pulled her tightly to his already aroused body. "She will think that the Master of the house needs his wife's company, and she would be absolutely correct."

Capturing her mouth in a torrid kiss, they were lost in their desires when a noise drew their attention. Quitting the kiss, they stepped apart, each glancing down the hall in an opposite direction, only to smile as they looked back at each other.

"We are safe!" Evan teased. "No servants witnessed the Master ravishing the Mistress!"

Georgiana's eye twinkled in the dim light of the candles lighting the hallway. "That, my dear husband, was **not** *ravishing*."

"Suppose we step in here," Evan pulled her a few feet further to the door of their bedchamber, turning the knob and pushing it open, "and I shall show you what constitutes ravishing!"

~~~*~~~

Later, satiated and content, Georgiana lay next to Evan, her head resting on his shoulder, one arm across his chest. He kissed her forehead. "I love you, Ana. You are the best wife and mother in the world."

She chuckled quietly. "Well, maybe not the world."

She could feel his suppressed laughter as his body shook. "Yes, even the world! And you are compassionate. When I see you with Miss Elizabeth—"

"I am only doing what William asked of me," she interjected.

"No. You would have taken care of her without being asked, I have no doubt as you are a kind person. But to see you ministering to the one woman who destroyed the dreams you had for your brother ... I know that must be difficult."

Georgiana sighed, confirming his belief that she might need to talk. After all, she was a Darcy, and they were experts at keeping wounds covered until they festered.

"I cannot hate her, though I confess to wanting to in the beginning. She is a good person at heart who had some awful things happen to her." Georgiana shuddered. "But for the grace of God, I could have been born into such a family. I cannot imagine a mother caring so little for her own daughter."

"I could tell from your dealings with Miss Elizabeth that you no longer resent her, but what of your desire to see Darcy marry, to have children? That is unlikely to happen if he is in love with her."

"A wise man once told me that I cannot live my brother's life for him."

"That was easy for me to say!" He chuckled, then sobered. "But even I worry that he may slip into another bout of melancholy."

Georgiana pulled herself up, rested on one elbow, then leaned over to plant a kiss on his lips. "I love the fact that you care so deeply for William, too."

"Darcy is truly my brother, and I do not wish him to be hurt. You were so distraught at his exile that I never mentioned my own sadness. I missed him terribly, oft times heading to the stables to ride over to Pemberley and getting half-way to the corral before I remembered he was gone. He was my advisor as well as my friend."

"I could tell you missed him, but I was so miserable that I could not help you." They were quiet for some time, each lost in their own thoughts.

Finally Evan ventured, "Do you think Miss Elizabeth has improved noticeably since Darcy has been gone?"

"I do. Each time I visit she is better, and she has resolved her concerns about my brother, at least in her mind. I believe she will talk to him when he returns, if only to thank him. She did admit, when I asked, that she loves him."

"I imagine he thinks she must hate him—since she would not speak to him."

"Knowing my brother, he has thought of the worst possible explanation for her refusal."

Evan ran the back of his hand over her cheek. "Will you tell him that she loves him?"

"No, I gave her my word, and I know that, as my confidant, you will not."

"It seems a shame that he should be ignorant of the fact. He was quite distraught when he left for London."

"If my brother really loves her, he will find out for himself. That is something I will not have to tell him."

"I suppose you are right."

She snickered. "The best wife and mother in the world is *always* right."

He grabbed her, rolling her over until she lay beneath him. "And she is always desired."

The rest of the night was not devoted to thinking of Ana's brother or Elizabeth's problems but to the furtherance of the Ingram's happiness ... which was significant!

~~~*~~~

Chapter 22

Pemberley

As William reached the bluff overlooking the valley where the great expanse of Pemberley lay, he pulled Onyx to a halt to allow Mr. Campbell time to come alongside him. Onyx, spirited as always, insisted on trotting ahead of the other horse. The mare that Mr. Campbell always chose to ride was old and slow, and William smiled, pondering the older gentleman's fear of horses. He was fearless in regards to everything but horses.

In a short time, the Scotsman's mount stopped beside William's, and for a long while, neither man spoke as they watched the sun begin to sink behind the tree line. Soon the purple shadows would give way to complete darkness. Both men were well aware that they needed to leave this area as quickly as possible, in light of what they had just learned.

William's day had begun before daylight with his steward, Mr. Sturgis, informing him of the particulars of the problems of a tenant who had lost his cow and calf the day before, both having been killed by a wild animal. The result was a family with four hungry children and no source of milk, butter, or cheese. William had instructed Sturgis to provide them a cow from Pemberley's herd, thinking that that would settle the problem.

However, Sturgis was just beginning his explanation. He went on to say that while William was in London, they had lost several lambs near the same area in like manner and that he had asked the tenant not to butcher the cow until it could be examined by Mr. Campbell. Roy Campbell, a groom and excellent marksman, was the man on whom William relied to rid the estate of pests—usually packs of wild dogs—whenever any threatened the livestock.

Campbell had surprised William with his assertion that the likely culprit was a wolf. Wolves had been numerous in England two centuries before and a menace to the populace, but the only credible sightings he had heard of in the last ten years were in Wales and remote parts of Scotland. Granted, Pemberley was situated in the north of the Peak district, but he had never heard anyone complain of wolves in the vicinity. Thinking on it further, he did recall that his father had mentioned seeing one on a remote corner of the estate before William was born. Nonetheless, he would not dismiss Mr. Campbell's contention, as the man was born in Edinburgh and grew up hunting the creatures.

"Are you confident enough in your supposition to merit the warning of my tenants and neighbouring estates?"

Mr. Campbell considered his answer carefully before replying. "I am. Some will make sport, maybe call you foolish. But even if it is not a wolf—and I believe it is— something is killing the livestock. It could just as likely have been a child killed as a calf or a lamb. I have seen no signs of a pack, and if it is a rogue—well, I have seen a few of those in my day. They are evil clean through, sometimes killing for the sport of it and not just to survive."

William shivered, thinking of the heartbreak that an animal such as that could inflict. "Send out the warnings among our tenants first thing tomorrow. I shall warn my neighbours."

He glanced at the man he credited with much of his success in the position he inherited at his father's death. "I trust you to take the necessary men and try and destroy it before it kills anything else."

The old man nodded, and they kicked their horses back into motion. If Campbell's suspicions were correct, the nightmare might just be beginning.

~~~*~~~

Elizabeth bolted up in bed, her breath coming fast. An endless night, filled with dreams, and replete with repressed memories had ended with a totally unexpected revelation. She had come to expect the discomfort but never dreamed it would come from another source—a source that, in some ways, brought a deeper pain. Instead of reliving the count's cruelty last night, she had remembered Mr. Darcy's tenderness.

"I love you, Elizabeth Bennet. I think I loved you from the first moment I saw you.

"I swear that only the grace of God allowed me to catch sight of a slip of a girl with ebony eyes and a head full of chocolate curls from the corner of my eye. When your eyes locked with mine, it felt as if a fire ignited. Did you feel it as well?

"Of a truth, from the moment I saw you, Elizabeth, I was drawn like a moth to a flame, and it frightened me. I had been hiding behind this mask for so long...

"If you remember Pemberley, you will remember how much I love you.

"I will spend the rest of my life loving you, if only you will stay with me. Please, Elizabeth."

Elizabeth was completely astonished. Amazed. She pinched her arm and flinched at the reassurance that she was truly awake. It was not comforting. Not only had she remembered his affectionate words, but her recollection had summoned a rush of love—tender feelings so profound that she felt embarrassed by them even now, though she was alone. Had she been responding to his embraces, his kisses, in this manner all along?

The bittersweet memories faded quickly and an image of Stefano came to mind. Tears filled her eyes at the thought of the last time she had been in *his* arms. He had forced her into an embrace, kissing her brutally, then held her at arm's length and slapped her. Issuing his usual threat of death if she left him, he had quitted the room, locking the door. Stefano's cruel, sadistic nature and threats left no doubt that she and those she loved would never be safe as long as he lived. Shivering, Elizabeth wrapped her arms around herself.

This can never be! How Fitzwilliam feels about me does not matter. I will never be anything but an encumbrance—a liability. He has shouldered my problems when it is not his place, and he deserves what Georgiana spoke of—a wife and children. I will apologise for my actions and then find a place to go. I cannot stay here.

A fleeting recollection of Fitzwilliam's lips sliding softly across her forehead, the smell of his sandalwood cologne and his hands smoothing over her back, made her close her eyes and breathe deeply, willing herself not to sob. *How can I abandon such a love?* She sighed. *You will, because you must.*

Having no strength left to face him straight away, the rest of the day was spent in her room—using a headache as the perfect excuse for her absence. Mrs. Drury kept her company for the first part of the day, but the evening found her alone on the balcony. Just as the shadows began to lengthen signalling the beginning of darkness, she caught sight of a lone figure approaching from the direction of the stables—his unusual height and noble bearing proof of his identity. Her heart began to beat faster, and she could not draw her gaze away from his long strides. She found herself cursing the darkness because it hid his beloved features from her, and an unfamiliar ache deep within reminded her of what she had learned only this morning. *He loves me as I love him.*

Nonetheless, even though she longed to see him, Elizabeth was determined not to act upon that desire. For now, it was better that she waited until she could face him without giving away her feelings. He would never know that she had remembered *Pemberley*.

The Study

After the first paragraph, William eyed the letter with suspicion. Though it seemed to have been written by Charles, splotches and all, there was something about the handwriting and wording that made him uneasy. Charles' usual straightforward manner had been replaced by a decidedly feminine approach. Never in all their years had Charles written of new furnishings, even if they were for his expected child's room. It was as though the first paragraph was to convince him that this letter was indeed from Netherfield.

William fingers slid over his chin in agitation, a niggling doubt now turning into outright disbelief as he read the next part. The paragraph regarding Miss Elise was not logical. Why would Charles ask when Miss Elise would be returning to her home and imply that he would love an invitation whenever she departed?

This letter was not written by Charles. He sat up straight, his brow knit. *Could Caroline be at Netherfield?*

It was evident that the author wanted him to issue an invitation to Pemberley, which pointed to Caroline. But how would she have known the name they used to refer to Elizabeth? Had she been reading Charles' correspondence?

Immediately, William took pen and paper, composing a letter to the Bingleys. He would enclose this missive. If indeed this letter was not from Charles, then someone else knew of their plan.

God forbid Caroline has found out about Elizabeth!

London
A Townhouse
Grosvenor Square

Wickham felt like a lowly servant as he waited, hat in hand, to see Count Stefano. The butler was not there to take his coat or hat, and even the maid who let him in had not offered to perform this most basic courtesy, turning up her nose as if in disgust. None of the servants, foreigners all, were civil to him. He would not have bothered to come at all if he had not lost all that he had accumulated in the last three months on one badly played hand in a card game.

Wickham could hear men shouting as he entered the house, and it had not subsided as he waited. He tried, but could not make out the words. Finally, the heavy doors to the parlour flew open and a well-groomed, older gentleman stormed out, marching towards the front door, without bothering to acknowledge him.

He watched in fascination as the man cleared the front door so quickly that he left it wide open and trotted down the steps to his waiting carriage. Being someone who envied the wealthy, Wickham noted that the waiting carriage was expensive, and the number of footmen suggested that the gentleman could well afford such luxury. Wickham was staring after him still when the count's voice rang out from behind.

"Are you going to stand there and stare, or do you have business with me?" Wickham whirled about, speechless, and the count smirked at his discomposure.

"My father, Frederick Warren Stanton, Earl of Essex," Stefano gestured towards the departing man. "It is too bad he only had the time required to make another demand, or I could have introduced you."

Since no servants had appeared, the count moved to close the door while Wickham considered what he had learned. Knowing that he really should not ask, he nevertheless enquired, "Another demand?"

"He demands that I leave his *beloved* England and my dissolute ways behind!" The count laughed menacingly.

Softening only a bit, he continued, "I suppose he still cares enough to warn me that the Earl of Matlock may have figured out the puzzle of my many aliases, and it will not take him long to realise that I have returned to London. I should never have bothered with that de Bourgh woman."

He fixed his glare on Wickham. "Remember, not all women are worth the things you steal from them."

Wickham's interest picked up considerably at the mention of Darcy's uncle and cousin, not to mention the intriguing remark about his many names. But he barely had time to consider those things before Stefano turned around, heading in the direction of his study.

He called over his shoulder. "Come! I have work to do and only a short time to spare for your concerns."

Reaching the room, he threw the door open and strode to the large mahogany desk, dropping wearily into his chair and propping his feet on the edge. "Now, what was it that necessitated your unexpected visit to my home today?"

Having followed him hurriedly, Wickham took the chair in front, barely seating himself before blurting out, "I have uncovered news of your wife." At the count's scowl, he added, "I believe it to be credible!"

He watched eagerly as Stefano's feet hit the floor, and he leaned forward across his desk, his eyes narrowing. Wickham knew he had his full attention. "My sources say there is talk she did not die in the fire but was spirited away and could possibly be residing at her sister's house."

"Which sister?"

Wickham almost stuttered in his haste. "Jane Bennet—Jane Bingley, I mean."

Stefano frowned, waving his hand as if dismissing the idea. "She lives in Meryton. My man specifically checked with her mother in that town. She firmly believes Elizabeth to be dead. If she were alive and tried to hide there, her mother would find out and pass the information to me."

"Her mother?"

Stefano's face became as hard as stone. "You are never to repeat any of this conversation. If my relationship with Mrs. Bennet should ever be ..." His voice trailed off, and his thoughts seemed to be in another place.

Almost immediately he recovered. "Nevertheless, I shall send my man to reassess your information. If anyone would dare to keep Elizabeth from me, it would be her sister Jane."

"But why would—"

Wickham's enquiry was interrupted. "Silence. You ask too many questions. I advise you of all you need to know."

Wickham's confusion made the count smile. "Let us just say that **Mrs.** Bennet was a great friend to me, whereas **Jane** Bennet, or whatever her name is now, was not."

Pemberley
William's dressing room

Nervously straightening his cravat, William addressed himself in the mirror. *It is past time. Just do it.*

Today, he would offer an olive branch and pray Elizabeth would take it. He was not willing to live the rest of his life trying to avoid the only other occupant of his home. She could spend her time alone, if she wished, but at least they could be cordial to one another when they met. Perhaps, if she became comfortable, she might even leave the confines of her room. It would especially please him if she availed herself of the library as he knew her to be an avid reader. Thus, cautiously he made his way down the hall to the door to the sitting area, adjacent to her bedroom.

Taking a deep breath, he lifted one hand, prayed for success, then knocked. Immediately the summons was issued. "Come in."

The voice was Elizabeth's, not that of her companion, and for a brief second, he considered the impropriety of entering her room. Thinking on all that had happened before, he dismissed it and opened the door. His gaze was immediately drawn to the window seat where she sat, knees drawn up to her chest, the tips of her blue slippers visible under the edge of her gown. A book was propped upon her knees. Immediately, she moved to sit properly, placing her feet on the floor and smoothing her skirts. Her cheeks turned a lovely shade of pink.

"Please excuse me, Mr. Darcy. I thought you were Mrs. Drury," she murmured softly, laying the book in her lap, and then studying him curiously. Instantly, all thoughts of his planned address deserted him.

"I ... Miss Elizabeth." He swallowed hard, trying to think of what he wanted to say as all he could think of was how lovely she looked at that moment. "I apologise if my presence disturbs you."

"No."

"No?" he repeated.

"Your presence does not disturb me, sir. I have wished to speak to you since your return." At his look of astonishment, she smiled slightly as she explained, "To apologise for my behaviour ... my refusal to see you, but frankly, I have had no luck locating you."

The corners of his mouth started to lift, and a great sadness welled up inside of Elizabeth. For the first time since gaining control of her faculties, she saw him as he truly was—no longer the young man of Kent. The grey in his hair and lines on his face spoke to her of heavy burdens and, perhaps, sorrow. Even as he tried to smile, his mien uncertain, she could barely hold back the tears that filled her eyes at the tenderness she beheld in his.

"Please." He stepped closer. "Do not trouble yourself for my sake as you owe me no apology. If anything, I should apologise to you. I swore to keep you safe, but you were subject to even more distress while a guest in my home."

She did not trust herself to speak without crying, so she remained silent as he continued. "I would never wish to cause you further discomfort. I know you requested to be left alone, but ..." He tilted his head, and he looked so childlike that her heart ached for him. "I had hoped you might change your mind and join me for dinner." After a moment, he added tentatively, "Tonight."

"Yes," she whispered, wondering if she could swallow anything with the huge lump in her throat.

Now, he smiled widely, and to his delight, she returned it. "Mrs. Reynolds has sent word that dinner has been prepared. If you should desire to change—"

Elizabeth stood. "There is no need. I am ready."

As she placed the book she was holding on the nearby table and slowly walked towards him, her eyes locked with his and William's heart began to pound. He held out his arm, and he barely felt her place a delicate hand upon it. Then, without words, they quitted the room side-by-side and wordlessly headed towards the grand staircase.

As the handsome couple descended the stairs, Mrs. Reynolds and Mr. Walker stood talking in the foyer and both immediately hushed and moved to their posts—she at the end of the steps and he just a little further away..

The housekeeper nodded to Mr. Darcy and smiled at Elizabeth as they reached the bottom. "I took the liberty of having the staff set the table for two."

William tried to sound unaffected as he led his heart's desire forward, but he could not suppress a smile as he replied, "Thank you, Mrs. Reynolds. You are most efficient."

Entering the exquisitely decorated dining room, resplendent with mahogany furniture, fine linens, mirrored walls and a king's ransom in crystal and silverware, William watched Elizabeth surreptitiously, delighting in the look of wonder on her face. Her eyes widened at the opulence, and she turned completely around in a circle, before coming to a stop facing him and colouring. As though her inspection were the most natural thing in the world, he proceeded to seat her on his right, taking his place at the head of the table as the first course was being brought in. Shyly, he glanced at her and smiled slightly, and Elizabeth reassured him by returning it with one of her own.

Even so, her mind rebelled against the pull of her heart. This lovely, magical place could never be her home and even as she gloried in the fact that he had smiled just for her, it screamed out a warning. *Leave now before you are in too deeply.*

Netherfield
The parlour

Caroline was near to screaming. She pulled her head back so that she could look down her nose at the other occupants of the room, taking aim at Jane's mother. *If she says one more thing about her nerves!*

Mrs. Bennet had indeed come again to see her daughter and grandchild, dragging her other offspring with her, just as she promised. Unfortunately for Mrs. Bennet, Jane was still not feeling well and hardly attempted to entertain her family, thus leaving most of the hostessing duties to Charles' visibly irritated sister.

Caroline asked through gritted teeth, "May I offer you another piece of cake?" *Anything to silence the harridan!*

Mrs. Bennet took the proffered treat, stuffing it into her mouth, and began to speak before fully chewing and swallowing. This made Caroline more nauseated than was her usual wont when faced with the Bennets' company, and she turned away.

"I came specifically to see Peter!" the older woman declared, putting a finger into her mouth to lick the frosting off. "Oh, where is the dear boy?"

Jane wanted to say that she was keeping the boy hidden. Peter was scared to death of her mother's raucous exclamations of affection and would invariably issue a piercing scream whenever she tried to hold him. Instead, Jane held her tongue. On her mother's last visit, she had claimed that Peter suffered with an earache. Now she was faced with choosing a different malady.

"Peter is sleeping, Mama. He was up all night with a stomach ache, and I prefer that he rest. I am sorry that you came so far."

"Far? Nonsense! We are but two miles apart. Besides, if you would use the remedies I have recommended, he would never suffer stomach ailments. But do you listen to me? No!"

Her eyes narrowed at her eldest as though she was beginning to wonder if Jane did not want her to see the boy. She exclaimed resolutely, "Well, if he is sleeping, I shall just have to continue to come often until I find him awake!"

Caroline groaned audibly, catching the attention of Kitty and Lydia who had been chatting without regard to the others since their arrival. The youngest Bennets collapsed in laughter, and none of Mrs. Bennet's pleadings could force them to explain the source of their amusement. During it all, Jane threw an exasperated glance at Caroline, who just shrugged.

"Mama, please wait until Sunday. We are to join you for dinner, and I am sure Peter will be well by then."

Mrs. Bennet huffed but did not reply, instead, standing to depart. Everyone else stood, and they all made their way towards the door. Lydia and Kitty managed to go through ahead of their mother, running down the steps and shouting for her to hurry or the shops would close before their arrival. Mrs. Bennet, however, stayed resolute at the door, staring at Jane. Finally, Jane reached into the pocket sewn into her dress and retrieved a few coins, looking back to see if Caroline was watching. Glad for the departure of the meddlesome Bennets, Charles' sister had stayed behind in the parlour.

As discreetly as possible, Jane dropped the coins into Mrs. Bennet's waiting hand, and the older woman pulled it back to examine the contents. A pleased look covered her face, and she smiled. "You take such good care of your poor mother."

She leaned in to give Jane a kiss, but Jane swayed back slightly, and Mrs. Bennet kissed the air. "You should hurry if you are walking into Meryton, Mama."

"Yes. Yes, you are correct." Mrs. Bennet hastened down the steps. "I shall ask Mr. Phillips to have us driven home in his carriage as soon as we are done visiting Mary."

She was completely out of sight before Jane realised she still stared in the direction they had gone. Silently, Caroline had moved to stand beside her, remarking dully, "A very *unusual* woman, your mother."

"Indeed," came the reply—equally as lifeless.

Ignoring Caroline, Jane shut the door and quit the foyer, mounting the grand staircase and heading for Peter's room. How she hated it when Charles was away, and she was left to deal with his sister and her mother all by herself.

Netherfield
Later that evening

Caroline went to Charles' study earlier than was her usual habit as her brother and sister had not come down for dinner, and she assumed they had retired for the night. She was exhausted by the visit of Jane's awful family and was resigned to retire early herself, but not before checking to see if anything had come in the mail. She had become accustomed to the feeling of accomplishment she had in knowing all of the Bingleys' affairs, personal and financial. What with Jane's being indisposed lately, she had half-convinced herself that she was not meddling, but instead, keeping an eye on their shared circumstances and she felt entitled to do so.

She had no more than locked the door and sat down behind the desk, when voices in the hall outside brought her to her feet. She could hear Charles as he addressed a servant. She ran to stand behind a tall bookcase that separated a small reading area from the rest of the room. Gasping for air, she took several deep breaths in order to calm herself. Almost immediately, she heard the sound of a key, the yielding of the lock and squeak of the door. Footsteps made their way towards the desk, and the squeak of the leather chair alerted her to her brother's presence as he sank into it.

She stood ramrod straight for several minutes, trying not to faint, all the while thinking of and rejecting likely excuses to offer if she were noticed. Her mind raced, and her heart pounded so loudly in her ears, that she did not hear softer footsteps enter the room, only the sound of Jane's strained voice.

"Charles, I have been so busy I have forgotten to ask. Was there a letter from Mr. Darcy today?" Caroline's ears perked up, and she leaned closer to the shelf in an effort to hear.

"No, sweetheart, but I expect a letter any day now."

To her chagrin, Caroline still could not make out every syllable of Jane's soft reply.

"I am worried. We have not heard a thing since Lizzy regained her senses. Do you suppose she has recovered completely and knows everything—her narrow escape and our efforts to hide her?"

Caroline became rigid. *Elizabeth Bennet? But ... but she is dead!*

"Part of me prays that she has, Jane, and the other part wonders if she can handle the truth of what happened. Living with the count must have been a nightmare, and if she thinks he may still be looking for her—"

Jane interrupted. "If my sister is back to her true self, she would not wish to bring harm to anyone, especially not Mr. Darcy. It has been admirable of him to help her, but she is stubborn, and I fear she will run away from Pemberley—from us all, if only for our protection."

Caroline could hear the chair squeak as Charles stood. She prayed they were leaving, and footsteps towards the door seemed to indicate that she was saved from exposure.

"Come, sweetheart! It has been a long day, and there is no need to borrow trouble from tomorrow; we have plenty for the day. Let us save this conversation until we hear from Darcy." With those words, a door shut and there was the sound of a key turning in a lock. Knowing that she was, thankfully, alone once again, Caroline stepped from behind the shelves.

This cannot be!! Caroline's face hardened. *The cousin at Pemberley is Eliza Bennet, not Elise Lawrence, and it was all a ruse to escape her marriage?* Resolve washed across her countenance. *I...I shall go to Pemberley and—no! Mr. Darcy would never allow me to confront her. I shall have to destroy this harridan's plans by sharing her ruse with the world!*

She stopped abruptly. *But might that destroy Mr. Darcy, too?* Then, a slow smile crossed her face.

No! I shall paint him as the innocent party. None shall realise that he had ever known her before she appeared at his home. I shall say that her claim of kinship— being a distant cousin he had never met—was cleverly done with the help of a common acquaintance, and he was too compassionate to suspect their motives. Yes, I shall spin a believable tale.

Mr. Darcy's standing with the ton could never be jeopardised because of who he is, and what fool would fault him for being too kind-hearted? Yes, Eliza Bennet, I shall tell the world that you ran away from your husband and saw opportunity to attach yourself to Mr. Darcy. Afterward, he will have no choice but to send you away!

Caroline huffed and strolled to the desk. *And to think, my own brother has been part and parcel of this whole affair, aiding and abetting the very woman he knows I despised at first sight!*

Quite satisfied with her plan, Caroline sat back down and took out pen and paper. She would write to Sarah Beeson immediately. Hopefully she could stay with her in London until the Hursts returned for the latter part of the summer, and if not, she would try Suzanna Carlson. Surely, between the two, she could be in London shortly.

In Town, I shall be able to spread the news of Eliza's shameful behaviour.

~~~*~~~

Chapter 23

Pemberley

After seeing the destroyed animals and listening to Mr. Campbell's warning about the wolf, William had mandated that all the men at Pemberley carry arms. Likewise, he stationed guards in various sites around the grounds with the sole responsibility of watching for signs of the creature. Though he kept a pistol in the pouch on his saddle, he tried to set an example by carrying his rifle whenever he rode out. Despite the fact that it was more cumbersome, it was also much more accurate, and as he left the house that morning, he was thankful to have such a weapon. He prayed that upon completion of this mission, all his servants would be able to settle back into their customary duties.

Hesitating just before quitting the terrace, he looked towards the east—purple skies were fading and the line of trees was black against the glow of the rising sun. Pemberley in the morning never failed to inspire. Then he did something he had done seldom since his return from Ireland, he paused a moment to truly take in the beauty of his home—the bucolic scene brought to mind the landscape his father had commissioned and which now resided on the wall of his study. Suddenly an unbidden smile broke across his face at the realisation that neither the beauty of the day nor his property was the cause of his contentment.

During the last few weeks, he had felt the stirrings of something he had given up hope of ever experiencing again—unadulterated joy. The presence of Elizabeth in his home was intoxicating, but he scarcely allowed himself to dwell on it. She would dine with him, and occasionally he could talk her into staying in the library when she came searching for a book. Nonetheless, she was more apt to accept his company if Georgiana was there.

Her daily walks around the lake were undertaken alone or with Mrs. Drury, though neither knew that two armed servants, just out of sight, accompanied every outing. Though he had broached the subject of showing her the grounds himself on one occasion, she had politely refused. The excuse she had given was quickly forgotten, though not the wound to his heart at her refusal. It was clearly evident that she wanted to keep a certain distance between them, and as much as he ached to be near her, he tried to respect her wishes.

By then William had walked as far as the stables and the sight of his men, mounted and waiting, quickly dispelled the warm feelings that had spread through him at the thought of Elizabeth. Of necessity, he began to focus on the task at hand—helping to rid the area of the wolf. When he had warned his neighbours about the animal earlier, he had pledged his support in pursuit of the creature, should they decided to ban together to dispatch it.

The number of livestock killed at Pemberley had dwindled in the week after the discovery of the cow and calf and then stopped altogether. The week after that, the killings began at the estate north of Pemberley and days later, at the estate north of that. Mr. Campbell was of the opinion that the rogue was migrating back to its natural habitat in Scotland. When a request came from his neighbours in the northernmost section of Derbyshire to join a hunting party, William consented. Deciding that he, along with Mr. Campbell and every man at Pemberley competent with a weapon, would join the quest to scour the countryside, he hoped that the sheer number involved would assure success.

After determining that everyone was armed and ready, William mounted Onyx and steered him towards the path that led to the front driveway and the others followed. Now that he was on his way, he could not keep his thoughts from drifting to his sister's visit that day. It was disappointing to know that as long as Georgiana was there, he could have spent the day with Elizabeth. She never objected to his company when his sister was a member of their party. Sighing heavily, he kicked Onyx into a canter.

The sooner we get started, the sooner I shall return.

The Conservatory

"I would love to have a picnic," Elizabeth proclaimed, forcing a smile as she rolled the ball to Millie. She and Georgiana had been playing with the child in the conservatory all morning, but she so longed to be out of doors. Especially, since it was a warm, gloriously sunny day.

If she were honest, she had to admit feeling gloomy since Fitzwilliam had left early that morning to take part in the hunt for the beast that had been terrorising the county. Watching him meet the others from the vantage point of her balcony, she had taken pains not to be seen observing him. At one point in his walk to the stables, he had paused and turned to stare in the direction of her balcony, and it had necessitated a quick step into the shadows lingering near the walls.

Nevertheless, after he mounted his horse and departed, a deep insecurity had engulfed her. Though he might spend the day in his study or in the library, while she made sure to be elsewhere in the house, the knowledge that they were under the same roof always gave her peace. And, peace was something she had enjoyed little of since her father's passing.

"I realise your brother is not here to ask, but do you suppose he would mind terribly? He has insisted we stay close to the house for weeks now."

A fit of giggles from Georgiana answered Elizabeth's question. "Mind? I assure you that if he were here for us to ask, he would find some reason to mind. He is very protective."

Elizabeth laughed. "Why do I feel that you love that about him?"

"I did not at one time," Georgiana mused soberly, then brightened with a small, mischievous grin. "I am afraid I gave my poor brother cause to worry for many years."

At Elizabeth's quizzical brow, she explained. "I was used to doing everything with him, conducting myself almost like a boy instead of a girl—catching frogs, swimming, riding recklessly across the meadows. When the time came that I had to start behaving as a *proper* young lady ... well, let me just say that I was not happy!"

She shook her head, remembering their arguments. "As my brother, and practically my father as well, he admonished me to act like a lady, lest I get hurt. As I matured, he included protecting me from everything else under the sun, including would-be suitors. I resented him very much. I felt as though I could take care of myself!

"It was not until my eighteenth year that a friend of mine, Miss Garret, mentioned to me how much she would love to have an older brother to protect her—someone like Brother. You see, she too lost both her parents at an early age and had only an elderly aunt to rely upon. If not for the intervention of a caring family friend, she would have been involved in a scandal involving an unscrupulous suitor, and her words certainly made me see my brother in a different light. For once in my life, I realised that he was not trying to be dictatorial, but he was trying to protect me because he loved me."

She giggled. "So, just remember, when he is domineering or tells you stories about tragedies that happened because someone would not listen, it is only because he cares for you."

"I have heard some of his tales."

William's sister laughed aloud now. "He has lots of them and will, no doubt, use that ploy for the rest of your life to keep you safe."

Elizabeth's smile faded, though Georgiana did not notice. Her words about *the rest of your life* brought home the bittersweet truth that Elizabeth would not be at Pemberley for much longer. Forcing herself not to dwell on it, she grinned, a trace of naughtiness in her eyes.

"So, we should be on our way before this domineering, fierce protector returns and forbids our picnic?"

Georgiana smirked, "Precisely!" Then she wavered. "Perhaps we should not go out of the house until William returns. After all, most of the men are with him, and the wolf has not been destroyed yet."

"I overheard him as he told Mr. Walker that the beast has moved further north, and they think it is heading back to Scotland." Elizabeth tilted her head and pouted. "Please! I am so tired of being in this house!"

Georgiana pondered the situation for just a moment, before rolling the ball back to her child. "If you will watch Miss Millie, I shall find Mrs. Reynolds and arrange for a basket of goodies, as well as blankets to sit on—oh, and for the phaeton to be readied. The ponies are easily handled, and we shall only go as far as the other side of the lake."

Georgiana vacated the room while Millie took her place in front of Elizabeth, red ball in hand.

"Eee Lee ... ball!" Millie declared, using her version of Elizabeth's name. Drawing the beautiful, tousled-haired girl into a tight hug before setting her back on her feet, Elizabeth took the offered treasure.

"Yes, darling. You have a bright, red ball. Watch it bounce across the room." Elizabeth made it skip across the wide, open area, and Millie ran after it, giggling the entire time.

~~~*~~~

The air was beginning to cool as the sun sank lower in the sky, and it was tempting to stay a little while longer. Having eaten hours before, Elizabeth and Georgiana were lying about on the blankets spread on the grass. Millie lay between them, asleep, and occasionally Georgiana would brush from her eyes the one stray curl that the wind would just not leave alone.

Various birds, having gotten their energy back with the lower temperatures, were now flitting back and forth from tree to tree in vigorous pursuit of each other, and Elizabeth was enjoying watching them as she lay on her back.

"It is so peaceful here," she sighed, rolling on her side and propping on one elbow.

Her gaze drifted to a small family of ducks playing in the pond that fed into the larger lake. The pond was situated just below a gentle waterfall that cascaded down a rocky slope. Overhead there were numerous outcroppings of large flat rocks that baked in the sun, but the little oasis below them was lined with large shade trees that offered a cool place to have their picnic and rest. To the right, a large meadow covered with all manner of wildflowers stretched as far as the eye could see.

"Yes, I barely remember it, as I was just a little older than Millie the first time I came here with my family. That was not many years before Mama ..." As Georgiana faltered, Elizabeth reached to squeeze her hand. Georgiana took a deep breath and nodded. They had developed a natural affinity, and words were not needed to communicate.

Elizabeth changed the subject. "It warms my heart to see Millie so happy, so loved."

Georgiana smiled as she turned to look at her child. "My heart aches with love for her, and I want to give her everything she could possibly desire. Evan and I could not love her any more if she had been born to us."

"So, when will your husband return?" The question brought a fleeting expression of sorrow that was not lost on Elizabeth.

"I am sorry. I should not have mentioned—"

"No, it is a perfectly normal thing to ask." Georgina interrupted. "Ignore my melancholy."

Elizabeth smiled wanly. "I will, if you ignore mine."

Georgiana nodded; Elizabeth's subdued manner that day had not gone unnoticed. It was evident that she missed Fitzwilliam, and that had been a primary motivation for Georgiana to arrange the picnic.

"To answer your question, Evan expects to be gone two more days. By then, his late father's wife should be settled in her new home, and he can return." She sighed heavily. "I do not understand it. I am not a weak person in any sense of the word, but I feel like such a child when he is gone. I feel lost."

Elizabeth reached to take her hand. "You love him very much ... that is all. It is only right that you should feel an emptiness when you are apart." Then staring into space as though seeing something Georgiana could not, she continued, "It is a void that no other person can fill."

"You understand me so completely." Georgiana sighed, and then sobered as she watched her companion divert her eyes to the distant hills in order to hide her tears.

Though the tears did not fall, Elizabeth's demeanour spoke of anguish. It was at that moment that Georgiana recognised the impossible struggle this woman was going through—that Elizabeth loved her brother as deeply as she loved her husband. Never had she looked at the relationship from that standpoint. She had only prayed that Fitzwilliam would overcome his love for the young woman in order to live a normal life, without considering how devastating all of this must be to Elizabeth.

Now it was Georgiana's turn to comfort. Using one finger, she touched Elizabeth's chin, directing the teary eyes back to hers.

187

"You share the same feelings for my brother—I know. You feel the void, too, even when he is away only for the day."

It was not a question, and Elizabeth examined Fitzwilliam's sister for a long time before speaking. Clearly, she no longer feared being completely honest with her, and she trusted the truth would go no further.

"I ... I have missed him, longed for him." Shaking her head as though doing so would rid her of the lump in her throat, she finished hoarsely. "By the time I returned to Hertfordshire from our encounter in Kent, I realised how foolish I had been, letting my pride overrule my heart. I recognised that I had rejected a man that I actually loved. Later, when the count ..." She breathed raggedly, waiting until she could master her voice. "I realised that Fitzwilliam was lost to me forever, and I wanted to die."

She met Georgiana's shocked look. "I was too much of a coward to do anything like that, but thereafter I lived with this ... this ..." She struggled for the words. "What do I call it? Ache? Relentless pain? There are simply no words dreadful enough to say how much I regretted him."

Georgiana moved to slide an arm around Elizabeth's shoulder. "And now that you are here?"

"It is unbearable to be near him but not *with* him. It is a sweet torture."

"Oh, Elizabeth. I am so sorry. Until now, I never really understood how deeply you love him."

Just then the ponies began to whinny, jerking their heads up, as if trying to break free from the reins that secured them to a nearby tree. Georgiana sat up. Something was not right.

"I shall check on the ponies," she stated as calmly as possible, reaching into a bag she had laid on the blanket to retrieve her pistol.

Seeing Georgiana retrieve the pistol brought Elizabeth up to a sitting position—alert. She cast a wary eye around the pastoral scene, before her eyes came back to rest on Millie, who was sleeping soundly. All of a sudden, the ponies broke free of their restraints and began to run, dragging the phaeton with them. Georgiana stared after them in shock, not realizing the reason for their flight. Twirling about, she froze. On the large rock just above Elizabeth and Mille, sat a huge, dark gray animal with its teeth bared. The waning daylight showcased the eerie yellow eyes that met hers, and her heart stopped. The wolf!

Seeing the alarm on Georgiana's face, Elizabeth turned slowly, her heart lurching as she locked eyes with the monster above her and Millie. It growled menacingly, moving closer to the end of the rock, preparing to jump. Georgiana began crying and running towards them, as Elizabeth instinctively rolled over to cover Millie with her body. The creature jumped just as Georgiana fired a shot, and it yelped in pain. But the wound she inflicted only served to make him land awkwardly before regaining his footing.

Back upon all fours in an instant, he leapt towards Elizabeth who hid her face in the blanket and screamed. Just as Georgiana leaned down to grab a fallen limb for a weapon, the crack of a rifle rang out. The shot brought her to a standstill, and before she could turn, William rushed past her. Brought out of her stupor by his appearance, she resumed her run towards her child, still holding the makeshift weapon and beginning to weep.

William reached Elizabeth first, leaning down to pull the dead beast away, and then kneeling with a strangled cry, "Elizabeth!"

As he rolled her over and off Millie, the child began to wail, frightened by being awakened so violently. Georgiana, trying to control her sobs, tossed the stick and reached down to pick up Millie. Sheltering the child in her embrace, Georgiana stepped a short distance away, continuing to comfort the girl as she watched her brother frantically checking Elizabeth for wounds. Her heart began to ache at the amount of blood now visible. Surely, that did not bode well.

There had been copious amounts of blood down the back of Elizabeth's gown, whether from the wolf or from wounds to her, William could not tell. When he turned her over, his hands began moving over her body in what would have been a scandalous display of impropriety had Georgiana not been the only witness. As it was, he halfway feared that the bullet that felled the wolf might have passed through the animal into her, but she appeared unscathed. He found no evidence of wounds except for the now rapid dampening of her sleeves. Tearing the flayed cloth away, his eyes involuntarily filled with tears at the bloody scratches covering her arms.

"Oh, sweetheart!" The absolute despair in William's voice, as he began undoing his cravat and ripping it into bandages, brought Elizabeth back to her senses. Seeing the silent tears sliding down his cheeks as he wrapped her arms, her heart broke, and as he finished, she reached up to cup his face with both hands.

"Fitzwilliam, look at me!" He obeyed, misery etched on his face. "I am not seriously injured. I have only these scratches. You have saved us."

For a moment, he seemed not to understand, still staring with a troubled mien, but all at once he did something that he had longed to do since discovering her again at Netherfield. Claiming her mouth, he kissed her thoroughly, deeply, unabashedly, endlessly. Knowing it was futile to try and resist, Elizabeth returned his kiss with equal passion, the strength of her love at that moment so overwhelming that she lost all ability to reason.

Georgiana walked away to give them privacy, the tender scene bringing even more tears. Whispering soothing words to Millie, she headed in the direction of the phaeton, which had stopped just past the pond, one wheel hung over a downed log, stopping their retreat. In the distance she caught sight of Mr. Campbell coming towards them as fast as his old mare could trot.

~~~*~~~

The trip back to the house seemed to take forever, and on the last two hundred yards, William galloped on ahead so he could send a footman after the physician. By the time the phaeton turned the last curve to the front portico, numerous servants were waiting alongside the master to help the women into the house. One long-time footman had seen the look on William's face, as well as the blood on his clothes, as he rode towards the front door and had immediately set out after Mr. Woodwright.

Mrs. Reynolds had descended the front steps as quickly as the front door was opened, and upon seeing the upheaval, began issuing orders. Even as William passed her with Elizabeth in his arms, taking the steps two at a time, she was right behind him and reaching for her bag of remedies from a maid hurrying towards her. Georgiana trailed after her brother but stopped to hand Millie to her nurse, Mrs. Calvert, who had heard the commotion and had hurried to the foyer.

Way ahead of the others, William reached the open door to Elizabeth's sitting area, walked inside and having no patience, kicked the partially open bedchamber door back to enter it. Heading straight to the bed, he laid her gently on the counterpane against her protestations that she would get it dirty. Without saying a word, he sat on the edge and began unwrapping his makeshift bandages in order for Mrs. Reynolds to apply some of her remedies to the scratches. He had had little time to examine the wounds at the pond and as the bandages came off, he flinched. Swallowing hard, he realised that a few were much deeper than he had first believed and began to worry that they might become infected.

Elizabeth inspected William with fascination. He was so completely focused on her injuries that he was not paying any attention to her, not even answering her complaint that she would bleed on the beautiful counterpane. Finally, he stopped long enough to notice her watching him. There was a strange look in his eyes as he leaned in to softly kiss her forehead, both eyes, then the tip of her nose.

"I love you, Elizabeth," he breathed into her ear before capturing her lips at last. They were lost in the kiss when Mrs. Reynolds arrived, having come through the sitting room. She respectfully turned and walked back into that room without making a sound. Unfortunately, Georgiana had not come from that direction and the bedchamber door flew open, causing them to fly apart.

"Oh, Brother, are her wounds very deep?" Hurrying closer, she could barely see Elizabeth's face over his shoulder so she ran to the other side of the bed, taking a seat on the edge. "Are you well, Elizabeth?"

Though her mind was still on William's kisses and his declaration of love, Elizabeth managed to answer. "Thanks to you, I will be." She sought William's eyes and a sharp pain pierced her heart at the look of love on his face. "And your brother."

Georgiana began to sob. "No. I had no part in your rescue. I could not have stopped that creature with just my pistol. I am so sorry that I put us in harm's way." She kept chattering nervously. "I believed the wolf had returned to the north, but I should not have taken the chance."

Elizabeth shushed her. "Please, do not blame yourself. I begged you for the picnic, so it is my fault."

William interrupted. "No! Everything is my fault. I took most of our men to Lord Burton's estate. I was too confident the beast had moved north, and we were just fortunate that Mr. Campbell discovered footprints showing that the wolf had backtracked and was returning to Pemberley. I pushed Onyx to the limit to get home. Finding that you had taken the phaeton out, I tracked you, albeit almost too late to rescue you. Can you both forgive me?"

Elizabeth caught his hand, bringing it to her lips and kissing the back of it. "You have always been swift to take the blame when you have done nothing to warrant it. Your quick actions saved us. Let us speak no more about it."

Just then, Mr. Woodwright, the physician came rushing through the door, followed by Mrs. Reynolds. Glancing between the furrowed brow of Mr. Darcy and the apprehension on Miss Elizabeth's face, he resolved to lighten the atmosphere.

"Well, well, Miss Elizabeth," he jested, "it seems you cannot stay out of trouble."

Elizabeth tried to smile bravely. "So I have been told most of my life, sir."

~~~*~~~

Chapter 24

London
The Beeson Residence

The dinner party was quite large, and Caroline Bingley had high hopes of turning a few heads after she had accomplished what she came for—spreading the gossip about Eliza. Sarah Beeson, an acquaintance from Mrs. Latimer's School, had granted her request to host her in London but it came with a price. She had insisted that Caroline and a number of their schoolmates attend her Grandfather Beeson's birthday celebration and ball, and make themselves available to dance with the men who would be present. Caroline had not been anticipating this soiree with delight.

"Thank you for the invitation to stay with you, Sarah!" Caroline declared with false sincerity, grabbing her friend's hand as they lead the parade back to the music room after dinner. As they slowly moved forward with the crowd, she justified their relationship. *At least the home is elegant, even if the occupants are not*, she mused, taking in the large bevelled crystal chandeliers, numerous gilded mirrors, dark mahogany tables, imported Persian rugs and other expensive furnishings.

While it was true that Mr. Beeson was in trade, a connection Caroline normally avoided whenever possible, they were wealthy. And after all, Mrs. Beeson's grandfather had been an earl and she was accepted among some factions of the *ton*, which in itself redeemed the family somewhat. Otherwise, Caroline would never have considered Sarah worthy of her time, as she was not fashionable, good company, or accomplished.

As she, Sarah, and their little coterie gathered in a small alcove near the open doors to the balcony, Caroline stood out in her tangerine gown, her choice of colours making all of the others look positively sickly in their pale pinks and whites. As always, she became the centre of attention in the less than stellar group and turned the conversation to her recent return from Hertfordshire seeing an opportunity to further her first priority–ruining the good name of Elizabeth Bennet.

"I do not think I could have endured one more day in Meryton," she said, waiting until all eyes fixed on her to continue. "There is no refined society in that awful wasteland. My brother's child whines constantly, and his wife is a shrew who ignores me completely—which is the only good thing I can say about her. As I have said many times before, she brought nothing to the marriage—no dowry, no connections. I cannot abide that Charles has forced me to associate with her and her equally appalling family."

Suzanna Carlson, another tradesman's daughter, wrinkled her nose in a look of contempt. "From what you have said, Caroline, they are people of the lowest sort. Why ever did your brother condescend to marry someone with such a family and no dowry, especially when he could have done so much better?" Left unsaid was the fact that she herself had chased Charles Bingley for over a year, but he had never given her so much as a sideways glance. Truth be known, not only was Miss Carlson very plain, but her disposition was too much like his sister's for Charles to be tempted.

"Two words, Suzanna," Caroline opined. Everyone quieted, anticipation building as they awaited the pronouncement.

"*Arts* and *allurements*," she declared with absolute authority. There was much murmuring among the group as everyone nodded knowingly.

Rebecca Watley, a mousey, thin woman interjected, "Mother says many strumpets use those very things to secure decent men—the very men who should have been courting *me!*" Her voice got higher as she became more flustered, waving her hands about. "I mean *us*—but for the temptations offered by these trollops, I might have been married already."

There was another round of mumbled agreement from the unattractive band, each now convinced that they were likely the victims of such women since they were unmarried.

"And that, ladies, is the very reason that I have hurried to London," Caroline trumpeted. Eyebrows rose in unison, as ears perked up again. "It is my Christian duty to warn a good and decent man of my acquaintance of a similar scheme being perpetrated against him at this very moment by a deceitful woman." She was very pleased to see eyes widen and mouths hang open in expectancy.

"Do tell us who, Caroline." Sarah whined. Caroline never understood Sarah's penchant for whining instead of speaking clearly as it always made her skin crawl. But she forgave the whining in this instance, since the high pitch of Sarah's voice drew everyone's attention.

Throwing her head back in righteous indignation, Caroline peered down her nose, as her eyes circled the group. "I expect you to keep this our little secret," she warned at full volume, knowing full well they would do as she wished and shout it to the heavens. "I intend to warn Mr. Fitzwilliam Darcy."

A chorus of gasps pierced the air.

"Fitzwilliam Darcy?" Marjorie Simonds lamented, almost moaning his name. "He is so handsome. My mother said if she were just a little younger—"

"Oh hush, Marjorie!" Gladys Pope scolded. "We have all heard how your mother would do this and that, if she were a little younger. Let us hear what Caroline has to say about Mr. Darcy."

A worshipful look suffused Theodora Berman's face. "If you ask me, he is simply divine. I used to swoon whenever I was in his company, though he has scarcely been seen in London in years."

"I agree, Theodora. I tried to get his attention in my first season. He was the most handsome man of my acquaintance," Muriel Burnett sighed. "Do tell us, Caroline, though I cannot help but wonder if he would even heed your advice. He is very much his own man according to my father."

"I have no doubt he will listen to me as we are such good friends. I have known him for years." Caroline added purposefully, "And it is that intimate knowledge that tells me his kind heart has led him into this unfortunate circumstance."

Caroline poured her heart and soul into the tale she spun about Mr. Darcy's distant cousin, so much so, that her performance would have put to shame many an actress on the London stage. Unbeknownst to her, there were two people not of her group, listening with more than benign curiosity.

Lady Gwendolyn Waltham was near Caroline, and upon hearing Mr. Darcy's name mentioned, moved close enough to hear everything. She began to wonder. *Could it actually be true that the unattractive little woman I observed at Pemberley with Fitzwilliam was not his cousin, but an imposter who fled her husband and sought to insinuate herself at Pemberley?*

An unbidden smile appeared as she contemplated this new intelligence. In some ways, this twisted tale offered her a ray of hope. *Or perhaps Fitzwilliam knows who she is but enjoys her ... hmm ... company.* Could his staunch sense of decency and honour have developed a crack in its facade or, with any luck, a large fissure?

Gwendolyn smiled for the first time in days. *If my dear boy is going to cast propriety to the wind, then why should I not be there to catch it? Surely he did not mean to cast me aside with that whore Leighton.*

Sudden thoughts of Count Francesco came to mind. Lately, he had been preoccupied with business matters and had neglected her, leaving her to find other escorts to soirees such as this, and he was no longer showering her with jewels as he had when their acquaintance was new. The presents had been a great incentive to tolerate his attentions—well, that, and his proficiency in bed. Still, he was so sure of himself that he expected her to be available whenever he deigned to visit. A return to Derbyshire would kill two birds with one stone—warning the count that she was not one who would tolerate being taken for granted, and, if she were lucky, relighting an old flame. The time was ripe to approach the reticent Mr. Darcy again. She smirked as she passed the roomful of insignificant people on her way to the man who had escorted her, the elderly Lord Greenwich.

Fitzwilliam simply must be tired of that ugly, diminutive toy by this time. In any event, there is nothing to be gained by staying here.

Also, within range of Caroline's diatribe was George Wickham, who had stepped out on the balcony to avoid a jealous husband. The sound of the name of his old nemesis being bandied about just inside the open doors garnered his curiosity. He moved closer, being careful not to be noticed by the small band of women gossiping in the alcove.

He was surprised to see someone he recognised holding court—Charles Bingley's sister. This was a woman whom he knew had used her brother's friendship with Darcy to chase after him for years now. As he listened, she wove an illogical tale of a married woman and the heir of Pemberley. Knowing Darcy as he did, Wickham was about to dismiss the tale as a fabrication when Miss Bingley mentioned the woman's name—Elizabeth Bennet.

Was not that the maiden name of the count's wife? This Bingley woman did mention that this cousin had run away from her husband.

His interest peaked, Wickham headed straight for the door to collect his coat and hat, eager to contact his man and have him investigate this visitor to Pemberley. Knowing not to make claims that he could not irrefutably prove, he was determined to ascertain the lady's identity before confronting the count with the evidence. A wide smile split his face as he practically ran out of the house to await his carriage. Five thousand pounds would go far towards settling his expenses and putting him back in the game, and he was determined that no one would collect that reward but him.

~~~*~~~

Pemberley
The Library

The house was silent except for the footsteps of Mr. Cravets as he made his rounds, checking the doors, windows and vacant rooms. Nevertheless, this night when the footman checked the library, he was startled to find Mr. Darcy still occupying the room with only one small candle and the fireplace for light. It was obvious that the Master was not himself, from his state of undress to the strong smell of liquor saturating the air, and he was not reading a book as he normally did. Undeterred, the long-time servant added more logs to the fire and asked the Master if he could perform any service for him. Summarily dismissed, he bowed slightly before slipping back into the hall leaving Mr. Darcy alone.

After an hour of tossing and turning, William had come downstairs clad in the clothes he had donned after getting out of bed—a shirt, which he had not taken time to button, and breeches. It was late, and he presumed no one would be awake to see him retrieve a bottle of imported brandy from the liquor cabinet. It seemed the only solution for sleep after his conversation with Georgiana. Her insistence on talking before they went to bed meant a sleepless night for him, as their conversation played over and over in his head.

"Brother, may I speak to you for a moment?"

William's brows raised in question. Something about the way she held herself made him wary. He was not sure that he could handle another difficulty after today's episode with the wolf.

"We are all exhausted. Can it not wait until tomorrow?" he proffered kindly.

She took a deep breath and blew it out, but did not meet his eyes. "I would like to say this while I still have the courage."

"That sounds ominous," he tried to jest, but she did not smile.

Standing aside, he motioned his sister through the door. Once inside, she glanced about as though she had not seen his private rooms hundreds of times when she lived at home. He waited. Finally, her eyes met his, and a lump formed in his throat at the pain clearly visible in the blue depths. He had always tried hard not to hurt her.

"I know you love Miss Elizabeth. Lord knows, even I have come to care for her like a sister. But it is obvious, after what I witnessed today, that you will never be satisfied to live together as friends, and I cannot fathom how this situation can turn out well for either of you. She is married. If she stays here, it can only bring the both of you terrible heartache. Surely you know that. Would it not be better to send her to your estate in Scotland or Ireland where she would be safe from her husband but not a temptation for you?"

William took one step towards her, and Georgiana fell into his embrace, sobbing. He laid his head atop hers, and they stood like that for some time, neither speaking. Finally, almost to himself, he whispered strangled words into her hair.

"I have tried not to love her." He gathered his strength. "I have no idea what the future holds, but it must include her. I cannot live without..." He trembled, struggling for control. "Please do not ask it of me."

Georgiana cried harder, and he held her even tighter. Eventually, she quieted. Sniffling, she stepped back to wipe her eyes, then smiled wanly, kissed his cheek and opened the door. Just before going out, she offered tenderly, "You have my support, no matter what you decide. I love you, Fitzy."

He made a great effort to smile. "I love you, too, Gigi."

Once in the library, meaning to have only one brandy and leave, William became comfortably ensconced on the sofa. Watching the glowing fire, he was lost in the flickering flames and his own contemplations as he swirled the amber liquor in the glass and mulled over his resolution to stop at just one drink. Instinctively, he realised that the oblivion to be found in a bottle might destroy him. Drowning one's sorrows might provide temporary relief for manageable struggles, but with unfathomable heartaches, one ran the risk of drowning along with them. Even so, he needed the oblivion tonight—so he poured another glass and then another.

Not a half-hour after Cravets left, the candle on the table had almost burned out, leaving only the light from the fire. Soon afterward, Elizabeth quietly opened the door to the library and stealthily moved inside in search of a book, a small candle in her hand.

William held his breath at the sight. She was dressed for bed—the front of her lace trimmed, yellow silk nightgown, a present from Georgiana, clearly visible. Over her shoulders she wore an eyelet dressing gown which was loosely tied at the waist. Her hair was loose and hung down around her shoulders like a silky veil. It was obvious that she had dressed as quickly and carelessly as he. Unmindful of his presence, she promptly made her way to the wall of books and held the candle higher to peruse the titles. As she did, the sleeves of the dressing gown fell back, revealing the bandages covering her arms. A deep sorrow pierced William's heart as he wondered if her wounds were keeping her awake.

Since he was in an alcove, Elizabeth could not see him reflected in the light from the fire until she reached a certain point on the bookshelves. Suddenly, he appeared in her peripheral vision, and she turned to gasp. He was half-sitting in the corner of a sofa, his legs and bare feet spread along the length of it. His hair was dishevelled, his beard dark enough to be visible, and his clothes were clearly rumpled. Though he watched her, he said not a word.

"I ... I could not sleep," she began to mumble disjointedly. "I thought to find ..." Her eyes dropped to his open shirt, where dark hair covered his chiselled chest. She swallowed hard. "...to find a book ... something to read." She could not seem to form another sentence or gather the strength to move.

William perceived the exact moment she became aware of his state of undress, and he was mesmerized by the way her eyes widened and got even darker. Though the amount of liquor he had drunk made him unsure if he was dreaming, he stood, steadying himself. In spite of all he had consumed, he was surprisingly graceful as he walked slowly towards her.

Elizabeth followed his progress, barely remembering to breathe until he finally stood inches from her. Without breaking eye contact, he took the candle from her hand and set it on a bookshelf. Blue eyes stayed locked with brown, as he ran one hand gingerly along the arm with the least injuries, stopping before he reached her bandages. She was not a dream.

"Are you in pain? Mr. Woodwright left laudanum if you need it to sleep."

"I am not in pain at present. Between Mrs. Reynolds' herbal draughts and Mr. Woodwright's salves, it is not too painful to bear. I shun laudanum, as I do not wish to lose my wits. I have spent too much time unaware, and I will not return to that state."

William nodded absently, his gaze never wavering.

"Then why?"

"My injuries are not what robbed me of sleep tonight. You were." His eyes closed briefly in exhilaration, before opening to devour her again.

"Please, forgive me. I should never have presumed to kiss you today. It seems I only bring you pain and suffering."

"On the contrary, sir, you have been my rescuer, and though we both know it can only lead to heartache, I welcomed your kiss."

Leaning in until their foreheads met, he groaned her name. His warm, brandy-scented breath was hot against her skin, and she shivered as he pulled her into a tight embrace. In spite of the bandages, she grasped his forearms as his hands slid around her waist, pulling her as close to him as he dared. A few seconds more and he could resist no longer.

He kissed her forehead and the tip of her nose before claiming her mouth, first tentatively, then with ever increasing passion. Lost in the kiss, his hands slid down to her bottom, drawing her hips hard against his. When at last he began feathering kisses across her jaw to the spot below her ear, she found the strength to speak.

"Oh, Fitzwilliam, I love you so." Her words instantly sobered him, and he began whispering endearments as his hands moved to safer places, and he buried his face in her hair.

"My love ... my darling ... my Elizabeth." Stilling his head atop hers, he waited for his heart to stop pounding and his ardour to cool. "I love you more than life."

It was several moments before he continued. "Forgive me, sweetheart, for I am a beast. You are injured." He barely touched one bandage. "While I thought only of—"

"Shhh!" she soothed, rising on tiptoes to brush her lips softly across his. This simple act of affection gave him leave to claim her mouth once more, and they were lost as William deepened the kiss with every answering move of her tongue. It was some time before they pulled apart, both panting with desire. She let her head fall back, her loved-filled eyes meeting his half-lidded gaze. "I know it is wanton of me to say, but I desire you just as much as you desire me."

A great sadness enveloped him, and he sighed. "I fear that if I were to truly show my love for you, it would only do you more harm. You deserve to be more than my mistress."

"You could never hurt me by loving me. It is you who would suffer, for you ought to have a proper wife and children."

"And you are worthy of a true marriage! If I cannot have you—have children with you—I will never have another." He pulled her closer, clinging to her desperately. "Do not ask me to let you go, for I cannot."

Elizabeth closed her eyes, tears slipping from beneath dark lashes. "We are both lost."

He kissed the tears away, and she tried to smile. "And I thought I was strong enough to leave you—"

"No, please," he whispered as more quick kisses from her stopped his protest. She took a deep breath, caressing his face, and studying it as though trying to memorise every part.

"If I were not selfish, I would have left days ago ... for your sake and for your safety. But, God forgive me, I cannot stop wanting your love."

Suddenly she leaned back, lifting her shoulders with new confidence. "I have decided. I will be your mistress, have your children. You can send me away to your home in Scotland or Ireland—anywhere—and no one will ever know. If I stay here, it will only cause your ruin and put you in harm's way."

He clasped her so tightly that she could barely breathe. "You would be mine, bear my children, knowing we cannot marry?" She nodded against his chest, so he lifted her chin up, willing her to look at him.

Seeing the concern in his eyes, she responded, "I will have your children ... no one else's."

He kissed her then, willing everything he felt in his heart into the kiss and feeling Elizabeth's love for him as she returned it with equal fervour. As he quit the kiss, he began talking animatedly.

"I know a vicar who I believe will perform a marriage ceremony for us, though he may not be able to keep official records. I shall write to him today. Until then, I ..." His lips curved into a small smirk. "*We* must check our desires."

He crushed her to his chest again. "You have made me the happiest of men, Elizabeth. I shall never love anyone but you, my darling. In my heart, you will be my wife. I shall provide for you and our children in my will. Georgiana and Evan will know everything, along with Richard. They will take care of you and our children if anything should ever happen to me."

"Do not speak of such things!" she pleaded. "I could not live without you ever again."

"Richard should be returning to London soon and when he does we shall travel together. It will give me the chance to meet with my solicitors to add provisions in my will for you and our future children. But, you must know this, wherever you decide you want to live— my estate in Scotland or Ireland— I will live with you. I have no intention of ever being parted from you again."

This time when his mouth claimed hers, it was with more tenderness than passion. He tried not to think of his own desires, and kissing across to her ear, he whispered, "Soon, my love. Soon."

~~~*~~~

Chapter 25

Pemberley
The Balcony

T he air was crisp and breezy, and though it was still quite dark, the first faint signs of dawn were underway by the time Elizabeth walked out onto the balcony. She dearly loved to watch the sun rise over this beautiful place, so she remained there, wrapping her arms tightly about her thin dressing gown to thwart the cold. Waiting patiently for the first rays of light, she considered for the hundredth time her decision to stay—to be his. She supposed she should feel ashamed, but that feeling was not the one with which she grappled this morning.

Being with William inspired feelings unfamiliar to her—a stirring somewhere deep within. It was ever-changing...sometimes a tingling and other times a fire. Her only certainty was that once it ceased, she longed to experience it again. She had known the anguish of unrequited love, the torture of a broken heart and despair so deep it had brought her to the brink of madness, but she had known little happiness. And never, *never*, had she felt anything so consuming as her craving for him. She blushed to acknowledge her malady—it was desire, pure blissful desire.

Naturally, she also contemplated the effect she had on him. That he desired her was obvious—his body betrayed that fact every time he held her close to him. Even now, butterflies took flight in her stomach at the memory of his hardness pressed against her. But beyond the physical attraction, what she found most fulfilling was the assurance that he truly loved her...had loved her for years. She could not hold back a smile from her lips. *Fitzwilliam Darcy loves me!*

Her thoughts returned to her earlier musings. If those warm, sensual feelings were just a prelude to the act of marriage, then she was certain that to love Fitzwilliam would not be a duty to dread as her mother had always lamented to her daughters, but instead would be a pleasure to anticipate. Unbidden, the image of another bare-chested man appeared to taunt her. Closing her eyes tightly, she tried to purge Stefano's face from her thoughts. He had been cruel, insisting she respond to his kisses when she felt nothing for him save disgust, and becoming more abusive when she did not.

In contrast, she welcomed Fitzwilliam's gentleness, his touches, his kisses. Forcing her thoughts to focus on her heart's desire, a strange thing happened—she felt his presence. Eyes still tightly closed, she pictured her beloved there with her and whispered his name almost as a prayer—*"William."*

Abruptly, two muscular arms slid firmly around her, one just under her breasts, the other about her waist, pulling her solidly against his broad chest. At once sure of her captor's identity, she melted into him. Warm lips found the juncture between her neck and shoulder and quickly kissed a path to her ear, causing her to shudder. A flash of desire so strong she almost fainted shot through her. She turned to brush her cheek against the coarse surface of his woollen coat and breathed in the scent of soap and sandalwood. The aroma calmed her as effectively as a drug.

A deep voice whispered roughly in her ear, tickling the sensitive skin. "You could not see me. How is it you knew I was here?"

She sighed contentedly. "I cannot explain it, but I can sense you...your presence." He kissed the top of her head at the revelation, and had she turned her face up to his, she would have seen a look of incandescent joy on his face.

"Since you found me, it is as though something within alerts me when you are near. I can remember, even when my mind was still unclear, that I would sense you close by and turn to find you watching. It gave me such peace to know my protector was always there."

"Oh, Elizabeth!" He kissed her hair again. "I will always be your protector."

When she turned in his arms, his mouth captured hers. This kiss was not gentle, as had been their final kiss last night, but full of want—of insatiable need. Immediately, she felt the now familiar hardness against her, and the knowledge of his desire rekindled her own. She slid her arms around his waist, trying to pull him closer. His response was to unbutton his coat and pull her inside its warmth. Quickly, she unfastened his waistcoat and slid her hands over the hard planes of his chest. The heat of her small hands was like a brand through the thin cloth of his shirt and he groaned. Sliding his hands down to cup her bottom, he lifted her and slowly rubbed back and forth against her, causing her knees to buckle. Picking her up in his arms, he carried her inside and gently lay her on the bed. His eyes were dark as pitch as he sat down on the side and leaned across her.

"If you only knew how much I desire you at this moment."

He climbed onto the bed, not stopping until he lay atop her, boots and all. Rising up on his elbows, he stared into her eyes as slowly he lowered his mouth to unite with hers. The kiss was achingly slow, each touch of their hungry lips progressively harder, until powerful, deep strokes merged their mouths, and they would not be parted.

Hands, both his and hers, found places they had longed forever to caress and lingered, lost in pleasure. He pulled her dressing gown fully open, and he found generous breasts soft beneath the thin nightgown, until under his manipulation, each nipple hardened. Her hands found entrance under his shirt, and he as she explored his body, beginning at his rock hard chest, before sliding down to his abdomen.

Unconsciously, their bodies fell into a motion, a rhythm, responding to desires as ancient as the earth, though their clothing prevented complete satisfaction. It was with great effort, that William finally rolled onto his back, pulling her onto his chest, his breath coming in pants, as did hers.

His voice was hoarse. "I find myself begging your forgiveness every time we are together."

"You did not hear me object, my darling," she sympathised, raising her head to admire his handsome face as she ran a finger along his jaw. "Please do not make me feel wanton by apologising for something I clearly wanted as much as you."

He smiled. "Then I shall simply say that I am sorry to have started something I cannot finish—at least not now. I love you, Elizabeth, and I cannot wait to make love to you."

She kissed him lightly. "I cannot wait either." His countenance changed, and she wondered if she had said something upsetting.

"Sweetheart, I worry that you have been so abused by *him*. I never want you to feel that I would use you or discard you, or ever harm you, or—"

A finger to his lips silenced him. "I have no such thoughts. You are *nothing* like him. When I rejected your offer, you fled England because you could not have me. When I rejected him, he took me by force." At the wretchedness etched on William's face, she continued. "It is time I told you."

"Never feel that you owe an explanation or that I require one."

"I know that I do not, and you are so kind not to ask, but if we are to be together, I must tell you. Otherwise, there will be a gulf between us, and I could not bear it."

William threaded his hands into her hair, lifting his head to place a kiss on her forehead, before dropping back to the pillow. "Then, tell me everything."

"When I said he took me by force, I was referring to the abduction." Elizabeth swallowed hard. "I was never his wife in *any* sense."

William tried not to show any surprise, focusing on keeping his breathing as normal as possible. "Do you mean he never—"

"No, though he tried to." She took a ragged breath. "I awoke in the middle of the night to find him in my bed. It only happened the one time, but he could not...he was incapable," she sputtered, blushing a deep red and diverting her eyes. "He left and never tried again, though he did force his kisses on me."

William closed his eyes and pulled her back to his chest, burying his face in her hair as the tears he could not hold back escaped the corners of his eyes.

"Oh, sweetheart, while I despise that he touched you in any way, I am so thankful you were spared."

"God must have meant for me to be only yours."

Instantly, he rolled over, trapping her beneath him, but this time he did not kiss her. Propping himself on one arm, he ran his hand gently through her hair, then began to trace along her brows, eyes, nose, jaw and eventually her lips. His eyes followed his fingers, committing each feature to memory. At last, he spoke with great purposefulness, gently raising her chin so their eyes held.

"Are you sure this is what you want...loving me, committing to me forever, having my children? You have been through so much, Elizabeth. Forced into a marriage against your will, abused, kept a virtual prisoner, your friend killed before your eyes, and your being so ill. You have borne so much pain in your short life, and God help me, I was part of it."

Shaking her head, she cried, "No!"

"Yes, I was. If I had not been so proud, so bound by duty when we met, perhaps you would have accepted my offer, and all the rest would never have happened."

"We cannot know that."

Releasing a weary breath, he rolled over on his back, staring up at the canopy. He sought one of her hands and raised it to place a loving kiss there.

"I need to know that you understand. You are free. You are no longer a prisoner. You have choices, and *you* determine your future."

She struggled to understand. "You said you would have no one if you could not have me? Do you still feel that way?"

"God knows my heart. I will never love anyone but you. If I cannot have you, I will remain single."

She sighed, closing her eyes in relief. "You have given me my freedom, and I have chosen you. Do you think that you are the only one capable of loving only one person?"

This time when he pulled her into his arms, his kisses were intense, and they were lost in a world of their own until a soft rapping on the door penetrated William's passion, bringing him back to reality.

He groaned, pulling back and apologising. "I forgot that I asked Adams to alert me when my horse had been saddled." Then he smiled adoringly at Elizabeth. "Please tell me all is resolved and we shall be together forever."

She lifted her head to brush his lips with hers. "It is settled. We shall love each other forever."

Another series of kisses and another knock on the door ensued before William slid off the bed, straightening his clothes. With regret Elizabeth watched him readying to leave. "Will you be gone all day?"

"I have many tenant problems to settle before I return, but I hope to be home in time to dine. If that is not possible, will you wait up for me?"

She slid off the bed to follow him to the door. "I would not dream of going to bed without a goodnight kiss."

He opened the door to find Adams waiting patiently and trying to look indifferent. Informing his valet that he would be down shortly, William quickly closed the door and swept her back into his arms. "Nor would I dream of leaving without this."

Bending her backward, his strong arms were the only thing keeping her from collapsing to the floor. He kissed her thoroughly, leaving her breathless before returning her upright. Still holding her tightly, he held her gaze for a long moment. "Remember, no matter what the future holds, I love you."

"As I love you."

With a squeeze of her hands, immediately he was out the door and walking down the hallway. As he reached the top of the grand staircase, her heart called out, *Look back at me.*[2]

As if in response, he turned, giving her a dimpled smile. Then he turned and hurried down the stairs, as her heart began a familiar ache.

Rosewood Manor
Morning

"Ana, have you seen my riding crop?"

Evan turned to see his wife watching him as he rifled though his closet. His smile widened. She had hardly let him out of her arms since his return from London last evening, and the gleam in her eyes signified that she was not done with him yet.

"What are you thinking, Mrs. Ingram?"

"I was thinking of waging another assault upon your person, Mr. Ingram," Georgiana purred, standing now so that her breasts were clearly visible through the thin, peach-coloured satin gown he had purchased for her in London.

Evan groaned, an arousal beginning again. "That gown should be outlawed."

Georgiana moved to stand in front of him now, sliding her hand along the rigid tent in his breeches. "You purchased the offending item."

"Oh, it does not offend me—exhausts me perhaps, but it does not offend me."

---

[2] *With a nod to Elizabeth Gaskell, North & South, my next favourite story.*

"So, are you no longer capable or willing to make love to me day and night for days on end?"

Bringing her roughly to his chest, he murmured into her hair, "Oh, I am quite capable and willing, if that is what you desire, but the estate may go to ruin while I am otherwise occupied."

"Yes, but to ruin for an excellent reason."

It was another hour before they left their bed to find Millie and her nurse in the music room, sitting side-by-side on the pianoforte bench. Mrs. Calvert, who had been a gentlewoman before circumstances forced her to enter a life of service, was skilful on the pianoforte and was encouraged by the Ingrams to incorporate music into Millie's day whenever possible. She was busy creating a simple melody for a poem that Millie seemed to enjoy. Georgiana easily picked up the tune and began to sing the words she knew by heart.

> When the green woods laugh with the voice of joy,
> And the dimpling stream runs laughing by;
> When the air does laugh with our merry wit,
> And the green hill laughs with the noise of it;
> When the meadows laugh with lively green,
> And the grasshopper laughs in the merry scene,
> When Mary and Susan and Emily
> With their sweet round mouths sing "Ha, Ha, He!"
> When the painted birds laugh in the shade,
> Where our table with cherries and nuts is spread,
> Come live & be merry, and join with me,
> To sing the sweet chorus of "Ha, Ha, He! [3]

At the sound of her mother's voice, Millie gasped and slid off the bench. She was a vision in blue with bouncing curls as she ran towards them. Spotting her father who had been absent for almost two weeks, Millie pulled up short, began to cry and instead of running to Georgiana, headed straight for Evan.

"Papa!" the child cried out as he stooped to pick her up. Tears gave way to giggles as he kissed every possible place on her face.

Finally, Evan pulled back to look at her. "My, how you have grown!" Millie beamed. "Were you a good girl for your mother and Mrs. Calvert while I was in Town?" The small, golden head bobbed up and down, as her blue eyes stopped tearing.

"Wonderful! I brought you some things that I thought you might like. Would you like to see them now?" Another round of silent head bobbing commenced.

"Has the cat got your tongue?" Looking astonished, Millie felt for her tongue and finding it, shook her head. Evan winked at Georgiana.

"Well, your presents are in the conservatory, along with some for your lovely mother." Holding out his arm for Georgiana, she took it straightaway as he smiled at Millie's nurse.

"Come, Mrs. Calvert, there are presents for you as well."

---

[3] _Laughing Song_ by William Blake (1757 – 1827)

The woman could not help but blush. "Oh, Mr. Ingram, that was completely unnecessary."

"Perhaps not necessary, but entirely warranted by your excellent care of our daughter."

Thus, the little troupe made their way down the hallway, singing the *Laughing Song,* which Georgiana had begun as soon as they started out. Several maids, amused at the antics of the Master and Mistress, followed as they made their way to the pile of presents in the conservatory. Mrs. Jenkins, the Ingram's housekeeper, brought up the rear, following those she had recruited to help with all the discarded wrappings and refreshments.

Pemberley
That Afternoon

In the bedroom she had occupied since coming to Pemberley, Elizabeth bustled about inside the closet. A huge storm with thunder and lightning had commenced after William left that morning and still raged. It was impossible to enjoy any diversion, as she could not concentrate on a book or the pianoforte while sick with worry about his safety. Thus, she had found another occupation to distract her.

When Mrs. Drury entered the room, she could not help but laugh aloud. Elizabeth was nowhere to be seen, but occasionally an item would fly out of the closet, though there was hardly space left on the floor for it to land.

At her companion's laugh, Elizabeth stuck her head out. "Mrs. Drury, do I remember correctly? Did Mr. Darcy bring my chest back from Northgate? I was in such a fog, but I believe I remember his saying something about returning my chest and that it should contain my Bible."

Elizabeth prayed that the vicar Fitzwilliam mentioned might agree to conduct a symbolic marriage ceremony and possibly read a verse from her Bible. It was the only thing she had left from her childhood—a gift from her father—and she wanted to record their names inside it. They might have to, by necessity, keep their relationship secret from all but a few—the Bingleys, the Ingrams and Richard, but she wanted it recorded therein for their children to read one day.

"Why yes, child," the elderly woman replied, turning to go back into the sitting room, "but I believe it is in here." Elizabeth followed to find Mrs. Drury entering the closet in that room. Presently she backed out, holding the small chest that Elizabeth remembered from her childhood

"There it is!" Elizabeth exclaimed, a myriad of emotions flooding through her at the sight of the present she had received on her eighth birthday.

"What will you do with so fine a treasure, Lizzy?" Mr. Bennet smiled. "I promised your mother that you would not fill it with clothes and try to run away again."

Elizabeth's smile dimmed. Memories of the whipping her mother had administered when she was found at the coach station made her wince. "No, Papa, but, I was only going to London to find employment. When I had lots of money, I would have come home."

He tried to smile. "We can get by without having you work, my dear."

Lizzy frowned. How could she tell her beloved Papa that she had heard her mother tell her Aunt Phillips she would like to send her to live with distant relations so there would be more for the rest of her sisters?

"I truly love the present, Papa. Now I have my very own chest in which to keep the clothes I made for Martha."

"Ah, yes. Martha." Her father sighed, remembering the rag doll that Elizabeth had fashioned by herself. "How is Miss Martha?"

"She is sad sometimes. But I talk to her, and I remind her that things will get better once she grows up." Lizzy swept a lock of unruly hair from her forehead, looking up with the dark, bright eyes her father adored. "That is true, is it not? Things will get better when she grows up?"

Mr. Bennet directed a long, thoughtful look at her. "Yes, Lizzy. Things will get better when Martha grows up. You see, this little trunk is called a dowry chest. Martha should put all the things in it that she loves, and the things she will want to take with her when she marries. One day a handsome prince will fall in love with her. They will marry and go to live in a beautiful castle. And they will both be happy for the rest of their lives."

Lizzy had smiled her lop-sided grin, jumped down and run over to get the bag that held all Martha's belongings from under the bed. Then she had sat by her father's feet on the floor and put everything in the chest.

The sight of the small case affected Lizzy more than she had thought it would when she set out to find it. It was the only familiar item she found among her belongings when she gained awareness of her surroundings at Northgate. Suddenly tears streamed down her cheeks unabated. Realising where her thoughts had surely turned, Mrs. Drury set the treasure down and pulled the young woman into her arms, rocking her as she smoothed her hair gently.

"Please do not cry, Miss Elizabeth. You are safe now, and there is a good man who wants to protect you. Do not let old memories ruin your present happiness."

Elizabeth pulled back, sniffling and wiping her eyes. She wanted so desperately to confide her plans to this wonderful woman, but she could not for fear of jeopardising everyone's safety, and if she were truthful, fear of her disapproval. After all, while choosing to leave a cruel husband might not be frowned upon by some, choosing to become another man's mistress would be condemned by all.

"You are correct. I should remember my old philosophy—think only of the past as its remembrance gives you pleasure."

Mrs. Drury patted her arm. "And look to your future. If Mr. Darcy has any part in it, it will be a bright one."

Pemberley
On horseback

As William travelled from one tenant's farm to the next he reflected on the letter in his pocket from Richard. It seems that Richard had had very little time to dwell on anything other than his duties since he had returned to his post and he was looking forward to a few weeks leave after his next trip to London and hopefully solving the mystery of the count.

He had related that he had heard from his father and the men hired by Lord Matlock had not been successful in locating the man who had married Anne. Other than repeating that he had apparently fled England shortly after he had cleaned out her bank accounts, these detectives had nothing to add. Their excuse was that the count had apparently used many aliases and it made tracking him difficult if not impossible and they believed that he would never dare to return to England.

William had often pondered the similarities between Anne's husband and Stefano, but Elizabeth never seemed to fit in the puzzle. He and Richard had both been of the opinion that the men were similar in character, but the time frame between Anne's marriage and Elizabeth's abduction was so close as to make it almost impossible for one man to accomplish. And while Anne had a fortune to plunder, Elizabeth certainly did not. Even so, the detectives William had his solicitors hire to investigate Stefano had not uncovered anything new and his whereabouts were still a mystery—just as mysterious as Anne's husband.

In this same letter, Richard went on to mention that one of his old army acquaintances now ran a detective agency and he was of the opinion that they should seek his assistance. At the end of the missive he had concluded, "I would enjoy helping you find Stefano and ridding England of the blackguard."

So would I, cousin, so would I, William thought as he kicked Onyx into a trot.

On the road to Derbyshire

They were still miles from Lord Greenwich's Derbyshire estate. Gwendolyn Waltham had thought it a streak of good luck when Lord and Lady Greenwich decided to return to their country home directly after she had resolved to try one last time to seduce Fitzwilliam Darcy. But now that they were caught in this monstrous storm, she was not quite sure it was luck after all.

It had rained steadily for the last five miles, and the roads were beginning to become impassable, as wheels slipped into deep ruts caused by the coaches that had gone before them. The horses were having trouble keeping their footing as well. As they pulled into the last coach stop before Lambton, the innkeeper informed them that the bridges ahead were likely to be unusable, as streams and rivers easily overflowed their banks in this type of deluge. The inn was old and quite small, and the only accommodations he could offer them was to spend the night sitting at the tables in the common rooms, as all the bedrooms were taken.

These circumstances cemented the plan that had been forming in Lady Waltham's mind as they got closer to the place she really wanted to be—Pemberley. There was no argument from the elderly couple when she informed them of the benefits of travelling on to Mr. Darcy's home. They were accustomed to Gwendolyn's taking charge of arrangements while they travelled, and that was one reason they encouraged her company. Thus, it was late evening when Lord Greenwich's coach pulled up to Pemberley's front entrance in a driving rain. Several footmen ran out to assist the occupants into the house, while Mr. Walker sent for Mrs. Reynolds and went to the library to inform Mr. Darcy.

William had come home just in time for dinner, as he had promised Elizabeth, and they had retired to the library afterward. They were sitting on one of the sofas, while William explained everything that had happened that day, from the newborn colt at Mr. Cramer's homestead, to his difficulty in finding a place to cross the swollen stream on his way home, when Mr. Walker interrupted their conversation with a knock on the door. Immediately, William moved to the sofa opposite Elizabeth and called out, "Come."

Mr. Walker entered and bowed. "I am sorry to have to disturb you, sir, but visitors have just arrived. I have shown them to the drawing room."

"Visitors?" William stood. "In this downpour? Good Lord, they must be drowned." He reached out to take Elizabeth's hand. "Would you rather not be introduced? I would introduce you to the world as the woman I love, if it would not offend you. But I do not wish to embarrass you or harm you in any way." He lifted her hand to her lips. "If you wish, you are my dearest cousin, Miss Lawrence." He smiled lovingly. "And until we remove ourselves from Pemberley, you shall be introduced as such to outsiders, unless, madam, you do not wish to be on display."

"I believe it is time to meet the world again."

He took her hand. "I am glad. Come, my love."

As William led Elizabeth towards the drawing room, they could hear the newly arrived party talking animatedly about their dilemma and upon reaching the interlopers, found Lord and Lady Greenwich standing in the doorway, effectively shielding Gwendolyn, who was inside the room, from William's view. At William's approach they both quieted and turned to face him.

"My lord?" William said, bowing to the elderly man. "What brings you to Pemberley in this storm?"

"We were headed home but got caught in the deluge and feared to travel further," Lord Greenwich replied as he tried to judge Mr. Darcy's reaction to their sudden appearance. "There were no rooms left at the inn, and I realise it would be impossible to cross the bridge that fronts my estate. It always overflows in this type downpour. We were hoping we could impose upon you for the night."

William silently cursed the fact that the guest rooms were being refurbished because a tree limb had fallen during the last storm, causing a hole in the roof squarely in that hallway. It had been his decision to close that entire wing and paint all the rooms during the repairs, especially since no guests were allowed while Elizabeth was in residence. Consequently, the unexpected company would, of necessity, have to be housed in the family wing.

As he pondered the dilemma, Lady Greenwich interjected, "Gwendolyn reminded us that your estate was nearby, and we agreed with her that it would be prudent to stop at Pemberley tonight and travel on to our estate tomorrow. We hope you do not mind our imposing on you, Mr. Darcy. After all, she explained that you and she are old friends."

A bad feeling began in the pit of William's stomach. "Gwendolyn?"

At that moment, Lady Waltham stepped from behind the open door and came towards him, grinning as though she actually believed she was welcome. "Fitzwilliam!"

She reached out to clasp his hand, but William stepped back, leaving her thwarted. Once more she stepped towards him, and again he stepped back. Now completely out in the hall, his hand went out to grasp Elizabeth's, bringing her forward, and alerting her to his discomfort by the stiff way he held himself, his iron grip and the tone of his voice.

"Lord and Lady Greenwich..." He hesitated as his eyes flicked to Lady Waltham. He continued after a few endless seconds. "Lady Waltham. Allow me to introduce my cousin, Miss Elizabeth Lawrence, from Essex. Miss Lawrence has been visiting us this summer."

Elizabeth fell into a perfect curtsey. "It is an honour to meet you, Lord Greenwich. Lady Greenwich." As she rose, she turned to greet the woman so obviously infatuated with William, and to her astonishment Gwendolyn huffed and walked several feet away, throwing orders over her shoulder.

"Fitzwilliam, I would like a word with you. I shall wait in the library." She started in that direction but stopped in a few feet when he did not reply.

Lord and Lady Greenwich looked stunned, not knowing what to make of Gwendolyn's behaviour. They chose to ignore her conduct entirely as they greeted Elizabeth politely, if hurriedly, and begged to be excused, citing their long journey and the lateness of the hour.

Ignoring Gwendolyn, William assured his guests that they were most welcome to retire and nodding to his housekeeper, added, "Mrs. Reynolds will send a tray to your rooms."

The Master's discomfort with this rude woman was not lost on Mrs. Reynolds. As his eyes sought hers, she nodded her understanding of how much this *lady* was welcome at Pemberley. She summoned Martha to escort the couple to their rooms. "Take Lord and Lady Greenwich to the green room."

After the elderly couple were out of hearing range, William turned to Lady Waltham. "We have nothing to discuss, madam. I suggest you retire as I intend for you to leave at the earliest possible moment tomorrow."

Mrs. Reynolds stepped forward instantly. "I shall show you to your room."

Gwendolyn huffed, "As you well know, I am quite familiar with Pemberley, since my late husband and I were great friends of George Darcy." She looked pointedly at Elizabeth. "And with Fitzwilliam. Just put my things in the blue room. I know where it is."

William was furious at her audacity. His response was quick and harsh.

"The blue room is out of the question!" Gwendolyn's chin rose, her anger clearly visible. "While I have no objections to aiding Lord and Lady Greenwich, I feel no such obligation to you! You will never be welcome here. Nevertheless, because of the severity of the storm, I will allow even you sanctuary for one night and one night only!"

Addressing his servant, though his steely eyes never left Gwendolyn, he declared, "Mrs. Reynolds, I trust you to decide on appropriate housing for this *lady*."

The housekeeper nodded in response. She understood exactly. Lady Waltham would be at the far end of the hall."

After Elizabeth had risen from her curtsey, William had grasped her hand again, caring not what his elderly neighbours or Lady Waltham made of his show of affection. Now, still holding it tightly, he turned to head back to the library with her. Having this harridan insinuate herself in his home shook him to the core, and he needed a few minutes alone with Elizabeth to regain his composure. As they reached the sofa where they previously sat, a sound caught his attention, and he turned to see Gwendolyn sweep into the room. Behind her, Mrs. Reynolds stood at the door with a look of consternation, her arms folded across her chest.

~~~*~~~

Chapter 26

Netherfield
The Drawing Room

As Charles Bingley arrived in the room, he immediately sat on the sofa next to his wife, slipping an arm around her shoulders. Jane was knitting something for their son and he waited until he had her full attention before he spoke. As she turned trusting violet eyes to him, Charles swallowed hard. How he hated to inform her of this news!

"I have something to tell you, sweetheart. I would have done anything to spare you this worry, especially in your delicate condition, but I know you would want to know." She nodded her agreement and he was encouraged to continue. "You remember the letter that came this morning as you were going upstairs to feed Peter?" Jane eyes widened, but she did not reply. "It was from Darcy."

His voice was strained as he began to tell her everything regarding the letter and the fact that it pointed to Caroline's involvement in trying to elicit an invitation to Pemberley. "It is a good thing that Darcy was not fooled and realised almost instantly that it was not from me. But Caroline did mention the cousin staying at Pemberley, Elise Lawrence, so she has evidently read our correspondence."

Jane sat stunned for several moments before saying softly, "Caroline knows." She shook her head side to side—as if by denying the words she could keep them from being true. "This cannot be. We were so careful. How could she—"

Charles interrupted. "I have no idea. I suppose she gained access to my study somehow and read my letters from Darcy, or she could even have eavesdropped while we were talking. Either way, she has proven once again that we cannot trust her. She does not care for our family or wish to be a part of it. If she had not left for London, I fear I would strangle her with my bare hands!"

"Heavens! Does she suspect that Elise is Lizzy? If she does, she will do whatever she can to harm her! She has always hated Lizzy!"

Charles sighed, taking her hand and squeezing it. "It is obvious that she wrote that letter to Darcy, but sometime between sending the letter and leaving for London, she must have ascertained that Lizzy and Elise are one and the same. When the letter was sent, she was merely begging an invitation to Pemberley. But I have just today been informed that she is spreading vicious rumours in London that Lizzy is the cousin staying at Pemberley."

At Jane's shocked look, he explained. "My friend, Jonathan Mattson, wrote me a letter which I received by special express just moments ago." Reaching inside his coat pocket, he retrieved the missive and unfolded it, beginning to summarize the contents.

"He says his sister—you remember Margaret?" Jane nodded absently. "Margaret told him that Caroline has, in her words, *been telling everyone that will listen that she has to warn Mr. Darcy of a woman who is trying to take advantage of him.*

Caroline indicated that the woman was already at Pemberley, pretending to be a long, lost cousin."

Jane began crying. "Why? Why would she do this, Charles? If she has read our letters to William, then she must realise that Elizabeth is not well, and that we are hiding her from...from *him*. Has she no compassion?"

"I can say with all confidence that she does not! She cares only for herself, sweetheart, and it looks as though she still will do anything to separate Lizzy from Darcy." He hugged Jane, rubbing her back solicitously as she wept. "It will not help tremendously, I fear, but I shall go directly to London to attempt to undo some of the damage."

"What can you do? The news has likely been spread far and wide by now. You know she is a part of that vindictive band of schoolmates who dearly love to tear people to shreds with their gossip."

Charles stood and advanced to a small writing desk, throwing the note from Mattson angrily upon it. "I have already informed Darcy of the situation in a letter, which will go out in the morning by express. The day after tomorrow I intend to travel to London to notify Caroline that her allowance has been cut off completely. She will be moving to York, as soon as I can make the arrangements to live with our aunt, Bertha Caulfield. There she shall perform in whatever capacity our aunt desires—even as a maid, for all I care. I shall give Caroline's allowance to Aunt Caulfield for her maintenance. And, as my aunt is always in need of monetary assistance, I am certain she will be happy to oblige me by taking in Caroline."

"You would cut off her allowance and give it to your aunt?"

"I shall explain to my sister that in order for her to regain her allowance, she must call on all of her friends and acquaintances before she leaves London and confess that her own jealously caused her to spread the lies regarding Darcy. She shall affirm that the woman at Pemberley is truly Mr. Darcy's cousin, Elise Lawrence, who is staying there to recover her health. If she does a credible job of making a laughing stock of herself and teaching others never to trust her again, then at the end of one full year, not one day less, I shall restore her allowance, and she can do with it as she pleases. In any event, she shall never get one penny more than the allowance from me or be welcome in my homes ever again."

"How will you know if she complies—if she confesses or even changes the confession to favour her?"

"I will make it clear that she has to confess exactly as I stated and I shall find out the truth of it. She knows that I have trusted friends in London, who have sisters that are her acquaintances. I shall be able to gauge the genuineness of it."

"And if she refuses? Caroline treasures her self-importance, after all."

"If that is the case, I will tell her that I shall inform my friends that she is very jealous of Darcy, and that accounts for why she made up this lie about his cousin, and I shall ask them to pass that information along to their families and friends. Caroline knows she can put a better light on it, perhaps even be pitied for her jealousy, whereas I do not care how she is perceived. Whatever the source, the end result will be the same—she will be ridiculed. However, if I am left to handle the situation, she will not have the opportunity to redeem her allowance."

"But what of Louisa? Will she not just take Caroline in?"

"Louisa shall be made to know that if she takes Caroline in, she will be aligning herself with someone who is no longer welcome in my homes, and therefore, she will not be welcome either. I daresay, Bertram will not be happy to have Caroline in residence, especially with no allowance, nor will he be happy to forgo my stock of imported brandy that he enjoys imbibing so freely. I do not think Louisa will be imprudent enough to choose her sister over me."

"Oh, Charles, are you positive you want to take this course of action?"

"Darcy is like my brother, and Lizzy is dearer to me than my own sisters. It will be no sacrifice never to see Caroline again. And, if Louisa wishes to align herself with her, then so be it. I shall be the richer for not having to restock my brandy so often."

London
Preston House

Wickham waited while two men backed out the front door, carrying a large settee, following their progress as they carefully made their way down the steps to deposit it in a large wagon. Shaking his head in wonder, he hurried up the steps behind them and into the foyer. There he stood for a moment, looking about, but Mr. Potts was nowhere to be seen. No one else appeared either to take his coat and hat. Hearing voices in the parlour, he quietly walked in that direction, taking pains not to make any noise with his heavy boots. In his line of work, keeping his presence a secret often came in handy. He had learned a good deal of useful information in that manner.

"I realise you have not been paid for three months, Clara. I am not a halfwit! I do intend to pay you—pay all the servants—just as soon as I receive the funds that I have invested. I have informed my banker, and I should have a draft this week. Please tell the others that they shall be paid by Friday, even if I have to get a loan from my uncle until I have my money."

Wickham could see the maid's face through the partially open door and she did not seem to be appeased. Striding into the room as though he were just arriving and had not overheard their conversation, he declared loudly, "Mrs. Preston, I hope I am not interrupting, but there was no one in the foyer to announce me."

"Yes, well—" Cecile began, but Wickham continued undaunted.

"I stopped to see Mr. Stratton at the bank, and when he learned I was to meet with you today, he asked if I would mind delivering this." With those words, Wickham pulled an actual bank envelope from the inside pocket of his coat. "He prays you will forgive him for not bringing it in person, as he would have been delayed until tomorrow."

Clara's eyes lit up upon recognising the envelope that Wickham handed to Cecile, who seized the opportunity. "You may go now, Clara. Please inform the others of our discussion."

"Yes, Mrs. Preston," the heavy woman replied, dropping a curtsey and nodding pleasantly towards Wickham as she turned to leave.

"Oh, and Clara?" The maid stopped and turned again. "Would you please ask Ives to take Mr. Potts' place at the door and then bring us some tea?" The woman bobbed again before swiftly leaving the room.

"You could not have come at a better time!" Cecile sighed, dropping into one of only a few chairs remaining in the large room. She held up the envelope in question. "I do not suppose this is actually mine?"

Wickham shook his head and reached for the object he had used to his advantage on many an occasion. Then, looking about at the nearly empty room, he inquired.

"What in the name of God are you doing? There are only half the furnishings in this room since last I visited. Are you selling your furniture to pay the bills?"

Cecile shrugged. "I never liked most of it anyway. The pieces were inherited from Mr. Preston's family and were not my taste. It is too bad the Prestons own this townhouse, or I could sell it as well."

"You have certainly made enough money procuring your friend's jewellery to be solvent. Instead, your wagers on the horses have you in dire straits. You should give up gambling, my dear, as you have not the head for determining winners."

She laughed mirthlessly. "And that from the man who gladly accepts my wagers!"

Wickham tried unsuccessfully to smile and it seemed more of a glower. "My associate would be quite cross with me if he found that I had refused a wager. However, as a fellow business associate, I hate to see you struggling when you have made quite a good income with our other little endeavour. Besides, it is essential that you keep up appearances, or you will be of no use to me in that enterprise. No one wishes to associate with someone who is on the brink of ruin, and selling your furnishings speaks of that. Can you imagine what the *ton* would think if they saw this room? And servants talk!"

Cecile dismissed his assertions with a wave of her hand. "When I marry Farthington, I shall have license to buy anything I want."

"Farthington? Lord Harold Farthington?"

"Yes, why?"

Wickham held back a laugh. "Well, I presume you have not read the society pages this morning."

Cecile's face first turned pale before beginning to redden in anger as he continued to stare at her. "Are you going to tell me what you are crowing about, or do I have to send for a paper?"

Giving up all pretence, Wickham's laughter rang out. "I hate to be the bearer of bad news, but Lord Farthington has announced his engagement to Lady Bumgardiner—you know the rather ugly woman who inherited sixty thousand pounds, not to mention three estates, when her husband died a year ago."

Cecile screamed, "How can he do this to me? He practically promised to marry me! Me! Not that unsightly, humourless chit!"

Wickham gestured. "Calm yourself, madam. You will alert the whole neighbourhood to your misfortune if you keep this up. Do you wish everyone to know of your humiliation?"

At just that moment, Clara arrived with the tea but stopped in the doorway, apparently wary of coming inside after hearing the mistress's outburst. She relented when Wickham gestured her forward. Gingerly moving into the room, she set the tea and biscuits on the liquor cabinet—the only place available in the nearly empty room. Wordlessly, she bobbed another curtsey, before practically running from the room. Wickham laughed, following her to shut the door, and after locking it, he turned to see that Cecile was still seething.

"My dear Mrs. Preston, do not pine for that old codger. I have a proposition that may very well make you a fortune. If you agree to help me, we shall both have enough money to live well—howbeit, we may need to move to another country."

Cecile's eyebrows rose in question, but she said nothing. Instead, she walked over to the liquor cabinet and proceeded to pour two cups of tea. Then she opened the doors below and removed a half-empty bottle of brandy which she used to lace her cup. Turning she held up the bottle.

"Only tea for me, with a little cream and sugar. I have a lot of work to accomplish, and I have need of a clear head."

Handing Wickham his cup, she assumed her former position, slipping into the upholstered chair and sipping the hot liquid as though deep in thought. Wickham was not pleased. Here he was offering her a way out, a way to keep her present standard of living, and yet she hesitated.

"Whether you decide to help me or not, you are never to tell anyone about this conversation. If I learn that you have told anyone, I will have you *eliminated*. Is that understood?"

Cecile swallowed hard, her mien reflecting her newfound anxiety. *This must be very serious indeed.* Not doubting that Wickham would do as he said if he suspected she had informed anyone, she was well aware that he had ample *friends* at his disposal to accomplish the task. "I swear I will not say anything to anyone."

"Good! In the past, you have taken *things*, jewellery and such, but this scheme involves taking a person—a woman. She will not be harmed—only held for ransom. A very handsome ransom, if you will. But if you do not want to be involved, tell me now, and there will be no repercussions, no hard feelings. However, should you agree to join me in this venture, there will be no changing your mind later. Is that understood?"

"I have your solemn promise that this person will not be harmed?"

"My solemn promise?" Wickham snickered at the thought of his promises being something of worth. "Of course!"

At Cecile's look of dismay, he tried to be more convincing. "I am a gentleman and not a ruffian. I do not relish harming anyone, especially as that entails much greater punishment if one is caught in the act."

Cecile frowned at the mention of punishment, making him chuckle. "Rest assured, I have an excellent plan and do not intend to get caught. Mind you, I will do whatever I must to protect myself. However, I feel certain all can be accomplished without any violence whatsoever."

Realising that there appeared to be no other solution to her predicament and with so little money that she would likely have to sell her estate next in order to satisfy her creditors, Cecile acquiesced. *After all, should Marvin learn that I have been selling the furnishings from this townhouse, I shall have no choice but to move back to my estate.* "I agree. What does this plan entail?"

"If my information proves true, I will have the exact location of a very wealthy man's wife. She ran away from him some months ago, and he wants to learn where she has been hiding. The woman could easily be worth a twenty thousand pounds reward, and if you agree to help me, half is yours."

"Why would she be hiding? Does he wish to harm her?"

"What he does or does not wish to do is none of our concern. Our only worry should be what this exchange means for us."

"Who is she?"

"You do need to know until the information is verified, and the time to take action draws near. The less you know until then, the better. If you have no knowledge of the details, then if something happens to thwart our plans, I will know for certain that you were not the one who betrayed me."

Cecile nodded. Ten thousand pounds would put her back on her feet quite nicely. "You know that I have no choice. Count me in."

Wickham smirked. "I knew I could depend on you. Let us hope the source proves accurate."

Pemberley
The Library

Lady Waltham was beside herself as Fitzwilliam Darcy completely ignored her, escorting his supposed cousin into the library, hand-in-hand. As Mrs. Reynolds began to lead her up the stairs, Gwendolyn turned and ran back down them, heading directly to the library as though she had not been rebuked. When William looked up at her entrance to the room, she declared, "What I have to say to you is private!"

Drawing himself up to his full height, William never flinched. "I told you that I have nothing to say to you, madam, nor do I wish to listen to your drivel."

Gwendolyn stood motionless for some time, her fiery eyes flickering between William and Elizabeth. She craved to hurl the gossip learned in London at her rival, but knew it would be more effective if she used it against Fitzwilliam...alone. Huffing, she headed towards the door.

"This is not over, Fitzwilliam. You will face me sooner or later!" With that pronouncement, she was out the door and a livid housekeeper escorted to her to the smallest, least comfortable guest room at the end of the hallway.

"What was that all about?" Elizabeth asked. Clearly the woman was acting the part of a jealous lover. At William's look of dismay, she laid a hand on his arm. "I am sorry. I should not have asked. If you do not wish to tell me—"

"I wish you to know everything, though I fear you will care less for me afterward."

Elizabeth cupped his face and brushed a light kiss across his lips, causing him to ache for more. "Nothing ... absolutely nothing could induce me to care less. Since we have found each other again, you have been all that is good and kind towards me, and that is as far in the past as I care to delve."

"A very wise person once said, 'If we are to be together, I must tell you. Otherwise, there will be a gulf between us, and I could not bear it.'"

Elizabeth smiled, though tears threatened as they filled her eyes. "As another wise person replied, 'Then tell me everything.'"

William smiled wanly, pulling her into his arms as if to keep her from escaping. He kept his head lying atop hers, fearing to look into her beautiful face as he explained his relationship with Gwendolyn Waltham. It took several minutes and, afterward, Elizabeth was deathly silent as neither moved. When he could bear it no more, William pushed her to arm's length, though he still clutched her forearms. "Please say you do not hate me."

Wiping the remnants of tears from her cheeks, Elizabeth tried to smile. "What happened to you was an injustice, just as surely as the one perpetrated against me. Lady Waltham took advantage of a good-hearted young boy, who has grown into the good-hearted man I love. That you turned your back on that type activity, when so many of your sphere would have embraced it without conscience, speaks well of your character."

William kissed her deeply then murmured, "Oh, my sweet Elizabeth. Hearing you speak well of me is all I ever desired. Thank you for being so understanding."

213

"I could also thank you for your understanding heart, but we would be all night singing each other's praises." She kissed him lightly again. "Now, if I remember correctly, you wanted to take a hot bath to soak you poor, aching back. Being on horseback most of the day must have been excruciating. Come, let us retire, so you may get some relief."

"I look forward to the respite of soaking in my tub, but knowing that you know everything and love me still is worth more than all the hot water in Derbyshire in allowing me to sleep."

Peals of delicious laughter filled the room, bringing a smile to his face. "Oh, Fitzwilliam, how do you always know just what to say to make me love you more?"

~~~*~~~

Once in her room, Gwendolyn had donned her most revealing nightgown, though she had no intention of sleeping. She sat down and waited for what she concluded was a sufficient amount of time for the household to settle down. Upon determining that everyone was probably abed, she donned a robe, blew out the candle on her dresser and opened the door barely wide enough to peer into the hall. It was pitch black save for the occasional lit candle in the sconces along the wall. As she moved down the corridor hoping to locate William's quarters, she heard footsteps coming and quickly tried a nearby doorknob. Finding it unlocked, she slipped inside an empty bedchamber and placed her ear against the door. Not hearing anything more, she opened the door slightly and was startled as William walked past in the dark. Not seeing her, he turned and greeted Adams, who was coming along behind him. They carried on a whispered conversation well within hearing distance of her hiding place.

"Sir, I have come from the kitchen. I am having more water heated for your bath, as what I brought up earlier has cooled. It is still warm, but not as hot as you like it."

"Thank you, Adams. It is entirely my fault for taking so long downstairs. I shall begin my bath with what you have here. Just bring more hot water up when you can."

"Very well, sir. I shall return just as soon as it heats." With those words, the servant retreated the way he had come, and William entered his dressing room, leaving the door unlocked for his valet.

Gwendolyn could not wipe the smile from her face. She could not have planned a better seduction. She would wait until William was in his bath to slip inside his room, and this time, he would not be able to resist her. Congratulating herself on her ingenuity, Gwendolyn looked about the room for a chair and finding one, sat down to wait. Fitzwilliam would have time to undress and enter his bath, and then she would appear.

~~~*~~~

Lord Greenwich was already in bed when his wife opened the door between their rooms and appeared at his bedside, candle in hand.

"Martha, my dear, what are you about? I thought you would be asleep by now."

"I cannot rest. There is something about Gwendolyn's behaviour that is does not seem right to me. Though she said she and Mr. Darcy were old friends, he did not seem happy to see her in the least. And did you see how she snubbed his cousin's greeting, almost as if she were jealous? I tell you, Harrison, there is more to this than meets the eye. I pray that we have not been ill used to upset Mr. Darcy."

"One could not help but notice the snub of Mr. Darcy's cousin or Gwendolyn's jealous behaviour, and the tension between her and Fitzwilliam was palpable. I, too, fear there might be a reason, other than the weather, that we were diverted to Pemberley."

"My thoughts exactly."

"But we cannot sort them out tonight, sweetheart. Please return to your bed; we shall make sense of this tomorrow. There is one thing for certain, weather permitting, we shall leave as early as possible."

"Of course, you are right. Forgive me for bothering you with my fears at this inopportune time, Husband."

Lord Greenwich reached to take his wife's hand and kissed it. "You are never a bother, love." A very close bolt of lightning lit up the room, as the rumble of thunder shook the windows. "On second thought, would you like to share my bed tonight? After all, it is storming, and you have never liked to sleep alone during storms."

Lady Greenwich blushed, though it was too dark to be seen. "Oh, Harrison, you are still the romantic, are you not?" With that, she set her candle down on the table, blew out the flame and crawled under the covers being held open by her mate of forty years.

Snuggling against his warmth, she sighed. "It is so sad that most young people never know the kind of love we have shared, sweetheart."

Lord Greenwich could not help smiling widely as he pulled his wife closer. "Yes, very sad. Now, go to sleep. I shall keep you safe, love."

Lady Greenwich instantly sank into a deep sleep, secure in the arms of her husband, while Lord Greenwich lay awake unable to do the same. His mind was occupied by thoughts of the rumours he had heard recently at his club. Oh, there had always been insinuations about women in general, and Gwendolyn Waltham in particular, but he had always chosen to ignore them. Most of the stories, he was sure, were invented in the imaginations of men who had no such liaisons but were eager for others to think they had.

However, recently there had been talk of some kind of confrontation between Gwendolyn and Mr. Darcy at the Matlock's ball held in honour of Leighton's birthday—talk that Fitzwilliam Darcy was not happy to be the object of Lady Waltham's interest. Apparently, in the tale going around White's, Darcy had told her so quite emphatically. After seeing Darcy's face when he realised that Gwendolyn was in his house, Greenwich now had no doubt that this was one rumour that was true.

His Martha had always dearly loved Lady Waltham's company, so he had chosen to ignore the woman's irritating ways. But convincing them to drive on to Pemberley when Mr. Darcy clearly was displeased with her presence was insufferable. Darcy had always been a good neighbour, and though Greenwich had been more comfortable with George Darcy than his son, he did not wish to injure that relationship by indulging Gwendolyn Waltham's whims.

With a heavy sigh, he concluded he needed something to help him sleep.

Making sure that his wife was still sound asleep, he gave her a peck on the cheek and then slid out of the bed. Surely, Darcy would not begrudge him a glass of brandy to calm his nerves. He was sure that George Darcy kept a liquor cabinet in the library, and Fitzwilliam had changed hardly a thing since his father had passed away. So once in the dark hallway, he headed in that direction.

~~~*~~~

Chapter 27

Pemberley

Tight muscles finally began to relax as William sank deeper into the warm water filling the oversized tub. After several moments of enjoying the sensation, he sat up straight and grabbed a cloth and soap and began scrubbing. Completely finished in a short while, he plunged under the water, re-emerging seconds later, wiping the water from his face. Then laying his head against a small, folded towel on the back of the tub, he closed his eyes, anticipating the pleasure of having more hot water added as soon as Adams returned. Exhausted, he barely noticed the opening and closing of the dressing room door. Without looking, he murmured, "That did not take long."

Waiting expectantly for the hot water to be emptied into the vessel, he was surprised when none came. Realising there had been no answer to his greeting and thinking it odd, he ventured, "Adams?"

There was still no answer. Looking over his shoulder, he could see no one as the room was only lit by a couple of candles, and the corners were left in the shadows. Perplexed, he stood and reached for the towel that Adams always placed on his dressing table. There was no towel on the table, nor was his robe hanging on the hook where it always resided. With a resigned sigh, he stepped out of the tub to obtain a towel from the linen closet. "What a time to forget ..."

His words abruptly halted as Gwendolyn Waltham stepped out of the darkness holding up his robe. Winking at him, she threw the article of clothing on a nearby chair and took a step closer, holding out the towel. In order to take the offering, however, William would have to move towards her. He hesitated.

"My, my, Fitzwilliam! The boy that I knew has become quite a man." Lust-filled eyes trailed from his face to his groin. "It looks as though you have ... *grown.*"

Trying to mask his uneasiness, William replied through gritted teeth, "Give me the towel and get out of my room."

She laughed. "I believe, sweetheart, that you are in no position to give orders." Untying the ribbon at the top of her dressing gown, it fell open and Gwendolyn shrugged her shoulders, causing the silky material to slide down her arms.

"Do you want to see what you are rejecting? You may change your mind." Still holding the towel, she slid first one arm and then the other out of the sleeves, sending the offending article floating to the floor. Beneath it, she wore a very sheer, silk nightgown and, clearly, nothing else.

A look of revulsion crossed William's face and his eyes narrowed. "My valet will return at any moment. I suggest you leave before he does."

Gwendolyn was not discouraged. "On the contrary, I think you are not so concerned with your valet's return, but you fear your little plaything may find me here?"

"I have no idea who you mean."

"Oh, my! Are we not protective? You are not fooling anyone. The story of your **cousin** has reached London, and everyone believes that she is your mistress, although I had hoped they were wrong. What could you possibly see in her? Honestly, I would have thought you, of all men, would choose a lover from your own sphere. I hear she is but a country chit, unlearned I am certain, and undoubtedly lacking in proper decorum. Besides, I have seen her, and she is certainly no beauty!"

William stepped forward, jerking the towel from her hands and quickly tying it around his waist. "You do not even know Miss Lawrence, yet you condemn her and call her a whore. I am not surprised. You, like most of the women of the *ton*, are conceited, selfish and lacking human decency and morals. Life is a just a game to you—a chance to see how many heads you can turn, how many men you can bed. You cannot conceive of a lady like my cousin—someone who is all that is virtuous, selfless and lovely—so you disparage her and try to ruin her reputation."

Catching him off guard, Gwendolyn quickly ran her hands up his wet abdomen to his chest, admiring the feel of the hardness under her palms. "Surely you do not mean that."

He pushed her away forcefully, taking several steps back. "I meant every word!"

The hurt she felt was evident in her eyes, but she was undeterred. "There was a time when you welcomed my touch, Fitzwilliam. Do you not remember our passion? We could still be good for each other, if you would only calm yourself and let passion have its way. I have never forgotten how fervent we were, but you would be astounded at the many ways that I have learned to please you now. Most men only dream of the sensuality I am offering to you. No other woman of your acquaintance can possibly match it. Let me live the rest of my life pleasing only you ... let me be your mistress."

"Fortunately our relationship was years ago, when I was young and naive. When your husband died, I only meant to help you—never to become your lover. Thank God, I am no longer a gullible boy and will never again be taken in by someone as vulgar as you. So please, do not embarrass yourself further. Go back to your room and stay there. I mean to post a footman to assure that you do. I want you out of my home at first light."

"And if I refuse?"

A decidedly angry voice came from the direction of the doorway, "Lady Waltham!"

Gwendolyn jumped at the sound of Lord Greenwich's displeasure and paled as he opened the door that she had failed to close properly.

"I have heard it all. Come, madam! I will escort you to your room. You have upset Mr. Darcy long enough, and I, for one, am ashamed of having brought you here."

Looking back at William, Gwendolyn realised that her gambit had failed. Huffing as she stooped to pick up her dressing gown, she donned it hastily before stalking to the door and stopping in front of the elderly gentleman. She hissed, "I need no escort, you old fool!"

Lord Greenwich watched her progress down the hall until satisfied that she was inside her room before addressing William. Without turning to look at his young host, he offered solemnly, "Please excuse me for insinuating myself into your business, Darcy, and for inadvertently bringing this woman here. Be assured that I shall remove her from your home tomorrow morning as soon as it is light. And you can rest assured that this matter shall never be spoken of by me." Lord Greenwich closed the door behind him, not expecting a reply.

Adams came into the room barely a minute after that gentleman had retreated to his own bedchamber. A quizzical look spread across the valet's face as he realised that William was not in the tub.

"Are you ready for more hot water, sir?"

"I believe I have been in all the hot water I can stand tonight, Adams. I apologise for the trouble, but I am going to bed. You may clean this up in the morning."

Adams observed the tired slump of his Master's shoulders as he headed into his bedroom. Scratching his head, the loyal valet poured the bucket of hot water into the tub and headed to his own quarters.

That is strange. The Master's bath did not seem to relax him in the least.

Meryton
The Vicar's Cottage

Mrs. Haversham found the former vicar where she often came across him, amongst the graves. He often tended his family plots, pulling weeds and tending to the flowers. Frequently, he would place wildflower cuttings by the headstones, as he had today. She watched as Mr. Williamson stopped at his parents' graves first and then attended to his wife's. But it was when he stopped at Elizabeth Bennet's grave and pulled a few weeds before placing some wildflowers on her headstone, that tears filled her eyes. It was well known in Meryton that Elizabeth had been like a daughter to the old gentleman and her death had taken much of his spiritedness out of him, but it had been a blow to her as well.

Ah, dear Elizabeth, how you loved wildflowers! My Julie would have been so happy to be sharing her wedding day with you. You were such good friends. Taking a shaky breath, she pushed away heartbreaking memories, as the dear man stood and made a display of straightening his back. When Mr. Williamson turned in her direction, she approached.

"Do you think the weather is going to stay rainy, Mr. Williamson, or will the Good Lord smile on us and let the sun break out for the wedding tomorrow?"

The old vicar smiled at the grey-haired woman who made sure the church was prepared for the services every week. "Well, now, Mrs. Haversham, I believe we must have faith that what we ask in prayer, believing, we shall have. And *I,* for one, believe that we will have sunshine. And you?"

Mrs. Haversham smiled, her lined face suddenly transforming with faith. "Aye, Vicar, I believe we will have sunshine as well."

"Good." Mr. Williamson smiled. "It only takes two to agree in faith for something to be done."

"Just as you have preached all these years." She grinned to see the vicar beam. "I just wanted you to know that I have finished preparing the church, and I am going home. I must help my daughter with the wedding breakfast, and we still have much to do. It is not every day that a granddaughter weds."

"No, indeed, my good woman, and I am proud to be the one chosen to conduct the ceremony."

"Well, we mean no offense to Mr. Clary. He is a good man and all, but you christened Julie, and nothing would suit her, nor us, but that you conduct the marriage as well."

"I assure you, Mrs. Haversham, that Mr. Clary takes no offense. He realises that years from now he will be marrying all the babies that he is christening lately. Now, if you will excuse me, I shall go home and practice what I shall say tomorrow."

The old woman laughed. "Practice? You have used the same service for as long as you have been here. Surely, you know it by heart."

Now it was Mr. Williamson's turn to laugh. "I am getting older and, believe it or not, I am more forgetful. So I like to prepare as though it were my very first time. If I am relaxed and confident that I know the words by heart, then I can concentrate on calming the bride and groom and ensuring that they enjoy the experience as well."

"Then that accounts for all the brides who sing your praises, Mr. Williamson."

A smile split his face, and his brown eyes lit up. "I do not know about that, madam, but I do enjoy a good wedding."

Suddenly, Mrs. Haversham saddened. "I could not help but notice that you placed flowers on Miss Elizabeth's grave. You know that she and my Julie were lifelong friends. It is so sad that she did not get to marry in our parish, or even come back home to visit—and then, to be taken from us so young, and in such a horrific way."

Mr. Williamson tried to blink back the tears that always appeared on remembrance of Lizzybet. "Yes, it was a tragedy. I find it hard to believe sometimes that she is gone." A ragged breath shook his gangly frame as his eyes sought Elizabeth's headstone over the others. "I suppose that that is why you may find me there so often, reading the inscription ... just to remind myself."

Mrs. Haversham touched his arm. "I apologise. I should not have brought it up. I did not realise your pain was still so tender."

He tried to rally. "You have said nothing amiss. I thought that I had come to accept her loss months ago, but a young man came looking for her grave a few weeks past. I am afraid that his pain was so fresh—so raw—that it stirred my own. I assure you that I shall be well, given enough time."

She smiled sincerely. "I shall pray that the Lord stays close to you in your sorrow and one day soon relieves you of it entirely, so that your only memories of her are happy ones."

"Thank you, madam. I shall believe with you that He will."

There was a rumble of thunder in the distance, and they both looked up at the dark clouds gathering. Mr. Williamson pulled his collar up, motioning towards the gate that marked the entrance to the small cemetery.

"Though there is sure to be sunshine tomorrow, for now I think it wise that we move along rather quickly, or we shall both get soaked."

Big drops of rain began falling, and each could hear the other's laughter as they ran in different directions.

~~~*~~~

Reaching his small abode, Mr. Williamson pushed opened the door and began wiping his shoes on the small rug just inside the door. With his dear Agatha gone, he tried to keep the little cottage as clean as possible. As he walked over to the kitchen table, he was surprised to find a letter lying there. It was normal for the young man who brought his letters to leave them on the table, but he had already heard from his brother this week and was not expecting any more correspondence. Noting the elegant script, he glanced up to see where the letter had been franked and was surprised to see the return—Fitzwilliam Darcy, Pemberley, Derbyshire.

How unusual to get a letter from him right after my conversation with Mrs. Haversham about Lizzybet. Are you trying to tell me something, Lord?

Carefully unfolding it, he began to read, his brow furrowing the further he read. Past the usual pleasantries, the letter was an invitation, almost a plea, for his presence. After reading though it once, he began again at the top, reaffirming the important parts.

...have much to talk with you about concerning Elizabeth...

...consider accepting my offer of a coach to collect you and bring you to Town...

...stay with me at Darcy House...

...if agreeable...travel on to Pemberley...

Scratching his head, Mr. Williamson wondered what more Mr. Darcy could possibly have to talk about regarding Lizzybet. He thought they had covered everything when the young man was in Meryton. Sighing, he knew he would never refuse someone in need and especially not a man he now considered to be a friend. Besides, he had insisted that Mr. Darcy contact him if he ever needed to talk, and if that poor young man still needed his help, then he must make himself available.

The fact that a change of scenery and a few weeks of a different occupation was part of the invitation only made his acceptance easier.

Pemberley

As is common after a terrible storm, the next day dawned sunny and beautiful. Only the broken branches and leaves strewn about the portico and grounds testified to the severity of the weather that preceded the bright blue skies and downy white clouds.

The visiting party practically fled from Pemberley at daybreak, though Mrs. Reynolds made sure Cook had plenty of food prepared to break their fast before they departed. Mr. Darcy had made a brief appearance in the dining room, speaking politely, though never acknowledging Gwendolyn, as he assured Lord and Lady Greenwich that he had been happy to provide them respite from the storm. Nevertheless, it seemed to the housekeeper that the Greenwiches were in a big hurry to resume their journey and took very little time to eat. Thus, by the time Elizabeth made her way downstairs, only William remained in the room, finishing a well-deserved cup of tea. Looking up at her entrance, he could not hold back a smile as he greeted her.

"Good morning."

Elizabeth tried to form a smile, but her expression changed to one of confusion. "Good morning. Have your visitors come down yet?"

"Our guests were up very early and left several minutes ago."

"Oh?" Elizabeth stated, her confusion changing to dismay. "I am sorry I did not get to see them before they departed."

Now William was curious. "And why, may I ask, would you care to see Lady Waltham again? I take it you were not that anxious to see Lord and Lady Greenwich?"

Elizabeth looked down nervously. "No, I wanted to see *her*. I was much too fascinated by her sudden arrival and her show of temper to actually look at her closely." Her voice lowered to a whisper. "I thought this might be my last chance to study her appearance ... to understand her appeal."

William stood and moved to take both her hands in his. Neither spoke, though she knew he was waiting for an explanation. Still studying her slippers, she let out a resigned sigh. "If you must know, I saw her go into your room last night."

William closed his eyes, irritated that Lady Waltham's antics might have upset Elizabeth. "And did you see her leave shortly thereafter?"

"No." She tried to cover her concern with a mirthless laugh. "I could not bear to know how long she stayed."

Pulling her into a tight embrace, he felt her hands surround his waist as he whispered in her hair. "She came in while I was taking a bath with intentions of seducing me, but I rebuffed her. However, had Lord Greenwich not come down the hall shortly after she entered, I am afraid I would have had to summon help to toss the trollop out. She was determined she was not leaving."

Elizabeth gasped. "How shameless! And his Lordship caught her?"

"Yes, Lord Greenwich heard everything, and he was quite upset, so I do not believe they will be escorting Lady Waltham around England ever again."

William pushed her to arms' length, noting that she would not look up at him. "Elizabeth, tell me what are you thinking."

She stuttered, "I—I can see why a man might desire her. From the short time I was in her company, I realise that she is very beautiful."

He cupped Elizabeth's face, leaning in to kiss the tip of her nose; then, he ran a thumb over each high cheekbone, as he thoroughly examined her face for some time. Finally, her eyes lifted to his and he smiled, satisfied to have her attention.

"I will admit that she used to be a beauty, but she never possessed that same beauty inside. What I need you to understand is that she was never—**in any way**—as beautiful as you."

She dropped her head, sighing with frustration. "Please do not say that, Fitzwilliam. I know that you find me desirable, but I am not beautiful. Mama said that I was passable, but that no man would ever find me beautiful like Jane."

He tipped her chin up. "Look at me." Finally, brown eyes, flecked with gold, met his. "You are the most beautiful woman I have ever known, and I intend to tell you that every day for the rest of my life. Please do not ask me to deny what I see ... what I feel. I have not looked at another woman since the day we met and never with the love that is in my heart at this moment. You take my breath away."

As he spoke, large tears formed and slid from the corners of her eyes. He leaned down to kiss first one, then the other, from her cheek.

"Oh, Fitzwilliam ... my William," she whispered. "I do not know why you love me, but please, do not ever stop."

Their lips met with great urgency, and the kiss quickly escalated, neither remembering where they were as they drank deeply from one another. He tried, but could not resist pulling her hips to meet his, to feel her body melt into him. When finally he remembered that a servant could walk in at any moment, he reluctantly broke the kiss, pleased to see both desire and regret in her eyes.

"Come, sweetheart, walk out with me." Leaning over, he grabbed a serviette and filled it with sweet rolls, before wrapping it and taking her hand. "Now, we are prepared!"

As they departed the dining room, William barely noticed the maids standing near each door. He had no way of knowing that Mrs. Reynolds had entered the room through another entrance and had quickly backed out, pulling the door closed. Discreetly, she stationed a servant to guard each entrance, giving William and

Elizabeth their privacy. Only the wide smile on the long-time housekeeper's face gave the maids any hint as to what might be transpiring between the two people inside, as neither dared to ask.

~~~*~~~

Lost in daydreams, William and Elizabeth walked nearly all the way around the smallest body of water without a word passing between them—simply enjoying being with each other and sampling the wonderful sweet rolls. For his part, William was content to have Elizabeth near. All too clearly, he remembered his despondency after Kent, and how, at that time, it was impossible to imagine anything would ever change—that one day she would forgive him and be living at Pemberley.

Finally, reaching the far side of the pond, a sudden movement in a nearby pasture drew their attention. A small black colt with white stockings was frolicking, running and kicking up his heels. A black mare with the same markings stood nearby, watching her young and when William came into sight, the mare whinnied. This caused him to call out, "Juno!"

Elizabeth laughed as they walked over to the fence, and William pulled a small apple from his pocket. The horse ambled to him, neighing softly, and he fed her the apple.

"Juno? Goddess of Marriage? And do you always have apples in your pockets?"

William rubbed the mare's head, glancing sideways at Elizabeth as he chuckled. "The answer is 'yes' to the first two questions, and I took two apples from the sideboard before you came into the dining room. Here," he held out the other apple, "it is your turn."

Elizabeth reached for the fruit and placed it on her palm. As the mare took it, she giggled as the velvety mouth nibbled on her hand. "She is beautiful." She stroked Juno's nose as she glanced at William. "Did *you* name her?"

"Never!" He broke into a broad smile, dimples flashing. "I told Gigi that we would be the laughing stock of Derbyshire if her choice for their names became known. But she insisted on naming Juno as well as Romeo, Juliet, Benedick and Beatrice, who are all around here somewhere."

Pointing in the direction of a magnificent, black stallion several fences over, he declared, "And that is Romeo, the sire of that little fellow entertaining us so earnestly." Nodding his head towards the colt, he offered, "His name is Cupid."

"God of Love?"

William looked sheepish. "If I should ever ride him, I shall be ashamed to call out to him, so it is likely I will resort to a nickname when he is older."

"Oh, please do not change it," Elizabeth begged, shyly touching William's cheek. "I love his name."

The smile faded, and he sobered as his eyes darkened. Turning into her touch and kissing the palm of her hand, he whispered, "You win. Cupid, it is."

She stood mesmerized, and though she retracted her hand, neither looked away. The love she felt was plainly evident, and at that moment, William knew he could never refuse her anything. His heart was beating wildly as he tried to continue the conversation. "I suppose now that you are here, Gigi will no longer insist on naming all my foals."

"Why is that?"

"She hoped that by naming them after symbols of love and marriage, they would bring good fortune to Pemberley." He brought her hand back to his lips before pulling her into his chest. "And they have. You are a Godsend, Elizabeth, and I am the most fortunate of men."

Brushing a soft kiss across her mouth, he discerned a whimper. Pulling back, he could not resist what he saw in her expression. Taking her hand he began pulling her towards a small copse. As they passed a large oak, he whirled around, pressing her against the trunk and capturing her mouth in a torrid kiss. When she moaned and arched into him, he shrugged off his coat and feverishly began to unbutton his waistcoat, letting it drop to the ground without quitting the kiss.

His hands slid up from her waist to her breasts and explored their softness. Not satisfied, he pulled her hard against him, away from the tree trunk, which allowed him access to the buttons on back of her gown. He began slowly unbuttoning them. Still lost in the kiss, he pushed the gown off her shoulders, caressing their softness. His shaft immediately hardened, and his resolve not to go this far instantly evaporated.

Need drove them—the need to touch, to possess. As his tongue slipped inside her mouth and she began a duel with her own, he slid a hand inside her décolletage, grasping one soft mound. The feel of her breast in his hand, the nipple hardening against his palm, was his undoing. Immediately, he pushed the gown further down and dipped his head, taking one hard bud into his mouth and running his tongue over and around it, completely absorbed in the pleasure he was experiencing. Her hands were in his hair, pulling him closer as she writhed. First one nipple, then the other, were privy to his kisses, nips, and suckles, until she could bear it no longer.

Sighing softly, she murmured, "Oh, my love, I am terrified that this happiness cannot last. Please make me yours while we have the chance."

Her pleas brought him back to the present, and he began pressing soft kisses around each dark circle before sighing and pulling her garments back into place. Their breathing was erratic as they came down from the peak of desire, and he leaned in, placing his forehead against hers. Once calmed, he gathered her back into his embrace, while he buttoned her gown. Having completed the task, he whispered into her hair.

"I understand how you feel. I cannot help but think something or someone will take you away from me, but I want you to consider me as your husband, not just your lover, when we consummate our love. I truly believe the vicar to whom I have written will agree to conduct a small commitment ceremony for us." He kissed her nose. "And despite my inability to restrain myself," another kiss on her forehead followed, "I want you to know I truly love you ... not just desire you."

She smiled wanly. "I know that you want to protect me, though I think it is *you* that needs the protection from me."

His eyes were serious, concern shining out of their depths. "I look forward to lowering my guard, then."

After leaning in for another soft kiss, he took a deep breath. "I hate to go to London without you, but I cannot take the chance of having anyone see us travelling together, since you, my dear cousin, are supposed to be recuperating at Pemberley."

Returning his kiss, Elizabeth murmured against his mouth, "Though, rumour is that your cousin grows stronger and more wanton each day."

Chuckling, he feathered soft kisses across her cheek, and nuzzled her neck. As she placed kisses in his hair, she sighed. "You have not yet departed, and already I am missing you. Please come back to me as soon as possible. I am only alive when I am in your arms."

William cupped her face. "And I am only alive in yours. I promise to return as fast as is humanly possible."

As he pulled her hard against him, another passionate kiss sealed his promise. With a sigh, he pulled her close and held her tenderly. Tomorrow, Richard would come down from York and they would leave for London. This one special moment would have to endure them until his return.

~~~*~~~

Chapter 28

London
Darcy House
Early Afternoon

As Richard preferred, there were no footsteps, creaking hinges or butler to give him away as he gingerly opened the door to the study. He often took the opportunity to examine his cousin off guard, as Darcy was prone to assume a mask in company—even in his company. Seeing the sombre expression on his cousin's face, the precise look William had worn since they left Pemberley, Richard felt completely justified in what he did next.

"Good Lord, Darce, you have not been this subdued since Father reprimanded you for trying to shave Mother's favourite cat!" William jumped at the sound of his cousin's voice, but Richard continued undeterred. "You hardly said two words on the journey here, and you have been isolated in this study since our arrival. You know what they say—all work and no play."

Now irritated at being startled, William laid down the papers he had been trying to read, to study Richard. He was leaning against the door frame, his raised brow an indication that he expected an answer. Though William appreciated that his cousin was only trying to cheer him, he simply could not find it in himself to be very jovial at that moment. This was his first full day in London, and already he missed Elizabeth so desperately that he could barely concentrate on the matters at hand.

"I did not try to shave Balthazar," William challenged, trying to assume a happiness he did not feel. "You did the deed and placed the blame on me!"

"Oh, wait! You are correct." Richard smirked, pushing away from the door and walking over to stand in front of William's desk. "But it was your comment that it was uncomfortably warm and that he would be much cooler without so much hair that gave me the inspiration. Thus, inadvertently, you were to blame."

William shook his head in wonder at Richard's convoluted reasoning. "As I recall, I often bore the brunt of your father's wrath, though your *ideas* were almost always the provocation."

"Well, of course, you did. I had to deflect the blame to someone. You were younger, and Mother felt sorry for you after Uncle George died, so she would not let Father apply the strap to your backside. Now, me? She clearly had no qualms about allowing Father to whip me into shape! So you should be proud to have served me so well as to have saved me from some of his fury."

"*'Proud'* is not the word I would have chosen."

"Pleased?"

"Puzzled is more like it."

William stood and stretched soundly before taking his seat again. "Usually, I had no earthly idea what Uncle Edward was talking about. It was only afterward, when you would confess to me exactly what you had done, that I would understand. But I think that somewhere deep inside his heart, he knew all along that you were the perpetrator."

"Nevertheless, you always watched out for me, Darce, and for that, I am profoundly grateful. That is why I try so hard now to share your burdens and make you laugh."

"I appreciate it ever so much, Richard," he said much more light-heartedly than he felt.

William took up the papers once more, trying to appear busy. He actually had much to occupy him now that he was in London. But truth be known, he had read this particular page several times and still did not know exactly what it was about, as his thoughts kept drifting to the last day he had spent with Elizabeth at Pemberley.

Richard continued to observe. Suddenly, he reached over and grabbed the paper from William's hand. "Tell me who this is from and what it is in regards to!"

William reached towards the missive. "Do not be silly. Give me the letter."

"Go ahead! Teach me to mind my own business—show me that you are actually getting some work accomplished in this drab room."

William looked flummoxed. "Very well! It is a letter from my solicitors!"

"That much was easy. Which partner?"

"Johnson. No, Grant!" His face contorted in frustration. "I cannot remember who it is, but it does not matter. I care not which one handles the matter."

"A good deflection, I must admit. And what is the subject of this letter?"

William turned in his chair to stare out the window. Weakly, he replied, "It has to do with the sale of ... of ... bonds." His voice got louder with his certainty. "That is it, bonds!"

Looking back to glare at Richard, they seemed locked in a battle of wills until, abruptly, everything changed. William sighed heavily, leaned back in his chair and began rubbing his eyes.

Walking swiftly around the desk, Richard placed a comforting hand on his shoulder. "I am sorry. I did not mean to pry." Then, with a mirthless laugh, he recanted. "What am I saying? That is simply not true! I did mean to pry because you are my best friend and more a brother to me than Edgar. It troubles me when you are in pain."

William was silent for a moment, then closed his eyes. "I miss her dreadfully—that is all."

Richard's face darkened. "That is all? Hell, Darce, you hung your head out of the window until Pemberley was completely out of sight, and you acted the part of a puppy too soon taken from its mother during the entire trip. If you cannot bear to be apart from her for such a short time, how in the world will you survive if she takes you up on your offer to live at one of your estates? Neither one is an easy journey from Pemberley."

William had not mentioned their decision to live as man and wife to his cousin, as he was determined to wait until everything was settled to reveal their plans. But just the suggestion that Elizabeth might move to another country caused his anxiety to rise. What would they do if the vicar would not conduct a ceremony? If truth be known, he was quite worried about the vicar's reaction to their pledge to share their lives in every way.

If only Mr. Williamson will understand how much we need each other—how much we are in love.

Glancing at Richard's furrowed brow, he tried to shake off his melancholy and paste on a smile. "I do appreciate that you worry about me. It is comforting to know that I have you to turn to if I need to talk. But right now, things are out of my hands, and you know how ill I become when I cannot control every facet of my life." William's attempt at humour made Richard grin.

"And I am truly sorry, but I do have a great deal to accomplish before I shall be able to return to Elizabeth. Now, would you please be so kind as to find a book and be quiet while I work?"

"Well, I suppose I shall just make myself invisible," the colonel complained, "though I cannot for the life of me figure out why anyone would rather look over those boring papers than have a brilliant conversation with me."

William did not reply, so Richard shrugged, declaring, "Come find me when you are finished."

Leaving the study, he headed in the direction of the billiards room.

~~~*~~~

Perhaps an hour later, Mr. Barnes knocked on the door. "Come," William called, rising to his feet in anticipation of greeting his uncle. However, it was not Edward Fitzwilliam, but Charles Bingley who walked into the room.

"Darcy! I could not believe my good luck! I am only in Town until tomorrow, and I heard that you were in residence."

William's brow furrowed. He had tried to keep his presence a secret, but since Charles was a friend, he held out a hand, enquiring, "How did you learn that I was here?"

Charles reached to shake William's outstretched hand. "One of our maids came bustling in this morning to report to Caroline, not knowing I was in the room. It seems Caroline has been paying the maids to report when you are here."

William scowled at the mention of Charles' sister. "And how would the fact of my arrival spread so rapidly?"

"I asked Bertha the same thing. Apparently, she saw your servant at the butcher's shop picking up a large order. All Mrs. Barnes need do is order a goodly supply of meat, and the rumours begin that you are in residence."

William seemed to ponder that a moment. "I see." Charles noted his distraction.

"I realise that you are probably busy, and I pray I am not disturbing you, but I had to enquire after Lizzy. Jane would never let me come back home if she knew you were here and I did not speak to you personally. Tell me truly, how is my dear sister?"

William could not help but smile widely at the mention of his love. "Elizabeth is well, Charles. In fact, she almost seems to be the lively young woman I first met in Hertfordshire. It is unbelievable how she has improved in the last three weeks."

Charles sighed with relief. "I am so glad that I shall have some good news to impart to my Janie. She has been so worried about Lizzy."

"I can see that you are well—how are Jane and Peter?"

"Jane is doing so much better. She has followed the doctor's orders and is improving daily. Now Peter ..." Bingley shook his head at the thought of his son. "Peter is a wonder—healthy and unruly as any two-year-old."

"That is how it should be! I wish all three of you could come to Pemberley for a visit—to see Lizzy's improvement for yourselves. I know it would do her a world of good to see her family."

"Hmm, well, the doctor has not given Jane permission to travel yet, but I will mention it to her. Mr. McGuire has hinted that she may be given permission to travel after her next examination. She has bent the good physician's ear about her determination to visit Lizzy, and I daresay it would lift her spirits to find her sister recovered. Her letters have really made a very positive difference in Jane's disposition already."

"Please let me know when Jane is free to travel, and I will send my best coach." William squeezed Charles' shoulder. "I know you have a good coach, but my latest purchase is far superior to other coaches, mine and yours, and I insist that she travel in as much comfort as possible."

"Thank you, Darcy. You are too kind, and I readily accept for Jane's sake. I will let you know as soon as we are given clearance. Now, for the other reason I stopped by today."

William's eyebrows rose in question.

"As I promised in my letter explaining Caroline's betrayal, I came to London to confront her."

William glumly sat back down. The mention of Caroline's treachery caused his stomach to begin to twist in knots. He motioned for Charles to take a seat. "So, did she accept your terms?"

"Not at first. But after I explained the alternative, she was eager to do whatever was necessary to have her allowance restored. I have given her until the end of next week to confess her sins, as it were, to her acquaintances. Then she shall remove herself to our aunt's home."

"I cannot imagine her confession, if she makes any, will do much good. The harm has already been done. People prefer to remember the scandals and not the retractions. I have already been confronted with the gossip that Elizabeth is my mistress."

"I am sorry, Darcy. I know her admission will never totally undo the damage, but I have to try. Besides, if it only serves to make Caroline the laughing stock of London, if not the surrounding counties, I shall be satisfied. Perhaps then she can do no more harm, as no one will take her seriously. She may well end up an old maid if this gets out. Then, I shall use her dowry, as well as her inheritance, for her upkeep."

"That could mean supporting her for the rest of your life."

"Yes. But Father left her enough in his will to live out the rest of her days, perhaps not comfortably, but adequately. And I will be most diligent to make sure she stays within her allowance in the future—no more supplementing her extravagant spending, now that she has shown her true nature. She hurt Jane as well as Lizzy, and I shall never forgive either offense. I am just thankful that you have not shunned me because of my sister's audacity. Your friendship is dear to me."

"Never think I would blame you for the actions of your sister. Besides, you have tried to check her during our entire acquaintance, but she refused to listen. She must now suffer the consequences of her actions."

Charles stood and walked towards the door with William following. Charles clasped his hand again. "I shall leave you to your work. I intend to retire early, so that I can depart for Netherfield first thing in the morning. I miss my family."

William's mind immediately flew to Elizabeth. *As I miss my love.* Shaking off this gloomy thought, he swallowed the large lump in his throat. "Can I not convince you to stay for dinner? Richard is here and his father will join us shortly. We could at least dine together."

"I am sure you have business to discuss, and I still have to make arrangements for Caroline's journey to York next week, as well as prepare for my departure."

"I understand. Then allow me to wish you a safe journey home. And please begin to make plans to visit Pemberley as soon as Jane feels well enough to travel."

"We will, Darcy. Tell Elizabeth that we send our love." Charles' face sobered. "I should thank you again for taking care of her. Her safety and recovery are entirely your doing. Jane and I shall be forever in your debt."

William shook his head. "It is completely the other way around. I shall be forever indebted to you for bringing her back to me."

Their eyes locked, each determined that **they** were the debtor and fully aware that neither would concede. Conscious that William was giving up far more than he, Charles clasped him in a hug.

"You are the one who is unable to marry the woman you love. I think you have made the greater sacrifice. God bless you, Darcy."

Determined not to let the tears filling his eyes show, Charles turned and was out the door before William could reply. Moving to the doorway, he followed Charles' departure from the house in silence.

What will he and Jane think of our decision to live as man and wife? Surely they will understand, even if no one else does.

~~~*~~~

It was only a few seconds later that Richard exited the billiard room, heading in the direction of the study. He was surprised to find William standing in the doorway, still staring in the direction in which Bingley had gone.

"Did I hear voices? Were you talking to someone?"

William shook his head absentmindedly. "Yes, Bingley stopped by to enquire about Elizabeth."

"You did not insist that he stay? I would have enjoyed his company."

"I would have as well, but he would not hear of it. He said he wanted to get an early start back to Netherfield. Jane has not been well since she is with child again, so I imagine it weighs on his mind. The situation with Elizabeth has not been easy on her or Charles."

"Did Bingley mention that viper, Caroline?"

"Yes. He carried out his plan, and Caroline has accepted his terms. Though I imagine the damage that harridan has wrought is irreversible."

"Maybe. Maybe not. Besides, when have you ever cared what the *ton* thought about anything that concerned you. That is one of the things I greatly admire about you—you are your own man. Would that I could be, also!"

William turned to consider Richard, before heading to the liquor cabinet. He poured two glasses of brandy, handing one to his cousin. "Is there something I should know?"

Richard shrugged, sinking down into an overstuffed chair. "If I were not a second son, I would offer for Mrs. Largin. But, alas, I shall have to settle for some woman with a large dowry."

"What does your father say about it?"

"I have not said anything to him. You know he would not understand. His counsel is always the same—it matters not what woman warms your bed, only that she brings a large dowry into it. It is a wonder that he and mother have such a good marriage."

"And your mother? What does she say?"

Richard smiled. "She would do everything in her power to see me happy. I have no doubt of that."

"But you have not told her either."

"No."

"Then confide in her. Aunt Evelyn is a formidable woman when she sets her mind to something. I am sure she will think of a solution."

A deep rumble of laughter burst forth. "That may be what I am afraid of, Darce!" Just as quickly, Richard sobered, stood, and walked to the windows to stare out into the garden.

William joined him, slipping an arm around his shoulder. "And you accuse me of being afraid to speak. You know I will help you in any way I can. I have offered you the estate in Scotland."

"And I appreciate it, but you know I cannot accept it." He took a deep breath. "It is just ... I do not want Mrs. Largin to want for anything. She is so beautiful, bright and kind, and she has her children to consider. I am sure she can attract a more suitable husband, someone with a grand estate and a large fortune."

"Without love, a grand estate and a large fortune mean absolutely nothing. Trust me, I know." Richard glanced sideways at William, noting a deep sadness on his cousin's face.

"I am sorry, Darce. Sometimes I am thoughtless. I forget that money does not cure every problem."

"Nor does the absence of money, apparently."

William held up his glass in a salute, and Richard returned it. Quickly they drained their glasses.

London
A Townhouse
Grosvenor Square
That same afternoon

As George Wickham strolled into Count Stefano's study, he found the man sitting behind the large carved desk as usual, feet propped on the edge. From Stefano's posture, one would assume he had not a care in the world, but Wickham knew better. Rumour among his seedier contacts was that the count was the object of several clandestine investigations, and Wickham wondered if that, more than anything else, precipitated his desire to return to Italy.

Peering about the near empty room stacked with boxes, Wickham offered, "There was no one at the door, so I let myself in."

"Yes, well my people are getting my things ready for shipment to Italy. I have very little staff still in London." Taking in Wickham's attire, he ventured. "To what do I owe the honour of this visit? I have paid you everything you are due, and from the looks of it, you used the money to buy a new wardrobe."

"I had a new coat or two made, but my reason for being here is to enquire as to whether or not you have located your errant wife?"

The smirk on Wickham's face clearly irritated the count. "Do not talk of my wife in that manner. I assure you, it is not appreciated."

Wickham sobered. He only intended to annoy the count, not make him angry. His breath quickened at the fire in the count's evil, green eyes. "I apologise. My jest was inappropriate. Forgive me."

The count studied him for a long moment. "The imbecile I hired has no earthly idea where to find her."

"You are still of a mind that she is alive?"

"Of course. I feel it here." He pounded on his chest. "If my Elizabeth were dead, I would know for certain."

Wickham could not keep from smiling. "I, too, believe she is alive, and I have a good idea where she may be found."

The count bounded to his feet. "Tell me! I must go to her."

"No. At least not right away. We must come to an understanding first."

The count sat back down, slowly reaching down to open a small drawer where he kept a loaded pistol and taking it out without any notice. "Are you trifling with me, Wickham?"

"I assure you that I am not. It is only that the place where I believe she is staying is a fortress. There is no way she can be taken from there against her will. The only hope of recovering her is for someone she trusts to convince her to leave. Afterwards, I shall have her under my control."

"And you are not going to tell me where she is?"

"I suppose it can do no harm. I believe she is at Pemberley."

"I have heard of it, the Darcy's estate in Derbyshire?'

"The very one."

"Why would he be involved?" The count's enquiry was quickly interrupted.

"He is the friend of Charles Bingley, Jane Bennet's husband."

"I see," the count said, a look of distaste crossing his features. "And what evidence do you have to lead you to believe that she is there? At Pemberley?"

"My spies tell me that a woman—a *cousin* has moved there in the last few months with her aunt. The cousin fits the description of Elizabeth Bennet. Conveniently, her name is Elizabeth as well, though they say her surname is Lawrence. Also, I had my man ply the currier, the one who delivers the post, with ale, rendering him very drunk. From him we learned that there have been many posts exchanged between Netherfield and Pemberley during the same time period."

"Is this Darcy in love with my Elizabeth? He must be; otherwise, why should he offer her shelter? She could only be a liability to him as a single man."

"That, I can neither confirm nor deny, but it does not matter. If you want her back, I can deliver her to you for twenty thousand pounds."

"Twenty thousand!" Stefano shouted, rising to his feet. "My Lord! Why would you think I would pay such an extravagant amount to you? I could always capture her myself."

"Not if you want to succeed. If you try to march into Pemberley and take her, you will die. Pemberley is a veritable fortress, with outposts and guards surrounding every square foot. I, however, cannot fail. I grew up at Pemberley, as my father was steward there, and I still have friends among the servants. Also, I have an associate, a woman, who is acquainted with your Elizabeth. She has agreed to help me deceive her into leaving the estate for half the money. So you see, I am not being too greedy."

The count seemed to consider the situation. His frown lightened just a bit and seeing this, Wickham continued.

"You can have a ship standing ready at Liverpool. I can deliver her to you there, as it is the nearest port to Pemberley. I do not believe they would look for you to sail from that port, even if they learn of our plans, since it is on the west coast. You could be on your way to Italy before Darcy learns she is missing. Of course, we would want to act while he is away, preferably in London. Once in Italy, I imagine that you can disappear. Only this time, you shall have your beloved wife with you."

There was no reply for some time, and Wickham became nervous as he watched the count shift from one foot to the other. Stefano clutched even tighter the small pistol he had slipped into his pocket. Finally, he lifted his cold, dead eyes to meet Wickham's.

"I will pay your price for my Elizabeth. BUT, if you try to betray me, be assured that I will hunt you down and kill you. Do we understand each other?"

Wickham let go of the breath he had been holding, swallowing hard. "I shall contact you the moment I know with certainty that everything is in place. You need to be ready to sail at a moment's notice."

"With my father's shipping business, that is not a problem. He is aware that I plan to return to Italy shortly, and though we do not see eye-to-eye, he would never deny me the chance to escape from England, especially if my life was at risk. His vessels sail out of Liverpool every week, not just from London."

"Good. Good. Now, if you will excuse me. I need to meet with my contact, who I shall instruct to depart for Pemberley promptly. She will need to convince *Miss Lawrence* that it would be in her best interest to leave Darcy's estate. I imagine if she cites tales of your anger at discovering her hideout, that shall suffice."

The green eyes turned dark. "You may invoke my name if it convinces her to leave. But know this—I do not like to be reminded of my past failures in regard to Elizabeth. You are treading on dangerous ground."

Wickham nodded, weary of the count's threats. "Again, I apologise, Count Stefano." Promptly, he changed the subject to his own concerns. "Now, all that is left is for you to procure the funds."

Stefano said through clenched teeth, "The money will be yours when I take Elizabeth's hand in mine. Not before."

~~~*~~~

Having stopped just outside the open study door, Gwendolyn Waltham quietly made her way back to the foyer, hoping to clear the front door before being seen by anyone. She had swallowed her pride to call on the count, hoping to find he still had some interest in her. Now, thanks to her eavesdropping, she knew that Francesco was likely not the count's real name since this man kept calling him Stefano, and that, whatever his name might be, he was leaving England forever with a wife she had not known about.

As she hurried along, Gwendolyn considered how this new information might be useful to her. She had no prospects for a new lover, and without being able to employ Lord Greenwich's coattails to meet wealthy men, it would be more difficult to find suitable companionship. She knew, however, that she would never be welcomed by him again, not after the debacle with Fitzwilliam.

Damn Darcy's lies! So he was sleeping with that woman all along!

233

Chapter 29

Mr. Scroggins moved to stand behind his employer. His mind was fixed on the pistol in his waistband as he scowled at the two gentlemen confronting Lord Stanton in his study. He recognised Colonel Fitzwilliam from having seen him about Town, but before now, he had only heard of the tall, reticent Mr. Darcy who stood alongside Fitzwilliam. He left off studying Darcy, however, when the Colonel replied quite testily to Lord Stanton's address.

"I care not for your diplomatic service or your reputation, Essex. My father has incontestable proof that your son, Stephen Arthur Stanton, is the man who took advantage of my cousin, Anne de Bourgh. He married and then abandoned her as soon as he drained her bank accounts. I assure you, it is to your advantage that my father agreed to let me negotiate this matter in his stead, as the Earl of Matlock is very displeased."

Lord Stanton sighed, motioning towards some chairs. "Please, sit down. Can we not discuss this rationally? After all, my son is eight and thirty, and I have had no control over him in years. And at this moment, I am uncertain of his whereabouts." Darcy nodded to Richard and everyone sat down.

Relieved that the Colonel had calmed, Stanton offered. "I would like to tell you about Stephen, as I feel you would understand the situation better if you knew his background. Would you agree to hear me out before we discuss the matter you have come to arbitrate?"

Richard crossed his arms. "We will hear you out, if you will answer our questions once you have finished."

"That is my intention," Frederick Stanton answered dryly.

William's eyes flicked to Richard's, and they shared a meaningful look—today they would know. Having listened last night to the investigator's report on Anne's husband that Richard's father had commissioned, they both concluded that the man who married Anne and Count Stefano were likely one and the same. They had convinced the earl to let Richard handle the matter, as they did not want his father to learn of the possible link between Anne and Elizabeth.

Lord Stanton cleared his throat. "I cannot tell my son's story without speaking of his mother. My wife, the Contessa Maria Issabetta de Cavour, and I met when I accompanied my father on a diplomatic mission to Italy. She was young and very beautiful, the daughter of a wealthy nobleman. Being not much older but quite foolish, I fell in love with her at first sight. Unfortunately, I did not realise that she was too immature to know her own mind or to move away from her family and her homeland. At that time, I thought love would conquer all, and we were married shortly before I was to return to England. Barely ten months later we were residing in Sheffield and awaiting the birth of Stephen.

"Being very spoiled, Maria never tried to adjust to England. She constantly cried to go home, and I indulged her by letting her visit for long periods of time during the first five years of our marriage. However, by the time Stephen was old enough to begin his education in earnest, she insisted he attend school in Italy. I disagreed. He and I were very close and, naturally, I wanted him educated here. I had hoped he might take over Northgate Manor, my family estate, when he was older. And, of course, I wished him to take his place among our equals in society.

"However, Maria was determined to return to her homeland with Stephen. When he was about seven, she succeeded in spiriting him out of the country while I was away on business. I tried to recover him from Italy, but it was made clear to me that I would never leave the country alive with Stephen in tow. Maria's family has great influence there, so I had to settle for visits and letters. As the years went by, those visits were fewer, and his letters stopped altogether.

"Our relationship suffered, as you can imagine. Near Stephen's eighteenth birthday, Maria's father died, and Stephen inherited his title and properties. Maria insisted that he be known thereafter as Count Stefano Gianni Montalvo de Cavour, ignoring his given name and the title he would one day inherit from me. I had no say in the matter and, unfortunately, Stephen was more eager to please his mother as he and I were practically strangers."

At the mention of Stephen's Italian name, Richard observed that William's eyes narrowed and his countenance darkened. He was beginning to wonder if bringing his cousin had been such a good idea. It had been a hard bargain talking his father into letting William and him handle the matter, and now it seemed his normally docile cousin was quickly becoming as infuriated as his father had been. Unaware of Richard's concerns, Lord Stanton continued his narrative.

"Sometime after his twentieth birthday, my son turned up on the doorstep at Northgate. He voiced his desire to live with me, and we had a grand reunion. For the longest time, everything seemed to go smoothly—or perhaps I did not wish to see the problems that concerned members of my family and my staff. Numerous times, my loyal steward mentioned incidences of Stephen's brutality regarding some of the animals on the estate. A beloved horse suffered a broken leg and had to be put down. My housekeeper's cat, which he despised, was found drowned and he even went so far as to bludgeon one of my favourite fox hounds, claiming the dog had gone mad and attacked him."

Lord Stanton was silent for a time, staring at something only he could see. "He always had a good explanation for his actions and, God help me, I wished to believe him."

He sighed resignedly. "Nevertheless, things can only be rationalized for so long I suppose. Within the space of another year, I had heard one discouraging report after another concerning my son. Only now it involved young women—maids and such. I tried to reason with him, to tell him he should not trifle with the servants or any woman for that matter. I suggested that if he could not control his desires, he should find a proper young lady and marry. He laughed like a madman." Stanton shook his head and repeated somberly, "Like a madman."

Seeming to recover, he continued, "That was when he declared that he could never marry one of those whores!"

At the shocked looks on the faces of his listeners, he clarified, "Those were his words, gentlemen, not mine. He went on to explain that he was already married and had fathered a child, a son, before coming back to England to escape a domineering wife."

Richard started to voice his disgust, but was stopped by an outburst from his enraged cousin. Standing with balled fists and blazing eyes, William declared, "All this time! He has been trifling with the lives of innocent women, and he is married!"

Alarmed, Stanton stood too, blanching as Mr. Scroggins moved between himself and Darcy. Surprised at his cousin's outburst and seeing the bodyguard's nervous grasp on the handle of his pistol, Richard stood and stepped between them, facing William.

He leaned in to whisper, "Calm down. We need to hear him out. Otherwise, how are we to help Elizabeth?"

William studied Richard for a few moments before dropping back down in the chair, a clenched jaw and steely eyes proof that he was livid still. Richard took the seat beside him as a precaution and nodded to Frederick Stanton to continue. The older man tapped Mr. Scroggins on the shoulder, motioning for him to stand down and then took his seat as well.

"The fact that he was married did nothing to curtail Stephen's pursuit of respectable women. His conduct was despicable and we parted company over his actions. Many disturbing reports followed—arguments, rumours of maidens ruined, duels, angry fathers and brothers. It was as though he had no conscience. Whomever he desired, he pursed with a passion, and once he had the woman, he no longer wanted her it seemed. I began to believe that Stephen was tempting fate, and that one day an angry father would finish him. It was not until his thirtieth birthday, however, that a cruel incident convinced me to intervene and commit him to Bedlam.

"I ... I had invited my niece to Northgate. Mary Catherine was to be married, and her mother, my sister, was determined that the wedding be held at our ancestral home. My niece was a lovely girl, barely twenty, with dark blond hair and green eyes. By this time, Stephen had been back in my good graces for about a year and often frequented Northgate. I remember thinking upon her introduction to Stephen that he acted the perfect cousin—respectful but not flirtatious.

"Apparently that was all an act as he was quickly smitten with Mary Catherine. My servants caught them together in a compromising situation so I went to him—asked him not to trifle with her affections. All he did was scoff! He implied that I had an evil mind—that he was only taking an interest in her welfare as any cousin should. The next day he eloped with her, taking a curricle and heading to Gretna Green. He was driving when it overturned, and she was killed. Everyone was devastated—everyone except Stephen."

A grimace crossed Stanton's face. "He laughed! Laughed! He claimed Providence must have intervened to save him from an imprudent union." He shook his head. "Our family was shattered, while he went on his merry way without so much as an apology. After that, I filed the papers to have him committed; but, in a twist of fate, someone alerted him, and he was on a ship to Italy before I realised he was missing.

"The next time I laid eyes on him, he was nearing four and thirty and much too clever for me to manage. Our relationship has been strained ever since. He knows I will not support him, but he insists on coming to my homes when least expected. That is how I learned of his new occupation—marrying widows for their money. I challenged him about his comings and goings at Northgate Manor, and he admitted as much to me."

Everyone was silent, as furtive glances were exchanged between the occupants of the room. Finally, William asked through gritted teeth, "How many women has he married?"

Lord Stanton lowered his eyes to the floor. "Actually, there has been only one actual ceremony of which I am aware."

William's voice was low and controlled. "What do you mean?"

"He carried out such a sham marriage to Lady Marlton, a wealthy widow, within a few months of his return. They eloped to Gretna Green. The poor woman died several months later under peculiar circumstances, and I was never sure of Stephen's innocence. After her demise, he began preying on other wealthy women—those who were most vulnerable—widows mostly, but anyone with no father or brothers to protect them. Sadly, most were not very intelligent."

"Once, I confronted him with what I suspected, and he did not bother denying it. In fact, he bragged of procuring blank marriage certificates, stolen from the magistrate in Gretna Green, and forging them. Apparently, Stephen and his victim would begin the trip to Scotland, and then along the way he would drug her. I suppose it was easy to keep her drugged for a sufficient number of days and then bring her out of her stupor to proclaim that they were *married*. He boasted of showing his new *wives* their marriage certificates while they were still quite groggy. The ring on her finger and the fake certificate was apparently proof enough. After a few months, they would find themselves back in their own homes, and Stephen would be gone, along with their money and jewels. I am sure they were too embarrassed to say anything, and who would champion them in any event?"

William gripped the arms of his chair, his knuckles turning white. Stanton swallowed hard, quickly adding, "You realise I could do nothing by the time I was informed about it. I knew that my son was not divorced from his first wife in Italy, so any subsequent marriages were illegal, including the one to Lady Marlton."

Seeing William's continued discomposure, Stanton sputtered, "Over the years, I have tried, given the resources I have, to help the women my son has injured. I will repay your cousin's dowry, though it may take some time. I know it is not much, but it is the best I can do under the circumstances. I cut Stephen's allowance off years ago, though I have allowed him to stay at my estates under certain circumstances, and I use the funds he would have received to reimburse what he has stolen."

He bowed his head. "You understand that one does not stop loving his child, just because he becomes someone who is unlovable."

Seeing Stanton's guilt, William hoped he might be willing to tell what he knew about Elizabeth. "What can you tell us of another of our acquaintances whom your son has apparently deceived—Elizabeth Bennet. She certainly would not fit the pattern of a wealthy woman or a widow, which you describe."

Lord Stanton observed Mr. Darcy, instantly recognising the place that Elizabeth held in his heart. "Yes, dear Elizabeth. You are correct in that she was not his usual target. I met her in Hertfordshire when I leased an estate there for hunting. I did not mean for Stephen to find me and join me there, but he did. Elizabeth was such a delightful girl and so smart—not fooled by my son in the least. I am afraid that her indifference intrigued him, and he was determined to have her. I tried to intervene and had great luck with her father, as Mr. Bennet was an old acquaintance from Cambridge. He listened to my council and soundly rejected Stephen's overtures."

"Mrs. Bennet, however, was as mercenary a woman as I have ever seen and she tried to force the match. Alas, Mr. Bennet died while I was in London on business, and when I returned, Stephen was gone and so was Elizabeth. I knew immediately what had transpired, just as surely as I knew she would never have agreed to marry him. She hated him, you see."

William swallowed the lump in his throat, as the earl continued. "When I returned to Northgate she was there but it was too late to help her. If I took her back to Meryton, her reputation would have been ruined and, besides, that horrible mother of hers would never have let her return home. Stephen paid the mother to have the daughter, of that I am sure!"

Without waiting for a reply, he stated, "I believe Elizabeth Bennet was the only woman that Stephen ever truly cared for, though he is not capable of loving anyone but himself. He told me that he loved her and accused me of turning her against him by telling her about his past. That was untrue, but he could never admit that she despised him. Then when he learned she had planned an escape from Northgate, well, you know about the fire I am sure."

Stanton turned to meet William's gaze. "If I am not mistaken, I believe you know everything that has happened to Miss Bennet since she disappeared from Meryton."

William nodded slightly, without speaking.

"I also believe that she did not die in the fire. You are hiding her, are you not?"

Astonished at the man's powers of deduction, William sat speechless, his eyes blazing, while Richard's gaze flew from one man to the other.

Unnerved, William had to know. "How did you ascertain she was not dead?"

Lord Stanton sighed. "Only my intuition. Something was not quite right in the account my housekeeper gave after the fire. She was evasive about the details, and I got the distinct impression that she knew a great deal more than she was saying. Then again, I recognised how difficult it had been for her to deal with Stephen all these years."

He shook his head tiredly. "I suppose some part of me did not want to know. So, I did not press her." Noting their uneasiness, he vowed. "I give both of you my word as a gentleman and as Elizabeth's friend, that I will never tell him that she may be alive. I thought a great deal of her and Mr. Bennet, and it sickened me to see her treated in such a manner."

William's agitation was palpable, so the earl persisted. "Nevertheless, let me warn you—though Stephen will get nothing from me, he has significant resources from his mother's family. If he were to ever to suspect that Elizabeth is alive—well, he is relentless in pursuit of what he desires."

William lifted his chin, his eyes like flint. "That makes two of us."

Stanton nodded. "Of that I have no doubt, Mr. Darcy. Keep her hidden. She deserves to be happy—to live as she desires, not as he wishes. Take care of her."

"You can rely on that."

~~~*~~~

The carriage ride back to Darcy House was very quiet, as the slow rocking of the carriage lent itself to reflection. Ever since departing Stanton's townhouse, Richard had silently studied the dark expression on his cousin's face, while William, deep in contemplation, was completely lost in his thoughts of Elizabeth.

William's heart beat furiously as his feelings fluctuated—from elation at learning she was not married—to despair at the complications created by Stefano's hoax and the continued threat he posed. One thought after another raced through his mind.

... Elizabeth was assumed dead ... Would it be legal to marry Elizabeth Lawrence? ...

... An announcement of marriage to Miss Lawrence would not draw attention ...

... And a special license would mean no need for banns...

... Mr. Williamson is likely to arrive soon... Will this change my plans? ...

... Will it be possible to locate this cad while I am in London? ...

A declaration from Richard interrupted his jumbled thoughts. "It must be awful to know the boy you loved is lost to you forever, and the man who returned is a reprobate—that all you have left to deal with is the devastation he leaves behind. Nevertheless, Stefano is truly a blackguard ... and I have met a few blackguards in my time."

William slammed his fist against the door. "That man should be horsewhipped then hanged!" Recovering, he stared out at the passing houses. "And Stanton shall not garner any sympathy from me. He should have tried harder to restrain his son, no matter his age. Had he at least warned more people of his debauchery, a lot of women, including Elizabeth, likely would have been spared."

"I cannot quarrel with you on that, though I dare say some people never listen to advice, or like Mrs. Bennet, would not have cared."

William exhaled loudly. "You are correct. There will always be those who fall prey to pretty words and a handsome deportment as well as those who care more for money than the well-being of their own children."

"Now, where does that leave us? I will tell Father that Lord Stanton agreed to repay Anne's dowry, howbeit, over a period of time. In addition, I shall inform him of the cad's propensity to elope without the benefit of a divorce and the likelihood that Anne was never married to him. Naturally, I shall not mention Elizabeth, but I assume you will want to locate this malefactor before he seeks her out."

"Precisely! Charles and Jane thought I could hide her at Pemberley, and I suppose I convinced myself it would work. However, if Stanton has figured out that Elizabeth is alive and living with me, Stefano could also have reached that conclusion. Since it is apparent that he is obsessed with her, as long as he is alive, Elizabeth will be in danger. I shall immediately advise my steward to double the guards again, and we shall intensify our search."

Conscious of William's reluctance to exact punishment in the past upon Wickham, Richard asked cautiously, "And you agree that he should be destroyed?"

William nodded. "I want the opportunity to call him out. Who is this contact that you believe can find him?"

"If anyone can locate him, it is an old friend of mine, Lieutenant Marbury. He has retired from the army and runs his own investigation firm. Rumour is that he has members of the Bow Street Runners on his payroll, so he knows where every scoundrel in London is at a given time, and probably over all of England. But, why would you chance a duel?"

"I would like the satisfaction of revenging Elizabeth. Do you worry that I am not capable?"

"Of course not! You are a better swordsman than I and an equal marksman. I have no fears in that regard, but I would not trust the man to fight fair."

"I appreciate your concern."

"I will help all I can, but I have to return to my regiment at the end of the month. What shall we tell Father if he asks why I am spending so much time with you?" Fitzwilliam looked at Darcy, and receiving no answer, ventured, "I thought we should say that we will not stop until we catch this devil and rid England of him. Agreed?"

"Agreed."

"This new intelligence—how does it affect your plans."

"It changes nothing. I still intend to marry her, only now I shall deal with Stefano first."

Richard chuckled. "I knew it! Shall I tell you what I theorized?"

William smiled wanly, shaking his head. "You are apparently going to tell me, whether I want you to or not."

"Well, first, I figured you never intended to let Elizabeth settle at one of your estates—at least not without you! And, knowing the honourable man that you are, I assumed you would marry her, with or without the blessing of the law or society."

He grinned to see William's eyes widen in astonishment. "It is not that hard, Darce. You are too predictable. When you love, it is with all your heart and soul; there is no half-way with you."

William tried unsuccessfully to smile. "I suppose I am transparent."

"That is not a bad thing, my friend," Richard jested. "You are honest, dependable and proper to a fault, so it is easy to figure out what path you will take. That cannot be said of many men."

William laughed mirthlessly. "I am hardly the saint you think I am."

Richard teased good-naturedly. "Oh, I do not think a *saint* would have considered marriage outside the law and the church."

At William's grimace, he promptly sobered. "Do not mind my kidding, Darce. Providence must have seen your selfless love for Elizabeth and intervened. After all, He provided a way out of this darkness."

Just then the carriage came to an abrupt halt, and they could hear the footman as he climbed down to open the door. As Richard prepared to exit, William grabbed his arm.

"Thank you for coming with me. Without your calming influence today, I might have gone completely mad. To hear what Stefano did," his voice faltered, "to my sweet Elizabeth."

Seeing his cousin's pain, Richard grasped his shoulder. "I am proud to have been there when you needed me, but know this—Elizabeth is safe right now, and you are the reason."

Darcy House
The next morning

Richard took a sip of his tea and a bite of a sweet roll as he watched William open a letter. It had just been delivered on a silver salver, along with several others, and William had rifled through the stack, picking out this one specifically. It caught Richard's attention, as William normally finished eating before bothering to look at the mail. A wide grin spread across his cousin's face.

"You look as though you were expecting that."

William gazed over the top of the missive. "I am sorry. I was going to inform you when everything was settled, but it is an answer from the vicar at Meryton, Mr.

Williamson. He was a great friend to Elizabeth, and he and I became fast friends while I stayed at Netherfield. I wrote him before I left Pemberley, asking him to visit me while I am in Town. He should arrive the day after tomorrow."

"So, Mr. Williamson from Meryton is the lucky fellow chosen to conduct some type of religious ceremony. Am I correct?"

"Yes."

Richard studied him carefully. "Does this vicar know she is alive?"

"No, when we met, neither of us knew. But he was like a father to Elizabeth, and I know he will be as thrilled as I. And it will please her immensely if he visits Pemberley, whether he chooses to help us or not."

"Let us hope that he fills the role nicely. By the way, I sent a courier for Lieutenant Marbury as soon as I awoke. We should hear from him by this afternoon, if I know my friend at all."

William looked genuinely pleased. "Good. I am eager to get things settled and return to Elizabeth. Lord, I miss her so!"

Richard laughed. "I know how you feel. I am going to make time to call on Mrs. Largin tomorrow."

"Am I to wish you joy?"

"Not yet, cousin, but I confided in mother as you wisely advised, and she has made it plain that she favours the lady. And she reminded me that grandmother left her a small estate in Derbyshire. Apparently, she and father have saved it for me all these years, hoping that at some point I would mature and marry."

"Well, one out of two is not bad," William smirked.

"Very funny, cousin!"

"In Derbyshire you say? What is the name of this estate?"

"Windmere."

"Windmere is not twenty miles from Pemberley, but I thought it belonged to Lord and Lady Perkins, though she abandoned it after he died."

"Apparently the Perkins had rented the estate from mother for years. With the passing of Lord Perkins last year, Lady Perkins moved to her daughter's home. Mother purposefully did not seek another renter in anticipation of my becoming a respectable married man!" At this pronunciation Richard wagged his brows.

"And Aunt Evelyn is not a woman to be thwarted!"

"No." Richard grinned from ear to ear. "No, she is not!"

William stood and embraced his cousin. "I pray that you have captured the lovely Mrs. Largin's heart if that is what you desire. I cannot express how relieved I am that you will be able to retire from His Majesty's service and become a poor working sod!"

"Such as yourself!"

"Precisely!"

They both convulsed in laughter.

That night

Soft curves yielded under his hands as he ran them over her body. She sighed, as deeply affected as he, and as he leaned in to capture her lips, he could feel her fingernails burrow into his bare back. Elizabeth!

William sat up abruptly, looking around the silent, dark room. This was Darcy House, not Pemberley. He groaned, disappointed to realise that he was only reliving Elizabeth's visit to his dressing room the morning he left for London.

Adams had left him sitting in the barber's chair while he went to sharpen his scissors for a quick trim of the Master's hair. Thus, eyes closed and clad only in breeches with a towel lying across his lap, William startled to hear Elizabeth's soft voice at the door.

"William?"

The dressing room door slowly opened and seeing that he was alone, she slipped inside. A vision of loveliness, she was clad only in a white satin nightgown and robe, her hair loose about her shoulders. Holding a finger to her beautiful lips, she smiled mischievously. "Shhh!"

Then she turned and locked the door before taking in the scene. Obviously the bath water had already been used, and for a brief moment she grieved that Gwendolyn had seen him in this tub, and she had not. However, as their eyes met, hers widened in surprise at how very nearly naked he was. Surprise was immediately replaced by a look of hunger as she followed the fine, dark hair across his toned chest down a trail that led across his slim abdomen and stopped at his breeches. When her tongue swept across her parched lips, William could not sit still any longer.

Throwing the towel to the floor, he had barely gained his feet when she ran to him. Her arms wrapped around him tightly and her fingernails began to trace patterns on his bare back causing him to shiver. Luxuriating in the feel of her, he buried his face in her hair and took a deep breath of the lavender scent wafting up.

"Elizabeth, my darling, what are you doing up at this hour? We agreed that you would not awaken to see me off. That is why we said our goodbyes last night."

"You agreed, not I!" She murmured into his chest, all the while placing kisses on every possible place. "I could not bear for you to leave me without another embrace, another kiss."

He was unprepared for the way his body reacted to her proclamation. Instantly aroused, he quickly untied her robe, pulling it off and throwing it aside before he kissed her hungrily. As they kissed, he backed her towards the wall. Once against the barrier, he cupped her bottom, lifting her as her legs immediately clasped around him. Holding her this way, his throbbing shaft was just where it longed to be, and as they continued to kiss, he rubbed slowly back and forth. She moaned softly causing him to harden even more.

A knock at the door and then a much louder one seconds later, finally broke the spell, if not the embrace. They quit the kiss to stare passionately at each other. Finally he let her slide down to her feet, and then stooped to retrieve her robe. After replacing the satiny clothes, he tried to dissuade his arousal but ended up opening the door for his valet holding a carefully placed towel. If Adams was surprised to find Elizabeth inside the room when he entered, he was well trained not to show it.

He began to apologise. "Excuse me, sir. I shall wait in the hall until you summon me."

"No need, Adams. Just wait here," William ordered, tossing the towel aside and grabbing Elizabeth's hand. In one fluid motion he pulled her past the surprised valet into the hallway.

Adams nodded absently as the door closed. Picking up the discarded towel, he sat down to wait as William swiftly led Elizabeth back to her bedroom for more pleasurable pursuits. At some point, lost in the ecstasy of her kisses, William remembered that Adams was waiting.

"I must go, darling," he said breathlessly. Elizabeth's head shook in disagreement as she brought his lips back to hers. A few seconds more and he pulled away to stare into her eyes, his own now black with desire.

"Know this, Elizabeth. The next time we are in this circumstance, I shall not stop until I have made you my own."

William thought of how startled Adams had been when he opened the door to find him dozing in the barber chair. He smiled wanly as he reached up to run his fingers through his long, dark curls.

I suppose I shall have Mr. Noble cut my hair while I am here.

~~~*~~~

Chapter 30

Pemberley

Elizabeth blinked several times at the papers in her hand, and unable to stop her legs from buckling, sank slowly to the floor. The papers had fallen out when she picked up her Bible, fluttering in all directions. As swiftly as she had stooped to retrieve them, she recollected why they were inside the sacred book in the first place, and for several seconds, she felt as though she were suffocating.

When William had brought her small keepsake chest back from Northgate, she had glanced inside it to ascertain that her Bible was still there before putting it aside. Later, after Mrs. Drury had helped her retrieve it from the closet to inventory its contents, she had chosen to spend time with William in lieu of tending to the task. But with William in London and Mrs. Drury visiting her ailing aunt, there was little to occupy her time. So this morning seemed the perfect opportunity to re-examine the contents of the small trunk that had once held symbols of her future—her dowry chest as her father had called it. Only after finding the papers did every detail of the impetus for her escape from the count become instantly clear, and she remembered in painful detail what had occurred.

Addie explained that she had been dusting the room next to Lord Stanton's study, when she heard shouting between father and son. Stunned to hear Lord Stanton call his son an adulterer and a forger, Addie had pressed her ear to the door. Though she could not make out all their conversation, some words were easily distinguishable— counterfeit marriage certificates, bigamy, Gretna Green. Already suspicious of Stefano, Addie had long been convinced that he was involved in illegal activities, so without delay, she hurried to share all that she had heard with Elizabeth.

Eager for the truth, Elizabeth determined to search for evidence of his father's charges the next time Lord Stanton and his son were both away. That opportunity came quickly, as both men abandoned Northgate shortly after their argument. Fortunately, Addie was able to pilfer a set of keys from Mr. Johnston, the steward, a clumsy, rather dour fellow, who had a habit of leaving the keys with which he was entrusted lying about. True to his nature, he said nothing to anyone about the missing keys, but simply had more made as it would not do for Lord Stanton or his son to find out he had been so careless.

With the purloined keys, the friends had access to all the previously forbidden rooms, and as luck would have it, the steward's set not only included door keys, but also keys to everything that had a lock within each room. Thus they began their search late one afternoon when the understaffed household servants were required for other duties. Fortuitously, on their very first foray they decided to search Lord Stanton's study. Elizabeth chose to begin with his lordship's desk, which she had found locked, while Addie went through an unlocked chest.

As Elizabeth rummaged around, she found what she was looking for in the bottom drawer, covered by an old ledger. Withdrawing a paper she vaguely remembered seeing once before—a certificate of marriage from Gretna Green—she was taken aback to see her name written upon it and to realise that the signature at the bottom was not her own.

"How can this be? This must be a forgery!" she cried, causing Addie to stop her exploration of a large chest and come to look at what Elizabeth had discovered. She pulled out several more certificates with different names, different dates, even completely blank certificates.

"My God, what has he done?" she asked, shuffling through the stack and stopping at one in particular to hold it up for Addie's perusal. "Anne de Bourgh—Mr. Darcy's cousin! He will be devastated to find his cousin included in this sordid affair!"

Finally reaching the bottom, she was confronted with a most incriminating piece of evidence—a fairly recent letter to Lord Stanton from someone in Italy. Elizabeth opened the letter and began to examine it, her face becoming colourless as she read further.

Addie, fearing she might faint, insisted Elizabeth sit down, and she slumped into a large chair that sat behind the desk. When she was finally able to speak, she explained to Addie that the letter was from a Countess Livia Canossa Ridolfi, who was plainly Stefano's wife. The countess discussed her fear that Stanton's grandson, and Stefano's son, Eduardo, would decide to move to England to be with his father.

Confused and beside herself with fury, Elizabeth took all of the papers she had discovered and secreted them in the back of her Bible, hoping to use it against the count. Thus armed, she vowed to Addie that she would leave Northgate immediately, on foot if necessary. Convinced of Elizabeth's resolve but fearful for her safety, Addie asked her to wait until she could send for an acquaintance, Mr. Robert Kilburn, and beg for his assistance.

Elizabeth had often heard Addie speak of the man, as Mr. Kilburn's family owned a small woodworking shop in Sheffield which produced and repaired tables and other small pieces of furniture. Over the years, he had often called on Northgate Manor and had become quite smitten with Addie. Kilburn, who secretly spent time with the maid, was well aware of Addie's loathing for the count and her concern for Elizabeth, so if her request for his help was made, Addie knew that it would not come as a surprise to him.

His business required that he drive a large, covered wagon to outlying towns and villages, hawking his wares along the road and not returning until the wagon was empty. Addie prayed that he would agree to hide Elizabeth in the conveyance, among his tables, and take her safely to Lambton. Lambton was the one place Elizabeth had mentioned that she might find refuge, as her Aunt Gardiner had lived there as a child and still had family and friends thereabouts. In the end, because of his regard for Addie, Kilburn would not be a hard man to convince, and a plan was formed.

But in spite of all their best laid plans, everything went horribly wrong. Instead of staying away for several weeks or months as Stefano normally did, he returned almost immediately. In fact, he had gotten no farther than an inn in a nearby village where he spent the ensuing few days drinking. Still quite drunk when he departed, he directed his coach back to Northgate, stumbling into the manor on the eve of Elizabeth's planned flight. She was already in Addie's room, awaiting the cue to slip out of the house to meet Mr. Kilburn, when Stefano found her.

He had gone to Elizabeth's room and not finding her there, had begun a search of the house. Finally, the count remembered Addie and determined to ascertain if the maid knew where Elizabeth might be. When he found Elizabeth in Addie's room in travelling clothes and with a bag at her feet, everything spiralled out of control.

As it was, in the aftermath of Addie's death, the fire and her debilitating injury, Elizabeth had forgotten about discovering the marriage certificates ... until now.

With this new discovery, Elizabeth's trust in her future with William began to crumble. Her emotions swung back and forth like a pendulum, with seemingly no way to put them to rights. On the one hand, she was ashamed to realise that she would be regarded as no more than Stefano's mistress, while on the other, she felt great relief to know they were never married. A niggling fear of William's reaction took root, and she wondered if it would be kinder just to disappear.

Lost in entirely new misgivings, Elizabeth had no idea she was about to have company.

~~~*~~~

"Good morning, Mrs. Ingram!" Mr. Walker declared enthusiastically and bowed as William's sister walked through the front door. He looked down the steps behind her to see a footman leading her horse toward the stables. "Are Mr. Ingram and Miss Millie not accompanying you?"

"No, my husband is working on a matter concerning one of his tenants this morning, and Millie has a slight cold and is taking a nap, so I thought I might visit with Elizabeth for a short while. I have not seen her since William left for London, and I promised him that I would look in on her."

Just then Mrs. Reynolds came out of a nearby room. "Mrs. Ingram! It is so good to see you. Where are Mr. Ingram and that lovely daughter of yours?"

Georgiana laughed. "I think Evan and Millie are more popular than I am."

The housekeeper blushed. "Oh, I assure you that is not true. It is only that you are rarely seen without them nowadays."

William's sister smiled brilliantly. "Yes, we are happiest when we are together, but I have the morning to myself, and as I was telling Mr. Walker, I would like to visit with Elizabeth. Is she available?"

"She is in her sitting room, I believe. Do you want to go on up, or shall I announce you?"

"I believe I shall surprise her, if you think she will not mind."

"Not at all."

Mrs. Reynolds sighed with happiness as she watched the woman she had helped to rear ascend the stairs. Mrs. Darcy never recovered completely from Georgiana's birth, and when she died, Mr. Darcy retreated into his heartache leaving the fragile little girl under her supervision. Thus they had formed a lasting bond.

Extremely proud of the woman Georgiana had become, the housekeeper was even more pleased to see the changes that Millie's presence in her life had wrought. Though Georgiana deeply loved Evan Ingram, the fact that she could not carry a child had stolen just a bit of her joy. However, once Millie arrived, Georgiana's lively disposition had returned in full-force, and now Mrs. Reynolds could clearly see Lady Anne Darcy's love of motherhood manifested in her daughter.

As Georgiana reached the landing and disappeared from sight, the long-time housekeeper wiped a few tears from her eyes and glanced around to make sure no one had seen. She had no way of knowing that Mr. Walker had come upon the tender scene, but had quickly retreated. He was well aware of Mrs. Reynolds penchant for appearing in control at all times and did not want her to know he had witnessed her lapse. Pleased that her display of emotion had apparently gone unnoticed, Mrs. Reynolds assumed her usual mien and headed towards the kitchen to order trays for the two ladies.

~~~*~~~

Reaching the door to the sitting room, Georgiana knocked lightly and hearing no answer, she turned the knob. The door swung open easily, revealing Elizabeth sitting in the middle of the floor, her head in her hands. She was weeping. Not considering decorum, Georgiana immediately dropped down beside her on the floor, sliding her arms about her and pulling her close.

"Elizabeth, whatever is the matter?" Georgiana could feel her trembling. "Should I call for the physician?"

"No!" Elizabeth said sharply, before softening her tone and pulling back to look at Georgiana. "No, please, I ... I need some time to ..." Her voice faded away as her eyes drifted to the numerous papers strewn across the floor.

Georgiana cupped Elizabeth's chin, commanding her attention. "We are friends. May I see what has upset you?"

Still sniffling, Elizabeth handed one paper to Georgiana, who began speaking as she read. "This looks like a marriage certificate from Gretna Green." As the contents became clear, her voice broke. "Oh, Elizabeth, it is yours." She squeezed Elizabeth's hand, trying not to cry as tears filled her eyes as well. "I am so sorry."

"But ... but you do not understand!" Elizabeth sputtered, starting to weep again. Then through copious tears, she related everything that she had just remembered. For a long time afterward, neither spoke as Georgiana held Elizabeth, rocking her gently.

Finally realising that none of this mattered—most certainly not to William, Georgiana declared, "This changes nothing! William loves you regardless of the circumstances you found yourself in before you were reunited. And if there is one thing my brother is—it is devoted to you. You do not know how often he told me that he could not live without you." Elizabeth's head lifted at that revelation, causing Georgiana to add confidently, "If anything, this only means that you are free to marry as soon as you wish, which will make my brother the happiest of men!"

Elizabeth tried then to smile, but it quickly faded. "I ... I do not know what to think. I am numb."

"Well, of course you are. You have had quite a shock. You have learned that the man you thought was your husband was not, and that he obviously took advantage of other women in the same manner. Who would not be numb?"

Georgiana watched Elizabeth closely, fearing the unusual expression on her face. "Please tell my brother about this. I assure you, he will know how to handle it."

Elizabeth's eyes widened, though she still wore a dazed expression. "No. Please, not yet. I ... I need to think of how to ... what to say. Please promise me that you will not write to him."

Georgiana considered the confused and evidently frightened young woman and reached out to smooth her hair. "I will let you write to him of this matter, but I expect you to inform him as soon as possible. Agreed?"

She swallowed hard and nodded. "Agreed."

Nonetheless, deep within, Elizabeth was not convinced she would tell William. Informing him of her added shame would probably only make matters worse, as he would be more determined than ever to shield her from society's condemnation. An honourable man could do no less.

London
Preston House

Cecile Preston walked back and forth in her sparsely furnished drawing room, considering exactly when she had lost control of her life. She had been happy as a child, but things had spiralled out of control after her father's death when she was sixteen. Choosing a marriage of convenience, she had never been happy with Owen Preston, but with her marriage had come adequate wealth and position—something that some could only dream of having. When had that not been enough? At what point had gambling replaced the emptiness in her heart?

She stopped pacing abruptly. *Now my seemingly easy way out of debt—working with Wickham—has evolved into a scheme to remove a woman from Pemberley. Remove? I am fooling no one. It will be deemed kidnapping. Kidnapping! How odious that sounds!*

After Wickham had explained her part in the plan, she had almost convinced herself that she was being noble. After all, she was only going to convince the woman that she should sail from England to protect Mr. Darcy from her husband's ire—that if she had any feelings for Fitzwilliam Darcy, surely she would want no harm to come to him. But, in the back of her mind, Cecile knew better.

She was disconcerted and her conscience would not be soothed so easily. Certainly, she was not above pilfering a few baubles from her rich acquaintances to support herself, but this scheme was malevolent. Why had the woman found it necessary to flee her husband in the first place? Was he violent? Would he kill her if she were in his power again?

Shaking her head to clear her thoughts, Cecile pondered the enigmatic Fitzwilliam Darcy. If he had not forsaken her for that woman, her gaming debts would long ago have been paid, and she would now want for nothing. As it was, she lived in a half-furnished townhouse with only a few servants left, and the proverbial wolf was at the door. She lifted her chin. *So why should I care one whit about Mr. Darcy or what he wants.*

Darcy's abrupt turnaround, followed by Lord Farthington's betrayal, had left her facing complete ruin. Nevertheless, she did not dislike Farthington as much as Darcy. She was never enamoured of him, as he had been merely a means to an end. Darcy, however, was very handsome as well as wealthy. No man of his looks and means had ever paid her any attention, much less offered for her. She had looked forward to parading him past the beauties of the *ton* who had tried to catch him for years. But alas, in the end, he had found her wanting, just as other men had.

Now, her funds squandered and her affairs in complete disarray, the empty room she occupied served as a symbol of her empty life, and Cecile hated it. She picked up a Dresden china cup and hurled it against the fireplace, watching it shatter it into a thousand tiny pieces. There was nothing to be done. She had no choice, if she valued her life, but to help Wickham spirit this woman from Pemberley. Besides, Cecile reasoned, she could leave the country with the ten-thousand pounds that would be her share and begin life anew.

Having made up her mind, she moved to the liquor cabinet where she poured herself a small glass of brandy. Drinking it down in one swallow, she sat down at a small writing table and took out paper and pen. A letter

Cecile received that morning from a friend in Derbyshire mentioned that Mr. Darcy had been seen returning to Town, and she knew that Wickham would want to set their plan in motion. Thus, she would share that bit of information with him.

After writing the short note, she rang for a servant, instructing him as to how to find the address of Wickham's current residence. As the man left the room, she rose and poured herself another drink. Quickly downing it, Cecile headed out of the room intending to commence packing while she waited for his reply. It would not serve for her to dwell on what she was about to undertake.

Darcy House
William's Study

Darcy leaned back in his chair, fidgeting with his pen and making his cousin nervous just watching him. "So Lieutenant Marbury thinks he has a good lead on Count Stefano or whatever he is calling himself this week?"

"Yes." Richard replied, chuckling at William's quip. "Marbury assures me that the count is in London. It is only a matter of time until he learns of the count's location. We have to be ready at a moment's notice, as he is a slippery snake and apparently changes addresses as often as most people change clothes."

William scowled. "No doubt he has people other than us on his trail." Closing his tired eyes and rubbing them, he took a deep breath. "I would like to get this matter behind me and go home to Elizabeth as soon as possible."

Richard smiled. "I have never known a man so eager to face an opponent. According to Marbury, the count is very accurate with pistol and sword."

William's eyes opened, fixed on Richard and then narrowed. "He had better be."

At that very moment, there was a commotion in the hallway. As Mr. Barnes' voice got louder, William stood and headed around his desk. It was clear that the butler was trying to explain to someone that Mr. Darcy was in a meeting.

Richard, however, realised straightaway that the person the butler was addressing was his mother. She must have learned that William was in Town, and nothing would do but for her to chastise him for not coming to see her.

The door flew open, and Evelyn Fitzwilliam walked in exultantly, Mr. Barnes close on her heels.

"Fitzwilliam, would you please inform Mr. Barnes," she reached William and tiptoed to place a kiss on his cheek before continuing, "that the rules of the house do not apply to me!"

William tried not to smile, but his lips refused to cooperate. "Mr. Barnes, you will have to excuse my aunt. Evidently, she does not expect to follow my rules, but I thank you for trying to enforce them, in any event. You may go about your duties."

Mr. Barnes bowed, cast a look of annoyance at Lady Matlock, then turned and left the room. Not taking her eyes off her nephew, Evelyn Fitzwilliam's brow knit until she saw the corners of William's lips lift slightly. Then she smiled radiantly.

"Well, Fitzwilliam, it seems you have once again come to Town without letting us know. What does one have to do to see one's own flesh and blood, especially when he is a few streets away?"

Promptly, William stepped forward to clasp his aunt in a tight embrace, picking her up and twirling her about.

"Fitzwilliam!" she cried, laughing, then instantly assumed a serious countenance and began smoothing her skirts when she was back on her feet. "Do not think, young man, that you can redeem yourself so easily. Why have you not been to call on me?"

Just then she noticed Richard, who had moved out of her line of sight the minute he heard his mother's voice. "And what kind of son will not tell his own mother when his cousin is in Town?"

Richard had watched the scene with great amusement but now sobered and shrugged, his eyes flicking to Darcy. He would not betray the fact that William asked him not to say anything to his family.

Not wanting to cause problems between mother and son, William confessed. "It was my request that Richard not say anything, Aunt."

He challenged his aunt's feigned glower, dimples flashing. "Will you not be seated and let me explain?" She nodded, so he guided her to a chair before returning to sit behind the desk.

"Whenever you are aware that I am in London, you plan several soirees to put me in the way of eligible women. I have much to accomplish in a short time, and I did not want to be distracted by attending dinners and balls. I would have called on you before I returned to Pemberley."

She smiled, though not too apologetically. "You are correct, but what if I promise it will be only a family dinner?"

"Then I shall accept, but I have to warn you that Richard and I are on the trail of the man who married Anne and abandoned her. Whenever the investigator sends notice, we must leave—even if during dinner."

"So, you have located that scoundrel? Does Edward know?"

Richard interrupted. "Not located yet, Mother. And no, father does not know, so please do not say anything. We would like to handle this ourselves, as father might get in the way and be hurt."

"And you and Fitzwilliam will not?"

"We will be very careful. I will tell Father once we have the blackguard in custody, not before."

At the resolve on her son's face, Evelyn Fitzwilliam nodded. She knew Richard was a fine officer and used to this type of exercise, and he was not one to take risks. She also knew that he was right.

"I will not tell him, but pray, be careful." She looked between them. "Both of you."

William interjected, "You may count on it. Now, when am I expected for dinner?"

His aunt's face softened. "Would day after tomorrow be satisfactory? Edgar will be home then, and I would like to have all the family together."

At William's worried look, she added, "You need not be concerned; Jacqueline does not accompany Edgar anymore."

William could not tell her that seeing just Edgar was not much better. "Day after tomorrow will be perfect."

"I suppose I should leave so you two can work on whatever you are planning." Neither man voiced an objection, so she stood and reached to take William's hand in one of hers, while patting it with the other. "I shall look forward to seeing you again."

She turned to wink at Richard. "You know you are expected. Now, would you please see your mother to the carriage?"

As Evelyn Fitzwilliam swept out of the room, silk skirts rustling, William and Richard exchanged concerned glances. Shrugging, Richard rushed and caught up with her as she donned the cloak that Mr. Barnes held. It was not until they began descending the front steps that she finally spoke.

"He has his heart set on someone." It was more a statement than a question and it caught Richard off guard.

He debated not being forthcoming, but seeing the resolve in his mother's manner he knew it was pointless. When she stopped to peer at him to ascertain the truth, he nodded.

"I have heard the rumours of this *cousin* that we both know is not any relation. I assume that this woman is—what did you call her—the love of his life?"

Richard nodded again, not sure what to expect, but his mother's only reaction was to stare past him for a few seconds before continuing.

"Fitzwilliam is a very intelligent man, and I have to trust that he knows what he is doing. I suppose you have met this woman and approve of her?"

"I approve of her very much. She is a gentlewoman, very kind and good hearted, but also extremely bright and well-read. She brings out a liveliness ..." Richard paused, trying to think of what to say. "When he is with her, I see glimpses of the boy that I knew before Uncle George died."

"And you are certain she is not a fortune hunter?"

"She refused his offer of marriage two years ago at Kent, so I would have to say no."

Her brow knit quizzically. "Refused? She refused Fitzwilliam Darcy? Is she mad?"

"Darce says she was right to refuse him because he was very arrogant in the way he made his offer."

She seemed to ponder that statement for a moment, then ventured. "Is she married, as is said of her?"

Since his mother already knew parts of Elizabeth's story, Richard thought he had no choice but to tell her more in an attempt to gain support for his cousin.

"Do you swear not to tell anyone what I am about to tell you?"

His mother squared her shoulders, drawing herself up to her full height—all five feet. "You have my word."

"I cannot tell you all the particulars, but Elizabeth's situation is closely associated with Anne's, and we will have all the answers when we find that cad." At her shocked expression, he added, "Please keep an open mind until the truth is revealed."

Her head dropped, and she seemed to be studying her shoes, so Richard lifted her chin with his finger. As identical blue eyes met, he volunteered, "I can tell you this. They are so much in love that no one will ever come between them."

Evelyn Fitzwilliam sighed heavily. "I will allow my nephew to find his own happiness and try to offer encouragement. If she loves him as he needs to be loved, then I can only champion her."

"I am proud of you, Mother, for not trying to force my cousin into something he cannot abide, as Father once tried to do. I pray he will understand as well."

"Let me handle your father." She tried to smile. "He has come down from his high horse after the disaster with Jacqueline and Edgar. I think he will surprise you," she paused for a moment, "at least, I hope he does."

"As do I, Mother." He leaned in to kiss her cheek. "I love you."

"I love you, too, my boy."

~~~*~~~

Chapter 31

A s the coach neared the centre of London, John Williamson observed his surroundings with great curiosity. At his age, he seldom visited, preferring the quiet countryside to the noise of Town, but it was interesting to venture forth on occasion and see what progress had been wrought in the heart of England.

On the outskirts, there were several new houses and a few new shops, but little had changed in the older, fashionable area of Grosvenor Square. As he progressed toward his destination, he remembered the summer, when he was in his early twenties, that he had stayed here with a friend whose widowed mother had married a much older man. That gentleman owned a townhouse several streets over, and he and his friend had enjoyed an entire month here all by themselves.

Williamson smiled, recalling a lovely park near the townhouse that turned out to be the perfect place to sit and watch the ladies parade about in their finery. Suddenly a park came into view out the opposite window, and he craned his neck to see if it was the one of his memories. He was still trying to decide when the coach came to an abrupt halt, and he turned back to peer out the near window. They had stopped outside a huge townhouse in a long row of townhouses, each grander than the next.

The elegant facade of the classical brick structure drew his attention, and his gaze traversed the three stories straight up to the roof, which was itself surrounded by an intricate ironwork parapet. That same ironwork decorated the long windows and a balcony that was partially visible on the side of the house. Certain that the interior of the home would rival the outside, he felt just a bit nervous; his friend's home, grand though it was, could not compare to this. He had no time to dwell on it, however, as at that very moment a footman opened the coach door and folded down the steps.

Williamson was pleased to escape the confines of the coach and stretched to relieve the stiffness in his back. He became aware that the footman was waiting for him, so he immediately turned and began to ascend the steps to the portico. The elaborate front door opened before he had attained it.

"Mr. Williamson, I presume?" Mr. Barnes declared, reaching out for his hat and gloves.

"Yes."

"Mr. Darcy is awaiting you in his study. Follow me, sir."

The dignified butler moved across the polished marble foyer. At the grand staircase, he veered to the left, headed down a long hallway and came to a stop at the first door.

At his knock, the vicar recognised Mr. Darcy's voice call out, "Come."

William looked up from the stack of papers before him to see Mr. Barnes step into the room with Mr. Williamson directly behind. William smiled and stood just as the butler announced the visitor.

"Mr. Williamson to see you, sir."

"Thank you, Barnes. That will be all."

The servant bowed slightly and backed out of the room, pulling the door closed. William reached out to shake the vicar's hand as he came near.

"Mr. Williamson, it is so good of you to come."

"It was kind of you to invite me. I have not been to London in quite some time and never in such a fine coach! It was almost as if I were sitting on the sofa in the rectory during the entire trip!" Both men laughed. "But it was a long journey, and being a tall fellow, I am pleased to have finally arrived so I can stand erect once more."

"I am glad that your trip was pleasant, and I certainly understand the problems of being tall." Mr. Darcy's brow rose as he chuckled. "I asked Barnes to show you in here first, as I wanted to greet you personally. Nevertheless, I imagine you want to freshen up and rest before dinner. My housekeeper can arrange a hot bath, if you so desire."

A smile lit the vicar's face. "A hot bath would be delightful! That is a luxury not often afforded at the rectory. My baths are usually lukewarm at best! Yes, I would dearly love to bathe and rest a bit before we dine."

"Then let me ring for Mrs. Barnes to show you to your room and order your bath. I shall see you at dinner."

"Dinner it is."

Preston House

Wickham was not surprised that Cecile Preston's home looked as if it were abandoned. There were no servants milling about, and goodly amounts of the furnishings were missing, all presumably sold to obtain operating funds. The last time they had talked, she mentioned that her late husband's brother had asked for a convenient time when he and his wife could visit. They would, of course, expect to stay at the family townhouse, and she dreaded their discovering how she had looted the house of its treasures. Between Marvin Preston's visit and her fear of Fitzwilliam Darcy's reaction, she intended to leave London just as soon as their little scheme was put into play.

Wickham chuckled to himself, wondering what the plain little woman would do once she realised that he had absconded with all the money promised for their part in the operation. That bastard Darcy was no dullard, and his cousin Fitzwilliam was a seasoned army intelligence officer. Once they discovered all the particulars, they would come for the woman who had been staying at Pemberley. He had no doubt about that.

And by the time they consider my involvement, I shall be on a ship bound for America.

Unable to wipe the grin off his face, he savoured the satisfaction of knowing that his old nemesis would suffer greatly when he learned that his lady-friend was taken right from under his nose—or at least the noses of his trusted staff. He sniggered to himself at the thought of besting his nemesis.

Even Pemberley is not impenetrable, Darcy!

His pleasant daydream was cut short by Cecile's declaration. "I am glad to see someone is happy." However, her gloomy expression did not support her contention. "I assume you received my message."

"Yes. I was surprised that you learned of Darcy's presence from a letter before my associates could alert me; although, I suppose avoiding discovery is his strong point." Wickham chuckled. "He has always been an expert at hiding in a crowded ballroom."

Cecile did not find it amusing. "No matter the source, he is in London. I shall leave for Pemberley tomorrow morning, but how can I be assured Mr. Darcy will not be returning on my heels? I do not relish the thought of his arriving while I am yet there."

"That is an astute observation, and one that I have considered." Wickham pulled a paper from his coat. "I have made this itinerary. You shall stay at these inns so that I will know where you are at any given time. My people will watch Darcy's house and notify me if he should suddenly decide to depart for Derbyshire. If he does, I will send one of my men on horseback to warn you. A man on horseback can keep ahead of a coach, and he will warn you before you get to Pemberley. In that event, we shall try again another time."

Wickham rubbed his chin thoughtfully. "I do not think that will be a problem, however. My sources overheard a conversation regarding a dinner at Matlock House later this week, and I assume Darcy will be obligated to attend. So, once you are at Pemberley, you must convince this woman to accompany you to Liverpool without delay. In our scheme, time is of the essence."

"And what shall be my tale?"

"Frankly, I do not care. However, I believe you need only mention that rumours abound in London that Darcy's *cousin,* who is staying at Pemberley, is married, and that *you* believe her husband to be Count Stefano. Tell her that a friend of yours has met the count and says that he is determined to recover his wife at any cost and is close to finding her. Suggest that if she stays, Darcy will be in danger. If, indeed, she has any feelings for him, she should flee without hesitation."

"Suppose she has no money with which to escape?"

"Inform her that you will fund her passage on a ship to America that is sailing out of Liverpool in a few days and give her one hundred pounds to live on until she finds work. That should further sway her."

"And what reason would I have to help with her passage and extra funds?"

"The oldest explanation for the behaviour of a woman—jealousy! Just say that you want Darcy for yourself, so it would be in your best interest for her to leave England. She would believe that. After all, it is true, is it not?"

Cecile glowered at the obvious insult.

"Oh, come now. Do not be missish. It is not like you and every other woman in England has not coveted him at one time or the other."

Ignoring his insults, she continued, "So I shall take her to Liverpool and await your instructions?"

"Yes, stay at the Landmark Inn. It is in the middle of the wharf district, but it is pleasant enough. I shall look for you there."

Wickham pulled an envelope from his pocket. "Here, you will need this." Cecile looked inside to see a large sum of money. "This should suffice until I arrive to join you."

"I do not see Fitzwilliam's allowing the count—or us—to get away with this."

"Do not worry. Darcy shall be so focused on recovering the woman that we shall be well away from England before he remembers us."

"I pray you are right, but somehow, I feel we are poking a hornet's nest with a short stick."

Wickham smirked. "Then let us do a good job the first time and run for cover!"

Darcy House
The Library

William sat amused as Mr. Williamson stood in the very middle of his vast library, a look of awe upon his face as he turned slowly in a circle. Finally, after making a complete circle twice, he stopped, and a smile graced his features.

"I can say only that I would be most happy to avail myself of your magnificent library whenever I have the chance to come to London. I could not have imagined that any home could boast of having this many books." He shook his head, chuckling. "I feel quite like a child in a sweet shop. I have no idea where to begin."

"Begin wherever you like. If you enjoy the library here, you will be even more pleased when we travel to Pemberley, as the library there is four to five times larger."

"Really?" At William's smile and nod, he continued, "How could a reasonable man refuse?" Suddenly, his features sobered. "But, enough about my interests. You asked me here to discuss Lizzybet, did you not?"

William's smile quickly disappeared. *Where to start? How much to tell?*

Seeing the trepidation on his host's face, Mr. Williamson moved towards him, taking the seat opposite and leaning forward. "Mr. Darcy, in all my years of counselling my congregation, I have learned that it is best to come right out with what is on your mind. Stewing about it will not change it or make it go away."

Looking up to meet the vicar's kind eyes, William tried unsuccessfully to smile, sure that it looked more like a grimace. Then taking a deep breath, he began his account of all that had happened regarding Elizabeth since last they had talked in Meryton—everything with the exception of their decision to live as man and wife and the discovery of Stefano's many marriages, details which would be revealed later. He finished, fell silent, and waited for the vicar's reaction.

However, the man who had so vigorously encouraged him to talk a few minutes ago, sat speechless, staring into space with a look of bewilderment on his face. After several seconds, William began to wonder if he should have told a man of his age something this unsettling. Standing, he clasped the older man's shoulder and shook it slightly.

"Mr. Williamson? Sir?"

Still he did not answer. Fearing the worst, William hurried in the direction of the library's double doors. Just as he opened them, calling out for Mr. Barnes, he heard a faint voice.

"That will not be necessary."

William hurried back to the elderly man, who was now lying back in the chair, resting his head against the upholstered cushion. His eyes closed as he murmured, "A brandy, please."

Barnes appeared at that moment to find Mr. Darcy leaning over the indisposed guest. "Bring Mr. Williamson a brandy, quickly."

The butler hurriedly complied, noting the vicar's pale complexion. "Shall I call for the physician, sir?"

"No!" Mr. Williamson exclaimed, adding in a softer voice, "Just let me rest for a moment, and I shall be well."

William studied the rector for a few moments before dismissing the butler. The trusted servant nodded and slipped out of the room.

Williamson opened his eyes to study the younger man. "My Lizzybet is truly alive? Then who is buried at Meryton?"

Remembering his shock at finding Elizabeth alive at Netherfield, he was sympathetic to the affect this news had had on her dear friend.

"Elizabeth is alive and well at Pemberley. That is why I asked you to accompany me there. The woman buried was a maid who perished in the fire. She had no family to mourn her."

Mr. Williamson drank one brandy and part of another before he felt well enough to comment. His colour had improved, and he sat up, no longer slouched down in the chair, which made William relax somewhat.

"I ... may I ask why you decided to share this with me, especially in light of the decision to tell as few people as necessary to assure her safety?"

William tried to keep his voice from trembling, but his discomposure was not lost on the cleric. "I needed to ask a favour of you; but to be totally honest, some things have changed since I wrote the letter asking you to come."

The vicar's brow knit as he gave William his undivided attention.

"To explain, Elizabeth and I are in love—have been in love with each other for years. We wish to spend the rest of our lives together and ..." He hesitated, wondering at the vicar's response.

Williamson's eyebrows rose. "And?"

"We want children."

To William's relief, the look on the man's face was not one of censure, but loving concern as he nodded solemnly. "Oh, I see."

He squeezed William's arm, studying him. "And you wish for me to conduct a ceremony?"

William nodded, his eyes imploring, "That was why I asked you to come—to beg you to let us pledge our love and devotion to each other in front of you and God, knowing full well that it may never be recognised by society or even by the church."

The young man's earnestness brought tears to the vicar's eyes. Seldom had he witnessed love so devout, though he had performed marriages for scores of people in his lifetime. Even so, his mind swirled with the consequences of what was being asked of him.

William interrupted his thoughts. "Although it does not change my intentions towards Elizabeth, since arriving in London, I have learned new truths concerning her *marriage*. My uncle has been searching for the man who married my cousin two years ago, stole her valuables, and promptly abandoned her. It happens that the man is Count Stefano, the same man who took Elizabeth."

The vicar's eyes blazed. "How did the blackguard accomplish that?"

"According to his father, the count used trickery to fool several women into thinking they were married to him, when they were not. He could not legally marry anyone, as he was a married man when he came here from Italy. In any event, he would convince his victim to start out for Gretna Green to elope, but during the journey, he would drug her, and take her elsewhere. Using a forged marriage certificate and wedding ring, he would convince her that a marriage had taken place.

257

After squandering her fortune and valuables, he would abandon her to begin again with a different victim."

"But Lizzybet would never have gone with him, and she had no fortune!"

William's eyes closed in torment. "No. Count Stefano fancied himself in love with her and forced her compliance for selfish reasons."

"I may be a man of the cloth, but should I ever encounter that—"

William swiftly laid a hand on his shoulder. "I assure you the pleasure will be mine. I intend to challenge him."

"Just beware. His proficiency with weapons was well-known around Meryton."

"I am not afraid."

Seeing the steely resolve in William's blue eyes, he responded, "No, I imagine you are not." The vicar's face began to soften. "You realise that if she was never Count Stefano's wife, then all your previous fears are for naught, as there is nothing to stop me from officiating over a marriage between the two of you. Of course, marrying Elizabeth *Bennet* could still invite gossip and possible censure."

"My only fear is life without her—censure, I would gladly bear," William stated decisively before a slight smile crept across his face. "Only my desire to keep her safe would keep me from shouting from the rooftops that Elizabeth Bennet is mine. But, in that regard, I have taken care to protect her."

Williamson's brow rose. "Oh?"

William walked over to his desk, opened a drawer and pulled out a piece of paper and a small box. He held the paper out to Mr. Williamson, who took it and smiled as the young man offered, "My connections were sufficient to procure this special license expediently."

The vicar read the paper, murmuring solemnly. "One life, held captive by greed, ends as another life, born of unselfish, unstoppable love begins. Fitzwilliam Alexander George Darcy shall be united in marriage to Elizabeth Elise Lawrence."

Glancing at the box William still held in his hand, he motioned. "And this is the ring?"

William opened the small case to reveal an emerald and diamond wedding ring set in an intricate pattern, with alternating stones circling the entire gold band. "It was my mother's."

"Lizzybet will love it, I am confident. Green was always her favourite colour." He sobered then. "May I say that my heart broke for you when I stumbled upon you in the cemetery that day? Your love for her was irrefutable and your grief so palpable that it prompted my own sorrow to return full force. You have no idea how pleased I am that you and she have found each other."

William coloured. "I believe I loved her from first sight, though, in my stupidity, I would not allow myself to consider offering for her."

At Williamson's questioning look, he added, "Simply because of her family, most especially Mrs. Bennet, I left Hertfordshire to try to forget her."

Wise old eyes fixed on younger ones. "But my Lizzybet is unforgettable."

Blowing out a breath, William quoted, "The heart that has truly loved never forgets, but as truly loves on to the close." [4]

"The Irish poet Thomas Moore?" Williamson ventured.

---

[4] *Thomas Moore, Irish Poet (1779 – 1852) The poem follows on Pg 260, This quote was also accredited to a Thomas More, who was an English Statesman, but I believe it belongs to the Irish Poet, Thomas Moore, as shown at http://theotherpages.org/poems/index.html Poet's Corner*

William nodded. "A hard lesson to learn! It would have saved us both a lot of heartache had I just accepted the inevitable."

The old vicar laughed. "But, the question is, would Lizzybet have accepted marrying you as inevitable!"

Remembering her wit, impertinence and disapproval of his attitude, William shook his head. "I believe I would have had to work long and hard to be the kind of man she could respect and accept."

"Then you should be proud." At William's quizzical brow, he grinned.

"Because you have become that man."

Rosewood Manor
The drawing room

Georgiana paced back and forth across the room, her actions so very reminiscent of her brother that, unbidden, a smile formed on Evan Ingram's lips as he sat watching. Quickly he suppressed it, fully aware that it would not do to let Ana see him smile while she was so upset.

"I am sorry. I should have been here when you returned. We could have discussed it then, and you would not have had to bear it alone.

"You cannot blame yourself because business with a tenant kept you away until after dark. Besides, I was so tired that I retired early. It was exhausting trying to convince Elizabeth that nothing has changed. She seems to be sinking into melancholy spirits again, and I do not know if she heeded my advice. I must send a note to William, for I fear what she may do."

"I think that is a good idea. Your brother has always been able to calm her when she gets upset. Are you sure that finding those marriage certificates has caused this reversal?"

"I believe so. She did not mention anything else. Though I reminded her of William's devotion, I think she is worried by the fact that she lived at Northgate for two years without being married."

"I would think she would be pleased to be unmarried. That means she and your brother are free to marry and—"

"Yes, she is pleased about that," Georgiana interrupted. "But ... but it is hard to explain. She feels as if she were a kept woman, a mistress, if you will. She fears the gossip, especially from William's sphere, if they hear of it. She is so devoted to my brother's welfare. It was she who pointed out that he will bear the brunt of any censure because he has to conduct business in Town."

Evan rubbed his chin. "I can see her point, but truly, will it matter? Perhaps no one will ever know, and if so, it will not change the way Darcy feels about her. I have seen how her love has changed him. He is more like the person I knew as a boy. Surely, she can see his happiness."

"For now, I am afraid she cannot see beyond the shame he may suffer. I pray she does not do anything foolish. I spoke to Mrs. Reynolds about keeping an eye on her, but I must be sure to check on her every day until he returns."

"Yes, love. Do whatever you think is necessary to assure her health and safety. Darcy does not need to lose her now that he is so close to finding happiness."

"Happiness." She sighed. "He has had little true happiness in his life, and I fear what he would do if he lost her."

Evan Ingram pulled his wife into a tight embrace, each closing their eyes. "Then let us pray that he never will."

Just then, Mrs. Calvert appeared in the doorway with Millie who, upon seeing her parents, struggled to be put down. The sound of small shoes tapping on the wood floors caused the couple to open their eyes and turn towards their child.

"Millie!" They called in unison. As the small bundle of energy in pale yellow reached them, Evan leaned down to scoop her into his arms. She giggled as he placed kisses on her forehead, and then held her out so Georgiana could do the same.

"How would you like to visit the stables and see the new colt born this week?"

Small yellow curls bounced up and down. "Yes, Papa. May I?"

"Excellent! Of course you may." Evan glanced at his wife. "If Mama will agree to join us, we shall be away. Ask her, sweetheart. Say, 'Please, Mama.'"

Millie grinned, crinkling her nose and displaying her small white teeth. "Please, Mama."

Georgiana chuckled, leaning in to nuzzle her hair. "I would not miss it for the world! Perhaps it is time to think of a name for him."

Evan's tone was sombre. "Darcy told me of the names you gave his colts, Ana, so I do not feel comfortable leaving the task to you."

Smirking, she leaned over to take Millie in her arms. "Come, love. We shall just ignore your papa and try to come up with a suitable name." Glancing at Evan mischievously just before she stepped out of the room, she ventured loudly, "Perhaps Petruchio."

A loud groan, easily heard by most of the house, caused Georgiana to break into a fit of giggles. Millie giggled as well, not truly aware of the reason, but simply because she loved to laugh ... especially when her parents did.

Believe Me, If All Those Endearing Young Charms

BELIEVE me, if all those endearing young charms,
Which I gaze on so fondly to-day,
Were to change by to-morrow, and fleet in my arms,
Live fairy-gifts fading away,
Thou wouldst still be adored, as this moment thou art,
Let thy loveliness fade as it will,
And around the dear ruin each wish of my heart
Would entwine itself verdantly still.
It is not while beauty and youth are thine own,
And thy cheeks unprofaned by a tear,
That the fervour and faith of a soul may be known,
To which time will but make thee more dear!
No, the heart that has truly loved never forgets,
But as truly loves on to the close,
As the sunflower turns on her god when he sets
The same look which she turned when he rose!

~~~*~~~

Chapter 32

London
The Castle Inn
Morning

Wickham was not surprised that the count now resided at an inn. The last time he had seen the man at his townhouse there were few servants in attendance, and boxes were stacked everywhere about the rooms, presumably awaiting shipment to Italy. Still, he was dumbfounded as to why the count had not kept him informed of his change of address. After all, how were they to work in partnership to reclaim the man's errant wife if he could not be found?

For a few moments after he arrived at the townhouse in Grosvenor Square to find it abandoned and locked securely, Wickham entertained the idea that the count might have left for Pemberley on his own to seize his wife. However, as he stood peering at the unanswered door, a man had stopped to enquire if he could be of service. That gentleman turned out to be a neighbour whose servant had overhead the former resident give orders for a coachman to take him to the Castle Inn. Slightly annoyed, George made his way to the inn and now stood before the count in a very agitated state.

"Did you not think I should have been notified of your move? After all, I was the one who located your wife and devised a plan to spirit her away from Darcy's estate!"

Count Stefano sat in the only comfortable chair in the small sitting area of his room, his feet resting upon a stool. At Wickham's exclamation, he stood, his eyes narrowing, causing Wickham to take a step back.

"I am well aware of your contributions to my future happiness, Mr. Wickham. However, it would be wise of you to remember that you answer to me and not vice versa. The only reason you were not notified earlier was my need for haste in vacating the premises of my former residence."

Wickham's brow knitted uneasily. "I apologise. I was upset that I could not find you. May I ask why you had to leave so hastily?"

"I was warned that your boyhood chum, Darcy, and his cousin, Colonel Fitzwilliam, were not only in Town but were actively searching for me. How is it that I learned of this before you? Were you not supposed to inform me when he was in London, so that we could begin our plan to recover my wife?"

"But he has only just arrived!"

The count scowled, apparently aware that that was not the case. He seemed about to challenge him anew, when Wickham quickly added, "One of my associates informed me yesterday that he was in Town. I immediately met with the woman who is to help us recover your wife and, as we speak, she is on her way to Derbyshire. I came as soon as I could to inform you that I leave for Liverpool in the morning."

"And when did you suppose I would leave for Liverpool?"

"You have not said, though I assumed you would most likely leave straightaway once you had heard from me that all was in readiness."

"I did not think it necessary to explain, given my devotion to my wife, but I had always planned to travel with you. I have very little baggage, as most of my belongings are already on the dock in Liverpool, and one of my father's ships sails from there shortly."

"Yes, of course. So you will sail from England with your wife as soon as she is brought to Liverpool?"

The count bristled. "What I do after I recover my wife is no concern of yours, and you would do well to remember that!"

Wickham grew cross at the count's attitude, but tried to control his temper by concentrating on the reward. "I shall endeavour to remember that for future reference. Now, as to our imminent journey, the coach I hired leaves early tomorrow. Keep in mind that as soon as your wife is convinced to leave Pemberley, the clock begins ticking and time will be of the essence."

"Let us hope, for your sake, that luck and time are on our side. I could not abide failing to reclaim my Elizabeth."

The evil expression on Stefano's face unnerved Wickham. He had dealt with many corrupt men, but the lack of feeling in the count's eyes made his skin crawl, and he was disquieted at having to share a coach and accommodations for the four-day journey to Liverpool with him.

Why do I think the reward will hardly compensate for being in your vile company?

Matlock House
A Dinner Party

When William arrived at Matlock House, he was surprised at the number and variety of people assembled. Aunt Evelyn had kept her word—there were only family members present, but she had failed to mention that distant relations might be among the guests. As he looked from one person to the next in the half-circle waiting to greet him, his discomfort increased substantially. Included in the group was a woman William detested almost as much as Lady Catherine—his aunt Gladys Fitzwilliam.

Gladys was the widow of Lord Matlock's brother David. From the time he was old enough to form his own opinions and live with his own decisions, William had avoided her company. The only exceptions were an unexpected visit to Pemberley after his father's death and an equally unexpected visit to his London townhouse shortly before he left the country.

During the London visit, he was quite sure that his aunt had tried to force a compromise by slipping her oldest daughter Florence into his dressing room late one night. Fortunately, William's valet was still in the room and opened the door to find Florence standing just outside in the hallway dressed in nothing but her nightgown. Consequently, their visit did not end cordially but with even more strained relations between them. William never told anyone but Richard about his suspicions.

After he had moved to Scotland, Richard wrote that Florence had married, and her husband had been killed in a hunting accident within six months of the marriage. And as William noticed this same cousin standing next to her mother, he could not help but feel some sympathy towards her. At the very end of the line was Edith, the youngest daughter, whom he hardly recognised, since she had matured so much physically in the last two years.

In thinking of his cousins, William had always tried to keep in mind that the daughters were probably only pawns in their mother's plans. After all, Florence had been very apologetic, if not honest, as to her reasons for being in the hallway in such a state of undress. Tonight, however, he cringed to consider why they had travelled to London, as they normally resided in Brighton this time of year.

Quickly recovering, he moved forward to address his aunt and uncle and then on to Amelia. His cousin was now eight and twenty and no longer the lively girl he remembered playing with as a child. Richard had informed him of the sad state of his sister's marriage, and the fact that she had not been able to conceive a child. It saddened him that she looked stressed and much older than her years. Even more disappointing was that, somewhere along the way, she had lost her lively disposition and smile.

William bowed. Taking her hand, he brought it to his lips, all the while looking intently into her eyes, willing her to see his concern. "Amelia, it has been too long. I have missed our conversations."

"Yes, it has been a long time, Fitzwilliam. I, too, have missed our talks, especially of books, plays and operas. You are the only cousin I have who can carry on a decent discussion regarding Shakespeare…umm…well, except for Georgiana, of course. But, alas, since she and I have married, we hardly see one another."

"Then you must come to Derbyshire. You and your husband are welcome to stay at Pemberley, but I know Georgiana would want you with her at Rosewood Manor as well. You could enjoy being together again, as you did when you were girls. She often speaks of you—in fact, she mentioned you just last week."

She smiled brilliantly for just a moment, and then the smile faded completely. "She has a child now, does she not?"

William squeezed the hand he still held, knowing this was hard for her. "Yes. A little girl—Millie. You would love her as much as we do. She is truly a blessing. She was an orphan, you know."

Amelia looked wistful. "Yes, I heard." Then she seemed to recover her guard, straightening and resuming the indifferent demeanour that she had exhibited when he entered the room. "I would love to see Georgiana again and you as well, but I fear that I cannot come. Marshall does not allow me to be away from home for very long, and Derbyshire is quite a distance. He is not fond of visiting family—mine or his."

William leaned in to whisper, "Perhaps it is time to do what is not allowed." He nodded at her slight smile and moved on to greet Colonel Fitzwilliam.

"Richard! It seems we are always meeting."

As everyone laughed, Richard flicked his eyes to the extra family members and back again, speaking softly. "Just remember, this, too, shall pass." Then he said for everyone to hear, "Are you not the lucky one?"

William could not hold back a smile, but it faded when he looked to the next in line. Edgar's eyes flashed defiantly. He had always been jealous of his cousin, and his wife's infatuation with William had only exacerbated the problem. Though he knew the flirtation was one-sided, Edgar still held to his dislike of the man he had always envied. Besides, he had entertained tender feelings for his cousin Florence for years, and she, like all women of his acquaintance, only had eyes for William. Bowing slightly, he spoke stiffly.

"Darcy."

William took his cue from his cousin and replyed stiffly, "Leighton."

Earlier, Edgar had delighted in informing Gladys Fitzwilliam that William would dine there tonight, thus securing her attendance. To add further to his cousin's unease, after he and William had exchanged cursory greetings, he declared loudly, "I say, Darcy, when you entered the room, you look unnerved—as though you had seen a ghost."

"Edgar," Evelyn Fitzwilliam warned in a low voice.

Instantly, Amelia switched places with Richard and pinched her brother's arm, causing Edgar to scowl at her and then shrug at his mother's look of disapproval. Proud of temporarily disarming Darcy, Edgar skulked away from the group. Amelia raised her chin as if daring anyone else to tease her favourite cousin and seeing this, Richard patted her arm lovingly.

Lady Matlock stepped to take William's arm, guiding him towards Gladys Fitzwilliam. She pretended a cough and covered her mouth as she whispered, "They were not expected." William only had time to place his hand over the one on his arm and give it a knowing squeeze before they reached his nemesis.

~~~*~~~

As they finished the main course, William looked up to find Florence, who sat directly across from him, smiling in his direction. Quickly he diverted his eyes to Richard, who happened to be sitting next to her. Richard, however, had turned to Edith, who was going on about something William could not hear.

Firmly fixing his gaze back on his plate, he tried to occupy his mind by considering the extreme differences in his cousins. Florence was approximately six and twenty, tall, with hair so light that it was almost white. Her complexion was fair, but she had dark lashes and brows, which brought out her features. She also had green eyes that danced when she smiled, and tonight she seemed to smile a great deal—at him.

Edith, on the other hand, was about one and twenty and a good bit shorter, with medium brown hair. She reminded him just a bit of Elizabeth, though when he chanced a glance her way, he noted that her eyes were blue, not brown. As he mulled over the puzzle of sisters being so dissimilar, he failed to hear Florence's enquiry. Finally, Aunt Gladys' strident voice penetrated the fog of his musings.

"FITZWILLIAM!"

As he looked up, her annoyance was obvious. "Are you listening? Florence asked you a question."

He coughed self-consciously as Edgar chuckled. "I am sorry. I was distracted." He looked towards Florence. "What was the question?"

Florence's green eyes lit up as though she were about to laugh. "I asked if it would be possible to beg a visit to Pemberley in the near future. I barely remember visiting the summer after Uncle George passed away. I do recall the general splendour of the property and how much I enjoyed your tour of the grounds."

William's eyes went to Richard, who was watching him somberely, and then to his aunt, who looked concerned. Realising that he could not refuse Florence after inviting Amelia, he struggled with what to say.

"It would be a pleasure to have you and your family visit Pemberley again." Florence's face beamed, as did those of her sister and mother. The delight quickly faded, though, at his next pronouncement. "However, I am afraid your visit will, of necessity, have to be delayed until next year."

Aunt Gladys interjected. "But, surely you are not so busy that you cannot entertain family for a short while."

"I assure you that I am quite busy at present."

"But, you invited Amelia!"

His eyes sought Amelia's. She nodded knowingly, so he continued. "Who will, no doubt, stay with Georgiana during her visit, as I have no time to entertain her."

Quite put out, Aunt Gladys declared, "And I suppose it is that *cousin* we have heard so much about that occupies all your time."

The entire table fell silent, making all aware of Edgar's snicker. Speechless, William glared at the woman. Even Florence, sensing that her mother had gone too far, recoiled at the fury on her cousin's face.

Evelyn Fitzwilliam quickly intervened. "William has been a pillar of strength for his cousin Miss Lawrence. She needed a place to rest and recover from a long illness, and he was kind enough to offer her the quiet of Pemberley. I daresay he would do the same for any of his relations, if their needs were similar."

Gladys Fitzwilliam was not to be challenged. "I have never heard of these so-called cousins—the Lawrences."

"Neither have I," Edgar rejoined, to the dismay of his parents.

Before William could reply, Richard joined his mother's ruse. "I would be most surprised if you had. The Lawrences are distant cousins of the Darcys, not the Fitzwilliams. They hail from Sussex, do they not, Darce?"

William was so angry, all he could manage was a nod, but Richard continued undaunted, fixing a formidable glare first at Edgar and then at Gladys Fitzwilliam.

"I had the privilege of meeting the Lawrences years ago when I was in Sussex, though I am sorry to say they have passed on—at least the older generation." He looked back to William. "I believe Miss Lawrence is your only Lawrence relation left, is she not?"

Grateful for his aunt and cousin's support, William rallied. "Yes. Yes, she is. Both of her parents are dead, and she was the only one of her generation to survive to adulthood."

His aunt sniffed, "How convenient!"

Edgar decided to deliver another blow. "And how is it that you met them Richard, but I have not? You have never mentioned them to me?"

"Unlike some, I have to work for my living, and I travel the length and breadth of England in service to the Crown. I meet any number of people that you never shall." Richard smirked. "As for telling you, when have you ever taken time to talk to me, a lowly officer, about anything?"

Edward Fitzwilliam had reached the limits of his patience. He had approached this dinner with the hope that his oldest son had gotten past his anger towards his cousin, provoked anew by Jacqueline's preference for Darcy. Long since accepting his part in the disastrous marriages of his son and daughter, he had tried to redeem himself by listening more and being less officious. Tonight, however, he could see himself in Edgar, and it was not a pleasant reflection.

As for Gladys Fitzwilliam, she seemed overly eager to skewer his nephew as well. He had no idea of what had caused the coldness between the two, but assumed it had to do with Florence. The fact that Edgar was apparently intent on helping her dress-down the boy made him furious. Finally, the Earl of Matlock spoke.

"Enough! Edgar, you and my sister have made quite a number of insinuations. I, myself, had occasion to meet George Darcy's relations, the Lawrences, many years ago. I can only add that I am proud of Fitzwilliam for taking in someone with no family left in Sussex to see to her care."

When Lord Matlock began his tall tale of the Lawrences, William, Evelyn, and Richard all turned to stare in astonishment. Never, in their wildest imaginations, would they have believed the earl would take up the story they had begun to protect William.

Seeing that she had angered the one person she feared most—Lord Matlock—Gladys rose to the occasion. "I apologise. I should not have voiced my reservations about this cousin, even if I believed the rumours to be true."

Edward declared, "Rumours are just gossip, madam! And you need not apologise to me. Apologise to Fitzwilliam!"

At that, William's aunt fixed him with an insincere smile. "I am sorry if my opinions brought you pain. Please forgive me."

William stood, his chair scraping the floor. "I accept your apology, madam, though I wish you to know that your opinions mean nothing to me. Whatever I decide to do with my resources is my concern and no one else's. And as to the future, I intend to please myself."

With that, he excused himself with a bow, as did Richard.

~~~*~~~

Later that night as Evelyn Fitzwilliam prepared for bed, she could not wipe the smile from her face.

It was not the grandest or liveliest dinner party the Fitzwilliam's had ever given, but to her it was one of the most satisfying. Tonight her family, save Edgar, had come together to protect the nephew she loved like a son. Her husband's vile relation—a woman she disliked as much as Lady Catherine—had truly been put in her place, and her dearest husband had proven himself to be the man she had always known he could be—a man worthy of all her respect and love.

And as she stood to inspect her person, having left her hair loose as Edward preferred, she smiled at her reflection in the mirror. Tonight she would slip into Edward's bedchamber. After all, he had winked at her when he left her to her preparations.

Darcy House
The Library

"So there you are!" Mr. Williamson strolled into the library—book in hand. "I heard a commotion and supposed it was you and the colonel returning from your dinner engagement, but I expected you would go directly to bed."

William stood and gestured towards the brandy carafe. Williamson shook his head. "No, thank you. I was just returning this book on medieval remedies, hoping to find something equally as absorbing to read."

"My cousin retired, and I was just thinking of doing the same." William stifled a yawn. "By the way, I apologise again for leaving you alone tonight."

"Think nothing of it. I have thoroughly enjoyed having time to myself. As much as I love being a minister, my little cottage is never free of parishioners needing one thing or another. When I am home, I can hardly finish a book."

Sitting down, William sighed heavily, gaining the vicar's full attention. Williamson now noticed the decidedly strained look on his host's face. "Is there anything I can do to help?"

William chuckled. "Can you do away with some of my relatives?"

Williamson guffawed. "If I could do that, I would be in greater demand for funerals and would be richer than you, I imagine."

At that, William laughed and the vicar studied him. "I take it that something unsettling occurred at the dinner party."

"You might say that." Blowing out a deep breath, William began to relate all that had occurred at Matlock House. Afterwards, they sat in companionable silence for a time.

Finally, the vicar ventured, "I can certainly understand the reason for your question about doing away with your relatives."

William grinned tiredly, rubbing his forehead. "Yes, but my uncle certainly redeemed himself, at least in my opinion. He has always drummed duty, family and responsibility into me and into his own family as well. It was a shock to see him stand up for me like that—most especially since he and I have not been close in years."

"I should imagine from what you have told me of Lady Matlock that she has been a great influence on his change of heart. And you, of all people, can understand the influence a worthy woman can have on a man who just needs to set his priorities in order."

William lifted his glass in salute. "I believe you have come to the heart of it."

There was a knock on the door, and the men exchanged glances. "Come," William called out, and Mr. Barnes entered with a letter in his hand.

"Sir, this was just delivered by a footman who would not tell me the name of his employer, but he did say that it was urgent that you read it as soon as possible."

"Thank you, Mr. Barnes. That will be all."

The butler nodded and quit the room.

Staring at the decidedly feminine handwriting, William knew exactly who had sent the missive, and for a brief moment, he hesitated. Glancing over to Mr. Williamson, the man's brows rose in question, and he knew he had no choice. Swallowing hard, he tore into the scented envelope.

Dear Fitzwilliam,

I have information regarding your dear cousin ... the one staying at Pemberley for her health. If you are truly interested in her wellbeing, you will want to hear what I have learned from two very interesting sources—a count who claims he is her husband and a swindler who says he was reared at Pemberley. They have great plans for Miss Lawrence.

You know where I live. Come to my house in the morning if you wish to know what I heard quite by accident. Perhaps we can work out an agreement whereby I can share it with you.

Gwen

The look on William's face was enough to convince Mr. Williamson of the seriousness of the situation. After several seconds of silence, he decided to get involved.

"If I may be so bold, I can only imagine from the look on your face that this letter is in regards to Elizabeth. I do not believe you would be afraid for yourself, but you look frightened for her."

Only his eyes moved to the vicar. "Yes, I am afraid an acquaintance of mine—a woman—has learned of some plan afoot to harm Elizabeth. She is not above using blackmail to enrich her coffers, and while I abhor paying for information, I will do anything in my power to protect Elizabeth."

"Naturally. Are you to meet with her?"

William stood up. "Yes, in the morning, and if I am to get started early, I will need to retire now."

"Certainly. Would you like me to accompany you tomorrow?"

"I appreciate your kind offer, Mr. Williamson, but Richard will insist on going with me, as he knows the woman well. And although she is prominent in the *ton,* I fear a man of your occupation would do well to stay clear of her."

Williamson smiled. "So people would talk if I were seen coming from her house?"

William chuckled. "The only way you could avoid the gossip would be if you had administered the last rites, and she were carried out dead."

"And what of your reputation?"

"I am Fitzwilliam Darcy." He smiled mischievously as he lifted an eyebrow. "I need no reputation."

"Oh?"

"Nevertheless, I would never call on her alone. I would do nothing to crush Elizabeth's faith in me."

The kindly reverend widened his grin. "I think Fitzwilliam Darcy worries more about his reputation than he pretends."

Mr. Barnes was checking the last of the doors when he heard the master and his guest laughing as they went up the grand staircase. He smiled to himself. He could remember a time not so long ago when Mr. Darcy never laughed at all.

~~~*~~~

Chapter 33

Lady Waltham's townhouse
The next morning

Willliam and Richard arrived at a decent hour for a morning call, but were forced to wait for over an hour without being afforded as a courtesy any explanation as to why Lady Waltham had not joined them. Other than the housekeeper who had brought in tea after they were seated, they had seen no one.

"I do not understand it, Darce! How could Gwendolyn Waltham be privy to information concerning the count and Miss Elizabeth?"

"Shhh," William warned, looking over his shoulder. The drawing room of Lady Waltham's townhouse was eerily quiet, and there was no one in sight, but the door had been left ajar by the housekeeper so he answered in a soft timbre.

"Lower your voice, Richard. We do not know who listens without, and we do not want her to think us disconcerted. Try to appear indifferent. I am quite sure from her note that she expects to reap a substantial reward for whatever information she thinks she has stumbled upon. I do not wish for her to think we are overly anxious and raise her asking price."

Richard nodded, calming somewhat. Had he been able to have his way, William would have stayed at home and allowed him to handle the woman. As far as he was concerned, Lady Waltham was a carnivore and his cousin her favourite entree. Glancing at William, he wondered at his ability to project such a calm demeanour, since he knew without a doubt that the man was worried sick about how this would affect the woman he loved. But before he had time for further reflection, a seductive voice purred from the doorway.

"I was not sure you would come."

Both men stood and turned. Lady Waltham wore a very revealing gown, not in any way appropriate for morning. Her gaze vacillated between William and Richard before she fixed on William, her eyes slowly moving up and down his body in an erotic manner.

"You look very well this morning, Fitzwilliam."

William kept his eyes on hers, refusing to let them wander to her nearly uncovered breasts. Richard, however, had no such reluctance. Trained to study his enemy thoroughly, he took in the entire vision that was Gwendolyn Waltham with a sly smirk.

Irritated by Richard's open inspection when his was not the attention she desired, Gwendolyn added, "I see you brought your protector."

With an air of certainty, Richard replied, "I am merely here in case you forget yourself, Lady Waltham. I understand that you have trouble grasping the meaning of the word *no* without the help of Lord Greenwich."

Gwendolyn's eyes hardened, and her mouth formed a straight line as she tried not to let either man see that her confidence had been ruffled. Taking a seat on the sofa directly across from where they stood, she motioned to them.

"Have a seat, gentlemen. This discussion may take some time."

With a deep intake of breath illustrating his impatience, William sat down, and Richard followed, his gaze now fixed on the sight of long, slender legs peeking from under her gown. Undoubtedly, she had pulled the hem up as she sat down.

"Let us get to the heart of it," William declared. "What information do you have about my cousin?"

"My, my, we are irritable this morning!" She leaned forward as she scolded William, affording both men a view of her ample cleavage. "Could you try to be a little more amiable, Fitzwilliam? After all, we were once—"

"Madam, as I stated to you at the Matlock's ball and again at Pemberley, what we were years ago is of no import to me in the least. Let us get to the reason for your imperial summons. How much?"

Irritated that her considerable attributes were even now of no advantage with William, she answered testily, "As you wish! Three thousand pounds!"

"You are mad!" Richard quipped. "How do we know that you have valid information? And even if you did, that amount is ridiculous!"

"I daresay it is a pittance to Fitzwilliam Darcy! I mentioned a count, did I not? What if I also mention George Wickham?"

Richard and William exchanged furtive glances, which did not escape Gwendolyn's notice, and she smiled like a Cheshire cat. "From the look on your faces, perhaps I should have asked for more."

William interjected, "Do not try my patience, Lady Waltham. As it is, you are inviting more trouble than you realise. Your request for money is blackmail."

Greatly offended, Gwendolyn sputtered, "But ... but I am only offering to pass along the gossip I overheard because it concerns you. I knew you would want to know."

"For a price!" Richard's voice escalated as he moved to the edge of his seat, leaning forward. "And if it involves harming a young woman—"

William gripped his cousin's arm, and Richard's head swung around. Seeing the look on William's face, he acquiesced, sitting back in the chair again with a smug look at the alarm now on Lady Waltham's face.

William proffered solemnly, "I will pay what you ask." Gwendolyn lifted her chin, glancing at Richard with the beginnings of a smile before he continued, "After you tell me what you know."

The smile vanished entirely, and William challenged, "But, if I find that you are playing me for a fool, I shall spare no expense in seeing you prosecuted. And you know that my uncle is well able to accomplish that."

Indignantly, Gwendolyn rose and began to pace, sputtering loudly enough to be heard, "Ungrateful!" She stopped, stomped her foot, then squaring her shoulders faced William.

"After the contemptible way you have behaved towards me recently, you do not deserve my help! One would think that we were never anything to each other!" As William started to protest, she held up a hand. "Even so, you are most fortunate in that I find myself uncharacteristically low on funds, so I will tell you what I know. I can assure you that you will not be disappointed in the information that has fortuitously fallen into my hands."

"If I am not, you shall have a bank draft this afternoon," William assured her. "Tell me everything that you know about the threat to my cousin."

She sat back down, assuming her pretentious manner. "First, I shall recount how I came to be acquainted with the count and how that placed me in the position to inadvertently learn of the plan to kidnap your cousin from Pemberley."

At the word "kidnap" William's entire countenance darkened. It was not lost on Richard, who began to consider what his cousin would do if someone were actually able to abscond with Elizabeth. He roused from his reverie though, as Gwendolyn began a recitation of the first time she met the count.

~~~*~~~

Richard was beginning to be concerned, as William had not uttered a word since leaving Lady Waltham's townhouse—not even in response to his statements regarding what they had just heard. Instead, he stared blankly out the carriage window.

He leaned forward to shake his shoulder. "Say something, or I shall assume you are in need of a physician and act accordingly. I know you are reserved, but this is ridiculous."

William's countenance did not lighten at his teasing, as was customary. Instead, his gaze never left the window as he seemed to study something that only he could see. Then swallowing with great difficulty, he replied hoarsely, "I was mistaken to leave Elizabeth alone at Pemberley. I should have kept her right by my side, so I could protect her."

"My Lord, Darce! You might not have been able to prevent this, even had you been at Pemberley or were she here with you. You cannot watch her every hour of the day and night. Now, quit thinking along such lines and begin to help me formulate a plan to deal with this blackguard."

William attempted to recover, fixing his gaze on Richard. "I have been trying to figure it out—make sense of it in my head—but I am not sure where to begin. Gwendolyn said they talked of abducting Elizabeth as soon as I arrived in London. If this is true, there may very well be an express on the way informing me she is missing. I am torn between racing to Pemberley to try to prevent an abduction and assuming that they have already taken her. My heart tells me that I should head straight to Liverpool to keep her from being spirited aboard a ship bound for Italy. If she were removed to somewhere that I could not recover her at once ..." William's voice trailed off, and he shook his head at the prospect, tears clearly visible in his eyes.

Seeing his anguish, Richard moved to sit beside him, slipping an arm about his shoulder. "Trust your heart. It would make sense to go to Liverpool first. When you send word to Pemberley and Rosewood Manor, tell them we shall be at the Landmark Inn in Liverpool in four days, and advise them to send us news at that establishment. If everything is well, we shall simply return to Pemberley from Liverpool."

William straightened, sitting up taller. "I shall send a special express to Mrs. Reynolds and also to Evan and Georgiana the moment I get back to the house. Meanwhile, if you will direct Lieutenant Marbury to inspect the address Gwendolyn provided for Stefano, perhaps we can learn if he actually has quit London. If we get no clear answer soon, I feel we have no choice but to head straight for Liverpool."

"Have you considered who this woman might be—the one who is to convince Elizabeth to leave Pemberley?"

"I have absolutely no idea."

Further discussion was ended as, at that moment, the carriage pulled to a stop in front of William's home. As the footman opened the door, a familiar face stepped towards them.

"Mr. Darcy, I came to inform you of what I lately have heard regarding Stephen. It appears that he has left London."

William mouth dropped into a scowl. "Please come inside. I have just received information regarding him as well."

Lord Stanton's voice was full of concern. "Of course!"

Once everyone was seated in William's study, he related to the count's father the entirety of Gwendolyn Waltham's early morning revelation.

Stanton sighed heavily. "I wish I knew with certainty his destination, but all my man could tell me was that he left in a coach with a Mr. Wickham, so it seems as though your source may indeed be correct."

"If he is with Wickham, I have to assume that they are headed to Liverpool to meet the coach that has Elizabeth. There is no way Wickham would be able to enter Pemberley."

"Are you confident they will succeed in persuading Miss Elizabeth to agree to leave your estate, Mr. Darcy?"

William reflected on the many times Elizabeth had expressed concern for his safety. "Whoever they sent to Pemberley has only to convince Elizabeth that my life, or that of my sister, is at stake and she would leave. She would never place either of us in jeopardy."

"I fear you are most likely correct. Miss Elizabeth was far too tender-hearted for her own good." Stanton breathed deeply. "Would that I could stop him."

William's steely eyes met the earl's. "I intend to stop him. I will find Elizabeth and take her from him for the last time."

Stanton lowered his head. "I understand. Your first concern must be for Elizabeth. Now, I should leave you to your plans. Do not bother rising, Mr. Darcy; I can see myself out." With those words, the elderly man exited the room.

Richard spun back around to William. "With your permission, I shall have Mr. Barnes inform the coachman to ready the coach with all speed and to send a groom ahead to make arrangements for fresh horses at the inns I will specify. I know that route well. I have travelled it many times in my service to the crown."

William nodded and Richard started towards the door, calling back over his shoulder, "We should be able to leave at dawn."

William's deep baritone rang out, "We shall leave within the hour."

Richard halted mid-stride, turning awkwardly. "Surely not today?"

"Within the hour, Richard."

"But how in blazes will the servants get everything ready in time?"

"My coachman is well aware of my propensity to travel at will. I am certain he has already checked the coach and is only awaiting my orders to leave. I have plenty of horses available, so in one hour I shall be on my way. Will you be joining me?"

Richard shook his head in awe. "We needed you in the last campaign! You are as hard a task-master as Wellington! Of course, I shall join you. After all, who is to keep you from meeting with trouble you cannot handle?"

William chuckled mirthlessly. "Who indeed?"

Darcy House

Mr. Williamson made his way down the grand staircase amidst the hustle and bustle of the servants' rushing to have everything ready for the Master's departure. Just outside his bedchamber, he had overheard William's valet giving orders to a footman regarding some trunks, so he was alerted as to what all the activity signified.

Spying William as he exited his study, followed closely by his steward, Williamson waited for him to conclude his business before heading in his direction. The minute William spied the reverend he tried to assume a smile.

"Forgive me for not speaking with you sooner, Mr. Williamson. Would you please step into my study?"

The vicar followed him and took a seat in front of the desk as William sat down behind it. He noted the worry lines now gathered on the young man's forehead and the fact that he did not look as though he had slept any last night. Assuming that the meeting William had had this morning was the cause for all the commotion, he was about to ask about it when his host began speaking.

"I am afraid that something very important has come up, and Richard and I have to travel to Liverpool straightaway. I would appreciate it very much if you would travel on to Pemberley in my other coach and wait there for my return."

"If your departure concerns Lizzybet, I respectfully request that you tell me what is happening."

Reading the deep concern in the reverend's eyes, William acquiesced and told him of the discussions with Gwendolyn Waltham the day before and Lord Stanton a few hours ago. The older man sat with his head in his hands for a moment before looking up to enquire, "May I not travel with you and the colonel?"

William's mien darkened. "If I find the count in Liverpool, the situation could quickly become very dangerous for everyone involved."

Mr. Williamson stood. "I was unable to help my girl the last time she was abducted. I would like the opportunity to be of service to her now."

William promptly came around the desk to clasp his shoulder. "I know how you feel. The last time I was not of any help to her either."

"But you have been her champion since finding her. So, let us focus together on how we can rescue her from this villain."

"Richard and I are leaving within the hour. I shall request that your trunk be packed quickly, if that is your wish."

"It is. Thank you for allowing me to join you."

"We can always use a man of prayer on our side." William's face sobered. "Thank you for loving Elizabeth so well."

"I could say the same about you."

Pemberley
The next day

The sky was quickly turning grey as the coach entered the longest section of the drive towards the manor house. It had been a tiring three-day journey, and Cecile Preston still could not rest until she had spoken with Elizabeth. As soon as she reached Pemberley, the hardest part began—convincing the woman she envied to accompany her to Liverpool.

As they neared the manor, Cecile began to fret that her brother and sister might possibly be visiting. It was certainly late enough that the Ingrams should be at their own estate, but there was always the possibility that they were to spend the night at Pemberley. In the pit of her stomach, a queasy feeling began and, just for a moment, she felt as though she might become ill. Summarily, she pushed the thought away.

Cecile Preston, you will do what you have come to do! You have no choice!

Suddenly the coach cleared the last stand of trees before the circular portion of drive began. The front entrance came into view, and she breathed a sigh of relief. There were no carriages or coaches in sight. Praying that Georgiana had not ridden over on horseback, Cecile held her breath as the coach came to a halt and the door opened. A footman was immediately there to help her alight. She watched Mr. Walker open the door as she began to take the steps.

"Mrs. Preston," he declared warily as she entered the front door, "I am afraid Mr. Darcy is not in residence."

Mrs. Reynolds rushed towards her, eyebrows raised in question. "Mrs. Preston, we were not expecting you. Mr. Darcy is not—"

Cecile interrupted her. "I came to see Miss Lawrence. Is she available?" For a moment the housekeeper stood staring at her, so Cecile continued. "I have a letter from Mr. Darcy that he asked me to deliver personally. I suppose, as late as it is, I should have travelled on to the Ingram's estate, but he seemed anxious for Miss Lawrence to receive it as soon as was possible."

A look of great relief spread across the housekeepers face. "A letter? Why, of course, I shall tell her." She motioned towards an open door. "Would you please wait in the drawing room? I shall send some refreshments while I locate Miss Lawrence."

Cecile nodded. "Excellent." All was going according to plan.

Waiting in the well-appointed room, Cecile breathed a sigh of relief. It seemed no one was visiting, and Mrs. Reynolds had been only too glad to fetch Miss Elizabeth when she mentioned the non-existent letter. A small part of her whispered that she should not go through with the ruse, but she cast that thought away as the door opened.

Elizabeth entered hesitantly. Georgiana had told her of Mrs. Preston's part in their ill-fated first meeting—the incident where Georgiana had confronted her because of Cecile's erroneous conclusions. Why this woman would agree to bring her a letter from Fitzwilliam was beyond her grasp, but she wanted to hear from him so desperately that she cast her apprehension aside. As she shyly moved forward, Cecile stood and smiled holding out her hand.

"Miss Lawrence. I am Georgiana's sister, Cecile Preston."

Elizabeth nodded, though she did not move to take her hand. "I know who you are, Mrs. Preston. Georgiana has spoken of you."

Dropping her hand, Cecile continued cheerfully. "I just came by to speak with you on Fitzwilliam's behalf."

"I understand that you have a letter for me."

Cecile's smile was more of a grimace. "Not exactly. Shall we sit down?"

Elizabeth stiffened, continuing to stand. "What do you mean, 'Not exactly'?"

Just at that moment, a servant quietly entered, deposited a tray with tea and cakes on a sideboard, and after bobbing a curtsy, departed. After she was gone, Elizabeth shut the door behind her and turned back to Cecile.

"Either you have a letter or you do not."

"I am afraid I do not, but if you will just sit down, I shall explain my intentions in coming." Each sizing up the other, they both sat down stiffly.

"I own that I fabricated the existence of the letter because I felt that it was the only way you would agree to meet with me. I have travelled many miles because of my concern for Fitzwilliam's welfare."

Elizabeth's chin rose. "You have come to counsel me to stay away from him?"

"I am here to appeal to your concern for his wellbeing. I pray that if you truly care for him, as I believe you do, you will leave Pemberley to assure his safety."

Elizabeth's dark eyes grew wider. "Continue."

"Your husband, madam, is aware of your ruse and is, at this very moment, formulating a plan to steal you away from Pemberley—by force, if necessary."

Elizabeth stuttered, "My—my husband?"

"Count Stefano."

Her face crumbled at the name, and her face paled with fear. "How—how would he know that I am here?"

"The gossip circulating in London is that a married woman, claiming to be a distant cousin of Mr. Darcy, has insinuated herself at Pemberley. It even has been said that she was hiding from her husband. The count was bound to hear of it since he apparently has people searching for you. When I learned of the count's plans, I immediately set out to warn you."

Elizabeth raised brows. "But why would you—"

"For Fitzwilliam!" Cecile interrupted curtly. "I still care for him very much, and I would not like to see him hurt or, heaven forbid, killed."

"How did you learn this?"

Cecile took several minutes to weave a tale of meeting Mr. Wickham and through him, the count. She said that the count had talked frequently of recovering his unfaithful wife and, only days ago, claimed that he had discovered her location. According to Cecile, it was only after she realised that he was speaking of Elizabeth and Pemberley, that she felt she had to take action. She ended the lies by repeating Wickham's words that the count threatened to extract his wife from Pemberley, even if it meant killing Fitzwilliam Darcy.

Seeing that Elizabeth was in shock, she added, "I instantly knew what I had to do—offer you a way out—a way for you to escape your husband and to keep Fitzwilliam from being harmed."

Elizabeth sat silently for a long time, overwhelmed by everything she had heard. The thought that Fitzwilliam could die because of her and knowing she could not live if that happened, forced her to compose herself.

"How do you intend to help me to leave?"

"I will personally escort you to Liverpool tomorrow morning. There is a ship there leaving for the Americas next week. I have taken the liberty of purchasing you a passage. In addition, I shall give you one hundred pounds, which should be sufficient until you find some type work when you land. Moreover, I will send an express to Mr. Wickham informing him that I called on you at Pemberley and learned that you were no longer here. He will be sure to pass the information to his friend, the count."

"But why would you help me—buy my passage and give me money?"

"Fitzwilliam thinks he is in love with you. Once you are out of his life forever, I shall comfort him and, hopefully, assume my rightful place in his life. After all, I was his choice before you appeared."

Though William had told her many times that she was the only woman he would ever love or have in his life, Elizabeth physically ached to hear Cecile speak as though it would be no challenge to replace her in William's affections. And for a moment, in her mind's eye, she could picture him with Cecile, entering a crowded ballroom, smiling and laughing as lovers do. Her tortured meditation was so vivid that only Cecile's raised voice could penetrate it.

"Are you listening to me?"

Elizabeth shook her head to remove the tormenting image. "Yes. Yes, I am listening."

"Then you agree that Fitzwilliam is too much the gentleman to let you leave, even if it is to protect himself. That makes it imperative that we leave before he suspects anything or, God forbid, Georgiana finds us out. We must leave at daybreak."

Elizabeth blinked, trying to stave off the tears. The woman was right about one thing—Fitzwilliam would never let her go, even to save himself.

"Daybreak? Yes, we should leave at daybreak. I shall inform Mrs. Reynolds that you are staying the night and that I will be accompanying you to the Ingram's home very early tomorrow. I shall not have my things packed, which would raise suspicion, but bring only a few things in my valise, which you can put with your bags."

"Excellent plan!" Cecile declared with relief. "By the time our story is proved false, we shall have a good head start to Liverpool. I only hope that by the time someone suspects we are gone for good, they will have no idea as to the direction in which we are headed."

Cecile concealed her unbridled happiness as she stood and moved to pat Elizabeth's arm. "I am heartened that you have listened to my counsel. After all, we are both only trying to protect Fitzwilliam."

Elizabeth stood to leave. "Mrs. Preston, I am not as naive as you believe. I know that your concern is strictly for yourself." Then she walked to the door, stopping to address her once more. "I shall inform Mrs. Reynolds to prepare a room."

Cecile fumed as she watched her rival quit the room.

At least I was not pretending to be his cousin!

~~~*~~~

Chapter 34

Pemberley
The next morning

With a heavy heart, Mrs. Reynolds stood on the front portico until the coach carrying Mrs. Preston and Miss Elizabeth was completely out of sight, disappearing down the long drive and seemingly into the surrounding forest. She was well aware that Mr. Darcy would not be pleased when he learned of Elizabeth's trip, but she had done her best, reminding her charge that the master would not want her to leave Pemberley while he was away. Nonetheless, her warning did nothing to dissuade the determined young lady.

Oddly, the housekeeper had begun to feel anxious the moment Miss Elizabeth had announced that she was going to accompany Mrs. Preston to the Ingram's residence that morning. Something about Elizabeth's demeanour was unsettling. Last evening she had been so excited at the prospect of a letter from Mr. Darcy that she had rushed downstairs to greet Mrs. Preston personally. In the morning, when asked if Mr. Darcy had mentioned when he might be coming home, Elizabeth had sounded oddly despondent when she had replied that he had not.

In addition, Mrs. Preston's feigned interest in Elizabeth's company was not in any manner believable. The housekeeper had not spent years observing the women who tried to impress Mr. Darcy without becoming quite adept at identifying the cunning ones, of which the Widow Preston was a prime example. It pained her greatly to see Elizabeth keeping company with a woman who obviously still fancied Mr. Darcy for herself.

Realising that she had been staring at nothing but the trees since the coach had travelled completely out of sight, Mrs. Reynolds steeled herself not to worry. *After all, worrying never changes anything except the number of grey hairs on my head.*

Turning back to the house, she noted Mr. Walker waiting at the ornate front entry, a frown evident on his face. She tried to put on a smile as she stepped over the threshold, and he closed the heavily carved door soundly behind her.

"I do not like the looks of this," Walker offered sourly as he glanced about to make sure no other servants were within the sound of his voice.

Mrs. Reynolds met his eyes in equal disapproval. "Nor do I, but what could I do, other than to remind Miss Elizabeth of Mr. Darcy's express instructions that she remain here until his return. At least they are only going as far as Rosewood Manor."

"Mr. Darcy will not hold you at fault. I heard your warnings, and you tried to make her realise the danger of leaving the estate. Yet, I cannot help but feel a strange uneasiness at her accompanying that woman. There must be a reason, other than friendship, that would compel the widow to take an interest in the young miss. For my money, the old hen still fancies the master for herself."

277

Mrs. Reynolds chuckled at his words before promptly sobering at the truth of them. "I am afraid that I heartily agree with your assessment. I shall not feel at ease until Miss Elizabeth is safely returned this evening."

Then trying to put a pleasant perspective on the situation, she added, "But on the other hand, perhaps a visit with Miss Georgiana, I mean Mrs. Ingram, will cheer her. Miss Elizabeth has been in poor spirits since the master left and much the worse since Mrs. Preston's arrival. I pray she will be back to her usual cheerful nature when she returns."

"I trust that will be the case, as well. It pains me to see the young miss with a frown on her lovely face. Now, I suppose I should get myself busy and try not to dwell on what could happen in the few short hours she will be away."

Exchanging wan smiles, the long-time servants turned and went in opposite directions.

Pemberley
That afternoon

In the early afternoon, a carriage carrying Evan, Georgiana and Millie Ingram pulled to a stop in front of Pemberley. As the Ingrams disembarked, they were certainly in good spirits. They had come expressly to cheer Miss Elizabeth, as seeing Millie always improved Elizabeth's frame of mind.

Evan descended the carriage first, reaching back in to take Millie from his wife's lap and then set her gently on the ground. While he was thus engaged, a footman assisted Georgiana from the carriage. Then each parent took one of Millie's hands and turned to ascend the steps three abreast. Almost immediately, they encountered Mrs. Reynolds, who was already coming down the steps at a quick pace—the look on the housekeeper's face instantly alerting them that something was amiss.

"Mr. Ingram ... Mrs. Ingram!" Mrs. Reynolds began breathlessly, looking over their heads towards the long drive as if expecting another carriage. "What a surprise to see you here. Are you escorting Miss Elizabeth back? Is she riding with Mrs. Preston?"

"Mrs. Preston?" Evan Ingram began cautiously, glancing at his wife. "Mrs. Preston is not in Derbyshire as far as we know."

The housekeeper's hands shook as she placed them over her heart, her face paling instantly. Stuttering now with fear, she could barely get out the words, "I ... I was led to believe she was accompanying Mrs. Preston to Rosewood Manor early this morning. Have you not seen or heard from them today?"

"No!" Georgiana exclaimed uneasily. "We came to see Elizabeth and had no idea she was not here! You say Cecile escorted her from Pemberley? When did she arrive?"

Seeing that the women's panic was beginning to draw the attention of the servants, Evan spoke up. "Let us go inside and discuss this matter rationally."

He scooped up Millie, and they all proceeded into the house. As they entered the foyer, Margaret, a young maid who often cared for Millie when they were at Pemberley, was coming towards them down the hall. Mrs. Reynolds motioned for her to come forward and enquired of Evan, "Would it not be best to let Margaret entertain Millie while we discuss all of this in the drawing room?"

"I believe that would be wise," he replied, kissing Millie's cheek before handing the child over to Margaret, who eagerly stepped forward to take her little friend.

"Go with Margaret to the conservatory, sweetheart. She will let you take some toys from the large box to play with while Mama and Papa talk with Mrs. Reynolds. You will like that."

Millie's eye lit up at the mention of toys, and she nodded her head in agreement. "Yes, Papa."

Everyone followed the two as they disappeared in the direction of the conservatory then swiftly made their way towards the drawing room. Georgiana had no sooner entered the room before she addressed the housekeeper. "Tell us everything that has happened with Miss Elizabeth since last I was here."

What followed was an account of the arrival of Mrs. Preston, including the woman's claim of having a letter from Mr. Darcy for Elizabeth, Elizabeth's insistence that Cecile stay the night, and her strange decision to accompany the woman to Rosewood Manor that morning.

"I had a dreadful feeling about her leaving with Mrs. Preston. I tried to dissuade her, reminding her that the master wished her to stay at Pemberley where he could be sure of her safety. However, it seemed to me that she had her mind made up. She was resolved to go regardless of what I said."

"Do you suppose my brother said something in his letter that upset her?" Georgiana asked, her mind reeling with possibilities. "You know he has a tendency to say things in the wrong manner."

Evan, who was too troubled to sit, interjected, "I am almost certain that there was no letter from Darcy. Frankly, I do not believe that he would send a letter to the woman he loves via my sister. I have to believe that the letter was a ruse to get to Elizabeth."

"I had not thought of that!" Georgiana exclaimed, the truth of her husband's observation sinking in. "Now that I think on it, my brother would never have trusted Cecile with something so close to his heart!"

Mrs Reynolds added, "I know it was not my place, but because of my unease, I took the liberty of searching Miss Elizabeth's bedroom after she left this morning, trying to determine if she might have packed a bag."

Georgiana brow knit anxiously. "And had she?"

"From what was left in the room, I could not make a true determination. She did not carry a bag as she left, but I suppose she could have hidden it among Mrs. Preston's items. It appeared, if my memory serves, that there were a few gowns missing but certainly not all of her clothes."

Mrs. Reynolds sighed heavily. "To tell the truth, I was just relieved to find so much still left in her room and wished to believe that the missing clothes were amongst the items waiting downstairs to be washed."

"What of the little chest she loved so much?"

"I did not think of that!"

Instantly, Georgiana stood. "Let us search her rooms. Perhaps we can find some evidence to settle our minds. I know we will have to inform William, but I want to investigate every avenue before I compose a letter of this import."

She glanced to Evan as she headed to the door. "Please come with us dear. You may notice something we do not."

Minutes later, the three were examining the closets and drawers in Elizabeth's rooms. Mrs. Reynolds had just located the small chest, which was sitting open on the floor, when Evan called out, "Here!" She and Georgiana hurried into the small sitting room next door to find him holding a letter aloft.

"It was propped against the lamp on that table," he nodded towards a small reading table in the corner. "I think you should open it, Ana. Darcy will certainly understand why you felt you needed to read it."

Georgiana nodded, taking it from his hand and reading her brother's name in Elizabeth's fine script. Then, after meeting the others eyes, she tore open the seal. As she read she did not comment, but grew increasingly pale. Evan pushed a chair close behind her and carefully pulled her down into the soft cushions, even as she kept reading. By the time she had finished, the room was deathly quiet.

Eventually Georgiana's softly voiced what they all feared. "Elizabeth is gone forever—to the Americas. My ... my brother surely will die of heartache when he reads this."

She began to sob, and Evan pulled her up from the chair and into his arms, soothing her in his tight embrace. His eyes met those of Mrs. Reynolds as he looked over his wife's shoulder, and the tears on the housekeeper's face caused his to well up. Still holding Ana, he reached to take one of the elderly woman's hands as she lamented, "This is all my fault. I should never have let her go."

Georgiana turned then to embrace Mrs. Reynolds. "No! You love her, too. You could not have known this would happen nor could you have prevented her from leaving."

Evan wanted to reassure the women, though his mind reeled with the implications of what his sister had done and how he might reverse the damage. Almost instantly, he formed a plan.

"Ana, send a special messenger to Darcy in London. Tell him I am making preparations to go after my sister and recover Miss Elizabeth."

Georgiana managed to speak even as she wept. "But ... but how shall we learn in which direction she was taken?"

Evan stilled for a moment. His voice as firm as his reply. "Money loosens tongues. I shall send men along all the main roads out of Derbyshire and have them question the people along the way. Someone observed a large coach leaving Lambton this morning. I pray that there was only one or, if more than one, that I follow the right coach."

Georgiana leaned into him, resting her head on his chest. "I want you to find them, but you must promise to take an adequate number of men with you. I fear Cecile is not acting alone. Something tells me that Elizabeth's husband," she swallowed hard, trying not to cry. "I meant to say the count, is involved. And he would not hesitate to harm you."

"I believe your assumptions are correct, my love. I will take men from Pemberley as well as my own, so do not be anxious." With a quick kiss on her nose, he began to pull her towards the door. "Come, sweetheart. We must collect Millie and return home. I have much to do and a short time to accomplish it."

He called to Mrs. Reynolds as he went out the door. "Keep Darcy informed and pray that I find Elizabeth before something dreadful happens."

They were out the door before Mrs. Reynolds could reply, so she moved to the doorway to watch husband and wife walk swiftly down the hall and begin the stairs to the foyer. Her heart aching with grief and worry, she turned her eyes toward heaven.

Lord, please help Mr. Ingram find her, and keep him and Miss Elizabeth safe. Bring them home to us soon. Please!

On the road to Liverpool

Richard and Mr. Williamson exchanged worried glances as they listened to William's slight snore. Both men were well aware that the young man on the other side of the carriage had a tenuous hold on his emotions, and the longer they had travelled, the worse the situation had become.

He had been the picture of control when they had left London the day before, however, today his companions noted that his voice would oftentimes break when he spoke of Elizabeth and, before he finally succumbed to sleep, he had fiddled endlessly with his gloves and his cravat. Apparently mortified that he could not regulate his feelings, William had chosen to say nothing for the last few miles, except to answer questions directed at him very briefly. His lack of conversation had led to his current state of slumber, for which they were most grateful. At least when he slept, he was not quarrelling over the slow pace of the journey or the quality of the horses.

As he watched his sleeping cousin, Richard reflected on what had transpired on the first leg of their journey yesterday evening.

Before travelling many miles, the sky had begun to turn grey as daylight faded, which was to be expected by starting out so late in the day. Up ahead, the first inn Richard had planned to utilise appeared in view.

"Ah, our accommodations for the night! Not perfect but better than most."

As they attained the inn and climbed out of the coach to stretch, William began to grumble. "Must we stop so soon? Surely we can travel a greater distance than this before the horses are too tired to go on."

Richard sighed. "Yes, we might, but it would be dangerous in the dark. Do you want to risk one of the horses suffering a broken leg, perhaps stranding us along the road? Besides, I am tired, and I am sure you are, too. We shall rest here and get a very early start. Tomorrow I mean to make excellent time."

Noting the take-charge look in Richard's eyes, William acquiesced. There was no use in arguing with him when he assumed his colonel persona, nevertheless, he seized the opportunity to assert his control over the next day.

"I expect to be on the road by the time dawn breaks," he stated flatly, brooking no opposition.

"Count on it, Cousin!" Richard laughed, turning to Mr. Williamson. "Vicar, what say you and I get some rest? I think our dear companion will probably sit up all night so as not to miss the rooster's crow, and it shall take both of us to carry him to the coach tomorrow."

William was not amused as he stood watching the other two enter the inn. Nonetheless, he followed soon after, determined to make sure they were back on the road as early as he intended.

~~~*~~~

William awoke with a start, looking somewhat disoriented until he laid eyes on the ones sitting across from him. He stiffened under their watch and sat up straighter, directing his gaze out the window.

"How long was I asleep? Where are we now?"

"Not nearly long enough and near Wilton, I would guess," Richard replied light-heartedly.

"How much longer until we make Liverpool?"

"I would estimate two more days after today."

"Blast! Cannot these horses make better time? When we get to the next inn, I expect to find much better animals awaiting us." He slapped his gloves against the window and then accosted Richard. "You did send a man ahead to arrange for fresh horses?"

Richard reminded himself to be patient, knowing his cousin's anger was not about him but about his worry over Elizabeth. "They are your horses, Darce. I do not think we shall find their equal in all of England. These animals were rested enough overnight to take us to the next post stop, and it is there we will change steeds."

"I could walk faster than this carriage is moving at present!"

Richard and Mr. Williamson both tried hard to abstain, but ended up chuckling. This caused William to flush with ire, which turned into embarrassment. Richard ventured serenely, "Calm yourself, Darce. You will be of no use to Miss Elizabeth in your present state. And should you have occasion to call out Count Stefano, you realize that you would have to be in a better frame of mind."

William's glare faded at the truth of Richard's words. "Forgive me. I cannot help but dwell on Elizabeth—what she must be thinking at this moment. Does she wonder why I was away so long? Perhaps she feels abandoned. And it worries me that she may not be in Liverpool as Lady Waltham directed us. Perhaps it was a ruse to keep us busy whilst they go in another direction entirely."

"Nonsense! Lady Waltham is not brave enough to cross you *and* my father. She told the truth—I would wager my life on it!"

"It is not your life that is being wagered," William said sombrely, turning to the window to hide the sting of his words.

Mr. Williamson interrupted. "It has been my experience, as a servant of God, that positive thoughts bring positive results. Let us take some time to be silent—to pray and reflect on how lovely the reunion with Lizzybet will be. We shall find her, and we shall take her home. Do not allow yourself to think any differently."

William smiled wanly, nodding silently. The vicar was right. Thus, closing his eyes, in a short while he was reliving the last time he had held Elizabeth in his arms at Pemberley and dreaming of their reunion.

Be brave, my love. You will be back in my arms again before long.

Left to his daydreams, William was entirely unconscious of the fact that the vicar and Richard were witnesses of that very moment when Elizabeth walked across his memory. As the face that had scowled for the last two days took on a look of utter happiness, they were astounded. And sensing that they were intruding on a private moment, they each turned to stare out the nearest window.

In another coach
On the road to Liverpool

Wickham gazed out the window with great indifference, watching the changing landscape as Stefano's voice droned in the background. Any prospect was preferable to looking into the face of that braggart—although there was no way to avoid listening to his self-important discourse.

From the way Stefano boasts, one would think he had done all the work of finding his wife's hiding place! And if my plan works, we will be pulling off a grand coup, absconding with this woman right from underneath Darcy's nose!

Praying that today passed more quickly than had the last two, he took comfort in knowing that he had only one more night to endure the torture of being cooped up in a room with Stefano before they reached Liverpool. He could not wait to rid himself of the company.

If we do not make Liverpool soon, I shall strangle him with my bare hands just to have some peace and quiet.

Meanwhile, Stefano continued to natter. "As soon as we arrive in Liverpool, I shall send my men to escort the women to the villa."

Wickham looked surprised. "My associate does not know your people, and she will not willingly go with them. I told her that I would meet with her when I arrived. Would it not be preferable for me to convince them that they should await the next ship in a comfortable villa, instead of a sparse room? After all, it would look suspicious to take two women out of the inn against their will."

The count seemed to be considering Wickham's argument. "I suppose it would be simpler, and my Elizabeth would be less wary. She is very intelligent; nothing escapes her notice." He stared out the window for a moment before continuing.

"In this instance, I shall defer to you, Wickham. Once we arrive in Liverpool, I shall have my men drive you to the inn. They shall pose as a postilion, driver and footman. You shall convince the women to come to the villa and after they are inside, there will be nothing Elizabeth can do to escape. She shall be mine once again!"

"And I shall have my reward and be on my way!"

Smiling knowingly, the count replied, "Yes, indeed. I imagine you shall be on your way in a short while!"

Wickham had begun lately to taunt the count with references to Darcy and Elizabeth—sweet revenge for the reprimands he had experienced at the madman's hands. Now that they were so close to concluding their collaboration, he could not resist another barb. "I intend to head to America on the next ship. Darcy will be so focused on recovering his lady love that he shall not think of me for quite some time, I imagine."

The count's voice rose in anger. "Must I remind you that Elizabeth is not his 'lady love?' She is my wife!"

"I should not have used that term. I do not suppose they were actually making love the entire time she lived at Pemberley."

Wickham's heart swelled with enjoyment to see the count's face turn bright red. "Do not EVER say such a thing in my presence again, Wickham, or you shall find yourself at the end of my sword. Do we understand each other?"

Wickham instantly wiped the smile from his face, though inside he laughed. "I am sorry. It will not happen again."

As if I would actually be so foolish as to duel with you! A pistol would finish you off quite nicely.

Just then, the last inn they were to occupy came into view, and the coach began to slow and then came to a stop. As he stepped out of the coach and approached the ordinary country inn, Stefano's thoughts once again flew to Elizabeth. There was no way his wife could have been interested in another man. Of that, he was certain. Straightening to his full height, he entered the establishment his head held high.

You will be back in my arms again before long, my darling wife.

283

Chapter 35

Rosewood Manor
Before dawn the next day

While Evan Ingram made preparations to follow Cecile, Georgiana stood mesmerized by the way her husband gave orders to the men gathered around their coach. Footmen were frantically loading trunks onto the conveyance. Meanwhile, several of the best marksmen from Pemberley as well as Rosewood, all dressed in travelling clothes, were systematically loading rifles into a trunk especially made to store them for travel and sliding pistols into pockets sewn into their jackets. She was full of pride at the way Evan took charge of the situation—sure and swift. It brought to mind memories of William. They were much alike, her husband and her dear brother—men who could be counted on to take command and inspire confidence when adversity arose.

Evan had heard from enough of his scouts to determine the direction the coach carrying Elizabeth was travelling—towards Liverpool. *Liverpool!* Georgiana cringed at the thought. Liverpool was a shipping port, and from there Elizabeth could be spirited out of the country in a matter of days, never to be seen or heard from again. Trying to calm her anxiously beating heart, Georgiana repeated the mantra she had clung to since Evan had decided to go after Elizabeth. *All will be well. All will be well.*

Having explained everything to his satisfaction, Evan glanced to the portico to find Georgiana standing in a shadowy corner of the large front entrance. Though it was still quite dark and the front door was closed, he could nevertheless make out her outline simply from her light blond hair. It reflected the glow of the torches on either side of the steps even though she stood perfectly still. Swallowing the growing lump in his throat, he took the steps towards her two at a time, well aware that he must get on the road immediately if he was to have any chance of overtaking the coach carrying Cecile and Elizabeth.

Reaching the portico, he gathered Georgiana in his arms, leaning his head atop hers and feeling her begin to shiver while he held her as tightly as possible. All he could think of at this moment was the way they had made love that night—as though he were leaving forever.

"You should not have come out in this cool air. You will fall ill."

Georgiana shook her head against his chest, trying hard not to cry. She pasted a smile on her face as she leaned back just enough to look into his eyes. "Evan Ingram, I have ridden across Pemberley at this hour since I was old enough to sit upon a horse. It has never made me sick."

"We both know that you were out at that hour only because you insisted on doing whatever your beloved brother did. Besides, I am sure he made certain you were well clothed for the weather. This dressing gown over your night shift is not sufficient to ward off this dampness."

"That is why I am hiding in this corner. I do not want the others to see me dressed as I am, but I could not let you go without saying goodbye."

Immediately, she pulled back from his embrace and grew solemn as she stared at him.

"Promise me." She took both his hands and squeezed them tightly as she brought them to her heart, all the while searching his eyes. "Promise me that you will send me posts all along the way—just so I will know what to tell Millie when she asks about her papa."

Evan knew just who needed reassurance. "I will, my darling. I promise."

He kissed her, pouring all his love into the endeavour. At length, he began to feather light kisses across her face before gripping her so tightly she could barely breathe. "I will return before long with Miss Elizabeth. I have no doubt that Darcy, and probably Richard, will be in pursuit as soon as they receive my express. We shall likely converge in one place to discover her well and bring her home. Try not to worry—just pray for us all."

Cupping his chin, she pulled his lips back to hers in a searing kiss. Then blinking back her tears, she whispered, "I love you more than life itself, Evan Ingram, and I shall pray for you every minute you are gone. Now, do what you must and return to me."

Grateful for Ana's courage, Evan touched his forehead to hers. "Take care of Millie, and tell her that her papa loves her dearly." Georgiana nodded and he pulled her close for one last kiss before whispering, "I shall see you both soon, my love."

"Soon, my love," Georgiana repeated, biting her lip as he turned and ran back down the steps. He was in the coach in an instant, and it began to pull away into the mist as soon as the others settled inside. Hanging partially out of the open window, Evan waved until they faded completely out of sight in the fog.

Essentially all alone now, Georgiana allowed herself the luxury of crying. Still standing in the damp night air, she stared at the long driveway that had taken Evan from her and cried until she had no more tears left.

Be safe, and come back to me.

The Landmark Inn
Liverpool
Morning

Glancing about the small, unattractive room, Cecile Preston had to wonder why the sign over the inn door boasted—*the finest accommodations in Liverpool.* If this was the finest, she would have been loath to see the worst! Granted it was clean enough, but it was obviously quite old and very plain, with only a few well-worn pieces of furniture gracing each room. The curtains and counterpanes were equally as old and quite faded. However, this was where Wickham said for them to wait, and wait she would! With the funds he had provided, she had reserved a suite with two bedrooms and a small sitting area. At least, she reasoned, each bedroom had a balcony overlooking the water.

The view of the sea was the only redeeming feature, and Elizabeth had hurried out onto the balcony that adjoined her bedroom as soon as she had arrived. At this moment, she was examining some ships in the distance, so Cecile moved to the doorway to observe her. The smell of salty air was invigorating, and Cecile took a deep breath. Then the wind shifted in their direction, and the smell of the fish market nearby replaced the more pleasant odour with one not so pleasing. Elizabeth seemed not to notice, her eyes never leaving the vessels on the horizon as she shaded them with her hand.

It had been awkward trying to study her rival for Mr. Darcy's affections in earnest whilst they faced one another in the carriage. Thus, Cecile was pleased to have this chance to observe her unnoticed. Sweeping Elizabeth's comely form with envious eyes, she began a mental inventory of her assets and liabilities. Miss Elizabeth was entirely too short—just over five-feet tall with a slender figure and full breasts, which undoubtedly made fitting her gowns difficult, she thought. Her face was pleasant enough, she supposed, with a small nose and straight, white teeth that, she had to acknowledge, were perfect. Furthermore, Cecile would concede that her dark hair was lustrous, and her equally dark eyes had merit, still her complexion was much too tan, obviously the results of excessive time spent in the sun.

No, she ultimately concluded, *she does not even compare to the quality of the women who have pursued Fitzwilliam Darcy!*

Cecile prickled at the recollection of the myriad of dinner parties and balls where she had stood in a corner, ignored, while the beautiful women in attendance threw themselves at every eligible gentleman, including Mr. Darcy. Well aware of her lack of desirability, she had never been foolish enough to attempt anything so bold with any man. Thus, she was reduced to being an observer and not a participant at those type endeavours. Releasing a heavy sigh, Cecile realised that this pattern had followed her throughout her life until Fitzwilliam Darcy had begun to notice her. And for a few short weeks, she had revelled in the jealousy of the women of the *ton.* For once in her life, she had been the one everyone envied!

Suddenly flustered by this bit of remembrance, Cecile concluded with a huff— *there is absolutely nothing about the physical appearance of this woman that would explain Mr. Darcy's enthralment!*

Unexpectedly, the second she settled on Elizabeth's unsuitability, Cecile comprehended what irked her most about the woman. During this entire trip, she had been unable to fathom why Elizabeth had agreed so readily to leave Fitzwilliam Darcy—to leave behind the safety of Pemberley for his sake. There was no doubt that she would have done the exact opposite, choosing to protect herself, so her disapprobation of Elizabeth was really an attempt to soothe her seared conscience. Elizabeth Lawrence, or whatever her name, had scruples—something she was sorely lacking— and it galled her.

Still observing her rival, Cecile began to ponder the man who called himself her husband. Wickham had never disclosed what the count had done to make her flee or what he might do to Elizabeth when she was returned to him. The few times that Stefano had been mentioned, Elizabeth had been more worried about his harming Darcy than any concern for herself. Would the man kill Fitzwilliam if he were to come after her? And what would Elizabeth do once she realised that she had been deceived? Quickly, Cecile pushed those worries into the same minuscule compartment of her soul that held her conscience. Reduced to her present circumstances, she reasoned, there was no room for sympathy for anyone other than herself.

A sudden knock on the door interrupted her musings. She opened it to find a maid holding a tray of tea and sandwiches—enough to suffice until dinner—so she stood back to let her enter. Surprisingly, as the maid set the tray down, Cecile noticed that it held delicate china cups with a matching teapot, something that seemed out of place in the barren room. Smiling, she sat down and poured a cup of the steaming brew before the maid could even exit, adding a lump of sugar before bringing it to her lips. It was just what she needed to calm her nerves, so she enjoyed another sip before rising to collect Elizabeth.

She was still staring solemnly out towards the sea, and before Cecile could speak, she enquired, "Do you suppose that ship is the one to take me from Fitzwil—" Her voice cracked as unbidden tears came, and she took a ragged breath, trying to recover. "From England?"

Cecile turned to find the ship that Elizabeth had indicated, shading her eyes from the sun's glare with her hand. She hoped that Elizabeth would not ask the name of the ship on which she was to sail to the Americas, as no passage had actually been purchased.

"I cannot tell for certain. There are too many ships in port. It could be any one of them, or it could already have docked, I suppose—or none of these at all. The ship to the Americas could yet be at another port in England picking up cargo. I understand it does not leave for at least a week."

"Oh ..." Elizabeth said desolately, the tears sliding from her eyes despite her best efforts to stem them. She swiftly wiped them away with the backs of her hands. "I hoped to sail right away. If he finds me, he will not allow me to leave."

"The count?"

"William ... Fitzwilliam."

Cecile frowned at the mention of the man she had coveted for so many years. "If I may be bold enough to ask, did you deceive Fitzwilliam as the rumours say?"

Elizabeth did not hesitate to answer, though she continued to stare out to sea. "Do you really think anyone could delude him? He is the most intelligent man I have ever met."

Cecile considered the proclamation. "Then, pray tell, how could you have married someone like Stefano or have convinced Fitzwilliam to help you hide from the man?"

"It is a story too long to tell, but know this—I did not marry the count of my own volition. As for Fitzwilliam, he and I have known each other for many years. At one time we were ..." Her voice faded away. "But when my sister told him of my escape from Stefano, he offered to help me."

"The count was so cruel that you had to flee?"

"Apart from the fact that I despise him, he is a cruel drunk and thinks nothing of striking anyone who disagrees with him. I was kept a prisoner, first with draughts and afterward, with locks. I was not allowed to see or hear from any of my friends or family. He threatened to kill anyone who dared try to see me and to kill me if I escaped."

"And yet you were a virtual prisoner at Pemberley, not allowed to leave there or be out in society."

Elizabeth's countenance grew wistful. "For Fitzwilliam Darcy, I would gladly be a prisoner ... for his love. He is the kindest, gentlest man I have ever known."

"Yet, you were willing to leave him."

"To keep him safe from harm, yes, I would do anything."

Cecile stammered, not understanding such devotion. "Yes, well, he certainly did not offer such kindness to me. True, he was civil, always the gentleman, but certainly never overly kind, nor did I see any extraordinary gentleness in his nature."

Elizabeth turned dark eyes on the woman who had tried to secure Fitzwilliam for herself. "He shows his true nature only to those who are well acquainted with him."

"Nonsense!" Cecile declared. "I have known him for years—he practically courted me for a time—and he has never been warm or very caring. Duty and honour are all that concern him. He has apparently duped you into thinking he is something that he is not—a romantic. You would do well to remember that all men are consumed with satisfying their own desires and cannot be trusted. Take my word for it."

Elizabeth's knowing smile made Cecile uncomfortable. "Then you do not know him, or you would not say such things."

Indignantly twirling around to return inside, Cecile called over her shoulder. "Our trays have been delivered. Come inside and eat if you wish, or you may stay out here and sigh wistfully over a man who exists only in your imagination."

Elizabeth watched her go with mixed feelings. Talking about William had renewed her longing for him tenfold. Moreover, now that she was close to leaving him forever, it was bittersweet to know that he had shown a side of himself to her that no other woman, including Cecile Preston, would ever know. Taking a deep breath and willing herself not to cry, she turned and entered the sitting room.

Liverpool
Evening

As the coach made its final approach to the villa that Stefano's father had purchased years before, the two men inside were equally glad to be parting company—or at least pleased not to be in such close proximity any longer. The house would provide ample space so that they would not have to see each other unless they wished to do so. During the trip, they had almost come to blows on several occasions, though each had refrained when recalling his greater agenda—Stefano's desire to capture Lizzy and Wickham's desire to collect his reward.

Now, as they halted outside the small but pleasant country house just outside of town, Wickham began to take notice of the number of servants who milled about. Including the men on the coach, he knew that the count had at least seven servants and perhaps more inside. Though a few were women, maids and such, the majority seemed to be guards—men who looked as though they could handle with ease any disturbance. A little nervous about how he would collect his money should the count decide to deceive him, Wickham pushed the fear aside.

If he tries to swindle me, I shall go to Darcy and offer to tell him where to locate the woman and the count. I just imagine he would be willing to pay the same price to get this woman back and avenge his pride.

Stefano had no more than climbed out of the coach, before he began laying out his plans as they walked up the steps. "I shall arrange for some warm water to be sent to your room at once. Get dressed immediately, as I shall expect you to call on the inn and retrieve my wife."

Wickham looked at the man as if he were mad. "I cannot call on them at this late hour nor expect them to remove themselves to this house tonight. It would be better to wait until the morning. Besides, it would cause much less notice if they voluntarily quit the place in the morning."

Stefano was not happy, but on closer deliberation, agreed with Wickham's judgment. "Very well, but first thing tomorrow, you *will* fetch my wife. Do you hear?"

Wickham causally called over his shoulder as he walked ahead of Stefano to the door, "Yes, I hear."

Entering the premises, he was pleasantly surprised to find a comfortable home. Stefano, who quickly caught up with him, explained that the house was mainly one level, with the bedrooms occupying the second floor. A young maid, who greatly resembled one Wickham had seen at the count's rented townhouse in London, appeared out of nowhere. Stefano nodded to her. "Florenza will show you to your room."

As he followed the maid through the house, Wickham tried to count the number of people he encountered. In his estimation, the number of servants was now up to ten—four women and six men. After showing him to his room, the maid was about to leave when Wickham addressed her. "Your kindness is appreciated."

The woman looked at him blankly and shrugged as if she did not understand. He assumed she did not, as she had the same dark characteristics of all the servants whom Stefano had bragged of bringing with him from Italy. He was frustrated to find that she probably spoke only Italian, as he hoped to bribe at least one of the servants to provide information about the count's plans. If all the servants were from his mother's country, that was unlikely to happen. Wickham cringed to think that he had allowed the count to replace the driver and footmen with his own men before they left London. In hindsight, he would have liked to have had a few men loyal to him close by.

Pemberley

Mrs. Reynolds was not surprised to see the express rider galloping up the drive and was most pleased that she happened to be on the front portico when she spotted him. Hurriedly, she descended the steps to meet the man, unwilling to wait until he came to her. After retrieving the post, she instructed a footman to see after the horse and motioned for the messenger to follow her. She was eager to share the missive with Mr. Walker, who was just as worried over the present situation. Though much younger, the rider had to do a bit of a quick-step to catch up with the housekeeper, who was definitely not standing in place waiting for him. As they mounted the steps, she assured the young man that he would be fed and given a place to rest, and that she would have some expresses of her own to dispatch.

Mr. Walker was busy in another part of the house when he heard voices in the foyer and immediately returned in the event he was needed. When he arrived, Mrs. Reynolds was hurrying towards him waving a post.

"It seems we have heard from Mr. Darcy at last!"

Quickly making her way to her office, Mr. Walker on her heels, she began opening the missive the minute they were inside the door. She scanned the short paragraph swiftly as Mr. Walker's eyebrows rose higher and higher in anticipation.

"What luck!" she declared. "Mr. Darcy and Colonel Fitzwilliam are on their way directly to Liverpool! Mr. Ingram will have help when he arrives to confront his sister and whoever else may be aiding her in this scheme. I am so relieved for Mrs.

Ingram's sake, as I know she must fear for his safety. Our dear boy will not let anything bad happen to his brother, nor shall the colonel."

"We should inform Mrs. Ingram as soon as possible to ease her distress."

"According to this, Mr. Darcy sent her the same information, but I shall send her a note in any event. I shall tell her that I am also sending an express to Liverpool to inform Mr. Darcy of Mr. Ingram's journey in that direction. The Master has given me an address to use while he is there—

Barnwell's Boarding House. It is where he stays before he travels to Ireland. If you would call a footman, I shall have a note ready for Miss Georgiana shortly."

As Mr. Walker left to find a footman, Mrs. Reynolds stilled, and her eyes searched the heavens. *You have answered my prayers to keep my dear boy safe so many times, Lord, but I am asking once again. Only this time I need to ask more of You. May it please You to keep my Master William, Richard, Evan and Elizabeth safe. I know You will not fail me.*

Wiping the tears that had gathered involuntarily, she took a deep breath and sat down to compose her notes, confident that all would be well now that it was in the Lord's hands.

It was no time at all until a man was mounted and on his way to inform Georgiana of the situation. Unbeknownst to Mrs. Reynolds, Georgiana was reading her own copy of the express about that same time. Luckily, the housekeeper's note reached Rosewood in time to keep Georgiana from sending a duplicate express to William in Liverpool.

On the road to Liverpool
Between Birmingham and Stafford

Several miles outside Birmingham, the rain began coming down in sheets while lightning flashed and thunder roared relentlessly. The howling wind blew against the coach with such force that it rocked from side to side as well as back and forth. More than once, William held his breath wondering if this time the coach would succumb to the wind. The roads were now dangerously slick, and Richard and Mr. Williamson exchanged worried glances. They had watched William clench and unclench his jaw for the last few miles as it became obvious that they had gone as far as they could. The next small establishment would have to suffice as there was no hope of reaching the more elegant inn in Stafford.

Not eager to suffer his cousin's annoyance, Richard had held his tongue but was aware that he would have to act soon. Fortunately, William's coachman, Mr. Burnside, took that judgment from his hands by pulling the coach off the road and into the yard of a small inn. He did so without hesitation, knowing the master would agree with him if he decided they were in danger.

William sighed audibly, and Richard responded in an attempt to soothe him, "Darce, you realise that we cannot chance one of the horses breaking a leg in this mud, especially since our next change of horses is in Stafford. If we continue in this deluge, we could all end up in a ditch." William closed his eyes, shaking his head in agreement though he was too disappointed to reply.

"Stay in the coach, and I will enquire if they have rooms enough for us," Richard commanded. Then he smiled and began to chuckle as a spray of water blew in the now opening door. "Pray we do not have to lodge in the stables, vicar!"

Several minutes later, the colonel ran back though the rain, his boots already thick with mud, sliding in the muck with each step. He almost fell several times before reaching them. Jumping back inside the coach, and shaking the water from his head, he cheerfully exclaimed, "The proprietor says he has one large room left which we may share. There is also room in the servants' quarters over the stables for the driver and footmen. Best of all, there is food and drink aplenty!"

"Then let us get out of this deluge, have something to eat and get some rest," William replied with more equanimity than he felt. "If we retire early, we may be able to make up lost time by rising even earlier than usual tomorrow."

Mr. Williamson raised his eyebrows in acknowledgement of Richard's slight smile. Both expected this to happen. "I think that a splendid plan," the vicar offered while managing to squelch a smile of his own.

The night found them sleeping on folding beds in a backroom normally used as an extra dining room—the large table had been moved to one end after they had eaten and still held some bread and such. Though the lodgings were not perfect, each was content to be dry and warm, due to the large fireplaces at both ends of the room. It seemed that Richard and Mr. Williamson were very weary as they nodded off first and were already snoring.

William, as usual, could not sleep. The weather reminded him of the night he found Elizabeth at Netherfield and how, even now, she was afraid of storms. Was she out there somewhere in this storm needing his reassurance?

Thoughts of her brought back memories of time spent in Scotland and Ireland, trying not to love her, and his heart began to ache. Those two years had taught him the cruelty of being without the one you love—no arms to embrace you, no lips to kiss. He closed his eyes and the softness of Elizabeth's lips, the scent and feel of her skin, the way she melted into his body came flooding into his senses, and for a few seconds, she was in his arms, her head under his chin; he could smell the lavender in her hair. Her delightful laughter had just filled the air when, all at once, a long sequence of thunder and lightning assaulted the inn, startling him from his trance. Disappointed that it was only a dream, he rose from the bed.

Walking to a window near the fire, he pulled back the curtain to watch nature's fury playing out in the darkness. As another bolt lit up the porch outside, he saw her face reflected in the pane, just as he had at Netherfield. Dropping his head in his hands, he cried quietly. *Will I ever find you Elizabeth? Can I live if I do not?*

A hand patted his shoulder, startling him. "We will find her, I promise," Richard said softly. "You need to lie down and rest, even if you cannot sleep."

Nodding his head in resignation, William did as his cousin instructed and lay back down. Finally, he drifted into a fitful slumber.

~~~*~~~

The next morning, neither Richard nor Mr. Williamson was surprised to be awakened before daylight by William, who explained that he had told the coachman to prepare to leave. Thankfully, the rain had let up, and the only trouble that lay ahead of them now would be the difficulty of traversing the muddy, rut-filled roads.

~~~*~~~

Chapter 36

The morning breeze was brisk and invigorating, but Wickham was indifferent to the weather as he slumped, half-asleep in the corner of the carriage. He was on his way back to town, under strict orders to escort Cecile and the count's wife to the villa. As it was his fate to have been awakened abruptly before dawn and made to dress hurriedly, he was still quite drowsy. Eyes closed and legs spread across the carriage seat, the back and forth sway of the conveyance had almost soothed him into another round of slumber by the time they reached town—almost.

Although his body was exhausted from all the travel in the last few days, his mind refused to stop replaying the events of the morning. Once awakened, all of his protestations of needing more rest had been for naught. The servant sent to carry out the count's wishes obviously did not speak English and continued to shake him until he relented and sat up in bed. Then the man crossed his arms, standing guard, to make certain Wickham put his feet on the floor and began to get dressed. Had the villain been smaller, Wickham's resistance might have been a little heartier, but when confronted with the tall, sturdy fellow who came to his room this morning, he had little choice but to comply.

Going about his morning ritual, he had pondered if the count was even awake at this ungodly hour, since it was still dark. That question, however, was answered the moment that same servant escorted him to the dining room. Breaking his fast as though he had not a care in the world, Count Stefano, dressed as elegantly as royalty, sat at the long ornate table. As Wickham entered the room, the count looked up from his plate, glaring at him, his distaste for his supposed late arrival evident.

"It is about time you were out of bed, Wickham. Did you consider that I would want to see my wife as soon as possible?" Wickham was too irritated to answer prudently.

"Humph! When I get to the inn, your wife will most likely still be sleeping, as well I should be! I do not relish having to wait while two women ready themselves to leave."

"Nonsense! After you have something to eat, it will be late enough to call. Besides, if they have not eaten yet, it will be a good opportunity to invite them to come here to break their fast. The food will be undoubtedly much better than that available to them at the inn."

Wickham sneered. "What better way to raise your wife's suspicions than to insist they leave straightaway without even taking time to eat? It is my intention to make her think that I own this villa, and that when I learned that her travelling companion, an old friend, was in town, I hurried to extend an invitation for them to stay with me. If you push me to arrive early and insist they leave straightaway, she may become suspicious and decide that she does not want to avail herself of my generosity. I can just imagine taking her screaming and kicking from the inn or trussed up like a fowl."

Stefano's countenance darkened, but he kept a civil tongue. "Then we shall do it your way. One more hour should suffice for them to be awake, to have dressed and eaten. You have until then to enjoy the hospitality of my table. Would you care for tea, or is something stronger needed to get your day started?"

Wickham bristled at the inference. "Why would you think I need something stronger?"

"Because nothing escapes me. I have noticed your fondness for strong drink."

"Perhaps I enjoy my brandy, but it never interferes with business! Tea shall suffice, unless you happen to have coffee. I do enjoy coffee in the morning."

Stefano turned to one of the footman. "Instruct Mrs. Delgrado to prepare some coffee for Mr. Wickham." He motioned to a chair. "Now fill your plate and sit down. We should discuss what will happen when you bring them back here."

Wickham took a plate from the sideboard and began to fill it. He had to admit that the wonderful smells coming from the array of foods displayed had awakened his appetite. With his back to his host, he took a small bite from a sweet roll, savouring the taste of the cinnamon and sugar. Then he placed the rest on his plate and made his way to the table. In an obvious display of his distaste for the count's officious ways, he took the seat at the opposite end, as far away from Stefano as possible.

Stefano sneered, "Can you hear me well that far away?"

Wickham continued to eat, keeping his head lowered and pretending not to care that the count was upset. "Well enough," he answered loudly, and then under his breath—*too well for my taste.*

"Then listen carefully. When you return with the women, none of my people shall be milling about outside, as I do not wish to raise Elizabeth's suspicions. A maid will be waiting just inside the door to escort the ladies to their rooms, and I shall make my presence known to my wife once she is situated. By the time she ascertains our intent, my men will have secured the exits and she shall not be able to escape, even if she wishes."

Wickham took another bite of his sweet roll. "How soon will I be able to get my money and leave?"

"I shall not discuss the reward until I have my wife here by my side. Is that understood?"

Wickham nodded. He was not happy with the rebuff, but he would bring the blackguard's wife to him, and then the count would pay him his due or he would go straight to Fitzwilliam Darcy. "Then let me be clear, Count Stefano. I expect to be paid in full once she is secured, as I do not plan to remain in Liverpool one minute longer than is absolutely necessary."

The count's steely eyes rested on Wickham while he finished his meal. Not allowing himself the satisfaction of replying, Stefano held his tongue. He would deal with this buffoon after Elizabeth was securely in his hands.

Once Elizabeth is mine again, I assure you that you shall not remain in Liverpool, or anywhere else, save hell itself, ever again.

~~~*~~~

293

The Landmark Inn

The tray of food and drink that Cecile had ordered before retiring last night sat nearly empty on the small table in the sitting room. A goodly array of food and a carafe of tea were delivered first thing that morning so that the two women could eat in the room instead of dining with the other guests. Each woman had eaten and then dressed leisurely. They now sat in the pleasant morning sun on the balcony, watching the many smaller boats swarm around the huge ships in the harbour.

Fortunately, this inn was not positioned directly behind the wharfs like many of the shops on this street, but was tucked away at the end—saved from most of the clamour of freight being loaded on and off the docked vessels. In addition, though the fish market nearby was already doing a brisk business, the wind was blowing in another direction this morning, leaving only the salty sea air to fill one's senses. Thus situated, they had an exquisite panorama to take pleasure in. *Tranquil*, Elizabeth thought as she took a deep breath, *but deceiving*. She had read enough books describing life aboard ships to be familiar with the dangers. From this viewpoint, she concluded, one might imagine the sea to be peaceful and inviting, but upon closer examination might find it savage and unforgiving. All of a sudden, more of Cecile's empty discourse interrupted her quiet contemplations.

"I would dearly love to be sailing somewhere far away," Evan's sister sighed wistfully. "Someplace to start anew, where no one knows my name or my situation. How liberating that would be!" For once, Mrs. Preston was being entirely truthful—she really did desire to start anew.

Elizabeth sighed wistfully as well. The only place she dearly longed to go was back to Pemberley ... to William.

Cecile continued to ramble, "I daresay **you** should be able to start anew in the Americas. I hear anyone with enough fortitude can succeed there." She added arrogantly, "And anyone who would do what you have done has to have gall. I will give you that!"

A knock on the door saved Elizabeth from replying to her crass comment. Unfortunately, this intrusion also set into motion a chain of events that would parallel her analysis of the sea only moments before.

At the interruption, Cecile stood. "I shall see what they want."

She swept her skirts aside to enter the narrow door leading to the bedroom and closed it silently, leaving Elizabeth to gaze at the water unaware of what would be said behind her back. The look of intrigue that passed between Cecile and Mr. Wickham was likewise unnoticed by the object of their conspiracy. In hushed tones, they discussed the woman on the balcony.

"Does she suspect anything?" Wickham enquired, straining to get a look at the dark-haired woman who, from what he could see, was very handsome. His heart beat faster. Too bad this woman was Stefano's—he would have enjoyed getting to *know* her better.

"I do not think so." Cecile shrugged. "She assumes that we are waiting here until the ship to the Americas arrives."

"Excellent. Go explain to her that your old friend George Walters has learned that you are in Liverpool and requests the honour of your presence at his summer home just outside town. Be sure and let her know that declining my invitation is not practical, as you have limited funds. You will know how to handle it I am sure. I shall wait like a proper gentleman for you to introduce us, once you have her assent."

"Walters?"

"She may have heard the name Wickham mentioned at some point while she stayed at Pemberley. I do not want to raise doubts."

Cecile nodded, turning to return to the balcony but stopped short. "What will happen to her when the count has her under his power?"

"Do not bother yourself with those details, my dear. I am sure you really do not want to know."

Cecile sighed, starting again to make her way towards Elizabeth. At one time, this type of deception would have been foreign to her nature—she would have found it revolting. *But that was when I still had a conscience.* Squaring her shoulders, she opened the door and stepped out to face her captive with forced cheeriness.

"You will never guess what has happened! What good fortune is ours!"

Turning to the sound of Cecile's voice, Elizabeth's brows knit as she caught sight of a man staring at her from just inside the room. He looked familiar, but she could not place where she had seen him. Nevertheless, something deep inside her cried out to be wary. Her heart began to beat faster under his continued analysis, while Cecile rattled on about the coincidence of Mr. Walters' learning they were in Liverpool.

... Old friend ... villa nearby ... guests of his ... save our funds.

All of a sudden, Elizabeth's attention was captured by a proclamation. "We shall be packed and on our way very shortly."

Elizabeth turned to stare at Cecile, totally ignorant of most of what she had been saying. "On our way? Where?"

"Have you not been listening? To Mr. Walters' villa, of course! We shall save the cost of rooms here."

Instantly, all manner of alerts began to assail her. The sound of footsteps close behind caused her to look back over her shoulder. She discovered that the stranger now stood only a few feet away, smiling self-importantly. Cecile waved him forward.

Seeing dread spread over Elizabeth's face, Cecile hurriedly exclaimed, "Elizabeth, may I introduce my good friend, Mr. George Walters. He owns the villa where we will stay while we await the arrival of your ship. Mr. Walters, this is Miss Elizabeth Lawrence, my friend."

Wickham smiled. Stepping forward, he reached for Elizabeth's hand and brought it to his lips, noticing the softness and the faint scent of rosewater. "It is a pleasure to meet any friend of Cecile's, especially one so lovely."

As their eyes met, a long-suppressed fragment of a memory came flooding back, and Elizabeth flinched without knowing the reason. She still could not recollect everything of the time she was ill, but instinctively she knew that she did not trust him. The man before her looked offended as she abruptly extracted her hand from his grasp.

"Thank you, Mr. Walters," she replied icily, as she studied him with a quizzical brow. "It is kind of you to extend an invitation for Mrs. Preston and me to stay at your estate. Nevertheless, I believe it would be best if I stay here until my ship departs. I would not want to chance missing it. I have no objections to Mrs. Preston's leaving me here alone."

"Nonsense!" Wickham declared, looking very irritated, his smile leaving as quickly as his temper flared. "My home is much nicer than this—" he motioned wildly with his hands, "this stark establishment. And as for staying informed, my servants will assure that you are notified well before the ship is to set sail. Meanwhile, you and Cecile can serve as chaperones for each other, as there are no other guests at my home at present. Surely, you would not deny Cecile the chance to visit, and she cannot very well come without you."

Elizabeth shifted from one foot to another as Cecile and this man coldly awaited her reply. Something was not quite right, but it was impossible for her to refuse the invitation as presented. "Of course not."

Wickham's pleasant mood returned at once, and he smiled brilliantly. "Excellent!" He turned to Cecile. "I shall have my men begin taking your luggage to the carriage so that we can be away from here as soon as possible. I have left instructions for my cook to expect company, and she always does a wonderful job when I entertain. I am sure the quality of the food will greatly exceed that which you have found here and on the road."

Cecile let go of the breath she had been holding and took Elizabeth's arm, guiding her towards her bedroom. "I am sure you will enjoy Mr. Walters' estate much more than this bare room. Come. Let me help you pack."

Liverpool
Downtown

Evan Ingram was already exhausted as he slowly made his way back to the centre of town. He had arrived in Liverpool early that morning with five trusted men, all expert shots. Each of them had gone in a different direction with instructions to frequent the local pubs, the wharfs, the shops—every place where people were known to congregate. They each had money aplenty to ply those they met with bribes or liquor, if warranted, to loosen tongues and stir memories regarding two women newly arrived from Derbyshire. Now with noon approaching, Evan was proceeding to a certain pub where they had agreed to gather to eat and discuss what they had learned. By nightfall, he hoped to know everything that he needed.

For his part, he had checked out the shipping offices, asking questions about all the ships in the harbour. He learned that three of them were leaving the next week— two for the Americas and one for Australia. When he enquired about any sailing today or tomorrow, the clerk was happy to point out that one had sailed that very morning for Italy and another had docked, set to sail tomorrow for Spain. Hearing of the departure of the ship to Italy, Evan cringed.

Cecile could not be acting alone in whatever scheme she had involved herself, and she surely had enough sense to know that if Elizabeth was anywhere in the British Isles or Ireland, Darcy would find her. Though he had said nothing to Ana, his first thought when learning of Cecile's ploy to take her from Pemberley was that his sister must be involved with the man who had taken Elizabeth from Longbourn— Count Stefano. He would certainly have had reason to put Elizabeth on a ship to Italy, and there had been ample time for Cecile to have travelled to Liverpool before that ship had sailed this morning. He prayed that was not the case.

Blast! He thought. *Darcy would move heaven and earth to find her no matter where in the world she was. Even Italy.*

Just as he was mulling over that notion, someone coming towards him from the opposite direction across the street waved to get his attention. "Over here, sir!"

Evan had to smile. If not for his voice, he might never have recognised Mr. Watson, his livery foreman. They had all dressed rather shabbily, trying to avoid scrutiny, each sporting a dirty face and a worn hat that covered much of it. Evan crossed the street, motioning him into an alleyway between two buildings. As Mr.

Watson entered the lane, a large carriage flew past on the street, and the servant could not contain his enthusiasm as he nodded towards the conveyance.

"That carriage that just passed may contain your sister."

Evan made to go after it, but a strong arm stopped him. "Wait, sir! Let me explain!"

Evan halted so Watson continued. "I met this fellow in a pub, who was very talkative as long as I paid for the brew, so I kept him from getting thirsty. He said there was talk of two women newly arrived in town, but did not know precisely where they were staying. We were nearing the Landmark Inn, when he excitedly pointed out the carriage that just passed. I saw the woman in question get aboard just outside the inn. He says the carriage belongs to the owner of an estate just a few miles outside town where he once worked."

Evan nodded at the truth of his words. "Are you fairly certain it was my sister?"

"I saw her only once from a distance when she was at Rosewood. However, if I were a betting man, I would say it was she. I did not see another woman with her, but I asked around the inn. Two women had been staying there, and someone said they both got into that carriage with a man—Mr. Walters, I was told. Personally, I only saw the one. According to the locals, this Walters is not a resident, though he has been staying at the estate I mentioned. I am sure that I can discover additional information, given enough time. I was headed to the pub to meet you and the others when I saw you coming."

"Well done, Watson!" Evan slapped his back. "We must acquire directions to this villa, as I want some of our men to steal onto that property today. We need to be crafty and see what we can discover. Also, it would help if we knew who owns the estate."

"If I can keep the locals drinking, I will find that out as well, sir."

"Excellent. You go ask some more questions, and I shall occupy myself with securing a nondescript carriage or two and some mounts to use while we are here."

Watson smiled, though his voice held a little trepidation. "Perhaps we might have that bite to eat first? I have not had anything since dawn, and I am sure the others have not stopped to eat either."

"Now that you mention it," Evan smiled warmly, "neither have I. Of course, we shall make time to eat first. I do not want anyone to faint from lack of nourishment!"

The large, brawny, liveryman motioned in the direction of the small pub where they were to meet the others, and with a satisfied smile, Evan took the lead, moving a little lighter now that some useful information had been discovered.

We have been here only one morning and have a lead to follow. Now, if only Darcy will arrive!

Liverpool
Later that afternoon

Weary to the bone, William, Richard and Mr. Williamson arrived in Liverpool late that afternoon. At William's insistence, they headed directly to the wharfs, though Richard tried to argue that they should not be seen about town until they knew exactly what they were facing. He reasoned that they really did not know if someone had actually taken Elizabeth to Liverpool or if she was still safely ensconced at Pemberley. Nonetheless, nothing would satisfy William but to check on the ships. He feared that Elizabeth might already be aboard one of them.

To appease Richard, William had brought several items of clothing—less expensive coats and hats borrowed from his steward, while Richard had brought along his civilian clothes, which were modest enough. Thus, when they finally exited their coach in a back alley near the wharfs, other than William's much too expensive boots, he and Richard were not as conspicuous as they might otherwise have been. They called on the shipping offices, while Mr. Williamson took the opportunity to check the nearest shops and pubs for gossip of new arrivals.

Unfortunately, at the shipping offices William and Richard learned more than Evan Ingram had learned only a few hours earlier. They, too, heard of the ship that was to depart for Spain the next day and of the ones leaving next week for the Americas and Australia. However, the news of the ship that had departed for Italy that very morning caused William even more apprehension than it had Evan Ingram. His request for a list of the passengers met with great resistance until some carefully placed pounds enticed the clerk to ask them into a private room. Once inside, the man not only provided the list, but also informed them of the last minute additions to the passengers—a man and a woman who had boarded right before the ship sailed. Alas, he claimed he had not personally seen them and could not provide names or descriptions. Unfortunately, while the passenger list did not include Stefano and Elizabeth, the last minute passengers could have been anyone.

Once they were privy to that information, Richard noted that William's entire countenance changed dramatically. Whereas before, William was simply too nervous to be quiet or patient and paced about endlessly, now it seemed he was too calm—almost unemotional. William was reacting in the same manner that he had when his father had died—he was shutting down emotionally. Richard knew he had to act quickly or all would be lost.

Tugging on his cousin's arm, he pulled William out the door and guided the now eerily passive man back to the alley where their coach waited. When they entered the lane, Richard whirled around, pushing William up against the side of the building. He put a hand on either side of his head and leaned in until he was within inches of his face.

"Get hold of yourself, man! You have not lost her yet! Hell, we are not even sure she is missing, much less on that ship! But if she was on it, you would bloody well just have to set sail after her!" Other than blinking, there was no response so Richard continued in this mode.

"Know this! If she is missing, we shall find her and bring her home no matter the distance. However, I cannot do this alone, and you will be of no use to Elizabeth or to me if you give in to your fears. Now, here is the question! Are you going to pull yourself together and help me or not?"

Richard's tirade finally pierced William's consciousness, and the deep-rooted bands of fear that had snaked themselves around his heart only minutes before let go. He took a deep, shuddering breath, closing his eyes and running his hands over his face several times. When he opened them again, the cousin that Richard had confidence in was back.

"You are right! I have not lost Elizabeth! Nor shall I ever let her go! I struggle against thoughts that I have lost my mother and father and I shall lose Elizabeth, too, but I shall conquer these demons. You have my word."

For a brief second, Richard gauged William's determination. "Very well, we shall put it behind us. Just remember, I have not lost a battle yet, and I do not intend to start now. What say you to staying at that boarding house you always frequent when you go to Ireland? I stayed there once, and they have clean beds and good food. We can rest a bit and make our plans."

Villa Tuscany

On the trip to the villa, Elizabeth had ignored the endless chatter between her companions. Instead, she feigned interest in the view of the countryside from the window. Now, several minutes after the carriage had turned from the main road onto the drive to the villa, her fears began to subside, and she wondered if she had over-reacted.

The prospect was certainly beautiful, and it was a relief to see that the only people in sight were an older man tending the shrubbery and a white-haired footman headed in their direction down the front steps of the white-washed villa. They certainly looked harmless enough, and the entire scene appeared pleasant and inviting, not at all foreboding as she had feared. She was most impressed with the house, which reminded her of the drawing of an Italian manor she had once seen in a book. Her thoughts must have been easy to read, as the gentleman passenger broke through her reverie with a comment.

"Now, this is not so bad, is it? I hope you will enjoy your stay at my humble home, Miss Elizabeth."

While he was speaking, the coach came to a complete stop, and the footman opened the door. Wickham exited first, turning back to help her out next. Elizabeth had no time to reply to his welcome, as Cecile exited the carriage right behind her, still talking constantly—a sign that she was nervous.

"Come, Elizabeth! Let us get settled in quickly, so we can rest before we dine."

In just a few short steps, they were inside the terra cotta coloured foyer furnished with marble floors and brightly coloured rugs and draperies unlike anything Elizabeth had seen before. While she was admiring the interior decorations, turning in an entire circle, a maid silently appeared before her and curtsied, then motioned for her and Cecile to follow. From the way she conducted herself, Elizabeth realised that the young girl probably did not speak English. She glanced at Cecile, who only shrugged and waved Elizabeth ahead of her. As they made their way up the curved stairs, Elizabeth happened to glance down and see her host following her actions with a strange look on his face. Wickham had just turned to go in another direction when, unexpectedly, she remembered where she had seen him. Her heart almost stopped.

She halted, causing Cecile to run into her. Swirling around, she ran past Cecile, back down the stairs towards the entrance. She had almost gained the foyer and the still open front door when Wickham stepped out to grab her around the waist.

Elizabeth began fighting and kicking with all her strength, but it only seemed to amuse him. He laughed, clasping her even tighter. In their struggles, he used his arms and hands to touch her in intimate places, and when he finally had Elizabeth immovable in his grip, one hand was across her breasts.

He could not resist and taunted her, whispering suggestively so no one else could hear, "What a beautiful body you have, Miss Elizabeth! Too bad I did not have time to take you the night I found you at the inn with Darcy!"

Thoroughly repulsed, Elizabeth renewed her efforts to twist from his grasp and was almost successful when a shot rang out. Wickham fell to the floor, letting her go and causing her to reel from being set free so abruptly. Shocked to see the one who had held her only moments ago lying on the floor, blood pouring from his temple, Elizabeth's eyes sought Cecile and found she was equally stunned. Suddenly, Mrs. Preston's screams pierced the air and were just the stimulus needed to remind Elizabeth of her mission. She twirled around, intent on escaping the manor, only to find two large men now standing in the doorway, blocking her way. A wicked laugh filled the house and her breath hitched.

Stefano!

Horrified— her eyes darted in every direction, but she could not locate him. Just when she had determined she must be mad, he stepped out of a shadowy doorway between her and the staircase, pistol in hand and his eyes glowing exactly as they had when Addie had died—like those of a demon.

"I told that fool that no one—NO ONE—touches my wife and lives!"

~~~*~~~

Chapter 37

Villa Tuscany
A bedroom that evening

Elizabeth sat in the large overstuffed chair in front of the hearth. With her head leaned back against the soft cushion, she closed her eyes in concentration. Only her bound hands and feet indicated her new status—she was a prisoner again. After making Stefano furious with her threats, he had decided to bind her as a sign that he was in complete charge and she was entirely at his mercy. She could do nothing he did not allow—except defy him. Just before quitting the room, he had stopped abruptly at the door to declare that they would leave at daybreak. She had not cowered at his decree as he expected, instead she lifted her chin, her dark eyes blazing in defiance. Her courage seemed to make him even angrier, though he continued out the door, slamming it in response and bolting it from the other side.

Now that the day was over, she relived the events in her mind, clearly proud of how she had responded. Today's horror had been ghastly, but the man who was killed was not a dear friend—only someone who meant to do her harm. Moreover, she was not despondent, though the manner of his death had evoked memories of that bleak segment in her life—a period that Fitzwilliam had helped her to confront and conquer. As she opened her eyes at last to fix on the embers of a dying fire, she considered how the man at the centre of her serenity had brought her though this utter chaos.

For just a moment, after Stefano's laugh, she had found herself paralysed—reduced to the frightened young woman who had watched Addie die. And though somewhere in all of this madness Cecile was screaming frantically, Elizabeth could not speak a word. Moreover, just at the moment when she feared she might faint, Stefano bounded up the stairs and grabbed Cecile roughly, causing her to shriek even louder. He slapped the hysterical widow then, but only his threats quieted her cries.

"One more sound out of you and you shall join your friend." Cecile immediately hushed, though she continued to whimper. "My sources say that you are Cecile Preston, the widow who has been helping Wickham steal jewels."

Cecile nodded, shaking so violently that it was obvious even from the foyer where Elizabeth stood, that the woman was frightened out of her wits.

"Now, Mrs. Preston, you may choose. Do you wish to die as Mr. Wickham did, or do you wish to sail to Spain with Elizabeth in the morning as her personal maid? I am sure she will appreciate having another woman along on such a long voyage."

Elizabeth looked at Stefano as though he were mad, but his gaze was fixed on Mrs. Preston.

Cecile's eyes flicked between Elizabeth and the count before replying in barely a whisper, "I shall be glad to accompany her."

"Excellent!" he crowed, smiling widely. "Most of my servants do not speak English, and I am sure my wife will enjoy having someone to converse with besides me." His air was very buoyant, and neither woman could fathom such joviality from a man who had just brutally killed the man who lay only a few feet away."

Noticing that Cecile's eyes kept returning to Wickham's body, the count declared to one of the huge men in the doorway, "Portalo via fuori da qui! Gettatelo in mare!" *(Get him out of here! Dump him in the sea!)*

Immediately, other men came forward to help the first, and they lifted the body and carried Wickham from the house. A maid immediately appeared with a bucket and began to scour the floor. Elizabeth had felt faint at the sight of so much blood, but forced herself not to succumb to the threatening darkness.

The count continued to address Cecile, as he motioned to a maid who immediately came down the stairs behind her. "Go with Maria. She will show you to your room. Do not unpack more than necessary, as we shall leave early in the morning. You both shall eat in your rooms tonight."

As Cecile meekly followed the maid up the stairs, Stefano focused his attention on Elizabeth. His mouth curled into a pretentious smile, the sight of which brought bile into Elizabeth's throat.

"Welcome back, my dear."

Slowly he descended to the foyer, his eyes never leaving hers as he steadily advanced until they stood face-to-face. She lifted her chin in a show of boldness, the glint in her brown eyes reminiscent of the Elizabeth he had met in Meryton—the one who had treated him with such contempt.

Irritated that after all this time she was still not subservient, he grabbed her arm and began to pull her down a long hallway. Finally, he came to a door and pushed it open to reveal a library stocked with numerous volumes, though the room hardly seemed used. He flung Elizabeth inside, followed and turned to slam the door closed. Then grasping her arm again, Stefano dragged her to a chair and pushed her into it, leaning over her menacingly.

"I am delighted that you could join me as I return to Italy forever. I am sure my family will be pleased to meet you at last, Elizabeth, especially my mother. She has often mentioned that she would like me to settle in Italy with my wife. Can you imagine how surprised she will be?"

Elizabeth stiffened, but refused to show any fear, instead gathering her strength for the confrontation ahead. "Surprised? I imagine she will be shocked! You forget that you already have a wife in Italy, and she will expect you to return to her!"

"How do you know of Livia?" His face darkened as he considered her barb. Then he remembered and smiled slightly, his brows rising in disdain. "Yes, of course! You must have found the letter from the countess when you discovered the marriage certificates."

"Yes. I read the letter from your wife, Countess Livia Canossa Ridolfi. She even mentioned your son, Eduardo."

Stefano's hands clenched into fists. "Do not say that! You were my ONLY wife— the only one I truly loved. All the others were just whores—a means to an end!"

"You lie! I was never your wife! We were never married and besides you were never ... capable!"

His breath was laboured as he slapped her across the face. "It has never been that way with any other woman. I have a son! It was merely the circumstances—the stress! Once we are away from this turmoil, everything will be as it should. You shall see! We soon will determine my *capability*."

Elizabeth rubbed her smarting cheek. "And what of your son? Do you deny him as well?"

Stefano's face softened, and he looked almost pensive. "My son is almost of age. He no longer has need of me, and his mother and I have been estranged for years. He will understand."

"Regardless of the circumstances, whoever you have married is nothing to me. I despise you, and I am not leaving with you."

The count's voice was low and full of fury. "Of course, you are going, Elizabeth. Do you not remember what happened the last time you defied me?"

"There is one important difference! There is no one here that I care for, thus there is no one you can murder to compel me to go with you!" Elizabeth laughed mirthlessly. "And let me warn you! You had best be on your way before those who do care for me realise where I am!"

The smile faded from Stefano's face. "I imagine you speak of that love-sick fool, Darcy. I doubt he will find out you are missing before we are well under way on our voyage. In fact, he is probably still in London, unaware that you are no longer at Pemberley."

"Fitzwilliam Darcy is no fool! You have no idea of the calibre of man you have pitted yourself against. He has a brilliant intellect, as well as being honourable and decent."

He began to pace in front of her. "While in Meryton, there were rumours that you despised him. What good did his honour and decency do him then in winning your favour?"

Elizabeth voice rose in anger and regret. "I admit to being foolish when I was young! But now I know his true worth as a man without equal."

He pulled her from the chair, clasping her forearms as he brought her to his chest. "If you cared anything about that man, you would never have come with Mrs. Preston."

"That is where you are wrong," she said through clenched teeth. "You know absolutely nothing of caring—of love. He is the only man I have ever loved! If I cannot be with him, then I do not care to live. You may force me to go with you, but you cannot force me to live."

"Oh, you shall live, Elizabeth. I shall see to that, even if I must have you watched day and night! You are mine, and I shall never again give you up!" He kissed her then, trying to hold her as her head wrenched back and forth. Finally, she succeeded in breaking the kiss, and he shoved her back down into the chair.

"I was never yours, and I shall never be yours!" she proclaimed vehemently. "My heart was his before I ever met you, and after falling in love with a real man, I could never have cared for the likes of you," she retorted.

Though still furious, Stefano looked truly confused as he shouted, "Then why did you leave the protection of Pemberley? I hear that no one could have torn you from there had you not wanted to leave!"

"To spare the man I love! I was convinced I could be rid of you forever by departing for Americas, and Fitzwilliam would be set free from the burden and responsibility he has assumed on my account. But, know this—he is not afraid of you!"

"If he dares to come after you, he will die!" Furious, Stefano turned over a table sending china figurines flying. "ENOUGH! We sail in the morning! And you will find that your paramour is nowhere to be found when we do!"

~~~*~~~

Now that she was away from her tormentor, Elizabeth wished with all her heart that she had never spoken to him of William. So incensed that he would think she would meekly accept her fate, she had lashed out with all the anger accumulated from years of abuse. In doing so, she had boasted of William's constancy, hoping the threat might persuade Stefano to abandon her.

There was only one thing in which she could glory—as this horror had unfolded, she had not slipped back into the abyss of despair that had swallowed her before. In the midst of all the turmoil, a sweet peace had surrounded her heart, and innately she knew that William's love had given her the strength to endure! It was now in her power to face whatever came without being overwhelmed. Tears filled her eyes at the thought of her true love.

Oh, my dearest! How could I have been deceived by Cecile's lies? And now, instead of protecting you, I have endangered your life.

The last thing she remembered before falling into a fitful sleep, still sitting bound to the chair, were their words of devotion they shared before William left for London.

"You have not left and already I am dreading it. Please come back to me as soon as possible. I am only alive when I am in your arms."

"As I am only alive in yours. I promise to return as fast as humanly possible."

Liverpool
Barnwell's Boarding House
Late that evening

The men were exhausted. William and Mr. Williamson were just settling into their rooms when Richard entered the sitting room situated between their bedchambers. He had taken a smaller room directly across the hall, allowing the older man and his cousin to have the larger suite. No sooner had he closed the door than there was a knock.

"I will see to it," Richard called out, assuming it was someone from the staff.

"Evan!" Richard exclaimed, shocked to find his cousin standing in the hallway. He opened the door wider to allow him access. "Come in, come in!"

The loud greeting caused William to walk back into the shared sitting room and Mr. Williamson to move to the doorway to see who had arrived. William was equally as surprised to find his brother standing there, dressed rather unkemptly and smiling widely as though he had just discovered gold while ploughing a field.

"Richard! Darcy! I could not believe it when I saw the Darcy crest on the coach in the stable," Evan declared, shaking first one then the other's hand. "I was counting on Darcy to analyse the situation and come here from London, but to find *both* of you here is excellent news indeed! I have been in Liverpool since early morning with three of my men." He nodded at William. "And two of yours from Pemberley—Mr. Judson, the farrier, and Mr. Allgood, a groom, I believe."

Richard looked perplexed, glancing over to William who was still digesting what Evan had said. "How is it you are in Liverpool? And at this very inn? You could not have received our express from London and journeyed here that quickly. And why are you dressed like a tenant?"

"One question at a time!" Evan chuckled. "You are correct in your assumption that I never got your express. After I learned what Cecile had perpetrated—taking Elizabeth from Pemberley—I simply decided that I would find them and bring her back. I had my men scout the roads around Derbyshire and learned that a fine coach had left Lambton on the road to Liverpool. As for being at this inn, it was strictly a coincidence. We had elected to stay on the outskirts of town, hoping to remain unnoticed. I trust you agree with me that Cecile probably did not act alone. I was unsure what we were facing."

William broke in, "Our express would have explained that some woman was working with George Wickham and Stefano to take Elizabeth from Pemberley, but we had no idea it was your sister! I swear I would like to—"

"She crossed my mind," Richard declared, interrupting William's search for some punishment harsh enough to exact upon her. "I have never trusted that spider." He glanced uncomfortably at Evan. "My apologies. She is your sister."

"Not as far as I am concerned!" Evan exclaimed. "I guessed Stefano was involved, but Wickham! It never occurred to me that that ne'er-do-well would have the nerve to do such as thing. But, on second thought, I do not know why I am surprised. He was always trying to wring more money out of you, Brother, and trouble always seemed to follow him."

William was bewildered. "What could have possibly possessed her to help Wickham – or Stefano, for that matter? Jealousy? Money? And why would Elizabeth agree to go with her?"

"Of course, she was jealous of Elizabeth, Darce, but my guess is that if she is in league with Wickham, it involves gambling. Word about London is that many influential women are indebted to him because they love to bet on the horses. As for getting Elizabeth to agree, all it would take is for Cecile to tell her that Stefano would harm you if she stayed."

"She may be your sister, Evan, but if Elizabeth is hurt, so help me God, I will see Cecile Preston hang!" William barked, hitting the wall with his fist.

Evan sympathized. "I would feel the same if it were Ana." Quickly he changed the subject, hoping to calm his brother. "I reserved a small dining room downstairs where we can discuss what we learned with all the men. The minute I saw your coach, I knew you would want to be included. How soon can you be ready?"

"If we can dress like you, we have no need to get ready," Richard smirked.

"Oh yes, my appearance." Evan spread his arms and turned in a complete circle. "You would be surprised how much I have learned dressed in this manner. It seems no one is afraid to speak to a poor farm hand," he chuckled, "or order him about. Already today I made a shilling for loading a large box onto one gentleman's coach."

Mr. Williamson walked into the room. "At least you have managed to earn honest wages, and you would certainly fit in any pub in that outfit."

William turned to face him. "I am sorry, Vicar. I completely forgot about you."

"Understandable, given the circumstances," Williamson replied, laying one hand on William's shoulder as he passed him on the way to shake Evan's outstretched hand. Meanwhile, Evan assessed the tall, lanky fellow with the kind eyes, while William recovered his manners.

"Evan Ingram, my sister's husband," William declared, waving towards his brother. "And this is a new friend of mine and an old friend of Elizabeth's from Meryton—Mr. Williamson. He was the vicar there for many years and knows Elizabeth well. In fact, he christened her."

Evan shook the hand even more vigorously. "It is a pleasure to meet any friend of Elizabeth's. She seems to have had so few people in her life who have truly cared for her well-being."

Williamson's chin came up, though he smiled. "I have done nothing to earn such praise, but this dear boy," his gaze softened as he regarded William, "has restored my faith in humanity. Not only was he willing to take Lizzybet into his home, he was willing to lay down whatever future he might have envisioned for himself in order to give her freedom and a life of her own choosing. Now, he is here to rescue her once again."

William coloured as he added, "We are all here to rescue Elizabeth."

Seeing William's unease, Evan declared, "Then let us get started! I shall meet you in a quarter-hour in the dining room."

A small dining room

As Evan closed the door, everyone was reaching for one of the plates of food the inn had provided—everyone except William. The table was laden with hearty fare, and Richard sat a plate of food in front of his cousin.

"I cannot eat anything, Richard!"

"Come, Darce! You like beef stew, and there is plenty of fresh baked bread! Eat! You will need your strength for tomorrow."

"I do not understand why we are waiting!" William exclaimed, slamming his fist on the table and rattling the dishes. The room got quiet as everyone stopped to look in his direction.

"Blame me, Cousin. I did not tell you that Lieutenant Marbury and several of his men left London a few hours behind us. I was not sure he would be able to arrive in time, given the bad weather. Nevertheless, this was waiting at the desk when we came down." Richard held up a post. "Marbury and four of his men will be here tonight. Not being sure of how many men Stefano has, I feared that we might have need of them. A good officer always makes sure he has enough men to do the job. And when this fight starts, I wanted to know we could finish it!"

William nodded glumly so Evan spoke up, commanding everyone's attention. "Let me begin then by explaining what has transpired since we arrived. I assumed that if Cecile brought Elizabeth to this seaport, it must be with the intention of taking her out of England. Thus, I started with the ships—their scheduled arrivals and departures. I learned much, including the fact that one sailed for Italy this morning and another is to leave port for Spain tomorrow. There are—"

William interrupted. "Are you aware that a man and a woman were last minute additions to the passengers on the ship bound for Italy?" If not for the look of anguish in his eyes, one would think William was unruffled.

Evan had been gathering his thoughts, hoping to tell his brother and cousin everything slowly ... deliberately ... without raising false hopes, should his assumptions prove incorrect. However, he now recognised that the longer he delayed sharing all his news, the more Darcy suffered. "Forgive me. I thought to wait to the last to tell you—to caution you—not to get your hopes up. But it seems I should just come out with it."

William grew more worried. "Out with what?"

"We may have located Cecile. If we are correct, she is staying at a villa just outside town."

William's jaw tightened, and his hands formed fists as he began to rise. Evan watched Richard place a calming hand on his back. After they exchanged glances, William sat back down.

"Patience, Darcy! Mr. Watson here," Evan nodded to the man on his right that William knew well, "was not entirely convinced that the woman he saw entering a carriage was Cecile, but he was concerned enough to bring it to my attention. He also learned that two women had arrived in town recently and were in the company of a man who is staying at this villa. By this afternoon, two of my men and two from Pemberley were already in the woods surrounding the place, trying to get an idea of the number of people who populate it. Two of them are still there on watch."

Evan then addressed Mr. Watson, "Did you learn anything more about the owner of the villa?"

Mr. Watson swallowed a large bite of stew, before answering, "Yes, sir." He cleared his throat. "A maid at the Landmark told me that it belongs to a Lord Stanton. She says he has owned it for nigh onto thirty years or more, and she told me the name—Tuscany."

As Watson began to answer Evan's question, William's eyes found Richard's, and he took a big gulp of air, remembering his promise to regulate his feelings. They were on the right trail!

Richard jumped into the fray, peppering questions at those who had been at Tuscany that day, asking about the number of guards, the lay of the land and the design of the manor. William listened intently, too affected to speak. The fact that their men were successful at getting onto the property and near the house, spoke volumes. Perhaps Stefano did not have as many men with him as they had feared.

Mr. Judson, the farrier for Pemberley, spoke up. "Other than about eight men who looked like guards, I saw plenty of servants, old and young men, and an equal number of women. The servants were easy to discern by their lack of weaponry."

William finally found his voice. "Thank you, Mr. Judson, for joining us. I have always been able to count on you."

Just then, Mr. Watson declared. "Tell Mr. Ingram what you saw, Avery."

A younger, red-haired fellow turned as crimson as his hair when every eye fell on him. Evan encouraged him, "Speak up. I need everyone to tell me what they observed. No matter how insignificant it may seem to you, it may help us. "

Avery swallowed. "Well, sir, I managed to get next to the house—at a window, precisely. When I looked inside, I saw this young lady sitting in a chair right in my view. I could hear some man shouting as though he was mad or arguing, though I could not see him. About the time his voice got real loud, as if he was near the window, someone came around the side of the house. Naturally, I had to move back to safety."

William leaned forward, his hands now resting on either side of his plate. "What did the woman look like?"

The look on Mr. Darcy's face made Avery a bit nervous. "She—she was right pretty, for all I could tell, only seeing her from the side. She had dark brown hair, and she was tiny." William's quizzical brow made him continue nervously, "I—I mean that she looked mighty small in that big chair—or short, you might say, not tall like Mrs. Ingram."

A sudden knock on the door caused everyone to jump. Being at the head of the table, Evan pushed back his chair, stood, and opened the door. There, looking very worn, stood Lord Stanton. Evan opened the door wider, and he stepped into the room.

"Do not look so surprised. I left London before you. Because my servants packed only my necessary items in haste, I missed most of the storm and have hidden at a friend's home, awaiting your arrival." Every eye studied him as he looked around the room.

"I have friends in all the seaports and shipping houses. Just after we parted in London, I learned that Stephen had booked passages for several people on the ship that left this morning for Italy." His eyes locked on William. "But he did not board that ship." William exhaled audibly as his eyes briefly closed. "He cancelled those bookings and bought passages on a schooner leaving for Spain in the morning. I believe he is taking Miss Elizabeth with him. He knows he can go to Spain and then over land to Italy, which might throw a lesser man off his trail."

William's face was as flint. "Why would you help me? You know I will stop him even if—"

"Even if you have to kill him," the earl finished solemnly. "I am aware of the possibility. However, I intend to go to my villa and convince him to let Miss Elizabeth leave with me. If he does, I want your promise that he will be allowed to sail from England unharmed."

William met Richard and Evan's eyes before answering. "No! There will be no more reprieves for your evil son."

Lord Stanton sighed. "But I had hoped to get him to release her without a fight. He may kill Elizabeth if you try to take her."

"And you cannot possibly believe he would release her to you! He is mad. More likely, he will kill you!" William barked angrily.

Lord Stanton smiled wanly. "I am not afraid to die, Mr. Darcy. However, I can no longer look myself in the mirror knowing I did nothing to stop my son from hurting Elizabeth again. I would like to do this for her and for Thomas Bennet. He was a good man."

"Your son will refuse!"

"If he refuses, then you must do whatever it takes to stop him. Make no mistake, I love my son. Nevertheless, I cannot—WILL NOT—let him ruin Elizabeth's life again." His voice grew quiet. "She has a future with a man who truly loves her. Mrs. Bennet and my son have stolen enough from Elizabeth. She deserves better."

William stated resolutely, "Your plan is unacceptable. Do not interfere, or we shall assume you are on his side and act accordingly."

The earl seemed resigned as he opened his coat and pulled a letter out of his pocket. "This is a letter to the captain of the schooner, Fernando Diaz. He is an old friend of mine, and he will help you in your plans to recover Elizabeth, should Stephen manage to get her as far as the ship. I suggest you station men aboard the schooner, in the event that should occur. Now, if you will excuse me, I shall return to my friend's home and await the outcome."

Nothing was said as the earl turned to leave. When he almost had the door shut, he stopped, looking back to William. "Love her, Darcy. She deserves some happiness in her life."

"You may rely on it," William replied, his voice rough with emotion. Stefano's father nodded and shut the door.

Richard jerked his head towards Mr. Judson. "Follow Lord Stanton. We would not want him trying to be a hero. If he starts towards the villa, let us know. Otherwise, meet us back at the drive to Tuscany at first light." Mr. Judson grabbed several rolls from the table and his coat and hat from the rack on the wall and slipped out of the room.

The vicar, noting the gloom on William's face, leaned in to whisper, "We shall recover her, son. Just remember that."

Abruptly William choked out, "I—I need just a bit of fresh air." With those words, he was out the side door leading to a porch that wrapped completely around the house. Evan started to rise, but Richard held up a hand.

"Please, let me."

The air outside was beginning to cool, and Richard shivered just a bit when he stepped into the night. It took a moment for his eyes to adjust to the darkness, but they soon did, and he walked around the side of the house. William stood at the end of the porch where a dim light glowed; he clutched a column as if his life depended upon it. Richard walked slowly towards him, trying to decide what to say.

"Darce?" William did not stir. "I—what can I say to ease your mind?"

After a few seconds of silence, William whispered, "I love her so much, Richard. What if Stanton is right and Stefano should harm her before we can set her free?"

Though William did not face him, Richard could see the evidence of tears reflected by the light. "You know, every time I have led my men into battle, I have felt somewhat like you do now—knowing what I must do but fearing the consequences. Oh, I realise it is not exactly the same thing, but I do fear for their safety just as you fear for your Elizabeth's. Nevertheless, I have no choice and neither do you."

He moved to stand beside his cousin, threading an arm about his shoulder. "God does not always give us the easy way out. Sometimes we have to be willing to fight and die for what we know is right. All we can do is trust Him to be on the side of justice. He is, you know. We enter the fray with that knowledge."

William turned to embrace his cousin, holding him for a little longer than most would deem proper, but he did not care. This man had always been beside him— closer than a brother—supporting him and saying just what he needed to hear. "Thank God, I have you, Richard."

Richard tried to be stoic. After all, soldiers were not supposed to cry. "I thank Him for you too, Darce."

Several minutes later, the cousins made their way back into the dining room, where everyone was busy preparing food to take with them in the morning. Mr. Watson and Avery were getting ready to depart in order to relieve the two who were still at Tuscany.

If anyone noticed that both men had red eyes, no one was unkind enough to mention it.

~~~*~~~

Chapter 38

Barnwell's Boarding House
The next morning

On the slight chance that Stefano might manage to get to the docks, Mr. Williamson, accompanied by one servant from Pemberley, had already left for the ship to confer with the captain and take their places alongside the ship's crew. Stanton had assured them last night that his old friend, Fernando Diaz, would cooperate in their plans to keep his son from leaving with Elizabeth. The captain had had a disagreement with Stefano years before over payment for some freight, and he had never forgotten the incident nor forgiven him his duplicity.

Lieutenant Marbury and his men had arrived late, as expected. After a few hours rest, they had taken their position about a mile up the road from Tuscany, where they would be a last outpost to stop any coach that might get past Richard and the others. Thus, the early morning fog enshrouded William, Richard, Evan and the others nearing the drive to the villa. As he rode behind his brother and cousin, Evan could not help but reflect on the conversation of that morning.

"Everyone check your weapons, even if you have done so already," Richard ordered. *"There will be no time once the confrontation starts."* He turned to William. *"You did bring your sword?"*

William nodded, reaching into the coach to grab the sword that his father had given him upon the completion of his studies at Cambridge.

"Strap it on. It will do you no good in there, and you never know when you may have use of it. Pistols are only good until they are empty. 'Be prepared,' my old sergeant always said!"

Evan laughed, strapping his own sword about his waist and saluting. "Yes, sir, Colonel Fitzwilliam!"

Richard smirked. "You may laugh now, but you will both thank me for the warnings before the day is finished. Now remember, keep your heads down while on horseback; it makes you a much smaller target, and do not allow yourselves to be separated. There is strength in numbers."

William and Evan exchanged smiles, which Richard noted. "I intend to take both of you back unharmed." Turning briskly, he walked over to the other men to issue the same caution to them.

"Richard is the consummate army officer, is he not?" Evan asked, following his cousin with his eyes. William stopped what he was doing to observe Richard, who was now expounding on military strategies for surviving this venture to the servants who were helping.

"Yes, but he is much more. He has not lived this long without being very clever. I know I would not feel quite so confident without him being here."

Evan laughed mirthlessly. "To tell the truth, neither would I. Take care, Brother. I would not like to be put in a position to explain to Ana why you got hurt."

William patted Evan's shoulder. "Nor would I like to explain the same about you. God preserve us all."

"Let us hope that He is as tired of Stefano as we are!" Richard declared, overhearing their somber conversation as he returned. Then he smiled warmly. "If your weapons are ready, inspect your horses and mount up."

As they arrived at the woods just outside the entrance to Tuscany, dawn was beginning to lighten the skies, and they could see two overwrought servants running to meet them.

Arriving first, Mr. Avery said breathlessly, "I was wondering what to do—send Hawkins to find you or wait until you arrived!"

"Just what has you so disturbed?" Richard queried.

"Another coach has arrived! It entered the drive not a half-hour ago! If not for the racket it made in passing, it could have passed us unnoticed as it was still pitch black."

"So you could not determine if there was a crest on the side?"

"No, sir!"

William growled, "Stanton never meant to wait! Somehow he must have escaped Mr. Judson's watch!"

~~~*~~~

Awakened while it was still dark, Elizabeth was untied and made to dress. She was then forced to accompany Mrs. Preston to the large front portico, which was illuminated by torches along the length of it and part way down the drive. Alongside them stood servants and guards, awaiting Stefano's order to board two coaches piled high with trunks. One coach was to transport most of the men, guards and servants, several riding as footmen. The other was to convey the count, Elizabeth, Mrs. Preston, and the young girl, Maria, as well as the other men.

Elizabeth and the widow exchanged uncertain glances, though they did not speak. In no humour to converse with the woman who had betrayed her, Elizabeth glared as Cecile lowered her head. It was obvious that she wished she had never been involved with Wickham or fallen so low as to help the lunatic regain control of Miss Elizabeth.

Visibly on edge, Stefano paced about nervously, giving orders and asking questions. After Elizabeth had championed Mr. Darcy, he had begun to suspect that he might have underestimated the man. If Darcy had already surmised that Elizabeth was in Liverpool, he could arrive before they departed England. Giving last minute orders to his bodyguards, Stefano was the last to notice that those about him had ceased their activities and were staring at something in the distance. Barely distinguishable in the torchlights, a lone coach rolled towards the manor.

Stefano held his breath. No one would dare arrive at this hour unless they had come to confront him. Glancing about, he was pleased to see that his men had already drawn their weapons, so he resisted the urge to do the same. He never liked to appear fearful, though unconsciously his hands clenched into fists. When at last he was able to read the crest on the side of the luxurious conveyance, he began to shake with uncontrollable anger.

311

Father!

As Lord Stanton's coach stopped in front of Tuscany's front steps, a visibly nervous footman climbed down to open the door. Stefano's father exited his coach as though he had not a care in the world, though his anxious eyes instantly swept the people standing alongside his son. Finding Miss Elizabeth and meeting her eyes, he noted that she did not appear overly frightened. He nodded. She looked perplexed as to his intentions but remained calm as she nodded slightly in return. Next to her stood the maid, Maria, who had grown up at Tuscany, and next to the servant, another woman who looked quite traumatized.

As he approached the group, Stefano reached to grip Elizabeth's arm and pull her close to his side. Stanton ignored his son as he addressed her. "Miss Elizabeth, I am so very grateful that you look well. Your welfare has been of great concern to so many."

Elizabeth's brows knit in uncertainty, but she replied solemnly, "I am well, Lord Stanton."

Stefano glared at her before he addressed his father. "Why are you here, Father? Have you not been sufficiently warned to leave me alone? Do you realise the dangerous situation you have created by coming?"

"May we go inside, Stephen? I would like a word with you in private."

"Anything you have to say, you can say now—in front of everyone."

Lord Stanton frowned, but shrugged his shoulders. "In that case, I am here to ask you to allow me to return Miss Elizabeth to those who love her."

"OUT OF THE QUESTION!" Stefano shouted, ignoring his father as he turned his back and addressed his men. "Let us get started!"

Immediately, servants began bustling about, finishing their tasks as Stefano clamped his hand around Elizabeth's arm and dragged her forward.

Lord Stanton stepped in front of his son. "I cannot allow you to take her with you, Stephen. You are already married; you cannot marry her. She deserves a chance for happiness, and I ask you again to please let me take her home."

"Home? To that fool Darcy, you mean. Or you will do what exactly, Father? You have not enough men to take her from me by force, and you do not see Mr. Darcy here, do you? She is mine! He has no right to her! She will sail with me to Spain within the hour."

"Do not underestimate Fitzwilliam Darcy or the lengths to which he will go to find you and recover Elizabeth. He truly loves her."

Tears shone in Elizabeth's eyes at Lord Stanton's declaration, though she was clearly trying desperately not to cry.

Stefano's voice escalated. "I have no doubt you and he have become allies in your quest to take Elizabeth from me!"

"Darcy is a decent man who will take care of her, which is more than you can claim!"

"Is that all you have to say?" Stefano sneered. "Get out of my way, old man."

Again the count started towards the coach, trying to shove his father out of his path. But Lord Stanton did not budge, instead pulling a small pistol from an inside pocket of his coat. "Release her to me or I shall ..."

Stefano let go of Elizabeth, who retreated several feet, while he fought with his father. As they wrestled more violently, a solitary shot rang out. No one made a sound as father and son halted in their struggle, still holding on to each other.

After several seconds, Stanton murmured weakly, "I never stopped loving you, Stephen," then sank to the ground, mortally wounded.

Stefano, purloined weapon still in his hand, stared at his father's body in astonishment. For a fleeting moment, his face took on the look of a young boy who had suddenly discovered that his beloved father had died, and his face contorted in anguish as tears filled his eyes. Those standing about were astounded at the transformation. Nevertheless, only seconds later, his expression reverted to its former state, and the man they were well acquainted with replaced the child.

Lifting his chin in defiance, he spit out orders. "Put him in his coach! No wait! Switch the coach from Northgate with the one that was to carry the women, and get his men aboard it."

As Maria quickly tried to follow Cecile to a coach, he shouted, "Mrs. Preston, wait where you are. Maria, come here!" Visibly frightened, both women turned slowly, afraid to hear what he might say. Having no alternative, Maria did as he said, moving forward. Stefano had caught up with Elizabeth and roughly untied the ribbons on her bonnet, jerking it from her head.

"Take off your cloak!" he barked, and Elizabeth did as he demanded. Bonnet and cloak in hand, he motioned to Maria to take them. "Replace yours with these!"

Maria obviously understood English even if she did not speak it, for immediately the girl replaced her own modest coat and bonnet with the more expensive ones Elizabeth wore moments before. When she was finished, Stefano motioned Maria to make a complete circle. As she did, he laughed, his eyes glowing in satisfaction.

"Excellent! Now, get in the coach with Mrs. Preston and sit next to a window, but do not show your face. With your head turned, they will think you are my wife."

Meanwhile, Stefano's men had finished depositing his father's body in his coach, so he marched over to the stunned driver and footmen. "Leave now! At the main road, take a right away from town. My men will be following and if you disobey, you shall be killed! Do you understand?"

Nodding vigorously, Lord Stanton's stunned servants took their positions, and with the driver whipping the horses into a run, they fled the estate in one of Stefano's coaches with their murdered master.

~~~*~~~

Learning of Stanton's arrival, Richard ordered the two servants to mount their horses. They had barely done so when a coach suddenly left out of the gate to Tuscany, racing as though the devil himself was chasing it. Having turned right at the end of the drive, the coachman lashed the horses into a frenzy as they sped past the group's hiding place—heading away from Liverpool. In the light of the early morning sunrise, it was easy to read Stefano's crest on the side.

"Come on!" Richard cried, and everyone pursued the pitching and swaying coach. As the men on horseback drew nearer, getting off a few shots, the unarmed driver and footmen were convinced to raise their hands in surrender. Richard forged ahead, managing to grab the reins of the lead horse, and pulling the carriage to a stop several hundred yards past the gate. As they gathered about the ill-fated coach, they realised it was not Stefano's men but only Lord Stanton's servants.

"My Lord, man! Why the devil did you speed past?" Richard barked to the thoroughly frightened driver. For a moment, the driver could not find his voice.

"Speak up!" Richard shouted, as William, who had already dismounted, opened the door to make sure Elizabeth was not inside.

"He killed Lord Stanton!" a footman cried. "That son of his—sorry bastard that he is! He told us he would kill us, too, if we did not leave straightaway and head right at the end of the drive! The others are supposed to be just behind us!"

William examined Lord Stanton for a pulse, but he was already dead. Shaking his head at the other men, he slammed the door. At that precise moment, two coaches flew out of the drive to Tuscany not two hundred yards back—both headed in the opposite direction.

"After them!" Richard shouted, kicking his horse into a gallop and easily taking the lead. The others were close behind, with Evan out front of that group. Since William had dismounted to peer inside the coach, he was the last to mount and was several yards behind everyone else when he passed the drive that turned to the villa. The same small voice he had heard in the past spoke again.

Elizabeth is still at Tuscany.

William pulled his horse up short, watching the others get smaller in the distance. He could hear the sounds of gunshots from afar as Richard apparently caught up with the last coach. Frantically he tried to decide what to do—keep going or trust the voice. He glanced to the skies. *Show me what to do!*

Instantly, he saw a vision of Elizabeth standing on the porch that night at the inn when the voice told him she was in trouble. Without another doubt, he turned the horse around and kicked it into a gallop as he hurried down the drive towards the villa.

~~~*~~~

After all the coaches had disappeared into the fog, Stefano turned to the two guards he had ordered to stay behind. "Now, let us prepare for Mr. Darcy! Do not stop him from entering the house. Let him find me in the ballroom, but do not let him leave the villa under any circumstances."

He spat out an order to an older man who did the gardening. "Have a curricle prepared now! Bring it around front." The man nodded nervously and headed to the stables. Then Stefano addressed Elizabeth as he began dragging her back into the house. "If my father was stupid enough to follow me, I have no doubt that your friend is equally as stupid!"

"Please, I beg you, just let me go! If you leave now, you can sail out of England before anyone knows your father is dead."

"So now you are willing to beg. Well, you may as well know that I have changed my mind. You and I are not sailing right now, but will be travelling to Scotland. Before we leave, however, I have decided it will be enjoyable to teach your friend a lesson. You need to see for yourself which of us is the better man!"

Elizabeth tried to resist, but it was futile as Stefano overpowered her, jerking her back inside and then from one room to another. Instead, she forced herself to focus on how she might help Fitzwilliam if he were to come.

Her thoughts flew to the very small, gold coloured knife that was hidden in a pocket of her gown. Early this morning, she had remembered that it was in her sewing box. It had been a simple matter to loosen a button on the gown laid out for her. After showing the button to the maid, she had quickly retrieved the sewing box from her bag, and while the servant was distracted, had slipped the knife into the pocket. She was relieved to realise that it was still there, as she felt the weight of it as she walked.

After tugging her down a long hallway, they entered a room that might once have been a ballroom but was now empty except for a small table and chairs that were stacked at one end. Looking about distractedly, Stefano walked to a window and jerked loose a piece of decorative braid that still held the curtain back. Dragging her to the table, he lifted one of the chairs and sat it on the floor, pushed her down into it, and began tying her wrists and feet with the braided rope.

Elizabeth tried to hold her hands as stiffly as possible, to leave room for manoeuvring, but once he was finished, she found that while she could easily move her fingers, her wrists were securely tied. Stefano left the room, and while he was away, she tried to free her hands. It seemed hopeless, as the rope made her skin raw where it rubbed. Nevertheless, she kept at it, ignoring the pain.

The count returned shortly with a pair of decorative swords, which he placed on the table, a jar of oil and an armful of linens that he proceeded to pile around the walls and under the curtains. A guard came in right behind with wood in his arms. Dumping it in the hearth, he had a good blaze going shortly, and with a wave of his hand, Stefano dismissed the man. Taking the jar of oil, he walked over one of the linens on the floor and poured some of the contents on the cloth. Then he picked it up and tossed it into the flames. It immediately caught fire, and his eyes danced.

Wiping his hands against his breeches as he stood, he jerked his head around to study her, almost as though he had forgotten she was in the room. "There you see! They burn exceptionally well!"

He strode in her direction. "After I finish with your Mr. Darcy, I intend to set this place afire and leave for Scotland. There shall be nothing left of the esteemed Lord Stanton's home or your honourable friend."

He forced a kiss on her as she shook her head back and forth. Unable to break away, she bit his lip, causing him to pull back. He backhanded her, his ring causing a gash on her cheek. She cried out in spite of her resolve not to react. Then still rubbing his mouth, he laughed as if he were possessed and began to tie a handkerchief across her mouth so she could not speak. Studying his handiwork, he was apparently satisfied and stalked out of the room.

Ignoring her aching cheek, Elizabeth managed to grip the small knife in her pocket, extracting it by the heavier handle, as she slid it between the constraints on her wrists. The blade of the knife sliced into her wrist, but she ignored the pain and persisted in her mission. Then she began to rub back and forth against the blade. Focused on this undertaking, she was stunned when the count raced back into the room and took up a stance in front of her. Facing the door at the far end of the room, he pulled a pistol from his coat. Elizabeth's heart raced, and she almost panicked. Had William come? Would Stefano kill him without a warning?

~~~*~~~

It did not take long for William to navigate the drive and arrive at the front of the villa, pistol in hand. While dismounting, he noticed an older man, who had evidently just brought round a curricle, jump out of it and race back towards the stables. William had no way of knowing if he was going to alert Stefano's men or if he was just afraid. Looking about, he could see no one else in sight.

Cautiously, he made his way up the steps to the front door, tried the handle and finding it unlocked, eased inside. Once in the foyer, he waited. Hearing nothing, he took several steps towards the grand staircase and was just about to climb them, when an older woman appeared to the left of the stairs. She shook her head as if to warn him that he was going in the wrong direction. Bringing her finger to her lips in a sign of silence, she pointed down the hallway from which she had just come and raised her eyebrows. William nodded, though he did not know if she was warning him or leading him into a trap. With no other choice, he went in the direction the woman had pointed as she hurried away.

Further down the hallway, another servant, possibly the butler from the look of his clothes, waved William forward, motioning that what he was seeking was inside the next door. Taking a deep breath, William did as directed, and with pistol drawn entered a room that looked as though it was once a ballroom. He was not surprised to find a man fitting the count's description standing at the far end of it, his pistol leveled at his heart. Elizabeth sat in a chair behind him, her hands and feet tied and a gag in her mouth.

"Well, well. We meet at last, Fitzwilliam Darcy!" Stefano crowed quite civilly. "I have heard far too many flattering things about you!"

William ignored him as his eyes met Elizabeth's, and he said gently, "Are you well?"

Smiling despite the tears that had begun when she first glimpsed him, she nodded her head. Her eyes told him how much she loved him, and he smiled as though he could read them, sending the same message with his own.

Stefano growled, stepping in front of her to block William's view. "Now that you have that little pleasantry over with, suppose you put down your weapon, Mr. Darcy." William hesitated, so Stefano roared, "You do not really have any choice in the matter as I have someone you want!"

With those words, Stefano pulled Elizabeth from the chair, holding her as a shield while he placed the pistol under her chin. As fortune would have it, he was so preoccupied that he never noticed the small knife still in her hands. William's countenance darkened, but he eased his pistol to the floor, never breaking eye contact with Elizabeth.

"Now, kick it over here!"

Once William had complied, Stefano pushed Elizabeth back down in the chair. Darcy glowered at his roughness, and Stefano laughed. It delighted him to see Darcy lose a bit of his storied self-control.

"This is your lucky day!" Stefano smirked as William's eyebrows rose in question. "I am predisposed to prove to Elizabeth that you are not the champion that she believes you to be and, most assuredly, not someone to esteem."

Stefano laid his own pistol on the table, methodically unbuttoning his coat. Discarding it, he donned a glove that he pulled from his waistcoat pocket. Then turning slightly, eyes still glued to William, he picked up one of the swords lying on the table. Gripping the handle, he pulled the blade from the scabbard and instantly whipped it about in several directions. The movements made swishing sounds in the air.

"You may use this one." He tilted his head at the matching sword on the table. "But I trust you would rather use the one you are wearing."

William did not answer, instead shedding his coat and donning the glove he had pulled from the pocket before throwing it in a corner. He had no more than pulled his sword from its scabbard when Stefano abruptly lunged forward with his right leg, while wielding his sword erect, his left arm lifted in a square. *"En garde!"*

Taking advantage of the fact that William had no time to take his stance, the count advanced without further warning, managing to slice through William's sleeve, leaving a small wound that began to bleed. Elizabeth paled at the sight. Nevertheless, William was able to lift his sword in time to thwart a following lunge, and their swords began clanking back and forth against each other. Both accomplished swordsmen, they appeared equally matched at first, though William's wrist moved the weapon effortlessly compared to the count's awkward strokes.

While they parried in a circular direction away from her, lunging and thrusting in turn, Elizabeth continued to work the knife against the ropes, managing to cut through enough to slip one hand out. Surreptitiously, she began untying her feet whenever the count's attention was well engaged. She left the gag in place, fearing he would notice its absence right away.

As the battle escalated, it became clear that William was the stronger of the two, and he scored several hits along Stefano's limbs as he began to move forward, forcing Stefano to retreat as he began to sweat profusely. For a long while, the swords clashed in rapid succession, and the fight went on for several minutes, as first one then the other scored light hits. Suddenly, Stefano's sword was whipped from his grip by William's blade, landing several feet away. Then as William advanced for the kill, one of Stefano's guards stepped out of the hall and moved to stand in front of his master, pistol in hand.

The count sneered derisively, "You did not seriously think I would let you win, did you?"

During the course of the match, Elizabeth had managed to free her feet and cautiously reached for Stefano's pistol upon the table. Neither villain paid any attention to her, but William was very aware of her efforts. He had to force himself not to look at her, knowing she could be killed if either man learned she was no longer bound. Stefano was totally caught up in his triumph and kept his eyes on William while taunting, "Watch, my dear wife, as the man you thought so highly of—the one who would be your saviour—dies like a dog."

He barked orders at the guard. "Shoot him!"

Just as the guard took aim, Elizabeth fired, killing the man instantly and causing Stefano to whirl around to look at her. The look of fury upon his face was so evil that he no longer looked human—just as it had been the day he shot Addie. Instinctively Elizabeth backed into the corner as he headed towards her, spouting venom.

"You have betrayed me! I killed all of them for you and—"

"Stefano!" William shouted, closing in as he kicked Stefano's sword back to him, "Defend yourself!"

Stefano snapped around thoroughly disoriented and seeing his sword sliding towards him, stooped down to reach for it. William's pistol still lay on the floor nearby, and as he pretended to pick up the sword he lunged for the pistol. With one last thrust of his sword, William ended the count's reign of terror as he plunged the blade into his heart.

As Stefano fell to the floor, William extracted his sword and stooped to pick up the guard's unused pistol. He stood just in time to catch Elizabeth as she rushed into his arms. He soothed her, rocking her back and forth and kissing her hair while he kept the pistol and his eyes trained on the doors. He was not sure how many guards remained or if the servants were loyal to Stefano. All of a sudden, the man and woman who had directed him into this room stuck their heads inside cautiously.

Seeing the count lying in a pool of blood, the woman exclaimed, "Thank God you have prevailed!" The man nodded his agreement, beginning to edge close to the count as though he thought the villain might rise from the dead.

A little puzzled at their reaction, William ventured, "Are there any more of Stefano's men here?"

"None that can do any harm!" the woman replied. "My husband and the gardener have the last two guards tied up in the stables. All that is left are servants, and we want no trouble. We were loyal to Lord Stanton—God rest his soul—not to this vile creature. Perhaps I should not be happy that he is dead, but I cannot pretend otherwise. At least now he cannot hurt anyone."

Focusing on Elizabeth, she added, "I am sorry we could not help you while he and his men were in charge. Are you well?" She reached out to touch Elizabeth's wrist. "You are bleeding too."

Noticing the blood for the first time, William exclaimed, "We need bandages!"

The housekeeper hurried out of the room to fetch them.

Elizabeth tried to smile. "The cuts are not deep." She examined his injuries, frowning as she declared, "Your wounds are worse than mine."

William smiled lovingly. "They are minor. Besides, I am perfectly well as long as I have you."

Several young men, all clearly servants, appeared in the doorway abruptly, and the old man motioned for them to come forward. As they began to help him remove the count and the guard from the room, Elizabeth took one last look at the dead men before burying her face in William's chest. He ran his hands up and down her back in comfort, until she leaned back to look up at him.

"I have killed a man this day, but God help me, I would do it again! I would kill anyone who tried to harm you."

William touched his forehead to hers. "My brave, brave darling. You saved my life."

"Just as you saved mine." Elizabeth sniffled, clutching him even tighter and beginning to place kisses wherever she could reach, murmuring, "I love you ... I love you ... I love you."

Deliriously happy, William lifted her chin until she was looking at him and they exchanged words of love with their eyes. Their lips met with great urgency, and for some time they were lost in their own world, oblivious to the stares of the servants now standing about. William broke the kiss by feathering light kisses across her face, stopping to whisper in her ear, "We need to find the others and let them know we are safe."

"Others?" Elizabeth murmured languidly, still in a trance from his kisses.

Just then, loud footsteps echoed down the hall towards them and suddenly someone was rushing into the room. William leveled his pistol at the intruder.

"Richard!" William shouted as recognition dawned and he lowered the weapon. "My Lord, I almost shot you!"

"That makes two of us!" Richard declared, holstering his pistol in exasperation. "You are going to be the death of me! You never follow orders!"

Once he had realised that Darcy was not with them following the coaches that had left the villa, Richard had shouted orders for the others to continue while he returned to look for his cousin. Having found the villa looking very much deserted, he had just reached the top step when the sound of a gunshot brought him to a halt. Frantic with worry, he stole into the house, stealthily checking room after room, until the sound of voices brought him down the correct hallway. He was just in time to see several men carry Stefano's body out of the room. With pistol raised, he had rushed past an old woman to find his cousin and Elizabeth both alive and well.

"If I had not seen Stefano's body, I might have thought he had prevailed! It would be nice if you had let someone know you were still alive!"

William smiled, knowing Richard's rants were only to mask his concern for his safety. "We were just about to come and find you."

"Right! After another kiss perhaps?" he retorted with a wry smile. "Please do not let me keep you from whatever you were doing!"

With a slight smirk, William pulled Elizabeth into his arms, capturing her mouth in a kiss so torrid that Richard began to feel a bit uncomfortable. He left the room quickly, loosening his collar which now felt entirely too tight and seeking some fresh air. Lost in each other, neither William nor Elizabeth heard the low whistle that echoed through the halls just before Richard lunged out the front door.

By then Evan and several men were running up the steps. "Did you find Darcy? Is he well? And Miss Elizabeth?"

Richard looked more flustered than Evan had ever seen him as he spit out, "He is fine. Elizabeth is fine. Stefano is dead. All is well."

All the men collapsed, exhausted, on the steps, except Evan, who started towards the door. "Then why are they not out here with you?"

Richard stayed him, grabbing his arm as he shook his head sternly. "You do not want to go in there just yet, Cousin."

Evan stopped, looking perplexed, until suddenly he understood. He grinned, dropping down to sit on the top step to take a well-deserved rest. Richard took his place beside him as Evan chuckled.

"Do you suppose we shall have to wait long? You know how slow Darcy is when trying to make up his mind what to do next."

~~~*~~~

Chapter 39

Liverpool
Barnwell's Boarding House
A bedroom

Mr. Williamson sat on the bed as if in a daze. He had just spent a few precious minutes with Elizabeth while the others met with the constable and checked on the injured. Even so, he had barely had time to talk to her before being asked to leave to accommodate the physician. Instead of returning to the room in which the others would reconvene, however, he had retreated to his own bedroom to collect his thoughts—to consider what he would say to William about Lizzybet.

Though he had known for some time that she was alive, a combination of relief and sadness had washed over him when he finally stood face-to-face with her. The young girl he had known was now a woman—not much changed in appearance, but very different in manner. Her dark eyes now held a hint of cynicism instead of sparkling with insatiable curiosity. The girl, who had once asked him how to know if she was in love, had been replaced by a woman who knew far too much of love from a madman's perspective.

When the vicar opened the door, a maid sitting in a chair just inside quickly stood and nodded towards the balcony. As he reached the balcony door, Elizabeth turned at the sound of his footsteps and, for a moment, neither of them spoke. She looked bewildered, so he offered, "Lizzybet?"

Convinced it was actually him, she began to cry and ran into his arms. "Father Williamson!" He cried, too, pulling her into a warm hug. She apologised against his chest, "I—I am sorry! I mean, Mr. Williamson!"

Pulling back to look at her, he soothed, "I know your father made you stop calling me that because he thought it was disrespectful, but I never felt it was—I cherished it!"

"I was a child. I heard Gregory call you Father, and I wanted to do the same," Elizabeth replied sheepishly. "I did not know it could be misinterpreted until my mother heard and scolded me. Then she told Papa."

"Since Gregory was lost at sea, there is no one to call me that endearment anymore. I would dearly love you to do so if you wish. I always thought of you as my daughter, and I know you called your own dear father 'Papa' so I do not believe he would mind."

She shook her head, sniffling as she brushed the tears from her face. "Papa always respected you and our friendship, so I do not think he would mind at all. You realise that I have no family now, other than Jane, Charles and Peter and, of course, my aunt and uncle in London. I would dearly love for you to be a part of my family, as you have always been a part of my heart."

"Then so be it!" Williamson declared, clasping her again in a hug. *"Henceforth, we shall be family in truth as well as in spirit."*

Elizabeth nodded vigorously against his chest, before leaning back to look up at him with a quizzical expression. *"How ever did you come to be here? With Fitzwi— Mr. Darcy?"*

It took several minutes to explain how he had met Fitzwilliam Darcy and the detour his life had taken afterward. Mr. Williamson began his story with finding William in despair at the cemetery and their shared sorrow, adding how much he had admired the young man from the very first time they had met. Then, his face transformed, his joy palpable, he spoke of learning she was alive and of William's invitation to visit Pemberley to see her again. Finally, he related to her how they had come to be in Liverpool and about their efforts to recover her.

At the end, he declared, *"I cannot believe it. My Lizzybet is alive! God is good!"*

Reaching to hold both his weathered hands, Elizabeth suddenly seemed reserved, and her eyes dropped to the floor. *"I—I cannot let you leave without telling you of my resolution. Please know that I contemplated the cost but have chosen my path. I daresay that you will not approve."* Her eyes found his again. *"But, as part of my family, you have the right to know."*

He nodded solemnly—conscious from her manner that she was talking of something very close to her heart.

"Every minute I was Stefano's prisoner—over two long years—I longed for the man I truly loved—Fitzwilliam Darcy. I know now that he felt the same way about me." Tears slipped down her cheeks. *"It was his love that restored me. I would never have recovered had he not taken me into his home—into his life—and shown me unconditional love. And, foolish as I was to fall back into Stefano's hands, I have been given yet another opportunity."* She squeezed his hands harder now, willing him to understand.

"I am resolved not to squander this chance. Who knows what tomorrow may bring? When William comes to me, I intend to tell him that I do not want us to be separated—not tonight, not ever."

Thinking of the implications, the vicar did not immediately respond, and Elizabeth let go of his hands, turning to walk away. *"I have shocked you with my boldness."*

Williamson placed a hand on her shoulder, stilling her progress and turning her around. *"Nothing on God's green earth shocks me, child. I am a man of the cloth, but I am also human. I understand, truly I do."*

"I am not a wanton. I have never—even with Stefano, I never ..." She took a ragged breath as she studied her shoes. *"I do not wish to disappoint you, but I love William so very much, and I have come to care less of what society thinks. Society would never have given me this second chance for happiness with my only love."*

"You could never disappoint me." He lifted her chin, and she smiled. *"And I understand your disillusionment with the dictates of society. Nevertheless, I believe I have a solution that will suit you and your young man. Do you trust me?"* She studied him with a puzzled expression before nodding. *"Then allow me to talk to Fitzwilliam before I send him here to you."*

A large sitting room

"What the devil possessed you to go to Tuscany by yourself, Cousin?" Richard growled, pouring himself a brandy and holding up the bottle to see if William wanted one. At William's nod, he poured another. "You could have very well have been walking into a trap and been killed!"

William took the proffered glass and resumed pacing about the small sitting room as he had done for the last half-hour. "But I was not! Someone, be it God or an angel, told me to go back to the villa. The same voice warned me once before that Elizabeth was in trouble—at the inn on the way to Pemberley." His face darkened. "You remember that I told you about that blackguard who tried to ..." Shaking his head to calm himself, he continued. "In any event, you and the others were so far ahead that I had no choice but to act as I did, foolish or not."

"How in the world did you convince Stefano to face you with a sword? I had imagined you would be shot on sight."

William shrugged his shoulders. "His pride, I suppose. In his arrogance, he wanted to show Elizabeth that I was not what he termed a *champion*."

Richard guffawed. "That cocky arse challenged the fencing champion of Cambridge to a duel? You held the title until you graduated, and a number of your records still stand—unparalleled in the history of the university."

William smiled despite himself. "Yes, well, Stefano never intended to let me win! He had an armed servant standing by, who appeared when I relieved him of his sword. It was only thanks to Elizabeth that I am alive to tell the story."

"Elizabeth?"

"Yes. She was bound hand and foot, but managed to free her hands with a small knife she had hidden in her pocket. Then she untied herself and grabbed the pistol Stefano had placed on a table. Just as the guard aimed his weapon at me, she shot and killed him. As Stefano lunged for my pistol which was still lying on the floor, I finished him with my sword."

"Amazing!" Richard exclaimed, raising his glass in a toast. "It seems the dear girl is no longer a victim but a victor!"

At that moment, Evan, Mr. Williamson, and all of the servants, walked into the room.

"How are Avery and Judson?" William enquired, finally calm enough to take a seat.

Evan sank into the chair next to him. "According to the physician, Avery must take to his bed for quite a while, but he should recover completely from the wound to his shoulder. I have been arranging for his care until he has recovered sufficiently to allow a move to Rosewood. Your man, Judson, is resting comfortably in a room across the hall. He has a large lump on his head and a dreadful headache. Luckily, he was able to return here after Lord Stanton's man knocked him out. From the size of the lump, it is a wonder the attack did not kill him!"

William began to stand. "Perhaps I should see to him."

Evan grabbed his arm, stopping him. "Do not bother! He was sleeping when I left but a moment ago."

William sank back into his chair as Mr. Williamson broke in. "Lieutenant Marbury has taken Stefano's men and Mrs. Preston into custody. After consulting with the local constable, who it appears is an old friend of the lieutenant, they agreed that Marbury would escort the guilty parties back to London to be charged. Some of the servants, who were forced to board the coaches but did not wield weapons, will not be held."

Then the vicar put a hand on William's shoulder, causing him to turn. "What has Mr. Kennedy determined about our Lizzybet?"

William did not have time to answer, as the door to the adjoining bedroom opened just then, and everyone focused on the man who appeared in the doorway. Mr. Kennedy, the local physician, stood waiting, eyebrows raised in question, and it was obvious that he was not sure to whom he should report.

Mr. Williamson addressed him. "Would you kindly step into the next room with me, Mr. Kennedy. I am Miss Bennet's vicar, and since she has no family here, I will be pleased to act on her behalf. I have known her since she was born—in fact, I christened her." He smiled to see the disappointment on William's face. "Mr. Darcy, since she has been under your protection for the last few months, perhaps you would join us?" Instantly, William brightened, jumping up to follow them into the empty bedroom.

After they had left the room, Richard leaned in to Evan. "What do you suppose Mrs. Preston's punishment will be? After all, kidnapping is punishable by death, is it not?"

Evan sighed heavily. "I shall have to discuss this with Elizabeth and Darcy. Personally, I would like to see her sent to the penal colony in Australia for the rest of her miserable life. I think that would almost be a fate worse than death to her, but I could not assume to make that recommendation without first hearing their thoughts. In any event, we can only suggest a punishment, as the ultimate decision is left to the courts. The way I see it, she deserves whatever punishment she gets, and she will earn no sympathy from me."

~~~*~~~

"Apart from the cuts on her wrists and on her cheek, both of which I treated, there is only one thing I can find wrong with her." Both William and Mr. Williamson stilled, completely focused on the physician's unsmiling face.

Suddenly Mr. Kennedy smiled and added, "I am afraid she is quite sick of me! She seemed terribly anxious for me to leave so she could see someone, though I shall not hazard a guess as to who it might be." He chuckled and grabbed his bag. "Now, if you gentlemen will excuse me, I need to check on Mr. Avery again before taking my leave."

Neither of Elizabeth's protectors stirred until the man was completely out of the room. But the moment the door closed, William whirled about, heading to the door to the sitting room, obviously determined to see her without further delay.

"May I have a word with you?" Williamson dared to ask, putting a hand on William's arm to stop him. "I had several minutes with Lizzybet prior to your return from your conference with the constable and Mr. Kennedy's arrival." William looked puzzled as he reluctantly halted.

"I know that you are anxious to see her, but I pray you will indulge me for but a minute. Will you?"

William could not object and as he nodded with a wan smile, Williamson chuckled. "I do not imagine I will have much opportunity to speak to either of you once you are reunited, so now must suffice."

The vicar's features softened at the look on Darcy's face. He knew that the young man standing before him truly loved his Lizzybet and would do whatever it took to protect her, even from herself. "Have you considered that she might feel more secure if you stayed with her tonight?"

William's eyebrows rose along with the colour in his face. The truth was that he had been contemplating how to sneak into her room tonight, just to hold her—to comfort her. *Was the vicar actually suggesting he do just that?*

Williamson chuckled at William's expression. "My boy, I am a man as well as a servant of the Lord. And I was married to a woman I loved, so I know how you feel towards Lizzybet."

Embarrassed that the older man had read his mind, William found himself stuttering, "I—I was going to see—to ask Elizabeth what she wanted."

"I already know what she wants." At William's discomposure, Williamson smiled. "She told me minutes ago that she does not want to be separated from you—not even for the night. However, I am sure you wish to do the honourable thing."

William's features darkened. "I love her—I wish to **marry** her."

"Excellent! You have the special license and your mother's ring; it would be no problem for you to marry—secretly if that is your wish—then you may simply repeat the marriage vows in a public display later. It is not completely unheard of to have two ceremonies."

By this time William was smiling broadly. "If Elizabeth agrees, you may arrange whatever you wish. I had her name legally changed to Elizabeth Elise Lawrence before I obtained the special license. My attorney assisted me in recording it; she had only to agree. As for keeping it secret, I think not. If there are public displays planned, let it be celebrations of our marriage in whatever manner Elizabeth desires—even a renewal of our vows."

"I have no doubt she will agree, and I shall be delighted to organize the event. Now, I imagine that she is very unhappy, thinking that you have forgotten her. Go and reassure her while I make the arrangements."

William reached the door in a very few steps. Before he opened it, he looked back over his shoulder. "If I am to marry today, I would like the ceremony to be as early as possible." A huge smile spread across his face, both dimples clearly visibly as he winked at the vicar, then exited.

With one hand Williamson stroked his face, puzzling over what he had seen. "I never knew the man had dimples!"

A private dining room
Early Evening

"And Richard had the coach in the rear pulled to the side of the road by the time we reached him. He had already managed to kill three guards, leaving only two servants, Mrs. Preston, and a young maid in the carriage. Naturally as soon as we rode up, he took off after the other coach as though his horse's tail was afire!"

There was laughter and kidding among the men as they enjoyed refreshments and relaxed in the one room that was large enough to accommodate all of them. Most of those present knew exactly what had transpired that morning, but they enjoyed hearing Evan and Richard recount the story to Mr. Williamson who had just joined them.

Evan took another sip of brandy. "So, we left one man as a guard and went after the other coach."

"It appears we were the lucky ones!" Mr. Williamson declared, nodding at the man who accompanied him to the ship. "We had only to wait until everything was over and arrive here unscathed."

"But had either of those coaches gotten past us, you might have been in the thick of it!" Richard offered in the vicar's defence before answering Evan's tease. "As for my horse's tail being afire, you caught up soon enough."

Evan shrugged. "That was only because Lieutenant Marbury had blocked the road with a carriage."

"Yes, Marbury deserves to be rewarded! He and his men had stopped the coach that held most of the guards and had managed to kill or wound half of them before ever I fired a shot!"

"And when we caught up with you once more," Evan poked Richard in the chest, "what did you do? You took one look and headed back in the direction from whence we had come—without a word of explanation!"

Richard chuckled. "I realised that my cousin was not among you—just as he is missing now! What did you do with him, Vicar?"

Williamson smiled. "I have not done anything ... yet."

"What is that supposed to mean?" Richard and Evan said almost simultaneously.

"You will just have to wait and see," the vicar replied with a knowing smile as he picked up a leg of chicken.

Elizabeth's Bedroom

"You really do not mind being married as Elizabeth Elise Lawrence?"

"No. Except for my association with Papa and Jane, my surname holds painful memories. I care not what is on the license. My only desire is to be Elizabeth Darcy."

"And you do not mind marrying on such short notice? I do not want to rush you or make you do anything you do not—"

Soft lips, driven into his, erased every syllable of William's speech from his memory as he succumbed to her spell. Their bodies melting into each other as Elizabeth ran her hands over his chest, eager to touch him, she began unbuttoning his waistcoat. At the same time, William traced the curve of her spine with his fingers before sliding them down to the soft roundness of her bottom. With a groan, he pulled her hips tight against his, lifting her slightly so she could feel his growing hardness.

"Oh, Elizabeth!" William gasped, as he scattered hot, wet kisses to her ear, down her neck and across her décolletage. There he tugged the neckline of her dress down a bit, attempting to savour even more of her soft skin. "Tell me to stop!"

Instead, she responded even more passionately. Having succeeded in unbuttoning his shirt, she ran soft hands over his bare chest, and it was with great effort that William remembered that they were only one door away from a roomful of people. Pushing her to arm's length, he pleaded hoarsely, "Please, darling, let me regain control of myself!"

Nonetheless, seeing the desire in her ebony eyes, his lips claimed hers again. At length he broke the embrace, pulling her across the room towards an overstuffed chair. Roughly, he sat down, drawing her into his lap and clutching her so tightly she could scarcely draw breath. For some time he sat with his head buried in the crook of her neck, both of them listening to his laboured breathing. Once it returned to normal, William lifted his head and pulled her forward so he could kiss the tip of her nose.

"Do you have any idea how much I love you? How much I desire you?"

Tears pooled in her eyes. "As much as I love and desire you."

Their lips could not stay parted, and they met again, but this time the kiss was gentle. "If we are to marry today, I must leave you to prepare." Elizabeth nodded. "I shall ask if there is a maid who can help you dress." Suddenly, he drew back to look at her. "Will you mind not having a proper dress?"

Shaking her head vigorously, she kissed him lightly, eliciting a small groan. "As long as you are the groom, I care not for the trappings."

His response was a passionate kiss. He ran his tongue inside her mouth, exploring every inch of the velvety surface before her tongue began to duel his. Close to losing control again, William quit the kiss and stood, causing her to slide off his lap. He caught hold of her, bringing her into a tight embrace and rubbing his arousal against her, smiling roguishly.

"If I do not leave this instant, I shall take you here and now, and Mr. Williamson's preparations will be for naught!"

Elizabeth giggled as he pulled her with him to the door. With a very quick kiss, he exited, closing the door behind him. She was still staring at it when a soft knock drew her attention. Opening it, she expected to find William, but instead, found the proprietor's wife, smiling from ear to ear.

~~~*~~~

Abby Barnwell was a very refined looking woman. She dressed in gowns that were more elegant than was customary for an innkeeper's wife, and she had an air about her that mirrored her upbringing as a gentleman's daughter. Though she was still quite handsome at fifty, there was noticeable grey in her dark brown hair. Her green eyes, however, twinkled with genuine friendliness and concern. Over the years, she had made preparations for many weddings, the Barnwell's personal parlour having been the site of many a ceremony among their family and friends, and she was determined that the small event she now supervised would be perfect—or as perfect as could be had on such short notice.

As she surveyed the still elegant space, she sighed to think of how things had changed. Her family had once been of Mr. Darcy's circle before her father had lost everything by gambling and had run off leaving them penniless. In fact, George Darcy, a Cambridge classmate of her father, Martin Burris, had helped her mother purchase this old manor and turn it into a boarding house so that they would have an income.

Now, examining her handiwork—the polished silver, the linens and flowers— Mrs. Barnwell smiled. Fitzwilliam Darcy probably did not know their connection, especially since they had changed the name of the establishment when she and Mr. Barnwell married. If he did, he had never given any indication of it. After all, he was just a small child when it happened whereas she was a young woman. But with her mother's constant talk of Mr. Darcy's intervention, Mrs. Barnwell would never forget and being aware of their connection, she was determined to partially repay his father's benevolence by hosting a wedding for his son.

"Finish with that silver now, Margaret!" she prodded one of the maids. "There is no reason the candelabrums should not shine as bright as the mirrors. Did Maddie find the vases for the flowers?"

"Yes, madam," the younger girl answered. "She is putting them in water, and then she is going to bring the linens for the tables. The pianoforte has already been dusted. Will you be playing some wedding music?"

"I believe I may, if the couple would like it." She smiled thinking of the times she had heard her mother talk of entertaining guests in this very room. "I have not played nearly enough this last year, so I shall practice the pieces quickly, if you do not object to listening."

She did just that, to Margaret and Maddie's delight, since the older maid returned in time to hear as well. After several minutes, it was evident that she still remembered the beautiful songs she had played for the last wedding. Satisfied, Mrs. Barnwell headed to the door.

"I must see how Carrie is coming with the gown, if Cook has finished the cake and how Aggie is managing with the cottage. Now, keep busy, girls! We have only until seven o'clock!"

As their mistress exited the room, the two maids giggled, Maddie declaring, "One would think the Mistress was marrying off her own daughter the way she is carrying on!"

"She even brought the young miss over to the family's rooms to get dressed. Well, we had better hurry," Margaret noted, placing one of the clean linen runners on the sideboard. "She will be back before we know it, wanting to know why we have not finished!"

A bedroom in the private quarters

Elizabeth stood on a small stool as the maid went around pinning up the hem of her dress—or rather, the dress Mrs. Barnwell had found for her. Upon learning that she did not have a decent dress in which to be married, the kind proprietor had insisted that she try on a satin and lace confection that once belonged to her daughter. Elizabeth had to admit that it was certainly lovelier than any of the muslin frocks that she had stuffed into her bag.

"My Pauline wore it only once! She outgrew all her clothes the summer she turned eighteen. She is almost as tall as her father now! I have kept it all these years, as it cost me a fortune, and I did not have the heart to have it redesigned. I was hoping to have a granddaughter who might need it." She laughed. "That will never happen."

She watched Elizabeth run a finger over the bruise and cut Stefano had left on her cheek. "Do not fret, dear. I have powder to cover that." She searched through a drawer, quickly pulling out a jar. "Here is what we need!" She took a very small brush and dusted a flesh coloured powder over the wound making it almost invisible.

At last the maid was finished with the hem and stepped back. Abby Barnwell sighed. "Oh, miss. You look like a princess!" Elizabeth blushed. "Now, where did I put those pins with the tiny flowers on them? They will look wonderful in your dark hair!" She began pulling items out of other drawers of the dressing table, first one thing out and then another. "Oh, here they are!"

"Carrie, take the dress and hem it quickly, while Suzanne and I arrange Miss Elizabeth's hair! Carrie laid the dress carefully over her arm and started from the room. "Make haste, girl! We do not have much time!"

A sitting room

Mr. Williamson joined Richard and Evan in the sitting room that connected their bedrooms. They were making plans to leave in the morning and wanted to discuss who would be riding in William's coach. He did not mention the plans that he had executed, nor would he, as it was not his secret to reveal.

"I assume I shall ride back with William, but I have not spoken to him about it," he replied casually in answer to Richard's query.

"Where is my elusive cousin?" Richard complained. "I imagine I shall have to forcibly remove him from Miss Elizabeth's room so that she can get some rest." Everyone chuckled at his jest.

"I, for one, want to leave at first light!" Evan proclaimed. "Ana will be worried, and I do not want her to suffer unnecessarily. Besides," he said candidly, "I miss my girls."

Richard chuckled. "I was about to say that, when you volunteered the information! You would never make a soldier—having to be gone for months." He had ordered a bottle of brandy and had just poured himself a drink, holding up the bottle. "Would either of you like one?"

Mr. Williamson stated, more calmly than he felt, "I would love a small glass." Richard proceeded to pour two fingers and handed him the glass just as a knock came at the door.

Evan opened it, revealing the innkeeper's wife, Abby Barnwell, smiling brilliantly and looking very satisfied with herself.

Seeing Mr. Williamson over Evan's shoulder, she raised her chin and winked at him, raising the other men's suspicions. And just as Richard and Evan exchanged quizzical glances, she made an announcement.

"The happy couple awaits you in the family parlour, Reverend. Everyone, just follow me, if you please."

Richard heard the glass shatter as his drink crashed into the hard wood of the floor.

~~~*~~~

Chapter 40

Mr. Walker barely had time to open Pemberley's front door before Georgiana flew through, Millie in her arms. She gasped for breath as she began addressing Mr. Walker animatedly before he could begin to greet her properly.

"They are coming home—Elizabeth, William, Richard, Evan! They shall begin their journey home tomorrow morning! Only two men were injured, Mr. Avery and Mr. Judson, and both of them are expected to fully recover. God has answered our prayers!"

Before the butler could say a word in reply, footsteps alerted them to the approach of Mrs. Reynolds who was coming from the direction of her office. Mille, having just been set on her feet, began running towards the housekeeper, and as the child got closer, the elderly woman stooped to catch the bundle of energy.

Rising with the child in her arms, she practically beamed with happiness. "Yes, we have received an express as well! It will be so good to have them home." She tilted her head to look down at Millie, "I imagine you will be glad to see your papa."

"Papa?" Millie responded and then craned her head to look behind at her mother. "Papa?" she repeated to Georgiana.

"Yes, we have talked about Papa coming home." Georgiana moved close to rub Millie's back affectionately as she addressed the housekeeper.

"Millie goes to the windows to look at the front drive when we are in the drawing room. She knows that Papa always rides up the drive when he returns from his morning exercise. When one of the servants asked me about Evan yesterday, she ran to the window and pulled back the curtain to peer out."

Both servants laughed aloud. "It does not take children long to figure things out," the old butler exclaimed. "I remember when Mr. Darcy had the servants search the house to find Master William one summer's day when he was barely four."

Mrs. Reynolds interrupted, "I remember that too! He was hiding because he thought he was going to be punished for breaking his mother's favourite vase."

"Yes!" Mr. Walker continued. "And all the time we were searching for him he was atop the ladder in the library, sitting partially on the ladder and partially on the last bookshelf. He was so quiet and still that no one noticed him. Thank God he did not fall."

"And, poor Mr. Darcy was so relieved that the child was found and that he would not have to report back to Lady Anne that their son was lost, that he never did punish him," Mrs. Reynolds finished as everyone had a chuckle.

Mr. Walker was the first to sober. "It will be so good to have them home, although I shall miss my good friend, Mr. Judson."

"Yes, and poor Mr. Avery, too. Evan explained that Mr. Judson agreed to stay behind with him until he is well enough to travel," Georgiana volunteered. "I have no idea how Brother and I could have been so blessed to have such loyal, trustworthy servants."

The butler and housekeeper both coloured. "We feel that we are the ones who have been blessed," Mrs. Reynolds replied.

Just then, Millie spied Margaret, a young maid who often played with her at Pemberley, coming towards them and began to point to her. "I suppose you want Margaret to play with you," Mrs. Reynolds stated, glancing at Millie and then her mother. "Do you mind?"

"Of course, not. Give Mama a kiss." Millie leaned in to kiss her mother's cheek, and then Mrs. Reynolds handed her to Margaret, who had halted when she saw the party in the foyer included her little friend.

"Take her to the conservatory and let her play," Mrs. Reynolds instructed, and as Margaret headed in that direction, she kept up a one-sided conversation all the while.

"What will you want to do first, little miss? Will you be riding the rocking horse or shall we find your ball and ..."

Georgiana followed their progress, smiling at Margaret's banter until they were out of sight, then enquired, "Could I have a minute of your time, Mrs. Reynolds?"

"Of course, you may. Would you like to go to my office or the drawing room?"

"The drawing room," Georgiana said, immediately heading in that direction with Mrs. Reynolds on her heels. They had no more gotten into the room and closed the door, before William's sister looked both ways, as though she was not sure they were alone, and whispered conspiratorially, "We shall have a wedding to plan very shortly."

The old servant smiled at Georgiana's enthusiasm. "You may be correct."

"I am correct! And after the wedding, I shall want to have a grand reception at Rosewood and invite everyone in Derbyshire and half of London. Will you help me to plan it?"

"Perhaps you had better wait until the Master informs us of his plans— cart before the horse and all that."

"I know I should wait, but I am so excited!" Her voice got higher as she continued. "Who would have thought when William brought Miss Elizabeth to Pemberley that she would become my sister? She is free—free to marry and have lots of children, so Millie will have plenty of cousins as playmates."

"My, my! We have gone from wedding receptions to children in two sentences," Abigail Reynolds chuckled.

"I am awful! I know I am! But I have waited for this day for so long!" Georgiana stepped into the middle of the room and began turning in a circle like a child, arms straight out and eyes closed. She practically shouted. "My brother is getting married! Do you hear, Pemberley? You are to have a mistress once again, and the sounds of children's laughter will be heard echoing down your halls!"

Laughing and crying at the same time, Mrs. Reynolds reached out to steady her as she came to a wobbly stop. "Well, in order that we both do not get into trouble, I suggest we wait until the engagement is announced, then I shall be more than willing to help you plan any number of soirees. Is that acceptable?"

Georgiana nodded her head in concurrence as she took hold of both the housekeeper wrinkled hands. "You have been like a mother to William and me, so I do not have to ask if you approve. You must be thrilled, as I can tell you love Elizabeth as much as William and I do."

"At first I was determined to like Miss Elizabeth because I knew the Master cared for her. Later, as I learned her story and saw her fortitude in trying to overcome circumstances that would have crushed most young women, I admired her. But, I must confess, it was her regard for our dear boy that made me love her. Though I did not agree with the solution, she truly loved your brother enough to put his welfare before her own—willing to leave Pemberley rather than risk some harm coming to him. And that is why I know she will be the perfect mate for him and the ideal Mistress for Pemberley."

"I could not have said it better. Elizabeth is the kind of woman I always wished my brother to marry. And to think that I was entirely wrong about her in the beginning, refusing to allow myself to see past her injuries and her circumstances—to see their bond. I am not sure if I actually professed my faults to either of them, so when she returns I shall confess my failings, ask their forgiveness and acknowledge that they are ideally matched."

Mrs. Reynolds reached to take Georgiana's hand. "That is one of your most endearing qualities—you have never been too proud to admit your mistakes."

A tear slid down Georgiana's face. "I always wanted you to be proud of me."

Mrs. Reynolds pulled her into a hug. "You have made it very easy, my sweet girl."

Barnwell's Boarding House
The Family Parlour

Abby Barnwell stood at the door to the parlour beaming at her handiwork. She was immensely proud to have put together a proper wedding, including a lovely cake and refreshments with very little notice.

All the furniture had been moved out of the parlour, except for the pianoforte, and a large sideboard holding the refreshments and some tables along the wall. A few smaller, wooden chairs had been added so that the guests could sit and enjoy the refreshments afterward. A latticework trellis, made by her husband for just such occasions, had been placed at the front of the room. It was painted white, and lace was interwoven throughout the lattice. She always added fresh greenery with every wedding, weaving it in with the delicate lace. That greenery, along with flowers in crystal vases on every available surface, made the space a veritable garden.

Having used most of her mother's best china, crystal and silverware, the entire room seemed to glow as candles reflected off every surface, including the mirrors along the walls and in the midst of all this finery stood a beautifully decorated cake. Initially meant for the family's dinner, it had been diverted with excellent results as the cook had been instructed to decorate it with white frosting and faux flowers, making it proper wedding fare. Punch filled a large crystal bowl, and plates of tarts and scones and small sandwiches surrounded it.

Tears filled her eyes, as they always did before a wedding. The thought that some young couple would once again pledge their troth in her home and begin their lives as one always gave her pause—that it was George Darcy's son and his bride made it all the sweeter. Taking a satisfying deep breath, Mrs. Barnwell set out to notify the vicar that all was in place, since Mr. Darcy had already been informed.

~~~*~~~

331

As Richard and Evan followed Mrs. Barnwell into the family section of the boarding house, Richard leaned over to whisper, "I will not believe any of this until I actually see it happen."

Evan chuckled. "I know what you mean, but why is it so hard for either of us to believe?"

"Do you realise how many years I have wished to see my cousin happy? I know that marrying Elizabeth will make him deliriously so, but for this event to be accomplished so quickly and at so unlikely a time—it is like a dream."

Before Richard had finished speaking, they reached the parlour and both stopped short at the entrance, amazed. The parlour had been converted to a wedding chapel. Their gazes fell on those standing along the side—the servants who had come from Derbyshire, evidently some Barnwell family members and a few of the Barnwell's servants. Mrs. Barnwell smiled at the people assembled as she passed through them on her way to the pianoforte.

As she began playing the music she had rehearsed earlier, Richard and Evan had still not moved and Richard breathed, "My word!"

"My sentiments exactly!" Evan whispered in return. "I did not expect to see anything this impressive. Now I am actually starting to believe that my brother is getting married." Their private conversation was cut short as an arm slid around each of their shoulders.

"Believe it! I am to be married today, and I am proud to have both of you to stand up with me." William was barely able to contain his joy as he pulled both men along with him to the front of the room. Just as they reached the altar, Mr. Williamson hurried around all of them, taking his place beneath the trellis.

"I was delayed, as Lizzybet asked me to find her Bible and use it to conduct the ceremony." He handed the Bible to William. "Would you hold this while I position everyone?" As he handed William the Bible, a paper fluttered to the floor unnoticed by everyone but William.

While Williamson was busy pointing out where Richard and Evan were to stand, William stooped to retrieve what had a fallen—a letter. Instantly he recognised his handwriting and knew it was the letter he had given Elizabeth in Kent. A sharp pang of regret pierced his heart to know that she had kept it all this time. At that very moment, Mrs. Barnwell changed the music to indicate that the bride was about to enter the room, so William could do nothing but place the letter in his coat pocket as he was afraid it might fall again during the ceremony.

As Elizabeth appeared at the door, all murmuring halted, and the room went silent except for the sound of the music. Mouths were agape at the vision of loveliness that was the bride. She wore a satin gown that could easily have been fashioned for her. The cap sleeves were off the shoulder and the bodice was low but not excessively so. Delicately embroidered blue flowers covered the bodice and sleeves, while a deep flounce of Brussels lace was featured on the hem and a smaller band edged the sleeves.

Elizabeth's dark curls were piled atop her head, except for three long tendrils, fashioned into curls that hung over her right shoulder. Interspersed in her hair were the small white, flowerlike pins that Mrs. Barnwell had discovered in the dressing room. She wore pearl earrings and a single white pearl on a silver chain—on loan from Abby Barnwell as well. For a few seconds, she stood perfectly still as though waiting for some sign.

William, resplendent in his black coat and breeches, had just handed Mr. Williamson the Bible and turned to see her. His dimples were impossible to hide as a wide grin split his face. This display of happiness by the Master of Pemberley was more than any of the servants from Derbyshire had ever seen, and instantly there were murmurings among them. As servants and family alike looked from one half of the couple to the other, the principals locked eyes. Seeing her hesitation, William held out both hands, and Elizabeth slowly began walking towards him—towards her destiny.

As their hands met, their fingers entwined and neither could look away from the other. Seeing their devotion, Mr. Williamson did not demand their attention but instead solemnly began the ceremony. "Dearly beloved ..."

Just as both parties had requested, unbeknownst one to the other, he kept the service very short. The words of the ceremony seemed only on occasion to penetrate the consciousness of the young couple, and he soon learned to touch an arm or hand when a response was needed. After a few words on the sanctity of marriage, he leaned in to tap William's arm, requesting, "Repeat after me."

"I, Fitzwilliam Alexander George Darcy, take thee, Elizabeth Elise Lawrence, to my wedded wife, to have and to hold from this day forward, for better for worse, for richer for poorer, in sickness and in health, to love and to cherish, till death us do part, according to God's holy ordinance; and thereto I give thee my troth."

As William concluded his pledge, Elizabeth began without prompting, "I, Elizabeth Elise Lawrence, take thee, Fitzwilliam Alexander George Darcy, to my wedded husband, to have and to hold from this day forward, for better for worse, for richer for poorer, in sickness and in health, to love, cherish, and to obey, till death us do part, according to God's holy ordinance; and thereto I give thee my troth."

The rector did not have to ask for the ring, as William had already taken it from his pocket and, as Elizabeth finished her vows, he gently slipped his mother's ring onto the third finger of her trembling left hand. So overcome with emotion that his eyes were now almost as dark as Elizabeth's, William recited his last vow with an intensity seldom witnessed in such a setting.

"With this ring I thee wed, with my body I thee worship, and with all my worldly goods I thee endow: in the name of the Father, and of the Son, and of the Holy Ghost, Amen."

Not disturbed in the least that the ceremony had been taken out of his hands, Mr. Williamson looked from one to the other with a full heart as he intoned in his most solemn voice, "Those whom God hath joined together, let no man put asunder!"

Everyone waited, but William and Elizabeth did not move. Before Mr. Williamson could prompt William to kiss his bride, Richard pushed his cousin towards Elizabeth, offering, "If you do not kiss her, I shall!"

Immediately William leaned in to capture Elizabeth's lips and cheers rang out among the spectators. After a few moments, it was obvious that the couple were caught up in their happiness, so Richard gently chided, "That is enough, Darce. Save it for the honeymoon."

Instantly remembering where he was, William pulled back, blushing furiously. For her part, Elizabeth coloured, too, but not from embarrassment in regards to the kiss. Knowing that he was finally hers and she was his brought a realisation of what was to come. And if making love with William brought just a small measure of the pleasure that his kisses created, she was not only unafraid, but eager to spend the night in her husband's arms.

Her husband!

Elizabeth's heart soared, and she held back tears of joy as she and William turned to acknowledge the well-wishers who surged forward to congratulate them. And as they spoke words of encouragement that she barely heard, she felt William's warm hand begin to slide possessively up and down her back—the gentle pressure of his fingers conveying the need he could not express. Her eyes almost fluttered shut at the contact, but she managed to recover as this same hand moved to her waist and pulled her to stand closer to him.

~~~*~~~

Chapter 41

Barnwell's Boarding House

Hand in hand, William and Elizabeth made their way down a torch-lit gravel path that wound its way through the pleasant gardens behind the boarding house and beyond the stables, finally coming to a stop in front of a picturesque masonry cottage. Mrs. Barnwell had taken them aside after the wedding to tell them of her plans for them to spend their wedding night in this special place.

"It was my mother's home during her last few years. She was tired of all the noise from the boarding house, so we sold the last of her jewels and built this especially for her. I allow only certain guests use of it, as it is very dear to me—all these furnishings were hers from before ..." Her voice caught and then she laughed self-consciously. *"Well, never mind all that!"* The handkerchief used to staunch the tears that had begun at the wedding was put to good use once more. *"There are only a few rooms, but they are excellently appointed, and you are welcome to stay as long as you like."* She reached to take a hand of each of them. *"You will remember tonight for as long as you live and cherish the memories. Do not be in a rush to leave in the morning."*

Before Elizabeth could utter a word in praise of the beautiful structure, William swept her off her feet, and she giggled as he carried her up the steps. At the door, he managed to turn the knob without putting her down and, once over the threshold, kicked the door shut with his foot.

Kissing her lightly, though not willing to put her down, he asked, "Would you care for a glass of wine?" As he spoke, he tilted his head towards a bottle chilling in a bucket on a nearby table, next to a plate of refreshments just like the ones at their reception.

Her gaze never leaving his, Elizabeth shook her head vigorously. "I had wine enough during the toasts."

"Something to eat?"

More determined shaking of her head was his only answer.

"Then do you wish to have the bedchamber to yourself for a short while to change?"

"No."

William's brows rose and he could not suppress a slight smile at his determined wife. "No?" he asked expectantly.

"No," she said firmly. "I have waited so long William ... dreamed of this so many nights ... I do not intend to wait a second more—no conversation, no wine, no food. In spite of what dear Mrs. Barnwell said, we leave early in the morning, so let us not waste a moment of our wedding night in a misguided attempt to be proper."

With this daring pronouncement, William was lost. He captured her mouth with such intensity that she could barely breathe, and not quitting the kiss, he began to make his way through the open door to the bedchamber, almost stumbling in his haste. Once inside, he set her down on the thick Oriental carpet, and both of their heads turned as they gaped at the large, ornate bed that took up the greater part of the room. A roaring fire glowed in the hearth, revealing an upholstered chair, an elegant bedside table and a lamp that completed the furnishings.

As each turned back to the other, smiling a little nervously, it was only a moment until they were engaged in another sensuous kiss, hands freely exploring previously forbidden places and before long, both were engaged in frantic attempts to remove what clothing separated them. William, however, found his fingers quite ineffective as he fumbled with the small buttons on the back of Elizabeth's dress, while Elizabeth's delicate fingers were almost as useless on the heavier buttons that held William's waistcoat.

With subdued laughter, Elizabeth broke their kiss, her eyes crinkling and her lips lifting in a crooked smile as she looked up at William. "I do believe, Husband, that we shall accomplish our tasks much more quickly if we each undress ourselves."

"Indeed!" William replied smiling broadly, dimples flashing. "I knew I married a very wise and accomplished woman!"

William continued to coax her lips with his as they simultaneously shed layers of clothing, thrilling at the feelings created and at her responses. Once down to her thin chemise and his breeches, they broke apart, both taking great gasps of air. Quickly William lifted her, setting her on the side of the bed, where he immediately dispatched her shoes, tossing first one then the other over his shoulder to her lilting laughter. Then he methodically began rolling one silky stocking after the other down her slender legs—all the while willing himself to control his ardour, even as he devoured her with his eyes.

Satisfied with his progress, William promptly pulled her to her feet and tight against his body. Mesmerized, she felt one large hand begin a slow journey down her body, the heat of it burning through the thin fabric of the chemise as it moved over her breast, down her toned stomach, still further to her thigh where he grasped the hem of the garment. In one fluid motion, he lifted it up and over her head, leaving her completely exposed. Entranced, he took a step back to drink in the magnificence that was his wife, her body bathed in the soft glow of the fire. She heard his slow, deep intake of breath as his eyes travelled from her generous breasts to her slim waist, flat stomach and still further. She found herself blushing in spite of her resolve not to do so.

However, emboldened by his continued inspection, Elizabeth slowly removed the flowerlike pins from her hair and shook her head, allowing untamed dark curls to fall down around her shoulders, her breasts now peeking through the silky curtain. William stood spellbound, so she stepped forward to take his hands and pull him back to her. As their bodies met, his hands slid from her waist to her breasts, where he began to slowly palm and then cup each soft mound. She sighed, closing her eyes and leaning into him as he ran a thumb over the dark centres until they hardened, causing his arousal to harden in response.

Driven from his spell by her soft sighs and his growing need, William picked her up and moved to the bed where the dark blue and gold counterpane and the silk sheets were already turned back, awaiting them. Laying her down gently, he placed one tender kiss on her lips before turning to perch on the end of the bed to remove his boots. Once accomplished, he hastily shucked off his breeches and lay down beside her.

Murmuring words of adoration, he placed wet kisses over every trace of her softly scented skin, the evidence of his passion leaving red marks on her fair complexion. "My love, my only love, you taste so sweet." He gently nipped, then kissed the place at the curve of her neck causing her to writhe and pleased by her response, spread more kisses across her collarbone before continuing down the valley between her breasts. "I have longed for you so long," he whispered, his voice rough..

Elizabeth moaned as a fire rushed through her, and she entwined her fingers in his hair. "I have loved you so long, my darling. Make me yours. Love me."

Without another word, William rolled atop her—a groan of pleasure escaping his throat as their bodies melded one into the other. He had felt her flinch the moment they became one, however, and opening his eyes in concern for her comfort, he found her dark eyes swimming with unshed tears, as well as unfathomable love.

"I love you so," she whispered, cupping his face and bringing his lips back to hers. Breathlessly, they continued their kiss as he made her his own.

Though he was determined to be gentle, William found it progressively difficult to concentrate on anything but the pleasure of being inside the woman he loved—to know that, from this moment on, every part of her was his to touch, to love. As he began to feel as though he had left his body, Elizabeth's responses brought him back to the present as a quivering deep inside her assured him that she had reached fulfilment. All else was forgotten then as he pursued his own release and found himself falling off a precipice into an ocean of exquisite waves of bliss, and from somewhere afar, he called her name.

For some time afterward, they lay joined together, neither willing to sever the connection as their breathing returned to normal and they floated slowly down from the pinnacle of their lovemaking.

At length, he bestowed a soft kiss on her swollen lips, very tenderly whispering, "You are everything to me, Elizabeth—my friend, my wife, my lover, the very air that I breathe. And from this day forward, we are one—husband and wife. Come what may, we shall face the future together."

Elizabeth wept, too overcome by his words and what they had just shared to form an answer. He understood the depth of her emotions as, without saying a word, her fingers dug into his back, straining to pull him closer still while she clung to him as though she would never let him go. He felt exactly the same.

Being fatigued from the events of the last few days, they were in the arms of Morpheus in a short while, despite both their wishes to remain awake. Each was soon lost in dreams of the other.

In a Coach on the road to Derbyshire

"What do you think Darce will do when he finds we have left them to come home alone?" Richard asked, leaning across to address Evan while trying not to awaken a now sleeping Mr. Williamson who sat next to him.

Evan smiled. "I think he will be delighted. After all, what man wants to spend the first day of his marriage in the company of a coach full of people—especially other men?"

Glancing out the window to make sure the coach he hired for his servants was still following along behind, Evan relaxed and trained his eyes on his cousin. "I think your idea to hire another coach and for you and Williamson to ride back with me was a splendid wedding present. They may have to travel back to Pemberley on their wedding trip, but they can certainly have the coach to themselves. I hope that we are able to have the inn hold their best rooms for them tonight."

Richard chuckled to himself. "The only thing I dislike is that I missed my chance to tease Darce this morning. I suppose I shall be forced to wait until he gets home. What a shame! I have waited almost ten years for this day to come, and I was not there to confront him after his wedding night! I would dearly love to have made him blush!"

"William blush? I do not know that I have even seen him do that. Scowl perhaps, but not blush."

"Oh, he has many times, believe me. Once I stood nearby at a ball when a young woman, newly widowed, made my poor cousin one of the most obscene offers I have ever overheard. And I am used to hearing all manner of talk in the army! It embarrassed even me!"

"And he blushed?"

"As red as my regimentals! Naturally, he had to leave the ballroom, and of course, he was angry, which always makes him even redder. But I have seen him blush on many occasions."

"My word! I would never have believed it."

"Believe it! In spite of his facade of worldliness, William has lived a very sheltered life. He has not taken full advantage of what his wealth and position could have afforded." Richard waged his brows mischievously. "You know what I mean— loose ladies, widows and such. He is still, in essence, very much an innocent when it comes to women, so he can be embarrassed quite easily. I would have loved to have teased him about his *enjoyment* of last night."

"I can only imagine!" Evan grinned. "Ana has often mentioned the many times, before we married, of course, that she followed him around at various balls and dinners to keep the ladies at bay. I just assumed he was immune to it by now."

"Never!" Richard crowed. "Your dear brother will never be used to being the object of the fantasies of the female masses!"

Evan laughed aloud, covering his mouth as he glanced over at the now stirring vicar. "I suppose Elizabeth shall now be in charge of protecting her husband's virtue."

Richard guffawed, causing Mr. Williamson to open one eye. He went on to declare. "Why do I have the feeling that Elizabeth can handle with aplomb anyone who tries to dally with her husband?"

"Perhaps, because it is true!" Williamson retorted, striving to sit up straight as he stretched to relieve his aching back. "My Lizzybet is a strong woman, and she will suffer no fools! Anyone, man or woman, who tries to come between them, or heaven forbid, harm Fitzwilliam, will find that out straightaway! Why, I remember her giving Martin Long a black eye once for pulling Jane's pigtails! She was fearless!"

"I do not think I would want to be in Lady Leighton's shoes if she ever tries a trick again like the last one she attempted with my cousin!"

Williamson nodded. "Lizzybet may be small, but she can be lethal with a weapon, and she is not above using one to even the odds. Once she hit John Lucas in the back of the head with a stone using only a slingshot. She must have been all of six years at the time, and she hit him from at least fifty feet away."

Richard guffawed, "And the poor boy's crime?"

"Trying to give her cat an unwanted swim in the pond."

As the vicar continued to spin tales of Elizabeth's prowess as a champion of the oppressed, whether man or beast, the coach erupted often with copious amounts of laughter, drawing the attention of the three footmen and the driver on the outside of the conveyance more than once.

Unknown to the Master of Rosewood, Colonel Fitzwilliam and Mr. Williamson, the servants raised their brows and smiled at one another with every loud outburst, though none were impertinent enough to remark on the merriment inside the coach. They were just pleased that the men were in good spirits, the weather was fair, the roads were passable, and they were sure to make their next stop, an inn within three hours of Lambton, before nightfall. They were going home!

Barnwell's Boarding House
The cottage

A feeling of numbness in his right arm brought William out of his sleep while the room was yet shrouded in darkness. As he tried to move, he realised that some type of weight lay on his arm and opened his eyes to find that he was clutching a soft, lavender-scented body tightly to his chest. Underneath a silk sheet, a naked torso lay half-way across his chest—while an arm and a leg stretched to his other side, as if trying to assure he could not escape. In the crook of his neck, hidden inside a halo of unruly, ebony curls, a face was buried. *Elizabeth!*

His heart swelled with love at the realisation that he would wake in a similarly pleasant manner for the rest of his days. A contented sigh escaped him then at the remembrance of the night's lovemaking. Loneliness was now a thing of the past! She was his forevermore!

Suddenly, reality invaded his euphoria. Shortly others would expect them to board a coach to transport them home to Pemberley. The thought of having to spend the entire day sitting next to her in a coach full of men, but not being able to touch her, made him begin to ache. Perhaps if they could make love just once more this morning, he would be able to survive until they reached the inn in the evening.

William's first thought was that he wanted their next joining to be slower and gentler than the last. Last night they were both lost in long suppressed desires and their lovemaking was fervent—impassioned. Today he intended to take his time while loving her. Placing a kiss atop the mass of curls he whispered, "My love?"

Elizabeth mumbled something unintelligible and tried to burrow deeper into him, her arm and leg gripping him even tighter. William smiled, profoundly content with her show of possessiveness. With one quick motion, he rolled to his right side taking her with him, so that she was lying on her back. Her eyes barely opened to observe him. The sight of her uncovered breasts instantly made him harden in desire, and as he captured one soft mound in his mouth, his tongue began a slow circle around the tip, causing it to harden as well.

As his attentions continued, her hands slid up to capture his unruly hair and she moaned, fanning the flames of his desires. In mere moments, they were joined again, only this time William made sure to keep himself under rigid control. Slowly moving in and out, he took Elizabeth to the heights of passion until she cried out for release, and only then did he allow himself to plummet into that same pleasure. Afterward they lay tangled, breathless.

"Oh, William, making love with you is so wonderful! I never dreamed it could be like this!" Elizabeth murmured, pulling his mouth down to hers for another passionate kiss. When she released him, he was grinning from ear to ear, and she laughed aloud at the look on his face. "Proud as a peacock, I see! And rightfully so, I might add!"

"Proud that you are my wife and that we are so well-matched. I want nothing more than to satisfy your every desire—whether it be in our bed or any other area of our lives. I truly want us to become one, Elizabeth."

"That is my desire as well," she answered contentedly before her dark eyes became sombre and began searching his earnestly. "This means there can be no secrets between us. Do you want to know what I wish for most at this very moment?"

"I will always want to know your heart's desire."

She touched his face tenderly. "My heart desires a child—your child, William." He could not conceal the love shining suspiciously like tears in his eyes. "I have waited years for you, my darling, and I want to proceed with the business of living—of filling Pemberley with our children. I need the sounds of laugher of family all about me—happy and content. And you, sweet William? What do you wish for at this moment?"

"We are no longer starry-eyed youths, and I am more than ready to be a father, Elizabeth," he said earnestly. "As long as you are their mother, I long for children, too."

She leaned in to place a soft kiss on his mouth, teasing, "Then, I believe, Husband, that all that is left for us to do is to practice. As Lady Catherine once told me, no one can be a proficient if they do not practice! And you would not want her to think us remiss in our commitment to excellence."

William could not help but chuckle. "I believe this is the only time that you shall hear me agree with anything my aunt has ever said. But I beg you, for the sake of our felicity, do not mention her name again on our honeymoon!"

He punctuated his request by tickling her, and their horseplay quickly became serious as they settled in to practice diligently what they had learned once more. It was long past the hour for them to meet the others at the coach when they finally were dressed for the trip.

The Barnwell's Boarding House

"Should I take a tray of food and drink to the cottage? The Darcys have not appeared to break their fast."

Maddie's question brought Abby Barnwell out of her daydream, and she turned to see the maid holding a platter of sweet rolls that was destined for the dining room.

Maddie continued with a sly grin. "They have not appeared in the dining room, and most of the guests have eaten, except a few stragglers. There may be nothing left by the time they remember to eat." Her slight teasing was not lost on the proprietor.

"What? Oh, heavens, no! Leave the newly wedded couple alone! It would be most improper to interrupt them. They will appear when they are good and ready. Our duty is to have plenty of food and drink available for them whenever that may be."

Maddie curtsied and left, a bright blush filling her cheeks at the thought of what occupied the couple instead of finding the time to eat. As she moved into the dining room, Margaret passed her on the way back to the kitchen as she returned with some dirty dishes.

"Have the Darcys come out of the cottage yet?" Margaret enquired, a big grin on her face. She knew full well that they had not, as she and Maddie had been going on about their absence all morning.

"You had better wipe that smile off your face before the Mistress sees it. She has just chastised me for asking if I should take them a tray of food. She says we should just let them be, as we might be *interrupting* them." They both giggled.

"*Interrupting?* What might we interrupt in the broad daylight?"

Maddie, who was nearly seven years older than eighteen-year-old Margaret, smiled knowingly. "You have much to learn about men and women. I have been here six years, and I could tell you many stories about what goes on in the broad daylight, newlyweds or not!"

Now it was Margaret's time to blush. "I ... I had better get these dishes to the kitchen."

As she hurried to finish her job, Margaret pondered the implications of Maddie's comments. Many times she had heard strange noises as she made her way down the halls of the boarding house. Once she had even summoned Mrs. Barnwell to the hall outside the last bedroom on the first floor, sure that the moans and groans coming from behind the closed door indicated that the guests inside were sick. The proprietress had promptly sent her to do another chore, insisting that she would handle the situation.

Her face now burned. *Perhaps they were not in any distress at all. Perhaps they were ...*

By the time she had placed the dirty dishes on the counter, she felt sure she would faint without a breath of fresh air. Heading into the garden through the back entrance of the boarding house, she almost ran directly into a tall gentleman and his lady. The Darcys!

"Good Morning!" William ventured to the obviously flustered maid.

If it were possible, Margaret blushed even redder, bobbed a curtsy and mumbled a slight greeting before running past them down the gravel path they had just come up.

Elizabeth chuckled. "My goodness! She was in a hurry. If I did not know better, I would think she was embarrassed to see us this morning."

"Indeed," William replied, his puzzled brow following the path the maid had taken before turning to find Elizabeth watching him. "Come, Mrs. Darcy, let us find the others and see if Mrs. Barnwell will be good enough to pack us a box of food and drink so we may be on our way."

"Mrs. Darcy will be happy to oblige, Mr. Darcy," Elizabeth jested, bringing a smile to her husband's face. He held out his arm, and she wrapped hers around it as they entered the door.

Inside, Maddie pointed them in the direction of her Mistress, who was overseeing the dining room staff as they cleared the room. As William and Elizabeth headed in the direction that the maid had indicated, they could hear Abby Barnwell instructing the help on the proper way to clear a table, when suddenly she appeared before them.

"Oh, Mr. Darcy, Mrs. Darcy, I am so pleased to see you this morning. I trust you found the cottage adequate?" She beamed as she looked from one to the other, awaiting their approbation.

"It was enchanting!" Elizabeth answered. "You will never know how much we appreciate your letting us stay there. It was as if we were the only two people in the world—so peaceful and quiet. We heard only the sounds of the birds this morning. I can assure you that we will wish to stay there again sometime in the future," she smiled lovingly up at William, "to remind us of our wedding and our honeymoon."

William raised the hand he was holding to his lips, and Elizabeth leaned into him affectionately. Abby Barnwell smiled at their devotion. "Of course! I make it available only to a select few but, rest assured, you will always be welcome to have the cottage whenever you visit Liverpool."

"And we cannot thank you enough for making our wedding day so lovely. You will always have a special place in our hearts for the many acts of kindness that you performed for us!" Elizabeth continued taking Mrs. Barnwell's hands as William nodded his agreement.

Changing the subject, William asked, "Could I trouble you to prepare a box of food and drink for Elizabeth and me to take on the coach? I fear our travelling companions have already eaten and are most likely tired of waiting for us. We were supposed to have left an hour ago."

"Do not worry about your companions, sir," the proprietress declared, a secretive look crossing her face as she reached into a pocket of her skirt to retrieve a piece of paper. "This note should explain everything." As she handed William the paper with his name on the front, he recognised Richard's handwriting.

"I believe you shall have plenty of time to eat, and I have a private room prepared just for you." She began to walk away. "If you will follow me, please."

As the older woman went in an entirely different direction, William raised his brows at Elizabeth's questioning look, took her hand, and began to follow their proprietress with his wife. Once they were inside the room, Mrs. Barnwell quickly left them saying she would send a maid with a tray shortly. Not bothering to be seated, he opened the note simply addressed to *Darce,* and read it aloud to Elizabeth.

"Finally! The lovebirds are prepared to break their fast and join us!

Well, it is too late. We have already departed, having decided last night that you deserve to spend the journey home alone with your lovely bride.

Though I had no doubt that you would miss my witty repartee and excellent company, I was unable to convince Evan and Mr. Williamson of that. Thus, I have joined the vicar in Evan's coach. We have hired a coach to take all the servants home as well.

We shall secure a suite of rooms for you at the inn if they have any available, assuming you intend to catch up with us sometime later today.

We wish you joy!

Richard

Tears filled William's eyes, and Elizabeth grasped his hand, squeezing it in solidarity. "Your family is all that is good and kind," she whispered as she slid an arm around him.

He chuckled quietly, thinking of Lady Catherine and Gladys Fitzwilliam. "Not *all* of my family, but the ones I care most for certainly are."

"I really have only Jane and her family and my aunt and uncle in Cheapside, but they are all that is good and kind, too, and I love them."

"And they shall be a part of my family—our family. You shall spend all the time you want with them, and they will be welcome at Pemberley or Darcy House whenever they desire to visit."

Elizabeth's brow knit. "Will I only be allowed to see them at Pemberley or Darcy House?"

"Of course not, sweetheart! But I intend to be very careful with you, my dear wife, and with where you visit. Those members of your family that are neither good nor kind may still mean you harm. I am determined that they shall never be near you again—or our children."

She smiled at the mention of children and nodded in understanding. "I never want to see them again, either."

William pulled her into his chest, and placed a kiss atop her head. "Then it is settled. We shall welcome the ones we love and those who love us into our lives and our children's lives. They shall be our family."

Elizabeth nodded as big tears rolled down her cheeks. "*Our family*. It sounds so wonderful."

~~~*~~~

Chapter 42

Going Home

The hypnotic sway of the carriage had rocked Elizabeth almost to sleep only an hour outside Liverpool, though the last time William had asked, she had insisted that she was not tired. He chuckled contentedly at the way she leaned into him. Moving his arm to wrap it around her shoulder caused Elizabeth to tilt precariously forward, so he gently pulled her back, and her head came to rest against his shoulder.

His low baritone was smooth as he whispered in her ear, "Lie down, sweetheart. Put your head in my lap and your feet on the seat. If you rest, you will feel much better by the time we stop for a change of horses."

"But what of you?" Elizabeth murmured sleepily, yawning and rubbing her eyes. "You must be just as tired as I am."

He laughed aloud, the deep sound reverberating through his body into hers and filling her with happiness. Smiling now, she looked back over her shoulder to study him.

And to think that I once thought him incapable of merriment!

Her thoughts were quickly interrupted by his declaration. "Surely you do not think I can lie down in this coach, sweetheart! While you sleep, I shall lean into this corner and doze as I always do while travelling." Quickly lowering his head to nuzzle her neck, he whispered seductively, "Now, lie down and rest, my love, as I intend to keep you awake again tonight."

Swiftly she turned her head to meet the lips now placing hot kisses on her neck, triggering another very passionate interlude. Not expecting such a response, William whirled her around so that she faced him. His eyes shown with unbridled desire, and she felt herself melting into him as he cupped her face and drew her mouth to his. If not for the driver calling out a command to the horses a few seconds later, William might have completely forgotten that they were not alone. He smiled sheepishly as he pulled back to look into her equally affected eyes. His desire had kindled hers, and she sighed audibly when he broke away.

"I forgot where we were for a moment."

"I … I forgot as well, my darling," Elizabeth murmured, resting her forehead against his. With such close proximity, their lips could do naught but join again, though this time there was not the previous urgency. After several minutes of deliciously tantalizing kisses, William loosened his grip and lowered her to lie in his lap.

"Rest, my love." One hand tenderly smoothed her hair. "Rest," he murmured with an exhaled breath.

Soothed by his tender caresses, Elizabeth closed her eyes. Last night had been both infinitely satisfying and totally exhausting. William was right—she should rest while she had opportunity.

As he observed the rise and fall of her chest, it was not long until William realised that her breathing had become steady. Once he was convinced she was soundly asleep, he reached into his pocket to retrieve the letter that had fallen out of Elizabeth's Bible just before they were wed. Though it had been forgotten in the euphoria of last night, he had caught sight of it when he had donned his coat this morning. And while he intended to return the letter, he wished to read it through once more before confessing that it had fallen into his hands. Written two years ago, he was unsure if he remembered correctly what he had said and was equally worried that he had.

Pulling the familiar paper from its hiding place, he noted first that it was well worn, almost falling apart at the folds, evidence that she must have read it often. His eyes flicked to Elizabeth's face, serenely beautiful in sleep. Determining that she was indeed unaware, he began to read the words that he had written in anger so long ago. The further he read, the more ashamed he was of his arrogance. Every word had been fashioned to defend his position with absolutely no concern for her feelings. Finishing the first page, he was convinced that she must have hated him more with every examination of it. But, as he moved the page to read the second, he discovered that someone had written on the back of the first.

Immediately, he recognised Elizabeth's delicate script, and his breath caught at the tenderness contained in the greeting.

My Fitzwilliam,

I blush to consider what you would think if you learned that I used that endearment in regards to you. But use it I shall, as I know you will never read these tender words from my contrite heart.

I am equally confident that it would shock you to find that your words have kept me sane during my long ordeal. I have been allowed no correspondence with my dear Jane, and your letter has been my only connection with one who cares for me—or once did. How often have I read it with the deepest of regrets!

I confess that I cared for you from our earliest acquaintance, and your statement that I was merely "tolerable" hurt me deeply. Thus wounded, I set out to find fault with your every deed. But no matter the number of imperfections that I laid at your feet, you always conducted yourself like a gentleman—even when you realised that I had heard the remark and apologised with kindness. Would that I had considered that kindness before I rejected your offer!

For after refusing your offer and returning to Longbourn, I was bargained to a man of no scruples, no kindness—a man I cannot respect—by my own mother. His hands never reach to me in kindness but instead are weapons used to force my submission. Even as he echoes my mother's words of my unworthiness to be a gentleman's wife, I have only to read this letter to be reminded that you once found me worthy of being yours. Reaffirmation of my value from a good and decent man has kept me from ending it all, though I was very near doing so many times. So, you see, you have been my saviour unawares.

I cannot say why I felt a great need to pen this reply. I suppose it eases my conscience in a small way, and I would beg you to indulge my folly were it possible to speak to you.

I can only end my letter in the same benevolent manner as you did your own. I ask the Lord to bless you, kind sir.

Elizabeth

By the time William had read the letter completely, tears threatened, and he swallowed hard to keep them in check. Glancing down upon the beautiful face of his wife, his heart shattered anew for all she had endured because of his failure to act. He leaned down to press a soft kiss on her forehead, and in her sleep, she smiled. The serenity on her face brought him a small measure of comfort, and he closed his eyes to make a vow.

Never again my love! Never shall you know the pain of not being loved and cared for—as long as I live! I swear this to you!

As though she had heard his silent oath, Elizabeth was staring up at him when he opened his eyes again. Her brows furrowed as in a sleepy voice, she whispered, "Whatever is the matter?"

Unhappy that he had once again caused her to worry, he pulled her back up and into his embrace with such intensity that she could barely breathe. Overcome with emotion, he murmured hoarsely, "Have I told you today how much I love you, Elizabeth Darcy? How much I have always loved you?"

Lying against his chest, his rapidly beating heart drumming in her ear, Elizabeth discerned the need in his voice and clasped him tighter. "You have, my darling, but I long to hear it again."

Subsequently bestowing warm kisses over every conceivable place on her face and neck, he whispered the words she never tired of hearing between each token of his affection. "I love you. I shall always love you."

When at last he found her mouth, he made a great effort to control his ardour, kissing her tenderly then situating her under his chin and gently running his hands up and down her back. Comprehending that he was trying to find the words to speak, Elizabeth lay perfectly still against him. Shortly thereafter, William began to share with her how he had found the letter and read her reply. Once finished, he lifted her chin so that he could look into the dark brown pools that had imprisoned his heart so long ago, willing her to understand.

"I realise now that there was never a moment that I did not love you, Elizabeth, though I was too stubborn and foolish to admit it. Be assured that I will love you until the last breath leaves my body. No! If God allows, I shall love you better after death—even throughout eternity!"

She wept, too affected to speak for some time, and finally murmured brokenly, "I never dreamed you would read what I wrote, but it is true. I loved you from our first encounter, and in spite of the terrible consequences of my refusal, my love and respect for you never wavered—nor shall it ever."

The rest of the journey was punctuated by kisses and whispered endearments, which kept them well occupied until they caught up with the rest of their party at the last inn they would inhabit before reaching Pemberley.

Netherfield
The Drawing Room

"Janie!" Charles shouted, hurrying into the room with a letter held high in the air. "We have heard from Darcy! The count is dead, and the long ordeal is over! Lizzy is safe at last!"

"Thank the Lord!" Jane exclaimed leaping to her feet. "When are we to see Lizzy?"

Charles read over the missive again as Jane waited impatiently. "According to Darcy, they will marry in Liverpool and then return to Pemberley. In fact, they are most likely already man and wife as we speak!"

Charles ended his speech in front of his wife, where he picked her up, swung her around, and kissed her soundly before putting her down. Suddenly realising what he had done, he stopped abruptly to peruse her swollen belly. "Forgive me! Did I hurt you? Are you and the child well?"

"Nonsense!" she replied, giggling with happiness. "I am not fragile, Charles. Now, permit me to read what William has written."

Charles handed over the letter, content to watch his wife's eyes light up as they followed each line. "How romantic! It seems that Lizzy was the instigator. She did not want to wait to be married, and fortunately, Mr. Williamson was in attendance. Oh, we must go to Pemberley straightaway so I can see her now that she is well!"

Promptly heading towards the door, she spoke aloud to herself. "I have so much to do—packing to oversee, letters to write, people to inform, and deciding what I shall bring for Peter."

As she continued, naming everything that she had to accomplish, Charles called out to her, causing her to stop in mid-stride. With a small amount of annoyance, she turned to learn just what her husband needed while she was so busily planning. The twinkle in his eye surprised her, and he chuckled softly at her dismay. She was not amused, lifting one eyebrow in a show of displeasure.

"Perhaps you would like to take Peter back to the nursery before you begin?"

Jane's gaze immediately dropped to the large basket of clothes sitting next to the sofa. It contained items that needed mending, and she had been working on them when he arrived. On top of the clothes lay her firstborn, fast asleep. Blushing to think that she might have forgotten him, she hurried back to the basket. Never intending to allow her to pick him up in her condition, Charles took up the task. Peter never stirred as his father lifted him, holding the babe gently to his chest while he snored lightly.

"How could I have forgotten one so dear?" Jane lamented, softly stroking her baby's angelic face.

"Blame it on the fact that you were thinking of the return of another who is dear to you—one that has been returned from the dead as it were. That is all, sweetheart."

Jane leaned in to place a soft kiss on Charles' lips, and when she pulled back, she recognised the look in his eyes and smiled slyly. "I do not have to see to the packing this very moment."

"Do you suppose Peter will sleep for another hour?" he ventured eagerly.

"I just imagine that he will."

With Jane's arm wrapped securely around his, they made their way up the grand staircase, first to the nursery where Charles placed Peter in his bed under the watchful eye of his nurse, and then, with hands clasped, to their own bedchamber. And for the next hour or more, they forgot all their cares as they celebrated the joys that came with being married to someone you dearly love.

Brenda J. Webb

An inn on the way to Derbyshire

"There you are, Cousin!" Richard strode forward to clasp William's hand as he and Elizabeth stepped down from the coach a good hour after dark. If not for the torches along the front of the inn, it would have been pitch black, as the clouds obscured the moon. On the breeze, the smell of rain in the distance made Elizabeth take a deep breath of fresh air.

"I was beginning to think I should send a search party out to find you!"

His eyes danced with delight as William scoffed, "Considering how late we left Liverpool, we made good time. I was determined that we would arrive tonight before the rain, as I want to reach Pemberley with the rest of you tomorrow."

Richard lifted his brows in mischief. "Were you afraid of the tales I would weave if I returned to Pemberley before you?"

William smiled knowingly. "No, I was afraid that if I did not reach this far tonight, you might decide to wait for me in the morning and ride back in my coach. As it is, I can now rest assured that you will travel with the others, and Elizabeth and I will be alone again tomorrow as we travel."

Richard grabbed his heart with both hands. "I am wounded!" Glancing over William's shoulder, he addressed Elizabeth. "Do you see how this reprobate treats his relations? Would that you had known this before you married the scoundrel!"

Elizabeth's musical laughter filled the night air, instantly reminding Richard of the young girl he had met two years ago at Rosings. Taking in her lovely appearance, he thought of how far she had come since William had brought her into his home—into his heart. Elizabeth Bennet had come back to life! No, it was Elizabeth Darcy who had risen from the dead.

His musings were interrupted by Elizabeth's impertinent retort. "I have firsthand knowledge of his kindness and generosity, sir. I shall never be dissuaded from my regard for him."

William smiled lovingly at his bride as Richard stepped aside to motion them on into the inn. "Then so be it, milady. Since you have been hopelessly hoodwinked by my cousin, there is nothing I can add, except to say that I wish you both joy!"

Elizabeth placed her hand around the arm that William extended, and they proceeded inside to find a clerk giving directions to several servants, while their trunks were being carried up the stairs by William's footmen.

Trying to hide a smile, William enquired, "Why are the others not here to greet us? Are they already asleep?"

"You have guessed correctly. They have long since succumbed to fatigue—neither is able to endure such weariness as often follows a career such as mine. Only an experienced officer could withstand such incessant travel and still function admirably at this hour." At William's raised brow, he guffawed, "Or a newly married man!"

"You should not have waited up either," William offered. "But I must confess that it was good to see your smiling face when we emerged from the coach." Richard shrugged at the tribute.

As the newlyweds started up the stairs, William threw a question over his shoulder. "Were you able to get us a suite?"

"Yes, though you shall be sharing it with me!"

Stopping in the middle of the stairs, William turned, his face now sporting a frown. Enjoying himself immensely, Richard commenced to explain. "There were

348

only so many rooms left when we arrived. The suite has two bedrooms with a sitting room between, so I told them I would take it!"

Because Richard had signed the register when he arranged for the room, the staff had no idea if the couple newly arrived were married, other than by their affectionate manner. And since Elizabeth wore gloves, there was no ring to placate their uncertainty. Thus the maid escorting their party coloured a bright shade of red at the mention of just who would be sleeping where.

Richard, having seen her disquiet, was much too amused to desist. Thus, he waited until she had escorted them inside the sitting room to say solemnly, "I just assumed that you and I would share a bedroom, Darce."

William choked as he swallowed, causing him to strangle a cough and Richard added, "Surely you do not expect the young lady to share!"

The maid was so taken aback that she immediately ran out of the room, slamming the door and causing Richard to laugh uproariously. William's first inclination was to be angry with his cousin for letting the maid think that Elizabeth might not be his wife, but as he glanced Elizabeth's way, he saw that she was not angry in the least. Her shoulders were shaking, and she covered her mouth with both hands, trying desperately not to make a sound. Meeting her eyes, they both laughed out loud, while Richard joined their merriment.

Hearing the occupants of the suite laugh so stoutly after she pulled the door shut, the maid gasped. Then she quickly went in search of the other night maid, wishing to share her experience with the party in the expensive suite with someone who would understand.

Finding Henrietta in the kitchen, she went through the entire tale before adding, "All I can say is that the lady did not look in the least offended at their discussion of the number of beds available."

Henrietta shook her head knowingly. "I do not believe I shall ever understand these rich folk."

Back in their bedchamber, William made a mental note to make certain that the entire staff of the inn would know he and Elizabeth were married before he had departed the next day. Perhaps adding a bonus for the first-rate service rendered on their return home from their wedding would serve the purpose.

Later that night

Alone in their bedchamber, Elizabeth sat on the edge of the bed listening to the sounds of the inn as she awaited William's return. He had stepped out to have another word with Richard, suggesting she prepare for bed and promising to be back shortly. As good as his word, he returned in a few minutes and began his preparations for bed, completely unaware of what had transpired whilst he was gone—something fated to affect him tremendously.

As Elizabeth had been waiting, the couple in the next room began to argue, and while she could not hear all the words, she could hear enough to be embarrassed for them as well as for herself. Apparently the walls were paper thin. That fact, along with the knowledge that Richard, Mr. Williamson and Evan were somewhere close by, caused her to reassess the activities that William had planned for that night.

As he slid into the bed beside her, she ran her fingers over his cheek. "Darling, perhaps—just for tonight—it would be wise for us to refrain from—" She stopped whispering, trying to judge his astuteness in ascertaining what she was trying to say.

Not liking the turn of this conversation, William tilted his head to study her. "From?"

"You know very well what I am talking about," she replied softly as he pulled her towards him.

Seeing that she was serious, he stopped and his brow knit. Surely she *was not* suggesting...

She scooted even closer, wrapping her arms around him and laying her head on his chest as she related what she had heard through the walls. "My concern is that if you are half as vocal as you were in the cottage—well, I do not relish the entire inn hearing your oaths of love. How would I ever face your family, much less the other guests, in the morning?"

Trying to be understanding, William had to admit that even he would not want their lovemaking broadcast throughout the inn.

Smiling wanly at the look of concern in her eyes, he proffered, "Do not worry, my darling. It will not be easy, but I am a not a beast, and I can certainly abstain for one night. Just allow me to hold you."

So spooning together, her back to his chest, they closed their eyes with the best of intentions. But good intentions often go awry. Needing the touch of her bare skin, he reached down to pull the hem of her gown up and over her head.

"William?"

"Just let me touch you, and I shall be satisfied."

His hands slid around to cup her breasts, believing surely that would satiate his desire for intimacy. He was quite mistaken. Almost as though they had a mind of their own, his fingers began to slowly manipulate each soft mound until the centres hardened.

"Darling," Elizabeth whispered, writhing against the arousal that had announced its presence by poking her. "We should not."

Her words stopped completely when he palmed both generous breasts and began to place hot, wet kisses along her neck and shoulders. A sharp intake of breath announced her most willing compliance.

William's voice was filled with desperation as he murmured, "Can we not make love very quietly? No one will suspect a thing if we do not make any noise."

Wanting him as desperately as he wanted her, Elizabeth replied hoarsely, "I shall not make a sound if you do not."

No further encouragement was needed and, not bothering to have her turn around, he quickly lifted her leg to lie atop his before he guided his shaft into her. The novelty of this position and the knowledge that they must be secretive only heightened their pleasure. The dilemma was—as their enjoyment increasingly rose— so did their exclamations of affection. And by the time they were in the throes of ecstasy, neither was concerned with what anyone might hear.

Afterward, they fell into a profound, restful sleep, so deep that neither knew that a thunder storm had developed and raged into the early morning hours. Only the considerable noise of servants pushing carts in the hallways the next morning succeeded in awakening them.

~~~*~~~

In the light of day, both Darcys were a little discomfited to realise that they had made considerably more noise than they had intended during their secretive activities of the night before.

"William? Do you suppose anyone ..." Elizabeth's voice faded as William's head instantly swung around and his gaze met hers. She was blushing a becoming shade of rose.

"No! And we shall not give anyone the chance to gloat, especially Richard."

Elizabeth puzzled over her husband's contradictory statements, but he only continued to make them. "Keep your eyes averted. No one can disconcert us if we do not acknowledge them."

Now fully dressed, they left the room to join the others. With their eyes lowered and their faces devoid of any expression, they arrived in the common dining room to find Evan, Richard and Mr. Williamson already there, breaking their fast. At their arrival, the three glanced up and then quickly back down, though William chanced to see a hint of mischief cross Richard's mien, before it quickly faded.

A bit of playful banter was exchanged as William and Elizabeth sat down at the table, but the men were very conscious of Elizabeth's presence, and none would dare say anything that would make her uncomfortable. After they all had eaten and the trunks had been loaded, the party filed out of the inn into the early morning light, anxious to board the coaches.

As Evan and Mr. Williamson entered their coach, William assisted Elizabeth into theirs and was about to climb aboard when he felt a hand tugging on his arm, keeping him from taking the step. He turned to face Richard, who had made sure that Elizabeth was securely inside before he began to pull his cousin a few feet away. Finally William halted, the look on his face a confirmation that he would go no farther.

Richard kept his voice low as he stated very seriously, "I hate to bring this up, but I am afraid that I had to inform the proprietor that I was somewhat dissatisfied with our accommodations. In fact, I threatened not to pay for the room!"

William was afraid to ask to what he was referring so Richard leaned in closer as though sharing a state secret.

"I told him that the walls are much too thin, as I could clearly hear other people saying their prayers!"

Suddenly remembering what Elizabeth had cried out in the throes of passion, William schooled his face to show neither recognition nor pride, the latter having surfaced unbidden.

"I was trying to sleep. It was the middle of the night, and suddenly a woman shouted, 'my Lord in heaven' only it came out as one word ... my-lord-in-heaven! Whatever do you suppose she was praying for, Darce?"

William never replied, nor did he glance back at his guffawing cousin as he strode back to his coach, climbed in and sat down next to Elizabeth. But inside, he was smiling.

Seeing her quizzical expression, he offered, "Richard wanted to know if he was staying at Pemberley or Rosewood Manor when we reached home."

"And what did you tell him?"

"I told him that he was welcome to visit Pemberley, but he is staying with the Ingrams until I decide that the honeymoon is over!"

The sound of the horses being whipped into action covered Elizabeth's giggles as she turned in the seat to face William, nuzzling into his neck before laying her head against him and closing her eyes as his arms encircled her tightly. Never would she learn what Richard had said regarding her cries of pleasure. Nor would she know that William was torn between being exceedingly proud and being slightly embarrassed that they had been heard.

~~~*~~~

Chapter 43

Rosewood Manor

A s Georgiana came down the grand staircase, servants were rushing to and fro, almost colliding with one another in their attempts to get everything accomplished before the coach arrived with the Master of Rosewood. According to the last express he had sent, he would arrive today. Being exceedingly anxious, Georgiana had already questioned Mrs. Jenkins regarding the progress of the preparations, and the housekeeper's assurances had calmed her somewhat.

For her part, Georgiana had awakened at first light, gone into the nursery to check on Millie and found her wide awake. She had lain down on the bed with her child, hoping a cuddle with her mama might lull her back to sleep, but after a half-hour of back rubs and lullabies, she gave up, and, with daughter in tow, headed below stairs.

Now three hours later, Georgiana sat anxiously watching the drive through the drawing room windows, while Mrs. Calvert entertained an increasingly heavy-eyed child by reading to her. *She will probably be irritable and sleepy by the time Evan arrives.* A big yawn from Millie just at that very moment confirmed her fears.

"Mrs. Calvert, please take Millie back to her bed for a short nap so that she will be well rested when her papa arrives home."

Millie's head swiftly whirled around to study her mother. "Papa?" she echoed.

"Yes, darling," Georgiana replied, smiling at the tow-headed child that she no longer remembered was not her own flesh and blood. "Your Papa will be home by midday, and our family shall be complete again! That will make you and Mama smile!"

Millie nodded, doing exactly that. "Mama smile."

Georgiana walked over and took her up in her arms, running her fingers lightly over her face. "Yes, Mama smiles when Papa is home." Then she handed her child to the nurse who had waited patiently and was now reaching to take the bundle of muslin, lace and beribboned hair. Millie's face crumpled, her bottom lip starting to poke out. Georgiana laughed.

"You will get nowhere by pouting, sweetling!"

She leaned in to kiss her daughter's soft forehead before the now whining child was carried out of the room. Her cries began in earnest once she could no longer see her mother, and Georgiana, stepping to the doorway, watched stealthily as Millie's tears of protest lessened the farther Mrs. Calvert walked, stopping completely by the time they negotiated the hallway upstairs. Then she walked back into the room smiling, remembering the nurse's assertion that Millie never cried for long.

As her daughter was now down for a nap, Georgiana focused her attention solely on the deserted front drive, sighing heavily. *Where are you, Evan?*

Pemberley

The scene at Pemberley was not unlike the one at Rosewood Manor. However, there was one difference—there was no one to question Mrs. Reynolds about the state of preparedness.

For years, she had been solely in charge of the house and often took care of a myriad of other tasks while Mr. Darcy was away for long periods—not because she particularly desired to do so, but because the task fell to her lot. Or at least it had up until now. The realisation that someone else would now be taking care of the matters previously ascribed to Anne Darcy stopped the elderly servant in her tracks as she crossed the foyer on yet another trip to the kitchen. Captivated by the notion, she felt the corners of her mouth lifting into a smile. *After all these years, Pemberley is truly going to have a mistress once more!*

When she was unmarried, Georgiana had often tried to function as hostess at dinners and such, even showing some interest in running the house, but she had never attempted to fill her mother's role. Thus, Mrs. Reynolds seldom dwelled on the possibility of someone else replacing Anne Darcy ... until Elizabeth had come.

Suddenly, something drew her attention to the top of the grand staircase, where an apparition of William's father and mother materialized, their eyes communing with hers. They were dressed exactly as she had seen them before the last dinner party that Mrs. Darcy had been well enough to attend. The housekeeper had had similar glimpses of them over the years, and each revelation reassured her that they were watching over Pemberley and their children. With shining eyes, she addressed them in her heart.

Fitzwilliam has married a good woman who loves him—Elizabeth Bennet. And just as when I spoke to you of Miss Georgiana's husband, I have no doubt that you would heartily approve of his choice, too. You raised them well, and I pray that you rest in the assurance that, because they are honourable, they have found the happiness that oft times evades those of their circle.

Suddenly the candles on the large chandelier overhead flickered, causing her to chuckle. *You need not remind me that, though I may be a sentry, I am never alone on my watch.*

A familiar ache remained as they faded away, and a quick swipe of her hand removed all traces of the tears that had suddenly surfaced. Straightaway, Pemberley's long-time servant resumed her duties as though nothing untoward had occurred. After all, there was much to accomplish before the arrival of Mr. Darcy and his bride.

Another post with explicit instructions from William had arrived yesterday, and in response, she had begun airing out the Mistress' rooms and moving the items that Elizabeth had left behind into the closets and dressers that had once belonged to his mother. Subsequently, all of the bed coverings and curtains in the Mistress' bedchamber were removed. Lady Anne might have preferred dark reds and royal blues, but William assured her that Elizabeth would prefer lighter colours—green, lavender and cream. These colours would work with the embossed ivory wallpaper with a delicate green vine woven throughout—until Elizabeth could select her own.

A quick trip to a shop in Lambton late on the previous day had confirmed that fabrics in those hues were available. The merchant, Mr. Thacker, long accustomed to Mr. Darcy's propensity to request that an item be made overnight, and equally aware of his habit of paying extraordinarily well to accomplish that, assured her that bed sheets, counterpane and curtains for all the windows would be ready today. Cheerfully, he spoke of calling in extra seamstresses to work through the night to accomplish the task. What he did not say was that he was conscripting an order begun for another estate, done almost entirely in those exact colours. He reasoned that he would just explain to Lady Throckmorton that some of the fabrics for her order had been delayed. The completed curtains needed only to be hemmed and an exquisite satin counterpane was not so far along that it could not easily be converted to what Mr. Darcy desired. Satin sheets in all of the requested colours were already stacked and waiting. And since Thacker was more than willing to put off the Throckmortons than fail his foremost customer, he was certain to deliver the items with time to spare.

In William's Coach
Near Pemberley

Knowing they were close to home, William smiled down at the dark head of curls resting under his chin. Long since convinced that she would rest most comfortably by sitting in his lap with her legs stretched along the seat, Elizabeth had taken advantage of the last hour to do just that. Her upper body was turned so her head lay on his chest and he wrapped her in his arms, holding her close. This pleased him tremendously, not only because he loved holding her thusly, but also because he had done nothing since they had left the inn but fantasize about the night to come, their first at Pemberley as man and wife, and he did not want her to be too tired to participate fully.

Suddenly smiling in spite of himself at the memory of Elizabeth's cries of completion which had alerted practically the entire inn to their activities, he just as swiftly frowned at the remembrance of the knowing smiles of those they had passed on their way to the dining room. For once, he was grateful that Elizabeth had brought a bonnet, which he usually forbade her to wear. At least the bonnet's large brim had hidden the smirks of the gentlemen they had encountered, including Richard's. Aware that his cousin would do more than tease him when they were alone, he was prepared for that eventuality. However, he worried that somehow Elizabeth might learn that their amorous activities at the inn had become general knowledge and be mortified. That she was so uninhibited in their lovemaking had been a wonderful discovery, and he wanted nothing—*absolutely nothing*—to affect that!

William ran a finger down the small nose peeking out from under the curls, finding himself aroused by that simple gesture. She did not awaken, so he took a deep breath to quell his growing need and tried again. "Elizabeth?"

This time his touch caused her nose to twitch as though a fly might have landed thereon, and he could not help laughing aloud. The sound of his guffaw woke Elizabeth, and she squinted up at him curiously.

"I apologise, darling!" he declared, hugging her tighter. "You look so sweet when you do that!"

Still sleepy, she resumed snuggling into his chest, completely unaware of how that simple act reminded him of their lovemaking. In fact, he admitted with some dismay that her every gesture reminded him of making love—biting her bottom lip, raising a quizzical brow, even smiling her crooked grin. He concluded that it was almost impossible not to desire her constantly, his hardening groin area demonstrating agreement. He took a deep breath, trying to gain control.

Hearing that sound and seeing the now familiar hardness, Elizabeth pulled back to study William. In his passionate gaze was raw desire, and it fuelled her own. She whispered desperately, "Do we have time?"

Lost in yearning, William could not think clearly as his pounding heart echoed in his ears. "You ... you will not think me a barbarian?"

Her lips crashing into his was the only answer he was to receive, and quickly she found herself lifted to sit astraddle him. Frantically now, both fought to remove the clothes that obstructed their joining, and it seemed only moments before they were united. At first content just to be joined, their desires quickly progressed into the rhythm of the act itself, and they made love to the rocking of the coach. Unbeknown to them, just as they had reached fulfillment and clung to each other in utter happiness, the coach entered the gate that began the long drive towards Pemberley.

Rosewood Manor
The foyer

"Do you suppose we should just find our rooms and ignore them?" Richard asked Mr. Williamson as Georgiana and Evan continued their endless welcoming kiss.

Hearing his retort, Evan pulled back to give him a pretend glare. "Wait until you are married, my friend, and see how you greet your wife after a long absence!"

"Yes, Richard!" Georgiana replied over her husband's shoulder. "I daresay you have much to learn about greeting a wife after you have been gone for days. You should watch my dear husband, instead of trying to disconcert him. I assure you that you will learn valuable lessons in how to have a happy marriage."

"Well I, for one, love to see married couples display affection. I have counselled too many couples who do not get along well to object to displays of affection between a man and his wife," Mr. Williamson interjected.

Then he bowed towards Georgiana's questioning gaze. "John Williamson, madam. I am the vicar at Meryton."

Georgiana smiled sheepishly at her visitor. "Please excuse my poor manners. Evan wrote that you would be staying with us, and I am indeed pleased that you are here. Elizabeth spoke of you quite often, and any friend of hers is welcome in our home."

"Yes. My Lizzybet is like a daughter to me."

"Lizzybet?"

"An endearment from her childhood which I have never forsaken. She will always be Lizzybet to me."

Displaying mock exasperation, Richard exclaimed, "So now that we are all acquainted, could you please desist these displays of domestic felicity long enough to direct me to my room? I am in great need of a hot bath and a bit of a nap before dinner."

Everyone chuckled, and Mrs. Jenkins stepped forward as Georgiana addressed her. "Please show my cousin and Mr. Williamson to their rooms and have hot baths prepared for them as well as for Mr. Ingram." She winked surreptitiously at her husband. "I believe they all will want to wash off the dust of the road and then rest before dinner."

"Please follow me, gentlemen," Mrs. Jenkins instructed, turning towards the grand staircase.

As the two men followed the housekeeper up the stairs, Richard's braggadocio began. "I love to stay with my rich relations, as it is the only time I am treated as a gentleman of leisure! I am sure you will get quite used to it and dread returning to your calling as much as I do mine!"

More outrageous statements followed, echoing throughout the two-storied foyer and then down the upstairs hallway, causing those listening below to shake their heads in wonder.

"Your cousin certainly has a way with words!" Evan chuckled.

"Yes, he does. And oftentimes I find myself wishing he were mute!"

"Speaking of mute, it is much too quiet in this house. Where is my lively sprite of a daughter?"

Georgiana chuckled. "She was up so early that she was getting sleepy, so I sent her back to the nursery for a nap. However, she has been asleep only for a short while."

Evan took his wife's hand, nearly dragging her up the stairs behind him. "Then let us get reacquainted, my darling. There will be time enough to awaken our daughter and tell her how much her papa missed her."

Near Pemberley

Elizabeth fumbled about, trying to find the pins lost during their interlude of passion and was becoming a little missish with the smug smile on her husband's face as he unhurriedly lent a hand.

"Hurry, William! We shall be expected to exit the carriage soon and my hair is not presentable!" With great frustration, she pushed another pin into the hastily reconstructed coiffure.

William hid his smile, aware that his nonchalance was beginning to unsettle her. "You look lovely, Elizabeth! Just put on your bonnet, and no one will be the wiser!"

"Except for all the curls that are not contained by the bonnet!"

"I love those curls! And I love that they do not stay contained!"

She huffed. "I am returning as the Mistress of Pemberley, and I look like a ragamuffin!" Then, unexpectedly her eyes filled with tears.

Seeing this, he immediately pulled her into a tight embrace, holding her until she relaxed and melted into him. Then he leaned back to cup her face so their eyes locked.

"Forgive me. I did not understand the extent of your distress. But, know this! You do not have to impress anyone, darling. Every servant at Pemberley already loves you for the kind, wonderful woman you are, not for who you married."

"But I want you to be proud of me! And I know nothing of being the mistress of so vast an estate! What if I—"

A kiss ended her protest, and she had calmed considerably when he continued, "I am proud of you just as you are. And you already know everything necessary to be the Mistress of Pemberley. For all I have ever desired is someone to share my love, bear my children and see to their welfare. Everything else is incidental. I care not if you take over the account books, supervise the cleaning, plan the menus or entertain guests. I will care if I want to be with you, and you are occupied with unimportant things. Do you understand?"

The glint in her eye suggested that she did not find that prospect unattractive. "So you are saying that you should be the main focus of my attention?"

"Exactly! I have been alone for far too many years to bury myself in the concerns of life or let you do the same. I intend to enjoy the wife that the Lord has so graciously given me." He nuzzled her neck. "At every opportunity I am afforded."

They were still kissing when the coach came to an abrupt halt, and a footman climbed down to take his position at the coach's door. Knowing better than to disturb the newly married couple until they wanted to be disturbed, he pasted an indifferent look on his face as he stood at attention and waited for the Master to unlatch the door.

On the steps, almost the entire host of Pemberley's house servants, led by Mrs. Reynolds and Mr. Walker, were waiting to welcome their new mistress—the double line progressing even into the foyer through the open front door. All eyes watched the footman intently for any indication that the Darcys were about to appear, when suddenly the door flew open. The steps were folded down, and the Master disembarked first, smiling as most had seldom seen. He reached back into the conveyance to take the hand of his bride, and in seconds, Elizabeth appeared. For just a moment, it was obvious that she was taken aback by the throng waiting to greet her.

She took a deep breath and put a smile on her face as William squeezed her hand and whispered, "Welcome home, *Mrs*. Darcy."

Netherfield
The next day

"Jane! Jane! Where is that headstrong girl?" Mrs. Bennet came stomping into the foyer, heedless of the trunks that were being deposited there in light of the Bingley's visit to Pemberley.

Charles left his study to meet Jane's mother, his steward wisely choosing to wait there, when he peeked out of the door to see who was making such racket.

"May I help you, madam?"

"Where is Jane? And why was I not told that she is going on a trip? Or that Peter is leaving, for that matter? I am his grandmother for heaven's sake! Does that not account for anything? I had to learn from the neighbourhood gossip that you are leaving today."

"My wife is in her rooms preparing for our journey, and as for our trip, we did not think it essential to inform you."

"Essential?" Whom do you think you are addressing, sir?" Mrs. Bennet tried to pull herself up straighter. "You have gotten high and mighty since you married my daughter! What right have you to talk to me in this manner? And just where are you heading?"

"That is none of your concern."

"Humph!" she grunted. "I shall know before Jane leaves." She turned to begin to climb the stairs, but Charles blocked her path. Allowing her growing anger to get the better of her, she called out, "Jane, come down this minute and explain yourself!"

Charles was about to say more when Jane appeared at the top of stairs and began slowly descending. He ran up the steps to take her arm, as she often got off-balance because of her delicate condition.

Mrs. Bennet looked quite smug as Jane came towards her, even going so far as to smirk at Charles. But when Jane finally stood before her, she noticed that her daughter's eyes were hard and unwelcoming.

"Why are you disrupting my home?"

"I have come to learn where you are going, and why you kept it a secret."

"From now on, where I am and whom I visit will be of no consequence to you. I intend to sever all ties with you and my sisters and move as far away as possible."

Mrs. Bennet paled, beginning to flap her handkerchief. "Why, you do not mean that! I am your mother and Peter's grandmother! Surely you jest! But that is a cruel jest indeed!"

Jane stiffened, and Charles slipped his arm around her waist in support. "I swear to you, it is no jest, as you shall soon learn."

"And what would give rise to this rejection of your family, even your own sisters?"

"You sold my most beloved sister into a loveless marriage to a madman. I think that is reason enough!"

"I ... I sold?" Her voice failed, though the look on her face indicated that she knew of what Jane was speaking. It was obvious that she was suspicious of how much Jane knew about Elizabeth's disappearance. "Whatever made you think—"

"Enough!" Jane's voice was eerily cold and her countenance colder still. "I know everything! Suppose you start by telling me why you would do such a horrible thing. Make me understand, Mama, how you could sell your own flesh and blood!"

Jane's demeanour was such that Mrs. Bennet knew she had no option except to lie. Her only hope was to garner sympathy instead of the wrath that now emanated from her eldest child.

"Can we not go into the drawing room? I should hate for our discussion to be gossip for the servants to spread."

Jane turned on her heel, and she and Charles unceremoniously led the way to the drawing room where, once inside, Charles shut the door with no little noise, causing Mrs. Bennet to jump. Jane had moved ahead to take a seat on a small sofa, and he joined her there, taking her hand and glaring at her mother.

Seeing her once-favoured daughter so resolute on having an explanation, Mrs. Bennet began a sorrowful tale of woe, explaining her dire straits after Mr. Bennet's demise and how all of them would have been living in the hedgerows had the count not made the offer she could not refuse.

"So, you see! I could have done no less! Lizzy was not likely to receive any other offers of marriage, as she was determined to be a scholar. Men do not appreciate women who flaunt what they know; they want someone compliant to warm their beds. You understood that. Why could she not?"

Jane's sharp intake of breath did not bode well, so Mrs. Bennet quickly added, "I was doing her a favour in securing her a rich husband. And the rest of you would be able to live well in the bargain! And how is it my fault that she died in a fire?"

"A fire set by the very man to whom you sold her!"

Mrs. Bennet did not look surprised. "Well, if that is so, and I have no idea how you would know such a thing; it is not my fault! He seemed a gentleman to me!"

Jane stood shakily, her eyes blazing and her breathing ragged. Charles rose to steady her. "A gentleman? A gentleman? What part of Papa's objections to this monster did not register in your hard heart? He rejected the man's offers for my sister because he was well aware of his faults, thanks to Lord Stanton. And I know he told you everything, as he said he had, and you would not listen!"

Mrs. Bennet could only stutter, "I—I—"

"No! You knew he was no gentleman! You did not care how he would treat Lizzy, only that you would be paid for her sacrifice! You are despicable! I no longer want to be known as your daughter; and as for Mary, Kitty and Lydia, they have never once shown any concern or love for Lizzy. Like you, they care only for themselves. So, it will be no imposition to cut them from my life as well."

Mrs. Bennet stood, shaking violently. "You do not mean that!" She attacked Charles. "You! You have done this!"

Jane resolutely stepped to within inches of her mother's face, instantly silencing her. "You drove me away—no one else! Now, kindly leave my house and never try to see me or my child again!"

Charles had walked to the door and opened it. He motioned for two large footmen to step forward, when Jane finished and stalked out of the room, her mother on her heels, crying and begging.

At his nod, the footmen each took an arm and escorted Mrs. Bennet from the premises, even going so far as to walk her to the edge of the property and stand guard as she turned to berate them and the occupants of Netherfield Park.

Quickly Charles caught up with his wife, helping her up the stairs and into her room. Watching as she lay down on the bed, the tears streaming down her face, he immediately sat on the edge, trying to determine what course of action he should take.

"Janie? Are you well? Should I send for the physician?"

She shook her head without speaking and lay quietly for a moment with her arm across her face. Finally she moved her arm to her side and spoke, greatly easing his mind. "I am not crying because of what has just happened. I have neither respected nor loved Mama for some time now. I am crying for all that Lizzy went through for so selfish a reason. Father did not leave much, but she would never have had to live in the hedgerows. Greed was responsible for my sister's dreadful experience. She nearly died!"

As Jane's tears began again, Charles leaned down to kiss her forehead. "This is not good for you or our child." He ran his hand over Jane's stomach. "Lizzy would not want you to risk your health or the child's when she is so deliriously happy."

Jane's mouth curved into a slight smile. "And how do you know she is deliriously happy?"

It was Charles' turn to smile. "Because she has loved Darcy since she first saw him. Did not her letters attest to that? And now they are married. How could she not be happy? I know what it is to be married to the love of your life."

With those words, Jane's tears instantly ceased. Charles was right! It was time to forget the past and look to the future. A future that included her most beloved sister!

She reached to cup Charles' face with her hands. "Are the servants ready to leave? Do you think we have time?"

"We have as much time as we wish," Charles murmured, leaning in to capture her lips in a quick kiss. "After all, we are the masters of our destiny!"

Her giggles were stopped by an all-consuming kiss, which was interrupted moments later by Peter's cries to be fed.

"Well, perhaps not the masters of everything!"

~~~*~~~

Chapter 44

Pemberley
Six Weeks Later

"Jane! You cannot hit the ball by holding the mallet in that manner!" Elizabeth smiled as the ball went scurrying to the left of the wire loop and all the way to the small fish pond, where it dropped unceremoniously below the water. "That makes two!"

Everyone laughed including the perpetrator. "Were I not so huge and cumbersome, I am sure I could do much better. You do remember that I was good at this game when we were young, Lizzy!"

Elizabeth winked at Georgiana surreptitiously before answering, "I remember that you knocked the balls into the weeds then, as opposed to into the pond now!"

"Lizzy!" Jane cried, putting her hands on her hips. "Surely you jest! I won nearly half our games as I remember. But now that I cannot see my feet, when I swing I am fearful of where the mallet will land!"

"It is not the mallet I fear for, dear Jane, but the ball!"

Georgiana was giggling uncontrollably as she lined up her next shot, but she managed to interject, "She has a point, Lizzy! I have never played Pall Mall with anyone who was as great with child as is Jane, though I did play with Marjorie Witt, who is grossly overweight, and it was just as diverting!"

Jane dropped her mallet and made her way to the cushioned chair brought onto the lawn just for her. It was impossible for her to sit on the ground now that she was eight months along, and even this slow game was making her exceedingly tired. Sitting down and heaving with the effort, she began wiping her brow with the lace handkerchief she drew from her pocket, feigning sarcasm as she replied, "I am so pleased that I could entertain you. I believe I shall just sit and watch now, as I shall knock all the balls in the pond if I take my turn."

Laughing, Lizzy dropped her mallet as well and walked over to sit down on the colourful quilt spread out on the lawn on this unseasonably warm day, and just as she did, Jade came from out of nowhere to lie in her lap. Then she lay back and studied the glimpses of blue sky through the limbs of the large oak tree that shaded their resting place while she stroked the orange cat's soft fur.

Georgiana dropped her mallet and joined Lizzy, lying on her back as well. "Perhaps we should just make an end to it! We have played three rounds, and none of us has won without cheating. Besides, Brother had the hoops set up too close to the fish pond. It is much too easy for the balls to go astray." She giggled. "I shall never forget the look on Mr. Cravets' face as he waded about the pond last week, trying to retrieve the ones that we lost then."

"You mean the balls that *I* lost last week," Jane replied, her face expressionless, causing a new round of giggles by her company.

A sly smile began around Georgiana's mouth. "Well, if we are to do nothing but rest, what shall we talk about?" She loved it when Elizabeth made her sister blush with her observations about married life.

"Lovemaking!" Elizabeth announced with such enthusiasm that Jade jumped up and ran down the lawn.

Jane looked about nervously for evidence of any men in hearing distance. "*LIZZY!*"

"Why, it is a perfectly natural part of marriage, Jane," Elizabeth said as the corners of her mouth lifted. It was not easy holding back the broad smile that threatened, as she delighted in making her staid sister blush.

"Yes, but not one we should be discussing amongst ourselves!" Jane continued, mopping her brow which was suddenly flushed. "That is private, only to be talked about between husband and wife."

"I was not suggesting we discuss the *mechanics* of the act, only such things as the average number of times. And how are we to know if we are *achieving* the average if we do not know what *is* average?"

Georgiana could barely control her laughter as she joined in, "Indeed!"

"Three!" Elizabeth proffered.

"Three? Whatever do you mean?" Georgiana smirked, knowing full well that Elizabeth would elaborate, and she would learn something she had always wanted to ask another woman. *Oh, to be as bold as Lizzy!*

"The number of times we make love on a given day ... well now that the honeymoon is over and the cares of life insist on their share of our lives." Elizabeth smiled dreamily. "In the first week we were married, we often made love that many times in a night."

By now Jane's face was bright red, and she tried to stand. "If you insist on embarrassing me, I shall just have to go inside and rest while Peter is napping."

Elizabeth rolled over on her side and studied her prim and proper sister with a slight smile. Jane was soon to be a mother again, and still she was not comfortable speaking of the act of love. But that was Jane, and she loved her very much just as she was ... as she would always be.

"Please do not go! I do not mean to embarrass you, Jane. It is just that I have no way of knowing if my life is ... average. Maybe I should just be grateful that it is wonderful and not care whether or not it is normal."

"Life with my brother will NEVER be normal, I fear!" Georgiana offered, as all three giggled again. "And I must admit that it is disconcerting to be discussing my brother in this context!"

"Then I shall change the subject. We can talk about courses!"

"Courses?" Jane sounded incredulous, looking about even more nervously. "Why would we discuss ..." A knowing look soon spread across her face, and she was speechless.

Georgiana, however, was not, her voice rising in excitement as she rolled onto her stomach and propped upon her elbows, she cried, "Are you with child, Lizzy? Pray tell us!"

"Shhh!" Now it was Elizabeth turn to sit up and look around. "I am a week past my time, but William has not noticed, and I do not want to get his hopes up just yet."

"Oh, Brother will be so happy if it is true," Georgiana said a bit too loudly, her enthusiasm hard to control. "He has wanted children for so long." She sat up and moved over to hug Elizabeth. "I want so much to be an aunt, and Millie needs cousins with whom to play. It would be a dream of mine come true."

Elizabeth beamed. "I just had to tell someone! The last time William was so disappointed when my courses came." Reflecting on that event, she took a deep breath as she continued. "Actually, I think he was more worried for me—because he knew how much I wanted to be with child. He told me not to worry, that it would happen all in good time. But, if I tell him now, and it is not to be ..." Unbidden tears filled her eyes.

Jane reached for her sister's hand. "Lizzy, you have been married such a short while; give yourself time. It will happen eventually."

"I know I am being silly, but I remember so vividly being in my room at Northgate, considering the madness of my life and wondering if I should just ..." Her voice trailed off, and she stared into the distance.

"It was in those times that I imagined I was married to Fitzwilliam—it was my only solace." She smiled, completely unaware of how her mien transformed when she spoke of her husband. "And when I dreamed of him, we were always sitting on a lawn, under a huge tree." She looked up to the strong limbs of the oak above. "And our child was lying in a basket between us."

Tears now flowed from all three women as Lizzy tried to recover her former cheerful mood. Suddenly, she remembered Georgiana's miscarriages and touched her hand. "I am sorry, Georgiana. I should never have mentioned—"

"Nonsense!" William's sister interrupted. "I have my Millie, and I am exceedingly happy. Evan and I are even talking of taking in another orphan; so do not fret for me. I have no reservations in praying that you are with child. I yearn for this for my dear brother's sake as well as for yours!"

Elizabeth took both her hands. "I have very little family left, and you have truly filled a place in my heart as a sister."

Touched, Jane held out her hands, one to Elizabeth and one to Georgiana. "And you have become like a sister to me as well, Georgiana. I could not love you more."

"Then we are all agreed!" Georgiana declared, sniffling. "I have always wanted sisters, and now I have two!"

Elizabeth and Georgiana stood and helped Jane to her feet. Then all three hugged as only women are prone to do—giggling and whispering. Their laughter could be heard through the upstairs window where, unbeknownst to them, an audience was watching.

The Billiards Room

While William and Evan finished one last game of billiards, Mr. Williamson slipped to the open windows to enjoy the breeze and take in the breathtaking view of Mr. Darcy's estate. As he did, he contemplated how much his life had changed since Mr. Savage, the young vicar of Kympton, invited him to move north and help with his growing parish. He had agreed, not only because Lizzybet had begged him to stay but also because his heart demanded it. No one had known the extent of his loneliness after Gregory had been lost at sea and Lizzybet had been spirited away from Meryton, and now that the Darcys had assured him that he was a welcomed part of their family, his joy had returned. He had a purpose! He was a father once more! He relished that title and looked forward to being a grandfather, which, were he a betting man, he would wager to happen within the year.

Even as he smiled to himself, as so often happened, his thoughts drifted to the small cemetery at Meryton where his parents and dear wife rested. He would never forsake them and had sworn over their graves that he would return often. It had eased his mind when Mrs. Haversham, blessed friend that she was, vowed to tend their graves in his absence.

"I will care for their graves just as I do my own dear mother's," she had assured him when he returned to Meryton to make arrangements to move. *"Rest in confidence that not one weed will flourish and fresh flowers will be present in season. In addition, I shall keep you informed of the goings on in Meryton, since I know you will miss us as much as we will miss you."*

Thus he had left half of his heart in a village that he had served almost his entire life, to move closer to the other half—to Lizzybet. A familiar giggle and soft trill of feminine chatter drifted up from somewhere below, and he stepped closer to find the source. At this angle, he could see Elizabeth lying on the ground with Georgiana, while Jane rested in a chair.

"What do you suppose they find to talk about?"

Evan's question startled the vicar, and he turned to find Evan standing on one side. William was behind them both, holding out a glass of brandy for each. He did not answer Evan, but instead took a sip as William moved to his other side and looked down as well.

"I suppose they are discussing the latest fashions," William offered confidently. "Elizabeth has finally decided on the wallpaper she wants in her bedchamber, and she and Jane were all aflutter about paint colours for the Bingleys' estate at last night's dinner."

"You are probably right, Darcy. Ana loves to talk of paint colours!"

Mr. Williamson smiled. He had waited to see what they thought before speaking. "I can assure you that that was not the subject, gentlemen."

Both young men eyed the older gentleman now standing between them, awaiting his further pronouncements. After all, he was the most experienced of the group, having been married for over thirty years before his wife had died.

"When women get together, they talk about us."

Evan and William both stiffened and sought their own wife's form below as their faces darkened at that revelation. This made the vicar smile. "Oh, do not look so troubled! I found that as long as my wife had another married woman in whom to confide, she was more content with me. More satisfied overall."

At their dubious expressions, he added, "Especially in our bedchamber."

At that pronouncement, the shoulders of both young men relaxed, and they each took a deep breath and smiled to themselves. At this point, Williamson felt free to put forward further advice.

"I always offer this counsel to married men, especially *young* married men. Remember to court your wife as though you were still trying to win her heart ... not only with gifts but with words of your devotion. Gifts are wonderful and certainly warranted, but sentiments will reward you long after the gifts are forgotten."

Mr. Williamson smiled as each man again peered out the window, seeking his wife in the group below. "I do not think that that advice was necessarily needed in your situations, as I have seen firsthand the devotion between you and your wives, but I feel a need to pass along what I have learned to the next generation."

William volunteered, "It is too bad that Charles was not here to be enlightened. I fear he has learned too much about my stock of liquor and not enough about his wife."

They were still laughing when Bingley came into the room holding an unopened bottle of brandy. "I found it, Darcy! This is the brand I was referring to last night. Mrs. Reynolds assured me that you have plenty left in the cellar, despite Colonel Fitzwilliam's designs to do away with every last bottle."

Seeing the smiles that spoke of secrets shared, he asked, "What?"

Later that day

Jane and Georgiana were resting, along with Peter and Millie, leaving Elizabeth to her own devices—finally!

It had been wonderful hosting Jane and Charles for the entire time they had been in Derbyshire, and now that they had moved into their own estate of Glendale, which was close by, there were frequent visits from her beloved sister. And since Georgiana lived as close as Jane, it made sense for the three of them to spend copious amounts of time together enjoying the camaraderie that she had always craved.

But, if she were to be truthful, she had to admit that sometimes ... sometimes she wished for the house to be free of everyone save her husband. She longed for the early, uninhibited days of their marriage when William had barred all the servants from the upper floors unless they were expressly summoned. She blushed, remembering the looks on the faces of the maids as William had rung for dinner trays, hot baths, and even changes of the sheets in her bedchamber as they took up residence in his freshly made bed.

All these memories kindled a need she could not suppress a moment longer; consequently, a quick search of William's bedchamber revealed that he was not upstairs. Swiftly she traversed the hallway and then the grand staircase in her quest to find him before someone demanded attention from one of them. As she did, a niggling thought crossed her mind—was he still ensconced with the men?

As she crossed off each successive room in her hunt, her hopes began to fade. It seemed he was nowhere to be found in the house, which meant he had probably gone riding. Her disappointment was so raw that she could not suppress the tears that suddenly appeared. She desperately needed to touch him, to hold him, if only for a moment!

A maid was coming towards her as she entered the hallway outside his empty study, so she tried to recover by walking away, into the quiet library. Without stopping, she crossed to the double doors that led unto the terrace and practically ran into the cool afternoon air. Taking a deep breath to calm herself and control her disappointment, she closed her eyes.

"Fancy meeting you here, Mrs. Darcy."

William's warm baritone caught Elizabeth by surprise, and when she opened her eyes, he stood before her, giving her no chance to wipe away the evidence of her distress. Having successfully convinced all the men to go riding without him, he had been walking up from the stables, when he saw her run out onto the terrace. Making short work of the distance between them, he was concerned to see the look of misery on her beautiful face and further distressed to find that she had been crying.

Pulling her into his embrace, he whispered, "Elizabeth? Darling, what is wrong?"

"You!" His brows knit in surprise. "I wanted you, but I could not find you and ..."

He was smiling now, for as he placed kisses in her dark locks, he understood. "I know, sweetheart. I want you, too." Leaning down, he captured her mouth in a burning kiss before whispering, "Let us not waste a minute of this precious time."

With those words, he took her hand and began leading her through the doors, into the library and out into the foyer. At the steps, he picked her up so he could take them faster. She giggled despite herself.

"What will our guests think if they see us?"

"Let them think whatever they like!"

William was aroused by the time he attained the landing and practically ran with her to his bedchamber. There he managed to open the door without putting her down, and once inside, kicked the door closed, as was his habit when overcome with desire.

They frantically undressed as he backed her towards his huge bed, and as they bumped into it, he picked her up and tossed her lightly onto the soft bedding and numerous pillows. She giggled as he joined her and was just as swiftly lying atop her.

Pulling back to look into her eyes and run the back of his fingers over her cheek, he breathed, "Have I told you today that I love you more than life, my Elizabeth?"

"Not in those exact words, my darling."

"Well, it is true. I do." His lips crushed hers and tongues fought for control as they collided and tangled. Without further conversation, they joined in the way they both desired, each voicing a loud groan with the joy of being one again. Not waiting, William began a fast, furious rhythm until they both cried out in release.

Elizabeth preferred that they stay joined, that he held her for a time after they made love, so lying sated in her arms, his breathing slowly returned to normal. Eventually, he propped up on both elbows to consider her.

"When were you going to tell me?"

Her brows first knit and then smoothed again as she realised to what he was referring. "You know me too well."

"Is there such a thing?" His expression held only love. "I thought we wanted to know each other completely."

She reached up to cup the face she loved and pulled his mouth down to hers in the gentlest of kisses. When she finished, there was unfathomable love shining in her eyes. "I shall never try to keep anything from you again. I only wanted to spare you any disappointment."

"I am only disappointed if we are not forthcoming with each other."

"Duly noted," she purred, having no idea that she had captured his heart again with her lopsided grin. "I am only a week past my time."

His pride was visible as he slid one hand down to rest on her stomach, and his fingers began a circle with gentle reverence. "We have a son. I just know it."

"Are you a soothsayer as well as a great lover?"

"I am a man violently in love with the woman who is carrying my child."

"I pray you are correct."

"While we were desperately searching for you, Mr. Williamson taught me a great deal about prayer—much of it by example. I have asked God for this, and He has heard my heartfelt plea and answered. Of this, I am certain."

Tears of joy appeared as her faith rose with William's resolve. "Then we should begin to thank Him for this gift!"

"I already have, my love. Last week I wrote a draft for the funds needed for the orphanage that Williamson has championed since he agreed to help Mr. Savage at Kympton."

Elizabeth shook her head in awe as she ran her hands over his beloved face. "Have I told you today that I love you more than life, my William?"

"Not in those exact words, my darling."

After Dinner
The Drawing Room

As was the custom, the men did not separate from the women after dinner, as they had been separated by different activities most of the day. At least, all had been separated except William and Elizabeth—who some noted had a certain glow about them this night.

It was decided that there would be no entertainment, cards or other games, as everyone wished to relax, and because Georgiana wanted to discuss the invitations they had received to Richard's engagement ball to be held in London in two months' time. Lord and Lady Matlock had been unable to attend the reception that Georgiana had given for William and Elizabeth after their marriage, but begged to be able to fete them in London at a later date. William had respectfully declined, saying that he and Elizabeth understood their dilemma, as the Earl had been ill. He explained that they would visit the Fitzwilliams in London soon and declared another reception unwarranted. Nevertheless, now that Richard was engaged, a trip to London seemed unavoidable.

"Well, whether or not we want to see all our relations in London, we owe Richard our allegiance and our support! We have to attend!" Georgiana exclaimed, all the while looking at her brother.

Elizabeth took up the cause. "We must go. It is their engagement ball, and we owe Richard so much. I fear to think what might have transpired during my rescue had he not been there to calm William."

There was gentle laughter, though Jane glanced to see if Lizzy's husband was enjoying the laugh at his expense. Seeing a frown, she tried to lighten the discussion. "I am just glad that Charles and I do not have to attend such a ball. I shall be glad to stay home with my newborn as I was intimidated attending the reception Georgiana gave you."

Charles interjected, "I have always been intimidated by Darcy's sphere, but I refuse to let it bother me now. I will rise to the occasion! If he is my friend, what does it matter what others think?"

Georgiana agreed. "Precisely! You and Jane are family now, so you shall have to get used to being invited to our events. Evan and I love you as much as Brother and Lizzy!"

Evan lifted his glass in acknowledgement. "Ana is right!"

He said nothing more, aware that Ana and her brother could settle the question of attending the ball in London without his intervention—after all, these were not his relations; his part was only to accompany Ana if she wished.

"Surely we will go, William," Elizabeth ventured again, a different expression now on her face—a change in mien that did not go unnoticed by her husband.

William put down the book he had been holding as an unreadable expression crossed his own face. Only Lizzy knew that he was trying to compose what he wanted to say, but he had everyone's undivided attention by the time he did.

"If you desire to go, Elizabeth, then we shall go. I am exceedingly proud of you, and I would love for London and the whole world to see my beautiful bride." He paused as she blushed, examining the handkerchief she knotted in her hands. William had read the unspoken question in her last comment. He was **not** ashamed of her.

"But, know this—some of my relations cannot be civil. I shall not tolerate any of Edgar's insults, whether aimed at you or anyone else I love. And, I should add, that applies to any of my relations who do not respect my choice. I am a man, not a boy to be ordered about. My only reservation is that I know that if some of them attend, and they might in hopes of insulting you, a confrontation is inevitable. I do not want it to be more than you can bear."

"I can bear anything with you near me, my love."

Elizabeth's expression as she looked towards her husband was so intimate that everyone else averted their eyes.

For his part, William wanted only to carry her directly to his bed, but all he could accomplish was to swallow hard, his eyes entreating her to read his mind. *Later, my love!*

Strangely, before another half-hour had passed, each couple declared their exhaustion and retired to their rooms, leaving the newlyweds alone in the drawing room. William and Elizabeth lingered there not a minute longer than necessary for the last guest to clear the grand staircase before they hurriedly made their way to the privacy of their bedchamber.

~~~*~~~

Chapter 45

London
Matlock House
Two Months Later

T he woman reflected in the gilded mirror no longer resembled the waiflike creature that William had brought to London from Netherfield so many months before—the one with lacklustre locks, dark circles under her eyes and a pale complexion. In her place stood the perfect example of a woman transformed by the love of a man and expecting her first child—she was radiant.

Her dark eyes sparkled, her skin had a healthy glow, and her lustrous dark locks, styled by Lady Matlock's French maid, were pulled atop her head then woven into an intricate design, featuring long curls down the back with diamond pins scattered throughout. She wore an emerald-green, silk gown with cap sleeves. Elaborate silver embroidery accented with glass beads surrounded the dress at the empire waist and were repeated on her white satin slippers and white, elbow-length gloves.

Though William had insisted that she order a new gown for this occasion, at the last minute, she had decided to wear this one because she loved the colour, and it was not too revealing—or it had not been when she had worn it at the reception the Ingrams had hosted three months before. Nevertheless, now that her breasts were determined to keep pace with the increase in her stomach, the décolletage appeared much more daring. As she studied the dilemma, her eyes were drawn to the very exquisite necklace adorning her neck—William's wedding present—and the corners of her mouth lifted in a smile.

At least most are more curious about my necklace than my breasts when I wear this!

For a brief moment, she had deliberated against wearing it, as she did not want to divert attention from the newly engaged Mrs. Largin. But remembering Lady Matlock's assurance that it was appropriate for tonight and that she had loaned Richard's fiancée an equally elaborate necklace from her collection, Elizabeth's misgivings had vanished. That matter settled, she was free to admire her lovely present, and her fingers slid effortlessly over the brilliant diamonds fashioned into five-strands and featuring a large teardrop emerald.

It was designed as a choker that dipped in the front, where the teardrop, surrounded by smaller diamonds, rested. Along with the matching earrings, it coordinated with her wedding ring. Truly astonished at the riches at her disposal now that she was Mrs. Darcy, Elizabeth recollected how William had insisted she select some jewels from the Darcy collection their first week at Pemberley. Afterward, he had secretly commissioned this necklace, in spite of her insistence that she had all that she would ever need at her disposal. Suddenly she pictured her husband on his knees presenting the gift as she had sat at her dressing table.

"I am not being extravagant, sweetheart. This is your wedding present, and it should be uniquely yours, not something passed down through my family. And please do not forbid me to shower you with such gifts, as I intend to do it for the rest of my life."

"But ...but, I have no gift to give you."

"You have given me a priceless gift—you have given me yourself. For you are worth more than any token I might buy."

She cupped his dear face. "I shall forever thank God that you took me back into your heart when you found me at Netherfield."

"You never left my heart, Elizabeth. It would not let you go."

"Neither would mine forsake you."

Remembering the way they had made love afterwards, she continued to finger the piece, considering its appeal. The majority of the *ton* would envy her these jewels, unaware of how insignificant they were apart from being tokens of William's affection. She, on the other hand, was well aware of her true treasures—William and their child. Thoughts of the baby made her turn sideways and, from habit, run her hands down her abdomen, seeking reassurance that there was indeed a swell where the baby lay. Her heart filled with happiness as she contemplated the child she had longed for, and she did not notice when Lady Matlock appeared at the door.

"No one will guess unless you tell them, Elizabeth."

Startled, she glanced to the corner of the mirror to see Evelyn Fitzwilliam behind her. As their eyes met, the expression on her aunt's face was the same as when she gazed at William—as a mother would regard her child. Tears came to Elizabeth's eyes, and she swiftly lowered her gaze, trying to keep her new aunt from seeing.

But Lady Matlock had seen the reaction and hurried forward to put her hands on Elizabeth's shoulders, their eyes meeting in the mirror. "Oh, my dear, I assure you that no one will recognise that you are with child just from your appearance. I would never have said anything if I had known it would upset—"

Elizabeth shook her head, tears escaping the corners of her eyes as she interrupted, "It is not the baby, and truly I do not care if they do guess. We were going to announce our good fortune to our family this weekend. It is just that you sounded so much like a ..." she took a ragged breath, "a mother."

Having long since heard of the events that brought Elizabeth into William's life again, Evelyn Fitzwilliam's heart broke, and she turned the young woman to face her, gently lifting her chin. "Elizabeth, if you will allow me, I shall be privileged to care for you as a daughter—after all, I have always loved William as a son."

No longer able to hold back her tears, Elizabeth began to cry softly, and Lady Matlock pulled her into an embrace—Elizabeth's head resting on her shoulder. "Now, now, dear, you must not cry. My nephew will want everyone to see his bride, and you are much too beautiful to ruin the effect with a red nose. William is so seldom in London that I am convinced that many came tonight just to catch a glimpse of him and the woman who won his heart."

She whispered conspiratorially, "But do not tell Richard, as he will think they all have come to see him!"

Elizabeth managed a small smile as Lady Matlock pulled a lace edged handkerchief from a hidden pocket of her beautiful ball gown and began dabbing at Elizabeth's face.

"There, there! You have a plethora of envious women to put in their places. Now take this handkerchief, and keep it with you in case you have need of it."

She studied Elizabeth's face and proud of her accomplishment, enquired, "When is the child due?"

"In the middle of summer."

"Wonderful! I knew it would not take long for my nephew to beget an heir, especially after seeing the way he looks at you."

At Elizabeth's blush, she chucked. It had not escaped her notice in the few days that they had been in each other's company how often William touched Elizabeth or she him. They were reluctant to be parted—clearly disappointed at being seated away from one another at dinner or separated afterward when the men customarily got together for cigars and brandy. And as soon as the men rejoined the ladies, William would seek her out, taking her hand and bringing it to his lips in a silent avowal of his love.

"Nor have I missed the way you gaze at him. The bond you have is practically sacred. I have no doubt that he has already made up for the nights he spent alone in his bed."

Elizabeth coloured even more when she spied William at the door, dressed elegantly in black coat and breeches, emerald green waistcoat with silver embroidery and a white shirt, all designed to complement her gown. His dark hair was longer, covering his collar the way she liked, and his blue eyes sparkled as he smiled at her. Straight white teeth cut across a perfectly tanned face, and Elizabeth's breath caught at the realisation that this Adonis was hers alone.

However, beholding Elizabeth's red eyes and the handkerchief still clutched in her hands, William's mien darkened, and his smile vanished. Instantaneously, he transformed from an amiable man to an irate husband and seeing the change, Lady Matlock sought to calm him.

"Do not stand there, Fitzwilliam. Come and escort my lovely niece downstairs. The ball will begin shortly, and I must check on my new daughter-to-be. Did you pass Richard in the hall?"

William, who had stiffened at the sight of his wife's discomposure, shook his head absently, not moving as he focused completely on Elizabeth. Crossing to him, his aunt laid a hand on his arm and stood on tiptoe to kiss his cheek.

"All is well," she whispered, then exclaimed aloud, "I was just telling Elizabeth that I have room in my heart for another daughter, and I am afraid I made her cry."

As she glanced between the couple, she marvelled at having seldom seen so deep a love. At that moment, the maid assisting Jenny appeared at the door, coughing to get her attention. She nodded to the servant before addressing William and Elizabeth.

"Though you would not assent to my sponsoring another soirée for your wedding, I wanted this event to be a celebration of your marriage as well as a celebration of Richard's engagement. I have explained that to him and Jenny, and they wholeheartedly agree. You and Elizabeth are as much my son and daughter as are my own children."

William pulled his aunt into a hug, unable to speak for the lump in his throat. When he released her, she hurried out of the room, leaving him to go to Elizabeth, who had turned back to the mirror to regain her composure. As he came towards her, she instinctively rested her hands on the baby, and when he reached her, his hands slid around her waist coming to rest in the same place.

"My aunt made you cry?" he whispered softly.

Elizabeth nodded, closing her eyes and leaning her head back against him. She took a deep breath before speaking. "I am not used to being regarded as a daughter—that is all."

"I understand perfectly. I am still not used to being thought of as a son."

She opened her eyes to study him, and as he smiled, she nodded at the truth of his statement. "I had never considered that we are both parentless. Your aunt is very kind to include me in her family."

"Yes, whomever Aunt Evelyn loves is indeed very fortunate."

Elizabeth turned in his arms. "Please hold me for a moment." He pulled her tightly against his body.

"Are you unwell, darling? For if you feel the least bit upset or nervous, we shall return to Darcy House. I do not want anything to disturb you," he kissed her forehead, "or our child."

She smiled dreamily. *Each time I think I could not possibly love you more, you say something to prove me wrong.*

With this declaration, he watched her carefully for any signs of distress and seeing her smile, he pressed her tighter against his now hardening member.

"Oh, Elizabeth, do not smile like that. I shall embarrass the both of us by making the entire assembly await our arrival while I make love to you again, or even worse, we may never get downstairs."

Elizabeth could not fathom that so kind-hearted a man resided in so handsome a frame or that he should love her. Indeed, his handsome mien had been her downfall that night in Meryton when she had fallen in love at first sight, against her better judgment and her will, with a man she knew was far above her station. Suddenly, longing welled up, and she felt that she simply must have his love this very moment.

She cupped his face, drawing his mouth down to hers. "I say we let them wait."

The Ball

London had not seen a celebration of this magnitude in quite some time. Matlock house glowed brighter than Vauxhall Gardens[5] during their fireworks display. Each room was exquisitely appointed, especially the grand ballroom which featured mirrored walls that reflected the lights of at least a thousand candles in the huge crystal chandeliers. The best shops in London had been depleted of all manner of flowers for the event, making the house a veritable Garden of Eden. And as carriage after carriage made slow progress to the front of the house to unload their passengers, an army of chefs worked to provide food and drink for the throng.

It seemed that half of England had been invited to celebrate Richard's engagement and had accepted, eager for a glimpse of the Fitzwilliams and the elusive Darcys. For their part, the Fitzwilliams and their extended family, decked out in their finest apparel, looked every bit the cream of society as they stood shoulder to shoulder, facing the world as a united front.

As usual, the Earl and Countess led the receiving line, followed by the Viscount Leighton who surprisingly, acted very civilly to everyone. Standing next to him was

---

[5] *Vauxhall Gardens was the oldest of London's pleasure gardens. Its twelve acres, containing shrubbery, walks, statues and cascades, were located in Lambeth, south of the Thames from Westminster Abbey. (The Regency Encyclopedia)*

Amelia, once again attending without her husband. Richard was next in line followed by his fiancée, Jenny Largin, then William and Elizabeth, and at the end of the line, Evan and Georgiana.

The entire process had gone smoothly, though it seemed agonizingly protracted because of the throng of people. As the line wound down to the last few guests, William began looking about for a chair for Elizabeth to occupy as soon as the last person was received and the dancing began. Being with child, she easily tired, and he could tell that she was weary. He motioned a footman forward and sent him in search of a chair. Even as she protested that she could stand, she acquiesced to his pampering, knowing it would help him to relax if he thought she was well.

She squeezed his hand, leaning in to whisper, "Do not think procuring me a chair will relieve you of your duty to dance with me. I intend to dance with my husband and make all the ladies green with envy."

William chuckled at her impertinence, releasing her hand to slip an arm around her waist and bring her close as he murmured in her ear. "I would not dare suspend any pleasure of yours, Mrs. Darcy. But you shall rest between sets. I insist upon it."

Georgiana moved closer to speak to Elizabeth, and as he watched her converse with his sister, he could not have been prouder. Elizabeth had held her own against the barbs of the *ton*. He had literally swelled with pride as she had answered every cutting remark with good nature and every intrusive question by changing the subject. There had been the expected scrutiny and patronization, but both were surprised at the number of people who seemed willing to accept her into their good graces, if not for her benefit, at least to appease the Fitzwilliams.

Now, with the line dwindling and the next couple involved in a lengthy conversation with Lord Matlock, Amelia pulled Jenny towards her for a chat. With Jenny thus occupied, Richard turned to his left to see concern on his cousin's face. He could not hold back a quip as he chuckled under his breath.

"If you keep making that scowl, Darce, your face will freeze like that, and you will scare small children for the rest of your life. Did your mother not ever tell you that?" Shaking his head, William chuckled, pleasing Richard. "There! You look much nicer, and you won't scare your lovely wife. By the way, when is the blessed event?"

Shocked that their secret was known, William's brow knit. "How did—"

He was cut off as Richard retorted, "Do not blame me; blame Jenny. Seems she has been watching Elizabeth and, well, she just knows these things—having had two children of her own. But, rest assured, she has told no one but me, though I doubt you have fooled Mother either!"

William glanced to see Elizabeth still talking with Georgiana and Evan, and as she was not attending to what he and Richard were saying, William began to clarify, "Elizabeth did not wish to announce our good news until after the ball. She insisted that she did not want to detract from your engagement, and I suspect, though she will not admit to it, that she also did not want all the old biddies counting up the months."

Richard chuckled quietly. "You would take away the old biddies' only enjoyment?"

"I care not if everyone knows she is carrying my child, but if I could possibly accomplish it, I would do away with all the gossip. However, I am afraid that gossip will go on as long as there are—"

"Women?" Richard offered.

"Human beings!" William finished. "Just consider all the gossip bandied about at Whites!"

"You have me there!" Richard chuckled, his face instantly sobering as he caught sight of the arrival of a few more guests.

"Put on your scowl, Cousin! Here comes Mrs. Hampton who is sure to have been insulted that you did not choose her ugly daughter to marry!"

~~~*~~~

"Did you see how Mr. Darcy ran his hand around his wife's waist to pull her closer!" Mrs. Graham sighed dramatically. "Would that Horace had ever done that to me in public! And I had forgotten how handsome Georgiana Darcy's husband is—quite a catch! Not that any woman would rebuff Colonel Fitzwilliam either!"

"Humph!" Mrs. Hinds retorted. "They are all handsome men, Colonel Fitzwilliam, Mr. Darcy, and Mr. Ingram. But I dislike how each of them shows affection in public. It is just not proper!"

"It would be proper if it were you!" Jane Mumford said under her breath, smiling when she realised that Mrs. Trentholm had heard her, because she betrayed it with a giggle.

"And, frankly, Margaret, I see nothing about Mrs. Darcy that is exceptional." Gertrude Hinds continued her critique, "She is a pretty creature, I will say that. But my Sarah is just as lovely, and when she was presented to society, he never gave her so much as a nod."

"Perhaps because Sarah has teeth that protrude and a crooked nose!" Lady Mumford whispered to her audience of one, who giggled again, only to quiet when Mrs. Hinds whirled around.

"Well, I, for one, am glad that Mr. Darcy never showed the slightest interest in Jacqueline Fitzwilliam or that Waltham woman! Though, heaven knows, they were ridiculous in their efforts to gain his attention!" Mrs. Harris sniffed haughtily.

"She would have chased after him, too, had she been given any assurance that he would have welcomed her advances!" Lady Mumford continued in her whispered conversation, to Mrs. Trentholm's delight.

Unaware of the censure, Mrs. Harris continued, "At least Mrs. Darcy is a refined lady. I have it on good authority that her family was well respected in Sussex, though they have all passed now. It is said they owned a large estate and several lesser estates, and she was the sole heiress when her uncle died."

"You are quite right, Martha," Margaret Graham replied. "I was informed at the reception that his sister hosted, that Mrs. Darcy was almost as wealthy as Mr. Darcy when they married. And it is evident from their behaviour that theirs is a love match. How very amusing to see the staid Mr. Darcy so enthralled!"

"She is not so much amused as vexed that it was not her!" Janet Mumford confidentially informed her willing listener. Then she declared for all to hear, "I understand that Jacqueline's father banished her to his country estate when she returned home. And our dear friend, Lady Waltham, fled back to her estate in Ireland since after Lady Matlock effectively made sure she was excluded from all the best parlours in London."

Patience Trentholm laughed, speaking for the first time. "That proves that it does not pay to cross the Countess!"

Standing behind a Roman column, Lady Matlock smiled to herself as she listened to the gaggle of gossips. Their discussion of her most beloved nephew and his lovely wife had taken the correct turn, and she was satisfied.

At least the rumours Miss Bingley started have been squashed and replaced by more complimentary ones!

Since she had been instrumental in creating those rumours, she could not help but smile as she proceeded to make her round of the ballroom.

Heiress indeed!

~~~*~~~

As Lady Matlock continued her turn around the room, she was slowed by those wanting to congratulate her on her son's engagement or compliment her on the splendour of the ball. However, nearing the end of it, she was met by Mr. Rutgers, the butler.

"Madam, there is a man at the door who says he is a servant of Mr. Darcy. He insists that he be allowed to speak to him right this minute, but he is wet and filthy. I barely convinced him to wait downstairs and have appointed two footmen to watch him."

Lady Matlock's eyebrows rose as she turned to find William in the crowd, and their eyes met. He had just finished dancing with Amelia, and was standing behind Elizabeth, who was sitting in the chair he insisted she occupy between dances. Elizabeth was sipping a glass of punch and watching as Georgiana and Evan danced, completely unaware of the drama about to play out downstairs.

Seeing his aunt's expression, William leaned down and spoke to Elizabeth, who nodded. It was obvious that she not was privy to his concern. He then said something to Amelia who quickly took his place next to his wife as he moved towards Lady Matlock. Richard, having witnessed everything and seeing the determination in William's face, instantly sent Jenny to join the ladies while he followed. As both men converged on the countess in the front hallway, she passed along Rutgers' message.

"Do you want Edward to come with you?" Evelyn Fitzwilliam asked, her eyes darting anxiously towards the ballroom, secretly hoping her husband could be kept unaware as he had not felt well that day, and she did not want anything to upset him.

William shook his head. "No, I believe I know what this is about, and I would rather not alarm the others, especially not Elizabeth. Just carry on as though nothing is amiss. I am hopeful that no one will notice that we are not in the ballroom, particularly my wife."

"Well, I am certainly going with you!" Richard declared, causing William to smile.

"I was counting on it," he replied, slapping his cousin on the back. Thus, with grim faces, the two descended the grand staircase towards the mud-encrusted man sitting on a bench in the foyer. Footmen on either side were still regarding him questionably, and when he saw William and leaped to his feet, each grabbed him by an arm.

"All is well; turn him loose," William stated, nodding towards a room to the right. "Let us go in here."

As the three filed into a small parlour, the man noticed Richard's stern appraisal and began talking nervously. "Excuse me, sir, for coming here dressed so poorly, but you charged me with keeping you informed as soon as I had any news! And once I heard you were here, I hurried right over."

"Yes, I certainly did. Now tell me why you are back so soon and looking as though you have rolled in the mud."

"I did as you instructed and followed that woman. She boarded a post coach, with one other passenger already aboard, that was headed to Hertfordshire, just as she swore she would, only ..."

"Only?" William's brow knit, and he wondered at why the man suddenly began to study his shoes.

"Only she never made it to Meryton. Ten miles outside London it began storming, the rain coming down with such fury that the sky turned black as pitch! Even my horse had trouble keeping to the road as we followed the coach. Then suddenly it happened!"

"What happened?" William's curt reply reflected his growing impatience.

"The accident!" The man took a shuddering breath, which caused his entire body to quiver. "The coach was going too fast for the muddy road. It rounded a curve, and pitched sideways and began to fall. Being next to a ravine, it tumbled over the edge and slowly began rolling to the bottom. I stopped to help, but there was nothing I could do. The driver was thrown to the ground and survived, but the passengers—the man that I spoke of and that woman—were killed."

"Mrs. Bennet is dead? Are you sure?" William's voice was toneless. Was it true that the woman who had abused his wife so cruelly was a victim of her own greed— coming to London to ask about Jane, and having seen Elizabeth, attempting to extort money from her?

"Positive! I checked her pulse myself before I went to the nearest village for help. The local physician pronounced them dead when he arrived!"

William stood mute, obviously pondering what effect this would have on Elizabeth. Thus, the servant glanced to Richard, unsure of what to do next.

Seeing William's discomposure, Richard addressed the man, "You have done well. Go back to Darcy House and have a bath, something to eat and a good rest. I am sure my cousin will reward you for your service as soon as he has had time to consider everything that has occurred."

The footman began to leave, but stopped as William finally found his voice. "Thank you, Bradley! You have done well and will be rightly compensated!"

The man turned to smile, cracking the dried mud on his face. "Just doing my job, Master!" But it was with a much livelier step that he exited the room. William closed his eyes then ran his hands over his face and through his hair as Richard had often seen him do when he was distressed.

A low whistle broke the silence. "I know that I have been occupied with my engagement, but when you find the time we need to talk." William nodded blankly. "Will you tell Elizabeth what you have learned tonight?"

"No!" William straightened, coming back to himself. "I shall pick a time when I believe she is capable of accepting it—not tonight." He went towards the door.

"Maybe you should take a minute to compose yourself. Would you like a brandy?"

"I have left Elizabeth alone far too long as it is. I must go to her."

"Then let us return together and hope that everyone will just assume we were having a cigar in the card room or out on the terrace."

As they re-entered the ball, Amelia and Jenny were still engaged in conversation with Elizabeth, assuming that they had kept her from realising that William was missing. And fully aware of their efforts, Elizabeth had dutifully played along. Unfortunately, neither knew of the special bond that united the pair. The weeks Elizabeth had spent in the recesses of her mind, lost in despair, William had been the only light to penetrate the darkness. And as her soul reached out to connect with his, she had learned to sense his presence. Thus the moment he entered a room, she could feel him, and subsequently, she also knew the minute he left.

~~~*~~~

Later that night, after all the guests had departed and the family had retired to their rooms, or in the case of the Darcys and Ingrams, to their own townhouses, Elizabeth asked the question that had been on the tip of her tongue since William had disappeared from the ball.

"What secret are you withholding until you believe I am capable of dealing with it?"

In the process of removing his boots, William stopped with one halfway off. Shrugging to himself, he wondered how he ever thought he could hide anything from this beautiful, intelligent woman. Still, he did not answer, but unhurriedly finished undressing under her watchful gaze. She would wait until he found the words—she always did. As he gathered his thoughts, he relived what had transpired two days before.

At the soft knock, he looked up to see Mr. Barnes at the door of the library.

"Sir, there is a woman at the door insisting that she is Mrs. Darcy's mother. I barely got her to wait on the stoop while I came to inform you. I would not let her in without your consent."

William quickly calculated how long Elizabeth would be gone on her shopping trip with his aunt. "Barnes, if Mrs. Darcy returns while this woman is here, I would not like them to meet." Barnes nodded. "Please escort her to my study and have a footman wait outside the door while I interview her."

Mr. Barnes quickly went back to the front entrance. Once there, he took a deep breath and opened it. "Follow me, madam."

Pleased to be allowed inside such an expensive house, Mrs. Bennet could barely follow the butler for surveying and touching the elegant furnishings. Looking back to see her dawdling, Barnes chided, "I said follow me please!"

She stepped up her pace and shortly found herself inside a study. As she turned in a circle, envying the splendour, William entered, motioning for the footman following to wait at the door as he closed and locked it. He then crossed to sit down behind the desk, his face an inhospitable mask as he eyed the woman he had come to despise. She stood looking about uneasily, as he never offered her a place to sit.

But seeing as she had the attention of the elegant Mr. Darcy that she remembered from Netherfield as being very wealthy, she began her prepared speech. "I am Mrs. Darcy's mother, Frances Bennet!" She dipped a low curtsy.

With no little disdain, William spit out, "Explain why you are here!"

"In London?"

"At my door!"

She smiled hesitantly, taking a seat on the edge of a chair. "I came to London in pursuit of the whereabouts of my eldest daughter, Jane Bingley. When I saw in the news that you were to be in London for Colonel Fitzwilliam's engagement ball, I rushed here. You and Charles Bingley are friends, are you not? You would know where he has taken my Jane."

"Why do you not know where your daughter resides?"

Mrs. Bennet cocked her head guiltily, not meeting his eyes. "Jane was helping to support me and my other daughters. Once Mr. Bingley found out, he spirited her away from Hertfordshire and cut off all communication. He is indeed most ungenerous."

Lifting shifty eyes, she eyed William to gauge his reaction to her next statement. "I was hoping only for information on my Jane when I arrived, but I found so much more! I found that my Lizzy is not dead, but alive, and I was equally shocked to find that she is your wife!"

"I can assure you, madam, that Mrs. Darcy is not your daughter. My wife is the former Elizabeth Lawrence, a cousin of mine from Sussex."

"Nonsense! I know my own daughter! You and she were leaving the bookseller on Centre Street when I exited the shop across the street. I could not get to your carriage in time, but I clearly saw my Lizzy." She shrewdly looked about the room estimating the cost of the furnishings. "And I know that with so wealthy a husband, my daughter would want to help her destitute family, since my Jane is no longer allowed to do so. Besides, you are so much wealthier than Mr. Bingley. It would not surprise me if you were to set us up in a much nicer estate and with an allowance."

William's jaw clenched as his hands formed fists. He stared coldly at her until she shrank back in the chair speechless.

"Madam, according to Jane Bingley, your daughter Elizabeth resides in a grave in the cemetery at Meryton, put there by your greed and selfishness."

Mrs. Bennet tried to assume an innocent look. "I assure you all those rumours of how I benefited from her marriage were not true! And now I learn that even my Lizzy's death must have been a lie meant to wound me. After all, I saw her for myself only yesterday!"

"ENOUGH!" William shouted, his voice vibrating through the room and silencing the harridan. "My Elizabeth's surname is Lawrence—Elizabeth Elise Lawrence. She is no kin of yours, I can assure you!" William's eyes darkened and narrowed as he leaned forward. "And if you persist in spouting this nonsense, do you know what action you shall force me to take?"

Mrs. Bennett's head slowly moved from side to side, her eyes widening in fright at the expression of hatred on his face.

"I shall be forced to have you arrested for threatening my wife and have your sanity evaluated. I assure you, with my friends in the medical field, that you shall be found insane. Then my uncle, the Earl Matlock, will begin proceedings to have you committed to Bedlam straightaway."

Mrs. Bennet took a ragged breath, her head still swinging slowly left to right as she wondered at the turn her mission had taken.

William stood, slamming both hands down on his desk as he leaned forward, making her jump. "Bedlam, madam! Where a delusional woman—one who has contributed to the death of her own child, whom she buried in the local cemetery and now insists is alive—should reside!"

"You ... you cannot!" Mrs. Bennet said, suddenly becoming flustered. "I ... I am not insane! I have friends and relations who testify as to my good character!"

William went around the desk to stand in front of her, leaning to within inches of her face. "I assure you that I most certainly can, and I will. My uncle can have anyone committed to Bedlam, even you."

Mrs. Bennet swallowed hard, her eyes darting about before finally coming back to settle on him, as he had not moved. "I must have been mistaken, Mr. Darcy. Of course my Lizzy is dead, and besides, she was never pretty enough to capture a fine gentleman like you. Why, you could have married the most beautiful—"

"Mrs. Bennet!" The fierceness of his bellow caused her to cover her ears, and he jerked her hands away from them so she could hear the rest of his declaration. "Your daughter is dead! Have you no regard for her even now?"

At her ignorant, vacant look, he continued, "If you know what is good for you, you will never contact anyone in my family or mention my wife ever again. If I learn that you have so much as breathed her name, I shall not hesitate to have you arrested and the process begun!"

Then he pulled her from the chair and stalked to the door dragging her with him. Opening it, he flung her into the hallway as he addressed the startled footman, "Escort this ... this thing out of my house!"

Mrs. Bennet recovered her balance as she was escorted towards the front entrance as fast as her trembling legs would allow. Once there, Barnes swiftly opened the door, and she hesitated only long enough to turn and meet William's eyes.

"I swear I shall never mention Mrs. Darcy again. You have my solemn vow."

"Do not mention Elizabeth Bennet either!" William shouted angrily.

"Of course! Of course! Not Lizzy either! You are right! Not a word! Not another word." She was still babbling as she backed out the door which was then slammed shut in her face.

So it was that William had to tell Elizabeth that night of her mother's visit to Darcy House and of the coach accident that claimed her life. As he feared, she broke down and cried like a child, so he gently picked her up and sat with her in his lap on the settee before the fire. There he soothed her with words of love and devotion as she hid her face in his chest, occasionally weeping anew. Finally having quieted, she looked up and he cradled her face, kissing all traces of tears away.

"I am not crying for my mother, though I suppose somewhere inside I should feel something. I am crying because I never had a mother."

William lovingly ran his hands up and down her back in a sign of his devotion, and she placed a soft kiss on his mouth before she continued.

"Just this day, your aunt offered me a place in her heart as a daughter. Do you know how often I wished to talk to my own mother as mothers and daughters do? How ironic that on the day that Frances Bennet died, I gained a mother."

~~~*~~~

Later, as she lay in William's embrace, his arms locked tightly about her as though by holding her in this manner he could protect her, she cried once more with the realisation that she was finally free. Elizabeth Bennet was no more. She could finally be put to rest along with the woman who had made her life miserable.

Chapter 46

Pemberley
Saturday
Eighteen Months later
1816, July 14

Mr. Williamson felt completely at peace as he climbed the grand staircase in the very early hours, knowing he was right where God wanted him to be. He nodded to Mrs. Reynolds who passed him heading the opposite direction in an upstairs hallway. She smiled, stopping to ask if she could be of service. But with his assertion that he did not need a thing, she went on with her duties, paying him no mind. After all, he was just another member of the family now. He smiled, reflecting on his good fortune.

Who would have believed that I would spend my last days surrounded by such splendour, in the company of the woman I have always regarded as a daughter and others I have come to love through knowing her?

Now that his health required that he retire from all but occasional pastoral duties, Lizzybet had insisted he reside with them, but he had refused to invade their privacy or to give up his independence. So William had a nice-sized cottage built not a mile from the manor. The vicar chuckled to recall the reason William had given for selecting the location, though he would wager that William had not repeated it to his wife.

"You will be far enough removed to have some peace and quiet and close enough to join in the chaos, if you dare, when all of our family converges! And, besides, I might need to visit you occasionally to enjoy the silence."

Yes, the cottage is so close that I may walk over anytime my legs decide to cooperate with my wishes, or use the ponies and phaeton that William insists on having at my disposal if they do not.

And he had to admit that when all of the Darcys' extended family—the Ingrams, Bingleys and Fitzwilliams—were at Pemberley, it could become quite boisterous.

And that is not even taking into account the clamour the children create!

Mr. Williamson considered the growing number of children that would converge on Pemberley tomorrow, and that brought to mind his namesake, Master Fitzwilliam Thomas John Darcy—the dark-haired blue-eyed miniature replica of his father, whose first birthday was being celebrated the next day. He marvelled at the realisation that this birthday would mean the arrival of almost every member of the aforementioned families—some already ensconced in the family quarters, while others who lived nearby would arrive in time for the church services tomorrow.

Mentally, the vicar began to tally the count. Charles and Jane Bingley would be there in the morning, bringing Peter, almost three, and Molly, nineteen months old. Richard and Jenny Fitzwilliam would also arrive tomorrow, accompanied by six-year-old Margaret, five-year-old Mary, and their son, six-month-old David Richard. The Ingrams, who had just had a son, Blake Evan, after years of barrenness, would bring him and Millie, who, at four, was already the leader of the group of cousins.

Lizzybet's uncle and aunt, Edwin and Madeline Gardiner, had arrived two days prior, bringing their brood—Jane, Sally, Benjamin, and Jonathan, ages fourteen, eleven, eight and five, respectively. Lord and Lady Matlock had arrived last evening from London, bringing their daughter, Lady Amelia Fairclothe, whose husband, Lord Daniel Fairclothe, was expected the next day as he had been detained on business. At Amelia's arrival, Lizzybet had been so excited that she just had to tell him of William's part in introducing his cousin to her husband. Fairclothe, it turns out, was one of William's closest university classmates, and when Amelia's first husband, Lord Cosgrove, expired shortly after Richard's marriage, William had played the matchmaker. They had fallen madly in love but had waited for her year of mourning to pass before marrying.

Chuckling, Mr. Williamson recalled how animated Lizzybet had been as she added, "The Fairclothes have just announced that they are with child! Is that not wonderful—another babe in the family!"

He chuckled. *As if they do not have more than their fair share of babies already!*

But the true star of the day would be his grandchild—Will. By the time Will was born, Mr. Williamson had almost forgotten how securely a baby could capture a large portion of one's heart just by smiling at the funny faces one made to entertain the child. And now that Will was old enough to cry when he had to return to his cottage, his love simply knew no bounds. Often the vicar found himself near to tears when it was time to go, as Will reminded him increasingly of time spent with his own dear son.

And on the occasions when the tears did come, they were not born of sorrow but from the surety that soon he would see Gregory again—once more clasp him to his bosom as he had often done in this life. As a vicar, he was well acquainted with the seasons of life as he had spent his life presiding over the rituals associated with them. Babies were born, grew up, married and formed families of their own—then they would die and the cycle would begin anew. That was as God intended. And as he neared the end of his own life, Mr. Williamson was content—pleased that he could honestly say that he had no regrets.

His musings kept him occupied, and before he knew it, he was standing at the door to the billiards room. There, he had been assured, he would find William. The door stood ajar, and upon a cursory look, it seemed that no one had been inside today, as everything was spotless and neatly arranged. Nevertheless, as he turned to go, he caught sight of William standing in the corner of the bank of windows that ran the entire length of the room. His blue coat and breeches blended in well with the blue drapes and had completely disguised his presence, given that he stood perfectly still.

Approaching him quietly, it was obvious that the Master of Pemberley was totally engrossed in watching something or someone on the lawn below. Since the windows were wide open, it was not long until Williamson heard Elizabeth's melodious voice drifting up from below. Stepping closer to peer below, he caught sight of her helping her curly-haired son walk on the smooth lawn by holding each of his chubby hands. She was leaning over him from behind, while he looked straight up at her, grinning from ear to ear—his few front teeth clearly visible as he smiled back at his mother.

"You are doing so well, Will. Now let us see how you do without Mama holding your hands." Elizabeth moved to kneel in front of the baby, helping him to balance and then scooting back a couple of feet, holding out her arms. "Come to Mama, sweetheart!"

A nimble-footed Will Darcy picked his feet up a little bit higher than was necessary as he lurched forward. Giggling, he took six steps in a row and fell into his mother's arms. Instantly, he received a plethora of kisses while she extolled his accomplishment.

"That was simply wonderful, sweetling! You are doing very well! Papa will be so proud of you!"

As she continued to alternately put the baby down to waddle a few steps, then pick him up to kiss, cuddle, and praise his every effort, Mr. Williamson could not help but swell with grandfatherly pride. This child had captured his heart just as surely as his mother had six and twenty years before. Suddenly remembering that he was not alone, he glanced to see that Will's father had never even noticed his presence in the room.

"A penny for your thoughts."

William whirled around, an expression of pure elation on his face as he exclaimed, "Did you see him?"

Though his dark hair was threaded with grey now, his light blue eyes were sparkling as his dimples cut deeper than ever before. The result was that William appeared so much younger than the broken man of the Meryton cemetery two years previously that the vicar was momentarily stunned. And caught up in his astonishment at the contrast, the vicar did not answer.

William grabbed the mute man by shoulders, crowing, "Will is walking!"

He studied the vicar eagerly, waiting for him to acknowledge the significance, and as Mr. Williamson came to himself, he offered, tongue in cheek, "What a splendid accomplishment! I never doubted he would!"

This served to appease William, so he began to elaborate on what his son's grandfather already knew. "Will has been pulling up for months, and the physician assured us that he would walk all in good time, but Elizabeth would not leave well enough alone. She has worked relentlessly to have him walking by his first birthday."

From down below came a raised voice. "William? Is that you there in the billiards room? Have you seen what your son has accomplished? No, wait! Stay right there, and I shall bring him up to show you! Come, darling. Let us go show Papa."

William had leaned over the window sill to hear Elizabeth, but before he could answer, she had scooped up their son and headed back inside. Seeing that she was no longer down below, William whispered to the man he had come to love as a father.

"Quickly, before she comes up, were you able to arrange everything?"

"Yes. It is all arranged for tomorrow morning."

"Good! Good! I do not think she suspects a thing!"

"Have all the other members of your family been told of your plans?"

"Yes. I informed all of them months ago. All that is left is to surprise Elizabeth."

Mr. Williamson grinned. "You know how Elizabeth can be about anyone hiding things from her. I pray she does not get upset with you."

William smiled knowingly. "She never stays upset with me for long. Besides, how can she be anything but pleased when she finds out what I have planned and why? I want the world to know how much I love her."

"Well, when you put it that way, I—"

Just at that moment, Elizabeth scurried into the room, her face flush with the exertion of carrying Will, who was already big for his age, up the stairs.

"William—oh, hello, Father Williamson! I am glad you are here, too. You both must watch Will walk!"

Placing her son on the floor, Elizabeth beamed with pride as the child she had prayed for took several energetic steps towards his doting father, who had already knelt and was holding out his arms. As Will fell into William's arms, he pulled him against his chest, then stood and hugged him, rocking him from side to side.

"I knew you could do it, Son! You had only to make up your mind!"

Suddenly overcome with love for this little person, he buried his face in Will's sweet-smelling curls and pressed kisses there before reaching for Elizabeth's hand to pull her, too, into his embrace. As the three embraced, lost in their love for each other, Will's grandfather grinned with the thought of something he now recalled—Richard's wisdom on why the boy had not walked yet.

Will does not walk because he is just like his father—he will not be cajoled into anything! And, besides, why should the child walk when everyone insists on carrying him around?

The Pemberley Chapel
Sunday
1815, July 15

"But I do not understand why William insisted I dress so grandly," Elizabeth complained to Jane and Georgiana as they exited the carriage that had just delivered the three—the last of the family—to Pemberley's chapel. As she stood, she smoothed the beautiful white gown replete with Belgium lace ruffles and appliqués. "Mrs. Reynolds brought this gown into my dressing room this morning, informing me that it was a present from William, and that he wished me to wear it today. I imagine my husband is quite pleased with himself for having it created without my knowledge, but I scarcely wear white since Will was born as he always manages to stain my gowns. And since he is to be blessed today for his birthday, he will probably manage to do that before we leave the chapel. Besides, this one is too elegant for everyday wear."

Jane and Georgiana exchanged cautious glances but did not reply, each praying they could finish their directive for William's surprise—getting Elizabeth inside the church.

"Does Mrs. Drury have the baby with her?"

"Yes, Lizzy," Jane sighed a little exasperated. "As I have told you twice before, Mrs. Drury has Will, so you do not have to worry about him."

As they neared the stained glass panel in the front door, she caught a reflection of the flowers tucked in her dark curls. She giggled. "And one would think I was going to a ball instead of the local parish church. I can only wonder at Lady Matlock's insistence that her maid style my hair today."

Jane and Georgiana still did not comment, and this time it did not go unnoticed. Elizabeth stopped and turned to study her sisters, one brow raised in suspicion as she eyed first one then the other. "Is there something that I should know?"

Jane sighed and Elizabeth looked to her, knowing she could get information from her sister more readily than from William's. "Tell me what you know that I do not!"

Jane bit her bottom lip and looked to Georgiana. "Jane? You know how I hate surprises. Does William have something planned for later today?"

Jane stared at her feet. Elizabeth glanced at Georgiana, noting that she was doing the same. "Well, I shall just have to ask him! Since it seems we are the last to arrive, I imagine it will be after services before I shall have the chance!"

As Elizabeth was speaking, she turned to open the chapel door with much more force than was necessary, due to her exasperation and took one step inside. The sight that greeted her, however, was so breathtaking that she stopped short. The ceiling of the chapel was decorated with layers of white tulle strung from all four sides to one central point just in front of the altar. There, it was gathered and tied with lace, and a small nosegay of white roses and baby's breath was tucked inside. These same nosegays decorated the ends of the pews, and dozens more roses filled crystal vases throughout the chapel. There were enough candles lit to brighten the entirety of Pemberley.

Stunned, Elizabeth began to look around the room, meeting the gazes of those who were now smiling at her. Among the throng, were not only their family members, but Mr. and Mrs. Barnwell, Mrs. Browning, her sister, and Arthur—all of whom nodded their greetings. Being in a trancelike state, Elizabeth would not be able to recall later the names of everyone in attendance.

Finally her eyes rested on William, standing in front and looking every inch the prince from one of her favourite fairytales. Her ebony eyes widened as she distinctly heard her father's voice in a bittersweet dialogue from the past.

"Ah, yes. Martha." Her father sighed, remembering the rag doll that Elizabeth had fashioned by herself. "How is Miss Martha?"

"She is sad sometimes. But I talk to her, and I remind her that things will get better once she grows up." Lizzy swept a lock of unruly hair from her forehead, looking up with the dark, bright eyes her father adored. "That is true, is it not? Things will get better when she grows up?"

Mr. Bennet directed a long, thoughtful look at her. "Yes, Lizzy. Things will get better when Martha grows up. You see, this little trunk is called a dowry chest. Martha should put all the things in it that she loves, and the things she will want to take with her when she marries. One day a handsome prince will fall in love with her. They will marry and go to live in a beautiful castle. And they will both be happy for the rest of their lives."

Georgiana, seated at the church organ, began the first notes of a wedding song, and it penetrated her consciousness causing her to recover from her reverie. Seeing her slight disorientation, William held out both his hands to her—just as he had on their wedding day. That gesture was all that was needed and Elizabeth smiled at her groom, the love radiating between them almost palpable to those watching. Sighs could be heard from all sides, and the next thing Elizabeth knew, Jane was pressing a bouquet of white roses into her hands, giving her a hug and then a little nudge towards the front. No other incentive was necessary as Elizabeth followed her heart to the one who held it securely in his grasp.

This ceremony was much longer than their first, though not any more heartfelt, as Mr. Williamson now used the entire marriage ceremony instead of the shorter version they had requested in Liverpool. The service progressed beautifully, the only incident to mar the solemnity of the occasion coming near the end when the vicar asked

Elizabeth to repeat her vows. Will, upon hearing his mother's voice, found that the toys Mrs. Drury had brought no longer entertained and began to call, "Mama!"

William and Elizabeth both instinctively turned to look toward their son, as the congregation chuckled quietly. Mrs. Drury, on the other hand, turned a lovely shade of crimson as every eye fixed on her attempts to capture the child's attention with a toy. Nevertheless, Will would not quiet now that he had seen his mother and began to whimper. William knew that that meant he would soon begin to cry, so he caught Richard's eye and nodded towards his son. Immediately Richard went to fetch the boy and bring him to his parents.

Thus, when Elizabeth began again—promising to love, cherish and obey, 'til death would part them—their son, content in his father's arms, smiled back at her, trusting that she was talking to him.

Sensing that he should hurry along now, Mr. Williamson promptly completed the ceremony and pronounced them man and wife. This time William needed no prodding from Richard and quickly leaned down to kiss his bride. However, upon seeing his parents kissing, Will leaned forward to receive his share. As the congregation laughed aloud, the couple quit their kiss to give Will one—a parent on either cheek.

There was not a dry eye in the chapel as the service ended.

~~~*~~~

Epilogue

In later years, Elizabeth and William would recall the day they renewed their vows as one of the happiest of their lives—in the same category as their wedding and the births of their children. And, by then, they had come to an understanding—while William still insisted that Elizabeth was the one responsible for filling their lives with love, children, and beautiful memories, she, in turn, insisted that it was he who had given her the chance to do so. As she so aptly pointed out, without his redeeming love, she would never have experienced any of it.

So it was that frequently William would find Elizabeth in the middle of some occupation, gazing into the distance with a certain faraway look in her eyes and a smile upon her lips. On occasion, he would question her woolgathering, and she would confess to recalling one thing or another. But more often than not, he preferred just to observe her beautiful face transform at some recollection, knowing that he had been instrumental in that alteration. And it was at those times that he would recall a special remembrance of his own, and his face would take on a wistful look as well.

With the arrival of Elizabeth Adelaide "Addie" Darcy in the summer of 1817, Will was no longer an only child. Named for her mother and Millie's, she had Elizabeth's dark hair and eyes, as well as her lively spirit. And while Mr. Williamson declared the baby to be the exact likeness of his Lizzybet when she was born, William was simply thrilled to have a smaller version of his Elizabeth to shower with everything he believed his wife should have had as a child; primarily, unconditional love.

Barely three years later, Evelyn Jane "Eve" Darcy was born, named for Lady Matlock and Elizabeth's sister. She had lighter brown hair, her father's blue eyes, and a quieter temperament, which suited her parents, as she complemented Addie's exuberance.

Two years afterward, Alexander Gerald Fitzwilliam "Alex" Darcy made his entrance into the world, the very likeness of his father, resembling his brother, Will, though his eyes were dark brown like Elizabeth's. And it was almost four years later that the Darcys learned they were to be blessed with a fifth and final child. Rosamond Elise "Rose" Darcy was born on William's birthday that year, as her father proclaimed her to be the most delightful birthday present that Elizabeth had ever given him!

Richard and Jenny had two more children after David: another boy, Edward Nicholas, and a girl, Jenny Ilene. Richard was very pleased to retire to life in the country, leaving the army a distant memory. They, along with her little girls, Margaret and Mary, whom Richard considered his own, resided at Windmere in Derbyshire, which was less than one day's journey from Pemberley. There Richard became a successful gentleman farmer under the guidance of his father and his cousin, the Master of Pemberley.

Georgiana gave birth to twins - a boy, Noel Darcy, and a girl, Anne Celeste - two years after Blake, completing the family that she and Evan had always wanted. Their little Millie became the happiest of sisters with their births, as she was a very good little mother and Blake was now at the age where he did not want to be mothered—well, at least not by a sister who tried to make him mind.

The Bingleys had one more child, Rachel Suzanne, the year that Peter was almost six. They lived as near the Darcys home as did the Ingrams, and all three families were frequently found at one estate or the other in the early years of their marriages. Elizabeth, Georgiana, and Jane felt the need to talk at least every few days, so there was a constant stream of carriages going back and forth, sometimes passing each other. At some point, William had insisted they make out a schedule of who would visit on which day of the week to reduce misunderstandings considerably. But, as with all things, the passage of time brought the arrival of more children, and because of the responsibilities that that entailed, the visits spread from weekly to monthly and then irregularly as circumstances dictated.

There were less frequent visits by their extended families, too, though the Gardiners were probably most frequently at Pemberley. Elizabeth loved her aunt and uncle and doted on her cousins, thus, they always visited Gracechurch Street whenever they travelled to London, and the Gardiners were among those always invited to Pemberley for Christmas.

As for William's relations, Lord Matlock's health began to deteriorate shortly after Will's birth, making it difficult for him to travel. Therefore, the Darcys would go to London on occasion to visit with them. However, William's cousin, Amelia, and her husband, Lord Fairclothe, often visited Pemberley bringing their three children. The viscount never married again, preferring to take a mistress, and upon his death at the age of forty, Richard became the earl, though he and Jenny continued to live at Windmere, eschewing a move to the larger Matlock estate.

Unfortunately, Anne de Bourgh continued to deteriorate mentally as well as physically and died only three years after William and Elizabeth married. Lady Catherine was distraught after the death and became a recluse, outliving her daughter by barely two years. In her will, Rosings was left to Darcy, as Lady Catherine had never changed the directive written when she assumed that he would follow her desires and marry Anne.

Father Williamson lived to see the birth of all the Darcy children except Rose, passing away peacefully in his sleep only six months after the birth of Alexander. It was a great loss for Elizabeth and William, as they had both loved him as a father, and the children had always considered him to be their grandfather. But it had been comforting to know that his last years had been spent with them in the manor house, where his every wish was fulfilled, as befitted a well-loved member of the family.

As for the people who had touched their lives in a negative manner, with Mrs. Bennet's death, Mrs. Phillips took in Lydia and Kitty, selling the house Stefano had purchased. She gave Mary a share of the proceeds, put aside a small portion for dowries and kept the greater part to offset the expense of seeing after the younger two. However, since neither Lydia nor Kitty aspired to more than securing a red-coat as their mother had often encouraged, each left town with a member of the militia the next spring. They were last seen heading in different directions and were never heard from again. Mary continued to live with her husband and two children in Meryton, inheriting the Phillips's property when her aunt and uncle died. She lived there until her death, completely unconcerned for Lydia and Kitty or the sisters her mother had alienated—Jane and Elizabeth.

After being caught in a compromising situation, Caroline Bingley was forced to marry a York farmer. She had seven children and worked a small tenant farm with her husband until her death. Charles never saw her again. Her sister, Louisa, however, had a much more pleasant life subsequent to her sister's departure to York. Bertram Hurst quit drinking after Caroline was no longer a large portion of their lives, and he and Louisa were blessed to have two children and live happily for the rest of their lives.

As for Mrs. Preston, after Elizabeth passed along to Lieutenant Marbury what she knew of Cecile's involvement with Wickham in the thefts in London, he discovered several valuable pieces of jewellery sewn into the linings of her gowns as well as in the luggage Wickham's left behind. Most of the jewels belonged to another of his noble clients, the Duchess of Rathburn, the last robbery victim in London. The discovery that Cecile had been a part of this scheme, along with her support of Stefano's plans to kidnap Elizabeth, effectively sealed her fate and she was sentenced to live out the rest of her life in a penal colony in Australia.

Thus our story comes to an end with our dear couple living in Derbyshire, in close proximity to those they loved and those who loved them. It was a peaceful area where the Darcys and, indeed, all their brothers and sisters reared their children in an atmosphere of unconditional love and acceptance. They would support one another through a future that would include much happiness and, as is life, some grief.

The life that our devoted couple created for their own family was a world away from that of Elizabeth's early years and the ugliness that had nearly swept her away from William forever—their story a constant testament to the power of one man's honourable heart. For as William had once explained to his Elizabeth...

"You never left my heart, Elizabeth. It would not let you go."

Finis

CPSIA information can be obtained at www.ICGtesting.com
Printed in the USA
LVOW092112270412

279463LV00025BA/93/P

9 781461 073147